THE LIE THAT BINDS THEM

By Matthew Ward

THE LEGACY TRILOGY
Legacy of Ash
Legacy of Steel
Legacy of Light

THE SOULFIRE SAGA
The Darkness Before Them
The Fire Within Them
The Lie That Binds Them

THE LIE THAT BINDS THEM

MATTHEW WARD

orbit

orbit-books.co.uk

ORBIT

First published in Great Britain in 2025 by Orbit

1 3 5 7 9 10 8 6 4 2

A CIP catalogue record for this book
is available from the British Library.

ISBN 978-0-356-51848-0

Typeset in Minion by M Rules
Printed and bound in Great Britain by Clays Ltd, Elcograf, S.p.A.

Papers used by Orbit are from well-managed forests
and other responsible sources.

MIX
Paper | Supporting
responsible forestry
FSC® C104740

Orbit
An imprint of
Little, Brown Book Group
Carmelite House
50 Victoria Embankment
London EC4Y 0DZ

The authorised representative
in the EEA is
Hachette Ireland
8 Castlecourt Centre
Dublin 15, D15 XTP3, Ireland
(email: info@hbgi.ie)

An Hachette UK Company
www.hachette.co.uk

orbit-books.co.uk

Dedicated to the memory of Jackie Ward,
who opened my eyes to worlds beyond our own.

Dramatis Personae

SKELDERS AND OTHER UNDESIRABLES

Katija Arvish	A woman adrift
Tanith Floranz	A daughter of two worlds
Tatterlain	Wearer of many faces
Rîma	Wise swordstress
Bashar Vallant	Notorious rebel
Zephyr	Veilkin navigator
Fadiya Rashace	Disgraced countess
Maxin	A reliable roustabout

THE ETERNITY QUEEN'S COURT

Yennika Bascari	The Eternity Queen, Nyssa Dominus
Ihsan Damant	A wayward man of honour
Yali	The queen's high handmaiden
Count Tuzen Karza	A rake of rank
Ardin Javar	Haunted traitor
Faizâr Kastagîr	Royal bodyguard
Malis Ethara	The queen's spymistress
Hargo Rashace	Furibund husband

| Igarî Bathîr | Hierarch of Alabastra |
| Emanzi Ozdîr | Member of the Queen's Council |

UPSTANDING CITIZENS

Mirzai Tzelda	Outcast engineer
Tarin Tzelda	Engineer's apprentice
Eri Gallar	Retired redcloak
Saheen Avaya	Burdened overseer

THE REGAL AND THE DIVINE

Nyssa Dominus	The Goddess Made Whole
Nyssa Benevolas	The Goddess of Benevolence
Nyssa Iudexas	The Goddess of Judgement
Tzal	Ancient enemy of the Issnaîm
Isdihar Diar	The Voice of the Eternity King
The Drowned Lady	Maybe a myth

ELSEWISE OF NOTE

Azra	A beloved betrayer
Caradan Diar	The Eternity King
Marida	A formless spirit
Hadîm	A man of wayward honour
Amakala	Forgotten queen

One

Kat had always hated Tyzanta, which was a symbol of everything she'd lost and every mistake she'd made along the way. A beautiful city – if one discounted the squalor of Undertown's slums and its rumbling factories – it was also a den of lies and iniquities that she'd barely had opportunity to address, much less correct. Yet for a time Tyzanta, last and greatest of the free cities, had stood for an impossible dream. A promise of freedom. Of hope.

Hope had always been the lie binding them together.

And as the streets beyond Manniqa Station burned, all Kat could think was that Vallant would have handled things better.

Beyond the soot-smeared glass of the station's arched roof, eerie wails and bright flashes against the rising smoke proved that a handful of Tyzanta's shrieker cannon batteries fought on. A redcloak dhow, black sails silhouetted against the setting sun and wreathed in vapour from the ruptured buoyancy tanks along its scorched hull, listed towards the lower city. Spars snapped and rigging thrashed as its starboard flank scraped a warehouse's third storey. Blackened rubble rained down on the station roof. Steel buckled. Glass crazed and disintegrated into glittering shards. Screams rang out along a crowded platform thick with the acrid stench of smoke and terror.

Kat stalked aft along the railrunner, jumping from one carriage rooftop to the next through the engine's billowing steam.

"Keep them moving!"

She shouted to be heard over the platform's sobbing, jostling rush of men, women and children. A crowd fed by the stream of refugees flowing past the makeshift barricade stretching from the stationmaster's office to the cargo exchange at the station gate.

The black-robed custodians labouring to keep order knew full well that time was running out, but speaking the words aloud held Kat's feeling of impotence at bay. It drew eyes to what she hoped was her calm, confident demeanour. Now more than ever she needed to live up to the simple black uniform and silver thread that marked her out as Tyzanta's governor.

The last of the city's great and good – those with the tetrams to buy passage on merchant skyships – had fled a week before, when the black sails of the Eternity Queen's war dhows had thickened on the western horizon. Most had headed east to Qersal even before that, when the shipyards at Azran had fallen and Naxos' ruling council had sued for peace. The sole remaining railrunner was for those too poor to make their own escape, or too loyal to abandon the failing dream. Twenty carriages and wagons scavenged from sidings across the city, most of them fit for the scrapper's yard. All of them already approaching capacity. And still the platform seethed with hundreds of lost souls fleeing the advancing redcloaks.

Many thousands more didn't want to leave. Too many welcomed the coming of the Eternity Queen, or were at least ambivalent to whom they paid their protection levies. They didn't know what Kat knew. About the Eternity Queen. About the Kingdom of Khalad. About the three-faced goddess Nyssa. The lies at Khalad's heart that promised the bleakest of futures.

As Kat approached the rearmost carriage a shadow rushed overhead. Shading her eyes, she craned her neck to see a second, smaller skyship augur in on the beleaguered dhow. Its cannons spat invisible flame, blasting blackened timber from the redcloak vessel's portside hull. *Sadia's Revenge*, one of only three skyships left in the city from a fleet now scattered to the winds.

The dhow's portside buoyancy tanks gave way with an aching sigh that set the station's surviving roof panes clattering. Lateen sail ablaze, it plunged, lost amongst the blocky adobe risings of factories and warehouses. *Sadia's Revenge* burst through its trailing smoke, filthy canvas blossoming on outrigger and spar to plunder every scrap of wind. Armoured keel plates scraped across roof tiles. A trailing spar set a weathercock spinning. And then the skyship soared away, ushered on by the chorus of desperate cheers and wild laughter echoing across Manniqa Station.

Kat cheered with the rest, marvelling at how readily despair became hope. How swiftly the lie took hold.

The ground shook with the dhow's impact in the unseen streets. The crowd's cheers redoubled. Kat's stuttered in her throat, the fires of the aetherios tattoo on her left forearm suddenly frigid as the souls of the dhow's crew brushed past her – *through* her – and hissed skyward, clawing for the Deadwinds and demanding with silent, nebulous voices that she bear witness. She closed her thoughts to them and tried not to wonder at how many had joined the battle only because the Eternity Queen had given them no choice.

She leapt to the last rooftop, her expression composed to conceal her discomfort from the tall, lantern-jawed man standing at the far end, hands thrust into the pockets of scarlet and gold robes whose splendour were an ill match for his tousled, unruly dark brown hair. Stockier than Kat – whose athletic frame had more or less survived the banquets of governorship intact – but not yet quite run to fat, he filled the carriage roof as completely as any actor owned a stage. It was as if all the uncertainty and horror of that moment had come into being merely to serve as a backdrop to some great performance not yet arrived. So it always was with Tatterlain, who smiled often and revelled in attention but somehow seldom lost his dignity in the process . . . unless, of course, it served his ends.

"It happened again, didn't it?" he said, without turning to look at her.

Kat grimaced. So much for concealing her discomfort. Then again, she supposed it shouldn't be easy to keep secrets from friends. "You know it did."

Thanks to the spider-work aetherios tattoo her father had inked on her left forearm, she'd talked to ifrîti – the fragments of souls that powered everything in Khalad from shrieker cannons to humble light-bestowing lumani – her whole adult life. Having those same ifrîti demand her attention was new, though it didn't take genius to know *why* that had changed.

His smile turned wintry as he gazed out across the crowds. "I hate to say it, but you can't save everyone."

"Vallant would agree. I'm not Vallant." Vallant, who'd vanished into the mists without a trace three months before. Which meant he was likely never coming back. The Veil devoured people, body and soul.

"You're certainly prettier, in favourable light at least. That doesn't mean I'm wrong."

It didn't, much as Kat wished otherwise. The railrunner was already well over capacity, the leading rooftops thickening with folk clutching tight to loved ones and thin belongings as harried custodians crammed ever more aboard. The score of custodians at the barricades wouldn't stop a determined assault – especially if koilos were loosed to the slaughter. Every minute gambled the lives of those aboard against those who might yet reach salvation. But what else was there? Choosing who lived and who died took more than she had.

This is folly. You should leave.

The graveyard sigh washed silently across Kat's thoughts. Conscious of Tatterlain's eyes upon her, she fought to keep her disgust concealed. She'd had plenty of practice. So far as most of Khalad was concerned, Caradan Diar, the deposed Eternity King, was dead. And so he was. Sort of. Almost. Maybe.

"We can wait a little longer," she said firmly.

Tatterlain twisted his lips, his left eyelid fluttering. Not for the first time, Kat wondered exactly what he'd seen in her expression. A master mimic didn't become so without a knack for observation. "We can."

The thin, stuttering wail of a distraught child pierced the cacophony.

There. Halfway along the platform to the thin barricade. A girl of maybe six or seven years with a threadbare stuffed paracat crushed to her chest. Her trailing ink-black hair flicked against the toy's tufted ears as she twisted to and fro in the suffocating press of bodies, searching for a familiar face in among the unfeeling strangers. With her dark bronze complexion and willowy build, she could have been Kat's younger self.

"*Kiasta.*" She murmured her father's favourite curse. Her tolerance for crowds was little greater than her love for heights – her perch on the rooftops wasn't *entirely* a contrivance of leadership – but she'd learned the hard way that selfishness gave the very worst of hangovers.

Steeling herself, she turned back to Tatterlain. "Watch the gate. If the redcloaks show—"

"Get the railrunner moving." He nodded. "Actually, I don't think you need go anywhere."

The seething crowd parted before a duster-coated woman whose white hair flowed from beneath her broad-brimmed hat to brush the long straight sword buckled at her shoulder. She walked on, priestly and unhurried, seeming not to notice as desperate evacuees, otherwise on the brink of a shoving match, somehow found space to let her pass.

Rîma thumbed a tear from the child's cheek, gathered her up and set out crosswise along the platform. Reunion between girl and distraught parents was as swift and inevitable as sunrise, mother crushing daughter to her chest as tightly as the child had her paracat. As a harried custodian ushered the three aboard an overcrowded carriage, Rîma raised her eyes to Kat's and offered a steady, shallow nod.

"Always the show-off," muttered Tatterlain, his tone absent of rancour.

Kat smiled. Even from her vantage atop the carriage, she'd not noticed the girl's parents until the last moment, and yet Rîma had somehow marked them from within the thick of the crowd. "She has cause."

You are out of time, breathed Caradan Diar.

She felt the heraldic's arrival as a cold prickle across her tattoo a heartbeat before it coalesced into a thin indigo shimmer a pace to her front, hovering above the crowds.

The ifrît's soulfire rippled into a passing semblance of a bodiless, featureless face, its lips barely moving as it breathed its message.

((Bad news, trallock.)) Its flat, emotionless tone jarred with the earthy colloquial Daric favoured by the captain of the *Sadia's Revenge*. ((Redcloaks just swarmed the Kairon Street watchtower. It's dirt to dinars that you're next.))

Message delivered, the heraldic shimmered, its meagre soulfire already dispersing. Convention held that they were only good for a single message before the Deadwinds claimed them, but Kat and convention had parted ways a long, long time ago.

She reached out with her left hand, indigo flame racing along the spiderweb lines inked on her forearm as she fed the heraldic enough soulfire to sustain it for the return journey. She felt the ifrît's pleasure and surprise mingle at the back of her thoughts – it was just aware enough to know how close it was to oblivion, and welcomed the chance to linger.

"Maxin? We're getting under way, but we could use some cover."

She wanted to add more, but the heraldic was already thinning, its indigo flames mingling with the backrush of steam from the distant locomotive. Gritting her teeth, Kat nodded to indicate that the message was done and withdrew her hand. "Thank you."

The heraldic bled away, already speeding skyward. Kat glanced at Tatterlain.

"I'll handle it," he said, already walking backwards along the carriage towards the distant railrunner engine. "Just make sure you're aboard."

She ran along to the access ladder linking roof and stoop, waving down at the platform and pointing towards the barricaded gate. "Rîma!"

Rîma straightened, nodded and set off in parallel, the press of bodies parting as readily as before.

For a mercy, the crowds had cleared almost to nothing by the time Kat stepped off the stoop and onto the platform. Maybe sixty or seventy more to get aboard. They might actually have done it. They might actually have saved everyone.

Better than Vallant had ever managed.

Kat winced. Was there anything more pathetic than rivalry with the dead? And she'd no doubt that Vallant *was* dead, even if Tatterlain and some of the others clung to hope. The hungry mists of the Veil had claimed him, the *Chainbreaker*, its crew . . . and all of it her fault, as she'd put him up to the voyage.

Throat thick with guilt, she rounded on a man dragging a weighty traveller's chest and falling further behind his fellow stragglers with every step. "Leave it!"

Stricken, he hesitated, but nodded. As the deafening blast of the railrunner's whistle wailed beneath the station roof, he ran towards the nearest carriage.

As Kat approached the mound of clatter wagons, broken furniture and abandoned traveller's chests that could generously be called a barricade, the nearest of the handful of custodians greeted her with a martial crispness that marked her as someone who'd begun her service under Tyzanta's corrupt Bascari regime. But for all that, Overseer Ayla Sinair was an honest woman whose insights into the petty rivalries, feuds and inanities of Tyzanta's daily life had smoothed the course of Kat's brief governorship. You found your place in Khalad or one was found for you, or so the saying went. Sinair, like Kat, had fought to choose her own path. That common ground had soon overcome the unpleasantness of a first meeting that had seen Kat in a convict's shackles. Long nights spent drinking away the frustrations of the day had cemented common ground into friendship.

"Lady Katija." No amount of friendship had ever made Sinair abandon formality, just as no amount of repetition could dull Kat's unease at being addressed as *Lady Katija*. Vallant had insisted that the title went with the governorship but, as far as Kat was concerned, titles were for the fireblood nobility, and she was as common a cinderblood as they came – even if her father had possessed ambition enough for a dozen noble houses. "I take it the situation's changed?"

There's no time for this, breathed Caradan Diar. *You—*

"Enough," hissed Kat. Death had done nothing to quell the Eternity King's persistence, nor his implacable pursuit of self-interest. If she died, so did he. It made for a reluctant alliance at best.

"Kairon Street's fallen," she told Sinair. "It's time we were gone."

Sinair grimaced. She'd never quite adapted to the fact that Tyzanta's custodians no longer donned the androgynous silver *vahla* masks commonplace elsewhere, and wore her feelings more openly than an overseer should. "You heard the governor! Get ready to move."

"Company's coming!" shouted a custodian perched on the cab of one of the overturned clatter wagons halfway up the barricade.

Kat clambered up to join him. Beyond Manniqa Station's gate, the lumani lights of the approach tunnel flickered, casting erratic shadows. Where the tunnel yielded to smoke-clogged skies, a dozen redcloaks advanced in loose formation, the stubby brass and polished wooden stocks of shriekers steady in their hands.

Sinair eased the barrel of her own shrieker over the makeshift rampart. "Vanguard patrol. They don't know what they're walking into. Not yet."

The railrunner engine loosed another blast from its steam whistle. In the tunnel, the leading redcloak stiffened and barked an order. The vanguard broke into a run, eponymous scarlet cloaks streaming behind.

"Stay low," said Kat. "Let them get close."

All along the barricade, custodians levelled their weapons. Kat did likewise, more for show than purpose. Long range or short, she was a terrible shot.

She let the redcloaks approach to within twenty paces before giving the order to shoot. The heart-wrenching wail of shriekers echoed along the tunnel, swallowing dying screams as bolts of flame burned cloth and flesh to ash. Only a single return shot found its mark, hurling a custodian from the barricade's summit, the fires fading and his soul fled before he hit the flagstones.

Kat grabbed at the barricade to steady herself as the souls of the dead

8

and dying rushed through her, the voices louder, more unsettling for their proximity. And beneath them, something else. Something *familiar*, though she couldn't quite place it. A soft, persistent pressure at the back of her thoughts. The feeling grew more diffuse as she tried to pin it down, her thoughts muddying . . . drifting . . . The past day and a half almost without sleep taking its toll.

Katija! snapped Caradan Diar, cold and clear.

Grateful despite herself for his intervention, Kat glanced back towards the railrunner. The platform was all but empty. They were the last.

"We're done here." She tried not to look at the dead custodian. "Sinair—"

She turned to find herself staring into the muzzle of Sinair's shrieker.

"I can't let you leave, Lady Katija."

Custodians twisted around. Some raised their own shriekers to cover the overseer. Most were frozen, conflicted.

I tried to warn you. Self-satisfaction crowded Caradan Diar's voice. A mentor indulging *Schadenfreude* for a student's oversight. *She's here.*

No need to guess who he meant. Not now. Not with Sinair's expression contorting as if a piece of her was surprised by her own actions. That scrap of resistance faded before Kat had chance to speak, sealed behind Sinair's eyes as unseen pressure warped her perceptions.

The Eternity Queen had a way of getting into people's heads. Those rooted in structure and obedience were most vulnerable of all, their longing for a simpler time a fulcrum about which their personality shifted. It transformed rebels into loyal soldiers and loyal soldiers into hardened fanatics . . . and all without them truly being aware of what had been done to them. The one failing that made resistance even possible was that it only worked if the Eternity Queen was close.

She was in the city. Maybe closer even than that.

"Azra . . ." breathed Kat.

"Come quietly, lady," said Sinair. "The Eternity Queen will forgive you."

"I'm sure she will." Kat held her gaze as the other custodians watched on, some with helplessness, some with outright horror. Each wondering who might be next to succumb. "But I won't forgive myself . . . so you're just going to have to shoot me."

Eyes still on Sinair's, she reached for her own shrieker.

Sinair's brow creased. Her finger tightened on her trigger.

She grunted and fell forward, eyes glassy, as the pommel of Rîma's sword cracked into the back of her skull, just behind the ear.

Kat lowered Sinair to the ground as gently as she could. So much for saving everyone. To die for the cause was one thing. Living to unwillingly betray it was something else. "You had to wait for the dramatic entrance, didn't you?"

Rîma scabbarded her sword. "You'll have to leave her."

Kat grimaced. "I know."

She steeled herself against heartache that begged her to indulge the familiar, hopeless dream that there was some way to bring Sinair to her senses. To rescue her friend from the madness that had claimed so many of those she loved. She'd wasted fruitless months on that dream. It had nearly killed her twice. But once the Eternity Queen had you, there was no coming back.

"Stars Below . . ." a custodian breathed further along the barricade.

The tunnel was no longer empty, but filled with a press of scarlet cloaks about a slender golden-gowned figure. Kat's heart sank another notch. Even at a distance – even gilded in regal finery and bedecked with gemstones – there was no mistaking that woman, whose black hair and bronze complexion were so alike to her own that in another life strangers had mistaken them for sisters. Khalad knew her as the Eternity Queen. Tyzanta had hated her as Yennika Bascari. But to Kat, who'd loved her more than life itself, she'd always be Azra. The false goddess Nyssa's first victim, and the vessel through which her ancient, malevolent spirit bent the mortal world to tyranny.

"Katija?" The Eternity Queen's voice echoed along the tunnel. "I know that's you down there. It's over, but it needn't be unpleasant."

Bad enough that she still looked like Azra. Worse that she sounded like her too, even at a distance. The languid self-assurance that bewitched or revulsed according to her mood.

But she wasn't her, not really. Azra was gone.

"Go!" snapped Kat.

The custodians raced back along the platform. Rîma, predictably, did not. Instead, she joined Kat at the barricade and regarded the scores of marching custodians with her customary calm.

"I confess, I worry about what you intend," she murmured.

As do I, breathed the Eternity King, rather more acidly. *Azra is not yours to save.*

"I know," Kat replied, the act of choosing her words to satisfy two parties – one of whom couldn't hear the other – having become second nature. The redcloaks didn't matter any longer. Even at a flat run they'd not reach the railrunner in time. But every step the Eternity Queen took increased the possibility of her seductive presence touching on the crowded carriages. And if that happened . . .

Barely bothering to aim – at that distance, it hardly mattered – Kat brought up her shrieker and fired a volley. Shots screamed along the tunnel, the echoes deafening in their backwash. Fire flared briefly against walls, roof and flagstones, filling the tunnel with dust and rubble. A single redcloak pitched forward, his cloak ablaze.

The column shuddered to a halt, its rear ranks retreating as they ushered the resisting Eternity Queen back towards the smoke-wreathed sky and out of range. Kat indulged a sharp smile. Thralls or willing servants, the redcloaks were the Royal Guard, with a bodyguard's duties and instincts – especially with the bodies of their vanguard littering the barricade approach.

The railrunner's whistle wailed three short blasts. Metal shrieked as gears bit and wheels shuddered to motion. With the yawning rumble of a slumbering giant rousing to wakefulness, the railrunner pulled away, the folk on its rooftops silhouetted against the roiling steam.

"Time to leave," said Kat.

With a last, unspoken apology to the unconscious Sinair, she turned her back to the tunnel and ran headlong for the departing railrunner.

Rîma overtook her without obvious effort. She leapt gracefully onto the stoop of the rearmost carriage and swung herself over its guardrail in a swirl of coat tails.

Pushing trembling legs to one last effort, Kat launched herself at the stoop moments before the railrunner left the platform behind. Rîma grabbed her by the wrists and hauled her unceremoniously aboard.

By the time Kat righted herself, they were beneath open skies. The slums of Undertown rushed past, the railrunner's acceleration banishing the glass and steel arch of Manniqa Station's roof to the middle distance. She barely noticed the sleek, scorched hull of the *Sadia's Revenge* swoop in from the south, pockmarked sails furling as she matched the overburdened railrunner's speed. Kat had eyes only for the burning city, and the black-sailed warships circling its ramshackle smoke-wreathed spire.

Tyzanta, last and greatest of the free cities, and everyone in it, now belonged to the Eternity Queen.

"This wasn't your fault," murmured Rîma.

Kat gripped the guardrail until her knuckles ached. "I know."

But as the city outskirts yielded to the arid red plains and black pine forests of the Zaruan lowlands, all she could think was that Vallant would have handled things better.

Two

"Nearly done. Just hold that grip-heel steady. I don't want my nose burned off."

Mirzai glanced down through the ladder's bowing, sun-bleached rungs. Tarin stood fifteen feet below, his grip-heel spanner wedged between the spokes of the governor valve's flywheel. For all that Mirzai loved his nephew like a son, the boy was reaching that difficult age where boredom and longing transmuted vital instructions into easily dismissed suggestions.

"Stop fussing," the fifteen-year-old called back. He'd inherited his waspishness from his mother, alongside the thick black hair cut short to hide its curl, and angular features that would have been the envy of any fireblood. "I know what I'm doing."

Mirzai stifled a smile. There were times when it felt as though Midria was still with them, speaking through her son. She'd never suffered fools gladly, and seldom laid eyes on a bigger fool than her younger brother. She'd have been unbearable but for the generosity her sharp tongue concealed. The reminder that Tarin was very much his mother's son was always welcome. They were the only family either had left.

But whether Tarin or Midria's departed spirit appreciated it or not, it was better not to take chances. The corroded pipe was a part of a feedline covered by a dilapidated planked roof and suspended above the ruddy plains in a tangled wood-and-steel trestle. It drew unprocessed vapours from the valley bore-rigs to feed the hungry refinery on the edge of town. Making a mistake on the *other* side of the refinery was costly – every breath of the precious eliathros gas that wisped into the winds was one that couldn't fill a skyship's buoyancy tanks – but all manner of mingled vapours churned within the feedline, blackfire damp among them. If Tarin's grip slipped – if the greased cork lining the sealant valve had begun to decay – then one spark would do more than burn off Mirzai's nose.

There was a reason the refinery was half a mile outside town.

Mirzai peered at the damaged section, which belonged to one of five pipes borne by the trestle. It was already a patch job in a superannuated system: one of three segments – each roughly the length and girth of Mirzai's stocky forearm, their ochre paint long since scratched and scored by the ruddy grit blown off the hills – that had replaced a much longer section at some point in the past. Just as well, because replacing a fully sized pipe would have needed six pairs of hands and a block-and-tackle to hoist the new section into place. The point of failure itself was a hairline crack along the pipe's upper slope. Just enough for the gases to seep away. Harmless enough to start with, will barely a whiff of dropped pressure showing on the dials to rouse worries. But so many things were harmless enough to *start* with.

With a last check that the ladder was secure, Mirzai reached through the tangle of pipes and support struts and groped blindly to connect his own grip-heel with the bolts securing the damaged pipe to its neighbour.

Neglected and battered by the elements – on the rare occasions the rainstorms of the Mistrali swept across Araq's hills, they did so with all the fury of an uninvited guest – the bolt refused to budge.

"Skrelling thing," muttered Mirzai. Even in late afternoon, the heat was punishing. He wiped calloused fingers across his sweaty brow and smoothed back his thick black hair to keep it from falling into his eyes. His hand was already filthy from hitching the replacement pipe in its rope slings above the damaged section.

14

Sliding his feet to the edges of the ladder's rungs, he looped his left forearm up and over the trestle's nearest strut and braced his right palm on the spanner's leather-wrapped heel, the better to put his weight into the next attempt. With a screeching, crackling sigh, the bolt gave to the tune of a quarter-turn. Flakes of rust trickled to the sun-bleached grass a dozen feet below, setting a startled mouse to flight.

The next bolt required the same persuasion, but the four that followed had clearly learned from their peers and surrendered without a fight. Ever alert for the telltale hiss and bitter odour of escaping blackfire damp, Mirzai loosened each in turn then shifted his attention to the pipe's far end. When these too were defeated, he worked the pipe through the gaps between its neighbours. It vanished into the grass with a rustle and a muffled *thump*.

Mirzai's nostrils rankled at the scent of blackfire damp. His heart skipped, but it was a wisp only, soon smothered by the bitter juniper borne down from the hills.

"You all right up there?" called Tarin.

"Just you worry about that valve." Mirzai winced, knowing he'd spoken too harshly. "Blackfire damp trapped in the seal, that's all. It happens."

"Any idea what caused it? Soiled alloy, maybe?"

Mirzai smiled at the hint of excitement. Soiled alloy meant that some greater force – greed maybe, or incompetence – lay behind the damage. Something Araq's custodians could pursue and punish. Much more interesting than the dull truth that maintenance was a long, tedious and necessary labour that never ended.

"Not this time. The metal's expanded and cooled once too often. Every inch of this line's seen better days."

"Like you?"

Mirzai ignored the jibe. Though he was barely into his mid thirties, that still left a ravine twenty years wide between them. Sometimes it simply wasn't for crossing. "I'll talk to Saheen about getting a crew up here to repaint it and fix the roof." Of the dozen or so planks that should have shaded his section of the feedline, most were sagging and three were missing entirely. Not a lot of use for fending off sun or rain.

Tarin snorted. "Like she'll pay for that. Cheaper to keep sending us to bake up here."

"Like I said, I'll talk to her."

Araq's overseer was famously tight-fisted – and necessarily so, given how few dinars there were to go around. But she was also a good woman and smart enough to know that no amount of patchwork would keep the feedline running for ever. No working feedline, no eliathros. No eliathros, and there'd be no coin in Araq at all.

Ignoring the sweat trickling between his shoulder blades, Mirzai set to work loosing the replacement pipe's rope slings a little at a time, always careful to never let it slope more than a dozen degrees out of horizontal lest it slide free entirely. The last thing he wanted was to winch the wretched thing back up again. Soon it was snug in place, and all that remained was to tighten the bolts . . . and hope the new pipe held better than the last.

He sang softly to himself as his hands fell into familiar patterns, the rhythm of the grip-heel's bite and swivel matching that of the song.

"*Thene voli ana meirionanna, nye. Ayin. Ayin.*"

The soft, sorrowful notes of the lullaby learned at his grandfather's knee were rendered more mournful still by a tin ear. Still, it seemed to him more beautiful than the blunt Daric tongue he used in conversation – even if he wasn't entirely certain what the words actually *meant*.

"*Thene allithara kene naranma, nye. Ayin. Ayin.*"

A prayer for better tomorrows, his grandfather had called it. More important to Mirzai was that it was a piece of his family's past not yet abandoned, stolen or given away. Perhaps the only piece, save for the silver and red-gold serpent pendant hidden beneath his shirt. Also his grandfather's, and like the song an inheritance that stretched back further than years could count.

"*Aethari myan te couri voreen. Ayin. Ayin.*"

16

He tightened each bolt in turn, the prickle of sweat and the afternoon heat lost in the quiet satisfaction of a job worth doing done well.

"Tell me you're almost finished," called Tarin. "It's bad enough that I'm melting out here without listening to that tuneless racket."

His good-natured tone couldn't quite hide resentment. He was bored again, most likely. Mirzai supposed he himself had been easily bored at that age, though he scarcely recalled. Life before Araq had been exciting for all the wrong reasons. "If you've no taste for engineering, they can always use more bodies in the mines."

Tarin snorted. "Better to get out of this place. Head west to Kaldos, maybe."

"Araq's been good to us."

"Araq's a silt-hole. In Kaldos they have ifriti to heat the water and light the dark. They have torch houses to keep the mists out, not a rickety torch fence that's always falling apart. Everything's always falling apart around here."

"If everything worked, they'd not need us." Proper engineers didn't come out as far as Araq and its humble comforts. "And you wouldn't like it in Kaldos. They have proper custodians there. You'll not run rings round them as easily as you do Saheen's geriatrics."

Even with his eyes still on his work, Mirzai heard Tarin's flinch. "I didn't have anything to do with what happened at Nyzanshar."

Mirzai's ears pricked up. Nyzanshar was a ruined fortress north of the town. In years long past, it had served as a toll house of sorts and a staging area for Kaldosi soldiers tasked with keeping the Qersali on their side of the hills. Nowadays, Nyzanshar's glories – like even the idea of an independent Kaldos – lay long in the past. It was just a crumbling sandstone relic, gusting further into history with every breath of wind. Only lately someone had felled the statue of stern Nyssa Iudexas that had stood guard over its collapsed barbican. Mirzai had put it down to simple erosion. Others blamed the Qersali, or Vallant's rebels – though why they should bother with a broken-down fortress like Nyzanshar, no one knew. Now another explanation beckoned.

Mirzai reached for the next bolt. "Uh-huh."

"Badran wanted me to go along. I turned him down."

"Uh-huh."

"Will you stop that?"

"Uh-huh."

"Fine. Name one person who says they saw me up there."

Even without the defensive tone of voice, the words were as good as a confession. Mirzai wrestled his grip-heel free of the trestle's tangle and sighed. "You want to go bashing lumps out of old statues, knock yourself out. I just wish you'd be careful. That place is a deathtrap, even before the mists come down."

"We had blesswood with us. We'd have been safe."

And there it was, the tacit admission. Knowing Badran, who was as shiftless a layabout as anyone Mirzai had ever met, the blesswood was likely stolen. Then again, Archon Serassa was a miserly old bag of bones who doled the precious timber out as meanly as good manners permitted. No tears there, not if the alternative was tragedy. Araq was right on the edge of Khalad, the billowing greenish-white of the Veil seldom more than a few dozen leagues from the town's eastern boundary. When the Aurora Eternis shone and the mists rushed in? Well, Nyssa help anyone not sheltering in the light of blesswood's magenta flames. Linger too long behind the Veil and the mists wore you away, body and soul.

More than that, Nyzanshar was perilously close to the fluid border with Qersal.

"And we weren't knocking lumps out of statues," said Tarin. "We were looking for the cloud qori."

Another bolt bit. Mirzai leaned into the grip-heel's handle to make it fast. "I've warned you about chasing scuttle-tales."

"She's real. Badran saw her up there, two Situsdirs back. That's why we had the blesswood. We were going to banish her."

"You can't even repeat the Drowned Lady's prayer without stumbling. Try exorcising a daemon and it'll have you for a snack." Not that a cloud qori was much of a daemon. Just a wailing, pathetic thing half

18

claimed by the mist. "Stick to fleecing your friends at skelder's whist." Tarin fancied himself something of a card sharp, and had a quick enough hand and eye to back the claim.

"You know Jedrah went missing up there. Aethri runs the same path taking provisions to the mine." Bravado just about won out over petulance. "I wanted her to be safe."

"Uh-huh."

A noble goal, if brashly pursued. Tarin had been trying to impress Aethri Talavi for weeks. Nice girl, once she scrubbed away the miner's grime. It probably had been about keeping her safe more than drawing her eye. Well . . . maybe a bit of the latter.

Better Tarin *had* been vandalising the fortress. That was the problem with the Veil: it offered a dreadful fascination. More likely Badran had seen a gloami wisp dancing on an unmarked grave. Araq's hills had had their share of bloodshed, which meant bad memories and unhappy souls. So close to the Veil, nightmares had lease.

Assuming he had seen anything at all, of course. "Badran's a shîm-head who'll say anything to drag you into his nonsense."

"I know better than to touch isshîm."

A tangent, but earnest enough that it was probably truth. "So that wasn't you I saw sneaking out of Qorral's place two nights back?"

"He had talent wisps of Aya Nazîd." Talent wisps were part of the swirl of spirit stuff the deceased left behind. Imbibing one let you embrace their skills and experiences for a time. Unchecked, they were as addictive as isshîm. "Aethri wanted to try one, but you know what her mother's like. She'd have gone berserk knowing she'd even spoken to Qorral."

Mirzai gave the last bolt a vicious twist and tried not to imagine Qorral's neck in the spanner's grips. "A woman of good sense."

"Qorral's not so bad."

"He's a parasite."

Everything bad in Araq began and ended with Qorral, who was likely the font of Tarin's tales of Kaldos and its bright lights, hot baths and myriad other pleasures. He ran the only courier service worth using, even though tales were rife that he read every letter that passed through his hands. He'd have been run out of town long before if not for the fact that he could get pretty much anything if you had the dinars. Talent wisps, last breath to spirit injuries away, tessence for birthday rituals, all of them common enough back west, closer to Zariqaz and the shores of the Silent Sea. Very little was common on the eastern border. Stars Below, but even the railrunner lines ended a dozen leagues to the west. Araq simply wasn't worth the trouble.

And yet the border brought freedom you couldn't find elsewhere. Rough comforts and occasional skirmishes with the Qersali were better than being under a fireblood's heel. No protection levies. No politics. No rebels. No redcloaks. A balance of power that suited everyone. Redcloaks were never good news.

But it was proving harder and harder to convince Tarin, who spent ever more of his waking hours daydreaming of laughter, silks and an easy life.

Frustration added weight to the grip-heel's final turn. Enough to set the ladder wobbling. Mirzai steadied himself against the trestle and eased his spanner out from the tangle of pipes. "That should do it."

"Should?" grumbled Tarin, still prickly.

"If the river flows to fortune," Mirzai replied.

An innocuous phrase unless you knew better, it nudged Tarin's not-quite-scowl to an almost-smile. "So I should open the valve?"

"Slowly. Just in case."

Tarin set aside his grip-heel and set to work easing open the flywheel.

The pipe groaned as the pressure built. Mirzai clung to his ladder just a little tighter. A metallic rattle ran along the trestle from somewhere near the governor valve and vanished westward. But there was no hint of blackfire damp and no breathy, winding yawn to betray hidden stresses in the pipe. Just the woody scent of the juniper trees further up the hillside and the dull, muffled rush of a flow restored.

He slackened his grip and fought the urge to wipe his brow again.

There was always risk to working on the feedlines, the danger rumbling beneath the surface. Just like his life if he forgot himself and started humming his rifted version of his grandfather's songs around folk who might recognise them. Or if people noted that he was fasting at the wrong time of year.

Maybe Tarin was right and they should move on. Perhaps not to Kaldos, but times were changing in Khalad. Supposedly an Eternity *Queen* now ruled in Zariqaz – unthinkable though that was after millennia of Caradan Diar's sole rule. Maybe history really did now belong to the past, old prejudices forgotten.

"What was it like?" he asked. "The talent wisp, I mean."

Tarin frowned, suspicious of chastisement. "I never said I tried it."

"You didn't have to." Tarin wasn't so blind to Qorral's failings that he'd have let Aethri imbibe a black-market talent wisp without precaution – the lad had the makings of an honourable man. Even if the wisp *had* been from Aya Nazîd, there was no telling just what other aspects of the legendary songstress had crept through with her talent.

Tarin's lip twisted at the reminder that his thoughts weren't always as private as he'd like. "I don't remember much. The colours were different, somehow. There was a tune in every rock and tree, but I couldn't quite reach it. I can sort of hear it even now. Nazîd must have been brilliant."

Mirzai grunted. "So I'm told."

He fought a hot swell of jealousy and cursed himself for even asking in the first place. Give him a mechanism and a span of moments and he'd see how to repair it or shatter it beyond recovery, because one was just the mirror of the other. Practical skills. Valuable enough that no one in Araq had ever enquired too closely about his past. But the intangible artistry of word, music or paint? It was another world. One Mirzai knew he'd never touch. He didn't resent it overmuch, and was grateful that the Drowned Lady had granted him any gift at all, but still . . .

Maybe the echo of Aya Nazîd could have unpicked the puzzle of his grandfather's lullaby, helped show him how to render the words with the beauty he remembered but could not imitate. Wouldn't that be something?

Now who was daydreaming?

The shadow was the only warning, and even that came too late.

The dhow swept in from sunward skies, so low that its scarlet keel passed within twenty yards of the feedline's trestle, close enough to set it clattering and rouse clouds of ruddy dust from the dry, rustling grasses. Mirzai snatched a glimpse of a sun-rimmed silhouette well out of trim, its port side dipping to give the deck a rakish angle.

Tarin spluttered and coughed as the dust overtook him. "What the ...?"

The ladder trembled as the backwash caught it.

Mirzai dropped the spanner and grabbed at the shuddering trestle just as the ladder slid sideways. His shoulders screamed a red wail as they took his weight. He hung, spluttering through mouthfuls of dust as the shadow passed, and prayed for the trestle to hold.

"Uncle!"

Forearm braced against the dust storm, Tarin scrambled towards the fallen ladder.

Mirzai clung on for dear life. He'd *probably* survive a fifteen-foot drop onto baked earth, but not with all his bones in the same number of pieces they'd started out.

Seconds scraped by like years before Tarin had the ladder upright again.

Another seeming decade passed before its uprights thumped against the trestle.

Mirzai hooked a foot around the ladder, then shimmied, hand over aching hand, along the trestle until he'd both feet and trembling legs secure. Moments later he had the baked soil of the plain firmly under his boots, and was glad of it.

Tarin, his simple green robes now mottled red with dust, stared away north towards Araq and the gradually shrinking silhouette of the distant dhow.

"That was a redcloak ship, wasn't it?"

"Straight out of the Deadwinds too." Shimmering aethersails billowed along the dhow's otherwise sleek flanks, worthless when it came to capturing the thin winds of the Araq plains, but vital for harnessing the vortex of swirling souls that crowned the skies above the Cloudsea.

"Heading into Araq?"

Mirzai shivered at the excitement in Tarin's voice. "I can't think where else they'd be going."

He couldn't blame the lad. It had been years since anything other than a blocky haulage carrack had put in to Araq's quayside. A redcloak dhow was something else – the sleek perfection of a skyship, gilded and gleaming, burst straight from Tarin's daydreams of a civilised, comfortable life.

Only in Mirzai's experience nothing stayed civilised when redcloaks were involved. In all the years he'd lived in Araq, he'd only ever seen one, and Eri Gallar had been retired so long she barely counted.

The winds were changing. Already the town felt less like home.

He pressed a hand against his chest, to feel the cold, hard pressure of his grandfather's pendant against his skin. "Help me get the ladder folded up. I want to see what all this is about."

Three

Araq wasn't much of a town, even as things were reckoned on Khalad's border. Barely a hundred weathered adobe buildings clustered about the sagging, wind-smoothed columns of the Alabastran temple. The tarnished golden statue of Nyssa Benevolas, her cracked skirts reddened by plains-dust that eddied and swirled through the tight alleyways, beheld it all with an eroded smile owing more to weariness than joy.

As Mirzai made his way to the overseer's mansion, he noted that the streets were emptier than usual. Those still travelling to and fro did so with downcast eyes, or offered furtive glances towards the elevated quay and the twin black masts of the redcloak dhow. Only the children seemed oblivious, playing hop-stone and quarrelling over everything and nothing as they always did until a tug on the ear dragged them back to lessons or chores. To them *redcloak* was only a word.

What was Saheen thinking? Did two decades of independence count for nothing?

Frustration began the long smoulder to anger as Mirzai crossed the low bridge at the centre of town. With his muscles aching from hillside labours and skin prickling from a long walk taken at haste in the heat of the afternoon, calm was an elusive companion.

Likenesses and scribbled particulars of ne'er-do-wells stared down from the bounty board at the mansion gate, each with a value tallied in dinars or tetrams according to notoriety. Wasted effort in Araq, whose slender comforts even fugitives avoided. Some posters had faded to match the long since dwindled reputations of their subjects. Others were fresh and dark, Bashar Vallant's latest amongst them. Ten thousand gold tetrams was a fortune in anyone's world, and a bloodgild tally exponentially grander than those of the ox-thieves, swindlers and brigands crowding the boards. It was challenged only by one other: a thin-faced woman with long black hair and noted as having hazel eyes. Katija Arvish – whose name was as unfamiliar to Mirzai as Vallant's was unmistakable – was worth seven thousand tetrams. Either one could have transformed Araq's fortunes.

The custodian at the mansion gate made a semblance of standing to attention.

"Is she in?" Mirzai growled.

Oshur nodded, his posture conveying unhappiness that his androgynous *vahla* mask concealed. Younger than most of his peers by three decades, he wanted to be liked more than a custodian should. He stepped aside, the trailing cloth of his black robes picking up a fresh patina of dust from the flagstoned path. "Tread carefully."

Mirzai stalked on, shoulders brushing waxy leaves and the feral tangle of black and white blooms spilling over the slatted fences to either side. Protocol should have insisted that Oshur accompany him, but protocol seldom held sway in a town small enough to be governed by a cinderblood overseer and not some fireblood noble – much less one whose grounds doubled as remembrance gardens for want of another patch of soil where the picky mandevillas would take root.

Besides, old comrades commanded latitude. They were also *supposed* to be afforded the benefit of the doubt, so Mirzai made a fresh effort to shackle his rising anger.

As was so often the case, the result was little to his liking. Thus his opening of the office door was more aggressive than was proper and his tone far short of politeness.

"You want to tell me what's going on, Saheen?"

The overseer turned from the crooked window, straight back and gloved hands loosely clasped at the base of her spine shaping the ideal deportment for a woman of her rank. But like the décor of the office, her clothes fell short. Both were too worn, the varnish on desk and wood panelling cracked and faded, the drapes tattered by moths despite sprigs of lavender bagged beneath the pelmets. What should have been the austere silver-chased black of her robes edged ever towards grey. Only her gloves, worn more to keep a barrier between herself and others than for comfort, retained any lustre.

She was harder and leaner than when they'd first met, growing responsibilities having chiselled the woman of today from the rough stone of her past self. Too many folk had underestimated her in those younger days, lost in green eyes that seemed all the brighter for the contrast with her rich dark brown skin and the tight black corkscrew spirals of her hair. But even back then those eyes had missed nothing. Nowadays they'd a knack for cowing those who earned her displeasure. But Mirzai had known her too long for that – long enough that the pang he felt so often in her company couldn't even really be described as regret any more. Some things just weren't meant to be.

"Mirzai?" For all that Saheen strove to look the part of a western overseer, her voice held no such pretensions. Though it was more gravelly these days, her fluid accent belonged to the border. "I thought you were out repairing the feedline."

"I was . . . until some reckless *jotri* knocked me clean off my ladder." He stepped deeper into the room, past the screen of the open door.

"I'm afraid I am the reckless *jotri* in question." The moustachioed redcloak *gansalar* stood at the room's far end, his back to the marble statue of some long-dead soldier that Saheen had rescued from the rubble of Nyzanshar soon after claiming the overseer's title. A vision in tailored scarlet and gold silks, he was about as out of place in that office as it was possible to be, his effortless decorum highlighting Saheen's for the imitation it was. Greying hair spoke to a man of middle years. The cut of his uniform to the wealth of a fireblood lineage. "We were patrolling to the south when one of the *Majestic*'s buoyancy tanks gave way. It made for quite the experience."

Mirzai grunted at the non-apology. "I'm sure." Buoyancy tanks were carefully balanced in order to *just* counteract a skyship's mass. If the ship was sailing swiftly enough, a small leak could be managed almost indefinitely through careful use of the pitching rudders. The bigger the hole, the faster things got messy. "So you're here for repairs?"

"Overseer Avaya assured us it wouldn't be a problem." The *gansalar*'s tanned cheeks twitched in a smile that didn't quite touch his eyes. The sort that the higher orders deployed when they felt they weren't receiving proper deference but deigned not to make an issue of it. "I'm sorry . . . I didn't catch your name."

"Mirzai. Mirzai Tzelda," Saheen put in. "He keeps most of Araq running."

The *gansalar* twitched an eyebrow. "Ah, an engineer?"

"Of sorts," Mirzai replied, reluctant to cede even worthless territory.

"From what I've seen of this town, you must be very busy indeed." The *gansalar* offered a shallow bow from the neck. "Gansalar Kard Shorza. I have the good fortune to captain the *Majestic* . . . though given its current state, I suppose that's a small enough honour." A wry smile accompanied those final words, the calculated self-deprecation of a proud man attempting humility.

Mirzai fought to stop a scowl spreading across his face. "Patrolling to the south? This close to the border, that means Qersali territory."

"There is no border." Shorza's urbane mask remained fixed in place, but his tone darkened. "The Eternity King brought Qersal into Khalad some time ago. The Eternity Queen wishes to remind the Qersali of that."

Saheen twitched, perhaps recalling kith and kin who'd sacrificed their lives to ensure there even *was* a border so far south and east; the screams and blood that had haunted the nights before an uneasy truce of coexistence. Too late to save Mirzai's sister Midria, who'd lost too much blood to Qersali arrows for even last breath to save her. Hers was just one of the many graves dotting the stony hillside above the town.

Mirzai offered a wordless prayer to the Drowned Lady and put his sister from his thoughts. "We don't want any part in your war. We have peace. That's enough."

"The *Eternity Queen*'s war," Shorza corrected smoothly, his equable gaze touching on Saheen, "which makes it your war as well. You've been allowed to stray, but you're still her subjects."

Saheen's cheek tightened. Just a little and just for a moment – a subtle enough gesture, but to Mirzai it was practically a scream. "That we are."

"Indeed." Shorza nodded. "And it might just be that you deserve better than unsteady peace with the zol'tayah's bandits. In any case, I have my orders . . . and I believe our business is concluded, overseer?"

"Of course," said Saheen. "I will make the arrangements."

"Then I shan't take up any more of your valuable time." Shorza's eyes touched on Mirzai's once more. "I'm sure you've much to discuss."

With a final crisp nod, he departed. Saheen sank against the windowsill, her shoulders sagging.

"Nice snake," said Mirzai. "Very shiny scales."

"He would be horrified to hear you say that." Saheen offered a weary smile. "He believes that he is charming."

"Most snakes do." Mirzai willed his muscles to unknot. With little success. "Just one more reason not to give them the time of day."

She glared. "What would you have me do, Mirzai?"

"Buoyancy tanks don't just 'give way'. Shorza only needs repairs because he picked a fight with the Qersali," Mirzai growled. "Do you really want us involved in that?"

Saheen pursed her lips. "The Qersali are on the other side of the valley. Shorza is right here, now." Her eyes hardened. "What am I supposed to do if he dispenses with charm and sends his redcloaks to take what we won't sell? Kill them?"

He met her gaze, his terse reply made harsher by old memories. "Maybe. Blood and freedom. We stand together or we stand for nothing, remember?"

Her eyes tightened at the oath, once shared by those of them old enough to remember what it had cost them to win peace with the Qersali: bitter nights filled with slaughter; mornings spent digging dead comrades from the charred embers of houses set alight by raiders. Back then, she'd spoken the words more often than he could count, a bottle raised in triumph or farewell. But those days lay long in the past, before the overseer's uniform had set her apart from her fellows.

Parted lips gathered to a scowl across gritted teeth. The silk of Saheen's gloves shifted as she gripped the windowsill. She could only be pushed so far. So could he. It was part of what had brought them together. And what had ultimately driven them apart. Someone had to lead Araq, and Saheen was no good at putting that part of her aside in quieter moments, just as Mirzai knew himself to be a terrible follower when loyalty was the only spur. On this occasion, however, Saheen's scowl faded into weary empathy. The storm blew itself out before thunder sounded.

"I suppose I cannot blame you for thinking that way. I would in your place." She was one of the few who knew enough of Mirzai's past to say such a thing and know what it truly meant. "See it from my side. Say I refuse repairs and Shorza forces the issue . . . even if I call up the militia to back my custodians, that's fifty blades. Most of them weary from a shift in the mines."

Mirzai shrugged, not yet ready to yield the point. "A ship that size runs mostly on motic ifrîti. Shorza has maybe a dozen crew. A score at the most."

"Even if it's only a dozen, they're rested. They have shriekers." She shook her head. "And if we do drive them off? That will not be the end of it. More redcloaks will come, and not to bargain."

"If the Eternity Queen's turning her eye to Qersal, these redcloaks won't be the last whatever we do," he replied bitterly. "What happens next time? What happens when they've gone into the Cloudsea and the Qersali blame us for what they've done? You don't get your buoyancy tanks holed for bringing smiles and goodwill."

Saheen flinched. "I cannot deal in ifs, buts and maybes, Mirzai. In the here and now folk will get hurt if I don't give Shorza what he wants. At least this way we get paid."

"That's really all that matters to you, isn't it?"

"He is offering more than dinars." She paused. "A pyrasti prism. A vibrant one. You know what a difference that can make."

The town had scraped together the funds to supply the derelict torch house atop Giriqan – the highest of the encircling hills – the previous year. Unfortunately, the tower was a two-hour hike away on a good day, and too close to the makeshift Qersali border for anyone to feel comfortable making it their home. If a pyrasti prism was installed, the ifrît inside would keep the blesswood fires lit for weeks, maybe months. Months of Araq, Nyzanshar and the surrounding hills protected from the clutching mists of the Veil. Months of returning miners not clinging to the temperamental torch fence as they made their way back to town. Months of Araq's townsfolk not flinging scraps of blesswood into their hearths and wondering if the juniper-scented flames would linger long enough for the mists to recede.

"Just happened to have one to spare, did he?" asked Mirzai.

Saheen snorted. "Shorza strikes me as a man who likes his comforts. Probably he did not fancy a long patrol behind the border without something to keep the night chills at bay."

She pushed away from the window and drew closer. "We have always been practical. That's all this is."

She pressed her hand to Mirzai's, her skin warm against his. Somewhere along the line, she'd removed her gloves and she *hated* doing that. The intimacy – the trust – might have convinced, if not for the lingering suspicion that it sprang more from manipulation than comradeliness. "If we get the torch house alight, we can open up that second shaft at Rhymsfalt, maybe even convince someone to lay

30

railrunner tracks into the centre of town. You know what a difference that will make."

"All right," said Mirzai. "Just don't expect me to help out with the repairs."

"I wouldn't dare." Saheen didn't smile, but her voice held a hint of mirth. She withdrew her hand. "But I hoped you would see your way clear to installing the pyrasti. Tonight."

"Saheen . . . I don't know. It's no small trek out to the torch house, and the aurora has been shining every night this week." When the emerald sheen of the Aurora Eternis lit the skies, Mistfall was seldom far behind.

"That is why I am offering double the usual rate." Her eyes gleamed. "Once the pyrasti is in place, it will be that much harder for Shorza to go back on his word."

Lost in argument, it was too easy to forget that Saheen was nobody's fool. Likely Shorza hadn't parted with the pyrasti willingly. And the extra dinars wouldn't be unwelcome. "He paid in advance?"

"He did. Gallar has the pyrasti. She's expecting you."

"Am I really that predictable?"

Sensing her argument was won – again, Saheen was nobody's fool – she at last softened to a smile. "Only to me."

Gallar's tiny store seemed just another unassuming frontage on the dusty road between temple and quayside. It looked for all the world as though it had somehow extruded into being – mud brick, narrow windows and all – squeezed tight into the space between the town's ramshackle granary to its left and the back wall of Elondine's Rest to its right. Come nightfall, the tavern's revelry seeped through the walls, juddering the shelves and their thin stocks in time to the thump of heel and the gusto of sozzled song. But with evening an hour or two away and the miners still at their shift, it was a cool – if dusty – hideaway. A place for Araq's Elders to pass judgement on the thousand trifling annoyances the younger generations ushered into being through laxness or wilfulness.

"I understand you've a pyrasti for me," said Mirzai.

Gallar nodded. "Oshur said you'd be over."

She never quite looked as though she belonged in Araq. Though her service in the redcloaks lay long behind, she retained the watchful eyes and stiff posture of her past employment. It should have roused distrust, but ex-redcloak or not, Gallar was an honest woman and generous with both her time and her fading strength. Whenever a roof needed retiling or the boundary fence needed another inevitable patch to keep jackals at bay, she was always first to volunteer. "He said you and Saheen were shouting again."

Mirzai drew up beside the counter and exchanged nods with the time-worn members of Gallar's tiny audience, each ensconced in a creaking wooden chair and nursing a battered mug of feldir tea, the aroma of apple and honey almost stifling beneath the low roof.

Archon Serassa's robes were as dusty as the steps of her temple were pristine – she swept the latter with a passion that far eclipsed that which she brought to her sermons. Qaba should have been lending his sour appraisal to the dockworkers repairing the *Majestic*, but had likely delegated such responsibilities to his daughter, whose appreciation for toiling sweat-sheened bodies was not wholly professional. Tarin was notable not just for the fact that he was a good forty years younger than the other three, but because he'd been granted neither chair nor tea, and was left to idly riffle the cards of his pentassa deck with a shoulder propped against a wooden pillar. Some things in Gallar's store couldn't be bought. They were granted only through acceptance.

"Oshur's a liar," said Mirzai, who honestly couldn't remember if he *had* raised his voice.

Serassa notched a polite eyebrow. Qaba stared into his tea.

Gallar handed Mirzai a mug and hefted hers in salute. "Blood and freedom."

"Blood and freedom." Mirzai clinked his mug to hers.

Gallar planted her elbows on the counter and threaded calloused knuckles together. "So you *didn't* argue?" Her words, weighted down by the earthy syllables of the Zariqaz slums, made it clear that she already knew where the answer lay.

Tarin snorted. "Of course they did. If they're arguing they don't have to *talk*."

Mirzai shot his nephew an unfavourable look. More of Midria shining through her son. She'd always read him plainer than he'd liked. And even the *suggestion* of gossip was red meat to the elderly wolves of Gallar's cabal.

Fortunately, Tarin also proved his saviour by leaning a little too insouciantly against the shelves. The motion set a handful of brightly glazed Qeramasi jugs rattling, provoking a not-quite-glare from Gallar and a throaty chuckle from Qaba.

"Are you going to give me the prism or not?" said Mirzai.

Gallar slid a leather-wrapped bundle across the counter. "Here."

Mirzai unfolded it. The black prism glittered like gemstone in the light from the windows. He ran a fingertip across the uppermost plane, vertex to vertex, marvelling at the precision of the craftsmanship. What few ifrîti prisms found their way to Araq were scuffed and battered by decades of reuse as successive inhabitants faded to nothing. This one had the sheen of something brand new and fashioned for elegance as much as function.

"Nothing but the best for the Eternity Queen's Royal Guard," he murmured, the title – the very idea of succession – still strange.

"Sometimes." A shadow deepened the laughter lines about Gallar's eyes.

"Zariqaz-made," said Serassa, joining them at the counter. "The shriversmen in the capital are always competing for the honour of supplying the throne immortal."

Mirzai touched the prism again. For all its beauty, it felt like ordinary glass . . . but then it took a rare and sensitive soul to make any kind of connection with an ifrît. Even the most accomplished shriversmen struggled to do so once they were bound to their prisms. He wondered briefly who the donor had been. Some hot-blooded sort whose passion had burned bright enough to endure past death. What would his own soul have to offer when his time came? Hopefully nothing, so long as he didn't die indebted to Alabastra. Which was why, despite seldom attending services, he always made the expected contribution to the temple's collections so that Serassa would have no reason to make record of his name in her white ledger. Better to go to the Black River whole than as waning parts and pieces.

"Did Oshur say anything about any glyph?" he asked.

"It's uncured," Gallar replied, confirming that it didn't need a soul-glyph to activate it. "Just put it in place. One whiff of mist and self-preservation will do the rest."

Ifrîti faded faster than people once the mists took them. While the pyrasti in the prism couldn't be said to be entirely aware, it knew that its only hope of survival lay in setting blesswood alight.

"I didn't think redcloaks used uncured prisms," said Tarin.

"We ..." Gallar's pinched lips chased the words away. "*They* don't. Too easy to steal." By contrast, an ifrît trained to respond only to the proper soul-glyph was a potent resource to those who had the proper tattoo inked on their skin.

"And yet Gansalar Shorza came all this way with one," said Mirzai.

"Maybe things are changing." Qaba cracked a smile. "It's been a while since Gallar roamed the Cloudsea."

"Or Shorza came prepared to trade." Mirzai scowled, a truth itching just beyond reach. With care bordering on reverence, he folded the leather covering back into place. "Either way, it's not doing us any good down here. I'd better get it installed."

"We're going up to the torch house *now*?" Tarin grimaced, petulance and disappointment fighting to dominate his tone. "That'll take all night. Aethri's expecting to see me at shift's end."

"And she will," Mirzai replied. "I can manage alone."

Tarin sagged, a smile tugging at his lips. "Thank you, Uncle."

"Go on, get." Mirzai allowed a little malice into his tone. "Before I change my mind."

Chased along by dry chuckles from the members of Gallar's cabal, Tarin beat a hasty retreat from the store. Mirzai gathered up the pyrasti prism and stuffed it into his satchel.

"You're too soft on that boy," said Serassa.

Mirzai nodded. "I am. But Aethri's good for him, keeps him grounded. They could both do worse. He deserves a chance to belong somewhere." He spoke the last words softly, more to himself than to the others.

Raised voices sounded in the street outside, followed by a *crunch* of splintering timber. Already moving towards the door, Mirzai picked up his pace, his mind's eye envisaging all manner of trouble for Tarin to have blundered into. Araq had no dearth of short tempers when the sun was merciless.

Tarin was nowhere to be seen. Beyond the shadows cast by the store's red and white awning, its pulley tines down against the dirt road, rested Qorral's cargo rickshaw. Qorral himself stood close by, arguing furiously with a pair of redcloaks, one of whom was busy picking her way through the packages stacked on the rickshaw's cargo bed. One such package – a wooden crate – lay broken on the roadway.

"Get your hands off!" growled Qorral, his weaselly face pinched tight with anger.

"You want to run goods to the quayside, you get inspected," said the male redcloak, stony-faced. "That's how it works."

"Never worked that way before."

"There wasn't a ship of the Eternity Queen's fleet docked there before."

Mirzai grimaced, spared the need to intervene by the sight of two custodians approaching along the street with as close to haste as their kind ever managed in Araq. No tears for Qorral and his dubious wares, but still . . .

"This won't end well," murmured Gallar at his shoulder. "It never does."

"Shorza said he's just putting in for repairs," said Mirzai, wondering why he was defending the *gansalar*. Wishful thinking, he supposed.

Gallar grunted. "I'm sure he did. They always do."

"Don't tell me, tell Saheen."

"If she didn't harken to you, she'll not hear me out." She stared at the growing disturbance, old ghosts gathering at the corners of her eyes. "Batten down, my friend. It's going to get blowy."

Four

By the time Mirzai gathered his gear and set out on the long, winding path up Giriqan's craggy slopes, the sweltering day had faded to a cool ochre evening, shimmering with the green fire of Aurora Eternis. Nose wrinkling at the camphor that had almost, but not quite, held the moths at bay from his threadbare cloak, he made a brief detour through the overgrown graveyard. Remembrance garden mandevillas might not have flourished on the arid hillside, but the choking gorse conquered all. He cast about, but he was alone save for an incurious crow pecking at a patch of dust, and the soft efflorescence of gloami wisps clinging to the newer gravestones, and so eased his scimitar from its sheath. He tapped the flat of its blade twice on the crest of Midria's simple stone so that her soul might take notice, were it able.

"*Ayin vanna enna*, Midria." Like the lullaby, Mirzai had only the haziest grasp of the prayer's meaning. *Loss and loneliness tinged with regret.* A plea for the Drowned Lady to offer protection to those in need, be they living or dead, and to bring retribution on their oppressors. Sentiment strong enough to bridge the gap between those who remained and those long departed. Always assuming that the Drowned Lady had whisked Midria's soul to safety before gluttonous Nyssa had claimed it, of course. "Tarin's doing just fine. You'd be proud. You *are* proud, I hope."

He swallowed, awkward as always when speaking to a woman no

longer there. Never certain if he did so for her sake or for his. He glanced back down the hillside to the subdued sprawl of Araq's dusty streets, to the *Majestic* lying in its scaffolded cradle, tiny figures working to repair its harms.

"You'll always be with us, even if we have to leave you behind." The wind gusted, the Aurora Eternis seeming to dance in response. No night to linger, not with Mistfall in the offing. He pressed a hand to the reassuring lump of his serpent pendant, hidden safe beneath his shirt. "Blood and freedom, sister."

He left the graveyard and rejoined the winding path.

Like the Nyzanshar fortress, the torch house on the Giriqan's summit had been abandoned in an earlier Age of Fire. The trail of weather-worn sandstone wayshrines, each with its statue of Nyssa Benevolas and offerings of desiccated flowers and tarnished copper coins, was seldom frequented. With dinars in short supply, restoring the upper section's crumbling steps or replacing bridges washed away by the Mistrali rain-storms had been no one's priority ... nor had taming the encroaching black pine trees. Thus it made for a frustratingly uneven ascent, punctuated by scrambles across broken ground, splashing through fast-flowing streams and, of course, the embrace of the gorse, which tugged at Mirzai's clothes and skin whenever it found opportunity to do so.

The bleakness that had driven Mirzai to bid conditional farewell at his sister's grave dissipated with the thinning air. It helped that Araq and its unwanted guest were now lost behind a fold in the hill. There was only the warmth of a body in motion and the crunch of soil beneath his boots, driving him on. Giriqan was a simple physical challenge to be overcome, unhaunted by nameless doubts of what might or might not come to pass.

He sang softly to himself, the words of his grandfather's lullaby made jarred and breathless by the uneven ground. Other songs followed, these learned around campfires with comrades who'd become neighbours, a bottle of calvasîr or sour Kaldosi red passed around to celebrate victory and commemorate the dead.

An hour after leaving the graveyard, his muscles aching in just the right way, he reached the craggy sandstone expanse of Giriqan Ridge. Even with the skies faded to purpled greys, the vantage offered a clear view across the fat, lazy meander of the Rhymsfalt river far below and the gentle sweep of hills beyond. Half a dozen men and women leading a pair of pack mules picked their way along the opposite ridge, silhouettes against the last flame of the setting sun. No more than two hundred yards distant as the hawk soared, but considerably further for those who'd have to make passage of the steep-sided valley and its treacherous river. Not for nothing had the Rhymsfalt become the border between Araq and the Qersali.

Not that these particular Qersali sought to reopen old wounds. A war party would have borne more than a pair of spears and a single shoulder-strapped sword. A hand on his own scimitar's hilt – old habits died hard – Mirzai raised the other and bellowed out a greeting. "*Ahada adahl!*"

Fortune be with you, ran the phrase when translated from Qersi to Daric, though he'd never learned if it referred to simple riches or a broader invocation of sympathetic fate.

Across the valley, a man peeled away from the shuffling convoy and offered a deep bow. "With you also," he shouted, in Daric. He raised his hand in mirror of Mirzai's own, then hurried to join his companions, leaving Mirzai relieved that whatever Gansalar Shorza had been up to over the border, it hadn't undone the hard-won peace. Better to trade greetings than arrows.

As grey skies slid into night, Mirzai lengthened his stride and drew his cloak tighter against the chill, letting aurora and starlight guide his steps as the gorse came alive with the chitter of insects and trilling nightjars.

As the torch house's slender white minaret – not sighted since leaving the graveyard –came into view atop the pine-choked crest, a vast black shape swept across the northern skies, sails unfurled as it climbed towards the Cloudsea. The dhow's silhouette swallowed the stars, displacing them with the yellow-orange pinpricks of lumani lanterns set along its flank.

A sigh gathered in the pit of Mirzai's chest and eased free into the night. Saheen must have roused half the town to get the redcloaks out of their collective hair before they became too comfortable. He'd worried over nothing.

He'd covered maybe half the remaining distance to the torch house, the patchwork dirt path finally giving way to flagstoned steps, when the smoky, bitter musk of the pines gave way to the scent of old memories, summoned up beneath starlight. The birdsong ceased, and the buzz of insects fell silent.

Mistfall.

Pulse quickening, Mirzai unslung his lantern from its haversack loops and worked at his tinderbox. The mix of oil and blesswood shavings in the lantern's reservoir caught light, the scent of jasmine and juniper rising to challenge the encroaching Veil.

The first skeins of mist showed beneath the trees, wending through the dry grasses. One breath, two, and the world drowned in luminescent greenish-white, the pines mere suggestions of shadow in the haze. Only where the magenta lanternlight ruled did the world have shape and substance.

Exhaling, Mirzai sifted through his haversack, double-checking that he had indeed packed a separate flask of oil and a waxed pouch of blesswood shavings. No matter how many times Mistfall caught him away from the hearth and from the bonfire Serassa routinely lit in the temple's portico – no matter how often he brought light of his own to bear against the hungry Veil – its onset was always a rush of ice through his veins. No one survived the mists, not for long. If he'd been too slow waking the lantern – if its fire faded now – then he'd have greater worries than the machinations of redcloaks.

That he wouldn't have those worries for long was hardly a comfort.

This time, at least, the Veil would be cheated of his thin soul. The lantern blazed merrily in his hand, and he'd both oil and blesswood to keep it fed for at least a day. Enough time to make the trip from the summit into town three times over, and all of it unnecessary as soon as he had the pyrasti in place. Assuming that the torch house's stocks of blesswood hadn't rotted.

With the torch house lost to sight, he trudged ever uphill, trusting to the path beneath his feet. His grandfather's lullaby came easily to his lips as he sought to keep unease at bay.

"Thene voli ana meirionanna, nye. Ayin. Ayin."

Skeins of mist roiled unhappily at the edge of the lanternlight, hissing into nothing where they strayed too close to the guttering flame. A shadow in the mists provoked a double-take, but it was just a way-shrine's spread-armed statue.

"Thene allithara kene naranma, nye. Ayin. Ayin."

The grasp of gorse, once annoying, was now a comfort. Worse was the silence, the myriad sounds of the waking world banished, all save those Mirzai brought himself: the scuff of boot on stone, breaths that were heavier and more hurried than he'd have liked ... a pulse more insistent than pride would admit. He wondered, not for the first time, if this was how ifrîti perceived existence beyond the cold, hard certainty of their prisms.

"Aethari myan te couri voreen. Ayin. Ay—"

A flagstoned step gave beneath his feet. Heart in his throat, Mirzai twisted as he fell. His quick thinking earned him a jarred elbow and the hot pulse of tomorrow's bruise on the outside of his left thigh, but it brought the lantern to a halt a foot clear of stone. "Too close," he muttered.

Indistinct shapes blurred and collapsed as the mist's currents took them, only to re-form.

Flexing his battered elbow, his good mood in full retreat, he started uphill.

Where was the wretched torch house anyway?

A wordless wisp of breathy song drifted up from somewhere downhill. A rich, honeyed voice, embittered by a minor key.

Catching his breath, Mirzai spun around, but caught no sight of the singer. Indeed, when the crunch of his booted feet faded, he no longer heard any trace of the song. If there had indeed been any such thing in the first place.

He turned this way and that, lantern aloft.

There was only the mist and the shadows of the trees. A scamper in the undergrowth too small to be anything of any threat.

Willing himself to breathe, he started uphill once more.

No sooner had he turned his back than the voice returned. "*Thene voli ana meirionanna, nye.*" She sang Mirzai's words back to him with a precision he'd never attained, every syllable thick with mockery and darker than sin. "*Ayin. Ayin.*"

Mirzai twisted on his heel and raised the lantern high. "Who's there?"

"*Thene allithara kene naranma, nye.*" The words grew darker still, beautiful with the promise of death. "*Ayin, ayin.*"

His blood cold, he put his free hand to his sword, recalling Tarin's tale of the Nyzanshar cloud qori. Tradition held that cloud qori were among the most harmless of daemons, mischievous at worst, luring the lost with soft words and laughter.

But then tradition also held that nothing – not mortal, nor daemon nor ifrît – could live in the mists.

The approximation of a mortal figure coalesced, recognisably neither male or female, not clearly defined nor wholly formless, the twitching strands of its long black hair streaming behind. Blood-red eyes burned.

Mirzai bolted for the torch house.

"*Aethari myan te couri voreen. Ayin. Ayin.*" The apparition's mocking song chased him on, effortlessly keeping pace.

The torch house's pockmarked walls parted the mists.

Heart pounding, Mirzai sprinted counterclockwise about the wall. He'd been part of the group who'd lugged blesswood up the hill the previous year, and the door had been solid enough then. If he could get inside and lock it shut, his pursuer could sing its heart out for all the good it might achieve.

Weathered stone yielded to sun-bleached timber. Mirzai fumbled the battered iron key from a pouch, set it to the lock and shoved at the door.

It shuddered and shrieked, the swollen timbers caught fast in the frame.

"*Finanar keli vess te couri lamal, cyanin, ayin.*" The unfamiliar words coiled out of the mist in continuation of a song the daemon knew better than Mirzai himself.

He set his back to the stubborn door and reached for his scimitar. Foolish to think a mortal blade could harm a daemon. Pathetic not to even make the attempt.

Distended, taloned fingers slashed through the mist.

Instinct raised Mirzai's lantern hand in self-defence. A blow meant for his throat instead shredded his shirtsleeve and sliced open his forearm. A hot rush of blood spattered his shirt and cloak, the roar of pain close behind. The lantern slipped from his numbed grip and shattered to dark fragments on a stone step. He caught the briefest glimpse of a cruel, haggard face, greyish and as bloodless as the mists, and fell backwards against the door. It burst open, pitching him into cobwebs and dust.

Thoughts thick with terror, he slammed the door shut, driving home deadbolts with enough force to bruise his good hand. The other hung nerveless at his side, his fingers clammy with cooling blood.

Skeins of mist no longer held at bay by lanternlight seeped in through the walls and oozed through the gaping floorboards like an ocean swell. Their gentle luminescence shaping broken crates and a wooden stair spiralling upwards towards the furnace and its fire platform.

Outside, the daemon's song gave way to a frustrated ululating screech.

Mirzai pinched his eyes shut. He was dead. Worse than dead, to be caught behind the Veil without a blesswood flame.

No. He wasn't dead yet. The daemon was trapped outside. And he still . . . He thrust his good hand into his haversack and closed his fingers around the leather-wrapped pyrasti prism. They'd stacked the furnace with blesswood last year. If it was still dry ...

Bring the fire, bring the light. The Veil would retreat. It might even take the daemon with it.

He bolted for the wooden stairway, cobwebs tugging at his clothes. A rotten step snapped beneath his foot, pitching him against the rope handrail of the outer stairway.

"Ammaro kevasta syella aro, ayin, ayin."

A greyish shape congealed upon the torch house threshold, fed by a flood of twitching, gauzy wisps and crowned by black hair writhing like serpents. Blood-red eyes fixed upon him.

Breath ragged in his throat, Mirzai took the steps three at a time, expecting claws in his back at any moment. He all but collapsed on reaching the floor of the furnace room and stumbled breathless towards the squat iron door. The oiled locking bar gave readily, revealing the furnace's charred interior. Baulks of blesswood sat counter-stacked across the small socket holding the ancient, long-faded pyrasti prism, the jasmine and juniper scent stifling in the confined space. Dry, thank the Drowned Lady, and begging for a flame.

"Tevalla kemorra salana teyo, ayin, ayin."

The daemon's mocking, bitter song ringing in his ears, Mirzai prised the dead prism from its socket and set the new one in place. In the moment he withdrew his hand he fancied that he felt a spark of warmth beneath the glass, a dry rolling chuckle on the edge of hearing.

The oil-soaked timbers caught light almost in the same moment he slammed the door, magenta and indigo flames licking at the base of the iron chimney that would usher them skyward. Already the mists were in full retreat, the greenish-white of the furnace room fading to magenta-tinged gloom.

Warned by an itch between his shoulder blades, he drew his scimitar and spun about.

The dull curve of steel swiped clean through the daemon's chest, the vapours of its being swirling cleanly apart only to re-form behind. It seized Mirzai's shoulders with taloned hands and bore him backwards against the furnace room's outer wall, the shock of impact driving the breath from his lungs and the sword from his grip.

It gazed into his eyes from inches away. The vaporous "skin" of its face ebbed and flowed, haggard cruelty melting to something softer, almost kindly, before malice returned. All hollow-cheeked hunger in one moment, revulsion in the next, magenta in the light of the furnace's inspection hatch. The rest of its body was the same, unshackled vapour coalescing to solidity, only to dissipate anew.

Only its grip remained unyielding.

"Please . . ." breathed Mirzai.

The pressure vanished from his left shoulder. A taloned hand lunged at his throat. He felt a tug at his neck and then the daemon was gone, shrinking away across the furnace room, no longer drifting like an untethered cloud but with uneven, stumbling steps. With a heart-wrenching wail, it sank to the floorboards.

Mirzai gulped down a breath and pressed his good hand to his clammy throat. It came away slick with sweat, not blood. His grand-father's serpent pendant was gone.

Still trembling, he stared at the daemon.

She – for the creature was now clearly a woman of early middle years, or at least woman-*shaped* – sat hunched in front of the furnace door, the vapour of her being drawn steadily inwards to seeming solidity. She rocked backwards and forwards on her haunches, breathing as fitfully as Mirzai, the leather thong of his pendant dangling between hands clasped tight to her chest. Her skin was no longer tinged grey, but the palest bluish-white. Unbound black hair glittered with the pinprick lights of captive stars.

The last dregs of Mirzai's terror receded into wonderment, for he knew her now – or he knew *what* she was.

"You're Issnaîm," he murmured, more to himself than her, "sent by the Drowned Lady."

Her eyes, their ruddy lustre faded to ice-white orbs bereft of iris or sclera, met Mirzai's. Her form rippled, and the final strands of mist flowed outward to become a close-fitting gown the colour of her skin. Haggard cheeks filled out to frame a heart-shaped face, its expression haunted by self-disgust.

"Sorry, am I. Couldn't control . . ." She pinched her eyes shut. "Help me. *Please*."

Pendant still clutched to her chest, she collapsed.

Five

Mirzai woke from murky dreams to a refrain of repeated hammering – Tarin's, by the cheery rhythm – on his front door. A second volley rang out before he lurched upright, swinging his feet out over the tiled floor, a chorus of aches and pains summoning up scattered memories of the preceding night.

The torch house. The Issnaîm. Had any of it been real? The bandages about his aching left wrist suggested so, as did the absence of the pendant from around his neck. He blinked blearily, sifting memories from dreams. A moment's peace, that was all he needed, just a—

The hammering sounded again, this time accompanied by a shout too cheery for the early hours. "Rise and roar, Uncle! Work to do."

Groaning, Mirzai pulled on a clean shirt, hauled the sash window open and flung apart the shutters. Light flooded in. Not the glow of dawn, but the bright sun of mid morning. Far to the west, beyond the town's boundary fence, beyond even the thin herd of sheep grazing Old Akiba's pasture lands, a sheen of greenish-white bridged the scorched-grass plains and the cloud-strewn skies. That and the scent of juniper and jasmine blowing down from Giriqan's slopes proved that the events at the torch house belonged to reality, not dreams. For the first time in who knew how long, the Veil had no purchase on Araq.

And if the torch house had been real, that meant that in his cellar . . .

It was suddenly *very* important to send Tarin on his way.

Mirzai propped his elbows on the windowsill and stared down at the path through the tiny, weed-strewn patch of scrub garden. "All right, keep it quiet. You'll wake the neighbours."

Unlikely. The nearest was a good quarter-mile down the dusty road. He'd selected the cottage for its isolation. Midria, preferring the bustle of streets, had demanded to know how he ever expected to fit in with the townsfolk if he were a stranger – a sentiment Tarin had readily echoed when he'd moved out the year before.

Tarin gazed up, his grin turning ashen. "What happened to you?"

Mirzai gingerly traced the outline of a bruise he didn't remember receiving. "Missed my footing on the way down Giriqan, didn't I?"

Tarin's grin returned. "Well, it was worth it. Saheen says she owes you a drink."

"I'll settle for the payment. What's this work that needs doing, anyway?"

"Quayside cargo elevator's thrown a cog. It's dinars to tetrams that Darashan's run the brake hot again."

"Sounds about right." The elevator that hauled trade goods and repair materials up to Araq's towering forty-foot-tall quayside was a simple crank-and-pulley machine, driven by an ageing motic – a rarity in the town. Slow, reliable and broadly idiot-proof though the system was, Darashan – the dock's chief foreman – was a better quality of idiot than the design permitted and notorious for using the emergency brake to "smooth out" the journey. "How urgent?"

"Enough that he's paying triple for the fix. A carrack's due in tomorrow, assuming it can dock. It leaving half empty cuts into the profits."

Mirzai frowned at his tone, which hinted at something unspoken. But he was too tired, his head too full of wool. Besides, he really *did* need to get rid of the boy. "Reckon you can handle it without me?"

Tarin brightened, surprised and pleased. "You're sure?"

"Are you?"

"If it's just a stripped gear."

"If it's not, come get me."

Tarin bobbed a nod, not quite managing to hide his proud smile. "As you say, Uncle . . . I'll even split the take with you. Get some sleep. You look like you need it."

"Thanks," Mirzai replied, his growl *mostly* for show. "Just try not to lose it all at the gaming table."

"I never do!"

Tarin offered a cheery wave and retreated down the street, the yew trees' mid-morning shadows tugging at his heels. Mirzai watched him a moment longer then withdrew inside. Entering the tiny wash chamber – the one room in the house he kept entirely pristine – he splashed the weariness from his eyes, pulled on a fresh robe and belted it tight. Belated morning ritual, practised a hundred, a thousand times. All save breakfast. Whether it contained wonder or horror, the cellar came first. He set his back to the traveller's chest that contained what few books he possessed and heaved it clear of the hatch.

Hand on the hatch's pull-ring, he hesitated. With sleep at last fully banished, he knew better than to mistake his trudge through the darkness for dreams, much less the burden borne during his descent. *Daemon*, he'd named her, then *Issnaîm*. Which awaited him?

He had to know.

The hatch came free with a rusty shriek, the disturbed air swirling dust to prickle his nose. Offering a last, hesitant glance at the sword belt hanging on its habitual hook beside the kitchen door – the weapon had done him no good during the night, so it was folly to expect otherwise now – he descended the broad, sagging steps.

The cellar lay heavily in shadow, not least Mirzai's own, lengthened to gangling proportions by the open hatchway. Here and there, golden shafts of light pierced the gloom at head and knee, infiltrators granted access by conspiracies of absent mortar and a sloping hillside. They touched upon strut and beam, set spiderweb and dancing dust shining silver . . . and at the cellar's back wall, where the deepest shadows lay, granted shape to slender gown-draped legs and bare feet the same bluish-white of recent memory.

"Thought you'd forgotten me, had I."

She leaned forward, fluid shadows retreating from a scowl. Though more solid than during the long, numbing stumble down Giriqan's slope, still she wisped and curled at the edges of her being, a daughter of mist in daylight as well as darkness. She'd been the slightest of burdens, never once stirring from unconsciousness.

She lifted her hands towards him, and the chains looped about her wrists went taut, straining at the eyebolt in the wall. "A kind host you are not, *ayin*." The soft mirth faded to sadness on her final word.

Mirzai fixed his eyes on the packed-dirt floor but stood his ground. A daemon might readily mimic the Issnaîm language – as she'd already echoed his song – to gain advantage. Besides, she'd plainly had freedom enough to reach the plate of food he'd left for her, which held only a few crumbs and a pair of stalks. A point against her being a daemon, as all tales agreed that such creatures didn't require mortal sustenance. Assuming, of course, that she hadn't simply hidden the food.

"I've learned to be a careful man," he replied, baring his bandaged forearm. "Especially when given reason."

"Where am I?"

Mirzai hesitated. "The town of Araq in the eastern reaches. My home."

"A prisoner, am I?"

"A guest ... I hope."

"An optimist," she replied wryly. "Why?"

"You begged me for help."

Her tone hardened. "Beg nothing of no one, do I ... Though had I done so, wonder why you showed me kindness, I might."

"Should I not? The Drowned Lady sent you to me."

She snorted. "Doubt that greatly, do I." The chains clinked gently as she leaned further forward. "Why won't you look at me? Am I not decent in my dress?"

Mirzai risked a surreptitious glance and stifled a gasp as her gauzy gown grew steadily more opaque, its scoop neck flowing upwards and narrowing to a tight frilled collar. Her starlight hair was a spill of oily smoke framing a heart-shaped face neither old nor young. Her lips crooked in the wisp of a smile.

"It's not respectful," he said, his eyes once more on the ground.

"*Waholi.*" She sighed, imbuing the word with aching contempt. "It's not respectful *not* to look at me."

"But you're Issnaîm."

"I know what I am." Brusqueness softened to curiosity. "How came you by the word?"

"My grandfather ..." Mirzai began haltingly, so used to keeping his family's past hidden that it flowed reluctantly even now. "*His* grandfather was at Anfai when the Drowned Lady sent your kind to offer us hope. The redcloaks marched from Kaldos to level our villages and salt our fields, to slaughter and scatter us. But my grandfather never once lost his faith. His dying breath was a prayer."

"I see." An unidentifiable note crept into her tone. "Do you have a name, grandson of a grandson?"

"Mirzai, *nasaîm.*" It felt strange to speak the secret language aloud.

"Zephyr, you may call me," she replied, "... but only if you look at me."

Still hesitant, he squared his shoulders and did so, meeting her glassy white stare for the first time.

"And now," she said with a wicked grin, "your soul is mine."

A cold fist closed about Mirzai's heart. A fool, a damned fool, and no one to blame but himself. He clamped his eyes shut and groped at the handrail for the cellar stairs, all the while knowing it was too late. He stumbled back, the lowest step taking him across the back of his calf and sprawling him unceremoniously.

Soft laughter danced through his self-imposed darkness.

"Mirzai ... Mirzai, a joke that was, nothing more." Zephyr's tone softened to something approaching chagrin. "Told in poor taste. I ... apologise."

He clung to the handrail, terror in retreat but uncertain whether to trust the Zephyr of that moment or the one of the moment before.

"I heard you singing, didn't I?" she said. "All else is nightmare, but that I remember. Sorrow of a lost home, and hope for the future. *Thene voli ana meirionanna, nye.*"

The familiar words soothed where reason had not. "My grandfather taught it me." Turning his back to the stairs once again, he risked looking upon her anew.

The corner of her mouth twitched in renewed apology, her otherworldly white eyes no longer cruel or mocking, but sad. "Drew me to you, it did. Lost in mist and hunger, was I, and still the words called to me."

"Nothing survives the mists."

"We do. *Akîa* gone and full of hunger, but we survive. Thinner and thinner, until there's nothing left worth the name. A brooch, I had, to hold me together. Lost it is. Lost to the mists." She stared down at her hands. Her voice, already soft, thinned to a whisper. "There a long time, was I. Parts and pieces gone for ever."

Mirzai edged closer, drawn by the heartbreak in her voice. "What happened to you?"

"I don't remember! Did you not hear me?" The harshness in her voice faded as swiftly as it had arrived. "Vallant . . . I was with Vallant, sails above and the wind racing. Then the air filled with fire. After that . . . it's gone. Lost to the mists."

"Vallant?" Araq wasn't so far removed from civilisation that he hadn't heard the stories. Saheen downplayed them, arguing that no one could survive the Eternity King's wrath, much less carve out an independent state from Khalad's heart. But then it had taken her a full month to accept that the Eternity *Queen* had ascended to the throne. Not that Bashar Vallant's state had lasted. Not after the redcloaks had levelled Tyzanta. "Then he's real?"

"He is." She sagged, the starlight dimming in her hair. "He was."

Mirzai thought back to the bounty board outside Saheen's mansion. "There's still a bloodgild on his head, if that helps."

"Proves only that they don't know *where* Vallant is, it does, not that he *is*."

"I suppose. His poster was a month old, while the one for the Arvish woman was brand new." So new, in hindsight, that Shorza must have brought it in on the *Majestic*.

Zephyr narrowed her eyes. "*Katija* Arvish?"

Mirzai nodded. "That's her. Seven thousand tetrams for sedition, murder, brigandage, arson ... It was quite a list."

A smile tugged at Zephyr's lips, the lustre and gleam returning to her hair. "Busy, busy, busy. Knew she'd take to it, did I ... What month is it?"

"Julas. It'll be Septros in a week."

She blinked, her cheeks tightening. "Six months behind the Veil? Fortunate am I to even remember my own name."

"I don't think you were always in the mists," said Mirzai, recalling again Tarin's stories of the cloud qori. "My nephew's friend saw you at Nyzanshar. They think you're responsible for Jedrah's disappearance."

She shuddered, extremities curling and wisping. "An old man, white hair."

Unease coiled in Mirzai's gut. "Yes."

She screwed her eyes shut, her face contorted with revulsion. "Had he kin?"

The words were as good as an admission of murder. Mirzai wondered just how close he himself had come to vanishing on the hillside. "Barely even a friend."

Zephyr stared blankly into the gloom. "Remember nothing, do I, save for drowning in the mists and hunger. Not until I saw your pendant. This pendant." She pressed her shackled hands to her chest, where the dull red-gold glinted atop her dress.

"It too was my grandfather's."

She laughed softly. "A wise man was he, to save us both so long after his passing. Rough was I when I tried to take it. Not myself."

"It seemed to bring you peace."

"It brought me together. As much as there was to find. Silver is truth, they say, but astoricum is certainty. Would you like it back?"

Mirzai had heard no other living soul refer to the red-gold metal by its true name, only the more common *oreikhalkos*. "Only if you wish to return it, *nasaîm*."

Zephyr drew herself up. "Trade it, will I, for freeness."

Mirzai hesitated, but while he remained afraid of the daemon he'd confronted in the torch house, Zephyr was plainly no longer that creature – if only because chains could never have held a thing that was solid only when it wished to draw blood. And she *was* Issnaîm, and thus a messenger of the Drowned Lady. To hold her any longer – to do so at all, even – was temerity bordering on apostasy.

Slipping the key from the pocket of his robes, he crouched and took her hands. He instinctively dipped his eyes as her cool skin met his, but not so soon that he missed her slight smile.

"Doing so well, were you," she murmured, not unkindly.

Having no ready response, Mirzai simply unlocked the padlock and stepped away. Zephyr flowed to her feet like rising steam, chains slithering clear of her wrists. She unlooped the pendant from her neck and held it out. Mirzai closed her fingers about it.

He willed his gaze to meet hers, and was surprised how readily it did so. "Keep it for now. In case you feel yourself coming apart again."

Her posture shifted, the change so subtle that he didn't notice at first, a guardedness that he'd assumed intrinsic to her nature melting away. But her stare's intensity redoubled, peeling back his soul layer by layer, in search of truth. "Generous I named you, and generous you are."

He bobbed his head, embarrassed. "I'm surprised you had no astoricum of your own."

Her cheek twitched. "I did. An heirloom of *my* kin, it was." She set fingers to the side of her neck, perhaps tracing the line of some vanished necklace. Her voice dropped to a murmur, losing almost a full octave. "What has become of you, Bashar? What became of *us*?"

"He's still alive, so the rumours say," Mirzai put in, her forlorn tone moving him to offer reassurance. "Fled to Athenoch after Tyzanta fell."

"And how would he do that without me to guide him?" snapped Zephyr. "Tales are not truth, whatever our wishes, and Vallant was always more useful as myth."

"I'm sorry." It felt impudent to offer sympathy to a divinity, but Mirzai, moved by her obvious pain, found it impossible to do otherwise. "What would you have me do now, *nasaîm*? What does the Drowned Lady wish of me?"

Zephyr raised her eyes skyward, or at least towards the cobweb-infested joists of the floor above. "Saves me, he does. Forgives my trespasses with barely a word, and still perceives that the scale of debt tilts only towards himself."

"As I should," Mirzai said stiffly. "You're a herald of the Drowned Lady."

She tilted her head and regarded him thoughtfully, a frown creasing her brow. "Mirzai..." She sighed. "What happened at Anfai... Not even a little bit divine, am I. Swear by moon's truth, I do."

He'd never heard of such a pledge, but she sounded sincere. "But the Drowned Lady sent—"

She gave a vicious shake of the head. "A story my kin taught yours to encourage revolt. We sold you a legend little better than a children's tale and tallied blood in the trade. And watched slaughter from safety behind the Veil, did we. Abandoned you and called it strategy. We used you, Mirzai."

A lump formed in his throat. "Why? Why would you say that?" He grabbed at the wall for support his shaking knees could no longer provide.

"Because ashamed of my kin, am I. Refused to fight their own battles, did they, and I will not lie to spare their sins. Save your reverence for the deserving."

No. It couldn't be true. If it was, then Anfai had been destroyed for nothing. Not just his family, but hundreds of others, decimated and driven into the wilds... and for what?

He glared at Zephyr. "You're testing me."

55

She stared back, unrepentant. "Played a joke on you just now, did I. A cruel joke, for no reason other than to make me feel better. The behaviour of a divine messenger, is that?"

She'd claimed to have stolen his soul. The greatest peril and punishment. A herald of the Drowned Lady would know that, would know its power and cruelty both. Mirzai took refuge in defiance as the foundations of his certainty crumbled. "You are Issnaîm!"

"That I am, but speak not for the Drowned Lady do I. You would not mistake those who do. Bleak are they, so stories tell, clad in weed and sweet with death." She drifted closer. "But a sharp tongue have I. The Lady is little more than a memory even to us, but perhaps watches you from beyond the Veil, does she. Maybe the river's flow brought me to you when I most needed a generous soul."

She didn't really believe it. He read it in her eyes. "I will not accept that we suffered for no reason."

"Always a reason for suffering, is there. Even if we cannot see it."

"I—"

The hollow pounding of fist on door sounded somewhere above his head. "Mirzai? Come on, I know you're home."

Saheen.

Mirzai's existential fears melted away in the face of rather more practical ones. While Saheen knew of his family's past, abstract knowledge was a far cry from being confronted with mortal truth. There was no telling how she might react. Alabastra and its jealous goddess taught that the Issnaîm – whom they named "veilkin" – were little better than daemons. And that was before Zephyr's allegiance to the notorious Bashar Vallant entered the mix.

He shot Zephyr a warning glance. "Stay silent, I beg you."

He left the cellar and heaved the hatch back into position, careful that the noise of its closing wouldn't carry. When he finally reached the front door, he found Saheen wearing both her faded overseer's robe and an expression of impatience that softened to concern before the door was fully open. "You're a mess."

Mirzai had never felt less like smiling, but forced one anyway. "I missed my footing in the dark. It'll heal."

Saheen narrowed her eyes, part in pity, part in despair, just as she always did when she thought he was being stubborn. "It would have healed already if you'd seen Haldia for some last breath."

"I prefer nature to take its course."

She cast a disdainful glance around the kitchen and its haphazard piles of cooking implements, ramshackle boxes and filthy tools. "I can see that. I swear this house looks more like a squat than a home."

"I told you, I'm fine."

"Lost your pendant, though." The corner of Saheen's mouth curled into a sad smile. "I'm sorry, I know what it meant to you."

"It'll come back to me."

"By way of the Black River?" She shook her head. "You're a good man, but you're a fool."

Mirzai suppressed a flinch, the jibe slicing deep. "Maybe the one has something to do with the other."

"Maybe."

She regarded him stonily, offering no clue to her thoughts. Imagination flourished unhappily in the silence. Had someone seen him bring Zephyr down from the hill during the early hours? It had been dark even with the torch house ablaze, but that cut both ways. Just because he'd seen no one didn't mean he'd not been seen himself. Was Saheen girding herself to deliver a warning, maybe even take him into custody for harbouring the Eternity Queen's enemies? Divine or otherwise, Zephyr was surely that. Before he knew it, his gaze was drifting to the living room door and the uncovered hatch. Saheen had been in his house enough to recognise that something was out of place. If she asked about it, he'd have to lie, and he'd never been good at that, not with her. Better to make an excuse now, better—

"Mirzai, we have to talk." Her worry was no longer an undercurrent, but the surface swell. "No . . . Better that I show you."

Now thoroughly perplexed, Mirzai nodded. "All right. And then you can buy me the drink that Tarin says you owe me."

"If you still want it."

He followed her from the kitchen and out into the morning's oppressive sunshine. "Saheen, what's going on?"

In place of answering, she set off along the narrow hillside path that eventually joined the long loop that climbed Giriqan's flank, the skirts of her robes swishing the dry grasses. Mirzai caught up to her at a gorse-choked overlook that offered a clear view across the town's mishmash of red tiles and slatted, paint-peeling roof timbers.

As he approached, Saheen set her back to the distant temple and its woebegone statue of Nyssa Benevolas. "I didn't want you to hear from anyone else."

Mirzai didn't understand what she meant at first. Araq looked much as it had on the previous day, the streets long emptied of workers trudging to the mines and the barge dock. Life went on, even with everything tainted by the faint magenta of the torch house's blesswood fires and the luminescent mists of the Veil lingering sullenly on the near horizon, but then wasn't that the point of the torch house, that life *could* go on, even through Mistfall.

It wasn't until he realised that the town looked a little *too* much like it had on the previous day that a new sense of dread descended. The black masts and furled sails of the *Majestic* still dominated the scaffold of the elevated dock.

Worse still, as he peered again at the humbled ruin of Nyzanshar, he realised for the first time that its bare stone was naked no more. Scarlet gonfalon flags hung from its walls; bright pennants from its two surviving towers. Even as he watched, a dhow rounded Giriqan's northern slopes and made lazy descent to join a sleek-hulled felucca and a blocky military carrack anchored level with the roof of the central keep.

Saheen moved to stand beside him. "The first arrived with the dawn. There was nothing I could do. Shorza says they'll keep to the fortress

58

but . . ." Her shoulders dipped, then she scowled and stood straight once more. "Just be careful. Please."

A dull, weary anger flickered to life in the pit of Mirzai's stomach as he looked down at Araq's empty streets. They'd not be empty long.

Six

Ihsan Damant clung to his washbasin and screwed his eyes shut as the bright peal of conclave bells trampled muffled thoughts. When the carillon faded, he splashed water into his face and peered again into the mirror with his one good eye. The reflection was little more to his liking on second glance than the first. He'd never counted himself handsome, and advancing years had only confirmed his suspicions. The laughter lines in his olive skin were deeper, the bags beneath his eyes heavier – his hair now white more than grey. Outward manifestations of internal weariness.

Or perhaps, he allowed, recalling the empty wine bottles clustered on his intricate ormesta-style dining table, it wasn't age at all, but indiscipline.

A third splash washed away the worst of the night, though it did nothing for the stubble he'd no time to shave were he to make conclave. He'd had no advance notice of the meeting, but that was no excuse. There'd been a time, and not so very long ago, when he'd risen with the dawn, not in the mid morning.

Silently pledging that this would be the last time he'd attend conclave in dishevelment – and trying not to think about similar promises long since broken – he pulled on silk gloves and castellan's robes and left his chambers.

Many of the Golden Citadel's passageways still bore scorches from shrieker fire inflicted during the Obsidium Uprising, which had claimed the life of the Eternity King, Caradan Diar, and freed the goddess Nyssa to seize his throne. Faithful repairs had ensured that the palace's original design prevailed, with gentle breezes wafting the sweet scent of honeysuckle through pillared cloisters.

Strand by strand, the cobwebs peeled away from Damant's thoughts. The silent salutes offered by the gold-masked redcloak sentries – salutes he returned with a crispness belonging to his much younger self – speeded the process along. A castellan should command respect.

The redcloak sentries guarding the conclave hall's heavy oak door were no slower to salute than their peers. Not so the portico's third occupant.

||You look terrible, old man,|| signed Yali, her fingers dancing through the Simah signs with an irreverence matching the broad grin plastered across her tawny-brown cheeks.

||And you're disgustingly cheerful,|| Damant replied, his own signs plodding and workmanlike, but then he'd never had to rely on the language, whereas Yali was deaf to all but the heaviest percussive sounds.

She blew him a kiss, the shimmering golden sleeve of her gown sliding back from wrist to elbow. ||I had a *very* good night.||

Which meant she'd been dancing somewhere down-spire until the early hours. Far from acceptable for a fireblood, but then Yali, like Damant, was as cinderblood as they came. Worse, she was a skelder, and while the Eternity Queen's friendship had raised her out of the lower city's vices and into the heart of Zariqaz's Golden Citadel as high handmaiden, no skelder ever truly escaped their past.

Not that Damant cared if Yali partook of her pleasures in the palace, on the dockside by the Silent Sea or anywhere in between. He only resented that even with her chestnut hair tugged back into a simple ponytail, and with maybe an hour's sleep behind her, she looked twice as presentable as he. Clad her in black silk and banish the mirth from her green eyes and she'd suit the part of castellan far better.

||I don't want to know.|| He softened the rebuke with a smile of his own. Outsiders had to stick together, even in the highest court in Khalad.

Especially in the highest court.

||You're right, you don't.|| Yali struck a haughty pose made angular by a rangy, athletic figure not yet grown into. ||And I wasn't going to tell you.||

Both redcloaks remained motionless throughout the exchange, their golden masks offering no clue as to their thoughts. It was entirely possible that neither spoke Simah, or at least couldn't read signing swiftly enough to follow the conversation. Damant hated not knowing, and felt a brief pang for his previous castellanship in service to House Bascari, where he'd known the names and capabilities of every custodian under his command. It felt like a lifetime ago, with a great many dubious decisions in between. The Eternity Queen had given him a second chance, and his gratitude was without measure.

At least in the daylight. Come nightfall, try as he might to do otherwise, he crawled into the nearest bottle to drown formless unease.

He winced away his discomfort, remembering too late that however deaf Yali might be to spoken word, mannerism and gesture screamed their secrets. ||Do you know why she's called this conclave?||

Yali shrugged. ||She doesn't confide in me like she used to.|| She turned a graceful step, setting her back to the two redcloaks. Even Damant, professionally suspicious though he was, wouldn't have given the motion a second thought had Yali's body not masked her next set of signs. ||Not since Kastagîr drew her eye.||

Damant grunted. Faizâr Kastagîr's meteoric rise from simple redcloak to *gansalar* to captain of the Eternity Queen's bodyguard invited rumour enough of its own. But if it wasn't Damant's business to concern himself with Yali's trysts, he'd certainly no right to meddle in the affairs of the reborn goddess, even if they had eroded his own authority. He just wished she'd shown better taste. Kastagîr's ambition burned brighter than the palace torch house.

A fresh peal of bells set his head ringing anew. "I suppose we'll find out," he murmured, forgetting to sign.

Yali's lip-reading was up to the task. ||After you, old man.||

Diligent labour had smoothed away the worst of the conclave hall's scars, the mahogany of its raised dais and concentric seating bright with gilded leaf motifs polished to a mirror sheen. Scarlet banners lent vibrancy, the grand segmented window overlooking the regal approach of the Golden Stair the necessary light to wake all to glory. Slumbering koilos – their mummified, robed remains armoured in the ceremonial lamellar of ember-saints – kept silent vigil from alcoves around the room, the criminals of the past become guarantors of present law.

Only two changes had been made during the refurbishment. One was the throne. Sited at the dais's northern compass point, it was a marvel of spiralled gold and silver, cushioned in rich blood-red velvet and set through with lumani, ensuring that it – and its occupant – shone fit to rival the sun. The throne immortal it was named, but the throne immortal it was not. That lay at the heart of the sanctum, whose vast, gilded door stood immediately to the rear of the throne. The door itself was the second alteration to the hall, for access to the sanctum, and the soulfire column by whose power Caradan Diar had caged a goddess, had remained hidden from sight during the Eternity King's reign.

Despite the unexpectedness of the conclave, the hall was as full as Damant had ever known it, the tiered seating full of worthies, guild representatives and custodium functionaries. Nonentities, paying homage and seeking preferment as was ever the way. The dais itself held a full council arranged about its circumference, neighbours conversing softly among themselves as they awaited the Eternity Queen's arrival. Moths courting her light, hoping to make a portion of its warmth and glory their own.

As Damant trod the perimeter, he rebuked himself for thinking ill of his peers. He'd no less chequered a past. The Obsidium Uprising had been a complicated time. Moving past it had required all sides to acknowledge intent more than deed.

Before the Eternity Queen's rise, he'd been allied to his old protégé, Bashar Vallant. That uncomfortable accord had never restored their friendship. Vallant would never forget how Damant had once commanded the ship that had grounded his behind the Veil, causing the death of his wife and daughter. Nor had Damant expected him to. The struggle to end Caradan Diar's tyranny had overridden all. But Vallant had been too long a rebel. After Nyssa's return, he'd manipulated Isdihar Diar – the Eternity King's Voice and heir – to legitimise an increasingly directionless rebellion. Vallant had fought not against the injustices of Caradan Diar's order, but against order itself.

"You look harried, Ihsan," drawled Tuzen Karza as Damant took his place at the throne's right hand. "Is our dear castellan so far out of favour that he didn't know there was a conclave?"

He shot a preening glance at the pasty-faced and rust-haired young woman draped across his right shoulder like a cloak, and was rewarded with a musical giggle. Her presence was a breach of protocol even before one took into account the gauzy collage of multicoloured silks that could only barely be said to be a dress, or the make-up-ringed and unfocused eyes that were the calling card of a shîm addict. Somehow the fact that she'd oiled and beaded her hair in a style made popular by Isdihar Diar – just as her heavy-handed make-up mimicked that of the Voice-turned-traitor – made it worse. She looked for all the world like a Saint Qamfel's Day effigy on the way to the pyre.

"You knew otherwise, I take it?" Damant replied, unable as ever to address Karza by the expected honorific of "lord" as a cinderblood should.

"You mustn't feel threatened." Karza kept his eyes on his draped ingénue, who stifled another giggle by burrowing her lips into his shoulder. "Some of us were born to these circles."

Yali – now kneeling with her back to the empty throne – shot him a flurry of signs. ||Ignore him. He didn't know either.||

Damant subsided, wondering if she'd caught something in Karza's body language that he'd missed, or was simply less prone to being

64

needled. Certainly, her sharp gestures conveyed contempt no less biting than Damant's own.

One of her closest friends in Vallant's band had been a man known as Tatterlain, but who preferred to go by "Tuzen Karza" when performing nefarious acts, which was often. Imposter and genuine article were as alike in lantern-jawed appearance as only brothers could be – save for the latter's vain attempt to conceal the creases of advancing years with make-up and his silvering hair and goatee with black dye. Brothers they were. Karza – the *real* Karza – had become master of the vast family estates at Phoenissa by dint of disinheriting his younger, illegitimate sibling some decades prior.

It had taken all of an hour in Karza's company for Damant to earn ironclad empathy with Tatterlain's desire to pile ignominy on his sibling's name, though Yali's disgust at a man who was her friend's ageing funhouse reflection greatly eclipsed his own. Accomplished mimic though Tatterlain was, no performance could have captured his elder brother's oily reality.

"Your companion looks tired, Lord Karza," said Malis Ethara, standing opposite. Her controlled posture and severe features made her seem less a woman and more some aristocratic likeness carved from volcanic rock. She'd fought against the throne during the Obsidium Uprising. Damant had argued against her appointment, but in the final analysis the cult's goals had been righteous, even if their methods had brought Zariqaz to its knees. And Malis *had* proven an effective enough spymistress. For some, subornment was in the blood. "Perhaps she'd be more comfortable in the stalls?"

The ghost of a frown faded from Karza's brow as his hurried glance found no ally worthy of the name. The paradox of courtly behaviour: firebloods had a high threshold for embarrassment, provided that they weren't called upon to acknowledge the *subject* of that embarrassment – especially when she was one of the Eternity Queen's small army of handmaidens. The palace was full of such young women, most of them the younger daughters of fireblood houses seeking royal preferment.

Not without effort, Karza unwound thin arms from around his neck and tilted back the young woman's chin until her scowl met his doting smile.

"This won't take long, Keti, I promise." He patted her hands soothingly. "Then we'll take a stroll through the market. I'll buy you a new dress for tonight. You'd like that, wouldn't you?"

Her scowl softened. "A Slarini, *darathi*?"

Damant shifted his appraisal of her age down a year or two, where it teetered on the border of acceptability. The Daric word encapsulating a daughter's affection for her father further highlighted a thirty-year age gap.

Karza's smile gained a touch of winter – a gown styled by the famous Slarini wasn't a trivial purchase even for a man of his means. "We'll see, poppet. We'll see."

Mollified, the girl stepped lightly – if unsteadily – from the dais and climbed the stairs to a seat on the lowest of the concentric tiers, hurriedly cleared by worthies less than eager to be seen in her orbit.

Karza arched an eyebrow at Malis. "Happy now?"

She favoured Keti – now slumped against her chair's backrest with the boneless quality of one soon to be asleep – with a disdainful stare. "Ecstatic."

A deep bellow spared Karza the need to reply. "Silence for the Eternity Queen!"

Hush descended on the hall, the conversations on dais and gallery falling silent as the occupants of the latter – Keti included – rose to their feet. The gilded sanctum door whispered open.

Yennika Bascari, Eternity Queen of Khalad, mortal host of Nyssa Dominus, in whom the goddess's aspects of judgement and mercy had found balance, swept into the room with her head held high, the skirts and sleeves of her off-the-shoulder white and gold gown trailing across the marble floor. Not for her the ostentatiousness of oiled, gemstone-set tresses and intimidating make-up once favoured by the absent Voice. She wore her long black hair unbound save for the silver circlet of her crown, and her dark bronze skin unadorned sparing a touch of eyeshadow lending weight to a stare that charmed or threatened according to her mood. Not that she needed such artifice. She was stunning by any measure, and moved with the confidence of a woman who knew that to be absolute truth. She strode with utter surety, as though she expected the world to remake itself around her should she miss her step. And perhaps it would.

Faizâr Kastagîr – owner of the voice that had announced her coming – marched two paces behind, a distance enforced in the first part by respect and in the second by the need not to set a boot to the Eternity Queen's train of golden silks. His uniform was a simple variation of a *gansalar*'s – though he wore his cloak inverted, scarlet within, midnight without – its seams straining against a chiselled physique cultivated far beyond the point of necessity. An oiled thatch of blond hair topped tanned rugged features that had remained unscarred through years of service by simple dint of the fact that he was as swift and murderous a swordsman as Khalad had to offer. He was as undeniably handsome as his queen was unassailably beautiful. And if he wasn't nearly so sharp as the jewelled scimitar belted at his shoulder, that didn't matter. She could do all of his thinking for him.

The Eternity Queen swept to the throne. Kastagîr took up position at her right shoulder, mirroring Yali's station at its left foot. A brief whisper of robes filled the chamber as the assembled crowds reseated themselves.

Silence reigned, the members of the royal council motionless as the Eternity Queen's gaze touched upon each of them in turn, her lips parted in what might have been prelude to a smile, or to a scowl blacker than thunder. So close, Damant found it impossible to mistake the flickering magenta halo that crowned her head and shoulders. Nor could he ignore the crow's feet at her eyes, the cheekbones that grew ever more pronounced as her features hardened, or the strands of silver threaded through once ink-black hair. These flaws did nothing to diminish her beauty. Indeed, they would only render her more striking as she ascended further into middle age.

Except Yennika Bascari had yet to see her thirtieth year. The strain of divinity carried a price not measurable in dinars or tetrams.

||"At long last, Tarakûn has fallen."|| Her proclamation echoed about the chamber, her signs firm and uncompromising and a voice given to sultriness during private audience awakened to ironclad authority.

Awe rippled through the conclave hall. Tarakûn had been the greatest of the eastern cities, its high walls reinforced year on year, the better to guard against the once ever-present possibility of invasion from neighbouring Qersal. Conventional wisdom had held it to be impregnable, but convention held little influence over armies charged by divine purpose.

The Eternity Queen waited for silence to return before continuing. ||"This night just gone, I sat in judgement over the souls of the ruling council. They yowled and pleaded, wretched and naked in the knowledge of their terrible arrogance."|| A smile touched her lips, not quite playful but not entirely stern. Even while shackled by her predecessor in the Stars Below, she had received the souls of the dead, ushering them to rebirth or atonement as merited. Freed, she now did so from her sanctum in the Golden Citadel, though so far as Damant knew, not even Yali had borne witness to the process. Some things were not for mortal eyes. ||"I offered what mercy I was able, which I daresay was more than they deserved."||

Another ripple swept the conclave hall, an echo of the Eternity Queen's own mirth. It faded with the retreat of her not-quite-smile, an uneasy silence settling in its wake.

||"Six months."|| Ambiguity of expression resolved to a scowl, her signs taut and angry. ||"Six months since I delivered you from the pretender's tyranny ... and what have we to show for it? A city in ruins. A sullen, rebellious kingdom. This is *not* the welcome I expected from those who claim to love me. My patience grows thin."||

Immediately to the left of the throne, Hargo Rashace cleared his throat and strove gruffly for courtly tone. As cheerless a man as Damant had ever met, his aged prizefighter's physique was scarcely less thuggish than his reputation. "As your majesty knows, I have overseen the reconstruction efforts personally. Your palace shines as bright as it ever did." The five ring-walls of the Golden Citadel had undergone diligent restoration before the first work gangs had even begun clearing the rubble from the lower streets. "As do many districts. Why, Khazli is unparalleled in its splendour."

"Your own palace lies in Khazli district, does it not?" put in Countess Emanzi Ozdîr, a woman of early middle age whose allies claimed as shrewd and whose enemies derided as opportunist. Like Hargo, she made no attempt to sign. Few of the council ever did, setting Yali the challenging task of keeping pace through lip-reading alone.

His gaze never wavered from the Eternity Queen. "A happy accident of geography, majesty, as Minister Ozdîr is well aware. I'm as frustrated by our lack of progress as anyone, but the spread of lethargia complicates matters."

||"And why is that?"|| asked the Eternity Queen sweetly, her regal majesty softening to playful, languid wickedness. The flawed mortal she'd once been had delighted in theatricality. That habit had scarcely softened with Nyssa's embrace. At moments like these, Yennika blazed brighter than the Eternity Queen's halo.

"Once a labourer shows signs of affliction, the entire work gang must be quarantined."

The sweetness sharpened, her halo darkening to indigo. ||"And why is *that*?"||

"I . . ." Hargo trailed off, eyes darting to the gallery as humiliation beckoned. Never the greatest intellect on the council – what he could not achieve through bullying and barracking he seldom achieved at all – even he recognised the snare.

"Lethargia is the goddess's will." Hierarch Igarî Bathîr clasped her hands to her chest. Her place at conclave owed everything to tradition and nothing to current status. Now that Nyssa spoke for herself, the once-domineering church was reduced to little more than a gaudy banking house, bartering in sin and souls rather than gold, forced to reflect on how smoothly Caradan Diar had twisted its traditions to imprison the very goddess it worshipped. "It has no claim upon the faithful. The swifter it spreads, the sooner Zariqaz will be purified."

A fine sentiment from a woman who'd spent much of the last year cowering in the tallest tower of Zariqaz's Xanathros Alabastra precisely so *she* wouldn't contract the lethargia, a wasting, enervating disease that gradually thinned the soul until it could no longer sustain the body. From the first, Alabastra's archons had preached its divine origin and punitive nature . . . and that it was a kinder death than sufferers deserved.

The Eternity Queen stirred. ||"Precisely. Lethargia calls to judgement only those no longer fit for this world. You're not concerned for yourself, I hope?"||

Hargo's cheek twitched. "Not at all."

She leaned back, the indigo flames softening to magenta. "A sinner's fate is not for changing. The afflicted no longer serve any purpose. If they are a burden, cast them beyond the city walls."

A murmur swept the gallery. Glances were exchanged. Far more firebloods than cinderbloods had fallen to the lethargia. Everyone in the chamber had a family member, a friend, a colleague touched by the disease.

||"You disagree, dear Ihsan?"|| said the Eternity Queen.

Too late, Damant banished an unintended grimace. He sometimes forgot that the goddess, for all her kindnesses, was an embodiment of judgement as much as mercy. ||"I was thinking only of your tenets of forgiveness, majesty."||

He caught Yali's grateful nod.

The Eternity Queen nodded thoughtfully. ||"As you were right to. Very well. Henceforth, Alabastra will ensure that any citizen afflicted by lethargia is eased into the Deadwinds, to end their suffering and hasten their journey to redemption and rebirth. Does that satisfy you, Ihsan?"||

70

It didn't, though it should. A lifetime spent second-guessing imperfect masters was not easily set aside, even in the face of divine grace and forbearance. Damant chided himself for faithlessness in the face of the goddess's love. ||"Yes, majesty."||

"But majesty, these people are sinners," Bathîr protested. "Do they deserve mercy?"

||"Mercy is a reflection upon the bestower, not the bestowed,"|| replied the Eternity Queen as if speaking to a child. ||"And in this case, it is repaid with opportunity. Koilos, in particular, have been in short supply since the uprising."||

"They have indeed, majesty," said Bathîr, her eyes alight with possibility. A soul harvested before lethargia had withered it to nothing could be sliced into many vibrant – and profitable – ifrîti. "I'll instruct the shriversmen. The finest specimens will come to the Golden Citadel, naturally."

||"Naturally."||

The small, rebellious part of Damant, lately in retreat, wondered darkly if the gleam in the Eternity Queen's eye suggested a conversation steered to an inevitable endpoint. The Obsidium Uprising had indeed seen many koilos destroyed, and however effortlessly the Eternity Queen won mortal men and women to her cause, they would never be as tirelessly loyal as the embalmed guardians. He scowled the thought away, headache returning. Such machinations were to be expected from Bathîr and her fellow archons, even from other members of the council. The situation was not of the Eternity Queen's making, but her predecessor's – a despot Damant himself had served, if at a distance. Transferring Caradan Diar's guilt onto her was unkind at best, and heresy at worst.

But still, in the silence of thoughts buried too deep to show, he wondered . . .

Hargo cleared his throat. "It will, of course, not address the worker shortages . . . unless some of the koilos were to be placed at my disposal."

Bathîr sniffed. "Such labours are beneath holy implements. If willing hands are needed to restore Zariqaz's glories, I suggest they be brought in from elsewhere. From Tyzanta's ruins, perhaps."

Malis sniffed. "Those gutter-camps should have been cleared long ago. They're a breeding ground for insurrection."

Across the circle from Damant, Ardin Javar scowled into his greying bushy beard. The black and gold templar's robes he'd once disgraced scarcely contained his bearish form. He'd teetered back and forth between rebellion and service so many times that no one should ever have trusted him again. Had his treachery not offered up the vital ship-yards at Nassos, literally stealing the wind from the rebellion's sails, no one would have done so.

||"They are what we made of them,"|| he rumbled, his words accompanied by heavy-handed signing.

Templar or gang boss, outcast or enforcer, Ardin had claimed Tyzanta as his home for much of his life. Its razing had hit him hard. So hard that Damant – wary of yet another volte-face from a man who'd made them habit – had assigned a significant portion of the Golden Citadel's custodium to keep careful watch on Ardin for any sign of disloyalty, or even reprisal; unlike Karza, Ardin was shrewder than he appeared. But the reports had turned up little, save for an intake of calvasîr liqueur that eclipsed Damant's own indulgences. Ardin didn't so much wash away his regrets as pickle them.

"Khalad needed an example of the consequences of following in Vallant and Arvish's footsteps," said Malis. "We provided it."

"The city had surrendered!" roared Ardin.

A gasp went up from the gallery. Malis met his stare dead-on. "And the next will know better than to let things get so far out of hand. That's how we hold the realm together. That's how the realm was *always* held together."

Ardin lurched towards her, too furious now to sign. "By slaughtering those who can't fight back? The goddess—"

||"The goddess can speak for herself."|| For all that the Eternity Queen didn't raise her voice, the threat was unmistakable. ||"Moreover, if she wished to speak of the past, she would have sent for a chronicler.

You know the decision to bombard Tyzanta was mine, Ardin. If you take issue with it – with *me* – you have only to say so."||

He rounded on her, eyes ablaze. The absence of a weapon at his side was suddenly of no comfort to Damant, not when a mere six paces separated him from a goddess who, divine or not, was half his size.

Shoulders hunched, Ardin took another step and then came to an abrupt halt, his brow furrowed and his eyes restless.

Kastagîr started forward, hand on his sword. The Eternity Queen touched his arm. "There's no need for ugliness . . . is there, Ardin?"

Ardin blinked and gave a slow shake of his head, a man trying to piece together the shreds of his dignity. Had he even arrived to conclave sober? Damant made a mental note to discuss the matter with the Eternity Queen. Ardin's name and chequered past carried cachet with skelders and others on society's fringe. But it increasingly appeared that he was so deep in the bottle as to make him not only useless, but dangerous.

||"Good,"|| said the Eternity Queen as Ardin returned to his place in the circle. ||"Then I believe we were speaking of the living, and not the dead. Hargo's work gangs offer them a purpose."||

"Why not?" Karza waved an airy hand. "I don't know how anyone survives what's left of Tyzanta in any case."

Malis turned her gaze on Emanzi. "House Ozdîr's custodians don't seem capable of preventing smugglers from running supplies into the ruins."

"My custodians can't chase gloami wisps," snapped Emanzi. "Those ruins are a warren. I couldn't lock them down if I'd a legion of redcloaks at my command. Worse, the smugglers know our patrols, our routines. It doesn't matter how often we change them, they're always one step ahead."

"A traitor in House Ozdîr?" muttered Karza, the words pitched just loud enough to be heard. "Surely not."

She glared daggers at him. "I'll gladly turn the responsibility over to you."

"Oh, that doesn't sound like my kind of thing at all." Karza turned to the Eternity Queen. "Besides, keeping the west running occupies my every waking moment."

The Eternity Queen favoured him with a thin, mirthless smile that left Damant in no doubt that she was fully aware of Karza's abilities, and their limitations. ||"Perhaps dear Ihsan could look into the matter?"||

Emanzi stiffened. "I can handle it. I just need more time."

The Eternity Queen's tone grew steely. ||"With respect, you clearly can't, and time – like my patience – is not without limit. You have been lax, Emanzi. Ihsan?"||

Damant gave a stiff bow. The last thing he wanted was a trek out to Tyzanta. Like Ardin, he'd too many memories buried among the ruins. Easier to blame Ardin for Emanzi's woes, as he surely had contacts in Tyzanta even now ... though with the man already under close surveillance and evidently less than stable, it was impossible to imagine how he could conceal such subterfuge. ||"As your majesty wishes. The *Stormchaser* should have resupplied by now. I'll leave tomorrow."||

||"Hargo will accompany you. I'm sure he's eager to recruit his volunteers."||

Hargo, a notoriously unhappy sailor of the Cloudsea, gave a rigid nod.

||"I will also provide you with letters of authority to Ursalar Bashan. The city of Azcadir has tested my patience too long, its council given every opportunity to embrace me. She is to bring it under siege, no one in or out. Let the good people of Azcadir gaze north to Tyzanta and in its rubble behold their future."||

"And if they do not?" asked Malis.

||"Then divine prophecy shall become truth, as divine prophecy ever should,"|| the Eternity Queen replied, her voice hard.

Uneasiness settled in Damant's gut. Bashan was newly risen to her rank – one that placed entire legions of redcloaks and dozens of warships at her command – and eager to prove herself worthy of its trust. She'd prosecute her orders with diligence bordering on ferocity. As for Azcadir, it was a fraction of the size of Tarakûn, or even Tyzanta. It had never been a wealthy city, and exerted little influence over its neighbours. ||"Is there no other way, majesty?"||

||"Perhaps, Ihsan,"|| said the Eternity Queen, not unkindly, ||"but it is necessary. Mercy motivates more in absence than in largesse. Even my patience has limits. I will waste no more of it on Azcadir. I trust that I am understood?"||

Damant cast a glance around the conclave, already knowing he'd find no support worthy of the name. Why should he? The Eternity Queen perceived the truth of the world in a way he never would. Though the moment remained fresh in his mind, he could scarcely credit that he'd challenged her decision in the first place. ||"Of course, majesty."||

||"Good. Then we are left with one other trifling matter."||

Damant stiffened as languid sweetness returned to the Eternity Queen's voice. An affection that suggested they were at last reaching the conclave's chief business. ||"Majesty?"||

Her gaze fell on each minster in turn. ||"When Katija Arvish escaped Tyzanta's fall, this council promised me that she'd be in custody within a week. That was three months ago. Since then, the East has been ablaze with stories of her victories and the wreckage of my ships. On the lips of malcontents and traitors, her name is second only to Vallant's. It would seem that anyone wishing to live a long and vigorous life at liberty can do no better than to make an enemy of this council."|| Her gaze settled on Malis. ||"I want her found."||

"My agents assure me that she hasn't returned to Athenoch," Malis replied smoothly. "We know that the Voice has accepted the protection of the Qersali zol'tayah, and that the borderlands are rife with sightings of Vallant's surviving ships. The zol'tayah may have thought better of directly provoking your wrath, but that hasn't stopped her from sheltering your enemies."

Vallant's brief alliance with the Qersali hadn't outlasted his disappearance. It seemed to Damant that the zol'tayah was waiting things out. Though its folk were tenacious, Qersal was a small enough nation. It had taken centuries for the Eternity Queen's predecessor to teach them caution, but the lesson had finally stuck.

"Skelders always stick together," Malis went on. "Arvish is no different. When we push into Qersal, we'll have her. A good war is like a rainstorm: it brings worms crawling to the surface."

||"Bring to bear whatever pressure you think fit. Squeeze the borderlands as much as you deem necessary. But no 'accidents', Malis. I want her brought to me alive."||

"Every effort will be made."

Her halo flaring to indigo once more, the Eternity Queen swept to her feet. ||"Alive. If she dies, you'll all follow her into the Deadwinds."|| She stared down at her hands, seemingly surprised to see her fingers curling and uncurling. "She's too important," she murmured.

Silence reigned, no one daring to chance the treacherous footing laid before them. All knew that Yennika Bascari and Katija Arvish shared a complicated past, bound by love and riven by betrayal. Just how much of that emotional tangle the Eternity Queen had inherited was an open question, and one that Damant had no stomach to ask.

"What of Vallant?" asked Malis. "Their followers?"

The Eternity Queen straightened. She briefly set a hand on Yali's shoulder and received a grateful smile in return. ||"From the moment of my rebirth, I forgave those who possessed the courage to embrace the future. I will always do so."||

Malis nodded. "And those who remained trapped by the past?"

||"May they find wisdom in the next life. Khalad cannot afford disunity."||

Malis bowed low. "Of course, majesty."

The Eternity Queen shifted her attention from the council, to the subjects crowded into the gallery. ||"I know these past months haven't been easy. We were all Caradan Diar's prisoners. I promised you freedom from his shadow, and freedom you will have. I *will* see Khalad reborn in unity and splendour such as you cannot conceive."|| She again stared down at her hands, scowled and raised her eyes to the gallery once more. ||"But rebirth does not always take the form we might wish, and it always requires sacrifice. Those we cannot forgive, we will mourn, certain in the knowledge that they will always be part of us. *Abdon Nyssa ivohê.*"||

"*Abdon Nyssa ivohê!*" bellowed Kastagîr.

"*Abdon Nyssa ivohê!*" rejoined the crowd, the mantra of the destroyed Obsidium Cult become a pledge of allegiance to the goddess reborn. "*Abdon Nyssa ivohê! Abdon Nyssa ivohê!*"

A smile playing on her lips, Yennika Bascari, Eternity Queen of Khalad, spread her arms wide and bathed in her subjects' adulation.

As the echoes faded, she stepped away from the throne.

She'd taken barely a step when her eyes turned up in her head and she dropped like a stone.

Seven

Headache forgotten, Damant rushed to the Eternity Queen's side as the conclave descended into uproar. She lay sidelong, unmoving but for fitful, shallow breaths, eyes closed and her cheeks drawn. A thin puddle of drool gathered where her lips mashed against polished timber. A seizure? It wouldn't have been the first. Her mortal and divine aspects didn't always sit as well as they might.

His gaze fell across her upper arm. A tiny dart, barely an inch long, burrowed deep. No blood, not yet, but the mottled greenish tint spreading from the wound told a tale all its own. Damant's own blood ran cold.

No. Not a seizure. At least not of the sort he'd first assumed.

Grateful for his gloves, he plucked free the tiny dart and palmed it in the same motion, as heavy footfalls trembled the dais.

"What happened?" demanded Kastagîr, in hushed tones calculated not to carry.

The aghast hubbub of the conclave hall washing over him, Damant cast an eye about the dais. Information was all now. Who had it – and *how* – would make all the difference. A stricken Yali was barely a pace behind Kastagîr. None of the other councillors had left their positions. Emanzi, Bathîr and Hargo looked on in shock, Malis with an appraising eye and Ardin with brooding suspicion. All entirely in character. All utterly useless.

Yali skidded to her knees, her eyes touching briefly on her mistress before finding Damant's. ||What's wrong with her?||

"Poison," said Damant.

Kastagîr went rigid, pallor creeping around the edges of his tan features. "What?"

One suspect fewer, unless he had masterful control of his blood vessels.

"It's *kerem* venom." Damant lifted his hand to allow a glimpse of the distinctive mottled stain beneath the skin of the Eternity Queen's arm.

||Stars Below . . . || Yali's eyes went wide, as well they might. *Kerem* killed with the certainty of omen rot, only without the telltale spasms. Once it hit the bloodstream, neither medicine nor last breath could arrest it.

Damant kept his voice low and his enunciation clear to ease Yali's lip-reading – and to impart authority. All the better to conceal the anger and horror swirling about his heart. "She needs the throne immortal."

Kastagîr gave a taut nod. "I'll take her."

The proper response for a bodyguard. But Damant was in no mood to leave Kastagîr alone with the Eternity Queen, just in case he *could* go pale at will. "Yali and I will handle that. Tell the others what I've told you . . ." he cast about the tiered seating, "and make sure we have the names of everyone present." Malis likely already had that information at her fingertips, but it never hurt to be sure.

"She's my responsibility," growled Kastagîr. "I—"

Damant let a little of the parade ground creep into his voice. "We don't have time to argue. Just do it."

Reluctance flickered across Kastagîr's expression, but in the final analysis he was a follower, not a leader. With the Eternity Queen incapable of issuing orders, bluster and a firm tone carried the day. "As you wish, Castellan."

The stiff reply lingering in his wake, he set out towards Hargo.

Yali chewed her lip. ||What do you need me to do?||

Damant slipped the dart into his pocket. Grunting with effort – the Eternity Queen was slightly built, but far from without weight – he gathered her up beneath shoulders and knees. ||Open the way for me.||

Yali in the lead and the Eternity Queen's skirts tangling Damant's steps, they left the dais, the murmurs of the crowd rising in pitch and energy, but the alcoved koilos remaining motionless and useless as they passed. A drawn blade would have roused the guardian ifrîti from slumber, but a silent dart had escaped their dimmed senses. Not that Damant was in any position to judge. Halting before the gilded door, Yali raised her hands and swept them out and downwards. The soul-glyph tattooed at the base of Damant's neck itched as the ritual gesture woke the army of hestics and motics that governed the mechanisms. Only he, Yali, Kastagîr, the Eternity Queen herself and a handful of the Royal Guard could come and go unescorted. The ever-watchful hestics turned the blood of all uninvited guests to fire.

As Damant ducked through the door, Malis's cold, clear voice cut through the conclave hall's chatter. "The Eternity Queen is unwell. Please depart in an orderly manner, and—" The soft *thud* of the closing door cut off the rest.

Damant followed Yali along the dimly lit passageway, the Eternity Queen's golden skirts seeking to entangle his legs at every step. Bas-reliefs of antiquity passed away to either side, their friezes of winged warrior women in red-gold armour and their battles against a dark coiling flame belonging to a history that had never been, or that at least lay so far in the past that it made no difference.

The Eternity Queen's eyelids fluttered. Her fingertips brushed his cheek. Even the passageway's flickering lumani-light was enough to betray the *kerem* venom's spreading stain, the greenish mottling now almost to elbow and shoulder. "Darling Ihsan ... does it occur to you that you might be ... wasting your time?" Even discounting her *kerem*-sent frailty, her words were soft, intimate. The mantle of divinity set aside for a friend.

"Try not to speak, majesty."

She gave a soft, musical snort. "Always the ... protector I don't deserve." Her hand fell back.

Yali repeated her gesture at the lower door, the presence of ifrîti even more suffocating and baleful here than in the chamber above.

The windowless sanctum was every inch as vast as the conclave hall, fashioned from polished black stone without seam or join. It was lit from within by a coruscating column of soulfire ten paces wide that rushed down from the glittering honeycomb ceiling far above, drowning the abyssal stone of the throne immortal in a storm of magenta and indigo flame. Thence the soulfire spiralled ever deeper through Zariqaz's stone, coming at last to the brooding caverns of the Stars Below, where Caradan Diar had once held the goddess prisoner. High above, where the flames met the ceiling, a meshwork sphere of silver and red-gold astoricum turned lazy rotations, its agonising slowness almost imperceptible.

Damant strode through the swirling Deadwinds motes bobbing a silent dance around the soulfire column like moths about candlelight, and stepped into the cold flames. With Yali's help, he righted the Eternity Queen on the throne. Her fingers gripped the armrests and she sank against the polished stone, a shrunken doll in a child's chair. The hollowness faded from her cheeks. For the first time since her collapse, her chest rose and fell in strength, not weakness.

Trembling with relief and exhaustion, Damant stumbled back out of the flames, glad as ever to leave their winnowing chill behind. But even in the soulfire's uncertain distorting light, the *kerem* stain was receding, the Eternity Queen's natural bronze asserting itself over the venom's grey-green.

Yali sank heavily to the floor at the throne's extent, skirts pooled about her ankles, and cuffed away a tear. ||How did you know that would work?||

||I didn't.|| The flickering soulfire lent Damant's signs an insubstantial, ethereal magic, their meaning lingering against shadows even flame couldn't wholly banish. ||But what else was there? The flames make her whole.||

He cast about the furniture gathered around the sanctum's walls, all of it incongruous in its modernity. The bookshelves laden to bursting with historical records covering all that had passed during her imprisonment in the Stars Below. The silk drapes to soften stale stone. The burnished tables and marble statuary. The vases and pedestals whose iridescent glazes sparkled in the soulfire backwash, and whose blooms lent a soft, musky fragrance to a chamber that would otherwise have stunk of nothing but dust and old memories. And the bed, which was itself larger than several of the palace's bedchambers – and whose construction had been the labour of a dozen blank-eyed koilos – laden with pillows and sheets of the finest samathine silk.

For all that the Eternity Queen maintained lavish staterooms elsewhere in the golden citadel, this was her home. Her sanctuary. Just as the souls of Khalad depended on her judgement to atone for their sins and rejoin the cycle of rebirth, so too did she rely upon their strength to knit mortal body to divine soul.

||How was it done?|| asked Yali.

Damant hesitated, but alone of the Eternity Queen's conclave, she had his full trust. Careful that the tip didn't pierce his glove, much less the skin beneath – the worst of the venom would have evaporated by now, but no chances – he produced the dart. ||Hisser dart.||

She frowned. ||A what now?||

He indulged a grim smile. For all her streetwise upbringing, it seemed Yali still had gaps in her knowledge. ||It works on the same principle as a shrieker, only instead of the ifrît flinging fire, it pushes air. That air pushes the dart. They're short-ranged, expensive and silent.||

||And small, I'm guessing?||

||If the artificer's up to it, small enough to palm or to be sewn into the helm of a robe.|| He shrugged. ||I've only ever seen one. Just owning it was enough to condemn a woman to death. Firebloods don't always fight fair, but some things are beyond the pale, even for them.||

She shot him a sour look. ||Firebloods don't do anything fair, honest and true. She could have died.||

||I'm sure that was the point.|| Glib tone disguised uncertainty. *Kerem* venom could kill the goddess's mortal host, but presumably not her divine spirit. What then would that mean for Khalad, whose people had already unknowingly conspired to her captivity in the Stars Below?

For all that the Eternity Queen claimed that the two halves of Nyssa – mercy and judgement – had found balance within her, that wasn't the same as a declaration of forgiveness. A mother's love lay equally in scolding as affection. ||Our old friends are getting creative.||

||This wasn't them.|| Yali's stony expression lent weight to heavy signs.

Damant sighed. For all her keenness of mind, Yali still had the stubbornness of youth. Old loyalties sometimes fought their way to the surface. ||They made their choice. Wishful thinking won't change that.||

||Kat wouldn't try to kill her. Certainly not with poison.|| Yali's cheek twitched. ||She loves her.||

||Maybe.|| Katija Arvish had loved the mortal Yennika Bascari, but who was to say that the regard had endured. Arvish had opposed the armies of the throne immortal ever since the Eternity Queen's apotheosis. Could she really fight one and not the other? Just because the Eternity Queen still showed flashes of affection for her mortal lover didn't mean they were reciprocated. ||Maybe not. But Vallant's fought a losing battle against the throne for twenty years. Do you really think he'd not stoop to such methods?||

||This wasn't them,|| Yali repeated. But this time Damant thought he caught a glimmer of doubt in her eyes. ||Short-ranged, you said. *How* short-ranged?||

He grimaced, his pride at her having read the situation so cleanly tempering a sudden sense of foolishness. He'd accused Yali of falling back into old patterns while having done the same himself. ||Short enough that only someone on the council could have done it.||

"Find them. Those who would harm a goddess ... should face her judgement." The soulfire column rippled in sympathy with the Eternity Queen's breathy proclamation, her tone no longer that of a woman speaking to her confidants, but a goddess addressing her servants. For all that her eyes remained closed, Damant had the keen sensation that little of his conversation with Yali had gone unnoticed. "I have endured captivity for millennia. I will not be denied. Not now. Not ever."

The soulfire column's magenta darkened to deep indigo as staccato passion displaced weakness, adding gravel to the Eternity Queen's already husky voice and power to her words. "All that you are, you owe to me. All that is endures only because *I* endure." Exhausted, she sank back, clinging to the throne's gleaming stone armrests as tightly as any drowning woman to storm-lashed rock. "Let all betrayers burn as Tyzanta burned."

Damant bowed. ‖"As you order, majesty."‖ Was it a trick of the light, or were there more grey hairs among the black than when she'd gone into the flames? He turned to Yali. ‖You'll stay with her?‖

Yali nodded, her pensive eyes on the throne and her expression unreadable.

The bitter purples of evening ruled the conclave hall on Damant's return, held at bay only where lumani prisms cast their warming glow across the polished timbers. The galleries had long since emptied, the almost great and not so good ushered out onto the streets – even Karza's companion, Keti, had possessed the sense to depart.

Only the councillors themselves remained: the councillors and a ring of a dozen redcloaks. The latter group had their shriekers holstered and scimitars sheathed, their expressions concealed behind their golden masks. All shared the curious stillness of men and women primed for violence. Kastagîr's embellishment of his instructions, Damant supposed. Unwelcome but hardly unexpected.

What *was* unexpected was that the council was shy one member.

Damant ascended the dais, eschewing his usual station at the throne's right hand for a position immediately to its front. "Where's Ardin?"

Karza sniffed. "He said he'd had his fill of 'all this damned theatricality' and that you'd know where to find him if you wanted him."

Even under ordinary circumstances it was poor manners to leave conclave without explicit dismissal. In the wake of an attempted assassination, many would have viewed it as a confession of guilt. But Damant had been too long a custodian to jump to lazy conclusions. Ardin's pride was hurting. Ill manners were to be expected . . . but still,

Damant wished he'd instructed Kastagîr to hold the council until his return. "His exact words?"

Karza offered a languid shrug. "I may have ... smoothed them over."

"Ardin's not the only one weary of theatricality," said Emanzi. "The Eternity Queen, Damant. She lives?"

A blunt question, but not unexpectedly so. "For now," Damant replied.

Bathîr offered a stiff curtsey. "I pray that she will recover." Such was the august reverence in her words that it almost distracted from their contradiction. To whom did one pray for a goddess's deliverance?

Karza and Hargo bowed their heads. Malis stifled a sigh. "You have suspects in mind?" Her eyes gleamed. She, at least, knew where this was going, but then she'd have been little use as a spymistress otherwise.

Damant straightened his back. "I'm addressing them now."

Hargo's head jerked up. "I beg your pardon?"

"Oh, be quiet, Hargo," Malis snapped. "*Kerem* venom, Kastagîr said. Is that so, Damant?"

"It is."

"Stars Below ..." murmured Emanzi.

"How did it happen?" said Malis.

"I have no information to share on that point," Damant replied, "at least for the moment." Uncertainty was a slender advantage to wield over the would-be assassin, but he'd take any edge he could get.

"I see." Malis threaded her fingers, a picture of dignified unconcern. Exactly the stance a woman satisfied of her own ironclad innocence might adopt. Or one guilty as sin and confident that no evidence would ever lead to her door.

"It isn't for you to withhold information from this council, Damant," rumbled Hargo.

"Hiding behind protocol?" said Karza airily. "How courageous."

Hargo rounded on him. "Something on your mind, Tuzen?"

"Only that I welcome whatever steps the good castellan deems necessary to bring the culprit to light." A peremptory smile touched Karza's lips. "I for one am pleased to offer my full cooperation."

"I'm very glad to hear it," put in Damant, "as with Captain Kastagîr's assent, you're all to be searched before you leave this room."

Hargo's cheeks ruddied to match a thunderous scowl. "You cannot be serious!"

Bathîr and Karza looked on aghast at the prospect of indignities to come. Emanzi's lips thinned to a slash. Only Malis nodded, stonily composed as ever.

Damant caught Kastagîr's eye. Receiving a sharp nod in exchange, he relaxed a fraction. Kastagîr's backing, and by extension that of every redcloak in the Golden Citadel, reduced the chances of the coming hours descending into mayhem. Each of the councillors had substantial private armies, whether custodians or simple mercenaries. Redcloak spears would stop soured pride mustering them against Damant's thin body of palace custodians.

Damant folded his arms behind his back, enjoying the moment. "I am *deadly* serious, Lord Rashace. How can I be anything else when the Eternity Queen was ushered to the edge of the Deadwinds by someone in this room?" Not that he imagined the search would turn anything up. Anyone with the wit to acquire a hisser in the first place would know to dispose of it at the first possible opportunity, most likely by palming it off to an accomplice before the gallery emptied . . .

He glanced at Karza. Perhaps Keti's departure from the conclave hall wasn't the concession to decorum he'd first thought. Had she whisked Karza's hisser from sight and was even now giggling with pride at a deception so easily accomplished? Someone who drew as much attention as Keti practically demanded to be ignored, lest the observer become tainted by association. He shook the thought away.

"You *will* be searched," he said, his gaze on Hargo once more. "I leave it to you how much dignity it costs."

"And what of Ardin?" growled Hargo. "He practically attacked the queen and now he's fled. The arithmetic couldn't be more obvious."

Damant stifled a grimace. Ardin's troubled soul and intemperate behaviour were damning, though hardly conclusive. Both Hargo and

Emanzi had been reprimanded during the conclave – Emanzi in particular for her failure to secure Tyzanta's ruins – and both were shrewd enough operators that they must have anticipated such criticism. Had one of them, fearing the Eternity Queen's wrath, taken extreme measures? "I'll speak to him when we're done here."

"Assuming he hasn't fled the city," said Emanzi, darkly.

"If he has, then he'll save me a deal of investigation." Flight would be as good as any admission of guilt.

She snorted. "True."

"And the deaf skirl . . . She is above suspicion?" said Bathîr.

Damant gritted his teeth. Between her deafness, her cinderblood birth and her irrepressible cheer, Yali existed at a confluence of the archon's prejudices. "I'm content that the high handmaiden is innocent, yes."

Malis stirred. "Are we permitted to know your reasoning?"

Because of everyone in this room, she's the only person who serves the Eternity Queen out of love, and not self-interest. Damant kept his expression carefully immobile. In truth, he'd no reason to exempt Yali from suspicion save instinct and friendship. Present either of those as "evidence" and the councillors would unravel his authority by those threads. "I would remind you that she above all others has unfettered access to the Eternity Queen—"

Malis nodded. "And such privilege breeds opportunity for wickedness."

"Indeed," said Damant, his attention given over not to her but to Kastagîr's fleeting scowl at the reminder that however high in the Eternity Queen's affections he might have been, he was by no means pre-eminent.

"Then by all means," said Malis, "let's have this over with. I, for one, have nothing to hide."

"And if nothing incriminating is found . . ." Emanzi's gaze lingered on Malis for perhaps a hair longer than necessary, "on any of us? What then?"

"Conclave will be suspended indefinitely. The inner palace and this hall will remain off limits while investigations continue."

Malis bristled. Without access to the Golden Citadel's palace, and by extension to the Eternity Queen, the ministers of the council were little elevated above the functionaries they oversaw. Rumour would spread, and the scrape of political knives being sharpened would echo through every hall in Zariqaz. "I see."

Damant inclined his head. "You'll cooperate, of course?"

"Do we have any choice?"

"No." The flat declaration was Kastagîr's, and brooked no argument. Defiant expressions slid towards resignation.

"And what of your trip to Tyzanta to investigate Emanzi's . . . short-comings?" asked Hargo.

Damant considered. He'd quite forgotten about that. "The Eternity Queen is my first duty. Tyzanta will wait. You should feel free to go on without me, Lord Rashace."

"And leave others to spread lies in my absence?" Hargo's eyes touched briefly – and not at all by accident – on Emanzi Ozdîr. "I think not."

Damant stifled a sigh. So the knives were being sharpened already? What did it say about the Queen's Council that they so readily turned on one another? What did it say about Khalad? The Eternity Queen deserved better.

Vallant, Arvish and the others, he understood. Unable to counte-nance the possibility that the Eternity Queen was indeed the goddess Nyssa, they clung to the pain of the past, perpetuating the cycle of rebel-lion. Had they but remained in Zariqaz after the Obsidium Uprising, they'd have witnessed her beneficence for themselves. They'd have understood. Even now, he hoped they might one day do so. They weren't wicked, simply misguided. Broken by Khalad's injustices as he'd once been. Fighting against a tyranny that no longer was. By contrast, the ministers of the council paid lip service to the Eternity Queen's vision, but continued as their kind ever had, seeking profit and influence wherever it could be found.

Perhaps it would be simplest to lock them all up ... or better still, send them to the Golden Stair, there to await the kiss of the executioner's blade. That had certainly been Caradan Diar's way. Order born of simplicity, practised with little mercy and less recourse, which had in turn seen cruelty fester in Khalad's ruling classes. That cruelty had driven Damant to join Vallant in rebellion; the certainty that the Eternity Queen would set things right and restore Khalad to what it should have been – and perhaps once *had* been – had brought him back.

Let the others bicker and jockey for position. He at least would remain true.

"Your lordship must do as you think best, of course." He rubbed the heel of his hand against his temple as the throb behind his eyes returned. "And if what you think best is to defy the Eternity Queen's command, then that is, of course, your prerogative."

Eight

Night fell long before Damant left the palace custodium behind, the chill air a welcome respite from the frustrations of a day not yet done. The scent of juniper and jasmine laced his cloudy breaths, born of the bright magenta and indigo flames leaping skyward from among the Golden Citadel's tangled streets. The Aurora Eternis had descended with the nightfall, its green shimmer contesting the cloudless starfields, and the keepers of Zariqaz's surviving torch houses were anything but lax. The Veil had swallowed too much of the city during the Obsidium Uprising for anyone to take the chance of repeating such days.

As he'd feared, searching the ministers had garnered nothing but sour expressions and silent promises of retribution. Subjecting his peers to a level of surveillance lately granted only to the absent Ardin Javar would likely yield more useful results, but setting the arrangements in motion had taken an inordinately long time. So had sealing the conclave hall – and by extension the Eternity Queen's sanctum – under the watchful gaze of hestics attuned to soul-glyphs borne only by himself, Yali and Kastagîr's most trusted redcloaks.

Some of those redcloaks were visible even now, patrolling the broad streets between the palace gardens and the ring-wall dividing them from the broader city. Always in twos or threes, their weapons polished to a mirror's gleam and their advance scattering servants and custodians alike from their path.

Setting a brisk pace and wrapping his cloak tight to keep the cold at bay – Zariqaz's nights were ever a contrast to its sweltering days – Damant crossed beneath the barbican portcullis and out onto the broad expanse of the Golden Stair. Polished flagstones shone in the reflected firelight, the blood of Caradan Diar's reign long since scrubbed away and the headless, carrion-gnawed bodies once strung beneath the arched roadway given decent burial. More of the Eternity Queen's largesse on display, and the citizens of Zariqaz had, by and large, repaid her in respectful fealty. Even the Undertown skelders were quieter than in any city Damant had ever known, and what little thuggery they indulged seldom trespassed on the spire's well-to-do streets. The Eternity Queen had brought order to Zariqaz, which made the day's attempted assassination all the more unthinkable.

Lost in unhappy thoughts, he left the Golden Stair behind and passed through the gatehouse of the second ring-wall. Here, as at the first, no redcloak stirred to challenge him. After months in the Eternity Queen's service his identity was well known, and anyone foolish enough to attempt impersonation would have to reckon with the dead-eyed koilos sentries, whose murderous ifrîti cared nothing for likeness and everything for the soul-glyph tattoo he bore.

Beyond the ring-wall gatehouse, the music and lights of the upper spire rose to meet him. While the palace belonged to the Eternity Queen alone, the lower four ring-walls were a tangle of fireblood palaces and townhouses, stretching out along arrow-straight roads of black marble and culverted streams that eventually emptied into the Silent Sea, far below.

Just down from the gate, crowds thronged in Temple Square. Lumani lanterns strung beneath the honeycomb archways woke bright silks to brilliance as drumbeat and lyre roused dancers to stave off the dawn. Ribaldry and mirth joined the clash of goblets and snatches of song. And all of it watched over by redcloaks and custodians unfortunate enough to have drawn duty that night, their presence a warning to any skelders who might have slipped spirewards from the lower city, or those firebloods who – like the ministers of the Queen's Council – needed ready reminder of virtue's rewards.

The heady fragrances of char-roasted meats and spiced wines swirling about him, Damant threaded his way past the golden minarets of Zariqaz's xanathros – the high temple of the Alabastran faith – and struck out for the darker quarter in the shadow of the sealed Qabirarchi Palace. Alone of all the Golden Citadel this had seen no mason's loving touch since the Obsidium Uprising, the Qabirarchi Council having allied themselves with Caradan Diar against the goddess. Transformed by their inner wickedness, the hierarchs of the council had become abominations more suited to nightmarish legend than waking life. Now the derelict palace was their only memorial; the palace, and several hastily rewritten verses of scripture by which the rest of the Alabastran church had distanced itself.

As the fire-blackened towers drew nigh, crowds that had once stood shoulder to shoulder thinned to conversation circles and amorous couples not yet drawn to the privacy of shadowed streets. The ragged edge of any gathering, where passion and vice were transacted beyond the unwelcoming gaze of custodium law. Twice in as many minutes Damant caught the gleam of copper and the clink of glass as dinars changed hands for talent wisp vials, as well as the hurried retreat of a handsome young man about whom the air buzzed with the sweet musk of isshîm powder.

The whip-crack of a slap sent a gaudily dressed man stumbling out of an alleyway, forcing Damant to a hurried sidestep. Arms flailing for balance, the unfortunate ricocheted off a small marble shrine on whose arch stone the wing-and-circlet emblem of the deposed Caradan Diar could still be seen, and struck a fountain basin forcefully enough to double him over and render a dunking from brow to neck.

As he rose spluttering from the waters, a slight rust-haired figure darted out of the alleyway, her bare shoulders and arms pimpled with cold against which her gauzy silk dress offered little protection. "*Darathi!* Let me help, please!"

Noticeably unsteady herself, she tugged at the man's arm with rather more enthusiasm than leverage. The ensuing tangle of limbs pitched her would-be rescuee twice more into the water before he at last surfaced for good, twisted about and slumped against the fountain basin. Blood oozed from twin scratches high on his cheek. His dark, unfocused eyes blazed with bleary indignance.

"Damant?" Karza's boot shot away on a marble slab made treacherous by his own flailing, forcing him to grab at the basin for support once more. "Blessed Nyssa, the very man. She attacked me! I demand justice!"

Damant, having already supped his fill of Karza's company that day, glanced at the shivering Keti, who now clung to Karza as much for her own support as his. Her watery eyes flitted hither and yon with the unmistakable skittishness of one emerging from isshîm's soothing dreamscape to bitter reality.

"Did she? This *child*?" The emphasis came unbidden.

"Not Keti, you imbecile," said Karza, himself no master of good manners in that moment. "Her!"

He jabbed an unsteady finger in the direction of a cloaked woman who, head bowed and hood drawn, was easing her way back along the street towards Temple Square.

Damant hesitated, but Karza's bleating had drawn too much attention, and custodial law enforced order only so long as folk believed it could do so.

He reached the would-be fugitive in two long strides. As his fingers closed around her arm, she tugged free and formed a fist. Her hood fell back to reveal cold green eyes and the collar of a golden gown.

Damant sighed. ||"Do you want to tell me what this was about?"||

Yali bit her lip, eyes unfriendly. ||His *lordship* said I looked lonely.|| An emerald band glittered on her ring finger as she signed, the breadth of its settings a good match for the bloody furrows on Karza's cheek. ||He suggested I might join them. When I refused, he reached for his purse.||

Still unsteady, Karza levered himself to something approaching upright, Keti hovering in his shadow. "I only meant—"

Yali buried her fist in his gut. He doubled over, retching, swayed a moment then toppled sideways onto the flagstones. Keti shrieked and shrank away as Yali hitched her skirts and rammed booted toes into his ribs.

She stepped back, signing furiously over Karza's twitching body, though it was doubtful he was by now in any state to take it in. ||I know what you meant! You think I didn't notice how you've looked at me these past few weeks? Those "accidental" little touches?|| Another kick elicited a fresh moan from Karza. Keti flinched as Yali jabbed a finger in her direction. ||Do you *really* think I'm like her? Really?||

A chuckle rippled through the growing crowd of onlookers. Odds were good they knew Karza's identity. Like each of the Queen's Council he'd delivered speeches aplenty to attentive crowds and no shortage of portraits in print and oils to acquaint subjects with his likeness. Though a servant of unparalleled status, a servant Yali remained. She held her status close and was likely a stranger to those present. But crowds had an instinct for taking whichever side was most entertaining, and Yali was certainly that. Prior even to her association with Vallant she'd proven herself a lock charmer of unparalleled skill. On the one occasion Damant had seen her at work, he'd found something oddly enchanting in the deft dancer's rhythm by which her lockpicks had coaxed the supposedly unpickable safe into giving up its secrets. Watching her attempt the same with Karza's ribs with nothing but a pair of wedge-heeled boots was scarcely less hypnotic.

But you could have too much of a good thing.

Stepping crabwise around the prone Karza, Damant again took Yali by the arm, tugging her sufficiently off balance that her latest kick wasted its force on empty air. He flashed an inverted fist-to-palm sign. ||"Enough."||

She glared up at him through red-ringed eyes bright with tears of rage. ||Not even close.||

94

At their feet, Karza moaned. "She's a madwoman ..." His arm buckled as he tried to push himself upright. He rolled over onto his back, his sodden and scuffed robes no longer close to the finest that Zariqaz's haberdashers had to offer. "And you're all witnesses! I want her in shackles!"

||Your brother was worth fifty of you.|| Yali's snarl could have curdled milk. ||Honest and true.||

Damant beckoned to Keti. "Help him up."

Still more terrified rabbit than girl, she nodded gratefully and darted forward. Flashing worried glances in Yali's direction the entire time, she lent brittle strength to help lever the downed Karza first to a sitting position, and then to his feet. A dutiful daughter helping her aged sot of a father. If only that had been the relationship. The onlookers offered a ragged ironic cheer as his lordship came fully upright. They voiced a rather more enthusiastic one as he swayed, staggered, then clutched at the fountain's rim and vomited noisily into the waters.

Ignoring the bittersweet aroma of undigested wine and Yali's triumphant smile, Damant fixed Keti with a basilisk stare she didn't deserve. He wondered by what blandishments and promises Karza had bound her. None of it illegal certainly, more was the pity. Powerful men seldom needed resort to such methods. "Can you get him home?"

"I ... I don't know," she replied in a small, trembling voice.

Damant turned on his heel, scanning a crowd of onlookers already thinning now the best of the entertainment had passed. "Custodian? I need you. Smartly now, woman."

Silver *vahla* mask gleaming in the lumani light, she left her station by the street corner. "Castellan?" Metallic reluctance shimmered beneath the words.

"Take his lordship home. Carry him if you have to."

Reluctance dimmed to fatalism. "Sir."

Arm still draped across Keti's shoulders like a scarf long past its heyday, Karza glared bleary daggers. "Not until I get resti ... restitution!"

95

Damant stepped closer and lowered his voice. "You know who she serves. Do you really want to antagonise her, today of all days? When your loyalty is already under question?"

Karza blanched, just sober enough – thank Nyssa – for the oblique threat to sink in. "I . . . I . . . I . . ."

"Fell over, your lordship?" asked Damant, deadpan.

Karza's mouth opened and closed, pride battling pragmatism in what little of his mind remained afloat on a sea of inebriation.

"That's right," said Keti, even her shîm-addled wits more apt to the moment. "Come, *Darathi*, let's get you to bed."

Karza nodded. With one final rheumy-eyed glare at Yali, he allowed himself to be led away into the night.

Otherwise alone now by the fountain, the night all the colder and its merriment further away than ever, Damant turned to Yali. ||Feel better?||

She stared at him in fragile, unblinking defiance, her eyes still red-rimmed but now empty of tears. ||No.|| The sharp, aggressive sign faltered and blurred. ||Maybe.||

||He'll need last breath.|| A guess, but a safe one. Even if Yali hadn't broken a rib, the raking blow from her ring would scar without swift treatment. ||You'll pay for it.||

||Fine. It was worth it.|| The last of the rage slipped from her expression. Shoulders sagging, she stared up the street to where Karza and his mismatched entourage had vanished into the crowd. ||That stupid girl.||

||She probably thinks she loves him. She wouldn't be the first to let a lie carry her through the day.||

Seeing that her right hand was trembling, Yali cupped it in her left until the tremors faded. ||No, I suppose she wouldn't.||

||You were supposed to stay with Yennika.|| When they talked in public – empty though the street now seemed, words carried in the darkness – she was never the Eternity Queen, and certainly not Nyssa. Her mortal name granted distance and protection against prying ears. A goddess was entitled to her privacy.

Yali scowled and tapped a clinking purse at her waist. ||She wanted wine. A Sessian red. Under the circumstances, should I really have fetched it from the palace kitchens?||

A touch paranoid, perhaps. An assassin who went to the lengths of acquiring a hisser would hardly rely on so haphazard a method as blind poisoning to get the job done, and they could have no way to narrow the selection down to a bottle destined for the Eternity Queen. But then he supposed Yali was entitled to a little paranoia. ||And Karza?||

||He and the girl were . . . having a moment in the alley. I practically walked into him, and he started . . . I didn't mean it to go so far. It just felt so *good* seeing him squirm. I wish I could have heard him scream.||

Damant grunted. ||Why do I feel like I just saved his life?|| And that he'd made a mistake in the process. No tears for Karza, whether he was a would-be assassin or simply a rake.

||I'm not Kat. I might wish I was, but I'm not.|| Yali sighed. ||I miss her, old man. All of them. Why did they abandon us?||

He met her gaze and reached for a reply, but found none. Before the Obsidium Uprising he'd been as close to peace as he'd ever known, freed of duty to a state unworthy of his service and in the company of men and women worthy of his respect, even of his friendship. Now? Now, he was surrounded by snakes like Karza. But what else could he have done? Kat, Vallant, Rîma . . . They'd taken arms against the Eternity Queen. Even now, months later, they were the ruin of the borderlands. Some choices were no choices at all.

||They chose their allegiance.|| He broke off to massage his throbbing temple with the heel of his hand. ||So did we.||

Yali stared at him a moment longer, her hands shaping the precursor to a sign that never found its form. Then she nodded, the hurt and loss locked behind her eyes once more. ||I'd better find that wine. You know how Yennika can be.||

Unforgivable to say such a thing of a living goddess . . . save perhaps between friends, and Damant had few enough of those left. ||I do.||

||And what about you? Don't take this wrong, but you look dead on your feet, honest and true. Get some sleep.||

||I will.|| He stared along the street, past the ramshackle palisade and the scorched, dilapidated walls of the Qabirarchi Palace. ||But first I have to see an old friend.||

Nine

The gates to Ardin Javar's mansion grounds were flung open to the night. The guards – a sallow and brooding trio who'd served their master in the streets of Tyzanta, and latterly during his oversight of the Nassos shipyards – scarcely acknowledged Damant as he stalked past into the manicured honeysuckle-fragrant gardens. Their disinterest spoke of an arrival anticipated and arranged for.

Had he been foolish to come alone? Possibly. But showing up at the gates with half the custodium at his back would have sealed Ardin's lips tighter than prism glass. He'd never responded well to shows of force. And besides, Damant reminded himself, he was hardly isolated, even now. A full dozen of Ardin's staff owed loyalty not to their paymaster but to Damant himself, their allegiance purchased with tetrams if the Eternity Queen's blessing proved insufficient.

Still, he took comfort from the weight of his shrieker resting against his thigh.

The steward who answered his knock at the mansion's front door offered a familiar face: Ryal, an ex-custodian with a blackened record that owed more to fiction than fact. He'd risen far in Ardin's service in a few short months.

Damant offered a curt nod. "Your master's in?"

Ryal jerked his head back towards the sparsely lit gloom of the main hallway. For a man whose abiding travail in life was to prove that a gutter-born cinderblood was every bit the equal of those who considered themselves his betters – no matter which side of the law he'd operated on at any particular time – Ardin was making a poor showing that night. The mansion seemed more a tomb than a dwelling, drowning in liquid shadows. "The south terrace. Up the stairs, third door to the left." More and more it felt like a trap. But even a trap had lessons to teach, if carefully sprung. "He's not been himself since he returned. Walk softly."

Damant offered the slightest nod – anything more might have endangered Ryal if another servant of less ambiguous loyalty was watching from the shadows – and began his twilit ascent.

The south terrace was neither so broad or so grand as the name implied, space being at a premium within the ring-walls of the Golden Citadel, its balustrade encompassing an area equal to the footprint of a modest townhouse. But the view offered ready compensation. Beyond the vine-woven trellis that provided shelter during the heat of the day, there was nothing save the shimmering haze of the Aurora Eternis and the stars of the night sky. The city's bustle felt a world away.

Ardin sat slumped in a wicker chair beside a low table, a goblet hanging from his hand and a brooding stare levelled at the night-swaddled horizon.

"Have you come to claim my head for our Bascari queen?" He spoke without turning, a liquor-leadened tongue furring his characteristic rumble.

"No."

He splashed a generous glug from a narrow-necked bottle into his goblet. "But she lives?"

"She does."

"Of course." He took a swig. "I've never had that kind of luck."

Damant flinched. "Those are dangerous words."

"This is a night for truth, and the truth is that I always hated that bitch, even before she had my dear Salenna killed." Yennika's youngest cousin had been but one victim of the vengeful feud that had ripped

House Bascari apart. Ardin stared down at his hands, the knuckles creaking as he flexed his fingers. "Ever since Tyzanta burned, I've had no happy thought that didn't end with my hands around her throat."

Damant suppressed a shiver. No calvasîr-laced bravado in those words. Not with that growl behind them. Not with black madness screaming humiliation and hurt beneath. More than ever, he was reminded of bodies broken in the gutter for House Bascari, for Vallant or for Ardin's own criminal advancement.

Hand on his shrieker, he stepped closer. "Did you try to kill her?"

"No. I'm just an ancient and impotent wastrel." Ardin quaffed, calvasîr dribbling through his beard. "But I'll toast whoever did."

Damant let his hand fall from his shrieker. He'd been ninety per cent certain of the answer even before he'd even asked – poison was too subtle a weapon for a man such as Ardin – but you never knew how that last ten per cent would fall. "Do it quietly and it can be our secret."

Ardin clambered unsteadily out of his chair and faced Damant. He looked five years older than he had even that afternoon, cheeks haggard beneath his beard and dark circles ringing bloodshot eyes. He tipped his goblet to his lips. Finding it drained, he reached for the bottle. On discovering that too was empty, he sighed like winter rain, set both down on the table and fixed Damant with a bleary stare.

"If you've not come for my head, why are you here?"

"To ask for your help." Damant scowled away a swell of disgust. He'd seen Ardin the worse for drink more times than he could count. Indeed, in his younger days they'd roamed the streets of Tyzanta's Undertown together. But this? This was different. As though there were a third person in the conversation that only Ardin could hear. "It will wait."

Ardin sank unsteadily against the terrace balustrade, his shoulders swaying even after the remainder came to rest. "Say that it won't. Humour me. For old times' sake."

This was feeling more and more like a waste of time. "The would-be assassin used a hisser. They're rare and difficult to make, much less restore if the ifrît's faded. No reputable shriversman touches that kind of work for fear of getting caught. But a *dis*reputable one . . .?"

Ardin grunted. "And you think I might know such an individual?"

"I imagine you can name at least three within the city walls."

His lips cracked a wolfish grin, a little of his old self shining through. "Why should I bother?"

"Because if you didn't try to kill the Eternity Queen, one of the other councillors did. And I know how much you hate them."

"Very good." Ardin tapped the side of his nose. "I'll tell you, but do something for me first."

His sudden mirth set Damant's nerves further on edge. "And what's that?"

"Here." Ardin patted the balustrade. "Tell me what you see."

Visions of being heaved over the terrace edge pushed to the back of his thoughts, Damant joined him. Far below, Zariqaz unfurled from the ring-walls of its central spire, a toybox upended by a thoughtless child, dotted with lights that wouldn't fade until dawn and magenta flames that would linger until Mistfall had come and gone. Even at that hour, dark silhouettes of cargo carracks and military dhows slipped sail from dockyard piers; columns of smoke from departing railrunners curled skyward. The Obsidium Uprising had levelled more than half the city, but diligent labour had smoothed away its wounds. Undertown's notorious slums were barely a memory, replaced by new construction and airier streets. Not paradise, not remotely so, but a far cry from how things had been before the Eternity Queen's enthronement.

"Well?" asked Ardin.

"The city. The lower ring-walls, Undertown." Damant shrugged. "Zariqaz."

"That's it?"

He frowned, unable to follow the tortuous path of drunkard's logic. Was Ardin even talking about Zariqaz, or about Tyzanta, whose ruins lay far beyond the south-east horizon? "That's it."

Ardin grunted. "You should drink more."

"I already drink more than I should."

A mirthless smile tugged at the corner of his mouth. "And why is that, I wonder?"

Damant frowned. What could he say? How to express the feeling of directionlessness that had haunted his every step of late? Better not to even try. "That's none of your concern."

"You were always rigid, from the very first day we met. I thought the streets of Tyzanta would fold you in half, but here we are three decades on. You're castellan to the Eternity Queen, and I . . ." Ardin lapsed into silence and gazed out into the night. "I am a fool."

"You're a minister in the Queen's Council."

"We are none of us what we seem, Ihsan," he said darkly. "Nothing is, not any more. Sometimes, when the calvasîr chases away the cobwebs, I think I see . . . No, not *see*. Sometimes I almost *understand* what we have become. Or perhaps even that isn't true. Perhaps we were always this way and never knew it."

"You're not making any sense."

Ardin rapped a knuckle against his temple. "That's the problem with drinking to clear the cobwebs. Lucidity retreats as enlightenment approaches."

"And drunk old men seek profundity in babble."

"I shan't weary your ears with it." He braced his palms against the balustrade and hung his head, eyes closed. "I *did* try to kill the Bascari Queen today, Damant. Oh, not with poison. But I would have snapped her in half with my bare hands and to the Deadwinds with the consequences. But when she looked at me, something *broke*." Fingers twitching, he massaged his chest with his open palm, smearing sweat across his templar's robes. "I was screaming the whole time, but I couldn't hear myself. Just like the night Tyzanta burned. Just like when I opened the gates of Nassos and ripped Vallant's flag from its spire."

So *that* was what this was all about? Ardin's conscience, buried so long beneath so many betrayals, was finally clawing its way to the surface? Knowing better than to say as much, Damant opted for an oblique path. "This is the calvasîr talking."

Ardin rounded on him, eyes wild. "It's only the calvasîr that lets me speak of it at all!" With a sweep of his hand he sent the table flying, bottle and goblet shattering on the terrace flagstones. "There's something inside me, Damant. It's twisting me inside out and I don't have it in me to live with it any longer."

So it *was* his conscience, wedded to the unhappy realisation that in the Eternity Queen he'd found the one person he could neither cajole nor bully.

Ardin sank to his haunches against the balustrade. "I don't expect you to believe me. I sound mad. I probably *am* mad." Low growl gave way to a mirthless laugh. "For all I know, you can't even hear me."

Damant crouched, wary of provoking another outburst. "I'm listening, Ardin. And I remember that you promised me three names."

Ardin sighed. "You only need one. Mezzeri. Works out of Tanleer Street. Shake her down with my blessing."

"I'll do that." Damant rose, the creak in his knees and back an unwelcome reminder of too many years behind. "What about you?"

"Enlightenment awaits, by one darkness or another."

Damant regarded him with pity, an old man in rumpled finery, haunted by deeds undone, and by others he wished he could unmake. Even as a templar, Ardin Javar had never been a good man. He'd always thought too much of himself, too little of others, and disposed of both accordingly. But he'd also taken a naïve young custodian under his wing when others would have let Tyzanta's skelders pick him apart. A capricious kindness, but one that had hardened to a firm foundation. Pity was owed for that, if nothing else. Even if Damant couldn't quite bring himself to lend it voice.

So he did the only thing he could, and left Ardin beneath the stars with his conscience and his failures.

Ten

Midnight had long since turned crisp by the time Damant found his way down into Starji district, but Tanleer Street was every bit as full as Temple Square had been. Subdued revellers clung close to street bonfires. Dogs skulked from one to the next, begging for scraps and growling to protect territory. Children who'd have been better served sleeping in the newly built townhouses on the street's north side huddled into their parents, mouths agape in the relaxed comfort of innocents and imbeciles. Older, cannier folk raised long faces and suspicious eyes from the flames, their conversation falling silent until he'd moved on. Though Damant was by no means as notorious as he'd been in Tyzanta, authority had an aura all its own.

Grateful for the directions provided by the local custodium, he picked his way along the row of awninged frontages to an unassuming pair of wooden pillars and a wide leaded window. A rare survivor of the Obsidium Uprising. Light glinted through a chink in the curtains.

Breath frosting, Damant hammered on the door. Receiving no answer nor any sense of motion from within the shop, he did so again, sparing a leisurely eye for the occupants of the nearest bonfire, two of whom were ignoring him with the rapt determination of folk paying the closest attention of all.

He knocked a third time with the same absence of result. The polite – not to mention *safe* – course of action was to retreat until sun-up and return with custodians at his back. But the cold had done little for his headache, and his investigator's instincts warned that time for answers was swiftly running out.

Besides, even at the best of times skelders had little claim on politeness.

He glanced up at the lintel. The flame-haired likeness of Nyssa Benevolas gazed out from a graven sentry crest. The black crystal of the prism serving as her eyes was cracked and dark, the hestic ifrît that had once watched the threshold long since dissipated to nothing.

So be it.

He slammed his boot into timber, just beneath the locking plate. The door practically leapt back off its hinges and slammed against the inner wall. Ignoring the sudden shouts of alarm from the bonfire, Damant pressed into the gloom.

The hooded lantern on the counter shaped a haphazard maze of shelves laden with trinkets and boxes. An armless statue of Nyssa Iudexas, armoured for war, stood sightless sentry in the far corner. The counter lay burdened with a dozen heavy ledgers, one of them open with a swan feather quill wedged in the gutter. A stack of coins, mostly copper dinars brightened by the occasional golden tetram. A whiff of spiced pipe leaf soured the air.

He took a step towards the counter.

Shadows seethed the aisle to his right, the scimitar barely a grey slash in the abiding darkness. He caught the attacker's sword arm at the elbow and rammed it against a shelf. She howled, sword clattering from a nerveless hand, and in the next moment found herself pressed up against the wall, Damant's forearm an iron bar across her throat and his eyes inches from hers.

"Mezzeri, I take it?"

She offered a vicious glare from a craggy, time-worn face that belied her true age. Life on the skelder's edge between outright criminality and honest employment took its toll. "You're dead."

A scuff of boots on the shop's threshold told the rest of the tale. Two of the watchers from the bonfire, possibly three.

Mezzeri's toes scrambled for purchase as Damant leaned in closer, raising his forearm to hitch her another inch up the wall. With his free hand he eased his shrieker from its holster and pressed its muzzle none too gently into her ribs. "Get rid of them."

Her expression froze, but her hand jerked a staccato series of gestures beside Damant's head. The footfalls withdrew, taking the prickle along Damant's spine with them.

He stepped back and dipped his shrieker. "Better."

Mezzeri massaged her throat and regarded him coldly. "What do you want?"

Progress, but he knew better than to hurry their conversation. Impatience was a useful ally. Folk would give up all kinds of information just to see the back of you. He glanced about, his eyes at last fully adapted to the sparse lighting. The shop's interior was a far cry from its external appearance, the shelves scuffed and sagging, the plaster coving pitted and rotting. "I expected something grander."

"You're hilarious."

"You know who I am?"

"The queen's castellan. I expected something grander too."

"It's an unjust world," Damant replied equably. "At some point in the past few days someone came to you with a spent hisser in need of a fresh prism. This afternoon, that hisser was used in an attempt to assassinate the Eternity Queen. Your only hope of not spending the next five centuries staring out of your own gilded skull as a koilos depends on what you tell me next."

"I don't know what you're talking about."

The expected denial, the opening to a familiar dance, but tonight Damant had no patience for its steps. Besides, for all her rote tone, Mezzeri had gone rigid, her eyes suddenly that of prey desperate for escape. Petty skulduggery was one thing. Abetting an assassination attempt on the Eternity Queen was something else.

"No games, Mezzeri. It's been a long day and I've a headache like you wouldn't believe. We both know that ten minutes of searching this warren will give any judicator cause to strip the skin from your bones." Damant shrugged. "I know who you are as well. A master shriver, disbarred from the guild after you were found slicing fireblood souls into talent wisps without family consent. Just how much of your own soul did you have to pledge to Alabastra to avoid execution?"

A rhetorical question, as the custodium records had been quite clear. Alabastra took the probity of its shriversmen very seriously indeed. Criminality ate into profit. That Mezzeri was still at large suggested she'd benefactors – or blackmail victims – within the church even now. Not that they were of any use to her at this moment.

He prodded her with his shrieker, ever an aid to flagging memories. "I want a name."

"I don't have one."

Damant grunted. He'd not expected her to buckle so easily. Then again, someone like Mezzeri only survived by being a ready reckoner of prospect and risk. "What *do* you have?"

"A custodian came by two days ago."

He frowned. "A custodian?"

"She wore the *vahla* mask and robes of one, anyway."

That was less concerning – such attire wasn't hard to come by – but also less useful. "Details, Mezzeri. What did she sound like? How did she move?"

"Taller than me. Walked as if she owned the place." Mezzeri narrowed her eyes, defiance kindling. "Lot of that going around. But she didn't say a word aloud. Simah only."

Smart enough to keep her voice hidden. More bad news. "Did she speak it well?"

"Had a stutter to it. I don't think it's her first language."

"And the hisser itself?"

Mezzeri shrugged. "Old. Beautiful. Inlaid with pearl. Probably an heirloom. I'd say you were looking for a fireblood."

Damant cursed under his breath and fixed her with a stony gaze. Her information wasn't worthless, but it amounted to little more than a dead end all the same. A fireblood woman taller than Mezzeri who spoke Simah as a second language? Once blurred by custodian uniform, the description applied equally to the female members of the Queen's Council. Certainly it eliminated Karza and Ardin from suspicion, but they'd barely been suspects to begin with. Nor was the choice of means helpful in narrowing the field. *Kerem* venom was easy enough to source – the snakes were everywhere in Zariqaz's upper sewer. All it took was camphor to block the effluent stench and a thick pair of gloves to blunt the fangs.

He toyed with the notion of leaning harder on Mezzeri. Instinct warned it was a waste of time. She'd already given up enough to get her killed if the assassin caught wind. If there was a magic question that would shake loose something useful, he couldn't even see the shape of it. "If you see her again – if you even hear of her – I want to be the first to know. Your service will not be forgotten."

Offering no acknowledgement to Mezzeri's mute nod, Damant holstered his shrieker and left the shop.

Several times in the long, slow trudge back up to the Golden Citadel he had the sense of being followed, but each time caught no glimpse of pursuit. Tiredness playing tricks, most likely, or else the erstwhile bonfire watchers were cannier tails than most of their ilk. In any case, the sensation vanished as soon as he passed the baleful stares of the koilos guarding the lowest ring-wall gate.

As Damant recrossed the Golden Stair, he was refused passage by a sentry piquet of no fewer than a dozen redcloaks. His mood, already tinged black, plunged deeper into the abyss during the interminable wait while a *gansalar* was fetched from his duty rounds, authorised his entry to the palace and imparted the information that Captain Kastagîr wished to speak with him in the conclave hall.

By that time, Damant very much wished to have words of his own, and gladly traipsed through a palace far thicker with redcloak patrols than on his departure, though happily ones disinclined to challenge his presence. Servants scurried from his path, eyes downcast, goaded on by a frisson in the air that Damant neither recognised nor trusted.

Try as he might to resist, his thoughts turned time and again to the Eternity Queen. Had she relapsed? Had there been another assassination attempt in his absence – impossible though that should be?

Sentries uncrossed their spears as he bore down on the conclave hall doors. Kastagîr stood in the centre of the dais, deep in conversation with two *sarhana* veterans, their redcloak livery heightened by golden gorgets and black sashes.

"What's going on, Kastagîr?" said Damant, cutting across their muttered conversation. "Is the Eternity Queen—"

"She's resting." Kastagîr dismissed the two *sarhana* with a wave and squared his shoulders. "Where have you been? I've had men looking for you."

That struck Damant as unlikely, given his reception at the gate. More likely Kastagîr deployed it as a shield against a reprimand. A dull soul he might have been, but one couldn't spend time at conclave without picking up new tricks. "I'm here now. What do you want?"

"The Eternity Queen requests your attendance."

Damant frowned. "Do you know why?"

"Oh yes." Kastagîr smiled. "Shall we?"

Damant followed him through the gilded door and down to the sanctum. The Eternity Queen still sat upon the throne immortal, though her regal, controlled posture belonged to a very different creature than the brittle woman from whom he'd earlier taken his leave. She was again a mortal goddess, implacable and enduring, the interplay of light and shadow from the all-embracing soulfire column lending terrible aspect to her beauty. Yali's absence provoked a flash of concern. Hopefully she'd come to no harm in her search for the elusive Sessian red.

Damant offered the Eternity Queen a low bow, and noted that Kastagîr did not. "Majesty. You're looking better."

"Thank you, dear Ihsan." She closed her eyes, white teeth gleaming behind perfect lips. "All thanks to your quick thinking."

"You do me too much credit. Majesty . . . forgive me, but it has been a long day, with another certain to fall hard on its heels."

Kastagîr stiffened, his expression unfriendly. One did not speak to the Eternity Queen thus. At least, he didn't.

The Eternity Queen opened her eyes. "You want to know why you were sent for?"

Damant shot a glance at Kastagîr, unable to resist a swell of petty satisfaction at having the gap in their status confirmed. "If it pleases you."

She nodded, solemn. Solemn, and a touch sorrowful. "Faizâr has caged the assassin."

Damant blinked. "He has?" The idea of Kastagîr outwitting anything swifter than a rock was a difficult proposition. "Who?"

"The queen's high handmaiden." Kastagîr's words rippled with contempt.

Damant glanced from one to the other. "You can't be serious."

"She's behaved suspiciously for some time, coming and going at all hours."

"That's it?" He shook his head, concern bleeding away into contempt. "She has a lover in the lower city. It's not a secret."

"His name?"

"I've never felt the need to pry." He glared at Kastagîr. "Is that really all you have?"

"She abandoned her post this very night."

"She abandoned nothing. The Eternity Queen called for wine, and Yali – sensibly – didn't want to risk something from the kitchens."

"Ihsan . . ." The Eternity Queen leaned forward. "I made no such request. She left while I slept."

Damant touched his eyes closed as a pit opened up in his stomach. Easy to see why Yali had chosen the lie. The Eternity Queen's wishes were not for gainsaying. Had she simply wanted an excuse to be away from the palace's stifling atmosphere, or had she darker motives as

111

Kastagîr clearly suspected? Unthinkable, but the lie made things damn difficult. "What else do you have?"

Kastagîr straightened. "Lord Karza deserves some of the credit—"

"Karza?" said Damant sharply. "What does that snake have to do with this?"

"Yali attacked him tonight. He petitioned me for redress."

"Did he mention that I'd already refused him that redress?"

Kastagîr frowned. "He did not. You witnessed the attack?"

"I did, and Karza deserved every inch of what he received."

"Regardless, he alerted me to her absence from the palace ... so I took the opportunity to search her chambers." He produced a folded square of paper from his pocket and handed it to Damant.

Glancing at the Eternity Queen and finding no help in her impassive expression, Damant unfolded the paper and peered at the scratchy, whirling sketchwork within: a spiderweb of lines trammelled by a bow-sided pentagon. A copy of a soul-glyph, meticulously captured. "What am I looking at?"

"I consulted Lady Ethara. She tells me it's the glyph for the palace koilos."

Damant turned the paper over. So Malis was part of this as well? Likely she was the one who'd planted the idea of the search in Kastagîr's limited brain. Not that it much altered Yali's prospects, which were growing darker by the moment. The koilos wouldn't care by whose authority that soul-glyph came to be inked, only that it was. Someone bearing the design could come and go as they wished. No wonder he'd been held at the gate. "You took this from Yali's chambers?"

"Two *sarhana* witnessed the search."

The two from the conclave hall, most likely. Kastagîr hadn't taken any chances. *Sarhana* veterans were as incorruptible as redcloaks could be. Either Yali was involved in something very dark indeed, or someone was working very hard to frame her. But then Yali *also* fitted Mezzeri's description, thin though it was. Had her imperfect Simah not been stuttered at all, but deliberately distorted?

"This doesn't prove that she's the assassin," said Damant.

"But it *is* proof of treason," said the Eternity Queen, a sorrowful note creeping beneath otherwise crisp words. "I don't welcome it either, Ihsan. I've always thought Yali faithful. I would hate to lose her service, but Faizâr's evidence is convincing . . . and her service needn't end with her death."

Damant stared again at the glyph. Easier to do that than grapple with what the Eternity Queen hadn't *quite* said. That someone was being played for a fool, he didn't doubt. Was he the fool in question, blinded by friendship and Yali's ready charm? Even if he was not, defend her too vigorously and suspicion would also fall upon him, hastened by chequered pasts too alike in the detail. Morning would come soon enough as it was. All he wanted was a stiff drink and whatever sleep could be managed.

But friendship brought duties of its own. "I'll speak with her."

Eleven

Kastagîr had ordered Yali confined to an unused guardroom in the north tower's barrack block, close enough to a torch house that the entire room was musky with juniper smoke and bare of furniture save for a serviceable bed. Better that than the palace cells, whose rancid mixture of fear and ordure no amount of fresh water or scrubbing could wash away. Yali sat on the bed, knees bunched up to her chest, her golden skirts wrinkled and scuffed.

||How are you?|| said Damant.

||I've had better nights,|| she replied, her eyes fixed on an unremarkable patch of whitewashed plaster. ||This isn't what it looks like.||

He grunted. ||I've never heard that before.||

||Why would I need to copy the koilos soul-glyph? I can come and go as I please.||

||To get an accomplice inside, to succeed where you failed.||

She shot him an angry glance. ||Did Kastagîr tell you that?||

||He didn't have to.||

Her signs grew sharp, furious. ||I have three rooms to myself. There are a hundred places I could conceal a scrap of paper in my bedchamber alone. Even you'd struggle to search them all in less than a day. Kastagîr finds it in few hours? Not a chance.||

She tugged a doubled fistful of her hair free of its ponytail, screamed her frustration at the ceiling and went back to staring at the wall with bloodshot eyes, rigid and trembling. ||You can't let them turn me into a koilos. You can't.||

||The Eternity Queen takes Kastagîr at his word.||

Yali snorted. ||So much for friendship.||

Though he understood her sense of betrayal, he deemed it misplaced. Yali and Yennika had been friends, or mostly so, but the Eternity Queen was *not* Yennika, or at least not her alone. She was Nyssa, and claiming friendship with a goddess was presumptuous at best. ||She can't show favouritism, you know that.|| But hadn't she done precisely that by taking Kastagîr's word over Yali's? Was the divine Eternity Queen even capable of feeling fear as a mortal might? ||You shouldn't have lied to me about the wine.||

Yali slumped, the last fight gone out of her. ||I know, but Yennika was sleeping and I wanted to see Qamar ... I knew you'd pack me back off to the palace if I didn't give you a better reason.||

He stifled a sigh. Foolishness on top of foolishness, every slab laying a path to the Deadwinds. But distant though the memory was, he'd been young once, and the lie should have been harmless enough.

||Qamar.|| Damant filed the name away. ||He's your lover?||

She shrugged. ||I don't see it lasting.|| Her expression grew pensive again at the realisation that the relationship might now end on a shriv-ersman's pyre. ||This is bad, isn't it?||

||It's worse than you think.|| Careful to keep his back to the door and his gestures close to his chest to curtail any possibility of being overheard by a redcloak peering through the keyhole, Damant laid out what he'd learned from Mezzeri. Yali's expression grew steadily more downcast.

||Have you told anyone else?|| she asked, lips pinched.

||No, but it's sure to reach Malis's ears.|| Ardin. Mezzeri. The toughs at the bonfire. Too many loose threads. ||I have not been subtle tonight. And besides ...||

||You can't be certain I haven't done everything I'm accused of?||

He hesitated. ||No, I can't.||

Yali offered a wan smile. ||I understand, I do.|| She sank back against the wall. ||If this comes before a judicator, I'm dead, aren't I?||

||You could ask for a trial before the conclave. The Eternity Queen might permit it.||

||And let Karza hold any influence over my fate? Worse, to have him think I owe him a favour?|| She grimaced, a woman beholding a fate worse than a koilos' grim shroud. ||Besides, it's still my word against Kastagîr's, isn't it?||

||It is.|| Until talk of Mezzeri's client got out, after which it would get a good deal worse.

||I think . . . I think I'd like to be alone now.||

There should have been something he could have said. Something to ease her pain or at least offer a ray of hope, but providing solace had never come easily to Damant, much less when the recipient was a woman a third his age. So he instead honoured Yali's request and left her alone with her thoughts.

Despite his intentions to crawl back to his bed, Damant found himself walking the palace's meditation cloister as the dawn began its inexorable conquest of the eastern horizon, though it was as yet barely a ruddy glow through the Veil's thickening mist.

The wider palace was gathering to the business of the day, the incense of Alabastran ceremony sanctifying the six chapels and driving gloami ifrîti from the headstones of the sunken graveyard. But there in the covered walkway wedged between the conclave hall above and the teeming functionaries' quarters and barracks below, he found something as close to solitude as could ever be found in the palace. Everyone else avoided the place, deeming it tainted by associated with the deposed Eternity King, whose Voices – female descendants tasked to deliver his will to conclave, and thus Khalad – had once held sole dominion over the cloister and its balconies. Damant had never cared for such foolishness, and counted it among his few refuges – even if the stonework had grown shabby for lack of a servant's touch and the flower beds wild for want of a gardener's attention.

116

And so he paced back and forth in the light of lumani lanterns as the Veil swallowed dawn's nascent glow and the air thickened with old memories, struggling to chart a course that wouldn't end in disaster.

That Yali *had* been framed by parties as yet unknown, Damant no longer doubted. In the first place, her particular mix of rage and fear was a tricky one to fake. In the second, the evidence – if such it should rightly be called – was a peculiar mix of circumstance and tidiness, lying unhappily against instinct and experience.

What then to do? First would be to speak to Halazni, the palace's chief shriver, so as to be absolutely certain the sketch was what it purported to be. While Damant didn't for a moment believe that Malis would easily mistake it, there was always the possibility that she'd lied. After that, talk to the *sarhana* who'd accompanied Kastagîr in his search. Maybe another visit to Mezzeri in the hopes of scaring something loose. With so many threads now entangled, it was less about opening up fresh paths of investigation than snipping off dead ends.

Even if Kastagîr *had* found the soul-glyph in Yali's quarters, the identity of who'd placed it there was another matter. The assassin, looking to muddy the waters as she readied another attempt? Kastagîr himself, seeing an opportunity to remove Yali from the Eternity Queen's circle? Karza, who was likely the unspoken source of Kastagîr's inspiration to make the search in the first place? Or even whoever was providing Tyzanta's smugglers with the details of House Ozdîr's attempts to curtail their activities? Always assuming that any or all of the above weren't the work of the same individual. The assassin's dart might not have slain the Eternity Queen, but it had thrown the palace into chaos. Opportunity was rife.

He ground the heel of his palm into his temple. Was this really the order he'd sworn to serve? Firebloods fighting like rats in a sack the way they always had. Bad enough if nothing had really changed, but Yali had cast off from her old life to serve at the Eternity Queen's side, and for what? To be hollowed out and serve for ever from behind a koilos' rictus when her mistress declined to offer so much as a word in her defence?

Head in his hands to ward off another swell of pain, he sank against the balustrade and drew down a deep breath to calm the galloping in his head. He couldn't think that way. The Eternity Queen had already done so much to restore Khalad to order. She wasn't responsible for the carrion pecking at her wake – and for all their looks and finery, carrion was all that Karza, Kastagîr and their ilk were.

Sleep. It would all be better when viewed with fresh eyes. Perhaps a drop or two of calvasîr to ease him on his way. Raging at the dawn did Yali no favours, nor himself.

He straightened, his headache at last receding.

All along the cloister the lumani went out.

"Don't move," a husky voice breathed. A woman's. Hard-edged and weary. Neither young nor old.

Headache forgotten and eyes struggling with the sudden gloom, Damant made to turn.

"I said *don't*," hissed the woman. "I have a shrieker. I'll shoot you down without a thought."

He froze. The voice was familiar, but he couldn't place it. The palace was full of redcloaks and maids, few of whom he knew well. He might have passed the woman a dozen times that very day. Certainty was a rare bird in the darkness with a shrieker levelled at his back.

"Your shrieker," she murmured. "Finger and thumb. Leave it on the ground."

"So you can shoot me?"

"I can shoot you anyway. Your choice."

Put like that, it was no choice at all. Careful to keep well clear of the trigger, Damant tugged his shrieker from its holster with forefinger and thumb and set it down between his feet. "What do you want?"

"To save the high handmaiden's life." Threat gave way to something sardonic. "If that's all right with you?"

"What do you know?"

"Follow."

Footsteps tracked away, the woman a dark shape in loose robes and

118

a heavy lace veil as she swept towards the cloister door and its still-lit lantern. It doused as she approached, rendering her but a shadow of a shadow.

Damant trailed her through the Voice's long-deserted chambers, the dust clinging to neglected antique furniture. No matter how he lengthened his stride he never drew close enough to glean more than the barest clue to her identity, and no lumani stayed lit long enough in her presence to offer more. Odd stumbles in her otherwise confident steps betrayed either age or infirmity, or else suggested she saw little better in the dark than he.

A dozen paces before the corridor terminated at double doors to the palace's main concourse, the woman turned. The brass muzzle of her shrieker a dull gleam as she trained it on Damant, she traced the fingertips of her free hand along the wall, tugging at the moulding here, pressing there.

With a soft click, a section of wall swung inward.

"Inside."

Damant eyed the darkness without enthusiasm. "I think I'd prefer you to just shoot me here."

"Don't be tedious."

Goaded by a jerk of the shrieker, he stepped over the low sill and into the narrow passageway. Glancing upwards, he glimpsed a flame-wreathed sentry crest, barely recognisable as such under layer upon layer of paint.

"Keep moving." She prodded him into darkness so complete that he'd no choice but to feel his way past worn brick and crumbling mortar.

"A secret passage?" he murmured. "I didn't think the palace had any."

The woman laughed softly somewhere behind him. "The great Ihsan Damant: all the imagination of a baked potato. The Obsidium Cult used them during the uprising. Probably they came and went for decades, scurrying like rats."

The disgust in her voice settled any doubt that she was Malis Ethara, who'd successfully petitioned the Eternity Queen for Terrion

Arvish – the Obsidium Cult's leader – to be added to the roster of ember-saints martyred in her name.

"Where are we going?" Damant asked.

"Afraid I'm leading you a merry chase to leave you dead in the darkness?"

"The thought had crossed my mind," he replied, as deadpan as headache and growing unease allowed.

"I wouldn't do that. Think of those poor maids going mad trying to find the source of the smell. Here."

For the first time, there was light in the gloom, a hazy glow emanating from two parallel horizontal cracks perhaps three inches apart. As he edged closer, Damant's questing fingers found a metal hinge and a tiny brass latch.

"Go on," murmured the woman. "Open it."

The latch gave readily. Light emanated from gaps in an ornate wooden lattice. Damant peered through, struggling at first to make sense of the arrangement of wood panelling and gilding in the chamber beyond. It was only when his eyes touched on the gold and silver throne, four paces away from the concealed hatch and directly below, that his weary brain made sense of what he was seeing.

The conclave hall.

"The nine hundredth and fiftieth Voice used this to spy on her husband," murmured the woman, sardonic delight back in her voice. "She thought he was having an affair with the chamberlain. Whenever conclave was held, she'd bring her own lover in here for reasons you'd not share in polite company, watching them both the whole time as a form of twisted revenge. I suppose it has a certain contortionist poetry."

Damant grimaced away the unwanted commentary and ran his fingers over the lattice. Easy to place it now. The design looped the conclave hall's rear wall about ten feet above the dais. With the hinged panel closed, this section would be invisible even under close inspection. Open, it offered a reasonable view of the back half of the dais through a trio of gaps, each barely wide enough to accommodate a finger. A shrieker's muzzle would never have fitted through … but a hisser's might. And the Eternity Queen's throne was just there, well within range.

The assassin hadn't been one of the conclave at all.

"Why are you showing me this?" he murmured.

"I told you," she replied, her voice hard. "To save the high handmaiden."

"This helps, but it isn't enough," he said, talking to himself more than to her. "I need something concrete. The weapon. A confession."

"The assassin will be at the Hanged Skelder in the Hazarid district at midnight tomorrow, expecting the second half of her payment. Emerald brooch and matching eyes. If you can't do something with that, I'll send for that baked potato."

Her payment. Mezzeri's mystery custodian. Assuming that he wasn't already talking to her.

Beyond the lattice, the conclave door yawned open and two red-cloaks marched inside. Wary of discovery, Damant pulled the spyhole panel shut, the stiff latch snapping back into place on his third attempt.

"How do you know all this?" he murmured. "Who are you?"

Silence was his only reply. He was alone.

Twelve

Mirzai arrived home as night fell, hands filthy and sore from an afternoon spent wrestling with the conveyor at Rhymsfalt Mine. Flush with dinars from Araq's recent expansion, Darashan had invested in a pair of motic prisms to drive the previously hand-cranked line, and true to form had insisted on running it at twice the rated speed. Two axles had given way under the strain, taking a section of belt with them.

The repairs had been straightforward enough, but enduring Darashan's self-pitying tirade would have drained the purpose from an ember-saint. Mirzai had found holding his tongue more draining than the work itself – especially with Tarin offering an uncanny imitation of Darashan's woe-is-me scowl whenever the foreman's back was turned.

Mirzai laid his satchel on the kitchen table. "Zephyr?"

Worryingly, a deadened echo was his only answer. Three weeks now, and she'd always been waiting in the kitchen on his return, save for those occasions when the tramp of redcloak patrols in the street or Tarin's knock at the door had driven her to seek shelter in the cellar. Some days she'd even greeted him with a prepared meal. Though her efforts were little more appetising than Mirzai's own, the results tasted less of machine oil and stale grease, which was a plus.

Had a patrol come by that afternoon? Their frequency had only increased with the growing redcloak presence. For his part, Tarin stopped by less and less, concern at his uncle's increasingly hermitic behaviour unspoken, but written plainly on his face.

The cellar was as empty as the kitchen. Her meticulously arranged bedding aside, only the pile of tattered books he'd bought to help her while away the hours offered any clue that she'd ever existed. Nor was she upstairs.

Shoulders prickling, Mirzai fought the urge to make a second, pointless search of the cellar. Zephyr was gone. But where? Shorza's redcloaks hadn't found her or they'd have been waiting for him too. Even without her connection to Vallant, her very nature as an Issnaîm made sheltering her a crime. More likely she'd grown impatient with his promises of help and struck out on her own. A reckless choice given the nearest town was two days away on bad roads, through hills teeming with redcloak patrols, but she'd become increasingly frustrated, with apology smoothing away sudden flashes of temper long after the fact.

What had begun as duty mired in reverence had given way to friendship in the intervening weeks. Though she'd spoken little of herself or her kin, she'd questioned Mirzai ceaselessly about his own, about Araq and about the prayers and rituals that had survived Anfai's fall. With her help, he'd pieced together the meaning behind the scraps of language he'd inherited, and learned that his grandfather's lullaby was in fact a lament for the dead ... and also that Zephyr had as little appreciation for his tin ear as Tarin, though that hadn't stopped her from murmuring along whenever he'd given it voice.

And sometimes, late at night when the stars shining in her hair dimmed with melancholy, she talked of days and nights spent roaming the Cloudsea, white sails billowing overhead. When she spoke of her comrades, she favoured all with waspish tone steeped in disappointment, the slow shake of her head shaping shortcomings forgiven by friendship. But fondness simmered beneath, and worry at what might have become of them during her time trapped behind the Veil.

She spoke of Bashar Vallant most frequently of all, and several times enquired as to whether a fresh bounty poster had been issued. Mirzai reluctantly confirmed that none had, though Katija Arvish had since seen two updates, most recently to the unthinkable bloodgild of fifty thousand tetrams – five times that of Vallant. Zephyr had borne the first piece of news with fragile stoicism, and the latter with grim glee.

"Proud of her, he'd be," she said. "Always was, and she hated him for it."

He supposed he should have resented how swiftly and completely Zephyr had demolished the cornerstones of a faith that had turned his family into fugitives. He'd spent the first two nights after her revelations staring empty-eyed into darkened skies, too heartsick even for tears. But he'd ever been a practical man, and faith was more than doctrine. However his ancestors and Zephyr's had become entangled, the tenets of hospitality they'd woven were sacrosanct. She'd needed his help, and now she was gone.

If the Drowned Lady had sent her to test him, as a stubborn piece of Mirzai still suspected, he'd failed spectacularly. At least he no longer needed worry about how to broach the subject with Tarin, whom he'd shielded from Zephyr's presence, and thus any consequences arising from her discovery.

He trudged back downstairs to the kitchen, poured a mug of water and passed outside.

The rear garden was no less neglected than the front, overgrown by waist-high grasses playing court to a pair of crooked yews that engaged in creaking argument with one another whenever the wind gusted over the low mud-brick wall. Propping his back against the nearer tree, he stared up at the magenta halo crowning Giriqan's summit.

"Take your bleak mood elsewhere," a voice called from above. "A surfeit already, have I."

Zephyr sat nestled among the yew's boughs, her vaporous skirts draped across the branches like shrouded cobwebs. A perplexed squirrel stared myopically down at her from the tree's upper reaches, uncertain what to make of its strange guest.

Mirzai's relief darkened to concern. "You shouldn't be out here. If someone sees you . . ."

"Needed to taste the wind, did I. Your house is a cage."

"There are worse cages hereabouts." A week ago he'd accepted Gansalar Shorza's commission to reinforce Nyzanshar's crumbing dungeon walls with metal bars and its doors with grated steel. Though the fee had been generous – as were all offered by Araq's growing redcloak garrison – he'd not wanted to take the work, but hadn't dared refuse lest it drew attention he couldn't afford. "You might want to end up in one of those. I don't."

Zephyr pushed away from the trunk and drifted groundward, restoring the squirrel to sole rule of the yew. She came to rest a pace in front of Mirzai, arms folded and expression unrepentant. "Happy?"

"It's a start." In truth, roaming redcloak patrols notwithstanding, the cottage's remoteness and the overcast night made it unlikely Zephyr would be observed, but an unnecessary risk was an unnecessary risk. Mirzai took a deep breath, recalling his worry at the prospect of her having left. "Please come inside, *nasaîm*."

Her lip twitched. "To squirm and scream as the walls press in around me?"

"It won't be for ever."

"Won't it?" she snapped. "Has there been *any* news?"

"None." He'd taken her letter to Qorral the day after he'd brought her down from Giriqan, but as yet no reply had arrived.

"Destroyed the letter, he has," she muttered darkly. "Or passed it to the redcloaks."

"I don't think so. Qorral's a rogue, but only when there's profit to be had. And if he'd sold it to Shorza, we'd be in adjoining cells by now." Assuming, that was, Shorza had somehow penetrated the true meaning of what had been to all appearances a singularly innocuous letter sent to a distant cousin Mirzai did not possess. Even he didn't know its true message, and treasured his ignorance. "You need to be patient."

"Patient? Tyzanta is gone! Athenoch is sealed away without me, and Vallant ..." Her scowl softened, her voice growing distant just as it always did when she wrestled with Veil-stolen memories. Her being uncoiled to translucence at the edges. She closed a hand around Mirzai's serpent pendant, which still hung about her neck. Little by little, solidity returned. "A poor guest am I," she murmured, "and you a more patient host than I deserve."

Mirzai sighed. "It's been tense in town since the redcloaks arrived. Maybe a reply *has* arrived but Qorral's had no chance to deliver it. I'll speak to him."

She laid her hand on his, the warmth of her touch as always a surprising contrast to her icy blue-white complexion. "But only if I go inside and scream silently at the walls?"

He offered a small smile. "You talked me into it."

With an uneasy nod to the checkpoint's redcloak sentries, Mirzai passed through the gate and into the market square. The commanding *sarhana* barely acknowledged his existence, her attention on a trio of redcloaks unloading a battered cargo rickshaw while its driver looked unhappily on.

Both sentries and gate were new, the paint nearly dry – a mirror to the checkpoint governing passage of the crumbling bridge on the Nyzanshar Road. A necessary precaution, Saheen had insisted, to keep order in the face of the newcomers who'd arrived in the redcloaks' wake: labourers drawn to employment in the newly opened shaft at Rhymsfalt or at the eliathros gas refinery now running night and day; hawkers, pedlars and street-nymphs who'd followed a trail of dinars itching to be spent.

Acting alone, Saheen's tiny custodium could never have kept order once the wine began flowing, and so Gansalar Shorza, who now had never fewer than two dhows tied up at Nyzanshar and at least as many more patrolling the Qersali border, had balanced the numbers with redcloak spears. What had been one town was now effectively three. Checkpoints had rendered the marketplace, temple, custodium and their adjoining buildings – including the two warehouses adorned by the scarlet gonfalons of the Royal Guard – a town in their own right, distinct from the remainder. And then there was the growing shanty of tents and lean-tos along the Araq–Nyzanshar Road, spreading as hungrily as brushfire. More and more, Araq resembled an open wound awash with the scarlet poison of redcloak patrols.

Mirzai pressed on through the empty town centre, ardent hymns soaring from the Alabastran temple vying with the earthier revelry from Elondine's Rest opposite. Two turnings later and the squat, dilapidated building that served as Qorral's shopfront came into view, the weather-worn scroll-and-arrow sign squeaking back and forth on its iron stanchion.

Two redcloaks stood silent sentry, their backs to the glazed half-arc door. Oil lamps above the shopfront that ordinarily blazed day and night – Qorral did his best trade when Elondine's Rest emptied and revellers sought pleasures more rarefied than liquor – were dark and silent.

A chill gathering about his shoulders, Mirzai walked quickly on. Reaching the end of the street, he looped back around to the marketplace, passing beneath the grim stone walls of Shorza's newly requisitioned residence, unconsciously picking up speed to match his racing thoughts.

There were a dozen reasons why the redcloaks might shut Qorral down, some more legitimate than others, but again and again Zephyr's letter returned to Mirzai's mind's eye. The letter, and its coded message he knew nothing about but that was signed with his name.

Blessed Lady . . .

Temptation to flee growing with every step, he veered towards the market checkpoint, determined to return home, pull shut the door and—

No. The redcloaks didn't know. Not about Zephyr's letter, and certainly not about Zephyr herself. Qorral had cheated a *sarhana* or bragged too loudly about his shîm trade, that was all. The redcloaks didn't know. They couldn't.

He had to be sure.

Up ahead, the doors of Elondine's Rest yawned wide in promise.

A wall of heat and light stole his breath as he crossed the threshold. Deafened by the din of a hundred conversations, he searched the room for a familiar face.

The sagging mezzanine, propped up by makeshift wooden pillars of dubious age and uncertain heritage, had the look of a barrack room, dominated as it was by so many carousing redcloaks. The banquet table, pressed to use during saints' days, served a crowd three deep, all paying rapt attention to the blur of dealt pentassa cards and the clatter of coins offered as stake.

The lower floor too played host to redcloaks, but here they mingled with other patrons, be they townsfolk of long standing, custodians, or newcomers from the growing shanty on the Nyzanshar Road. The newcomers – readily identified by robes that the plains-dust hadn't yet dulled to unsalvageable red-brown, greatly outnumbered the Araq natives. The redcloaks outnumbered both.

As he approached the bar, Mirzai sighted a presumably off-duty Oshur, *vahla* mask clipped to his belt and a broad sotted grin on his face, sitting nose-to-nose with a slender blonde redcloak, her hair twisted back in tight plaits and her eyes darkened to inky wells by make-up. One glance and Mirzai abandoned any hope of getting his attention. Unfortunate, as he was the best-informed gossip in Araq. If anyone knew what had happened to Qorral . . .

"Mirzai?" Beneath the mezzanine, Gallar thumped her table with enough force to set the cluster of goblets juddering. "Careful, my friend. There are *people* here." Beside her, thin-faced Qaba offered a theatrical shudder, then broke into a fit of wheezing laughter.

Accepting the jibe with what little grace remained to him, Mirzai threaded his way past the enraptured Oshur and slid onto the bench beside Gallar. "I must have taken a wrong turn."

"Haven't we all, my friend?" said Gallar, suddenly serious. "This brings back too many memories, and none of them good. Did you see that Qorral's out of business?"

Mirzai nodded, his chest tight. "What did they get him for?"

"Isshîm trading, so the warrant said. Saheen signed it herself, but it's corpse rot." Qaba shot a sidelong glance at the nearest redcloak and shuffled closer. "Half of this lot are adrift on the clouds already, or will be before the night's done."

"Then what?" Mirzai asked as calmly as he could manage.

"Refused to pay the protection levy is what I heard."

Mirzai frowned. All businesses in Araq owed a protection levy to fund Saheen's custodium. He paid it himself. Most Alabastrans treated it as a symbolic offering to Nyssa Iudexas. Refusing to stump up was a good way to make oneself a pariah. "There has to be more to it. Qorral's too smart to antagonise Saheen."

"Wasn't her levy," Gallar said heavily. "It was Shorza's. Twenty per cent, right off the top. He's not the only one who refused to pay. They seized Raya yesterday and commandeered her barges. Tamaz the day before that. There's a *sarhana* running his farm now."

"Can they do that?" asked Mirzai. Raya and Gallar weren't friends exactly, but they'd all stood together against the Qersali. So had Qorral, for all his many faults.

Qaba snorted. "They have shriekers and scimitars. They can lock us up, confiscate our holdings, load us down with 'official' fines. Maybe even pack us off to Kaldos for Hierarch Ethrîm to bind us with Alabastran debt, figuring we'll be so desperate to buy back our souls that we'll stay nice and obedient."

"Won't work with Raya," said Gallar. "She never bent the knee to no one. I don't see that changing now."

Qaba shrugged. "Maybe, but it's not just here. Had a family pass through from Ettra yesterday. Redcloaks shut down their custodium two weeks ago, the wife said. They got out when the *gansalar* started talking conscription. They'll be halfway to Kaldos by now, and good fortune to them."

Mirzai closed his eyes, the warmth and cheer of Elondine's Rest in full retreat. All too similar to his grandfather's tales. But in Anfai it had made a cruel sort of sense. There had been a revolt – however justified – to put down. Araq hadn't been in revolt. It had just wanted to be left alone. "Why are they doing this?"

Gallar gulped from her goblet and leaned across the table. "Troops have been slipping across the border for the past week. Burned a Qersali village four days back. It's just the start. The legions are gathering, and legions need food, supply lines . . . and fortresses to protect their retreat. They learned that down on the Copper Road. It'll be blood and freedom all over again, except it'll be blood for all and no freedom this side of the Deadwinds."

"I haven't . . ." Mirzai dropped his voice to a whisper as Gallar put a cautioning finger to her lips. "I haven't heard anything about this."

But then preoccupied with his own private treason, he'd had eyes and ears for little else. Things had been quiet with the Qersali for so long. Not friendship exactly, but a quiet co-existence. If the redcloaks were stirring the pot, Araq's future looked bleaker still.

"Of course not. Redcloaks close ranks around civilians."

"But not around other redcloaks? Ex-redcloaks?"

Gallar shrugged and drained her goblet. "It's your round."

Emerging from the fug of his own concerns for the first time, Mirzai realised that Gallar wasn't half as sober as she first appeared. Her bleary eyes belonged to a woman staring into the future and seeing only flames.

Mirzai didn't want to buy a round. He wanted to walk out the door, leave Elondine's Rest and its infestation of redcloaks behind. He glanced around a tavern filled with strangers; scavengers and opportunists come to pick over and reshape a town so many had died to protect, his sister Midria foremost among them. Even when he'd walked past Qorral's empty shop, heart in his throat and visions of interrogation echoing through his thoughts, Araq had felt like home. No more.

Time for him and Tarin to leave, even if that meant leaving a piece of himself behind.

But try as he might, he couldn't bring himself to begin the long walk back to his cottage. So instead he threaded his way through to the bar, dizzy with what-ifs and maybes. Had Tarin noticed how the town was changing? Would he even *want* to leave? Maybe, if Aethri agreed to leave with him. But she'd a family of her own. And where would they go? From what Qaba said, it wasn't just Araq but the entire frontier.

And what about Zephyr? Even travelling by night to stay hidden from patrols and redcloak skyships, she'd little chance of reaching safety. Be she mortal or divine, he'd offered her hospitality, placed her under his protection. Could he really abandon her?

What price might he pay if he didn't?

The lights and laughter of the tavern spun. He gripped the bar for support and breathed deep. The room steadied.

"Buy me a drink?" A guttural, honeyed voice penetrated his maudlin reverie. The blonde redcloak who'd so lately been the sole focus of Oshur's attention slipped between Mirzai and his immediate neighbour and fixed him with a hopeful smile. "I spent my last dinar yesterday and payday's not until the end of the week."

She didn't look much older than Tarin: too young to be a killer in service to the throne immortal. Then he looked into her eyes, sparkling blue and burdened with cynicism that sat ill with her delicate, pale cheeks and winsome air. He wondered briefly what she'd seen – what she'd *done* – to make her so. Then he remembered that she was a redcloak – with the black sash of a *sarhana*, no less. A heady rank for one so young. He dreaded to think how she'd earned it.

He broke her gaze and made a vain attempt to catch the server's eye. "Oshur would have bought you the whole bar."

She slid closer. "Maybe, but he's just a boy. And he *never* stopped talking. You look like someone who appreciates the value of silence. We could talk about that, if you'd like ... or *not* talk at all?" Her smile broadened with promise. "But it all starts with that drink."

She was persistent, he gave her that. More than that, it was working. As unsettled as he was, something about her called to him. He couldn't look away from that smile – those eyes. And it had been a very long time since any woman had looked at him with that kind of interest. Certainly not since whatever he'd not quite had with Saheen. The clamour of Elondine's Rest dimmed, suddenly a world away. Instinct screamed objection, warned that the redcloak's smile was just a little too predatory for comfort.

Despair howled for something – someone – to cling to.

She slipped her arms over his and about his waist, close enough for the soft fragrance of her scent to tantalise. Not the earthiness of a woman who'd spent the day patrolling under the baking sun, but then a *sarhana* drew lighter duties. "Is it the uniform? Don't let it bother you. It's just cloth. It comes away easily enough. Just say yes, and maybe the night will take us somewhere private. Your home, perhaps?"

More and more he wanted to say yes. Would have, maybe, but for the discomfiting realisation that the piece of him that wanted the woman didn't belong to him at all. Where it had come from, he couldn't say. He knew only that he couldn't trust it. And no matter how her eyes shone, she was a redcloak. Whatever her words, the uniform wasn't cloth alone. Its bloodstain went bone-deep. Desire – if desire it truly was – went only so far.

"I'm sorry."

Her brow furrowed, her sapphire eyes losing their lustre. She rose up on her tiptoes and pressed her cheek against his, her embrace suddenly cold and rigid. "Not yet, you aren't," she said, breath warm against his ear. "I don't take rejection well, Mirzai."

Ice washed away the last dregs of desire. Mirzai's world regained crispness and colour, a drowning man cresting the waves with the dregs of his last breath. "How do you know my name?"

"Hmm ... I must have seen it written down somewhere." Her tone was still laced with playfulness, but with threat lurking beneath. Offence that he'd even *thought* of refusing her screamed loudest of all. "I have so *many* questions."

132

The room spun. The letter. Zephyr's letter. Qorral *had* sold him out. Now that seduction had failed to free the truth, blood would follow.

Frantic, he pulled away. Her grip tightened, crushing his arms against his ribcage. "Don't be stupid. We don't want ..."

Commotion from the mezzanine swallowed her words. The dull thud of a punch thrown chased along by the crunch of a breaking chair. Drunken cheers broke out from one corner of the tavern, a woman's shriek from another. Directly above Mirzai's head, the battered banister gave way, broken spars, pentassa cards and copper coins falling like rain around two plunging bodies.

"*Kiasta!*" hissed the redcloak. Shoving Mirzai in one direction, she dived in the other.

Winded, he hit the floor in the same moment as the mezzanine's debris. By the time bystanders had helped him upright, one of the bodies was on his feet, swaying drunkenly, his left hand clapped to a brow slippery with blood. His eyes darted from the male redcloak lying motionless on the floor to the split knuckles of his right hand, then to Mirzai.

"Uncle?" Tarin swallowed hard. "He started it, I swear. Called me a cheat then came at me with a dagger." Trembling, he stared at the unnatural angle of the redcloak's neck, a thin croak of horror and anguish escaping his lips.

The cheers faded as Mirzai started forward, the mezzanine stairs thunderous with the tramp of boots as redcloaks flooded the lower floor. A grizzled middle-aged woman with the gold-trimmed sash of a first *sarhana* strode forward, two redcloaks at her back. The crowd shrank back, leaving Tarin and Mirzai alone in a sea of splintered wood and scattered coins.

Her lip curled as her eyes fell on the dead man. "We're beyond card-filching now, aren't we? You, you and you." Her gloved finger picked three redcloaks out from the crowd, Mirzai's erstwhile temptress among them. "Take him."

"No! You can't!" Mirzai started forward, fists balled.

The first *sarhana* folded her arms. The redcloak at her back snatched his shrieker from his holster. His own plight forgotten and fear blazing to ash in the flames of protector's wrath, Mirzai barely saw it. Gallar's insistent tug held him back.

Stepping across Mirzai, she stood to attention and offered the first *sarhana* a salute. "This is a matter for Araq's custodium."

"No," the first *sarhana* replied. "He goes to Nyzanshar."

At the clap of her hands, the redcloaks dragged Tarin away.

Thirteen

Mirzai lost track of how long he sat in Saheen's office, head in his hands and trapped in self-recrimination. He knew only that at some point the sun had risen and that beyond the unshuttered window life had returned to Araq, the streets crowding with clatter wagons and labourers going about their daily routines. He'd given up pacing, unable to face Nyzanshar's grim silhouette, plainly visible to the north. Nyzanshar, where Tarin huddled behind a cage's bars – alone, abandoned and terrified.

His fault. Not all of it perhaps, but enough. He'd scarcely spoken to his nephew outside of work these past weeks, hadn't taken the time to impress on him how the redcloak presence brought a hundred unseen perils. He'd told himself that Tarin didn't need the warning. He'd kept seeing a man and not a boy, forgetting how much guidance he himself had needed at that age, even if he hadn't known it. But it was one thing to fear a naked sword and a writ of authority. Recognising the threat behind a ready smile was something else.

Saheen entered, her green eyes weary and her face drawn from lack of sleep.

"Well?" asked Mirzai, throat tight with hope and apprehension.

"I have seen Tarin." Her voice, ordinarily full of verve in friendship or wrath, was as deadened as the rest of her. "They are treating him well."

Mirzai's heart sank. She was dissembling. She was usually direct. "That's not what I meant. What did Shorza say?"

"He was inspecting the front-line patrols all night. His second sent a heraldic for him."

The front line, not *the border*. Did the Qersali yet know they were at war? Would they make a distinction between the townsfolk with whom they'd shared an uneasy peace and the redcloaks who'd sought confrontation? "Just tell me. What did he say?"

Saheen's lip twisted. "That a dozen redcloaks attest to Tarin having started the fight."

"I don't doubt that."

She winced. "I am not surprised either. Shorza was apologetic . . ."

"I bet he was."

". . . but very clear. There has only ever been one penalty for killing a redcloak. By rights, Tarin should be dead already."

By rights. A farcical phrase when it came to redcloaks. Mirzai could have wept, had he not spent all his tears before the dawn. "You *know* Tarin, almost since the day he was born." The words tumbled out in a barely intelligible flood, racked by stuttering breaths. "He didn't mean for this."

"What he meant does not matter, only what he has done." Saheen pinched the bridge of her nose and stared out of the window. When she spoke again, she was rock solid, the personal sealed away beneath her threadbare overseer's robes. "Does Aethri know?"

"Not yet. She's with her parents." That she'd not been at Elondine's Rest with Tarin was the one saving grace. "I'd hoped to bring her better news." He knew the accusation in his voice to be unfair, but it was a small injustice by the standards of that bleak morning, and easily forgiven. "I'll go to her now."

"I can handle that."

He lumbered to his feet, joints creaking like a man twice his age. "No. It's my responsibility." What would he say? What could he? Tarin had been – *was* – her future as much as his. More. Could he really look her in the eye and scatter her dreams to dust?

"Mirzai ..." Saheen turned from the window, her jaw set. "Talk to Shorza. Tarin is your blood. I could not sway him, but you might."

He rested his palm against the door and closed his eyes, the blonde *sarhana*'s face dancing in the darkness. Thanks to Qorral, she knew – or at least suspected – that he'd something to hide. Why he wasn't in the next cell along from Tarin he could only guess. Who knew what might happen if he showed his face in Nyzanshar? "It won't help."

Saheen threw up her hands, the first hint of anger touching her voice. "Stars Below! He is your nephew. Surely it is worth the attempt?"

"I said it won't help!" Shame seethed his sorrow to hot sludge. Had it been him alone, he'd have gone up there in a moment, but there was Zephyr to consider. She was a stranger, and by her own insistence no more divine than Mirzai. Tarin was his blood – his *only* blood. What if it came to a choice between the two? What if Shorza or the *sarhana* had planned this, the redcloak's death an unforeseen accident as the trap snapped shut? "It might even make things worse."

Saheen folded her arms and glared at him with naked contempt. "You want to tell me what is going on with you, Mirzai? You have been distant for weeks."

He flinched. "And you'd know all about distant, wouldn't you? Running around playing Shorza's errand girl while he pulls this town apart?"

"The only errands I have run tonight are yours, and I ran them happily. Because we are friends ... or because I thought we were. Do you have any idea how many promises I have made these past few weeks to keep the peace?"

She cast her arms wide, emphasising each point with a chopping motion. "Only the night before last the Talyaz brothers got into a brawl with some redcloaks. Like Tarin, they swore blind they did not start it, but there are witnesses stacked against them, all of them in shiny red uniforms. The only reason they are walking around free is because their father put up his pitiful savings as collateral. Then yesterday the redcloaks dragged Helia Vahaz from her children. Apparently possessing a handful of Qersi-language books is proof of spying." She bore down with gritted teeth, her eyes flashing and her words guttural with mounting frustration. "Every family in this town has had a run-in with the redcloaks and they all come running to me to put things right. As they should. As is my duty. But I cannot. I wish I could. I have worn out my knees begging that bastard for clemency. How *dare* you sit there and tell me that you are not prepared to do the same."

Fists clenched, she broke off and spun on her heel, head bowed and shoulders heaving.

"I didn't know," Mirzai murmured.

"There is a lot you do not know." She sagged against the desk. "But you were right, back when this all started. We should have fought. Now all we can do is stay low, survive until Shorza gets his thugs killed fighting the Qersali . . . and pray that there is still anything left of this town."

For all that her words held hope, her voice was hollow. Tarin and Aethri's future was not the only dream crumbling to dust.

"I'm sorry. I . . ." Mirzai screwed his eyes shut and shook his head. "Thank you for trying."

He opened the door, only for Saheen's voice to bring him up short on the threshold. "Shorza did make one other offer." She spoke softly, steadily, unfurling the words with aching reluctance. "He set a bloodgild on the man Tarin killed. Meet it, and he will commute the charges to indentured service."

While the coin vanished into Shorza's pockets, no doubt. "How much?"

"Two hundred tetrams."

"That's impossible." Two hundred tetrams equalled some forty thousand dinars. If he worked night and day for the rest of his life, he might perhaps earn that much.

"Not if you borrow from Alabastra with your soul as collateral."

"Is that your suggestion, or Shorza's?"

"He offered you passage to Kaldos on the next supply carrack."

"He doesn't trust Serassa to make the arrangements?"

"In her dusk sermon two days ago, she railed against 'the power of the unchecked sword'. She is fortunate not to be in a cage herself."

Something else he'd not known. Serassa's status as a priest protected her, at least for now, but Shorza would never trust her to draw up the soul contract correctly.

"I can't do it. You *know* I can't."

"I know. But I promised to pass on his offer. And so I have."

Bartering his soul to Alabastra was more than symbolism. It granted the church licence to flense it into whatever ifrîti held value after his death. More than that, it would sever his ties to the Drowned Lady for ever, and bind him to Nyssa. Despite Zephyr's claims of his goddess being a fiction, even the *idea* of it wrenched him up, down and sideways. It was the deepest transgression possible. He'd become a walking shell, a damned mockery of everything his family had ever fought for, had ever believed. He couldn't do it, not even for Tarin.

But what did it make him if he couldn't? Did he love his nephew so little? When his time came, how could the Black River bring him to the Drowned Lady if he broke faith with kin so readily?

"How long do I have to decide?"

"Until tomorrow. You do not want to know what I had to offer up to get even that much time. Drowned Lady watch over you, Mirzai."

The Drowned Lady. Not the goddess. Not Nyssa. Three simple words worthy of an apostate's sanction in the wrong ears. They'd been friends so long, almost more than friends, and for all their recent distance it was increasingly apparent that he'd lately had the better of the deal.

"Thank you, Saheen. For everything."

Mirzai tapped the flat of his scimitar twice against the top of Midria's gravestone and drew his cloak tight. The bright morning had blossomed to an unseasonably bitter day. What little warmth the sun had brought now joined it in retreat beneath the western horizon. He wondered if the redcloaks had bothered to provide Tarin with a blanket to fend off the chill, or if they'd left him shivering in the corner of his cell.

No. Saheen had said they were treating him well, and she wouldn't lie about something like that. Even if it wasn't true, he had to believe it, if only for a little while, otherwise he'd have no strength to spare for what had to be done. Weathering Aethri's tears had almost been the end of him. In the end he'd made his excuses and slunk into the streets for fear that his might join hers and in the mingling never cease.

"*Ayin vanna enna*, Midria."

The tremor in his voice faded. A sign, perhaps, that her soul had heard and lent its fading strength to his. He hoped so. He needed strength now as never before.

"I . . ." He laid his hand on the grave, treasuring the rough scrape of stone beneath his calloused hands. "I don't know what to do. This town . . . You'd not recognise it any longer. It's everything Grandfather fought to escape."

He scowled. He was dissembling.

"Your boy did something foolish . . . They're going to kill him for it." The words scratched at his throat, but he somehow got them out. "It's my fault. I should have been there for him, but that won't change anything now. I failed him. I failed *you*. I'm so sorry."

The wind rustled the gorse, waxy green needles tip-tapping against the cemetery's stones. He bowed his head, listening for a reprimand, a sigh . . . anything to prove he wasn't speaking to himself alone. He heard only the croak of a frog singing its throaty song in the nearby stream.

"Whatever I do from here, it's going to be bad." He stumbled, the next words as hard as any he'd spoken that morning. "I don't think I'll be able to visit you any longer. But my blood is in this soil, same as yours. Wherever the river flows, a part of me will always be here, with you."

He gripped the stone tighter, imagining for a moment that Midria might feel the pressure of his hand. "Farewell, sister. River keep you."

Hearing no reply but the wind, he sheathed his sword and walked back among the graves, the fresh-tilled soil of Helia Vahaz's grave marked with mandevillas plucked from Araq's remembrance garden, and by a small doll left by one of her daughters.

Gallar was waiting at the lopsided wooden gate, shoulders hunched and eyes broody. "Well?"

Mirzai forced a smile. "Would you believe she didn't have anything to say?"

"What did I tell you? Sisters always hold their advice until after the fact." She stamped her feet, red dust curling against her boots. "Qaba says he's in. So are Ravli and Seram."

"I told you I didn't want anyone else involved."

"And I told you I didn't care. What is it you always say? We stand together or we stand for nothing. If this goes your way, they'll come for us all anyway. May as well make it count. Blood and freedom, my friend. Nothing's changed." She gazed out to the west, past the low, mismatched silhouettes of Araq's buildings. "It'll be dark soon. Are you ready to do this?"

"Not yet. One last farewell."

Zephyr rose from the table as Mirzai entered the kitchen, her expression flirting with concern before settling to a rigidity that belied her inconstant, vaporous physique. "Where have you been? Worried, was I."

He held out a dark grey cloak. "You'll need this. You have to leave tonight."

She narrowed her eyes, her brow creasing. "Why? What's happened?"

"The redcloaks. I think they intercepted your letter." He'd rehearsed this a hundred times on the walk back from the cemetery, but still the words rattled away from him. "Even if they don't know you're here, by this time tomorrow it'll be like someone kicked over an ants' nest. You need to be as far away as possible before that happens."

"Before what happens, *ayin*?" She set the cloak down on the table and folded her arms. "Slow down. Breathe."

"I ..." Quelled by Zephyr's less than friendly glare, Mirzai drew down a deep breath. "Tarin got into a quarrel over cards. A redcloak died. He's to be executed."

The words stirred a spark of panic. Some things would never be easy to say – *should* never be easy to say.

"And free him you will, or die in the doing?"

He blinked. "How did you know?"

"Not strangers are we, not now." She offered a musical laugh in a minor key. "Not so *waholi* am I to miss that look in your eye. Family is family."

She reclaimed the cloak from the table and tugged it on. It fitted closer than it had any right to, though even with it drawn tight, vapour curled from beneath its lower hem. She left the hood down, her starlit hair rippling against the woollen fabric as she tilted her head to and fro, examining its fit. "Do well enough, this will . . . even if it itches like the bite of a starving skarabi beetle."

"It belonged to my sister," said Mirzai. "Take it, and anything else you need."

Zephyr sighed, her disdain so complete in that moment that it wasn't just the cloak that belonged to Midria. "Never said I was leaving, did I."

"You have to. It isn't safe here."

"A daughter of the Issnaîm am I, Mirzai. Seldom have I known safety, beyond the mists or within them. When I was nothing but hunger you gave me back to myself. Repay my debts, do I." She threw back her head and fixed him with a level stare, her sudden smile as wicked as any she'd worn atop Giriqan, her self and soul unravelled in the mist. "So tell me, *waholi*: did your sister once carry a sword to match this cloak?"

Fourteen

Nyzanshar's south wall had suffered across the centuries. Though the gatehouse overlooking the winding approach road remained more or less intact, much of the adjoining stonework had long since crumbled into the valley. Scaffold and canvas marked ongoing repair, but gaps aplenty remained. Even from half a mile out, clinging to a stand of trees with his companions, Mirzai glimpsed enough of the courtyard to tally the silhouettes coming and going against the watchfires.

"Sixty, give or take," Ravli murmured over the shrill crackle of courting cicadas. She slid one of her many daggers from its sheath and turned it over and over in her hands. "A challenge."

A dour smile accompanied her words. Her husband had died in a skirmish with the Qersali shortly after Araq's founding. For years after, she'd been the terror of the frontier, slipping beneath the night sky to slit throats and leave warnings etched in blood. Though she wore the intervening years lightly enough, her auburn hair having scarcely gone to the grey, she'd never remarried. Townsfolk joked that death itself had taken her for a bride, though never in earshot.

"It's too many," said Seram, the shaft of his long-handled axe braced between his feet. Mirzai would have struggled to lift the weapon, let alone wield it. Seram stood well over six feet tall and, though his sixtieth year lay far behind, still felled trees and split pinewood for his living. "If we'd twice the number, it would be too many."

"I thought you wanted to avenge Helia." Gallar's eyes never left the distant fires. Where the other five wore mismatched skelder's garb chosen for its aptness to blend with the night, she wore her old uniform cloak inverted, faded scarlet within and black lining outward. A point of pride and disavowal. The shrieker buckled at her waist was another souvenir of those times. Its stock and barrel were polished to a proud sheen, though its prism was cloudy. Still good for a few shots, she'd insisted. There wasn't any way to be sure until she pulled the trigger.

"I do." Seram kicked at his axe haft, his stubble beard twisting to a scowl. "But getting shot down like a stray dog isn't going to settle debts. I told you the veilkin was bad luck."

A nightjar trilled deeper in the woodland. Mirzai exchanged a glance with Zephyr and received a rippling shrug in return. Gallar and Ravli had accepted her readily enough. Life on the border demanded a readiness to embrace unlikely allies, and without the baggage of Mirzai's Anfaian faith, they cared only that Zephyr had the will to fight. Seram's prejudice ran deep. Though he was the first to deny being influenced by Zariqaz propaganda, decades of Alabastran archons declaiming the Issnaîm as vermin, apostates and worse had left scars.

"Patience," said Mirzai. "There's still time."

And there was, but impossible to say how *much*. The dhows usually moored at the east tower's jetty had slipped sail with the dusk, but there was no way to know how long they'd be absent. If they returned, sixty redcloaks would become a hundred, and all hope would be lost.

As if on cue, bright flame blazed into being against the southern skies. A thunder crack sounded, a hollow rumble hard on its heels. The flames flickered hungrily across the skeletal mast and rigging of a redcloak dhow tied up at Araq's elevated dock.

"What a shame," said Gallar, deadpan. "They've been priming the buoyancy tanks all day. Must have been blackfire damp in with the eliathros. I told Saheen she was working the refinery crews too hard."

Seram's scowl broke into a wolfish grin. Ravli offered a thin smile – for her an outrageous display of emotion.

Overwork hadn't caused the explosion; Qaba had. Too old to take an active role in the night's business, he'd found his own way to contribute ... by means that only his status as Araq's dockmaster could have provided. There weren't many things short of outright rioting guaranteed to elicit a panicked response from a fortress full of redcloaks, but the prospect of losing a valuable warship – two, if the fires weren't brought under control – ranked high among them.

Already Nyzanshar's humbled southern battlement was alive with gesticulating figures. A horn sounded as a secondary explosion shook the night. The fortress gates crashed open and a ragged column of redcloaks ran down the approach road, heading for the town. Gansalar Shorza's moustachioed presence was unmistakable atop a dappled grey steed – a rare and expensive indulgence even for a man of his rank.

Thirty redcloaks gone to quell the flames, maybe more. The thirty left behind were still too many to fight, but Nyzanshar's walls were long, and thirty pairs of eyes kept slacker watch than sixty.

Mirzai jerked his head towards the fortress. "Come on."

They picked their way through the musky gorse, aiming not for the broken south wall, but the intact western one. Wincing at every rustle of branches and lamenting the brightness of the stars, Mirzai kept one eye ever towards the road and its draggle of redcloaks. But for all his fears the river flowed towards fortune and no cry of alarm rang out.

He scrambled into the shadows beneath the south-west tower, close enough now to scent juniper ash from the bonfire and catch snatches of conversation. Elation melted into apprehension at what was yet to come.

He glanced back at the others, dark links in a chain reaching back to the valley stream. The commotion on the roadway was all but spent, the last stragglers stumbling on towards the dhow's funeral pyre. Even if he could pass the fire off as accidental, Qaba would pay a heavy price. But there'd been no dissuading him, and there was no mistaking a spectacle sure to draw every eye in Nyzanshar.

Adjusting his scimitar to stop its hilt digging into his ribs, Mirzai set out along the western wall. The gorse rustled. Seram grabbed his arm. "Where are you going?" he growled. "The drainage ditch empties beneath the bridge."

"Change of plan," Mirzai replied, though in truth it wasn't. He trusted the others, but secrecy had kept him alive. "We go in that way we'll come up in a chamber off the courtyard. One idle glance and the Deadwinds will take us all."

"Then what?"

Zephyr breezed past, her footing on the treacherous slope more confident than Mirzai's own. "Hush, *waholi*. Already as subtle as spirefall are you." Her sweet smile held more than a hint of winter.

Seram glared, but he hefted his axe and followed. Ravli trod silently in his footsteps.

Mirzai offered his hand to Gallar, who was making heavy weather of the slope.

"Thanks," she whispered, her wrinkled face flushed. "Too much time propping up a counter and not enough spent stretching my legs. Never grow old, my friend."

"You could have stayed behind." Mirzai fought to keep concern from showing. Gallar was breathing too hard for his liking. "You could go back now."

"And spend the night fretting over what's become of you? One day you'll wake to find that the world is no longer the one you remember, and for all that you'll mourn the loss, it'll bring you clarity." She shrugged, a muscle in her cheek twitching as she stared back at Araq's flames. "I'm precisely where I mean to be."

He opened his mouth to tell her he'd come to exactly that conclusion the previous night, but her eyes warned of a meaning deeper still. Gallar had never talked about her time in the redcloaks, not even during the not infrequent occasions when she'd drunk the balance of Elondine's Rest under the table.

She shifted her attention from the flames to regard Zephyr's pale outline. "Are you sure she can do what she says?"

Mirzai grunted. "You don't question an Issnaîm."

She smiled. "Spoken like a heretic."

Halfway along the western wall, Ravli took the lead, her eyes ever on the rampart above. A dozen paces on, and she held up a hand. "Here," she hissed.

"You're sure?" asked Gallar.

A stare fit for an open grave was Ravli's only reply.

"Believe her, do I." Zephyr peeled off her borrowed cloak and sword belt and tossed them to Seram, her extremities wisping in the open air. "Mirzai?"

Nodding, he unwound the trusser's cord strung between his shoulder and waist. Finger-thin, its hemp woven through with steel, it was light enough to carry and strong enough to rig a felucca's sails.

Zephyr plucked the end from his hand. "Three tugs, then climb."

Her outspread arms and skirted legs growing indistinct to the point of translucency, she rose upon a gust of wind, a woman-shaped cloud, hazy fingertips brushing at Nyzanshar's worn sandstone and the trusser's cord trailing behind her.

"Stars Below," murmured Seram.

The cloud that had been Zephyr flowed across the battlements. Mirzai's straining ears caught a brief scuff of stone, all but lost beneath the faint crackle of the courtyard bonfire.

The trusser's cord leapt in his hand. Once. Twice. Three times.

Taking a deep breath, he gripped the rope tight and began to climb.

Halfway up the wall, his boots braced against stone, creaking fingers and burning shoulders reminded him that Gallar wasn't the only one to have let her strength go to seed. But the thought of Tarin shivering in his execution cell loaned strength to flagging muscles.

As he reached the battlement, Zephyr's fingers – again as solid as they ever were – closed around his. A redcloak lay huddled beneath her foggy skirts, bloodshot eyes staring skyward and his face contorted in unspeakable terror. There wasn't a mark on him.

"What happened to him?"

Zephyr shrugged. "Could not breathe, could he."

Her glassy white eyes shone with malice. Mirzai shivered despite himself. Zephyr might have been neither daemon nor divine, but nor was she mortal as he understood the term.

He jerked his thumb along the rampart. The north-west tower was twenty feet taller than the battlement upon which he stood, and the interplay of angles and distance made it unlikely that its sentry would see anything of what occurred beneath his feet. But no chances. Zephyr nodded, and swept towards the tower's overhang, her vaporous form soon swallowed by shadow.

Staying low against the outer wall so as to remain concealed from watchers in the courtyard, Mirzai unclasped the dead sentry's cloak and set its folds, scarlet out, across his own shoulders. After checking that the trusser's cord was tight about the crenellation – which indeed it was, and by means of knots expected of a seasoned Cloudsea-farer – he drew up the slack. With the trailing end secured tight about the corpse's waist, he pitched the fellow over the battlements, playing out the rope until unseen hands took the burden from him.

Squaring his shoulders in his best approximation of a redcloak's stance, he at last crossed to the inner side of the rampart. His earlier estimate of thirty redcloaks he swiftly downgraded to an even score, although that didn't count the five sentries dotted around the battlements. Three of those were spread along the scaffolding and what remained of the southern wall, their eyes on the distant burning dhow. There'd certainly be redcloaks in the belly of the towers and in the squared-off keep sited against the north wall. The dungeons lay in the keep's cellar, and would have at least one guard.

A wrinkle he didn't care for was that neither the courtyard nor his memories of the crowded road held the blonde *sarhana* from the previous night. Shorza aside, she was the only redcloak likely to recognise him. Though odds were good she'd departed on one of the fortress dhows, her absence was a wild card that left him ill at ease.

Gallar's imitation of a nightjar's hoot drew him back to the tower overhang, which was no longer refuge to Zephyr alone, but all four of his companions.

||A neat enough trick, I'll grant you,|| Seram allowed with heavy-handed Simah. ||What now?||

||We cross to the north wall, and head down through the keep. Anyone gets in our way, we take them out, but *quietly*.|| Mirzai stiffened his fingers to add emphasis to the final sign.

The corner of Ravli's lip twitched. ||Quiet I can do.||

||We free whoever we can, get them over the wall – hopefully before anyone's any the wiser. We'll deal with the rest as it comes.||

Mirzai's tentative plan was to double back to the Rhymsfalt, hijack a cargo barge and be leagues away by sun-up. With Zephyr on hand to remove the trusser's cord – and thus the only evidence of their trespass – Shorza would turn his command inside out looking for traitors within his ranks. But that depended on so much; Tarin's fitness to travel, for one.

||What about hestics?|| asked Seram. ||Koilos?||

||No sign of any koilos. And there weren't any hestics two days ago.|| With so many troops arriving at Nyzanshar – and likely more to come – managing any number of hestic soul-glyphs would have been a logistical nightmare.

Seram gazed unblinkingly down into the courtyard. ||Good.||

Gallar shot Mirzai a hooded glance and tugged on Seram's shoulder. ||What is it?||

He grunted. ||The *sarhana* by the keep's stairway.|| His signs, never the most fluid, grew vicious. ||He took Helia.||

Gallar's tug tightened to a squeeze. "We're here for the living, not the dead. Don't forget it."

Seram's knuckles tightened around the axe haft, but he nodded.

Mirzai eased open the tower door and slipped inside. Like much of Nyzanshar, it had seen better days, with a section of its north wall crumbled away to leave a man-sized gap open to the night. No redcloaks in sight, just supply sacks and crates packed floor to ceiling, leaving space only to access the ladder leading to the rooftop hatch, the spiral stair to the courtyard and the northern rampart. The door to the latter opened without quarrel onto an empty run of wall-walk.

Despite the shadows, one upward glance from the courtyard would have spelled disaster, and Mirzai's shoulders itched with every step he took across the crumbling stones. He didn't dare even breathe until he slipped inside the keep. Cots and hammocks – stripped from the sky-ships of Shorza's small fleet – hung from the rafters in as neat a set of rows as the not-quite-square room allowed. Discarded clothes, books and pouches spoke to the hurry in which the off-duty custodians had departed. Every bed was empty.

He padded to the heavy door opposite that led to the next section of rampart and bolted it shut, then doubled back to the foot of the tower staircase and repeated the exercise. Should anyone start wandering, consternation at a barred door was preferable to being walked in on.

He turned around just as a pair of redcloaks emerged from the head of the stairway leading to the entrance hall.

Instinct screamed at him to run. Calculation knew better. With his skelder's garb concealed by his borrowed cloak, he'd pass well enough. The rapidity of the garrison's expansion made it unlikely every redcloak knew each other by sight.

Offering a nod of greeting, he struck out towards the eastern rampart door – opposite the one by which he'd arrived.

"Hold there," barked the taller of the two, her voice crisp with the authority of a *sarhana* in the making. "I don't know you."

Mirzai halted halfway to the door. "Guardsman Kerazai," he replied, suppressing his guttural Kaldosi vowels as best as he could. "From the *Majestic*."

The woman's scowl deepened. "I know every face aboard. Yours isn't one of them."

Typical. Four ships under Shorza's command meant four-to-one odds, but he'd beaten them all the same. He took another step towards the battlement door, his face crowding with chagrin. "I meant I'm *due* to be assigned to the *Majestic*. I just came in from Ettra this morning."

"Nice try." The redcloak reached for her sword. "Let's have the truth."

Her companion shuddered and toppled forward, his flailing arms entangling in a hammock and a dagger's hilt protruding from his back. Mirzai's interrogator turned and fetched a second dagger in her ribs. An accusatory shout sputtering to a hacking, wheezing gasp, she sank to her knees. Ravli stood in the doorway behind, the blade of a third dagger already balanced between finger and thumb.

Setting his axe aside, Seram strode past her. Brushing past the surviving redcloak's outstretched arm, he clamped her head between his forearms and twisted. With a rippling, gristly crack, the redcloak jerked once and went still. Without missing a beat, Seram gathered her up by knee and shoulder and tipped her into the nearest hammock.

As Zephyr closed and bolted the door, Mirzai tugged the dagger from the first redcloak's spine and tossed it back to Ravli. "Nearly missed that other one. Getting rusty."

She stared back, impassive. "I reckon I'll be getting plenty of practice soon."

"Could be." Gallar stripped the corpse of its cloak and passed it to Ravli before helping Mirzai heave the body into another hammock. "Let's hope it waits for tomorrow."

With both bodies concealed beneath blankets and Seram and Ravli arrayed in their cloaks, they threaded down the spiral stair to the lumani-lit entrance hall. This too was stacked with provisions, so much so that the doors to the inner hall and the dungeon stair were barely visible. By contrast, the outer gate was open to the night, its stones framing not only the courtyard bonfire but the distant flames of Qaba's sabotage. Even from that distance it was clear that the dockyard fires had spread to the second moored dhow.

Zephyr took cover among the crates. ||An expensive night for the Eternity Queen.||

||I'm heartbroken.|| Gallar sank down beside her and eyed the two

151

redcloaks standing sentry two dozen paces away at the keep's open gate. ||Seram. Ravli. Watch our backs. Stay out of sight if you can. Bluff if you have to. Kill quietly if there's no other way. Mirzai? You take the lead.||

||And if you're challenged again?|| said Seram. ||Be more convincing.||

Ravli's left eyebrow twitched. Mirzai shot Seram a sour glance and considered pointing out that he'd deliberately made himself more suspicious once his bluff had been called, but decided against. Seram already knew anyway.

||And me?|| asked Zephyr.

||Follow, but hang back,|| Mirzai replied. ||You're hard to explain away.|| But during their preparations she'd also proven herself a sufficiently accomplished lock charmer to impress Gallar.

Receiving Zephyr's solemn nod, Mirzai crept across the hall, keeping to what shadows the tightly packed supplies permitted. Gallar followed, far lighter on her feet.

Mirzai ran his fingers over a crate's leading edge, the shipper's brand easily legible in the lumani light. The Natari Brewhouse. Nothing but the best for the Eternity Queen's finest. ||It'd be terrible if there was a second fire tonight,|| he signed.

||Wouldn't it? But let's not be greedy.|| Gallar's hands went still, her wrinkles curling with determination and reluctance. ||When we get down there ... What we find may not be pleasant.||

Tension seldom absent that night returned to Mirzai's stomach. ||I know.||

Ceding his position to Zephyr, he struck out for the dungeon stair. Gallar knew better than any what the redcloaks were capable of – what she herself had done before abandoning that life. Tarin was alive. He had to be.

But if he wasn't? Nyzanshar wouldn't be the only thing to burn.

There was no guard at the base of the stairs. The heavy door hung ajar.

"I don't like this," whispered Gallar. "You're sure there's no hestic?"

Mirzai glanced up at the wall above the door. "Still no sentry crest."

Which didn't mean Shorza hadn't had one positioned on the inside, but half the point of sentry crests was to dissuade intruders. "We'll have to chance it."

He eased open the door.

No sign of a guard in the corridor beyond, which from his earlier visit he knew formed the crossbar of a T-shaped room, with two cells along each arm of the T – each with stone walls and a door of steel bars. Three more lined each side of the upright. The stench of sweat and bodily waste rankled the chill subterranean air.

He edged out along the corridor, ears straining for a clue as to what awaited him deeper in. They caught only shallow breaths and the soft scuffs of what small movement might be made by prisoners in cells barely four feet wide and six deep.

The first cell was empty, its door-bolt drawn and the compacted straw on the floor undisturbed. The second held a figure in filthy, torn robes doubled over with his head on his knees. He wore heavy shackles about his wrists, and the right side of his face was a single mottled bruise, his eye swollen almost shut. It wasn't until he glanced up and offered a flinch in recognition of the redcloak uniform that Mirzai recognised his nephew.

Tarin's good eye went wide. Mirzai, his soul seething with anger at the boy's injuries and relief at finding him alive, pressed a finger to his lips.

Surprise retreating, Tarin drew his shackled hands as close to his chest as the chain allowed. ||Care. Redcloak.|| He jerked his head towards the T-junction.

Mirzai looked the cell's cage door up and down. It possessed all the complicated levers and barrels necessary for a motic ifrît to govern the steel bolt, but no prism had yet been installed, leaving a heavy padlock as the sole obstacle . . . and no obstacle at all for a determined lock charmer.

||Sit tight. We'll get you out.||

He drew his scimitar with a sweaty hand and glanced back at Gallar, whose sword was already in her hand. No time now for chances. The guard would be on edge for trouble. They might even have a soul-glyph bound to a hestic hidden elsewhere in the keep. Give them even a moment to think and they'd raise the alarm.

He rounded the corner. The redcloak sat crouched outside an open cell at the far end, an unsheathed sword on the flagstones at her side and her eyes staring through the bars.

Not just any redcloak. The blonde *sarhana* from Elondine's Rest.

With soundless strides honed stalking Qersali hunters, Mirzai edged along the passageway and implored the Drowned Lady to ensure that none of the other prisoners – Raya, Tamaz and two others languished in the cages he passed – did anything to give him away. He'd not killed in over a decade – had prayed fervently that he'd never be called upon to do so again – but wrath kindled by Tarin's injuries washed that old, imperfect resolution aside as if it had never been.

Redcloaks dealt readily in death. They deserved only death in return.

He was two paces away when the *sarhana*'s head jerked up.

"*Kiasta*," she hissed, coming to her feet.

Fifteen

Mirzai lunged with his scimitar, almost glad that apprehension had at last given way to action. Off balance with surprise and her sword still on the floor, the *sarhana* was as good as dead.

She twisted and sidestepped, the palm of her left hand smacking into the flat of his scimitar, pinning it against the stone wall between two cages. Even as Mirzai tried to wrest it free, she bunched the collar of his borrowed cloak in her right hand, jerking him closer as if he weighed nothing. A wicked smile twitching her lips, she rammed her head forward.

A dull thud drowned Mirzai's world in red-black darkness. Groggy, he barely felt the tug that pulled him off balance. The jarring impact of knee and elbow against stone was scarcely less distant. Steel chimed. As the darkness cleared, he saw Gallar stumbling away from the *sarhana*. She cried out as the redcloak's blade sliced a bloody spray from her thigh.

Head throbbing, Mirzai stumbled to his feet. It was only then that he realised he no longer held his sword. Another moment and he saw that the *sarhana* had it. Which meant that *her* sword . . .

Still swaying, he snatched up the *sarhana*'s scimitar – lighter and thinner than his own – and bore down on her from behind.

"Mirzai, no!" shouted Zephyr from the dungeon's crossway. "Tanith! Allies, they are!"

The authority in her voice rooted Mirzai to the spot. Sapphire eyes glittering coldly, the *sarhana* – Tanith – glanced from Zephyr to Gallar to Mirzai. "Well how was I to know? He's dressed like a redcloak, and she fights like one."

Breathing hard, Gallar pressed her free hand to her wound and stared at her bloody fingers with distaste. "Does someone want to tell me what's going on?"

Tanith rolled her eyes. "I came to this armpit of a town looking for her." She turned to Zephyr. "The idiot of a courier got your letter soaked – the ink had run. I'd only the town and the name 'Mirzai' to go on. The redcloaks snatched my contact, so I started asking around . . ."

Mirzai thought back. "Oshur told you who I was."

She offered an eerie saccharine smile. "When you proved . . . uncooperative . . ." her smile darkened with affront, "I at least discovered where they'd taken my contact."

"Your contact?" Mirzai stared into the cell she'd crouched outside. Qorral lay huddled in the unmistakable shapelessness of death. Or at least, what was barely recognisable as Qorral after a heavy-handed beating.

"A distasteful man but a useful one," Tanith replied without obvious sorrow. "Apparently he's been sending interesting titbits to Vallant for years now. Knew enough of our codes to use them himself, when it suited him."

"He didn't talk," murmured Mirzai. Qorral read everyone's mail, always had. Had he passed on the contents to Vallant out of ideology, or for profit? Had the water damage to the letter truly been an accident, or a means of leveraging dinars out of the recipient for the full story? "Otherwise I'd be in the next cell along."

Raya shuffled to the front of her cage. A stocky woman, skin and soul weathered by Araq's unforgiving climate, she'd aged five years since he'd seen her a fortnight before. "Gallar? Is that you?"

Gallar reached through the bars to clasp her hand. "It is."

Tamaz, huddled in the cell opposite, barely stirred from his slump against the wall, but a thin parched chuckle eased from his lips.

156

"Uncle!" Tarin pushed past Zephyr and enfolded Mirzai in a crushing embrace. "I'm sorry ... I didn't mean ..."

Mirzai pulled free sufficiently to clasp the back of Tarin's head in one hand. Careful of the lad's injuries, he pushed his forehead to his nephew's. In his heart he'd never expected to get even this far, but now the moment was upon him, he found no joy – only the challenges they'd yet to face. "All that matters is that you're alive."

"But for how long?" asked Tanith acidly. "I had a nice *clean* plan. One that didn't factor in three lumbering oxen."

Zephyr fixed her with a cold stare. "Hush, *waholi*. We'll manage. Go quicker, it will, if I don't have to charm *all* the locks. A key you have?"

Tanith met her glare ice for ice and spread a hand to encompass the cells. "*Seven* oxen? I'm not a drover."

"Nine. Two more watching our backs, there are."

"We can look after ourselves," said Gallar, her eyes still on Raya. "And we don't leave anyone behind."

"How did you get in?" asked Tanith.

"The ramparts," Mirzai replied.

Tanith sighed and reached for her belt. "Fine. Then we'll go out the same way. But you do as I—"

The piercing wail of a shrieker split the air overhead, followed by a dull crash of breaking timber and a bellow of pain. Seram's. Angry voices rushed after. The hollow boom of a slamming gate swallowed it all.

"*Kiasta*," hissed Tanith.

Raya snatched her hand back through the bars. "Go. Leave us."

"No," Mirzai snapped. "Blood and freedom, remember?"

Gallar pinched her lips and straightened. "It was always a hope, never a promise."

She left without a backward glance. Mirzai hesitated, but already slim odds had gone slender as a blade of grass. He shoved Tarin towards the end of the passageway. "Stay close to Zephyr."

Zephyr had already gone for the stairs, a billow of vaporous white a trail to mark her passage. Tarin blinked as the evidence of his eyes at last meshed with old tales, and stumbled on.

Tanith tossed Mirzai his sword. He caught it cleanly and held hers out by the blade.

She took it with a nod. "Should have bought me that drink."

With a last heartsick glance at the cells, Mirzai ran for the stairs.

The keep's entrance hall was a mess of broken boxes, wine amphorae and packing straw, the remnants of a stack of crates toppled across the outer archway. One of the two gates sat closed. The other hung inward, helpless to bar a bellowing mass of redcloaks barely held at bay by Gallar and Zephyr's flashing scimitars. Even as Mirzai cleared the stairway, Tarin dragged Ravli away from underfoot the melee, his arms under her shoulders and her heels furrowing the wreckage.

A shrieker wailed out. Gallar fell back into the entrance hall, her shoulder ablaze.

Roaring to banish a sick sense of unfolding disaster, Mirzai vaulted Gallar's body and ran to Zephyr's side. A parry more instinct than reason turned aside a redcloak's spear thrust and he rammed his scimitar forward. Warmth spattered across his fingers as his hilt met the dull resistance of meat. He planted his foot against the dying redcloak's hip, twisting the blade free of her body as she tumbled down the slope into her comrades.

All a heartbeat too slow. Fast enough to duck a scimitar's wicked edge, but not to stop its flat chiming against his temple.

The world drowned in red-black gloom, the scrape of steel and the screams of the wounded muffled and dim. Mirzai swayed, aware of a voice shouting his name, of a snarling redcloak drawing back his elbow, steel glinting in his hand. He strove to raise his own weapon, but it was too heavy.

A hand yanked him backwards, and a slender figure stepped in front of him. A scimitar flashed in the clearing darkness. A redcloak slumped wheezing to his knees, hands clasped to a bloody throat. Another screamed and fell backwards into the mass gathering on the slope.

Tanith's insistent voice pierced the red-black darkness. "Mirzai? You still alive?"

He blinked. The pain lingered, a dull knife at his temple, but the last of the gloom cleared. "... Think so."

Tanith scraped a parry and brought her heel down against a red-cloak's knee. He howled as his leg buckled with a crunch like rotten timber. "Then get this skrelling gate closed!"

Abandoning his sword, Mirzai grabbed at the gate's inward edge. He braced his back against the wall and a boot against timber. "Tarin!"

"I'm coming."

As Tarin joined him, the neglected hinges and ponderous bulk started to move, picking up speed as inertia joined the unequal struggle. A shrieker shot scored the wood black. After kicking a redcloak down the slope, Tanith left Zephyr to hold the shrinking gap and put her shoulder to the closing gate. Accelerating faster than it had any right to beneath so slight an assist, it slammed shut, the backwash of air setting Zephyr's form rippling and writhing.

"It will not hold them long, *ayin*," she cried.

Every desperate breath sending another dull spike through his temple, Mirzai helped Tarin wrestle the hinged crossbar into position. "What happened?" he yelled over the flurry of hammer blows from the far side.

"Seram ... went after the redcloak ... took Helia," said Ravli, slumped against an intact crate with her legs twisted beneath her in a pool of spreading blood. Her left hand held a dagger in a tight, brittle grasp. Her right was spread across a livid and angry wound at her waist. "Couldn't stop ... Seen ... Tried ... block gate."

Gallar rose painfully from her knees. Her hated scarlet cloak was black and flaky with ash at her shoulder. The right side of her face was red raw and stretched from the shrieker shot's burns. Her right arm hung limp against her ribs. Even a glancing shot was nothing to joke about. "Well, this hurts."

"Not ... a competition." Ravli's humourless laugh faded to a wheeze

159

that speckled her lips with fresh blood. The gate shuddered. "Be through . . . any moment. Leave . . . me."

Mirzai scowled. The gate wouldn't hold, and it was only a matter of time before the redcloaks woke up to the possibility of approaching across the tower's ramparts. "Tarin, help me with her."

He started forward. "Yes, Uncle."

Tanith scowled. "But—"

Gallar grabbed Mirzai's arm with her good hand. "She won't make it. She can't climb."

He gritted his teeth. Nothing but a vast dose of last breath could save Ravli now. He wasn't even sure how she was still conscious. It was one thing to leave Raya and the others in the cells, but Ravli had followed him there. "I won't leave her to die alone."

"She won't. I can't climb either."

He stared at Gallar in horror. "No!"

The clamour at the door slowed from a cacophony of thumps to a deep, slow pounding. The crossbar lurched with every blow.

"If we stay here much longer, it's not going to matter," snapped Tanith.

"It's all right, Mirzai." Letting go of his arm, Gallar unhitched her shrieker from its holster, her eyes full of pain that had nothing to do with her wounds and owed everything to a past of which she had barely spoken, save by its absence. "It's a better death than I deserve."

Throat tight, he nodded. He couldn't even begin to understand how she was so calm, but supposed that some certainties couldn't be argued with. Some paths could only be walked, not avoided – not if you wanted to remain true to who you wanted to be. He cast about for something to say, something that would tell Gallar that he understood everything that had gone unsaid, but words had never been his strength. "Nyssa keep you."

She offered a peaceful, determined smile. "River flow to fortune. For both of us."

The shuddering gate a drumbeat chasing him on, Mirzai took the barracks stairs two at a time, Tanith behind, Tarin behind her and

Zephyr bringing up the rear. He darted for the rampart door and peered out. No redcloaks. Not yet. If Gallar could hold the pursuit for just a few minutes, they might have a chance.

Ducking back inside, he found Tanith staring out of the window towards Araq's flame-lit silhouette. "You provincials really don't do 'subtle', do you?"

"It wasn't our ship anyway," he replied with humour he didn't feel.

A crackle of breaking timber sounded below. A flurry of shrieker shots screamed out.

"Where now?" shouted Tarin. The boy's eyes shone with terror. That none of it touched his voice spurred pride to banish the worst of Mirzai's own dread.

"Through the tower," said Mirzai. "There's a rope on the western wall."

A final shrieker shot sputtered into silence below, its dying wail replaced by running feet.

Mirzai ran for the rampart door and out into the night. The tower door opposite creaked open. A redcloak stood framed beneath its archway, a shrieker already levelled.

"Down!" shouted Tanith.

Her heavy shove sent Mirzai sprawling face-first onto the rampart walkway. The redcloak's shrieker bucked, the shot felt more for its heat than the rippling haze left in its wake.

Tanith screamed. Not just in agony, though there was pain enough in the cry. Its rage set Mirzai shivering, piercing his soul without touching his ears.

As his fingers scrabbled in the rampart dust, she swept past him, her ribs crusted and seared black by leaping flames. Not just the raging red-orange of a shrieker's blaze, but the cold magentas and indigos of something that had no business existing in the mortal world. She seized the redcloak by the throat and heaved him over the battlements without even slowing. Magenta flames overtaking the orange, she collapsed through the open door.

Feet skidding dangerously on the rampart and shrieker shots from the courtyard whining around him, Mirzai stumbled inside the tower. Tanith lay on hands and knees by the ragged gap in the inner wall, disintegrating plaits framing her face with a spill of golden hair, crackling and singed at the ends. Beneath the charred remnants of her uniform's robes her chest and shoulder were a blackened, scaly ruin. She'd taken the shot full-on. She'd no business being alive, let alone moving. The tiny chamber stank of burning meat.

"I . . . need a moment to pull myself back together," she gasped without looking up, her cultured Kaldosi accent darker and more guttural than ever.

"What *are* you?" asked Mirzai.

She shuddered, her fingers clenched like claws against the stone floor. "Very, *very* angry." The last of the orange flames sputtered out, swallowed by magenta. "Why couldn't you just have bought me that drink?"

The sight made sense of Mirzai's muddled emotions in Elondine's Rest the night before. Of Tanith's speed. Her strength. She was a soul-sucking amashti. A daemon. An abomination.

But she'd saved his life.

Taking Tanith at her word – and uncertain of the wisdom of touching her even if he could not – Mirzai reached the door leading to the western wall. A redcloak crouched beside the escape rope while two others gazed over the wall.

A fourth turned and stared directly at him. "They're in the tower!"

Mirzai wrenched the door shut and rammed the bolt home.

Zephyr did the same with the door leading back to the barracks. "Not the rescue I had in mind, was this!"

Tarin's gaze lingered on Tanith's huddled smoking body. "What do we do? Uncle?"

"What do we do?" Still on hands and knees, Tanith coughed and spasmed, bones creaking audibly back into place. Ash trickled across the floor. "We're done."

Impossible to miss the accusation. Lumbering oxen she'd called them, and lumbering oxen they'd been. Mirzai cursed himself for not recognising the rage in Seram's eyes. Twenty years back he'd been as cold as Ravli, but in the years since, Helia had become as close as a sister. Or perhaps it hadn't been that straightforward. Ravli had been barely coherent. Perhaps she'd described not how it started, but how it had ended. She'd have struggled to topple the crates without help, much less bar the door. She'd have needed Seram for that. Not that it mattered now. The odds had always been against them. Now they were all going to die.

I'm sorry, Midria.

Mirzai's gaze settled on the gap in the tower's north wall. Another rope and they could have climbed to the ground. Without one it was too far to fall.

At least, for most of them.

Voices echoed up from the spiral stairwell. The westward door shuddered and bucked.

"Zephyr." Mirzai pointed at the gap. "You can still escape. Please don't argue, *nasaîm*."

Her face pinched tight, not quite unfriendly. "Saving me again, you are?"

"What else can I do?"

She nodded and flowed into the gap between the stones, a bluish-white apparition against the night.

Footsteps sounded on the stairs. The north door creaked beneath a hidden impact.

Tanith stumbled to her feet, black cinders trailing as she fought for balance. "Zephyr ...?" She coughed and spat away a gobbet of something black. "Fourth arch of the bridge, five courses up, loose stone ... Take it, with my blessing."

Zephyr gave a sharp nod and was gone.

The westward door gave a heartbeat before the northern one. As redcloaks flooded into the room, Mirzai threw down his sword and raised his hands.

"Well, this has been fun," muttered Tanith.

Sixteen

Like most taverns in the Hazarid district, the Hanged Skelder was still doing brisk business as midnight approached. Its three above-ground storeys loomed over the squat adobe townhouses to either side, the light from their stained-glass windows infusing flagstones and passers-by with bright shards of colour.

Damant still found it impossible to believe that the wounds of the Obsidium Uprising had been banished so swiftly from the district. He'd walked these streets soon after the Eternity Queen's ascension and they'd been little more than fire-blasted rubble. But Zariqaz had done what it ever had: raised new buildings upon the remnants of the old and struck out for fresh prosperity. The result was a far cry from the luxury of the Golden Citadel, but it was impressive enough.

He beckoned to Overseer Jarana, who like himself wore a heavy cloak to conceal her uniform. ||The cellars go all the way down into the Underways,|| he signed, careful to shield his gestures from onlookers. Jarana was slightly hard of hearing, and in the hubbub of the streets, Simah made for more reliable communication. ||Six custodians. Hold anyone who tries to get out that way.||

||Yes, Castellan.|| Jarana nodded – after three admonishments she'd finally understood the importance of *not* saluting that night – and peeled off through the crowd.

Damant stifled a sigh and rubbed at his aching temple, longing once again for Tyzanta's experienced lawkeepers. Jarana was so very young. As were most of the Golden Citadel's custodians. The best candidates went to the Royal Guard, not the custodium. Redcloaks paid better and asked fewer questions.

He stepped deeper into the cover offered by the vine-hung trellis and its sweet dusk primrose.

"You're certain this is the place, Damant?"

Even with his scarlet cloak replaced in favour of the softer yellows and greens of a Frola Clan merchant, Kastagîr looked every inch the soldier. He was too stiff, his stare levelled with impunity. Even in semi-respectable streets, Zariqaz's citizens tended not to make eye contact, whereas Kastagîr scrutinised everybody with a mixture of impatience and contempt. A redcloak's stare, in other words. The only reason it hadn't given them away was the fact that there'd be plenty of redcloaks carousing inside the Hanged Skelder.

"My informant was very clear. The Hanged Skelder, midnight." Damant nodded at the tavern and jabbed a finger at the guildhall clock halfway back along the street, its burnished dial showing fifteen minutes to the appointed hour. "The Hanged Skelder. Midnight."

Assuming the shadowy woman was on the level, of course – something far harder to believe beneath open skies than in the conspiratorial hidden passageways of the royal palace. But what else was there? With the Eternity Queen's life at stake, no judicator would dare believe Yali's innocence without proof – nor would conclave, were he able to get the trial conducted there. Even with Hargo Rashace journeying westward to Tyzanta, the odds were against acquittal. Damant had no allies to speak of, and Yali none at all.

That meant finding the true culprit.

"Then we lock the place down," said Kastagîr. "I have a company of *sarhana* and four koilos over in Ghardi Square. It's more than enough for this ... nest."

He turned to go. Damant grabbed his arm. It felt like knotted teak beneath his sleeve. Even at his most circumspect, the man had all the subtlety of a Mistrali gale. But strategy required his presence, all the same. Catch the assassin and Kastagîr would be forced to drop his accusations. Even a failed attempt at capture might convince him to do so.

"You do that, and folk will think it's a raid. There'll be uproar, maybe even a riot, and our target will slip away in the confusion."

Kastagîr pulled free. "You don't even know who we're looking for."

Ardin would have cowed the bodyguard with bluster, but Ardin had been a far grander presence than Damant knew himself to be. Besides, Ardin was in no position to bluster, not any longer. His servants had found him dead that morning, his skin full of calvasîr and enough isshîm to drive a herd of oxen to soporific dreams.

Given their final conversation, Damant entertained no doubts that Ardin had been his own murderer – one final attempt to flee smothering clouds of melancholy and guilt. But he'd used the pretence of investigation to hold the shriversmen at bay long enough for the body to cool and the last of Ardin's soul to reach the Deadwinds unmolested by their spirit-knives. For all that he and Ardin had seldom seen eye to eye in later life, they'd once been friends. You paid your debts where you could.

He shook away a lingering grief that had more grasp on his soul than it should. "I'll know her when I see her."

"How?"

Emerald brooch and matching eyes, the informant had said. Hopefully a rare enough combination, and certainly not information Damant was ready to share with Kastagîr. "Because I've been at this a long time. Folk betray themselves if you give them the chance."

Kastagîr grunted. "She's already had too many chances. I speak for the Eternity Queen. We'll do this my way."

The words, spoken not to an elder or even an equal, but to an underling with temerity above his station – not that Kastagîr routinely dealt in words like "temerity" – scattered the last of Damant's patience. He drew in closer and craned his neck to fix the captain with a withering stare.

"You speak for the Eternity Queen? You just crawl into her bed when she crooks a finger. *I've* known her long enough to know that she hasn't a single drop of sentiment in her heart." An unwise – even impious – thing to say, but with the dull red double-thump at his temple gaining in fervour moment by moment, tact was not uppermost in Damant's mind. "When we return to the Golden Citadel with nothing but a sad tale of an assassin escaped because you roused the district to madness, how do you think she'll react?"

Kastagîr blinked and took a half-step back. "And she'll be delighted if we return empty-handed because your mystical skelder-charming powers don't work?"

"That's different."

"And why's that?"

Damant shrugged. "Because it'll be my head on the block, not yours. I'm prepared for the consequences of my choices." An untruth, for one of those consequences would be Yali's execution, but he was an accomplished liar. "Are you for yours?"

Kastagîr glared back with what he must have supposed was impassivity, either unaware of the muscle leaping in his cheek or hoping that it went unnoticed. That he was a brave man, Damant had no doubt. Face him with a sword and only death would end things. But Kastagîr was just bright enough to realise that he was out of his depth.

"I'll give you until a quarter past midnight," he said stiffly. "Then we do it my way."

Damant nodded. "Agreed."

In any case, he'd either have the assassin in his grasp by then, or she'd have slipped away, payment from her as-yet-unknown client firmly in hand. If Nyssa was with him – even months after her descension to mortal form, silent prayer remained second nature – he'd catch both parties together. A quick squeeze to shatter the prism in his pocket, and the parheraldic ifrît's dissipating wail would alert Kastagîr and Jarana to move in. That, hopefully, would be that.

With an unobtrusive pat at his pocket to ensure the parheraldic prism was indeed in place and a swift tug to re-site the shrieker belt hidden beneath his cloak, he set out towards the Hanged Skelder.

Kastagîr grabbed his upper arm with a grip like stone. "I won't forget this, Damant."

Damant. Not *castellan*, and the formality of title. Not *Ihsan*, and the illusion of equality. So much for recruiting an ally, but events – and his lately fractious temper – were seldom easily controlled, and in Kastagîr, as in so many others, a dearth of wit was no barrier to a surfeit of pride.

He pulled away rather less easily than Kastagîr had done moments before. "I wouldn't want you to."

Second thoughts surfaced as he crossed the threshold's wall of heat onto the stained, uneven floorboards, granted life by the drone of a hundred drunken conversations, arguments and snatches of song, all of which conspired with the flickering spill of light and shadow to redouble the drumbeat behind his eyes. Too little sleep on too much wine. Too many indistinct, tantalising thoughts creeping unannounced and unwanted at the edge of reason. He longed to escape the press of bodies, to leave the stink of sweat and the sour aroma of spilled drinks in favour of the open skies. But Yali was counting on him. And besides, Kastagîr wasn't the only one with a surfeit of pride. The sense of being adrift couldn't be cured by wilfully drifting further.

Gritting his teeth, he began his search.

The Hanged Skelder hewed to an open-plan design common to such establishments, with a central double-helical stair to serve the upper floors. Wood-panelled booths dotted around the outer walls offered semblance of privacy to those who desired it. Simah was as much the language of choice as spoken Daric, for spoken words sank readily into the cacophony of voices. A few such exchanges could have given Damant a busy night had he wished it, and he made a mental note to speak with the high overseer of House Ozdîr's custodium, under whose jurisdiction the Hanged Skelder technically fell, as to why criminal business was so openly transacted within those walls.

After burning a precious minute to purchase a goblet of wine at the bar – nothing aroused suspicions amid revelry more than abstention – he made a circuit of the outer booths. He didn't expect it to be that simple. They promised the prospect of an quick exit in case of trouble, but they were too easily surveilled. But process was everything, and assumption an arrogance.

In this case, however, assumption proved itself correct. Sidelong glances caught no sign of the green-eyed woman, nor her emerald brooch. Minutes ticking away, he eased himself past an overly made-up middle-aged woman lost in loudly declaiming a meritless husband to her circle of friends, and ascended the sagging steps of the nearest staircase.

The first floor proved more of a warren than the one he'd left. Save for a handful of private rooms at the very back, its partially demolished partition walls offered a series of semi-private spaces, softened by silk shrouds and low planters, for anything from couples to small groups. Most were already claimed, their occupants lost in their shared company, by one means or another. Those that remained held tables groaning beneath the weight of goblet and tankard, ringed by carousal that cut across the Hazarid district's varied mix of status and class, redcloaks and slumming firebloods alongside dockworkers and likely skelders. Licentiousness and drunkenness seldom noted social boundaries, as the harried serving staff likely knew all too well.

Even as that particular thought formed, the *crack* of a slap drew Damant's eye. A hassled-looking server in a dark jacket and skirt had somehow managed to keep her tray balanced at her waist while fending off the unwelcome attention of a fireblood Damant tentatively identified as Lallari Ozdîr. Flicking her unbound hair back across her shoulder, she stalked away to a chorus of jeers.

Snorting under his breath, Damant turned on his heel, resigned to another booth-by-booth search. A sinking feeling crept in over his bones. Instinct warned that it would prove as wasted as that of the floor below. Pragmatism insisted he make it all the same.

It was then that she appeared at the head of the other stairway, white hair trailing across the shoulders of a threadbare duster coat and a broad-brimmed hat jammed on her head. Not the green-eyed woman he'd been warned to seek, for even with her back to him he knew her eyes to be as grey as troubled skies.

Rîma. Erstwhile queen of the lost city of Tadamûr. A woman Damant might have counted among his closest friends but for her insistence on rejecting the Eternity Queen's order in favour of Bashar Vallant and Katija Arvish's doomed crusade.

And now she was here. In the Hanged Skelder. At the appointed hour.

Damant drew back into the shadow of a fluted column. All to the good in one sense, for he could now tail the paymistress to the assassin rather than the other way around. On the other hand, Rîma wasn't an opponent to underestimate. She didn't appear to be armed, but a long coat could conceal all manner of unwelcome surprises. Sword in hand, she was death incarnate. Crowded as the Hanged Skelder was, a single misstep could lead to slaughter.

Another glance. Rîma peeled away along a corridor between two of the half-sealed booths, the amorous couples within paying her no heed. Damant waited until she dipped out of sight around the corner, then followed, striking as nonchalant a pose as his pounding head allowed.

As he rounded that corner, a black door whispered shut ahead, the mutter of voices beyond muffled and indistinct. Two paces and he had his ear to the door.

"You're positive she's nae here?" A woman's voice. Young, careful and with a darkly musical northland burr. Familiar, but frustratingly hard to pin down.

"Certain." This one was Rîma, her priestly tones heavy with concern. "We must accept that something has happened to her."

So the assassin hadn't showed? Damant winced away his disappointment. That left Rîma's capture the best – the *only* – chance Yali had of living out the week. Taking her alone was out of the question, so that meant alerting Kastagîr and Jarana, certainly provoking the chaos he'd sought to avoid. The only positive was that even Rîma couldn't fight her way through a company of *sarhana*.

Probably.

He stepped back from the door and reached for the parheraldic prism.

The brass muzzle of a shrieker pressed against his neck.

"That's enough," breathed a stranger, as the first chimes of midnight rang out.

Seventeen

Damant froze, the parheraldic prism inches from his grasp.

"Not a sound." The stranger's voice was maddeningly familiar: crisp, cheerless and cultured. "Let's keep this civilised, shall we?"

"By all means," Damant said evenly.

Shrieker's muzzle still buried into his neck, she reached into his pocket and removed the prism. "A parheraldic? So you weren't so foolish as to come alone? You were always practical. Dullards always are."

The venom made her voice even more familiar. Maddeningly so. Not Katija Arvish, whose fireblood-tutored vowels had a tendency to lapse into pure Undertown once emotion broke through. He made a silent tally of the women he'd met while serving alongside Arvish and Vallant. No match presented itself.

His belt lightened as his captor tugged his shrieker from its holster.

"A Qarradin?" She murmured the craftsman's name with reverence. As well she might. Gazra Qarradin had worked solely on commission and commanded the steepest of fees.

"A gift from a friend." One of a pair, though the other had been taken from him in the depths of the Hidden City of Tadamûr.

"I told my mother that you weren't worth such expense. She never listened to me where you were concerned. Still using the old Bascari glyphs, I take it? That's an unexpected bonus. Turn around, but keep your hands where I can see them."

Damant obeyed and found himself eye to green eye with Mirela Bascari. Eldest daughter of Countess Elinor Bascari, who he'd served so loyally for so long. Yennika's cousin, who she'd framed for all manner of crimes, murder among them. Older and leaner than he remembered, her soft tawny skin lined by hard years until she resembled her mother in her final days, eaten inside out by the parasitic qalimîri daemon Yennika had set loose on her soul. But then she'd no right to be this side of the Deadwinds at all. Summoned to Zariqaz to answer for her "crimes", she'd been due to die on the Golden Stair. Inevitably, an emerald brooch glittered at the lapel of her jacket.

Mirela exchanged his shrieker for hers, which she slid into a holster concealed beneath her jacket. She tossed the parheraldic prism into an aspidistra's planter. "I might have known you'd come looking. Always my dear cousin's lapdog."

Awash in chagrin, Damant realised he'd already seen her in the Hanged Skelder that night, only he'd mistaken her for a server as she'd surely meant him to. The best way to vanish was not to be seen at all, but drawing unnecessary attention ran it a close second: the mind discarded the obvious. The simplest of subterfuges, and he'd fallen for it. That Mirela possessed the skills to perform it so smoothly was unexpected. But then she'd likely learned all manner of skills to stay among the living.

"What happens now?" he asked.

Mirela draped herself across his left shoulder, her shrieker hand slipping under his cloak to grind the muzzle against his ribs: an inebriated woman gazing gratefully up at her supportive companion. Only the brittle smile broke the illusion – she'd never been much for affection or warmth. "I've had too much to drink. Gallant as you are, you're going to walk me straight past whatever friends you have nearby."

So she wasn't going to hand him over to Rîma? Then again, for all her front, Mirela had to be desperate, and desperate assassins tended not to trust their employers. Loose threads were better off cut. "I should warn you that I'm a terrible hostage," said Damant. "Kastagîr doesn't like me very much."

"Nor do I. So don't push your luck." She jabbed the shrieker against bone. "Move. And put your hands down, for both our sakes."

He set out towards the stairs. Mirela kept pace, her blissed-out stare never leaving his face and her steps not so stumbling as they appeared.

"What happened to you?" murmured Damant as they passed the first of the half-sealed booths.

"I don't want to talk about it," she hissed. "But I survived."

Even without the shrieker digging into his ribs, he'd have struggled to spare sympathy for Mirela. Being unjustly accused of specific crimes wasn't the same as innocence. Like the rest of her family – her mother included – she was as wicked and manipulative as they came. "And your husband? Your children?"

"They won't even talk to me. I'm stained to them, outside and in. And they're right." Her smile flickered to an angry scowl. "What hope I had of clearing my name died when Yennika took the throne. Revenge is all I have left. I'll die before I let you take that from me. But *you'll* die first."

Rîma had chosen well. Fanatics made the best assassins, provided you weren't choosy about who else got hurt along the way. Dinars and tetrams were as nothing to a jilted, vengeful soul.

He'd never have got himself taken like this back when he'd run Tyzanta's custodium. The intervening months had softened him, just as they'd sharpened Mirela to a blade. Worse, he couldn't quite determine when his decline had begun. He knew only that in that particular moment he was a lesser man than he'd once been. Or maybe that was pride talking. How had Ardin put it? *Perhaps we were always this way and never knew it.*

Mirela's shrieker and hollow drunken laughter ever goading him on, he descended the stairs. At times, she rose up on her toes to giggle and whisper in his ear. At others, she sagged and babbled, using the transition to turn a leery eye on their fellow patrons. Never once did the shrieker's muzzle stray.

Damant played his part the whole time, careful to do nothing that would provoke her to premature murder. That murder was in the offing he didn't doubt. Regardless of any personal hatred she held for him – that he'd remained ignorant of Yennika's scheming almost to the last would hardly factor into whatever passed for Mirela's reasoning – he knew too much. He was as good as dead as soon as she was clear of the Hanged Skelder, which meant he'd a minute, maybe two, if he convinced her to leave via the cellar.

But as he rounded the last turn in the spiral, he realised that he didn't have even that.

Redcloaks lined the street beyond the tavern's expansive windows. Four koilos in dark cloaks and gleaming ember-saint lamellar towered above them, vast ceremonial flamberges held at saint's guard, hilts clasped to their chests and points skyward. Kastagîr had broken his promise, or had at least anticipated failure.

The denizens of the Hanged Skelder were pointing and staring – all save those beating a timely retreat towards the cellar or the side door. The only consolation was that with her eyes still on his through a combination of threat and play-acting, Mirela hadn't yet noticed. The slimmest of opportunities beckoned. The only one he was going to get.

His gaze still on the unfolding disaster, Damant smiled. "Let's not do anything rash, *darling*."

Her eyes narrowed at the barb of the carefully chosen honorific – Yennika's favourite, though he'd heard it little in recent months – only to widen as they darted to follow his and beheld the doom unfolding in the street. There wasn't much to signpost her wavering attention. A sharp intake of breath. A tremor in the drunkard's smile. The slightest crease of the brow. They amounted to barely a flicker – whatever lessons life had taught following her escape from the executioner's blade, she had learned them well – but Damant had been waiting.

He twisted as the pressure of the shrieker's muzzle slackened with Mirela's waning attention and rammed the heel of his hand into her breastbone. Winded, she shot back, her boots skidding on the worn

175

step. Damant's shoulders screamed as he took her weight, one hand locking about her gun wrist and the other over the shrieker's barrel. In one smooth movement he twisted the weapon free and let her fall.

Mirela plunged backwards down the spiral stair, patrons scattering from her path. Her desperate grab at Damant snared a handful of his cloak but succeeded only in snapping its fastenings clear. Shoulder by shoulder, she rolled down the remaining steps in an ungainly cloak-tangled heap, and struck the floor with a heavy thud.

Lying full stretch on her back and glaring murder up at Damant, she yanked the cloak free and reached for her holster.

"Don't!" snapped Damant, his own weapon already levelled. At barely six yards, even his underwhelming marksmanship would prove sufficient. Nearby patrons, unwilling to take the chance, shrank away, leaving Mirela in a clearing.

Mirela raised her hands, her jacket sleeves slipping back to reveal an intricate spiderweb of tattooed soul-glyphs too dense and unseemly for a fireblood of any standing to have tolerated.

Damant turned his attention to a redcloak *sarhana*, who moments before had directed his full attention to the scantily clad street-nymph now cowering behind a waist-high planter. "You know who I am?"

"Castellan Damant, sir."

Damant nodded, thankful for the unintentional flourish that had robbed him of his cloak and thus left his uniform in full view. "You'll want at least a dozen men." Easily done in the Hanged Skelder that night, even if not all of them were strictly fit for duty. "Upstairs. Black door. There are at least two more fugitives. If they're still there, take them. Alive."

The *sarhana* flung a salute and made for the second stairway, barking for others to follow him. As the tavern shook to the sound of running feet, Damant tried not to think about the fact he'd likely ordered them to their deaths. Perhaps it would be better if Rîma *had* fled already. She was certainly resourceful enough not to let a detail like blockaded doors trouble her.

Kastagîr marched inside flanked by two redcloaks. His smug scowl dissolved to a thoughtful frown as he stared down at Mirela. "So you *did* find our assassin?"

Damant couldn't help but revel in his consternation. "Mirela Bascari. The Eternity Queen's cousin."

Kastagîr grunted. "Family."

Mirela sneered. "You think this is over?"

Kastagîr shot a pointed glance at his redcloak escorts. "It is."

She touched her eyes closed. Damant might have taken it for resignation, but for his instincts shouting and Mirela's sly smile.

An other-worldly screech sounded in the street. A tavern window shattered inwards beneath a redcloak's bloodied body. Patrons scrambled for cover. Beyond the ruined window, a koilos' flamberge battered aside a pair of scimitars and swept their wielders into the Deadwinds. Screams rushed in from outside, quickly joined by those from within. The koilos stomped on, redcloaks and citizens streaming from its path.

Damant tore his gaze back to Mirela's self-satisfied smile. "The koilos! She has glyphs for the koilos!"

"Impossible," snapped Kastagîr.

Damant forgave him his disbelief. Bad enough that a miscreant might acquire the soul-glyphs to lull the palace koilos as Mirela had. But to possess those that not only *commanded* koilos but overrode their true handlers' wishes – much less those assigned far beyond the palace, and thus guided by different soul-glyphs entirely – had hitherto been unthinkable. Arvish had been the only woman Damant had met capable of such a feat, and her aetherios tattoo was one of a kind, able to reshape itself according to her need. From what he'd glimpsed of Mirela's tattoos, they were ordinary ink. That meant planning, patience ... and above all a contact at the very heart of the Golden Citadel.

He yanked her to her feet and rammed the shrieker up under her chin. "Call them off!" he bellowed over the screams and the thunder of running feet.

"Why? I'm dead anyway."

The tavern door broke apart. A koilos barged through the wreckage, its armoured shoulder scattering Kastagîr's redcloaks and flinging Damant sidelong into the bar. The countertop's leading edge crunched into his ribs, the impact blurring his vision and jarring his shrieker from his grasp. A redcloak screamed.

By the time he prised himself upright, Mirela was a dark shape in the open door. Kastagîr lunged between him and the koilos, his jewelled scimitar braced two-handed at hilt and tip to block the flamberge's brutal downward arc. Steel met steel with a dull metallic ring. Kastagîr's sword bucked and sparked. Brave or foolish in the extreme, but for all his faults, Faizâr Kastagîr had never lacked for courage.

"After her!" he roared.

Damant ran for the door.

Already the street was a charnel of moaning and bloody bodies. Shrieker fire wailed through the darkness. One koilos was already down, its robes burning bright beneath the stars. Another hacked one-handed at a knot of redcloaks as if its massive sword weighed nothing, wielding a blazing corpse as a shield in the other. As for Mirela ...

There. Disappearing into an alley on the north side of the street.

Damant urged his weary bones to pursuit.

The alley narrowed almost at once, its zigzag course and the skyline typical of Zariqaz's haphazard expansion and renewal. Flagstones gave way to cobblestones, the gentle slope to plunging, sheer-sided steps.

Lungs burning, knees creaking and his aching head roused to a blazing double drumbeat, Damant forged on, following Mirela's star-strewn shadow while it was within sight, and the echo of her footsteps when it was not. A final turn, and she vanished beneath the cast-iron archway of a walled remembrance garden, lost to the tangle of mandevilla trellises with their waxy black-and-white blooms.

Damant's flush of triumph mingled with the clammy warmth of pursuit. One way in, one way out. She'd trapped herself.

His exhausted feet missed a step, pitching his shoulder against the crumbling remainder of a wayshrine. He caromed clear and ran on, cursing youth for hiding so far in the past. Worse, by the time he reached the arch, he became aware of heavy footfalls somewhere in the alleyway behind, too rhythmic to belong to anything mortal. One of Mirela's tame koilos, come to protect its mistress. If he followed her into the garden, he'd be trapped just as surely as she.

But what else was there?

He slowed to a brisk walk. Koilos or no, trapped prey was doubly dangerous – especially one with a shrieker and enough of a head-start to find the perfect ambush spot.

Ears straining for a telltale rustle, he edged into the maze of heavy trellises, gnarled yews and alabaster columns, past the remnants of spent candles fused to alcove and stanchion; the sad, decaying scraps of memorial pinwheels jutting among the mandevilla stems. Nyssa Iudexas towered above the open cloisters, her sword braced point-down at her feet and her face shrouded. Her presence made the garden a memorial to the forsaken dead, to criminals and outcasts. Fitting, given the deeds of hunter and prey. Did the Eternity Queen know they were there? Did she stir in her sleep, her dreams haunted by trespass on holy ground?

With every step Damant took, the pursuing koilos loomed larger behind. The crunch of the gravel path beneath its boots. Yew branches crackled as it shouldered its way through the overgrown canopies.

Ducking behind a column, he caught brief sight of it, gilded skull shining beneath the stars and indigo fire blazing in its empty eyes. It had lost an arm in the carnage outside the Hanged Skelder, a mess of splintered bone and mangled metal scales trailing from its left shoulder. Damant held his breath as the koilos' gaze swept the column, expecting a shrill scream of triumph to split the air. Then it stalked away along a side path, shoulders hunched and flamberge point scoring a furrow in the gravel behind.

Damant raised his shrieker. He'd never have a clearer target. But the koilos was already a dozen paces away. He might place a single shot before it bore down, but if he couldn't strike it clean in the head, nothing short of blasting it apart would stop it.

Better to find Mirela and compel her to set it sleeping. Even fanatics feared dying with their work undone.

One turn, two, and there she was, crouched low between a mandevilla trellis and an ornamental rockery crowned by a thicket of woebegone memorial pinwheels. A well-chosen position from which her shrieker covered three of the four entrances to the clearing. Damant wondered if good fortune had guided him to the fourth, which emerged beneath a low-hanging yew branch a little behind Mirela's left shoulder, or had the Eternity Queen roused from slumber long enough to bless his purpose?

Either way, he'd take it.

Careful not to breathe, he edged towards her, placing his steps with care on the parched soil of the trellis bed. What sound his footfalls made vanished beneath Mirela's low, hurried breaths.

She flinched as he pressed his shrieker's muzzle to the back of her neck, and dropped her weapon. An indecipherable Qersi mutter no fireblood should know laced the night air.

"Last chance." Damant kicked the shrieker into the undergrowth. "Call off the koilos."

The trellis exploded in a shower of broken spars and mangled stems as the flamberge hacked through from the opposite side. Damant twisted about. His hurried shot whined away into the night, the heat of its passage blistering and melting the left side of the koilos' gilded skull. Then the upper half of the ruined trellis crashed into his chest. The weight of it bore him to the ground, pinning him in place.

He'd the briefest sense of Mirela fleeing, her boots spraying gravel in her wake. Molten gold dripping from its skull to sear its armoured robes, the koilos stepped onto the remnants of the trellis, crushing the breath from Damant's body and trapping his shrieker hand against the gravel path.

With a screech of triumph, the koilos straightened and reversed its sword, the point aimed down at Damant's chest in grim one-handed parody of Nyssa Iudexas's imperious pose.

It froze and shuddered, the soulfire of its eyes blazing with impotent fury. A vicious hiss issued from between its gilded teeth. Black vapour, somewhere between smoke and flame and almost intangible beneath the night sky, coiled about its limbs.

"Do you have it?" called Rîma from somewhere behind Damant.

"I have it." Her co-conspirator from the Hanged Skelder. "But I cannae hold it long."

"No need."

Moving with unhurried grace, Rîma stepped into sight, the tails of her duster coat snagging on trellis scraps and a long straight sword naked in her hand. It flashed out to strike the koilos' head from its shoulders. The skull scattered memorial pinwheels as it bounced across the rockery, the fires of its eyes extinguished before it clattered to a halt. As the black vapour uncurled from its body, Rîma set a careful – almost gentle – hand to its chest and pushed it backwards.

"Rest now," she murmured. "Be free."

Relief yielding to a renewed sense of danger, Damant heaved against the trellis. "Rîma, I . . ."

She whirled about, sword across her shoulders, her expression riven between anger and pity. "Hello, Ihsan. I've missed you."

The stomp of her boot swept him into darkness.

Eighteen

I *hsan. They are coming for you.*

Damant opened his eyes onto darkness neither warm nor cold. A wave of nausea drove him to his knees, the muddy drumbeat of the ever-present headache pounding behind his eyes. Lost in private pain, he barely heard the voice that was not a voice – that was recognisably neither male nor female – whispering through his thoughts.

Ihsan. I cannot help you if you don't wake up.

He screwed his eyes tight. Faces danced in the dark, flashes of emotion unmoored from recollection. Little by little, the red drumbeat faded to near black, permitting subtler sensation. The ground offered no texture as he rose. Hurried breaths brought no prickle of air.

Ihsan.

Magenta fires lit the middle distance. The Eternity Queen stood tall within them, her being an extension of the flames. She cooled to the familiar likeness of bronzed skin and dark eyes. Yennika Bascari's sharp features melted into the rounder, wholesome beauty of Nyssa Benevolas. As her welcoming smile blossomed, her features flowed anew. A stern male face coalesced, subsumed as Yennika's likeness bubbled to the surface.

You are almost out of time.

Damant spun around and stared into a darkness somehow bleaker than before. At a boiling, suffocating presence lurking just beyond sight.

He *felt* it move, coiling through the fluid logic of dreamscape, rippling towards him. He stared transfixed, limbs numbed and immobile.

IHSAN!

The Eternity Queen's silent cry returned strength to leaden limbs.

Damant lurched towards the flames, the living darkness clutching at his heels. The Eternity Queen extended a hand, her expression taut and her eyes on the darkness behind him.

Hurry. You have protected me. I will protect you.

A feathery chill brushed the nape of his neck. He broke into a stumbling run.

((*It's nae good.*)) The new voice was barely a whisper, audible only because Damant's footfalls made no sound. It issued from everywhere and nowhere. Pervasive. Insidious. ((*She has him too tight. He was always a follower at heart.*))

((*I will not accept that.*)) The third voice was as disembodied as the second and achingly familiar. It bore the weight and disappointment of ages. ((*I will* not *allow it.*))

Damant forged on towards the magenta flames, his head throbbing with every step.

The Eternity Queen's smile broadened.

((*It's too late.*)) The second voice thickened with impatience. ((*You're putting us all at risk.*))

((*I want to try something,*)) said the third voice.

Black-robed figures blurred into being in front of him, silk-veiled golden masks glinting beneath tatter-edged hoods.

A gloved hand grabbed at his arm. He shoved. His would-be captor staggered away, mask falling free from a withered, desiccated face. Even as Damant forced his way past, figures bled out of the darkness. One seized his arm. Others gripped his shoulders, his forearms, his neck. An undulating mass of arms and glinting masks guided by a single purpose, a single will. Dozens. Scores. And still more mustered in the dark. Ignoring his struggles, they hauled him around to face the living darkness.

"Nyssa . . ." he croaked, at last finding his voice. "Help me!"

"She will nae. She cannae." The darkness spoke – truly spoke – with the second voice. A woman's voice. "It seems there yet be powers in this world that even a false goddess must respect."

The darkness paled, abyssal greys shaping a weather-worn duster coat and a broad-brimmed hat. A long sword glinted where the woman propped it across her shoulder. No. Not glinted. *Shone*. It was the light by which Damant saw anything at all.

As he thrashed vainly, she drew closer, her stride measured, unhurried.

Jumbled memory matched a name to the face. "Rîma . . .?" He winced as the headache thundered back full-flood. How desperate he sounded. All that mattered was to break free. To reach the goddess and the safety of the flames. "Please. I have to go to her."

Rîma swept the sword from her shoulder. With a sad smile, she brushed his cheek with the back of her hand. "You're better than this, Ihsan. Let me show you."

Steel flashed. Agony flared, icy cold close behind.

And then Damant simply felt nothing at all.

The second time Damant awoke, he narrowed his eyes against the painfully bright chink of light from the bedchamber curtains. His muscles ached with the aftermath of exertions. But wonder of wonders, the headache was finally *gone*. In fact, his whole being felt lighter. Even in the gloom, the world felt realer – crisper – the stuffy air laced with just a hint of rose water.

It took him a moment to realise that he was lying atop the bedsheets, still fully clothed, clutching a sword tight to his chest – the very portrait of an ember-saint in deathly repose.

"Welcome back." The chamber's greys resolved themselves to a familiar figure sitting at his bedside, the meanest hint of relief tugging at Rîma's otherwise impassive expression. "You've been gone a long time."

Blinking away sleep's last grasp and feeling more than a little ridiculous, Damant set aside the sword – Rîma's sword – walked his elbows toward the headrest and swung out his legs into a sitting position. A part of him screamed that he was in danger, captive of a notorious traitor. But it was a quiet part, and growing steadily fainter. "It feels like it was only last night."

"It was," said Rîma, effortlessly following the unspoken half of the conversation. She'd always been good at that. "But that isn't what I meant."

More memories surfaced. Months spent on the Eternity Queen's council. Assent given to actions that he could no longer see as anything other than reprehensible. The men and women he'd dragged before the judicators for no other reason than they'd protested harsh decisions taken at conclave. Silence, most of all. Silence as the council dispatched redcloaks to crush those whose protests transcended words. As the redcloak fleet levelled Tyzanta and buried its people. As he helped peers he despised hunt those he'd counted as his friends. A word from him might have made no difference, but that didn't excuse the lack. Nor the fact that he'd never even made the conscious choice to withhold it. He'd kept silent because it hadn't occurred to him to do otherwise.

He peered at himself in the tiny bedside mirror. He didn't *look* any different, but still the reflection belonged to a stranger of whom he was achingly ashamed.

He sagged, inside and out. "What have I done?"

"It wasn't your fault," said Rîma. "The Eternity Queen's glamour twists people."

He hung his head, nauseous. "No. That's not it. I didn't serve. I *believed*. She was the only one who could bring Khalad to order . . ." The words turned stale on his tongue.

"That's how a glamour works. It steals the piece of you that asks awkward questions."

"No. I did this. I *wanted* it. I had to."

Rîma crossed to the window. "You were in Starji district not so long ago, yes?"

185

Running down the woman who'd repaired Mirela's hisser. Mirela, whom Rîma had been waiting for at the Hanged Skelder. "How did you know that?"

Rîma ignored him and drew back the curtain.

Beyond the scuffed and filthy glass, the mid-morning sun shone down on devastation. Perhaps half the houses still stood, flanked by rubble spoil or burnt-out ruins that trailed away down-spire along refuse-strewn streets. Every wall still bore scorches from the fires of the Obsidium Uprising. Of the surviving houses, every other lacked a roof, fit for nothing but the roosting crows that cackled and squabbled over scavenged scraps. The few that remained had seen repair with mishmashes of broken tiles and sheet timber. And everywhere in sight stood the wreckage of old bonfires lit to keep the night's chill at bay. Little traffic moved along the dislodged cobbles, but the streets were far from empty. Filthy figures huddled in doorways and wherever an alley's remnant offered shelter from the brilliant sun. Tyzanta's Undertown had looked better. The shanties of Tyzanta's Gutterfields had scarcely been worse. And yet the contours of Tanleer Street were unmistakable, matched to the hulking wreckage of what had been the Alabastran temple at its centre.

"I imagine it looks a little different to how you remember it," murmured Rîma.

Damant stared, searching for the newly built townhouses that existed only in memory. In his mind's eye, he still saw the revellers clustered about the bonfires. But memory lied. Tanleer Street – likely the entire district – had never risen from the rubble of the Obsidium Uprising. He thought back to Ardin's terrace. *Tell me what you see*, the older man had asked, and had been disappointed by the answer. He recalled too the Eternity Queen's frustration with the slowness of rebuilding. She, at least, saw the city as it truly was.

"Do they know?" he asked, unable to tear his eyes from the squalor of the streets.

"Some. Others live in the same fool's paradise as you, and wonder why family and friends regard them askance. Just yesterday I saw a man wolfing down gutter scraps and proclaiming it a feast. No hint of irony or awareness. He believed the Eternity Queen's reality . . . so did you. Now I've broken the glamour, you'll see things differently."

Rîma set her back to the window and stared stonily at the opposite wall. For the first time, Damant wondered if the curtains had been closed for her benefit, not his. "You were lost from the moment Azra entered the flame. The thing that walked back out brought all your worst instincts to the fore. The Eternity Queen sealed the Ihsan Damant I knew beneath the version she wanted." She offered a not-quite-smile. "You always did love order a little too much."

"Thanks a lot." Ardin Javar had known that too, hadn't he? *You were always rigid, from the very first day we met . . . We are none of us what we seem.*

But perhaps he'd done himself a disservice. He hadn't *always* been silent. He'd spoken out against the Eternity Queen's decrees at the most recent conclave, if mildly. And the headache that had plagued him for so long; the nights lost to calvasîr. Another sign that a piece of him had been trying to resist? A slim point of pride, but it was all he had. "How many? How many others has she turned inside out?"

"Not as many as you might think. Khalad's hierarchy attends to the rest." Rîma shrugged. "When you're at the bottom of the pile, it matters little what motivates your betters, just as those at the top seldom lose sleep over those trapped beneath them. She doesn't need to control everyone. Habit and selfishness bridge the gap. And the redcloaks act as they always have."

"Why me? What makes me so special?"

"I don't imagine you are. The wind doesn't care what it gathers and what it leaves behind. It simply acts according to its nature." She shrugged. "Or perhaps Azra wanted it this way. We've never determined just how much influence she has over Tzal."

Tzal. That was right. Nyssa wasn't really Nyssa at all. She was just a name and a face past generations had given to a cruel and ancient god.

A Cold Flame imprisoned by the Issnaîm who'd once served it and held captive by an Eternity King whose tyrannical reign had served a single purpose: to ensure that it never broke free. Nyssa Iudexas. Nyssa Benevolas. Tzal. Three separate faces of the same goddess . . . only two of those faces were nothing more than lies.

Parts and pieces of the semi-distant past flooded back. Gritting his teeth, Damant sifted them as best as his jumbled thoughts allowed. The Obsidium Cult had freed Tzal from the Stars Below, but he'd needed a body to complete his escape. He hadn't wanted Azra – as Yennika had called herself at the time – at all, but . . . "Where's Arvish?"

"Tzal nearly took us all at Tyzanta. With the rebellion in pieces, it seemed better to split up."

"That's not what I asked."

"We don't have much contact. Couriers can be intercepted and we can't be certain that Tzal can't pluck heraldics from the Deadwinds for interrogation."

He grunted. "That's still not what I asked. You're worried that I'll relapse, aren't you? Give up your secrets? Or that Tzal still has me, even now?"

"My associate is. I'm not. But I *am* careful."

"Understood." Damant scowled, frustration battling what remained of his professional pride and losing by inches. "How *did* you free me?"

"Your tiny soul scarcely holds room for one reality, let alone two. We created another to dislodge Tzal's, then withdrew it."

"We?" That made sense. For all that Rîma was an unusual specimen, she'd never claimed to possess a mystical bent. "Your associate?"

She nodded. "In part. One soul alone could never have broken Tzal's hold. My associate opened the gate. I provided the army."

The robed figures. Lost in the dreamscape's murky reality, he'd not made the connection before. Now it sang to him.

"The souls of Tadamûr." Founded by the long-dead Queen Amakala as an enduring memorial to her people, Tadamûr's city soul had steadily sapped the will from its living inhabitants, to the point that only

Rîma and a handful of others had any longer possessed personality of their own.

As Amakala's heir, Rîma had destroyed Tadamûr to prevent its untended evils from consuming nearby towns, and then only because Damant had saved her from the city's madness ... or more precisely, had enabled her sword – *Amakala's* sword – to do so. The same sword Rîma had run him through with in the dream. The one he'd grasped so tightly on waking that his knuckles still creaked. "I thought they were lost to the Deadwinds when you destroyed the city."

"Many were. Most anchored themselves to me." The not-quite-smile returned, though there was little humour in it. "I remain their queen. There's barely a glimmer of awareness among them – I suspect even the palest lumani perceives more of the world than they – but in some contests, quantity matters more than quality. It's not easily done. I've spent months learning how."

Damant caught the echo of weariness in her voice and wondered at the burden Tadamûr's errant patchwork souls placed upon her. He found no clue. Rîma's body had long since gone to dust and leather, as embalmed and bolted together as any saint's corpse. What youth her face maintained was owed solely to last breath.

"From your associate ... who would be Tanith?" For all that Mirela Bascari had recently demonstrated skills he'd never suspected her of possessing, he couldn't imagine her being Rîma's silent partner. But as a soul-sucking amashti – a daemon in thought and nature – Tanith Floranz was no stranger to glamours, or to the twisting of men's souls.

Rîma shook her head. "I haven't seen her since Tyzanta either ... and as I said, I'm being careful until I can be sure about you."

"You might be waiting a long time."

She laughed softly. "And what would you know about the passage of time, glint?"

Damant's stomach rumbled. When had he last eaten? He shook the unspoken question away. Some things were more important than food. "Tell me how I can convince you."

"You can start by telling me what's happened to Yali," Rîma replied. "She was supposed to meet us last night. She never misses a contact. When she didn't show and you did, I elected to renew our acquaintance. To your good fortune, as it transpired."

Damant blinked as the tower of his recent assumptions wobbled. "Yali *is* with you?" Which meant that she'd resisted Tzal's glamour as readily as he'd been caught up in it. He wasn't sure how he felt about that. "Then Kastagîr isn't so far off track as I thought."

Rîma narrowed her eyes. "What do you mean?"

"Yali's under house arrest and bound for the cells. Captain Kastagîr's always been jealous of her access to the Eternity Queen, so after your assassin botched the job, he planted copies of the palace koilos' soul-glyphs in Yali's chambers and—"

Rima's scowl became a full-on glare. "*My* assassin?"

"Mirela Bascari. The woman I was chasing last night. You were waiting for her at the Hanged Skelder, only she decided to get the drop on me instead."

"Since when would *I* need to retain an assassin?" asked Rîma mildly. "If I want someone dead, they die."

"Even the Eternity Queen?"

"Killing her does no good. Tzal will just possess another host. Maybe you, Ihsan."

"Perhaps you thought it was worth a try."

"If our only profit from the trade was a dead Azra, Kat would never forgive me."

"It might yet end that way," Damant replied, thinking back to how the Eternity Queen had aged in the aftermath of Mirela's poisoning. "He's burning through her fast."

"I know. So does Kat. But love goes deeper than reason. She won't let Azra go until there's no other choice . . . Maybe not even then."

Kat wouldn't try to kill her. Certainly not with poison. She loves her. So Yali had said. Different words, but the sentiment was too close to be coincidence. Damant's tower of assumptions toppled in on itself.

Rîma hadn't been waiting for Mirela at all, but for Yali. The rest was all coincidence and sloppy thinking. "Oh, damn it ... I have to get back to the palace."

Rîma folded her arms. "I'm not so sure that's a good idea."

"If I don't, Yali will end up before either a judicator or the Queen's Council without someone to speak for her, which means that she's as good as dead."

"Didn't you just say that the only evidence had been planted by this Kastagîr?"

"I did, but I was wrong." The words rattled out almost of their own accord, given momentum by inevitability. So many assumptions and disconnects, and he'd tangled himself tight in both. "Yali *did* steal those soul-glyphs, but not for Mirela. Mirela didn't need them – she proved that last night. Which means she was stealing them for you. Stars Below, but I used to be a custodian."

"Don't take it to heart. It's hard to walk straight when you've one foot in a dream."

Damant grunted. "I don't suppose you'd like to tell me why you wanted them?"

"What do you think?" Another not-quite-smile softened the words. "She told us she had them but didn't want to risk being caught with them on her person."

A wise decision, given how poorly her encounter with Tuzen Karza might otherwise have gone. "I suppose you're going to tell me that Tuzen Karza really *is* Tatterlain after all?"

"Tuzen Karza is Tuzen Karza, for better or worse."

"Shame. I could have used an ally on the council. As it is, I don't know what I'm going to do now that Mirela's in the wind – if she has any sense, she'll be halfway to Phoenissa by now – but I have to try."

"What if I can't let you put everything else at risk just to save Yali? She's no innocent. Khalad stripped that from her long ago."

So there *was* something else afoot? What could be so important to be worth sacrificing Yali to protect it? The Rîma he remembered would never have made that trade. Then again, Vallant had always sold the lives of his followers cheaply when he'd seen the need. Perhaps Rîma had taught him.

"Maybe not. But she is my friend. If anything of these past months is true, it's that." And englamoured or otherwise, there'd been little enough truth to be had. "I'm leaving, whether you want me to or not."

Rîma glanced at her sword, still lying atop the bedsheets. A good two feet closer to Damant than to her for whatever that was worth, which was almost nothing. "Are you sure you wish to go through with this?"

Damant squared his shoulders at a phrase that promised death. But for the first time in recent memory he realised he'd made a decision he could live with, if maybe for not very long. "If you want to stop me, stop me. I have things to do."

She tilted her head, the not-quite-smile broadening to something genuine, and raised her voice. "Well?"

The door swung open. A slender young woman – a girl, really – stood beneath the arch, her arms folded and her posture confident but contained. The orange and emerald shimmer of her Kaldosi sari was a perfect complement to rich bronze skin and the unbound bar-straight black hair brushing at her waist.

"Ye should probably let him live." A northland burr contested the clipped Zariqaz pronunciation and won more than it lost. "We neither of us have many friends left."

Damant eyed her warily. Though he'd met her only twice before, and then but fleetingly, there was no mistaking Isdihar Diar, Voice and heir of the departed – and largely unmissed – Eternity King. When speaking for her ancient grandsire, she'd invariably used a crisper, formal accent, but her father's northland growl suited her. "Aren't you supposed to be in Qersal?"

Though Vallant's coalition had long since disintegrated, the fire-bloods who had once taken arms against the Eternity Queen slain or humbled, there was still a rich bloodgild offered as reward for the

Voice's capture. Not for herself necessarily, but for what she represented: the possibility of a return to the old regime, or perhaps – as Vallant had once proclaimed – something newer and fairer than anything Khalad had ever known.

"I am there," Isdihar replied. "As is well known."

Which likely meant she'd been in Zariqaz some time, with tales told and rumours spread to suggest otherwise. "I take it you're the associate Rîma mentioned?"

"Or she's mine."

"And it was you who stopped that koilos last night?"

Isdihar offered the thin, pleased smile of a girl glad to have done the impossible. "Aye."

That begged the question of how she'd done so, but with so many questions swarming for attention, Damant was simply content that she had. He shifted his attention to Rîma. "How much of this was a test?"

"That implies ye can pass or fail," said Isdihar, her regal past shimmering through the words. "Life is nae that tidy."

Rîma retrieved her sword from the bed and swung the blade onto her shoulder. "It is to me. If Tzal had any hold left, Ihsan would promise anything, *say* anything, in the hopes of learning more. He wouldn't throw his life away by picking foolish fights." She shrugged at Damant. "No offence."

"What happened tae being careful?" said Isdihar.

"Yali happened," Rîma replied. "In any case, with Tzal's power growing as it is, it's only a matter of time before he swallows us all."

"What do you mean?" said Damant sharply.

"Tzal perverts the Deadwinds." Isdihar spoke softly but fervently, every word a curse roughened by her accent. "My sire siphoned naught but what was needed, leaving enough for each soul tae heal itself in the Stars Below before returning tae this world of flesh and sensation. The Cold Flame gluts himself daily and leaves scraps. He has made the promise of reincarnation a lie. Worse, he grows stronger with each plundered soul. Surely ye've marked his spreading influence?"

"You forget, I've been living a nightmare."

Rîma folded her arms. "When the Eternity Queen took the throne, her glamour affected only those in the palace and the first ring-wall. As recently as a month ago, it held sway only in the upper districts. It spread in fits and starts with every town and village the redcloaks razed. When they began culling those infected by lethargia, it accelerated. Now it touches on the outer edge of the Gutterfields."

"How can you know that?"

A shadow of pain touched her eyes. "Because my contacts in the city have gone silent. I have lost more friends in a month than in two of your lifetimes. Those who did not turn were betrayed by those who did. Mark my words, Ihsan, we are running out of time. Those who do not serve will become the fuel that feeds his flame. The cruelty is no by-product, it *is* the purpose. Every death makes him stronger."

Damant nodded slowly, liking little of what he heard but unable to muster an argument against. It chimed too well with all he'd seen, and lent further horror to the fate bearing down on Tyzanta's refugees. "It certainly makes you yearn for the tyranny of Caradan Diar, doesn't it?" He glanced at Isdihar. "No offence."

She inclined her head. "My sire's every deed was tae keep Tzal caged. Even morality must cede tae survival." Her expression softened. "But that disnae mean we have tae like it. Tzal grows impatient. He's nae longer content with forgotten towns and fading villages. Clearing Tyzanta's gutter-camps is only the beginning."

Damant winced at the reminder of Hargo Rashace's mission. *Clearing the gutter-camps* sounded straightforward enough if you said it fast and didn't linger on the implications of slavery and murder. Yet another abhorrence he'd condoned. "But why? There has to be more to it than that."

"Why do the wealthy chase riches they can never spend?" asked Rîma. "Sooner or later power is its own purpose. It was so for the city-soul of Tadamûr. Likely it is the same for Tzal."

In Damant's experience, those in power always had rationale for their deeds, however twisted or incomprehensible it was to those who suffered – but he allowed that his very mortal perspective might not apply to an ageless entity like Tzal . . . or Rîma.

"Yali warned you about Tyzanta the night she was arrested, didn't she?"

Rîma nodded. "She's brought us messages out of the palace ever since Tyzanta fell. Plans. Schedules. Cargo manifests. She won't even tell *me* where she gets them, but it would appear that you have at least one ally on the council."

Unlikely, given the candidates. More plausible that the self-proclaimed *finest lock charmer in Khalad* had purloined all manner of secrets or had simply eavesdropped by means of lip-reading. It explained the source of Emanzi Ozdîr's woes when it came to Tyzanta's smugglers.

And then there was Mirela. Someone had paid her to make the attempt on the Eternity Queen's life. They'd supplied her with the necessary glyphs to give her the run of the palace. Was her paymaster on the council? Would she make another attempt? Did he even care? Rîma and the others stayed their hand out of loyalty to Arvish, but what was Yennika Bascari – or Azra, if there was any longer a difference – to Ihsan Damant?

Something to consider when time wasn't against him. But Yali came first. Malis Ethara – he'd start with her. Even without Mirela in hand, he'd a compelling tale to spin. The spymistress's instincts would do the rest . . . assuming that she hadn't set Mirela in motion to start with.

"So I'm free to go?"

Rîma nodded her assent at once. Isdihar after a brief hesitation.

"Aren't you worried I'll fall back under Tzal's influence?" Damant loathed the tremor in his voice, but if anything were worthy of fear, it was that. "Won't he *know* that I'm free?"

"Not so long as you do nothing to give yourself away," said Rîma. "Tzal can't read minds. Otherwise Yali would have been caught long ago."

It made sense ... even if it offered little in the way of reassurance. "And if I *do* give myself away?"

"Then he'll smother ye deep in your own mind, or have ye killed." Isdihar smiled without mirth. "My advice would be tae not let that happen."

"You're still taking a risk."

"Sometimes risk is all we have."

"Assuming I can keep up the act ... how do I contact you?"

Isdihar shook her head. "Ye don't. Be assured we'll nae set foot in this house or the Hanged Skelder ever again. But we'll be in touch." She turned her painted gaze on Rîma. "Perhaps ye should give him our gift afore he leaves?"

Taking his cue, Damant followed Rîma down the creaking stairs to a windowless room. Slumped on a chair at the very centre, securely bound and blindfolded, sat Mirela Bascari. A livid bruise and crusted blood marred the left side of her face from temple to cheek.

"She made the mistake of swinging at Isdihar on her way out of the remembrance garden," said Rîma. "For a pampered princess, she's learned to handle herself well."

Someone with a bloodgild in the high hundreds of thousands would have reason to. "I'm sure she had a good teacher," Damant replied. "Another pampered princess, perhaps?"

The exiled queen of Tadamûr flashed a not-quite smile. "Perhaps." She nodded at Mirela. "She's all yours. Save Yali ... then we'll speak again."

Nineteen

Every staggering step along Araq's high road disturbed injuries barely healed, jolting agony through Tanith's back, her legs, her chest. The livid shrieker burn across her shoulders was the worst, her body's attempt to heal itself interrupted time and again before the dawn as the redcloaks had worked at her flesh with the garrison archon's silver-edged dagger. They'd kept at it long after they'd realised no amount of pain would coax forth answers to their questions.

Each step beneath the baking sun reopened those lesser wounds two or three at a time. The flickering magenta flames that served as her blood drew wary murmurs from her redcloak escorts and gaping, horrified stares from folk watching the procession from the long shadows beneath the mismatched buildings. She'd been the first daemon most of Araq's unwanted garrison had encountered, and they'd striven to make their time together memorable.

So what? She'd been hurt before, and by folk more expert than they. With every slice of silver, every finger the redcloaks had re-broken – every hurried, apprehensive glance – they reasserted her power over them. Fear couldn't hold a candle to adoration, but it had a brilliance all its own.

She hoped her wounds didn't scar. She liked being pretty. It made everything easier.

Of course, if something didn't change, she'd make for a pretty corpse, and that wouldn't make *anything* easier.

Her right knee buckled as the procession entered the main square. She flailed for balance, the chain linking the silvered wrist cuffs going taut. Biting back a scream as the hated metal seared her skin, she toppled, her shoulder crunching against a flagstone and her lungs gulping down a mouthful of dust-laden air. A murmur rippled through a crowd standing sullen behind a cordon of redcloak spears. Empathy was relative. Apparently the good people of Araq had more for a daemon in plain sight than those who draped their sins in scarlet silks.

"Get her up." Gansalar Shorza's crisp, authoritative voice rang out across the morning, rising above the *clop-clop* of his horse's hooves. Hardly anyone rode horses any longer, hadn't for decades. They were expensive to keep, uncomfortable to ride. But some folk went to any lengths to look down on others. "Get her up, or we'll drag her the rest of the way."

Mirzai crouched at Tanith's side. In Elondine's Rest, he'd struck her as good-looking, if in an unassuming way. Not so now, with his face mottled and swollen from his own beating and his black hair thick with crusted blood. "Can you stand?"

She stared past him to the scaffold that was all that remained of Araq's elevated quayside, the charred ribcage hulk of a redcloak war dhow grounded beside and below it. Whatever else could be said of Mirzai's comrades – one or two choice words sprang to mind – they didn't do things by half-measures.

"I said get her up," snapped Shorza.

Mirzai proffered a hand as best as his own shackles – steel, not silver – allowed. "Tanith?"

She nodded mutely. Not for lack of anything to say, but in an attempt to blot out the lavender soul-scent thickening with proximity, stronger even than the stale sweat that clung to them both. A muscle leapt in her gut, her mouth watering as her body responded instinctively to the nourishment it craved. She could have drained him dry then and there, gulped him down to the last glint. Except . . . she was trying so hard not to be that woman any longer.

Just because folk called her a daemon didn't mean she had to be a monster.

Not unless she chose.

Not that she could do much about it while bound by silver. She couldn't even feel the ifrîti in the redcloaks' shriekers, much less twist them to her purpose through her aetherios tattoo. Not while the silver had her.

She took Mirzai's hand, noting his concealed wince as the effort strained an arm otherwise gingerly held. The third such wince, for it was the third time he'd helped her up on the long walk from Nyzanshar. Tarin, Raya and the other survivor of the cells shuffled along at what little distance the redcloak escort allowed, the boy watching with fearful eyes every time his uncle approached her. Tamaz had slipped quietly into the Deadwinds during the night. His cellmate with rather more fury, her teeth in an interrogator's throat before the guards had shot her down.

Good for her.

At least Zephyr had escaped. Assuming the redcloaks hadn't found it, the heraldic hidden beneath the bridge would let her contact Kat. It might take a few days for them to arrange a rendezvous, but she'd get clear of Araq's misery. And not before time. They'd given her up for lost. Vallant too, though he mattered more for morale than practicality. Without Zephyr, they'd no one to navigate the Veil. Even the familiar voyage to the mist-fallen city of Athenoch had become slow and perilous. There were worse causes to die for.

Yes, Zephyr was safe. Mission accomplished. Maybe – just maybe – folk might remember her as a hero, not a monster.

"You really *should* have bought me that drink," she murmured as Mirzai hauled her upright. It had long since become a dour joke.

"I know." He craned his neck to look up at the line of *vahla*-masked custodians atop the scaffold quayside, some forty feet above the ground. His gaze lingered on the maskless Saheen, her weathered black robes shabby, her expression flat and unreadable. Not so Mirzai's own. "Can you make it? We wouldn't want to disappoint anyone, would we?"

199

Tanith swallowed to moisten a parched throat – they'd been given neither food nor water since their capture. A piece of her drifted away into the succulent, enticing lavender scent of his soul. "I'm trying not to think about how hungry I am. You wouldn't like me when I'm hungry."

Not true, of course. He'd *love* her when she was hungry. Her glamour didn't give them any choice.

Everyone loved her. And then they died.

Perversely grateful for the silver at her wrists, she prayed to a non-existent goddess that she could keep herself together long enough for the redcloaks to execute them. Mirzai didn't deserve what the monster she *mostly* wasn't would do to him.

The heavy thump of Shorza's boot sent her staggering against Mirzai.

"Keep them moving," he called to the *sarhana* at the column's head. "I want this done before Ursalar Hannim arrives."

Hannim was the recipient of the panicked heraldic sent from Nyzanshar during the night. Bloody to the elbow in his interrogations, Shorza had bragged of the reinforcements arriving with the dawn. Between escort and cordon, he now had over a hundred redcloaks at his command, all of them armed and itching for a fight.

Favouring his prisoners with a last disdainful leer, he set his heels to the horse's flank and spurred into the heart of the square, a petty king puffed up and proud. Anyone would feel confident with an army of redcloaks at his back and a scarlet-sailed war dhow making a lazy circle of the town perimeter. One of two survivors of the previous night, the second still out on patrol.

"That one deserves the monster," murmured Tanith.

Mirzai's puffy brow wrinkled in confusion. "Eh?"

"He reminds me of my stepfather," she said tiredly, awash in lavender. Six months she'd gone without eating anyone. Six months of sifting soulfire from the Deadwinds. Part of her promise to Kat. To *herself*. But Shorza would make a worthy exception. To feel him go limp beneath her, terror and adoration fading from his eyes as she drained him to the dregs . . .

Curse the shackles, anyway.

The leading edge of the crowd broke apart as the procession reached the quayside elevator, the cordon parting to allow passage of a second column of prisoners and escorts. Some Tanith knew from her brief masquerade, the ageing Qaba among them. The hawk-faced woman beside him could only have been his daughter, for the sour expressions and the features that bore them were too similar for any other explanation. Seven more prisoners for an even dozen, and twice as many guards. The elevator, a motic-driven crank-and-pulley designed for hoisting cargo and repair timbers up to the quayside, could have handled twice that and more.

More concerning than the infusion of redcloaks were the two koilos. Tanith hated koilos. Their thin, malevolent souls had nothing to englamour, no empathy or desire to exploit. And they died hard. So it was to her relief that they made no move to board the elevator's cast-iron cage. A redcloak might stand too close, might get sloppy. Then all she needed was a moment and a key. Hands free among captors that bled and breathed, she had a chance. Against a koilos, she had none. And there were at least a dozen more in the cordon.

As Shorza dismounted and boarded the elevator, an old woman in dusty archon's robes pushed her way through the cordon, oblivious to shriekers and spears. It took three redcloaks to hold her back.

"Nyssa will judge you for this," she bellowed, a stubby finger levelled at him like a lance.

He shrugged. "She judges us all, does she not?" He beckoned to the dockworker manning the elevator. "Why aren't we moving?"

The dockworker touched his palm to the glinting motic prism embedded in the cage's back wall. With a scraping moan, the tarred rope cables lashed at the corners went taut and the cage began to rise, swaying slightly as the morning breeze took it. As it rose above the crowds, Tanith appreciated the scale of the gathering for the first time. Out of choice or coercion, most every soul in Araq had come to watch them die. Kat would have hated it, her vertigo leaping and screaming

201

every time the cage twisted. At least the breeze dispelled a little of the lavender.

"Fame at last," she muttered. Notoriety, at least. Close enough.

"Shut it," growled a redcloak, hand on his shrieker.

The cage shuddered to a halt level with the quayside. At Shorza's barked command, the redcloaks goaded Tanith and her fellow prisoners through the tangle of crates and barrels intended as cargo before the night's sabotage. They stationed their captives always at the edge of the quay, above the blackened ruin of the dhow far below – two paces apart from one another and six in front of the row of custodians.

Mirzai and Tanith's path took them past Oshur – the spiced jasmine of the young custodian's soul recognisable even though a *vahla* mask hid his face – and beneath Saheen, a stony presence standing atop the makeshift rostrum of a stowage crate. Above her head, the vast red and gold flag that Shorza had raised atop a pulley crane barely stirred in the breeze, though its failure to flap courageously did little to strip away the trappings of ceremony. Tanith snorted. Having been humiliated by Mirzai and his comrades, Shorza wanted to humiliate Araq in turn. A small man aspiring to mediocrity.

Just like her stepfather.

Mirzai glowered at up Saheen. "So much for blood and freedom."

Saheen's gaze never left the temple's statue of Nyssa Benevolas, whose beatific likeness was more or less level with the quayside.

"Keep moving." A redcloak's hand propelled him forward.

A heavy shove set Tanith in her place, two paces to Mirzai's right, feet either side of a fire-blackened mooring bollard. Careful not to give her any opening, the redcloak spun her about to face across the quayside, her back to the plunge. The wind shifted as he withdrew, the lavender of Mirzai's soul replaced by the dusky heather of the masked custodian who stood, shrieker levelled, immediately to Tanith's front, the woman's scent sweetened by her fear as she strove to keep the swaying barrel trained on Tanith's chest. The redcloaks, escort duty done, retreated behind the custodian line.

All save Shorza. He clambered atop the stowage crate to stand beside Saheen, who acknowledged his nod of greeting with the same cold silence she'd offered to Mirzai.

A dozen custodians. A dozen prisoners. The tally was too exact for chance.

"Khalad is built on order!" shouted Shorza. "Duty brought us to your town. Duty to protect the Eternity Queen's realm from enemies without and within. We extended every courtesy. We sought to provide the protection that is your right as citizens of the throne immortal. To usher in a new era of peace and prosperity for these troubled borderlands. But some . . ." The crowd's hubbub rose to a growl, drowning his words. He raised his voice. "But some would rather be brigands, no better than the Qersali!"

Tanith risked a glance over her shoulder as the growl faded. Redcloaks moved among the crowd, scimitars drawn. Shorza's peace and prosperity unfolding before her eyes.

If only he could manage it with boring them all to death.

Blinking back the sun's glare, she eyed the shaking custodian to her front. One shrieker shot *probably* wouldn't bring her down. Or would it? Silver made everything chancy. On the other hand, dead was dead, however it took you. Better to fight. She shifted her feet and coiled aching muscles.

Shorza waited until silence reigned before speaking once more. "Overseer Avaya has convinced me that these miscreants poorly represent the good, loyal people of this town. If that is so, then let their deaths usher in a new beginning. Overseer?"

He stepped back, allowing Saheen to take his place. For a long moment, she said nothing. Then, with a fleeting glance down at Mirzai, she took a deep breath and spoke in a voice thick with unidentifiable emotion.

"You all know me. Some of you your entire lives. Others fought beside me when this town was barely a name on a map, forgotten by Zariqaz and left to rot. Together we built something worth more than gold. You trusted me to lead you, and I have failed. I saw the poison spreading through our town, and I had not the heart to burn it out. I was afraid of losing my friends. And now those friends stand before me, traitors to the throne immortal."

The growl returned to the crowd. One thing to hear accusations from Shorza's lips, another to hear them repeated by one of their own. Saheen glanced at Shorza and received a gracious nod in return. A man in his element, revelling in the pride creaking in her voice. The crowd's growl thickened to a dark, throaty rumble.

"What happened last night was my fault. I remained deaf to the warnings. I stayed silent when I should have spoken. I mean to atone." Saheen tore her attention from the crowd and stared down at Mirzai, whose frown bolstered Tanith's growing sense that something was amiss.

Shorza, standing a little behind and to Saheen's side, couldn't have caught the softening of her expression, nor the determination that ushered it back to rigidity. When she spoke again, she did so in a voice imbued with all the passion her earlier words had lacked. "There is wickedness in this world that cannot be reasoned with. It cannot be contained. It can only be fought. And it is *never* too late to fight."

At last Shorza heard the shift in her tone, his mouth agape as his brain caught up with his ears.

"Blood and freedom."

Saheen's final words were barely a whisper, but they carried across the rising tumult of the crowd where the others had not.

Her shrieker was already in her hand. The shot flung Shorza backwards off the makeshift rostrum, his chest ablaze. As he hit the ground, the line of custodians turned as one and opened fire. Redcloaks fell, their robes burning. The survivors scrambled for what cover the scattered cargo allowed.

The air blazed with shrieker fire and shook with the roar of the crowd.

Two shots struck Saheen in the same moment. Haloed in flame, she fell, a last spasm of her trigger finger loosing a skyward bolt that set the listless flag ablaze.

Tanith dived for shelter as the custodian she'd thought her executioner fell dead, skinning her knees as she slid into the shelter of a stowage crate. Mirzai was already there, shoulders hunched against the crate while Oshur, his *vahla* mask gone, knelt over him, fumbling with a key.

The shackles snapped open. Mirzai rubbed his wrists and nodded at Tanith. "Now her."

Oshur stared without enthusiasm, his amorous advances of two nights before forgotten in the light of the soulfire blazing from her wounds. "She's a daemon." He flinched and ducked lower as a shrieker shot blasted the corner of the crate to blazing splinters.

"We stand together or we stand for nothing." Mirzai snatched the key and wrestled Tanith's shackles clear of her fused and blistered wrists.

Sensation flooded back. No longer dimmed by the silver's touch, the morning was suddenly brighter, louder. Hunger thundered in her ears, the lavender of Mirzai's soul choking, intoxicating. *Irresistible.*

Six months since she'd eaten anyone.

The redcloak edging around the stowage crate towards Mirzai never stood a chance. His panicked shot slammed into Tanith's gut, setting flesh and robes alight. She screamed from habit more than sensation. Lost to the hunger's fury, she'd have waded through molten ore and not felt it. Not with a hearty meal right *there.*

Still burning, she slammed the redcloak bodily to the ground, her lips to his and the piece of her she loathed reaching out to claim him. He thrashed, spasmed and went still, the harvest of his soul made artless by haste and need. Wasteful too, the better part of it hissing away into the Deadwinds. But it was more than enough. As the flames from the shrieker shot faded, the snap returned to her limbs, her wounds closed and the hunger receded just enough that she could think straight once more.

Rising, she cast about. The battle atop the quayside, such as it was, had already tipped in the redcloaks' favour. Most of Saheen's custodians were already down, as were many of the prisoners. A dozen redcloaks stalked through smoke raised from shrieker near-misses. Qaba died in the moment Tanith laid eyes on him, cut down by a redcloak scimitar. A heartbeat later, Tarin shouldered a redcloak off the quayside and dived for cover behind a barrel as two others closed on him, scimitars drawn.

Fortunes were scarcely better in the square below, flashes of shrieker fire and screams rising from the press of bodies. There at least the redcloaks were outnumbered, but they were well armed and better trained. Worse, the skyship had shaken free of its lazy patrol and now brought its broadside to bear. The quayside shook as a shrieker cannon salvo slammed into the crowd, sending smoke and flames rushing skyward. A stray shot smashed through the temple statue. Fragments of Nyssa fell like rain.

Like Saheen, Araq had found its courage too late. Not so long ago, it wouldn't have bothered Tanith. People died, often for the meanest reasons. That was simply how Khalad was. But she'd made the mistake of learning empathy, and empathy, it seemed, fed fury like nothing else.

She snatched up the redcloak's fallen shrieker. Just because it was a lost cause didn't mean you couldn't fight. It wasn't like she'd anywhere else to go.

"Tarin! Stay down!" shouted Mirzai. "I'm coming!" A dead custodian's scimitar in hand, he charged into the smoke.

Tanith rose smoothly, the shrieker inert under her hand for want of a soul-glyph to command it. But that didn't matter. Kat would have wasted precious moments twisting her aetherios tattoo to mimic the proper design, but Tanith lacked that patience. Ifrîti were only slivers of soul, more emotion than they were anything else. They responded to kinship. Shriekers in particular were born of fury. They were incandescent with it.

In that moment, so was she.

Reaching out through her tattoo, Tanith made contact with her shrieker, and favoured it with a glimpse of her own wrath. The ifrît recoiled, a candle before the sun, and begged to serve her.

She dropped one redcloak as he took aim at Mirzai. The drifting smoke betrayed a second kneeling atop a bleeding custodian, the two battling for control of a dagger. Tanith shot him in the back and strode on, caring little for the shrieker fire hissing around her so long as her own shots found their targets.

Off to her right, a redcloak howled his last as Mirzai ran him through. To her left, a shackled prisoner flung herself at another, sweeping both off the quayside and into gravity's remorseless embrace.

Tanith sent three shots wailing at a redcloak cowering behind the stowage crate-turned rostrum, gaining nothing for the trade but black-ened timber and a shrieker suddenly cold beneath her hand.

She flung her spent weapon at him as he broke cover, and threw her-self into a headlong dive. His shot screamed overhead. She rolled back to her feet, snagged her toes under the blade of a discarded scimitar where it met the hilt and flipped it up into her waiting hand.

Her backhanded slash took the redcloak's throat before he could line up a second shot. She indulged a bitter smile as his body hit the ground.

Not bad. Not good enough to impress Rîma, but Rîma wasn't there, was she?

She cast about for fresh prey and found no redcloaks living, save those mewling their last. Oshur was still on his feet, his left sleeve sheathed in blood. Raya too, as well as two of the townsfolk from Qaba's group. And Mirzai . . . ?

The quayside shook as another salvo from the drifting skyship slammed into the square. A fresh chorus of sobs and screams chal-lenged the fading roar of the crowd. Flames clawed skyward from buildings fronting the square.

Away over the eastern streets, a second sail darkened the skies, a red and gold silk flag streaming behind. Shorza's other surviving dhow back from patrol. Maybe a minute out from the square.

Impeccable timing.

"Tanith!" Mirzai shouted from somewhere behind her. "Help me with him!"

She spun around and found a bare-chested Mirzai kneeling amid the dead, his nephew's bloodied body cradled in his arms. Cursing under her breath, she sprinted through the drifting smoke. Halfway there, she knew that no amount of her help would make any difference.

"I was too late," he breathed, his teary eyes touching briefly on two redcloaks lying close by, the man missing most of his sword arm and the woman's neck hacked almost through. Vicious work, especially from a man who'd thus far shown no hint of savagery. Tanith eyed him with new-found respect, understanding for the first time why Zephyr had put herself on the line for him.

Tarin clutched at his uncle's arm with trembling fingers. "The river doesn't . . . have me yet."

"And nor will it," Mirzai stuttered. "*Ayin vanna anri.*"

The lad's lower torso was a slick mess, the bleeding barely stemmed as Mirzai stuffed the remnants of his shirt against the wound. Tanith grimaced and looked away. Last breath might have saved Tarin, had they possessed it in great quantity; or perhaps Kat, given some of the tricks she'd picked up in recent months. But with neither in the offing and death looming overhead on scarlet sails . . .

One chance. The elevator. Ride it to ground level, and . . . She scowled. And *what*? Araq had become a battlefield. But some problems you took one step at a time. Tarin would find no help where he was. None of them would.

"Mirzai?" she said. "He needs last breath. There has to be some in the town."

He showed no sign of having heard.

"Gallar," said Oshur, lurching closer. "Gallar kept a stock in her shop."

Tanith nodded. "Get him to the elevator."

"We'll never make it! Not through all this!"

As if to punctuate the point, the nearer dhow fired another salvo into the square. A house-sized chunk of the quayside slid away into the smoke as a section of supporting scaffold collapsed. The uneven battle below was long since ended, Araq's surviving citizenry fleeing south from hungry redcloak scimitars. Corpses choked the roadways and alleys. Some wore redcloak scarlet, but not enough. Not nearly enough.

"Then stay here!" Tanith started towards the elevator.

But the elevator was gone.

Kiasta. She hadn't seen it leave, but then she'd missed so much in the chaos of recent moments. She glanced along the suspension arm to the winch drum, its cables steadily re-spooling as the elevator rose.

Not good.

She peered over the edge, directly down to the elevator cage. Three redcloaks. Four koilos in full ember-saint armour.

She retraced her steps to where Raya had joined Oshur and Mirzai. The latter was still lost in his own private world, striving uselessly to stem blood that wouldn't and muttering in what sounded suspiciously like the Issnaîm tongue.

"We're getting company," said Tanith. "Don't make it easy for them."

Trying to not let the tremor in her hands show, she snagged a shrieker from beside a redcloak Mirzai had butchered, but every time she tried to make contact with the ifrît, her thoughts wandered. Four koilos. *Four.* Concentrated fire might bring down one – maybe two – but the others would be on them too fast to make it count. No chance of disabling the elevator. The cables were as thick as her wrist. Better to jump and take their chances on the fall. Head-first, to make certain it was quick.

She could run. Stars Below, but now she was free of the silver, she could climb down the scaffold, providing that she wasn't shot during the descent. But that would mean leaving the others. Dying a hero meant you had to live as one first, didn't it? Curse Kat for coming back into her life and challenging her to be better. And Enna, wherever she was. *I wanted to see who you wanted to be,* indeed. She should have ignored them both.

The shrieker's ifrît acquiesced with a silent sigh. Tanith tossed it to Oshur. "Another! Quickly."

Behind her, the elevator rattled to a stop.

Tanith turned just as her end of the quayside drowned in the shadow of the second dhow, coming in low – too low – from the east. She made a hurried calculation of the clearance between the quayside and the dhow's keel and found it wanting.

"Get down!" she shouted. "Get—"

Pinion sails unfurled along the dhow's outrigger masts as the pilot at last realised his mistake and clawed hurriedly for altitude. Canvas bloomed with captured wind, dragging the keel clear of the quayside.

The stern, not so much.

With a sound like a dying forest, it crashed into the elevator assembly, shattering the header crane like twigs and crushing the cage against the quayside's leading edge, cutting off the trapped redcloaks' screams as soon as they began.

Tanith ducked as the keel roared over her head, koilos bones and mangled cast iron scattering in its wake. "Mad! He's drunk or mad!"

But as the dhow climbed higher, rising to match the larger warship still firing on the crowd, she at last realised the pilot was neither of those things. Neither was he a *he*, but a vaporous presence at the ship's wheel, her hair shining with the light of captive stars. The red and gold flag of the throne immortal was gone from the stern, replaced by a stylised sunburst.

Mirzai snapped out of his reverie and gazed skyward as Zephyr's laughter danced through the smoke.

Still the dhow rose, gunports creaking open as it stalked oblivious prey. If the captain of the first dhow recognised the danger, he gave no sign, his shrieker cannons still pounding the wreckage of what had once been Araq's town square until the moment the rebel dhow spat flame.

A second salvo cracked home as the redcloak captain tried to manoeuvre clear. Precious eliathros gas wisped skyward from the aft buoyancy tanks, and the skyship dipped to starboard, dark figures flailing vainly for salvation as their stricken vessel tipped them overboard. A skilled pilot could have compensated, bringing a measure of stability through clever balancing of his ship's pitching and lateral wheels. But this pilot hadn't the knack, or perhaps had already gone overboard himself.

In any event, a third salvo made ruin of the last of the starboard buoyancy tanks. A sheer deck became vertical, became an inverted slope as the buoyant portside clung stubbornly to the skies that the starboard side had rejected. But gravity would not be denied. Even as the dhow's keel rolled perpendicular to the ground, its masts and rigging snagged on the remains of Nyssa Benevolas and snapped away. Masterless and dying, the ship ploughed a furrow through Araq's streets, sending great plumes of dust to further choke the smoke-laced skies.

Tanith was still staring at the wreckage when Zephyr looped back round, bringing her dhow to rest alongside the creaking quayside with impeccable skill. Shrieker fire arced up from the redcloaks in the square, achieving little more than charring the heavy starboard bulwark. As sailriders returned fire with crossbow and the occasional shrieker, others belayed the ship and extended a gangplank. Zephyr waited for neither, drifting down from the quarterdeck, her face stricken as she looked upon Tarin.

First across the gangplank was a woman who shouldn't have been within a dozen leagues of Araq, but somehow Tanith wasn't surprised to see her. Taller than Tanith and as dark as she herself was fair, she wore a simple black tunic modelled on a Tyzantan overseer and moved with a confidence Tanith hated herself for envying.

Was that always the way between sisters? She'd no way to know.

"Kat? You shouldn't be here."

Kat offered a not-quite-smile. One of many aggravating habits picked up from Rîma. "You needed me. There's nowhere else I should be."

Knowing she hated displays of affection, Tanith embraced her. "But the fleet—"

"There's still time for that." Kat pulled away and stared down at the charnel of Araq's square. "*Kiasta* . . . I wish we'd arrived sooner."

A frown crowded her expression. One that wasn't really hers at all. It belonged to another of her mentors, though she'd never admit it. The frustration that arose from the knowledge that no matter how hard she fought, however thin she spread herself, her deeds would always fall short.

"Sails to the north!" bellowed a voice from the quarterdeck. "Closing fast."

Ursalar Hannim, for a certainty. Wouldn't *she* be in for a surprise? Scant consolation. One way or another, Araq was gone. Tanith glanced back to where Mirzai and Zephyr knelt beside Tarin. Oshur and Raya stood a little to one side, regarding the new arrivals with a mix of dread and relief. "The boy's dying. Can you help him?"

Kat cocked her head, the frown now one of rapt concentration, almost as if she heard something Tanith couldn't. "Maybe . . . I don't know. Let's get them aboard."

Twenty

Mirzai stood alone atop the high aftercastle of *Sadia's Revenge* as the fires of Araq faded into the distance. Long enough to watch the pursuing dhows abandon their chase, but nowhere near enough to untangle his emotions. Twice now the throne immortal had taken everything from him. Redcloaks had razed Anfai and salted its fields even before his birth. Now Araq too was gone.

And Tarin? Tarin could yet join friends and comrades in the Deadwinds. Might be that he already had, and no one had yet mustered the courage to say. At least Oshur and Raya would live. Both had been taken below to have their wounds tended. Mirzai had aches enough of his own, but none more recent than the interrogator's beating. The Drowned Lady had seen fit to bring him through Araq's final hour without a scratch and had visited disaster on his enemies. For all Zephyr's claims that the Lady and the river were nothing more than myth, faith offered sorely needed comfort.

"*Thene voli ana meirionanna, nye. Ayin. Ayin,*" he croaked, the faces of the dead rising behind his eyes. Saheen. Gallar. Qaba. Seram. Ravli . . . "*Thene allithara kene naranma, nye. Ayin. Ayin. Aethari—*"

His brittle voice shattered, the fragments of the lament stuck in his throat. Another voice – softer and sweeter than his – took up the refrain, imbuing the final words with the melody that ever eluded him.

"*Aethari myan te couri voreen. Ayin. Ayin.*"

213

Zephyr drew close enough for comfort without intrusion. "Once soothed a god to slumber did that song. Ease the passage of dead it yet may."

Mirzai nodded mutely, too close to tears to trust himself to speak.

"Sorry for all that occurred, am I," she said softly. "A curse on your kind have mine always been."

She'd never looked less a part of his world than at the moment, vaporous against cerulean skies and lit through by sunlight. Her unbound hair danced in the wind, its stars glittering like gemstones. More than ever, he felt unworthy of her presence. Wary of provoking another lecture, he refrained from saying so. "This wasn't your fault. This was power doing what power always has. Araq was doomed from the moment Shorza arrived."

She propped her elbows on the balustrade, pupil-less eyes fixed on the distant horizon, lips a thin slash in her bluish-white face. "True spoken, but still sorry am I."

Grief lent her solidity, mortality. It made it easier to speak to her as a woman than as a herald of a half-forgotten religion. "Shouldn't you be at the wheels?"

She twitched a vaporous shoulder. "Any *waholi* can hold a course. A friend you needed."

"What I need is for Tarin to live," he said, unable to keep the bitterness from his voice. "But there never was much hope of that, was there?"

Zephyr faced him, sudden sternness awakening an echo of divinity. "Lost in the mist was I, hungry and alone. But found me, you did. Showed mercy, though it was little deserved. Always hope, there is."

Mirzai stared down at his hands. Though Tarin's blood was long since scrubbed away, still he felt its warmth. "I wish I could believe that."

"Mirzai . . ." She sighed, though not unkindly. "Hope is the deed and the will to see it done. Carry as much as we wish, do we . . . only we do not always bear it for ourselves. It is our greatest gift to others and a fire that must never go out."

He nodded, recognising the wisdom in her words, even if he could not yet take them to heart.

"Is he bothering you, Zephyr?" Tanith joined them at the stern. "I'm sure he'll gladly jump over the side if I smile at him *just* right."

She favoured Mirzai with one hungry enough to send a shiver down his spine. Not quite the temptress from Elondine's Rest nor wholly the cold-eyed killer of the quayside smoke, something about her called to him despite the blood matted through her blonde hair and the grime smearing her pallid cheeks. Beautiful as gold and treacherous as greed.

"Forgive her," said Zephyr, her voice colder than the breeze. "More feral than *akîa* forsaken in the mists are some."

"Relax, veilkin." Tanith's smile broadened as Zephyr bristled. "I'm not even a little bit hungry. Besides, Kat wants to talk to him."

Mirzai swallowed, not wanting to ask for fear of the answer. "Tarin, is he . . .?"

"It's complicated. Kat will explain."

Mirzai followed her down the quarterdeck companionway, scarcely noticing sailriders busy with the endless chores necessary to keep *Sadia's Revenge* Cloudsea-worthy. *It's complicated.* Khalad held few truths – indeed, recent days had sundered many of those he'd once considered inviolable – but nothing good ever came of those words. Fortunately, the dhow was too small for any journey to last long. Another companionway took them belowdecks and a narrow passage to a small cabin abaft of the mainmast.

Tanith halted by the door and twitched what might have been a supportive smile. "Don't worry. I bite, but my sister doesn't."

Mirzai was about to explain that it was Tarin's fate, not Kat's manner, that troubled him, but realised that Tanith's misplaced humour was meant in distraction, not mockery: a daemon not entirely certain how people worked, but trying her best to offer comfort. So instead he simply nodded, pulled open the door and passed inside.

The cabin stank of copper, dusky aromatics and sour oils common to curative salves. A pile of bloodstained sheets lay jumbled between the raised cot and a shrouded porthole. A basin of bloody water rocked gently back and forth on a low, narrow dresser. And on the cot, his battered body covered in a clean sheet and his eyes closed . . .

"Tarin?" Receiving no answer, Mirzai rushed forward and grasped his nephew's hand. The fingers were warm to the touch, but the pulse at his wrist . . . "No . . ."

Kat unfolded herself from the shadows by the porthole, barely a shape in the wan light. "We gave him all the last breath we had aboard. The ship's physician stitched his wounds as best she could – Imini has had much practice of late – but he was in too much pain. His soul was already leaving his body. We had to try something . . . unusual."

A vein leapt under Mirzai's fingers, the pulse slow and thready – barely one beat every five seconds. But it was *there*. He tore his eyes from Tarin's immobile face and stared at Kat. "I don't understand."

"The soul doesn't always wait for the body to die. When the pain grows too great, it begins its passage into the Deadwinds." Her eyes touched on Tarin. "Then the body perishes or else lingers in sleeping death until strength fails. His soul was screaming. I had to separate them to give him a chance."

Mirzai blinked back a tear and traced his fingers across Tarin's cheek. But for the warmth of his skin and the painfully slow pulse, he could have been a corpse. "Separate them how?"

Kat held up her left arm and smoothed back her sleeve. Magenta flame rippled between elbow and wrist, coursing along a tangled webwork of black lines. "His soul is with me. Safe, for now, while his body heals."

Mirzai's breath caught in his throat. He pinched his eyes shut to blot out a room suddenly spinning around him. To steal a soul, and speak of it as if it were nothing? Tanith's words whispered through the darkness. *I bite, but my sister doesn't.* They were family? He saw little resemblance in likeness and none at all in colouring. Kat was clearly the elder, perhaps part way between Tanith's age and Mirzai's own, though she carried herself with quiet confidence where her sibling oozed fragile bravado.

But was the older sibling any less a daemon than the younger?

Nausea receded, bitter thoughts alongside. Tarin was still alive. That was enough ... wasn't it? The part of him that was an engineer – that lived by the laws of cause and effect, however strange – took the reins, burying the part that was kin deep inside.

Yes. It had to be. For now.

He opened his eyes to find Kat watching him closely. "Is he aware of anything?"

"I don't know. Souls don't see the world as we do. Without a body, they lack the necessary context."

"You've done this before?"

"On occasion."

A sour taste gathered at the back of Mirzai's throat. "With success?"

She hesitated. "Sometimes."

At least she was honest. Or at least clever enough to feign it. "Back there, at Araq, I saw what your sister ..."

"*Half*-sister."

"... really is." He stifled a shudder at the memory of her victim's pitiful dying gasp. "Are *you* a daemon?"

She pulled her sleeve back into place. "My father was a man of curious interests and unhappy secrets. The tattoo was his 'gift' to me. I'm still learning what that means. Tanith ... is an acquired taste." She smiled without humour. "Sometimes I think we both are."

Another evasion ... or was it? Mirzai wondered if her caginess might be kin to his own: not evasiveness, but discomfort at having to talk at all. "What happens next?"

"That's up to you. Tarin can't stay with us, not where we're going. We'll rendezvous with another ship at noon. Zephyr will take him back to Athenoch. He'll be safe there."

"His *body* will be safe. What about his soul?"

"It'll be as safe as I am, and I've no plans to die." She offered a not-quite-smile. "You'll be welcome in Athenoch too. From what Zephyr's told me, they could use you there. It's not luxury, but it's a living."

"Where are you going?"

Her smile faded. "Araq isn't the first town the redcloaks wiped off the map this month. It's the sixth, making for ten that I know of in the last eight weeks. They arrive all smiles and conciliation. Little by little they turn the screws. Then all at once, nothing is so little any longer."

Mirzai glanced down at Tarin, recalling the tavern brawl that had sent everything off the rails. "Sounds familiar."

"It's deliberate. And it's accelerating. In three days, the hammer falls on what's left of Tyzanta." She set her jaw, fire in her eyes. For the first time, she looked as though she belonged in that uniform. "I can't let that happen. Tanith and ... one other ... disagree. She thinks the Eternity Queen's trying to lure me out into the open."

"Because you're the face of the rebellion now that Vallant's gone?"

"We have a history. Let's just say that she hopes we have a future."

"And what's that?"

"She wants me for my body." Kat's tone hinted at deeper meaning beneath the statement's bawdy simplicities. Her vicious smile discouraged enquiry. "Let her do her worst. If I'm not willing to die for one person, then I've no business being here at all. There are *thousands* on the line at Tyzanta. I shouldn't have come to Araq, not really, but you know how it is with family ... even when they're an acquired taste."

Mirzai squeezed Tarin's hand. "I do." He closed his eyes. "Hope is our greatest gift to others."

"That sounds like Zephyr. You're lucky she likes you. She doesn't let many people get close."

"I'm Anfaian. Her people aimed mine at the Eternity King like a spear. No matter how she tries to disabuse me, I still see a divine herald when I look at her."

"She must like that."

"Actually, I think she feels guilty. But divine or not, she understands hope." He drew down a deep breath. "Tarin will be safe in Athenoch?"

"As safe as anyone can be in Khalad."

"Then I'd rather stay."

She levelled an appraising stare. "Why?"

"Because only one piece of Tarin is going to Athenoch. The other is here with you. Because you've given me hope, and the only way I know to clear that debt is to pay it forward."

Kat opened her mouth and closed it again. When she finally spoke, Mirzai had the sense that she'd intended different words at first. "Be careful, Mirzai. This isn't a path you follow; it's one that leads ... and not always to places you might wish to go."

"I've spent most of my life running or hiding. If I hadn't, maybe Tarin wouldn't be lying there." He met her gaze. "I have to do this. Do you understand that?"

To his surprise she nodded, her expression softening to approval. "Yes, as it happens."

Kat set the door to behind Mirzai and waited until his footsteps faded into the gentle creak of shifting planks and the distant burr of sailrider shanties. She was alone. Or at least as alone as she ever got these days.

Tarin's soul was a ... not a weight, but a *presence*. Already growing stronger now, it was sheltered from the harms of its body. Impossibly more vibrant than the thin tessence she used to charge her tattoo with soulfire. Richer than the strongest ifrît. Intoxicating.

Soul-tethering, it was called. Forging the connection had almost killed her the first time she'd tried it, weeks before. Even with physical contact, she'd badly botched the attempt. The second occasion had gone more smoothly only because she'd surrendered control to the unwanted passenger in her thoughts. By the third, she'd enough of a grip that the tethered soul survived the process. But tethering Tarin had been almost second nature, her subconscious mind having learnt what her waking self could not. She'd not even had to touch him. In fact, she'd the sneaking suspicion that she could have fashioned the tether from the far side of the ship.

I told you it would become easier with practice. The Eternity King's graveyard sigh was proud more than it was smug, for whatever that mattered.

"I'm not comfortable doing this," she murmured.

There was no other choice. Not if you hope to save the boy.

Hope. The fragile lie that made any of this work. "I don't want to end up like Tanith." Or like whatever Tzal had made of Azra. She tried not to think about that, but it was always near to the surface.

You will not. You possess a degree of self-control she will never know. It is in the blood.

So he always said. Kat was never certain she believed him. They'd been bound together so long that she couldn't really remember what it was to simply be herself.

But you can feel its power, can you not?

"Yes." Even though she was mostly sure he couldn't read her thoughts, lying took an effort of will she could seldom afford. "It's beautiful."

How long had it been? Mere minutes, and all she wanted to do was scratch the itch at the back of her mind, dissolve Tarin's soul into hers and bathe in its glory. The prospect turned her stomach, but temptation lingered. His mere presence offered a glimpse of . . . what? Kat had no name for it, or the shadowed sensation it cast. She knew only that the simple act of perception had changed her in ways she didn't understand.

Imagine a hundred such souls in your keeping. A thousand.

"I won't fight that way."

You may have no choice.

220

Twenty-One

Even without the Eternity Queen's glamour colouring Damant's perceptions, the Golden Citadel remained as beautiful in moment as in memory. If Khalad's history proved one thing alone, it was that a tyrant and her comforts were but reluctantly parted.

Doubt grew with every step through cloister and garden, a match to the pressure building at the back of his mind. The Eternity Queen's influence was surely stronger up close than from afar, else all of Khalad would have slipped under her spell. Resisting her in the city was one thing, in the wider palace another ... but in direct audience? There was no way to know. Would he even notice if his mind ceased to be his own, or would the world simply slide away, unheralded and unacknowledged?

By the time the conclave hall's sentries parted, he found himself wishing that Rîma hadn't been so free with her words. Alone of the Queen's Council, he now knew that the rebellion had an active presence in Zariqaz. Should he have fled the city with that knowledge to pre-empt betrayal? He'd been tempted from the moment he'd delivered Mirela to the Starji district custodium. But he'd been a bystander too often. Rîma's trust demanded more of him than silence. Yali was just the start. She had to be.

But the start of what would depend on whether he survived the coming moments.

The emptiness of the conclave hall stood stark contrast to the growing pressure at the back of Damant's thoughts. Faizâr Kastagîr was the only other living soul present – the koilos standing guard over the sanctum entrance scarcely counted.

He offered a shallow bow. "Castellan." *Castellan*, not *Damant*. A bow, rather than a nod. Somewhere along the line Kastagîr had learned a measure of respect. All the more ironic given that by any measure the subject of said respect was now a traitor to his beloved Eternity Queen. "You look terrible."

A wry smile softened the words' offence. Damant couldn't blame him for simply stating truth. A long night on little sleep had left him haggard and bloodshot.

"So do you." Bruises and scrapes marred Kastagîr's handsome face, a limp his habitually crisp stride. The palace was rife with whispers of how he'd fought the rogue koilos to a standstill long enough for shriekers to be brought to bear. No small achievement. "You could have been killed."

"Better that than stand back and let innocents die." The words held no arrogance, no self-aggrandisement. Kastagîr meant them in their simplest form. A sentiment rare to the point of vanishing when spoken by a redcloak, and a far humbler one than Damant might have expected. He'd been wrong about Kastagîr framing Yali. Had he been wrong about more besides? "The Eternity Queen awaits you."

The descent from conclave hall to sanctum was the longest of Damant's life, the growing pressure at the back of his thoughts rousing fear to brink of terror. He sought safety in old patterns: the implacable tread of a custodian on patrol, the wooden expression that had safeguarded his private thoughts through all manner of Bascari family intrigues. What if Rîma was wrong? What if the Eternity Queen *could* divine who had fallen to her glamour?

The rap of Kastagîr's knuckles on the sanctum door echoed back along the passageway.

The door whispered inwards under a motic's guidance. A racing heart urged Damant to make his excuses and leave. He crossed the threshold anyway. His breath caught in his throat when the Eternity Queen beckoned to him from the throne immortal, the flickering magenta tongues of the soulfire column rippling and re-forming about her upturned hand.

"Ihsan." Her expression and voice were unreadable.

He bowed, as much to conceal his own gnawing uncertainty as from protocol. "Majesty."

Her soft laugh was bereft of humour. "You needn't be formal, Ihsan. We've known one another too long."

Had they? Was any part of the Eternity Queen any longer Yennika Bascari, or was she Tzal in all manner save name and mortal flesh? Certainly that flesh bore recent ravages plainly. Though the spiderweb of *kerem* poisoning had faded, the grey hairs among what had once been inky black had grown too prominent to dismiss as the work of imagination, and her laughter lines were more pronounced than ever. She was still beautiful, but for the first time Damant had the impression that beauty owed more to something not seen with the eye, but was instead recognised by a soul unable to readily express what it beheld. Her dark eyes met his, and the sense of otherness grew, as though a piece of her existed beyond his senses.

She smiled and the pressure at the back of Damant's mind redoubled, squeezing out thought, stifling even his fears. Soothing, seductive voices whispered on the edge of hearing, the words indecipherable. He felt pressure at his shoulders, on his arms: gentle tugs, drawing him onward to his beautiful, irresistible queen. He could almost *see* them – gossamer shapes bereft of all but the haziest imagining of mortal form, pale steam twisting on a dying breeze.

Colour bled away, the bright magentas and indigos of the sanctum fading to listless grey. Only the Eternity Queen remained vibrant, wicked and beautiful in a world turned ashen.

Damant's final conscious thought was a silent apology to Rîma, whose trust he would soon surely betray.

And then, as suddenly as it had arisen, the pressure receded. The ifrîti faded and colour returned to the world. Damant blinked and breathed deep, the perfumed sanctum air sweetened by the sudden, euphoric certainty that the Eternity Queen's glamour had found no purchase on him. Rîma had warned that he'd see things differently, though he'd not understood how much until that moment.

"I'm told that I am in your debt once again," said the Eternity Queen.

Damant read no suspicion in her voice or expression. No sign at all that she knew he was no longer her puppet. The last of his fears seeped away. "It's my pleasure to serve, majesty."

"Poor Mirela. She would have done better to let matters be. I had forgotten she even existed."

That struck Damant as unlikely. Proof, perhaps, that Tzal had long since displaced what was left of Yennika's soul, or had at least buried it deep. But then Rîma thought otherwise, and her belief could only have been shaped by Yali, who'd had more opportunity than most to examine the Eternity Queen's foibles.

"As had I, majesty." Damant glanced at Kastagîr. "I assume that the prisoner is secure?"

"In the deepest, darkest hole the palace has to offer. Six guards on her at all times, and no koilos anywhere close." Kastagîr grunted. "The only place she's going is the Golden Stair."

For execution, in other words. Damant stifled a flash of guilt. Though other hands would wield the sword that took Mirela's head, her blood would stain his just as readily. But his loyalty to the Bascari family was long since done, and Mirela herself a poor beneficiary of mercy. She'd destroyed hundreds of lives well before Yennika's schemes had unmade her own. Yali came first. "She hasn't denied her actions?"

"Denied them? She talks of nothing else. But she refuses to say who paid her."

All for the best as far as Damant was concerned, as it neatly side-stepped the matter of his informant's identity. The word of an unknown woman, unseen save by silhouette and encountered by chance, hardly made for an unimpeachable standard of proof.

"She doesn't know." Isdihar and Rîma had left the Starji townhouse before Damant and, suspecting little opportunity after, he'd availed himself of the opportunity for a private interrogation. Rightly surmising that she'd been betrayed, Mirela had spoken freely – and bitterly – at some length. "The initial contact came by letter to Kezedi a month ago. A second included a series of soul-glyph designs and a writ of authority over a considerable sum of tetrams held in the coffers of the city xanathros. I suspect we'll find that the account was opened under a false name. Alabastra's munificents are not above bribery."

"Then how did she know to be at the Hanged Skelder?" said Kastagîr.

"A pattern of lumani lit in the lower palace, facing the city," said Damant. "A prearranged signal, calling for a meeting. Mirela went to demand the rest of her payment."

"How very convenient," sneered Kastagîr.

"Faizâr . . ." The Eternity Queen had made no effort to raise her voice, but he flinched and hung his head all the same. "Is there no possibility that she's lying?" she went on.

Again her stare fell upon Damant, easier to bear now he knew it to be powerless. For him, at least. Kastagîr, it seemed, was another matter. "Mirela was always more arrogant than capable. There was only one Bascari of any real cleverness, and I'm speaking to her now."

The ghost of a smile touched the Eternity Queen's lips. "Flatterer."

"Not at all, majesty." In their first dealings, Yennika had fooled him completely. She'd had *everyone* fooled, including Arvish. Azra hadn't simply been a role; she'd practically been another person. If Mirela's patron was equally deft at conspiracy, it would be a long road to the truth.

Damant froze as a fresh angle of investigation beckoned. An absurd one perhaps, born of wishful thinking more than proof, but one worth chasing down. Later.

"Mirela doesn't concern me," he said. "Yali does."

"Why? She had copies of the same soul-glyphs." This time, Kastagîr kept his tone respectful. "Clearly she sent the letter."

"And kept those copies lying around for another month, knowing they'd tie her back to Mirela? They were a decoy, planted by the real culprit." Damant stifled a yawn. "My apologies ... I didn't sleep much last night."

"He makes a good point, Faizâr," said the Eternity Queen. "And Yali *has* served me faithfully."

Kastagîr stiffened. "I'm thinking only of your safety."

Damant frowned. Like it or not, Yali would remain implicated in Mirela's assassination attempt at least until the true architect was identified. That she *had* stolen the soul-glyphs made proving her innocence that much more challenging. "Then let me suggest a compromise. Yali goes free, but we assign a koilos to watch her."

"Koilos can't speak. How's it supposed to report?"

"*Most* koilos can't speak. Raith Bascari commissioned one that could. A paratîr – a watcher – he called it: an experiment in proofing the Tyzanta custodium against corruption."

"What happened?"

"He quickly realised that an incorruptible custodian that couldn't investigate crimes was of far less use than one that occasionally did so despite the bribes. Besides, his wife hated the thing. I'm certain First Shriver Halazni can re-create the experiment. It is, after all, simply a case of leaving the ifrît's soul a little more intact than usual." Damant shrugged. "It will require the two of us to have specialised soul-glyphs inked, but with the palace glyphs compromised, we all face a turn under the needle anyway."

Everyone save the Eternity Queen herself, who needed no such crutch to communicate with ifrîti. The process had already begun, betrayed by the lack of koilos in the palace halls while their control glyphs were altered and the associated tattoos re-inked. Between that and the business of tearing the inner palace apart to seal up or secure hidden passages of the sort Mirela had used, the disruption would continue for days, perhaps weeks.

The Eternity Queen pursed her lips. "That seems acceptable."

Kastagîr grimaced, echoing Damant's distaste at the reminder of frustrating hours in a chair while a shriversman etched a new dinar-sized design alongside those faded across long years of service, but he nodded. "Agreed."

"Ihsan, you'll instruct First Shriver Halazni to procure a suitable ifrît for this paratîr." She favoured Damant with a warm, enticing smile that did nothing to lessen the horror behind her words. "A *sarhana* would be suitable. See that one volunteers."

By now practised at such things, Damant kept his unease from his expression.

Not so Kastagîr, whose sudden scowl dispelled any notion that the Eternity Queen's glamour had any sway over his soul. "To be made a koilos is a punishment for criminals, not loyal soldiers! 'Let those who reject Nyssa's will earn redemption through service.'"

"Do not presume to quote scripture at me," snarled the Eternity Queen, rising from the throne immortal. "A people who entrust the safety of their goddess to reanimated skelders *deserve* to have her taken from them, as she so nearly was in recent days. And you will of course recall that scripture also records how the ember-saints of old had no need of punishment to rouse their virtue? They served willingly in life and death. Surely you can find just one *sarhana* to match their selflessness?"

Kastagîr wilted. "Of course, majesty," he murmured, eyes downcast. "I'll supervise the selection myself."

Damant swallowed to clear a parched throat. Did Kastagîr understand the door that the Eternity Queen had just wrenched open? If one redcloak could be called to serve as a koilos, then why not more? Why not all of them?

The Eternity Queen's snarl parted. The tip of her tongue flickered across her teeth before slipping out of sight once more. "Then we are agreed."

Damant nodded, glad to hurry the conversation along. "Yali will be free to attend to her duties and the koilos offers a guarantee that she'll attempt no mischief." Rîma wouldn't like it, as it would end Yali's usefulness to whatever she had planned, and he'd no doubt that Yali herself would hate the effective halt to her romantic proclivities – passion could hardly thrive beneath a koilos' dead-eyed stare. But then Damant was increasingly of the mind that such proclivities had, at best, served as a reason for Yali to slip away from the palace to contact Rîma. It was entirely possible that they'd been fiction, front to back. "In the meantime, we let it be known that Mirela framed Yali and that her execution will conclude matters."

"You're hoping to lull the real culprit into making a mistake?" Kastagîr was still visibly shaken, but the colour had returned to his cheeks. Just how often had he suffered the Eternity Queen's wrath in this sanctum, away from prying eyes? Why did he tolerate the humiliation? Damant dismissed the question even as it formed. Though his best years lay far behind, he wasn't *that* old.

"That's my hope. There's still a traitor in the palace. Likely a member of the Queen's Council." The irony wasn't lost on Damant. By the strictest definition, there were now at least *three* traitors in the palace. But sowing a little discord never hurt. Nothing increased the value of truth more than being the only person who held it.

And to think that only days before, he'd despaired at the council's lack of unity.

"Malis," said Kastagîr. "Malis or Karza or Bathîr."

"And you say that because . . .?" asked the Eternity Queen.

"Because Count Rashace and Lady Ozdîr will almost be in Tyzanta by now," said Damant. "It's a reasonable assumption, but I'm certain the culprit isn't one to sully their hands directly. Count Rashace could have orchestrated the entire thing as handily from the deck of his yacht as from his Khazli district mansion."

"Are you accusing Hargo?" She seemed amused more than appalled.

"An example only, majesty. I've no proof he's involved."

"Which isn't the same as him being innocent," said Kastagîr grimly.

"Indeed," Damant replied.

Hargo Rashace lacked both the subtlety and the wit for conspiracy. Which wasn't to say he couldn't be offered up to the Eternity Queen. It would not only absolve Yali, but also put the true traitor in the clear ... which if they could be persuaded from ceasing their attempts on the Eternity Queen's life – and therefore Yennika's – might work to everyone's benefit. Whether one of the council acting directly or through a surrogate, the culprit clearly came and went at will, and had access to parts of the palace off limits to most, such as the hidden passageways.

But then, he'd already spoken to someone who'd known of the hidden passageways, hadn't he? That same someone had set him on Mirela's trail. Damant tilted the puzzle pieces of his clue sideways, then tipped them entirely upside down. For the first time, they took on a shape that made sense. A twisted sort of sense, but his world increasingly answered to no other kind.

Yes, he *definitely* wanted to hear back from the Kezedi custodium. In fact, it might well be worth the cost of a second heraldic.

The Eternity Queen's gaze settled on him once again, her brow creasing to a slight frown. But the pressure at the back of his thoughts remained in abeyance, her glamour disinterested in re-engaging a battle already lost. "Then we can consider the matter closed for now, and trust to the traitors' own arrogance to deliver them to my judgement." She turned her attention to Kastagîr and offered a smile that on another woman might have been taken for vulnerability. "Please stay, Faizâr. I spoke harshly just now. Indulge me the opportunity to apologise."

Her deeper meaning required little by way of interpretation, but Damant saw nothing of anticipation or eagerness in Kastagîr's expression, only the rictus of a hound who dared not disobey the tug on his leash. Ambition might have brought him to the Eternity Queen's service and attraction to her bed, but neither they nor glamour kept him there. She'd broken him much more personally than that.

Twenty-Two

Aware that he was coming to the end of what scant reserves a broken night and nerve-jarring morning had left him, Damant passed up the opportunity of delivering the good news to Yali in person. With his grip on the waking world increasingly tenuous, he trusted himself neither to ask nor answer the inevitable questions in a way that wouldn't put either of them at risk.

Instead, he sequestered himself in an otherwise empty room in the palace's signal house and dispatched a second heraldic to Kezedi, a single clear question burned into the ifrît's thinning soul. Then he scavenged a simple meal of cardamon-spiced lamb from the palace kitchens and retired to his quarters, just about clearing his plate before sleep took him.

He woke into a night heavy with the nostalgic scent of a Mistfall soon to come. Donning fresh robes, he returned to the signal house and was gratified to learn that the high overseer of the Kezedi custodium had issued replies to both heraldics. Far from bearing a false name, the account that had financed Mirela's assassination bore no name at all, simply a line entry in a scriptorium ledger. But in light of the second reply, that hardly mattered.

In the end, she kept Damant waiting in the meditation cloister just long enough for him to doubt that she'd show at all. But as midnight passed and the first skeins of mist blurred the distant skies, the lumani along the cloister winked out, drowning the filthy stone and overgrown flower beds in darkness.

"Thank you for joining me," he murmured, his elbows on the balcony and his gaze on the ravaged city, twice the ruin in the magenta backwash of its torch houses. "I hoped you would."

"I gave you Mirela so you could clear Yali's name," she said, her unseen frown carried in her words. "She remains a prisoner."

Still he didn't recognise her voice. An impressive trick. "She'll be free tomorrow."

"Having a koilos lurching at her heels *isn't* what I'd call freedom," she replied.

"Had I known yesterday what I do today, she wouldn't even have that."

She drew closer behind him, the soft scuff of her boots the only sound. "You're different. Something's changed." The words framed an accusation, but her tone was curious. She'd never been one to appreciate events spinning out of her control.

"Let's just say I'm seeing things more clearly than I have in a long time."

"I thought so. *She* doesn't know you well enough to tell the difference, but I . . ."

"If I turn around, are you going to shoot me?"

"Always so suspicious, darling." The words carried a hint of weary amusement, but only that.

Damant pushed away from the balcony, turned about and found himself face to face with the Eternity Queen. Or at least a woman who bore a passing resemblance. The same dark eyes and deep bronze skin. The shoulderless golden gown. The same ink-black hair shot through with silver. But where the Eternity Queen was imperious and confident, this woman was withdrawn and restless, her shoulders bowed and her pinched expression weary beyond words. More telling, she wore no halo of flame. Not a wisp. A shrieker dangled from her hand, almost an afterthought.

"I can't stay," she murmured. "I can already feel her waking up. Kastagîr can normally be relied on to wear her out, but after that brawl last night, he's not exactly at his best."

Damant nodded, grateful to be spared the details. "Her?"

"Yennika. The Eternity Queen. The pieces I allowed Tzal to take so that he'd leave the rest of me alone. The pieces I'm better off without. I'm her. She's me." She laughed without humour. "Except for when she's sleeping. Then I'm just me."

"And who are you?" Damant cocked his head. "No, don't tell me ... Azra."

It wasn't much of a leap. Azra was the name of the skelder Yennika Bascari had once pretended to be. Who'd loved Katija Arvish and been loved by her in return. What happiness – maybe even what nobility – she'd ever possessed belonged to Azra, not to Yennika. Enough, it seemed, to live a double life.

"I'm trying to be. I thought I could be." She touched her eyes closed and shivered, her bare shoulders raised to gooseflesh by the night's chill. "How did you know?"

"I didn't know. I didn't even suspect. But then I got to thinking about our time in Tyzanta. How easily you took to being two people. I remembered what you said to me immediately after the poisoning. *Always the protector I don't deserve.* I thought it odd even then, though I didn't know why. With Yennika on the brink of death, you were free to speak."

She gathered her skirts and perched on the edge of the flower bed. "That's your proof? You couldn't hang a dog with that."

Damant grunted. "I contacted Kezedi about the funds Alabastra disbursed to Mirela. No name on the account, but the original deposit was made in tetrams. Crystal tetrams, bearing the mark of House Jovina. There aren't many of those in existence any longer. But then we never did recover everything you stole." That theft had been the opening gambit in Yennika's attempt to wrest Tyzanta from her hated family. It had been particularly memorable: the worth of crystal tetrams sprang from the sheer concentration of soulfire caged within. It made them lethally volatile. Yennika's plot had scythed several storeys off Tyzanta's Xanathros Alabastra. "That's when I knew. What I don't know is *why.*"

The corner of Azra's mouth twitched. "One hand on the tiller. That's what Nyssa – what *Tzal* – promised me when I stepped into the flames. He told me I'd be a queen. That I'd never be afraid ever again. He was right about that last part," she said with sudden venom. "There are things I can face now that I never could before."

No need to ask her meaning, not after she'd gone to such lengths to arrange an attempt on her own life. "What changed?"

"Don't be coy, Ihsan. It doesn't suit you." She brushed at the silver strands in her hair and snorted. "One hand on the tiller? He never even gave me that. Do you know what it's like to be a passenger in your own body? To see yourself say and do terrible things without even the consolation that it was by your choice?"

He winced, reminded of how the glamour had distorted him. "I've some notion."

"Then you have your answer." She shrugged as though to suggest the matter was of little account. "Better to end it than exist that way. There aren't many who'd dare assassinate the Eternity Queen, even for a fortune in crystal. But I knew Mirela would walk through fire to murder Yennika Bascari."

"Yali sent the letter for you, didn't she? I know you've been using her to relay the council's secrets to Rîma."

Azra nodded. "I employed one of the old family ciphers so she wouldn't know its contents. She'd never have sent it if she had. She'd think she was protecting me from myself."

But Yali *had* looked, hadn't she? She might not have made sense of the letter, but she'd recognised the soul-glyphs for what they were and copied them for Rîma. "And the signal that brought Mirela to the Hanged Skelder. Also you?"

"Please, Ihsan. I have servants for that." For a moment, she looked and sounded like the woman he remembered, dazzling and confident. But only a moment. "I never meant to put Yali in harm's way. She's helped me keep what little sanity I have left."

"Then why not simply kill yourself? Why go to all this trouble?"

"You think I haven't tried?" she snapped. "Yennika doesn't sleep deeply enough. If I die, so does she. She won't allow that." Her eyes turned glassy, unfocused, haunted by memories Damant could only guess at. "I have to be taken from her. And from him."

"You said Yennika *is* Tzal."

"She is and she isn't. I don't think he's alive in the same way that you and I are. On some level, he's incomplete. He *needs* a body in order to exist. A perfect host. One that can't resist. That won't burn out. Until he finds her, he'll make do with me ... for as long as I last."

Damant shook his head. The Yennika he'd known had originally invented the Azra persona as a means to survive familial abuse that had left her a broken woman. After her schemes to claim Tyzanta had fallen through, Yennika had taken to calling herself Azra again and thrown herself into supporting Arvish in an attempt to re-earn the trust she'd broken. Indeed, that was when she'd first taken to treating Yennika as a separate person. Someone to bear her formidable sins.

At the time, he'd assumed it was a new take on an old pretence. Now he wondered if it was something more, the sign of a personality fracturing beneath the twin pressures of love and self-loathing, her every wicked deed shackled to "Yennika" and buried beneath Azra's newly dominant psyche. It might explain why Azra had any measure of freedom at all. To all intents and purposes, Azra *was* a different woman. One over whom Tzal had no claim. She'd even said it herself: she'd "given" Yennika to Tzal.

In the time he'd known her, the woman who'd been born Yennika Bascari had by turns earned his admiration and his hatred. He'd never pitied her as he did now.

"A perfect host? You mean Arvish, don't you?"

"Tzal won't stop until he finds her. But he can't have her. I won't let him." She bit out the words, defiant and passionate. "Not this side of the Deadwinds."

"And if he does?"

She sagged. "Then the suffering he'll inflict on Khalad will make Caradan Diar's worst excesses seem like a golden age."

"Why?"

"I don't know." She spread a hand across her breastbone. "But I can feel it here. It's not anger, but calculation. Cruelty with a purpose. It's already begun. With Yali's help I've blunted what I can, but the redcloak legions are grinding the Kaldosi/Qersali border to rubble. Hargo Rashace isn't inbound to what's left of Tyzanta so he can scour it for new workers, but to finish what Yennika started months ago. Tzal wants you angry. Desperate."

Rîma had claimed that Tzal had no reason for cruelty save cruelty itself. Damant had distrusted that analysis, but perhaps she – and Azra – had the right of it. Applying mortal motivation to something plainly *other* could prove a costly mistake. "And all those who die along the way make him stronger still."

Azra looked up in surprise. "Yes. We're all of us the food at his table."

"What will he eat once we're all dead, I wonder."

"I hope to be past caring by then," she said bitterly. "How did you know?"

Better not to mention that Isdihar Diar was back in Zariqaz. All evidence pointed to Azra and Yennika being as separate as the former claimed, but risk remained risk. "Rîma."

"Of course, I should have—"

She broke off, troubled eyes hardening. An indigo shimmer flickered to life about her shoulders. Barely a breath, but growing steadily brighter.

"She's waking up. I can't stay." But instead of beating a retreat along the cloister, Azra drew closer. She took his hand by the wrist and pressed her shrieker into his palm. Warmth spread across Damant's fingers as the ifrît recognised the authority of the tattoo inked at the base of his wrist. "Kill me. Before it's too late."

He pulled away, repulsed. "No."

"Don't be coy, Ihsan. We both know I deserve it, and more besides."

"Then do it yourself."

"You think I'd go to all that trouble with Mirela if it was that easy? I can't tell you how many times I've put this barrel in my mouth or a knife

235

to my wrist. Then I blink, and it's an hour later – even a day – and my thoughts are full of Yennika's laughter. If I try to kill myself now, she'll surface. She'll see you and she'll know that you're free of her glamour. What good does that do either of us? You stopped Mirela. You *owe* me this." She pinched her eyes shut. "Back in Tyzanta you were a better friend than I deserved. Do this for me now. Yali's safe. That's all I care about."

He shook his head. "Rîma says that if you die, Tzal will simply find another host. It won't change anything."

"She's guessing."

"Rîma doesn't guess." He cast about for more. "What about the people you've helped? You've saved hundreds of lives at Tyzanta alone, and I'm betting I don't know the half of it."

"I don't care," she hissed. "Not any longer. Don't you see? I can't live like this."

How to persuade her? Did he even have the right to do so?

A gut wound might do it, something beyond last breath's ability to cure but that would give him precious minutes to get clear and thus avoid becoming Tzal's next host. But who *would* Tzal possess in her stead? All evidence pointed towards it being someone who wouldn't resist as Azra had. Someone incapable of blunting his malice.

What swung it in the end was his last memory of Ardin Javar, sitting on his terrace half awash in calvasîr, lost in the Eternity Queen's glamour and begging for help in every way but words. He'd failed Ardin that night. He'd never be able to make that right.

He gripped the shrieker tight and levelled the muzzle at Azra's belly. She sagged, relief parting her lips as a stuttering sigh. "Thank you, Ihsan."

"Tell me one last thing."

Her eyes hooded with suspicion. "I'm listening."

"What would Kat do in your place?"

She recoiled and glared at him with murderous eyes. For the briefest of moments, she was again the Yennika he remembered. The cold-blooded plotter who'd sought to grind Vallant's rebellion into dust. But the moment passed, and with it her defiance.

"That's not fair," she murmured.

"This is Khalad," he replied, his voice hard. "There's no fairness here. You find your place or one's found for you. Isn't that what you used to say?"

She swung at him with an open palm. He caught her wrist before the blow could land.

"That's what I'm trying to do!" she snarled, struggling in his grip.

"No," he ground out. "You're running away. That's what Yennika would do. Azra would stand by her friends. She'd make Tzal pay for what he's done to them. To her."

She shook her head, disbelieving. "He's a god. We can't beat him."

"The Issnaîm did. They caged him."

"For all the good it did them."

"No one ever thought the Eternity King could be cast down, but he's gone. There's always a way. Arvish, Rîma and the others taught me that. I thought you'd learned the same lesson."

Azra's expression contorted with conflicting emotions. But she stood a little straighter, a little taller. Damant released her wrist. As her hand fell, he held out the shrieker.

After the briefest hesitation, she took it. "That was unkind, bringing Kat into it."

"Sorry."

"Don't be. I needed to hear it." She sighed. "I really do have to go. I've run things too close already. But we can talk tomorrow night, if you're willing."

Damant nodded, at last permitting himself to feel something approaching relief. "Count on it."

Twenty-Three

Come morning, *Sadia's Revenge* was no longer alone in the Cloudsea. A hundred yards off the port bow, visible through the bobbing swirl of Deadwind motes, a lateen-rigged dhow shadowed the rebel flagship. The unfaded and patchwork green paint along the newcomer's buoyancy tanks marked recent repairs, while the pockmarked port edge of its mainsail told a tale of battles survived, if not necessarily won. Qaba would have tutted to see it, and begun tallying the repair docket in the same breath. Mirzai's more practical eye noted the tight rigging and even trim, the lack of loose stowage on the deck and the smoothness with which the motic winches rearranged the pinion sails to better harness the majestic pull of the Deadwinds. *Amarid's Dream* wasn't a pretty ship, perhaps, but looks weren't everything.

It was certainly easier on the eye than the blocky, square-sailed transport carracks sailing even farther out. With their high fore- and after-castles, they put Mirzai in mind of dead woodlice ... and he knew they were about as good in a fight. But they could haul cargo with the best of them.

"The glory of the rebellion," said Zephyr. "Behold it and weep."

Still weary from the escape from Araq, but the worst of his harms soothed away by last breath, Mirzai failed utterly in his attempt to determine if she spoke in seriousness or jest. Another two warships hung off the port bow of the *Sadia's Revenge*, and five more transports – a mix of carracks and low-gunwaled barges – trailed astern. "It seems to have worked out so far."

"Named for a fallen friend, that ship is. Fallen family. This one too." She shook her head, captive stars gleaming amid the inky black cloud of her tresses. "They fight with us, even now. But a price, defiance has. Many debts will fall due in coming days."

Mirzai hesitated. "Do you think Kat can win at Tyzanta?" No one referred to her by surname or title. In fact, as far as he was aware, she didn't *have* a title. She was simply *Kat* to friends and followers alike.

"Surprises everyone, she does. Especially herself." Zephyr sighed. "Be coming with you, should I, but Athenoch has been lost too long."

Athenoch. The mythical city, claimed by the Veil and yet flourishing. Tarin's refuge-to-be. He stared down at the clouds drifting lazily past the keel of the *Sadia's Revenge*. "Can no one else navigate the mists?"

"Kat did once, long ago, but a muddle have they been since Caradan Diar perished. Changeable. Malicious. A-swirl and a-dance. Takes the clear head of an Issnaîm to chart a course."

"That can't be right. Even in the time you were lost to the mists, I heard the stories of rebel ships striking redcloak patrols and vanishing into the Veil."

She twitched a wry smile. "*Waholi* love to make mystery out of failure. Always Vallant's secret weapon, was I." The smile faded to a flat expression more sorrowful than any frown. "And then his death I became."

"You don't know that."

Zephyr scowled. "Gone is he, yet I remain. How can it not be my fault?"

A pang assailed Mirzai's heart, the shallows of his limited interpersonal skills long since abandoned for deep and treacherous waters. "If I hadn't gone to Nyzanshar, Gallar and the others might still be alive. Maybe Araq would still be a town, and not just a name on a map. But I'm not responsible for what the redcloaks did."

Zephyr pursed her lips, her cold white stare finding his. "And believe that, do you?"

Realising that the fingers of his right hand were working anxiously against his leg, Mirzai clenched them to a fist. "I'm trying to." He offered a warmthless smile. "What else is there?"

Tanith joined them at the bulwark in a whisper of skirts. "That's easy. We make everybody pay. For their terrible deeds, and for ours." In the bright morning sun, unplaited golden hair streaming behind and her ravaged *sarhana* uniform exchanged for a pale blue gown, she was more beautiful than ever. But Mirzai could smell the blood on her hands, long since scrubbed away though it was. "Listen to you two, gobbling hungrily after blame when there's a literal daemon in your shadow. You don't know what guilt *is*."

Icy fingers brushed Mirzai's spine. Tanith was personable enough when she wanted to be, but try as he might, he couldn't shake the feeling that the gap between ally and prey was a terrifyingly narrow one. From the sudden tautness of Zephyr's expression, she felt much the same. Apparently the gap between ally and friend was a larger one.

"The felucca's ready to take you to *Telthi's Pride*," Tanith told Zephyr, apparently unaware of the discomfort she'd provoked. She turned to Mirzai. "Tarin's body is already aboard, if you have any final farewells."

Mirzai shook his head. "If your sister told me the truth, everything important about Tarin is with her." Which hadn't stopped him spending the night in the same cabin as his nephew's soulless body, babbling apologies until sleep had taken him.

"I don't think Kat has it in her to lie." Tanith's tone made virtue the most shameful of vices. "But she did send for you, so if you're ready . . .?"

"Of course." He glanced at Zephyr, uncertain what to say. In the short time he'd known her, she'd bled from monster to divine herald and finally to friend, perhaps the closest friend he'd had in a good many years. For all his awkwardness, the parting felt almost like losing a piece of himself. "May the winds be kind, *nasaîm*."

She pressed something small and cold into his hand. His

grandfather's serpent pendant. "Yours, this is. Metal retains an echo of soul, so I was taught. May a piece of mine bring you comfort in need, as your kindness did for me."

He looped it around his neck, glad to feel its weight once more. He'd quite forgotten she'd still had it. "It was my honour."

She gave a small nod and the ghost of a smile. "River keep you, Mirzai."

He frowned, thinking at first that he'd misheard. "I thought you said the Black River was only a legend?"

"What does it matter if it brings hope? Not complain, shall I, if the Drowned Lady proves real. Maybe brought me to you after all, did she. Maybe she will again." She shifted her attention to Tanith. "Hold tight to your *akia*, amashti."

"I mean to," she replied, not entirely coldly. "Tell my mother I'll see her soon."

"Of course."

Zephyr glided away across the deck towards where a felucca's single bare mast could be glimpsed through the rigging, the tails of her vaporous skirts rippling over and through a deck scrubber's bucket before seamlessly re-forming. Throaty song broke out towards the prow as a dozen sailriders worked timber planks into position to replace a section of damaged bulwark.

"What was that about a river?" asked Tanith, her guttural voice thoughtful.

"The Black River flows beneath the world. It bears away innocent and guilty alike to the Drowned Lady, so that she may offer protection to the innocent and bring down vengeance on the guilty." Mirzai shrugged. "At least, that's what I was raised to believe. Zephyr told me it was all a lie, fed to us by the Issnaîm."

Tanith snorted. "You should never trust a veilkin."

"Or a daemon?"

"*Especially* not a daemon. We are terrible people." Mirth faded from her voice. "I saw a black river once. In the Stars Below."

241

"*You* were in the Stars Below?" he replied, unable to hide his scorn. More myth intruding onto reality. Or she was lying.

"Is that so unbelievable?" The smile was back in her voice now, if not on her face, though it wasn't especially kind.

"I suppose Nyssa judged you and set you free?"

Another shrug. "Judged maybe. I found pieces of myself I never knew I had. But there *was* a black river – dark and glimmerless and ... peaceful. It offered no reflection. It simply ... was. Perhaps I should have let it carry me off?" She pressed on, quiet and intense, without a hint of the mockery that was otherwise so present. "Does this Drowned Lady of yours look kindly on lost souls?"

"So we are taught," he said cautiously. For the first time since they'd met, Tanith's manner matched her slender years. She was uncertain, almost vulnerable – or at least as close to vulnerable as he expected she might ever come – a soul burdened by weight he could only guess at. "Why?"

"Because you're the not only one who could use a little hope. I really *have* done terrible things ... and Nyssa offers no comfort that I want." Asperity crept into her voice and expression, the vulnerability gone. "You talk too much, and my sister's waiting."

Given the modest size of the *Sadia's Revenge*, the gloomy, wood-panelled compartment that did double duty as the ship's wardroom and Kat's outer cabin made for a cramped meeting. Worse, with the outer doors closed to reduce the possibility of eavesdropping – Kat trusted her crew rather more than Tanith would have in her stead, but the Eternity Queen's glamour made treachery an ever-present threat – the air was already musty with the press of bodies crushed close on a sunny day.

At least the sweat went some way to smothering the soul-scents of the half-dozen men and women. Though Tanith had sated herself on Deadwind motes earlier that day, such feasts were thin, passive echoes of the real thing. They offered no triumph. No exhilaration. It robbed the meal of its visceral flavour. She loathed that part of herself – even now, the memory of the redcloak she'd devoured and discarded at Araq burned her cheeks – but she was honest enough to admit the power it held over her.

So as Kat called for quiet, Tanith took care to hold her breath whenever the spiced lavender of Mirzai's soul threatened to overwhelm earthy sweat, and tried to forget that her mouth was watering.

Kat set an upturned plate on the wardroom table, whose dark green tablecloth was practically black in the sparse light creeping in through the aft windows. "The Eternity Queen has decided to make another example of Tyzanta."

Her cheek twitched. It always did when she spoke of Yennika, though Tanith doubted anyone else noticed, even in that room. Maxin, perhaps. The squat, bald fellow was more perceptive than a broken nose and a past as one of Ardin Javar's leg-breakers might suggest. Maybe Vathi, who morosely insisted on seeing shadows in even the brightest sunlight. But then they'd known Kat longer than the rest. Longer than Tanith herself, truth be told.

Kat spread a handful of shucked almonds halfway between the plate and the table edge, the tip of their teardrops pointed at the plate. "Her fleet arrives at noon tomorrow. Officially, its orders are to recruit labourers from the refugees, but you don't send a man like Count Rashace to offer kindness and favourable employment."

Bleak laughter rippled around the room. Tanith stiffened. To the others, Hargo Rashace was just a name. To her, he'd been a cruel step-father consumed with rage at his wife for her unfaithfulness and at Tanith for being proof of the same.

"It will be a massacre," Kat went on. "Or it would be, if we weren't going to stop it."

"With three dhows and a bunch of broken-down cargo hulks?" rumbled Vathi. "Dying in solidarity's all very well, but I'd rather make a fight of it."

"*Five* dhows," said Maxin, from across the table. "*Galadin's Lament* and *Timmara's Sword* should be with us later tonight."

243

Vathi nodded at the almonds. "They still have eight, and all of them bigger than this one."

"Fifteen." Kat set another seven almonds at even spacing around the plate. "You're forgetting House Ozdîr's blockade."

Vathi glowered across the table. "I'm forgetting nothing. I'm trying to be an optimist ... and I'm assuming you have a plan for those."

"I have a plan for everything," said Kat. "We'll be arriving at dawn. That gives us a good five or six hours to slip in, evacuate anyone who wants to leave and get clear before the Eternity Queen's ships arrive. Sorry, Tanith."

Tanith nodded, understanding that there'd be no opportunity to bring Hargo to justice for his crimes, both familial and far-reaching. "I'm learning to defer my pleasures."

"Six hours sounds like a lot," said Aklia Tzan, a heavyset and grizzled Qersali bondswoman: one of a few hundred who'd rejected the zol'tayah's call to leave the floundering rebellion to its fate and return home. A veteran of the border wars, she was known for being as analytical as Vathi was downcast. "But even if nothing goes wrong, that's a lot of people to move. And unless something's changed there's another six Ozdîr warships anchored at Hazali. One whiff of trouble and the blockade ships will send up a heraldic. We'll be staring down the wrong end of two-to-one odds."

Kat set a smaller plate a handspan away from the large and set six almonds atop it. "The blockade ships don't worry me. Their patrols are meant to stop refugees getting out and smugglers getting in." She grabbed five dates from a bowl and set them on the opposite side of Tyzanta from the Eternity Queen's fleet. "We'll gobble up the two nearest ships before the others get close. Better still, the *Ancestral* is with us. Its captain had a change of heart after he was ordered to level Tyzanta's last functioning torch house. Once the fighting starts, he'll strike his colours and join us. That's three-to-one odds in *our* favour."

She scooped up two of the almonds on the plate's circumference, swapped another for a date. She tossed one of the almonds to Maxin, who caught it in his teeth and crunched it down.

"Sounds good to me," he said through a mouthful of nut fragments.

"Then our warships keep the rest of the blockade honest while the hulks evacuate?" Aklia mused. "It's still not much time."

"We've people on the ground already organising the refugees," said Tanith. "Those who want to go will be ready to move as soon as the first carrack ties up at Kazzar's Quay."

"You're sure about that?" asked Maxin. "No one's been in or out of Tyzanta for weeks. Not since Ozdîr really started locking down. We lost three ships on the last supply run."

"I was there six days ago." Tanith smiled as a hiss of surprise echoed around the room.

"Stars Below," murmured Vathi. "How d'you manage that?"

She blew him a kiss. "Folk just don't like saying 'no' to me."

Her smile soured at recollection of wretched souls clinging to what buildings remained, shivering beside fires fed by scavenged timber. Two of the city's aqueducts had survived mostly intact, but what little water they provided was closely rationed by the knot of custodians and Undertown enforcers who'd banded together to offer an imitation of governance. It was the children that had gotten to her. Thin and ragged, digging around in the unstable rubble for anything that might be worth trading, careless of half-buried bodies of those who'd pushed their fortunes too far. Most of them younger than she'd been as a feral thing in Kaldos.

Empathy took the fun out of life. Worse, it made you do *really* stupid things.

Kat shrugged. "We have eight carracks, six barges, three *maravhas* ..." *Maravhas* were shallow-keeled Qersali skyships, as slow and strong-backed as drowsy oxen and crewed by yet more bondsmen and women sickened by their zol'tayah's cowardice. " ... and a dozen smaller ships. Packed to the gunnels, they can handle three to four thousand. It won't be pleasant, but it *will* work."

"I'm still waiting to hear how we deal with the ships at Hazali," said Vathi. "Ask them nicely to stay home? The smallest one's twice the size of the *Revenge*."

"Not quite," said Kat. "That's where you five come in."

"Lucky us."

His eyes still on Kat, Maxin drove an elbow into Vathi's ribs. "Listen to the trallock, would you?"

"Hazali's an old cargo waystation. Railrunners more or less put it out of business a few years back, but since the blockade it's functioned as a dock for House Ozdîr." A not-quite-smile touching her lips, Kat set a sixth date on the table, halfway between her fleet and the smaller plate. "Hazali's eliathros reserves are low. They're expecting a tanker, but likely not the one that's going to arrive tonight. This one has a provocative quantity of blackfire damp mixed in with the eliathros. We've got all the documentation you'll need to tie up at the dockside."

"Then we set a fuse and run like hell?" asked Maxin.

"You do that and you'll get an impressive fireball, but an unfocused one. You'll be lucky to take out more than a couple of ships. The ships tied up there are the blockade relief, working a three-day-on, three-off rotation. They'll have just finished serving their turn on the blockade and will be settling in for resupply. Buoyancy tanks are always leaking and redcloak procedure is to flush and replenish, not merely top off. Normally the tanks on dhows that size can take a few cannon salvos before there's a loss of altitude. Not good for us – as Vathi's mentioned, we're hilariously outgunned – but if there's enough blackfire damp in with the eliathros and we get the first shot . . .?"

"Boom?" asked Tanith.

Mirzai grunted. "More like a hollow roar and a lot of screaming. *Then* 'boom'. After that, you don't hear much of anything at all."

"You've seen it happen?" asked Maxin.

"One of the filterage tanks at Araq had a crack in its seals, and one of the refinery workers liked smoking isshîm at unsuitable times. They found the remains of the tank halfway up Giriqan. Looked like a giant hand had torn it open." He grunted. "They never found enough of the worker to bury. The rest of his team wasn't much better. That was pure blackfire damp under pressure, but even mixed with eliathros it'll be impressive enough."

"What sort of ratio?" asked Aklia.

"Eighty/twenty," said Mirzai. "Anything higher and you'll lose too much buoyancy. Doesn't take a sailrider to know that a ship's dragging down the dock because it can't support itself."

Kat exchanged a thoughtful nod with Maxin. "I have someone embedded at Hazali – he's the one who made the suggestion – but he's not what I'd call technically minded. Consider him to be a contingency if required. In the meantime, I need someone there who is. Zephyr suggested you. Can you handle it?"

"There'll be a central silo hooked up to the individual berths. At least, that how Qaba used to run it at Araq. It could be configured any number of ways, but it won't be complicated. Complexity leads to errors." Mirzai nodded. "Get me in. I'll see it's done."

"Good," said Kat. "Then you'd better be going ... unless there are any questions?"

"Not from me," said Vathi, in the tone of a man staring into his own grave. "It's a terrible plan, but aren't they all?"

Tanith couldn't help but agree. Superficially, it made sense. Five fighters to neutralise six whole dhows. *If* the eliathros/blackfire damp mix worked as Mirzai said it would. *If* he could operate the supply systems at Hazali. *If* they weren't caught. And, of course, *if* Kat's fleet got off a salvo before the larger, better-armed Ozdîr ships blasted them to pieces. It was, in short, exactly the kind of plan that Vallant would have come up with.

"This would be easier if Tatterlain were here," she said. "He'd have talked the dockers to blowing up the ships for us."

Kat scowled. "Well he's not. I wish he were."

Tanith knew the sharpness of her sister's tone wasn't aimed at her. Kat didn't make friends easily, and she didn't like being reminded of the ones she'd lost to Deadwinds and distance. So she simply nodded and waited for the others to leave.

"Do you think Mirzai's up to this?" asked Kat, as the door swung closed.

Tanith took her first deep breath since the meeting had begun, glad that the air no longer tantalised. Kat's soul-scent was barely a wisp beneath the darker, brackish presence that had swamped her own ever since Caradan Diar had fused his deathless spirit to hers. No one else knew about that. But then Kat could hardly have kept it hidden from her.

"If you'd asked me that when I'd first met him, I'd have said no. But when things got ugly ...? I think he's been holding back for years, terrified of what might happen. Not that you'd know what that was like."

"According to the voice in my head, I'm *still* holding back." Kat rubbed her brow. "Even for a disembodied soul, he's not happy. He says this is all a waste of time and effort."

"Of course he's not happy, he's dead." Tanith rounded the table. "I just hope you know what you're doing."

"That's easy. I'm doing whatever I can to keep people alive while Rîma strikes the real blow. The more the Eternity Queen is looking towards Tyzanta, the less attention she has to spare for what's right under her nose."

Tanith heard the catch in her voice. It was always there when she spoke of Azra. "That's not what I meant."

"I know what you meant," snapped Kat. She shook her head, her voice softening at once. "He's helping me understand what I can do, and we need every advantage."

"I used to think our father was helping me, and we all know how that ended, don't we?" Tanith shook her head. "Just be careful, Kat. I've only just got used to having a sister. It would be annoying to lose her now."

Kat offered a wry smile. "That almost sounded affectionate."

Tanith returned it with a mock scowl. "Don't push your luck."

The waiting was the worst part, Kat decided as the wallowing *Lumberfast* sailed off into the gathering dusk. Not that she looked forward to actually being in the thick of a fight, especially not a sky-ship battle – though she'd commanded more than her fair share since Vallant's disappearance, familiarity hadn't so much bred contempt as attenuated her fears – but at least the chaos of battle left little time for regrets and second guesses.

Calm yourself, sighed the Eternity King. *This worrying is a waste of effort.*

"It's my effort to waste," said Kat, careful that her words wouldn't carry to Larsi, the *Revenge*'s captain, busy at the ship's wheels. The last thing she needed was to have folk wondering why she was talking to herself. Well, almost the last thing. That would be them knowing who she was talking *to*. Loyalty went only so far, and the revelation that their leader – fearless or otherwise – was sharing soul-space with Caradan Diar invited disaster. They'd not care that his advice, his experience, had helped transform a street skelder into a woman capable of defying the Eternity Queen. They'd remember only that he'd been the Eternity King they'd once fought and send for an exorcist to shake him loose from her soul.

She stared aft to the ragtag trail of barges, carracks and scows gathered beneath Vallant's sunburst flag to save the Tyzantan refugees. Now *Galadin's Lament* and *Timmara's Sword* had joined them, there were near a thousand sailriders under her command – and that number was so low only because the skyships' motics and helmics handled most of the work. Had they been prismless hulks like the original *Chainbreaker*, this rescue would never have been possible.

But even a "mere" thousand souls was a weighty burden. A gambler's stake, levied in the hope of saving thousands more. A wager that desperation and optimism could make truth of a lie.

Even if all went well, some would die today. Friends, perhaps. Maybe even her sister. Ironically, Mirzai's nephew Tarin was safest of all, with his soul nestled deep inside her aetherios tattoo by means she still didn't quite comprehend. Or maybe it wasn't Tarin who was safe at all, but her own conscience, because he couldn't pass to the Deadwinds while she still lived, and thus she'd never know guilt at his death.

As for everyone else . . .

She'd often accused Vallant of being cavalier with his responsibilities. More and more, she didn't understand how it hadn't crushed him flat.

Because leaders sacrifice, breathed Caradan Diar. *They wield their followers like a weapon because they perceive a greater truth that may endure through no other means.*

Kat scowled. She'd almost forgotten what it was to have her thoughts to herself. But without him she'd have been dead a dozen times over, first from the omen rot his deathless spirit had driven from her body, and the others from battlefield dangers her inexperience had missed. "Is that how you justify what you did to Khalad?" she murmured.

The old argument, refought time and again, and yet she never grew weary of it. She hoped she never did. That would mean that she'd become as cynical as her formless mentor. As Azra had been, before she'd started to understand there was a better way. It had been a brief enough flowering, cut short when Tzal had possessed her. Another unkindness in a world replete with them.

I served a greater truth. What is necessary must be. There is no other law.

The Eternity Queen doubtless thought the same. At her worst, Yennika – the real Yennika – certainly had. "At least you're honest."

It pleases me that you think so.

"So I'm just a weapon?"

You were born to be a weapon. You all were.

It wasn't the words that grabbed Kat's attention, but the way in which he said them – like a mortal suddenly regretting his tongue running away with itself. But she supposed he'd spoken truly enough. Through her aetherios tattoo her father had deliberately fashioned her to be the perfect vessel for Tzal's malevolent spirit. If that wasn't a weapon, then what was?

"Was Isdihar?" Unease granted the words more bite than she intended. Or perhaps not. Allies they might have been, but there was pleasure to be had in goading Caradan Diar, and no surer means than speaking of his descendant. She was the only thing in Khalad that roused him from dispassion. He might even have loved her.

Isdihar Diar at least was safe, or as safe as could be, for she had Rîma as a protector. Kat hadn't heard from them in months, not since they'd returned to Zariqaz with a dream of carrying the battle to the Eternity Queen herself.

It felt longer. Rîma was part of her in a way she couldn't explain. Her absence hurt more than all the other friends lost along the way. Damant. Yali. Tatterlain. Amarid. Vallant. The dead, the gone and the merely missing. It wasn't love, not exactly – or at least not as she'd loved Azra. *Old souls bound together across lifetimes* was how Rîma had put it, and Kat had found no better way to express the bond.

Time to fight for them.

Twenty-Four

||This really isn't necessary, honest and true,|| said Yali, her signs cutting through the marketplace clamour of the azasouk. ||I just wanted some fresh air. Even one minder is overkill.||

She shot a frustrated glance at the koilos trailing a pace or two behind. Even stripped of its ember-saint's finery and clad in the nondescript robes of the palace custodium, it cast a long shadow. Not for nothing had Yali – somewhat bitterly – named her watcher "Gloom".

Damant raised his hands to a series of fumbling signs. ||I'm not a minder. I just wanted some fresh air as well. This colour would suit you, I think.|| He unhitched a gown from the stall's awning frame and smoothed the burnt-orange skirts until the golden tracery of interwoven vines shimmered. ||It compliments your lovely green eyes.||

Yali narrowed those lovely green eyes and twisted so that her back was towards Gloom, concealing her signs from him. ||What are you up to, old man?||

Damant nodded his thanks to the stallholder and hooked the dress back in place. ||Up to? I just want to make sure you're all right.|| Lying was so much easier in Simah, where tone couldn't betray you. ||You don't look well.||

In fact, he saw a little too much of his recent self in Yali. Ordinarily irrepressible, her recent captivity clung to her, revealed in hooded glances and dark circles beneath her eyes. House arrest or cell, incarceration and isolation took their toll.

Her expression softened. ||I'm not very grateful, am I?||

||I hadn't noticed.||

||I have, and I really do appreciate everything you've done.|| She offered a wry smile. A sign of the old Yali breaking through. ||But – and I can't believe I'm saying this – I don't need another dress.||

||In my experience, that's no barrier to buying one.||

She narrowed her eyes further. ||Very funny.|| She sighed and turned to glare up at Gloom, her signs no longer concealed. ||What I *need* is to get rid of this . . . thing.||

"You'll hurt his feelings," Damant said without looking at Gloom. "Won't she?"

NO, intoned the koilos, his voice an impersonal rumble that made the base of Damant's spine ache. After a lifetime surrounded by voiceless koilos, there was something unspeakably unsettling about one that talked. So he *was* listening? It made things damn difficult. He had to assume that the ifrît was paying attention, and that every word would be conveyed to Kastagîr soon after. Concealing conversation by hiding the signs could only do so much. Indeed, under the wrong circumstances, the very fact that a conversation had taken place could condemn as readily as the words themselves.

"Have it your way." Damant switched to signing. ||He says he's very upset.||

Yali glowered her opinion of that and folded her arms.

He glanced around out of habit – Simah was as prone to being eavesdropped as the spoken word, especially in a crowded marketplace where half the traders used it to rise above the noise – but one advantage of Gloom's presence was that no one wanted to get too close. A castellan's uniform demanded respect, but a koilos commanded fear.

He tapped Yali on the shoulder. ||Humour me. There's one dressmaker in particular whose style would be perfect for you.||

She regarded him warily. It was ironic, in a way. Damant knew that

253

he could trust Yali, but he was just another blinkered puppet of the Eternity Queen so far as she was concerned. Anything he said or did was suspect.

He didn't blame her. He'd spent entirely too much time wondering at the decisions he'd taken – the man he'd become – while trapped in the Eternity Queen's glamour. So many of his memories were thick with fog, and he wasn't ready to trust those that he did recall. Custodians quickly learned not to trust strangers, and the Ihsan Damant who'd served the Eternity Queen *was* a stranger. He had to be. But was he truly free of her?

Could he be free of her?

||Fine.|| Yali stuck out her tongue. ||Though how a man who only ever wears a uniform knows *anything* about dresses, I'll never understand.||

||I have eyes ... and I was young once, hard though it may be to believe.|| He nodded towards the azasouk's western edge, where the ruins of the Qabirarchi Palace dominated the skyline. ||It's not far.||

Striking as casual a gait as he could manage – it was impossible to be *entirely* casual with Gloom in tow – Damant struck out through morning sunshine thick with spices and the warm, soothing aroma of freshly baked bread.

Before long, they reached a crossroads at the azasouk's outer edge. Damant drew to a halt as a grocer's clatter wagon lurched past and headed downhill towards the ring-wall gate, a trail of children scrambling behind to grab the apples tumbling in its wake.

||"Wait a moment,"|| he said, speaking aloud for Gloom's benefit.

AS YOU ORDER.

Again the shiver gnawed at Damant's spine. ||"I think we've taken a wrong turn."||

||Some castellan you are, getting lost in your own city,|| said Yali.

||"It's not my city,"|| he replied with rather more bite than intended. *Tyzanta* had been his city, and with his memory unreliable, he'd no notion of how much he was to blame for its woes. How did you atone for something you didn't know you'd done? ||"This way."||

The last of the children streamed past, a mongrel dog chasing excitedly at her heels. Damant crossed the street, ducked into an alley and took a flurry of turnings. Yali hurried to keep up, while Gloom simply continued his sonorous, implacable tread.

||This is where your dressmaker works?|| said Yali, without enthusiasm. ||Do they stitch up corpses as a sideline?||

Damant allowed that it didn't look the most reputable street, drenched as it was in the shadows from the nearby Qabirarchi Palace. It was barely wide enough for him and Yali to walk abreast, and most of the shopfronts were closed up, the paint peeling from their facades. More importantly, there wasn't another soul in sight. Not even a minute's walk from the busiest marketplace in the city, and they were as isolated as could be.

||"You're right. Definitely a wrong turn."||

A shutter creaked off to his left, a face briefly glimpsed beyond the peeling blue paint.

Damant grimaced. "I think we'd better get out of here before someone—" He stared back down the street, his good eye wide. "There! Look!"

Yali, still scowling with the effort of lip-reading in shadow, took a moment to follow his gaze. Gloom lurched about at once. Not that Damant had entertained any doubts on that score. He *had* to obey.

No sooner had the koilos turned than the door beside the blue shutter eased open. Isdihar stepped softly out into the street, her long unbound hair draped across her shoulders like river weed and her fists clenched and level with her hips. Still facing away down the street, Gloom went rigid as black vapour coalesced about his head and shoulders, the magenta fires in his eye sockets dimming to nothing.

||"Ye're late,"|| said Isdihar.

Damant cocked his head in Yali's direction. ||"She was stubborn."||

Yali's confused expression resolved to something that flirted equally with recognition and annoyance. ||I *thought* you were behaving strangely. You might have told me!||

255

||I might have done a great many things.|| He turned to Isdihar. ||You're sure this will hold him?||

She nodded. ||For as long as we need. But we should get off the streets.||

He reached into a pocket, withdrew a long fold of black silk and handed it to Yali. ||Blindfold him, would you? You're taller than I am.||

She shot him a sour look, but left it at that. When she was done, Isdihar, her expression taut with concentration, crooked a finger at Gloom. The vapour about his head and torso pulsing, he lurched towards her.

They picked their way through the blue-shuttered shop – which was as derelict inside as out – and crossed into an empty street thick with refuse. Gnarled, thorny weeds forced their way up through the flagstones to wind around the fire-blackened boundary wall of the Qabirarchi Palace. Isdihar led the unresisting Gloom through a gap in the stones. Damant and Yali followed through overgrown grounds filled with the skitter and scrape of unseen rats, arriving at last before an ornate archway whose grandiose flame-haired sentry crest was cracked and smeared with soot. A heavy bolt clacked, followed by the rumble of something heavy being dragged across stone.

The door creaked open on pained hinges.

||"You are late,"|| said Rîma.

||"It has been mentioned,"|| Damant replied heavily.

Once they were all inside, Rîma put her shoulder to the marble statue of Nyssa Iudexas and heaved it back across the door. Then she led them down a short corridor choked with blackened debris and into what had once been a small antechamber.

There she swept Yali into a heartfelt embrace. Discomfited by the display, and with no other option than to look at Isdihar and the blind-folded koilos she led by the hand – an uncomfortable sight for so many other reasons – Damant glanced around the room.

He'd not been in the Qabirarchi Palace since the fires had taken it. Supposedly no one had. The city folk considered it cursed ground, the site from which a cabal of Alabastran traitors had conspired with the Eternity King to keep their goddess caged. All of which was true, after a fashion. The Qabirarchs – former hierarchs and priests all – had been misshapen, pallid creatures, transformed by rapacious greed into glistening, leech-like siphons of soul energy. They had served as Tzal's captors in the Stars Below, lulling him to sleep with ancient Issnaîm song and suckling on his soulfire to keep him weak. All had perished in the Obsidium Uprising, but Damant struggled to rouse himself to regret.

This room at least had survived reasonably intact, though a coronal smoke stain darkened what had once been white plaster walls and the golden statue of Nyssa Benevolas that stood opposite the door had lost her looks to the flame. Someone – presumably Rîma – had assembled a mismatched but not unhomely collection of furniture atop the charred mess that had once been a carpet: bookcases, chairs, a low bed and a table strewn with scorched books and loose pages. What light existed came not from lumani – a wise precaution under the circumstances; if Arvish could press lesser ifrîti into service as spies, Tzal certainly could – but a handful of sputtering candles whose greasy light was a perfect match for the aura of conspiracy, and whose bitter aroma haunted every breath.

When Rîma had finally consented to tell him of her real base of operations – a secret hitherto known only to herself and Isdihar – he'd not believed her. Now it seemed the perfect choice. Curse-touched and shunned as it was, only skelders and stray ifrîti would bother them.

||"I thought we'd lost you,"|| said Rîma, at last pulling away.

Yali struck the same haunted grin Damant had seen several times already that morning. ||Me? No. I'm indestructible.||

||"I'm sure you know best,"|| Rîma replied, her wry tone a poor match for her words. ||"Thank you, Ihsan."||

||"Just paying my debts."|| So much of what he'd done over the years – for the Bascari, for Vallant . . . even for the Eternity Queen – he'd explained away as duty. For once, that concept fitted without caveat.

Seeing Yali and Rîma reunited was a good memory to cling to among the bad. ||"To business. We'll be missed eventually."||

Letting go of Gloom's hand, Isdihar rose on her tiptoes and kissed his forehead. The otherwise inflexible koilos sagged, his shoulders stooping. ||"For safety. I'll bring him back when we're done. He'll remember naught of this. The memories will flow together."||

She shrugged as if nothing remarkable had happened, then settled into the least threadbare of the surviving armchairs, feet tucked beneath her. It didn't escape Damant's notice that her selection gave her the clearest view of the slumbering Gloom.

Yali frowned at Rîma. ||Business?||

||"With Ihsan's help, yes ... and with Azra's."||

||So you know?|| It was Yali's turn to sag, and she did so all the way into a creaking chair. That left Damant nowhere to sit save on the low, uneven bed, so he elected to remain standing.

Rîma settled against the book-laden desk. ||"You should have told me."||

||She asked me not to, and she doesn't have anyone else. I wanted to keep her trust.||

||"She didnae keep yours awful well,"|| said Isdihar. ||"She must have known Mirela's attempt on her life would track back to ye."||

Even now, Mirela's body hung by its ankles from the underside of the Golden Stair. Damant had signed the order with a granite hand. What loyalty he owed the Bascari family – save perhaps one – lay long in the past, and keeping Azra's secret mattered more than mercy.

He thought back to his conversations with Azra across previous nights. She'd been more determined – less desperate – glad to have something to work towards, but there was no way to know when the horror of her situation would overtake her again. ||"I don't know that we have the right to judge,"|| he said, careful that his signs were as slow and legible as he could make them. Lip-reading in the candlelight's heavy shadows had to be nearly impossible. ||"Hers is a fate I'd wish on no one."||

Rîma nodded. ||"I would never have thought her strong enough to resist, let alone work against Tzal. And now it transpires that what remains of the rebellion survives as much because of her as Katija. She is lesser than she was, but greater than any of us. There is hope to be had in that . . . but we have to move beyond survival while we still can."||

||"Then you'd better tell me what you have in mind."||

||"I had hoped that the Issnaîm might have the answer. They imprisoned Tzal in the first place, in a silver pearl woven from his own obsessions."||

Damant nodded. He'd never decided if he thought the talk of pearls and obsession were truth or a metaphor for the encircling Veil. Arvish had once described Khalad as a giant snow globe, sealed from the wider world by mist rather than glass. ||"And the Qabirarchs used Issnaîm song to keep him sleeping."||

Rîma's cheek twitched. ||"Precisely. But after Zephyr disappeared, consulting the Issnaîm ceased to be an option."||

Isdihar shook her head.||"It would nae have worked. He's too strong tae be bound thus any longer."|| Her tone turned vicious to match her sudden scowl. ||"Besides, veilkin cannae be trusted."||

||"I don't need to trust all the Issnaîm,"|| Rîma replied in what was for her an unfriendly tone. ||"Just Zephyr . . . not that it matters now she is lost to us."||

||"I'm hearing a lot of talk about what won't work, and not much about what will."|| When no answer came, Damant stared at Rîma, Isdihar and Yali in turn. ||"Either you trust me, or you don't. I'm getting too old for half-measures."||

||"'Tis nae a matter of trust,"|| said Isdihar. ||"For as long as I can remember, my sire impressed on me the importance of his secrets and of the danger were they misused."||

||Your sire's dead.|| A deep furrow of her brow lent bluntness to Yali's signs. ||If his foresight didn't help him, we shouldn't let it hold us back.||

Isdihar's scowl smoothed away, the arch expression Damant had come to associate with the Voice blurring to the uncertainty of a girl striving to comport herself as a woman. ||"I know, but as with all secrets, they dislike being uprooted."|| She touched her eyes closed and sat straighter, the pursing and softening of her lips betraying inner turmoil.

Damant opened his mouth to speak, but closed it without a word at Rîma's small shake of the head.

"The throne immortal is as much mechanism as majesty," Isdihar murmured at last, her eyes still closed and her hands working against one another in her lap. "Built intae its spine is a unique prism, infused with the Dark of Creation and bound with astoricum. It was the means by which my sire sifted the Deadwinds tae prolong his life and bind his prisoner. Now Tzal employs it for the same purpose. Without it, he'll burn through what he's stolen. His influence will fade. This will again be a war of swords and shriekers, nae glamours and lies. If Azra is as determined as ye believe, she may even reassert herself for good."

Damant waited for Rîma to finish signing a translation for Yali. ||"Then we steal the prism. Better yet, we destroy it."||

Isdihar screwed her eyes tighter. "'Tis old magic, fashioned in a realm far beyond the Veil. It is quite impervious tae anything ye might bring to bear. Ye cannae destroy it ..." she took a thready breath, "but I can."

The realm beyond the mists. The world from which the Issnaîm had banished Tzal, dooming Khalad to his tyranny in the process. Arvish had spoken of it. Enna, alongside whom Damant had fought in the Stars Below during the Obsidium Uprising, had claimed it as her home, and had finally returned there – or so Tanith had said. Damant still didn't know that he believed it existed, and what Isdihar meant by the Dark of Creation, he'd no idea. ||"How?"||

Isdihar hung her head.

||"You have to trust them,"|| said Rîma, ||"or all of this is for nothing."||

Isdihar swallowed and sat bolt upright. Trembling, she raised her left arm and drew back her sleeve to the elbow, revealing a smooth expanse

260

of bronze skin, marred only by the darker splotch of a birthmark just below her wrist.

||I don't understand,|| signed Yali.

"Watch," said Isdihar, her voice taut.

She twisted her forearm about, the interplay of candle-cast shadows and contours of muscle and bone awakening reedy black lines across her skin. But as she brought her arm to rest, the shadows crept outwards, at first tracing the pattern of artery and vein before settling into fading, frond-like swirls. At the same time, similar designs crept across her cheeks and brow, in imitation of the tentacular make-up she'd worn as the Voice.

"What Terrion Arvish did to his daughters he did in imitation of what I already am," she said softly. "I am the vessel of my sire's blood. Part of me doesn't belong to this realm. It's how he speaks ... *spoke* through me. Through it I can command the prism. If I have the strength."

Yali stifled a grimace. Damant nodded, careful to keep his own discomfort concealed. She was a living aetherios tattoo, or as close as made no difference. ||"I don't understand why you needed the palace soul-glyphs in the first place. I've seen Arvish manipulate ifrîti on the fly."||

More than that, she'd been accomplished at twisting the behaviour of the ifrîti governed by the glyphs, setting them asleep so that others could pass undetected. Some of the palace redcloaks had complex soul-glyphs that allowed them to do the same in limited and carefully assigned areas of the palace, but Damant's own tattoos were simple pass-glyphs. They gave him freedom to roam, but wouldn't protect anyone with him unless they were accompanied by someone with broader authority.

"Even she would struggle given the density of ifrîti in the palace. Dozens of hestics and motics, scores of koilos. What Katija does ... it takes an artistry I lack. I have the blood, but not the skill – until the uprising, I never had need to learn it. I can smother a lone koilos – until we saved you the other night, I wasn't certain I could do even that – but

I cannot cajole. My sire saved Katija from her omen rot because he hoped, in time, tae learn how she came by such control. I think I may even be a mite jealous."

Damant supposed that it was typical of the Eternity King's arrogance that he'd assumed there was some trick to what was simply practice. That no low-born skelder could possibly achieve what his own descendant could not. Arvish – and later Tanith – had learned to manipulate their tattoos in order to survive. The luxurious life of the Voice would hardly have demanded the same of Isdihar. ||"The make-up you wore during your public appearances . . . that wasn't just for pomp and ritual, was it?"||

"It took years before I learned tae keep this hidden. My mother used golden powder to hide the worst of it and ink to blunt the meaning of anything that showed. Concealment became habit." She clenched her fist. The darkness seeped from her skin, leaving bronze behind. "I know it's nae pleasant tae behold, but some things can only be seen, nae explained."

The last of her grimace melting away into shame, Yali crossed the room, knelt before Isdihar and took her hand. ||Don't apologise,|| she signed one-handed. ||You are not responsible for how others see you. Honest and true.||

||"She's right,"|| said Damant, striving to match Yali's generosity of spirit. Isdihar's appearance troubled him less than the reminder of what she'd done in the Eternity King's name. But he himself was far from guiltless in such matters, and could only imagine how Isdihar's upbringing had twisted her. She'd never had a chance to be normal – whatever *normal* was. ||"Only our choices matter."||

A fragile smile flickered across Isdihar's lips. ||"Perhaps that's part of it,"|| she said, one hand still in Yali's. ||"Ye're both kind, but ye dinnae understand. I hope that ye never do."||

||"All this time, Tzal's been chasing Arvish to be his host,"|| said Damant. ||"Why not simply possess you during the uprising?||

||"Vallant took me beyond his reach."|| Her tone thickened with

regret. ||"Had he not done so, I might have destroyed the prism when this all started."||

Damant's custodian instincts warned of gaps in her story, but mysticism had never been his forte. One thing was clear, however: Isdihar had abandoned the relative safety of an exiled monarch in Athenoch or Qersal and returned to Zariqaz, all the while knowing that Azra's fate might one day be hers. Whatever her misgivings and the tenderness of her years, there was steel in her spine.

Rîma straightened. ||"Then we will give you your chance to do so now."||

||But we don't have the glyphs,|| said Yali. ||Kastagîr took my copies. Besides, they'll all have been changed by now. The important ones, at least.||

||"True,"|| said Damant, the nape of whose neck still itched from a shriversman's needle. He patted his pocket. ||"I can come and go as I wish, of course. But for the rest of you? I have the new glyphs, boiled down to their essence. None of that fancy additional linework the shriversmen use to disguise the functional part of the design from ill-intentioned skelders."||

She gaped. ||How?||

||"Azra penned a letter that gave me full authority and swore First Shriver Halazni to reveal nothing of the matter. To anyone."||

Rîma arched an eyebrow. ||"Or else?"||

||"Or else."|| Orders came and went, but fear was for ever. Yennika had enough of a turbulent reputation in the palace that Halazni would be unlikely to risk defying her instructions. ||"The Eternity Queen's seal doesn't care whose hand wields it, and Azra's handwriting is eerily similar to Yennika's."||

||"Does Azra know what we're trying to do?"|| asked Rîma.

||"She didn't want to. I don't think she trusts herself very much. But she wishes us good fortune."||

Yali narrowed her eyes. ||How did *you* know what they intended?||

Damant smiled at the jealousy in her frown. ||"Rîma didn't ask you to acquire the soul-glyphs so she could steal the palace silverware and graffiti the walls. It had to be the sanctum . . . I just didn't know why."||

||"We still have tae get the Eternity Queen out of the sanctum,"|| said Isdihar. ||"Even if Azra is with us, we cannae trust that she'll remain in control long enough for me to do what I must."||

||"Already attended to. Hierarch Bathîr is determined to have her offer a Redemptor's Feast blessing at the xanathros tomorrow."||

||"Your idea?"|| asked Rîma.

||"I had something to do with it."|| Igarî Bathîr had seized on the idea with all the desperation of a woman whose influence was waning alongside that of her church. By the time they'd parted, she'd quite forgotten that the notion hadn't been hers in the first place.

||What if the Eternity Queen refuses?|| asked Yali.

||"You underestimate Igarî's talent for grovelling. Besides, the Yennika of today is every inch as vain as the one of old. She'll welcome the opportunity to show off . . . I *may* have suggested that rumours were growing in the lower city that she'd been disfigured during the attempt on her life."||

Rîma folded her arms and levelled an approving stare. ||"You have been busy, Ihsan."||

He indulged a small smile. Stars Below, but it was good to feel useful again. Better still to have impressed Rîma. ||"I've a lot of time to make up for."||

A not-quite-smile ghosted across her bloodless lips. ||"Haven't we all?"||

Twenty-Five

Viewed from a distance in the red glow of the fading sun, Hazali was equal parts wonder and abomination. A mass of trestles, brickwork and pipes assembled according to no real plan Mirzai could readily identify, it clung to the ash-clogged slopes of Mount Kiral like some monstrous misshapen spider. The splayed legs running along the sheer cliff face were actually streets of slit-windowed buildings, belayed to the rockface by buttresses and scaffolds thick with sparrow nests. The body was a single massive skyship dock, protected from the elements by a humpbacked glass and girder canopy and backed by a cluster of warehouses. The sides of the dock were a timber cage open to the mountain winds, and the motic-and-piston gates that could be closed to prevent captains departing with their tithes unpaid a latticework rather than solid wood.

An engineering marvel it might have been, but it was also irredeemably ugly.

Maxin hauled on the tanker's lateral wheel, the dozenth correction since they'd descended from the Cloudsea. Ropes rasped in their pulleys as the tanker's motics obediently let out more sail to catch the dying wind. True to its name, the *Lumberfast* was an ungainly beast and held a heading with supreme reluctance. Worse, it required constant correction of its pinion sails to counteract the cargo of buoyant eliathros gas that no amount of water ballast tanks could offset. "Not surprised the trallock didn't want this job for herself."

265

He spoke of Kat with rough fondness, as one might of a treasured opponent in the prize-brawling ring.

"And why's that?" The ash-laced air prickled at Mirzai's throat. Every surface in the quarterdeck wheelhouse bore a grey-white coating, blown in from the mountainside. According to legend, the Zaruan Mountains had been the conduit by which Nyssa had sent fire from the Stars Below, sweeping away old and heretical orders so that the new might flourish. The resulting ash still lay on the mountainside millennia later. Hazali's rooftops were thick with it, and no ship that put into dock escaped its embrace.

"Look at the place," said Maxin. "Put a foot wrong and it's three hundred feet straight down. She's not good with heights."

Mirzai wouldn't have pegged Kat for a phobic, but then irrational fears were called precisely that for a reason. "I can't say I blame her."

Even for a man who'd never experienced a twinge of vertigo, Hazali was a grim prospect. Fully half of the central dock – which could easily have swallowed Araq's town centre whole – jutted straight out from the cliff, with nothing but a sagging trestle and divine grace to prevent it crashing down the mountainside.

Maxin grinned and rubbed at his pate. His palm came away white with dust. "Nor me, but don't you tell her I said so."

"Been with her long?"

"On and off. My boss threw in, so I went with him ... but I was leaning that way before."

"Why?"

"Because one day you stop thinking about survival and start thinking about the world you leave behind. Thought I was in the running to take over from Javar, I did. King of Tyzanta's Undertown, and all that good stuff." Maxin shrugged, but his tone darkened. "I used to have two nieces. That one's still this side of the Deadwinds is thanks to Kat. Got her out to Athenoch before the hammer fell and for no other reason than because I asked. I owe her a life, simple as that."

The words reminded Mirzai of how Kat had taken Tarin's soul into safekeeping while his body healed. Maxin was right: life had to be about more than survival. Araq had burned for want of learning that lesson. "The redcloaks have harried and hunted my family since before I was born. Murdered and chained us for our part in a feud built on lies. Tarin's all I have left. I'll do whatever it takes to give him a chance."

Maxin grunted. "That's how I am with Ezri. She deserves a future. Way I see it, the rest comes second."

Far ahead, a customs felucca emerged from behind the lattice gate. Lateen sail billowing as it caught the wind, it climbed towards the *Lumberfast*, a forest-green pennant bearing the Ozdîr lion fluttering behind.

"That's our welcoming committee." Maxin gave the wheel a nudge. "Better get the others up here."

Heart aflutter – convincing documentation or not, the customs inspection marked a point of no return – Mirzai left the wheelhouse and set off for'ard along the narrow walkway that bounded the triple hump of the *Lumberfast*'s deck. The tanker was less a ship and more a series of vast pressurised metal barrels rendered skyworthy. Unlike most of its kind, there was little pretence of seaworthiness. It didn't even have a mainmast, just a series of outrigger sails set along its flanks.

Tanith and the others met him halfway to the cramped crew quarters. Like him they wore nondescript sailriders' uniform: shirt, trousers and a woollen greatcoat to stave off the cold of the upper Zaruan, all of it already speckled with ash. The garb added suitably to Vathi's woebegone air. Aklia Tzan bore it with fortitude. Tanith less so. The life of a drab didn't suit her. Judging by her muddled scowl, she knew it.

"Time to go to work," said Mirzai.

"We saw." Tanith brushed at her shirt and stared in disgust at the grey-white trails left by her fingers. "Kat never mentioned anything about this."

"Slipped her mind," said Vathi. "She's always forgetting things."

"And what would you know about having a mind?" she asked acidly. More proof, Mirzai supposed, as to why Kat had put Maxin in command. Tanith either found the company of others intolerable, or delighted in pretending that was so. Either way, it was hardly the stuff of leadership.

"You have the paperwork?" he asked Aklia.

She brandished a leather folder. "Travel permits, docking pass, proof of transfer duties paid and a receipt for the outbound protection levy."

"Maybe hold that last one back," said Mirzai, offering a wry smile. "We don't want them wondering how we've paid that already."

"You think so?" she replied drily.

They made it back to the wheelhouse just as the customs felucca tucked in a little above the portside bulwark with a precision that spoke to long practice. As Maxin surrendered the wheel to Aklia, an Ozdîr overseer, his *vahla* mask marked with a diagonal green stripe, stepped lightly aboard, two custodians at his back. All were fully armed with shriekers and scimitars. Mirzai – who'd spent more time around shriekers in recent days than he hoped ever to do again – felt the *Lumberfast*'s paucity of armament as never before. Scimitars aside, they had a single shrieker concealed beneath the wheelhouse planks – uncured, so that anyone could use it, come an emergency. Not nearly enough to make a fight of anything.

But then if they *had* to make a fight of it, they'd already lost. Even two hundred yards out from the canopy watch house, shrieker fire would draw all manner of attention.

The overseer looked Maxin up and down. "What's your business?"

"Eliathros shipment from Nassos," said Maxin.

"You're not on the schedule."

He shrugged. "I told Overseer Rezli that, but she didn't want to risk sending a heraldic. Said that those skrelling rebels have been reading them right out of the air." He lowered his voice to a conspiratorial level. "Me, I think she didn't want the expense." He held out the papers – sans the outbound receipt, still safe in its folder.

The overseer made no move to take them. "She should have spent the dinars. We'd have told her there's no berth clear. Count Rashace has taken up every inch of dockside."

Behind the overseer and with her back to the felucca, Tanith's expression sharpened to a pinched scowl.

"Count Rashace is here?" asked Vathi.

Stiff with contempt, the overseer looked him up and down. "And what business is it of yours?"

"Not mine, but he owes Rezli for two eliathros shipments. I'm sure she'd like me to have a word."

The overseer snorted. "Good luck getting near him. He brought three barges of redcloaks in with his yacht. Took over the upper dock and most of the neighbouring streets. Rumour has it he's bound for Tyzanta tomorrow. You'd better hope so, because it's your only hope of getting a berth."

His gut tight at the prospect of failure, Mirzai drifted towards the wheelhouse door. One fireblood yacht and three troop barges fell far short of the eight war dhows Kat was expecting at Tyzanta the following noon, which meant that Count Rashace had likely come on ahead, preferring Hazali's thin comforts to another night on the Cloudsea. But a dockside crawling with redcloaks didn't matter if they couldn't dock.

He glanced at Tanith. She shook her head, which meant her amashti glamour wasn't finding purchase on the overseer.

Careful that he wasn't in view of the overseer or his custodians, Mirzai flashed a brief sign. ||Keep him talking.||

Maxin gave the smallest of nods. "Don't do this to me," he growled at the overseer. "The Deadwinds weren't kind. Four days aloft and one behind schedule. Rezli's going to have my teeth for her maracas as is it."

"Not my concern," said the overseer. "You'll just have to . . ."

Mirzai left the wheelhouse and hurried down the companionway into the tangle of pipes and walkways that constituted the aft ballast hold. Arguing with custodians – Saheen excepted – had never brought him much fortune. Machines were a safer bet.

Snagging a grip-heel spanner from behind a pipe, he made his way to the pressure control board. Every dial hovered comfortably clear of the red zone.

269

Couldn't have that.

It took less than two minutes' careful work with the grip-heel – tightening a connection here, loosening one there – to send the pressure gauge for Tank Three into a slow but steady freefall. It had to be Tank Three, because that was the only one filled with eliathros. The blackfire damp in others would have caused more trouble than it solved. The smell would have been the least of it.

He gave it another half-minute, then yanked on the chain linked to the warning bell in the wheelhouse and reached for the speaking tube. "Captain, you'd better get down here. We've got a problem."

Maxin arrived barely a twenty-count later, the overseer close behind. "What now?"

Mirzai tapped the dial. "The seals on number three are rotten. I guess the repair gang didn't do as good a job as they said."

The overseer stared at the dial. "It doesn't look that bad."

"Never does at first." Mirzai borrowed a little of Vathi's morose outlook and found it a surprisingly good fit. "But when they go, they go. It's good for a few hours, but after that? If the pressure drops too fast and there's even a hairline crack in the tank, it'll implode. We could lose half the ship."

None of that was true, of course. Even discounting the fact that what he'd gimmicked could easily be ungimmicked, there was no risk of implosion and, so long as they jettisoned enough water ballast to counteract the loss of buoyancy, no danger to the *Lumberfast* at all. But Mirzai had seldom met a custodian with a head for engineering.

Maxin glowered at the dial. "All I bloody need. We'll have to jettison Tank Three. Still ... at least it's paid for."

"Yes, better to be safe ..." The overseer tore his attention back to Maxin. "What do you mean, *paid for*?"

"You saw the paperwork. All settled in advance. Rezli runs a hard bargain when she wants to." Maxin shrugged. "Pity about the cargo."

Even through the expressionless *vahla* mask, it didn't take much to read the overseer's thoughts. A single tank of eliathros was worth ten years' wages, and *definitely* more than the overseer's career. "We haven't accepted delivery. Your employer will have to bear the loss."

"No, but you *did* just sign to confirm that we attempted delivery and were turned away through no fault of our own," said Maxin. "A judicator might see that as the same thing."

"I will not be blackmailed," the overseer said stiffly.

Maxin held up his hands. "Not my meaning, I swear ... but look, there has to be somewhere we can tie up. Doesn't have to be proper. We've got a quarter-mile of hoses on this tub. Just snag us in wherever you can and we'll get emptied before there's a problem." He flashed a knowing smile. "We'll pay full fees, regardless."

The overseer sighed. "Very well. There is *somewhere*, but it won't be pretty."

Maxin favoured him with a broken-nosed smile. "Do I look like I care about pretty?"

With a final curt instruction to follow them in, the overseer returned to his felucca, which quickly pulled away on half-sail.

"Don't they usually stay aboard to guide us to the berth?" asked Aklia, as the *Lumberfast* pulled in through the lowermost of the colossal lattice gates. Constructs of timber and steel, they resembled giant dragonfly wings when open, as they were now. Closed, they barred passage for all but those skyships small enough to slip between their spars.

"He's lining us up for a redcloak broadside," rumbled Vathi. "Doesn't want to get caught in the blast."

As Kat had promised, the sleek dhows of the Ozdîr relief fleet dominated the dock – three moored to each side of the lattice gates on tiered, offset trestle cradles that ensured each could easily catch the wind when it came time to depart – their tall shadows blocking what little sunlight found its way through the canopy of ash-smothered glass. Even the smallest dwarfed the *Lumberfast*. A flotilla of smaller craft – cargo scows, tankers and merchant carracks – filled what berths remained, tucked in among the cranes, ratlines and gangways.

"At least it'll make a sight to remember," said Maxin. With three tanks full to bursting with blackfire damp, it would certainly do that. "But maybe keep us away from open gun ports, just in case."

Aklia muttered an unidentifiable Qersi phrase and spun the pitching wheel a quarter turn, lifting the *Lumberfast* up and out of the line of fire from the dhow immediately to starboard.

Keen to focus on anything else, Mirzai left the wheelhouse and lost himself in the astounding nest of cantilevers and cables that kept everything suspended off the mountainside. Less impressive was the rotten and rusted state of much of which he beheld. Flaking paint and bowed stanchions betrayed neglected maintenance. Sloppy welds warned of repairs hurriedly undertaken. The sigh and creak of it all was readily audible even over the industry of the dockside.

Maxin joined him at the bulwark. "Impressive, isn't it?"

"I've never seen anything like it." Just keeping the dockyard safely maintained would have been the work of a hundred engineers, maybe more.

"There's four like this at Nassos, but at least they're built into the city's spire. This lot looks ready to go tumbling down the mountain."

"It's stronger than it looks."

Maxin grinned. "So are we all, until we break." He cupped a hand to his mouth and shouted to Tanith, standing alone beside the wheelhouse. "That stepdad of yours doesn't like company."

He jabbed a finger at the distant canopy where a narrow-hulled yacht had tied up at the base of the watch house, comfortably distant from the three neighbouring black-hulled troop barges.

Tanith twisted three fingers into a plunging Simah sign that forever dispelled any misapprehensions Mirzai had about her gentility and turned pointedly away.

"Count Rashace is her *stepfather*?" said Mirzai.

Maxin nodded. "An even nastier piece of work up close than from a distance, so I hear."

The customs felucca led them deeper into the dockside. So deep that the crosswind dropped to barely a breath and Aklia had to fully unfurl the sails to keep the *Lumberfast* moving. A jetty loomed from the shadows. Or rather, the *remains* of a jetty. It was barely half the length of the *Lumberfast*, ending in a mass of broken planking that dangled down the mountainside. The stairs leading up to the dockyard proper were scarcely better, with aching gaps where individual steps had collapsed and a handrail already half torn away.

"He's having a laugh . . ." said Maxin, aghast.

Mirzai glanced at the felucca, already circling around on the febrile breeze. The overseer stood at the prow, a finger stabbing back towards the collapsing jetty. "I don't think so." He stared down at the ashen slopes below and, for the first time in his life, felt something tug at his gut.

Maxin clapped him on the shoulder. "Let's get to it, then. Vathi! Get your miserable arse over here!"

As the *Lumberfast* closed, Maxin clambered up onto the bulwark and leapt to the jetty. Mirzai followed, never gladder to have something solid beneath his feet. Vathi tossed the mooring rope to Maxin and jumped to join them. But even with the tanker's sails furled to lessen drag, no amount of hauling could convince it to close the distance.

"It's no good." Vathi wiped a claggy mix of ash and sweat from his brow. "We'll just have to tie it off like this."

"You fancy climbing hand over hand to get back aboard?" said Maxin. "Because I don't. Go on . . . *heave.*"

Mirzai braced his feet and pulled with the others, again to no avail. Tanith landed lightly in front of him, pushed him aside and took his place. Though she pulled one-handed, without seeming to brace herself in the slightest, the *Lumberfast* at last began to move.

"Honestly . . ." she said sweetly. "Where would we be without big, strong men?"

Mirzai held up his hands in surrender and silently added another entry to the ever-growing list of reasons not to cross her.

Soon after the *Lumberfast* was tied up fore and aft – or aft and *mid*, given the state of the jetty – an overalled dockworker descended the stairs and favoured the tanker with an appraising eye. "You must be desperate." Mirzai noted that he made no attempt to move out onto the jetty proper.

"In a hurry, that's all," said Maxin equably. "Wasted time is lost profit, and all that. So if you can tell us where we can get hooked up to the central silos . . .?"

The dockworker shrugged, the weight of the world shifting on his shoulders. "Can't do it. I mean, there's a transfer valve on the dock above," he pointed up into the shadow of a merchant carrack, some six flights of uneven stairs up the mountainside, "but it's for topping off, not unloading. The foreman can authorise reversing the flow, but he's gone for the evening."

Vathi kicked idly at the jetty. Mirzai exchanged a look with Maxin. "When's he back on shift?"

"Dawn."

Too late by far. The dhows were scheduled to refill their buoyancy tanks overnight.

Tanith took the dockworker's hand. "Why don't you take me to see him?"

"I don't know . . ." Reluctance creaked beneath his uncertain smile. "He was very clear."

Sapphire eyes sparkling, Tanith leaned in close and flashed a winning smile. Even from three paces away, Mirzai felt the air thicken. The ash-bittered air grew sweet as honey and Tanith beautiful as sunrise after rain, despite her filthy, tangled hair and ill-fitting garb.

She rose on tiptoes, her lips level with the dockworker's ear. "Please?"

He nodded mutely and stumbled up the steps, Tanith's fingers threaded through his.

She winked at Mirzai. "Don't wait up."

Aklia watched them go with barely disguised contempt. "Always cutting out when there's work to be done."

"She'll be back," said Maxin. "Let's find that transfer valve."

Even if Mirzai hadn't known what he'd been looking for, the cluster of transfer pipework, with no fewer than three cut-off chambers and associated flywheels, would have been obvious enough. Even better, the captain of the merchant carrack had no desire – or more likely, given the beaten-up state of his ship, couldn't *afford* – to have his own buoyancy tanks topped off and so ceded the valve for the *Lumberfast*'s use.

Getting the transfer hose into place was another order of difficulty entirely. Thicker than Mirzai's thigh and fashioned of tri-walled oiled leather, it uncoiled reluctantly and fought every attempt at manipulation. Even after rigging a block-and-tackle on the upper jetty, and working in pairs – first Mirzai and Aklia, then Vathi and Maxin – it took the better part of half an hour to wrestle the hose into position, and another fifteen minutes for Mirzai, whose forearms and shoulders were now leaden and sore, to bolt the metal dock plate into position on the transfer valve. The crew of the merchant carrack, watching from the aftercastle, bellowed encouragement and what might have been meant as helpful advice throughout.

Tanith returned just as the last of the evening light had doused to purpled greys and the docks were awash with the pinprick lights of lumani lanterns. She stepped off the motic cargo elevator – unlike the *Lumberfast*'s battered mooring, the one at the merchant carrack's berth still functioned – and swayed noticeably.

Mirzai close behind, Maxin took her by the arm and drew her behind a tarpaulined cargo stack, out of sight of the merchant carrack. "Took your time, didn't you?"

She hiccuped and favoured him with a disagreeable stare. "I just spent an hour drinking the vilest rotgut calvasîr this side of the Zariqaz slum with the foreman – sorry, with *Ithaq* . . ." she attempted a besotted ingénue's vacant stare to match her briefly saccharine voice, "drooling down my neck while the street-nymph he'd hired for the evening glared daggers at me for stealing her client."

"Serves you right for being gorgeous," Maxin replied with a dry smile. "Get what we need?"

She handed him a rolled-up sheet of paper. "Letter of authority to reverse the outflow to our berth. He'll not remember signing it. No ifrîti to worry about. All that stray eliathros corrodes the prisms. But you'll have to find someone who knows how to actually reverse the flow. He had his mind on other things and his hands in places that were liable to get them chopped off. He's lucky I left him breathing."

"I can handle that," said Mirzai. "It won't be a complicated system."

"Sounds good," said Maxin. "Aklia, you stay with the ship. We may need to leave in a hurry."

"That thing's not taking us anywhere in a hurry," said Vathi. "Except straight down."

Tanith shrugged. "I can find something better."

"We don't have the glyphs for something better," said Maxin.

She tapped her left sleeve. "Don't you worry your pretty head about that."

"We'll need clearance to leave," said Mirzai. He'd no idea how quickly the dockyard's lattice gates could close if the alarm was raised.

She fixed him with an impatient stare. "Pretty sure I just said that I'd handle it."

They rode the cargo elevator in silence to the lowest street level and parted ways, Tanith heading – somewhat unsteadily – towards what passed for the better part of town and Mirzai following the others towards the girder-clad central silos at the dockyard's heart.

Twenty-Six

Tanith drew her new belt tight over her equally new robes and reached down to pat the unconscious custodian on the head. "Never mind. There are worse fates to find in the Zaruan Mountains."

Time was, there had been worse fates to find in her company. Not so long ago she'd have drained the man dry and tossed him over the side, not left him trussed and gagged in his underclothes in a dockside rope store.

It wasn't just that she'd drunk well from the Deadwinds only a day before. It wasn't just that Ithaq's rotgut calvasîr had set her thoughts spinning more than she liked. The act of feeding had grown … distasteful. A less than ideal development, as the longer she went without slaking her needs, the more monstrous – and the more irresistible – she became. Abstinence heralded madness, and madness left an indiscriminate trail of bodies. But even the redcloak she'd eaten at Araq – a situation born of the direst need – had left her feeling wretched.

Was this empathy?

She hated it.

She pulled the custodian's *vahla* mask into place, her nose wrinkling at the unmistakable aroma of a garlic-heavy *presika* curry. Unpleasant enough, but doubly so to be presented with the reminder that the joy of a simple, sustaining meal would be for ever denied her.

Smoothing her robes – they were too large, but the belt disguised the worst of it – she left the custodian dreaming addled dreams amid the coils of rope and went back out onto the dockside. The Rashace felucca her victim had lately guarded bobbed gently in the dockside crosswind, its buoyancy tanks so finely balanced it had no need of a scaffold cradle. She reached out with her aetherios tattoo to cradle its helmic, and the ifrît practically purred in response. No chance of it fighting when the time came to take control. It just wanted to be loved, but then didn't everyone?

She stared up at the underside of Hargo Rashace's yacht. No, not everyone. Some folk just wanted to make others miserable because it eased their own inadequacies.

Ship acquired, so that just left getting the necessary clearance from the watch house and waiting for the others. Or at least sabotaging the lattice gates so it didn't matter either way.

But once again, she found her gaze drawn to her stepfather's yacht. The *Tempest*. A rich man's toy more than a warship.

She pursed her lips. She *shouldn't*. She really shouldn't. That she was even considering it told her that she'd imbibed too much calvasîr. But when would she get another opportunity like this?

If past events had gone Hargo's way, she'd have been sliced up, shriven and sold for parts, a baying crowd shrieking for her death even while half of them lusted after her and wondered why. And her mother . . . Fadiya Rashace would have died in a distant land, denigrated and destroyed to salve her husband's fragile pride.

Leaving the dockside behind, Tanith wended her way up through Hazali's mismatched, ash-smothered streets. She saw barely a civilian, save for those tending the docks or slaking the appetites of the redcloaks who'd transformed Hazali from a decaying backwater to a garrison town. So like Araq, in its way. Not for the first time, Tanith wondered why the Eternity Queen – she didn't like to think of her as *Yennika*; their shared past was too complicated for that – relied so much on physical conquest when she commanded a glamour that made Tanith's own look like a sideshow illusionist's mesmerism.

No one challenged her as she ascended through the gust-blown ash. *Vahla* mask in place, one custodian looked much like another, and it was a simple enough matter to charm the few hestics set as sentries along the way. The sight of patrolling koilos at the boundary between the dockyard and the upper city almost turned her back – the bleak-souled ifrîti were more resistant to her cajoling than their lesser kin – but the lingering warmth and bravado of the calvasîr goaded her on.

Past the verdigrised remnants of what had once been Hazali's grand xanathros – and which was now as ashen and miserable as everything else in the town – she made enquiries as to which of the minareted palaces Hargo Rashace had taken as his own. In the end, a woman who looked entirely too young for her redcloak uniform, her eyes adrift on clouds of adoration, offered up the grandest as his lair.

The palace's sentries caused Tanith even less trouble than those in the dockyard, though the hestic at the main door bent to her will with the utmost reluctance. On the way up to the main state rooms, she relieved a servant of a tray of freshly roasted beef, crusty bread and pickles destined for her stepfather – no coercion required, as even Hargo's servants loathed being in the same room as him – and entered the sumptuous inner chambers.

The scent of lavender and juniper awoke fresh disgust. Typical of the man to pile his hearth high with blesswood for simple warmth and light while so many rode out Mistfall with only the meanest stocks to keep them safe from the Veil.

Hargo himself was alone in the chamber, his stocky ex-prizebrawler's frame silhouetted against the flames, his eyes downcast as a fortune in blesswood charred away. "Well?" he barked without turning. "What is it?"

"Your supper, my lord," said Tanith, careful to smooth her guttural Kaldosi vowels to something rounder. Even with her voice further distorted by her borrowed *vahla* mask, it would have been safer to englamour him. But even at its most predatory, the glamour was intimate – it revealed what was hidden – and though she and Hargo had no shared blood, there were some sides of him she'd no wish to see.

279

"Very good," he growled. "On the table."

He made no move to turn from the flames. A guilty conscience, perhaps, seeking solace in fire? Tanith snorted. Easier to believe that Hargo Rashace had grown wings. Whatever horrors he meant to inflict on the Tyzantan refugees come the morning, his only sorrow would be for himself.

She stepped closer. How then to do the deed? She'd wondered at crafting something demeaning, some perversion gone wrong behind closed doors, but to be truly memorable, such a death would have required the involvement and demise of a third party – possibly a fourth – and with the moment at hand she found she couldn't stir herself to tainting her revenge with a dose of relatively innocent blood. Empathy again, she supposed.

There was always hanging him from the chandelier bracket by his belt, perhaps with a suitably remorseful note for his misdeeds left nearby. But then unless she rendered him unconscious first – and where was the fun in that? – it ran the risk of becoming a very noisy episode indeed.

That left opening his wrists. Messy, but effective. Certainly memorable.

Or she could just open his throat and have done.

Setting down the tray on the low table, she took a deep breath and started forward.

Her right leg buckled at the knee, pitching her sideways.

She'd barely a chance to register the cold flood of horror in her veins, much less time to arrest her descent. The table shattered beneath her. The plate clattered across the tile floor, trailing food in its wake.

Hargo spun around from the fire, an iron poker in his meaty grip.

Tanith braced a hand against the floor. Her elbow buckled as readily as her knee had moments before, the sensation muddy, distant. Breath stale in her lungs and panic rising, she scrabbled at her mask as Hargo bore down. It came free on her third attempt. She whooped down a ragged breath.

She felt the mistake as soon as the scented air hit the back of her throat. Hidden beneath the woodsmoke, beneath the lavender and juniper of the blesswood oils, the musky bitterness of blackthorn blossom. As poisonous as silver to a daemon. To her.

"No ..." she gasped. Even her voice was distant. Plaintive. A beaten child's.

Somehow, senses swimming on clouds of blackthorn, she made it to her feet.

The poker blurred. Tanith heard the *crack* of it against her skull before she felt it. And then she was back among the ruins of the table, the chamber's bright colours dimming as they swam about her.

"I knew you'd come back for me one day," roared Hargo. "I knew!"

The poker blurred again, black in a greying world. Tanith felt something break under its strike, but sensation was now so distant she'd no idea what. Leaden limbs refused to obey. Her tongue was thick and limp in her mouth, stifling her scream.

Somewhere in the grey world, the poker clanged to the floor. A door slammed back, heralding the muted thunder of running feet.

"No, Batani," rumbled Hargo, "there's no danger, not now ... but send a runner to High Overseer Jannir. I'll lay tetrams to dinars that my stepdaughter didn't come to Hazali alone."

Mirzai snapped the last of the levers into place and glanced back over his shoulder. "How about now?"

"Could be worse," said Vathi, in what was for him the most positive of endorsements. "Pressure's building in Silo Three. This might work. *If* that hose doesn't come apart on us."

"Just get it done, would you?" said Maxin, his back to the door and a fading lumani lantern in his hands. The ifrît was already fading, the glass of its prism being steadily eaten away by the hiss of eliathros from an imperfect seal. "I've been in prison cells roomier than this."

The control room was of a generous size, large enough to house the feedlines and control gauges for each of the Hazali's three eliathros silos. Except they weren't in the control room – they'd lingered there only long enough to hand the foreman's letter of authority to start unloading the *Lumberfast* – but an inspection chamber half buried into the mountainside.

"I'm going as fast as I can," said Mirzai. "Unless you want a smothering in blackfire damp?"

"No thanks."

He grinned. "That was by way of being a rhetorical question."

"Funny man."

Occupying the control room would have required killing or knocking out three engineers and their supervisor – all of whom would likely be missed long before the eliathros/blackfire damp mix in Silo Three reached the proper proportion. Certainly long before the planned flush and replenish of the Ozdîr war dhows' buoyancy tanks. The inspection chamber was cramped, but with the *Lumberfast* busy emptying its belly into Hazali's pipe network, it gave Mirzai all the access he needed.

All told, it had gone faster than he'd expected. Five more minutes, maybe ten, and they could slink back to whatever skyship Tanith had "acquired" and let redcloak procedure do the rest.

The door crashed open. Lumani light glinted off *vahla* masks and shrieker muzzles.

"Let's have you out of there, shall we?" called a sharp, authoritative voice.

Twenty-Seven

Consciousness returned fleetingly, the amber glow of dawn prising apart Tanith's leaden eyelids. Sensation returned. A warm breeze against her cheeks. A weight about her shoulders, constricting her chest. Another at her wrists. Something hard and unyielding beneath her knees. And pain so diffuse that she could tell neither where it began nor where it ended. Not just the aftermath of blackthorn blossom. It was too sharp – too new – for that. It urged her to stay still, keep her eyes shut, draw no attention.

But she'd never been smart enough for that, had she?

She eased her eyes open. A ship's deck stretched away towards the prow. Shackles at her wrists. A chain wended four times about her shoulders and tight across her chest, both anchored to eyebolts in the deck with barely enough slack for her to stand. Two *vahla*-masked custodians equidistant from one another and her, the leftmost with a shrieker aimed, the other with folded arms. And between them, clad in the rich red-gold silks of a royal councillor, her stepfather watched her with a turbulent eye and a scimitar in hand. A low metal brazier puffed merrily to itself behind him, filling the air with the hated scent of blackthorn. And beyond them all, beyond the prow of the *Tempest*, the broken stump of what had once been Tyzanta sat jagged against the horizon, growing closer all the time.

Hargo crouched before her, eyes welling with hatred. "So you're awake?"

Lost in fumes of blackthorn blossom, Tanith barely saw his backhand blow. Heavy rings ripped at her cheek. The indigo fire of her blood hissed free.

Stifling a gasp of pain, she fixed him with as defiant a stare as swimming senses allowed. Bones clicked and groaned in her spine, her hip, her knees. The skin of her hands was mottled and dark. They'd beaten her while she'd been unconscious, or more likely Hargo had. He wouldn't leave something that personal to servants.

She'd never been so helpless in his presence, not since she'd been a little girl.

If he'd had the wit or resource to bind her with silver, she'd already be dead. Blackthorn sapped her strength and addled her glamour, but silver burned like fire and unmade everything she was. Even without it, her body was racing through precious reserves of soulfire as it fought to keep her alive. Would the madness of hunger take her before Hargo killed her? She prayed not. Better to die as a woman she recognised, rather than the daemon her nature had made her. But to whom did a lost soul beseech when the goddess was the greatest daemon of all?

"Couldn't afford silver chains, *Darathi*?" She laced the term of affection with all the contempt she could muster. Better that than to let him see her afraid. "I'm disappointed."

His eyes warned of the next blow a heartbeat before it fell, but with the mooring rope already tight from her previous stumble, she'd no option but to ride it out. She dropped, bones jarring at her left shoulder as her elbow struck the unforgiving deck.

"You're no daughter of mine," he growled.

"No," she gasped. "My father was a real monster. He hurt me in ways you never could. Impotent even now ... *Darathi*."

He towered above her, anger receding and the petulant, explosive temper that had forever cowed his household retreating behind the urbane mask seen by the wider world. "I've burned a fortune in blackthorn and blesswood every night this past year, knowing one day you'd return. I prayed to Nyssa that you'd find me ready, but this is sweeter than I dared imagine."

He stared out towards the ruin of Tyzanta and the scattered pin-pricks of its blockade fleet.

"The Eternity Queen's fleet is to rendezvous with us at noon. When it arrives, I will reach out my hand and cleanse Tyzanta of its last dec-adence. *That* is strength. *That* is greatness. Not seductive wiles and daemon's trickery. When this dust settles, those who mocked me will at last see me for who I am."

They surely would, though most would not perceive the conquering titan Hargo believed himself, only the overcompensating wretch who mistook cruelty for strength. A man whose self-regard had been so thoroughly broken by his wife's infidelity that he'd gladly drown the world in blood to silence mockery that only he heard.

Tanith might have laughed but for the fear that something would tear loose in her chest. Because in preaching his strength, Hargo had revealed something without price: he was afraid of her. And if he was afraid, he wasn't really in control. She was. All she had to do was find a way to make that count before he finally tired of showing off and decided to kill her.

"Sails to the south!" bellowed a sailrider from the *Tempest*'s topmast.

A custodian hurried forward with a spyglass. Hargo snatched it and trained it on the southern horizon. "The coincidences pile up. Vallant, perhaps … He was always a master of doomed gestures. Maybe even that sister of yours? There's nothing the Eternity Queen won't give me for Katija Arvish." He snapped his fingers at the custodian. "A heraldic to High Overseer Jannir. He's to cast off and make for Tyzanta with all speed. We'll follow him in."

Of course they would. The *Tempest* didn't even *look* like a warship. No shrieker cannons and only seven crew, including Hargo himself. Then again, Tanith doubted her stepfather had ever entertained the notion of joining the actual fight. Supervise and claim the credit, that was the Rashace way.

The custodian bowed and hurried away. Bell chimes and bellowed orders rang out across the deck as sailriders made the *Tempest* ready for battle.

"Kat will blast you out of the skies," said Tanith.

Hargo snorted. "With that pitiful flotilla? You don't understand, do you? Your friends at Hazali are taken. Their sabotage is being undone. Your sister is sailing into a battle she cannot win."

An icy pit swallowed Tanith's stomach. Mirzai and the others captured? Kat's plan had relied on Hazali's dhows being taken out of the fight quickly. Had relied on *her*. She'd let everyone down, all out of petty revenge.

She might not have been Hargo's daughter, but she'd learned from his selfishness all too well.

No. It couldn't end like this. She wouldn't let it.

Holding her breath to blot out the enervating blackthorn fumes, she flexed her wrists against her bonds.

As outriggers bloomed along the flanks of the *Sadia's Revenge*, Kat moved to the quarterdeck balustrade and stared out at Tyzanta, growing ever closer. No trace remained of the Bascari estate or the neighbouring Xanathros Alabastra. During the Eternity Queen's bombardment months before, most of the spire's throughways and tunnels had simply collapsed, the well-to-do streets caving inward or falling as stone rain on the Undertown slums. Mansions and tenements, torch houses and custodia, all had crumbled beneath fire from the skies, leaving few dwellings safe enough to offer shelter.

The ruins stirred uneasy melancholy. Kat had never liked the city. Too many painful memories. Too much injustice. But its people had been *her* responsibility, even before she'd assumed command of what remained of Vallant's fleet. It didn't matter that most of those who scrabbled for survival in the ruins had chosen to stay. She'd failed them. Today would make that right, if anything could.

She thought back to the frantic, naïve echo of herself who had first arrived in Tyzanta years before, on the run from Alabastra. What would past-Kat think to see her now? There was no way to know. All she could do was try to make her proud.

She stared along the deck, at sailriders standing ready with crossbows, scimitars and what precious few shriekers they possessed.

They're your weapon, breathed the Eternity King. *Wield them.*

Kiasta. Kat grimaced, but the time for doubts lay long in the past. She nodded to Captain Larsi, a solid, dependable presence at the ship's wheels who'd learned her trade and earned her grey hairs piloting a merchant carrack during the Bascari–Jovîna trade war. *Sadia's Revenge* was her pride and joy. "Let's make this count, shall we?" Receiving a grim nod in return, Kat craned her neck and raised her voice. "What have we got, Aldhad?"

The lad ran to her side, thick black curls threatening to burst free of the dog-eared bandana that constrained it to a semblance of order. A boot on the bulwark's sill, he peered out towards Tyzanta and flashed a grin.

"Seven Ozdîri, all laid out like you said they'd be, boss. Two nor-nor-west of the city, two to the south." His grin broadened. "And three right in our path, already stringing out line abreast to meet us head-on."

Arrogance at play. The Ozdîr dhows might have been larger than anything under Kat's command, but three-to-five odds were nothing to take lightly. But then, one of the three captains had more reason to be bullish than the others. "Which one's the *Ancestral*?"

"Westernmost," said Aldhad. "Hanging a little behind, but it's on the move."

Kat beckoned to the young signalwoman on station behind Captain Larsi. "Run out the flags. *Galadin's Lament* and *Timmara's Sword* to take the easternmost Ozdîri. *Amarid's Dream* to follow us down the middle. *Bescal's Wake* to stay with the transports in case something gets past us."

The motley collection of carracks, barges and scows hadn't a single shrieker cannon between them. Bravery counted for a lot, but not enough.

The signalwoman nodded, expecting something more. Kat felt eyes on her from across the quarterdeck and stifled a wince. Vallant would have made a speech, sombre and earnest to remind them of the stakes and chase them to victory. But vertigo was only one of Kat's phobias. People were the other. Yet she could at least make the attempt.

She raised her voice to carry clear. "And wish them good hunting. Let's make Vallant proud!"

Cheers rang out along the deck. Even the taciturn Larsi joined in.

The signalwoman grinned and ran for the aftercastle so that the ciphers of her bright semaphore flags would carry to the warships trailing behind the *Sadia's Revenge*. Heraldics were all very well, but at this range the flags were faster. She was barely halfway done when the Ozdîr lion vanished from atop the *Ancestral*'s lateen sail, replaced by a patchwork of white and yellow cloth that a charitable soul might have taken for a sunburst.

But sunburst or not, there was no mistaking the deathly wail and bright bloom of fire as the *Ancestral*'s eight-cannon broadside pummelled its immediate neighbour. The cheers on the *Sadia's Revenge* redoubled. Captain Gorahm had kept his word to Tyzanta's dead.

Time for the rest of them to do the same.

Far beyond the *Tempest*'s prow, the leading blockade dhow burned like a candle in the dawn, pounded by the cannons of Kat's vanguard and by the traitor off his starboard bow. The second loyalist dhow, its captain recognising odds well and truly against him, pulled away south, clawing for altitude and the illusion of safety. Even Tanith, her mind very much on other things, could see that he wasn't going to make it.

Hargo gripped the *Tempest*'s bulwark and leaned over the side, as if his fury alone could sweep the rebel ships from the skies. "I'll have Gorahm's hide for this!"

With the custodians to her fore distracted by the distant battle, Tanith twisted her right wrist until the shackles bit the back of her hand, tucked her thumb to her palm and tugged her left elbow down and away as far as the chains around her shoulders allowed. She revelled in the hot red scrape as the shackles' metal dug into the fleshy ball of her thumb. Pain didn't matter. Harms would heal. Let the whole thumb come off if it had to. She'd had worse.

A heavy hand yanked her head back by the hair. Her senses swam as she took an involuntary gulp of blackthorn-laced air.

"Enough." The custodian kicked away her right leg and shoved her forward.

Tanith's knee cracked against the deck, the words sultrier in intent than spluttered reality. "Such a flirt," she gasped.

Even in failure, she'd learned something. Upper arms bound tight, she hadn't the leverage to cheat the shackles. Escape required a greater sacrifice. Her gut tensed at the thought. But it wasn't just her life at stake.

It was of some consolation that by the time her vision cleared, the second of the two blockade dhows was plunging towards the Tyzantan plains, scarcely visible through a thick column of smoke.

"Better get your excuses ready!" she spluttered. "Yennika always liked a good grovel!"

The wind snatching at his robes, Hargo stalked back from the prow through the greyish-blue blackthorn smoke. The strike of his boot crunched a rib and hurled her backwards. Anchor ropes went taut against their eyebolts. The chains about her shoulders dug into her flesh.

"There's ... the sparkling wit ... I remember." Tanith gave a thin, wheezing laugh and collapsed awkwardly onto her haunches. "Only little girls ... can't fight back ... can they?"

Hargo flinched. Then his lips gathered to a snarl and he snapped out another kick. Tanith rode out the blow but played the impact for all it was worth, sagging as much as the chains allowed.

"No ..." A thin moan escaped her lips. "No more."

She even offered up tears. No difficulty there – a part of her had wanted to weep since she'd awoken aboard the *Tempest*. Defiance was strength, but weakness bought time. Carelessness.

Hargo's snarl bled to a self-satisfied smile. Standing taller and straighter, he rounded on the yacht's captain. Through lidded eyes, Tanith glimpsed the telltale shimmer of a fading heraldic.

"Where's Jannir?" he demanded. "Why aren't the ships away yet?"

"Hazali Dock's saying that the rebels tainted the buoyancy silos with blackfire damp," the captain replied with the stony manner of a woman well used to weathering her master's splendid rages. "They're running checks on the ships. So far, only the *Intemperate Wind*'s been cleared as skyworthy."

"Then tell them to have it launch!"

"Yes, my lord."

Smoke from the dying blockade dhow streaming across its deck, *Sadia's Revenge* descended towards the remnant of Tyzanta's ruined spire. Kat took in the slighted city – the streets she'd once called home. The folk emerging from rubble-drowned buildings, some cheering, most shuffling. The toppled statues and crumbled warehouses choked with wind-blasted shanties. The jagged mouths of severed aqueducts dribbling green-black weed and filthy water onto buried streets. She'd sensed the crews of the two destroyed blockade dhows pass into the Deadwinds and felt . . . nothing. No mercy, not for those who'd kept the Tyzantan refugees in squalor.

Let the Deadwinds take them all.

"Bring us about to Kazzar's Quay," she said. "Signal the transports to follow us in."

The young signalwoman, beaming with the flush of a victory not yet earned, let the order shine out through the skies.

Galadin's Lament and *Amarid's Dream* glided gracefully up and away to join up with the flame-marred *Ancestral*, now missing a chunk of its mainsail, as Captain Gorahm redeployed to confront the two southmost Ozdîr dhows. The blockade ships to the north were more reticent, wallowing about on an unfavourable wind. All to the good as far as Kat was concerned. Divide and conquer was easier when the enemy divided themselves.

The remains of Kazzar's Quay hove into sight. The warehouses Kat remembered were long since gone, as was most of the quayside, but three narrow piers remained. A point of pride for the refugees' leader, who'd taken defiant pleasure in ensuring that Tyzanta would be ready if the river flowed towards fortune.

Kat frowned, uncertain where that phrase had come from. That, and the sudden reverence for a veiled woman, her dress glistening with river weed.

So the boy is Anfaian? breathed Caradan Diar. *I thought we'd wiped them out.*

The boy? Tarin, of course. His soul – his memories – were bleeding into hers. Anfai, Kat knew only from her father's stories. A town drowned in heresy, he'd said, though given his own secret leanings, that judgement was hypocritical at the very least.

She closed her eyes and gripped her left wrist with her right hand, the cold flame of her aetherios tattoo flowing over her fingers as she gently probed Tarin's captive soul. His outrage at Tyzanta's fate was a pressure beneath her own, hot and unfocused as suited his slender years, stories of an obliterated Anfai he'd never seen brought to bitter life in the ruins below. The ship of history charting a familiar course, though a different hand now worked the tiller.

He's restless, said Caradan Diar, his voice simmering with disdain. *Anfaians always were.*

Reassured as she could be that Tarin's captive soul was safe, Kat opened her eyes as *Sadia's Revenge* slowed into Kazzar's Quay. Not to the piers already crowding with ragged men, women and children – those were better employed by the lumbering carracks and barges arriving behind – but beside a toppled statue of Nyssa Iudexas so vast that it lay across the ruins of three pulverised and fire-blackened warehouses. At Larsi's order, sailriders leapt aground with mooring lines. The prow capstan rattled a dance as the drag anchor plunged to find purchase in the rubble.

A woman with dark brown skin stepped aboard as the *Sadia's*

Revenge shuddered to a halt, a coil of waist-length black braids spilling across the shoulders of her close-fitting skelder's gear. Sailriders shrank away, eyes downcast, as she stalked aft, the ripple of fear cold even beneath the morning's baking sun.

Kat met her at the top of the quarterdeck companionway and nodded a greeting. Though she didn't fear this woman any longer, she would never feel entirely comfortable in her presence. "Marida. It's been too long."

Marida inclined her head to mirror Kat's nod, her glossy black eyes – the eyes of a qalimîri daemon – glinting with ... amusement? Approval? Disgust? Disdain? Uncertainty clung close to her, as befitted one who'd once been Ardin Javar's chief rival for control of Tyzanta's criminal underworld. Like all qalimîri – like Tzal – she'd no physical form of her own, only a smothering soul capable of possessing another's mortal body. At their first meeting she'd worn a much younger woman: a shîm-head waif with flame-red hair and elegant limbs. Marida invariably chose her hosts for their beauty, realised or potential.

But unlike many of her kind – and contrary to common rumour – she only went where she was invited. Shîm-heads and other addicts were her chosen vessels, their self-destructive urges a hearty feast for one such as she. By the time she moved on, body and soul were cleansed, the former through abstinence and the latter supped as one might a fine wine. Kat hadn't believed it at first, not until she'd spoken to Marida's previous host, now a young woman reborn into fresh purpose, pursuing her own duties in the fight against Tzal.

"Katija. I thought you'd forgotten about us."

"It took longer to organise than I'd wanted. There's not as many of us to go around as there used to be."

Marida swept a hand out towards the nearest broken-down dock. Already the pier was thick with refugees. "Maybe that's about to change."

"That's not why I'm doing this."

Then you are a fool, breathed Caradan Diar.

"Indeed," said Marida. "That's why I stayed."

After the city had fallen – after Kat herself had fled – Marida had stepped up to the challenge of leadership, protecting supporters and detractors alike. The old truth at play: that you either found your place in Khalad or one was found for you. Marida – like Kat herself – had made her choice.

You do not need that creature's *aid*, murmured Caradan Diar. *Send her away.*

Kat ignored him. "Are your people ready—"

"Kat!" bellowed Larsi. "Heraldic!"

Kat reached the ship's wheels just as the ifrît fully coalesced from an indigo swirl of Deadwinds motes.

((This is Elhin.)) Elhin was the captain of *Amarid's Dream*. ((We have new sails to the . . .))

The heraldic wisped away, gusted skyward by a breath of wind before it could finish.

"New sails?" said Marida.

"The reinforcements from Hazali," Kat replied. "All planned for."

No, said Caradan Diar. *This is something else.*

"Sails to the west!" Aldhad scrambled down the aftercastle companionway two steps at a time, frantic pointing lending weight to his words. "Redcloak sails!"

"*Kiasta* . . ." Kat's breath caught in her throat. "No. It's too soon." She stared down at the streets, at the men and women who'd pay the price for misfortune.

Fighting to keep the horror from her face, she swallowed. "How many?"

"Four, boss," Aldhad replied breathlessly. "Closing fast."

Only half of Emanzi Ozdîr's redcloak fleet? That was something, at least. Almost nothing, but you worked with what you had. Caradan Diar had been right. *Leaders sacrifice.* With thousands of lives on the line, that truth weighed heavier than ever. The rebel flotilla had space enough to empty what was left of Tyzanta, but only if they had time.

"Go!" shouted Marida, already running to the gangplank. "Leave the evacuation to me."

Kat forced herself to stand tall and filled her voice with every scrap of confidence she could muster. "Larsi? Cut moorings, get us back up there." She beckoned to the signalwoman. "As soon as we're clear of the ruins, signal the other ships to form up and follow us in. If the redcloaks want to reach Tyzanta, they'll have to get through us."

Twenty-Eight

T he city bells pealed bright and hopeful to match the brilliant sunshine. From the window of Yali's suite, Damant had a clear view
of the crowds milling at the xanathros, the ragged shoulder to shoulder
with the regal, all of them desperate for a glimpse of the Eternity Queen.

Igari Bathîr would be delighted.

Redemptor's Feast marked a turning of the year and a chance to
move forward unburdened by old failings. Even now, the Abidtzal con-
fessional chambers far below the city would be full of folk spluttering on
clouds of incense and pledging pieces of their souls to offset lingering
sins. Damant pulled back from the window. *Abidtzal.* Tzal's Abode, as
old Daric would have it, the chambers buried deep in the rock so that
the petitioners' promises might find their way to their deity's ears in the
Stars Below. Language remembered where people forgot.

||"Half the city's turned out to see their queen,"|| he said.

||As they should.|| Yali rose from her ormesta-style chaise and tucked
her hands into her chest, the subsequent signs concealed from Gloom,
who stood silent watch beside the antechamber door. ||Time to go.||

Fighting a grimace, Damant struck a long, looping course
around the sitting room. This was a conversation he'd hoped to
avoid. Yali had excused herself from joining the Eternity Queen at
the xanathros, blaming a galloping headache. She looked no better
than when they'd drawn up their plans the day before. This close,

the shadows beneath her eyes were visible even through her meticulously applied make-up.

||I need you to stay here.|| Damant's back itched beneath Gloom's baleful magenta gaze.

Yali glowered. ||People are always leaving me behind.||

"The Eternity Queen is concerned for your health, she wants to give you the chance to recuperate," Damant replied, but he kept his hands low and drawn in as he signed. ||Rîma wants you safe, and our friend by the door makes things difficult.||

Isdihar had enough to concentrate on without worrying about keeping Gloom sedated.

||I'm sure she does,|| Yali replied, her expression bitter. ||*I* want to be useful. Kat never left me behind.||

"I wouldn't let the Eternity Queen hear you say that." Once again, Damant's signs didn't match his words, though the strain of speaking near simultaneously in two languages made them even more stumbling than usual. ||If this goes wrong, it'll be up to you to carry on the fight.||

She sighed. ||I know. I'm sorry.||

||"Get some rest,"|| he replied, letting his signs show again. Gloom likely wasn't capable of suspicion, but it would be foolish to assume that of whoever ended up questioning him about Yali's movements. The thicker the veneer of truth, the better. ||"You'll feel better soon."||

||I hope so. I don't know how much longer I can live with this *headache*.||

In other words, how much longer she could continue living a lie. Damant winced. Whatever he'd done in the Eternity Queen's name, he could blame on the glamour. Yali had always acted of her own accord – that it had secretly been in service of a noble cause was likely little comfort. ||"I understand. It might get louder later."||

||If it does, I'll take a walk. You know where.||

||"I do."||

Rîma had arranged for a felucca to be waiting at the seaward dock if everything went to pieces. But then, if things went *that* badly, Damant expected that he'd be dead – or as close as made no difference. One more reason to keep Yali at arm's length. She still had a life ahead of her, whereas he'd already wasted so much of his own.

"Get the door," he told Gloom.

AS YOU ORDER.

The koilos hauled back the panelled antechamber door. Passing close enough to him for the faded aroma of charred bone to catch at the back of his throat, Damant halted on the threshold. Yali was at the window, her back to him. Perhaps that was better. Farewell was a prophecy that tempted fate.

He entered the corridor to a clamour of banging and cursing. A thoroughly dishevelled barefoot Tuzen Karza, his hair in disarray and his rumpled, stained shirt open to the waist, hammered the heel of his palm against a door twenty paces away on the opposite side of the corridor.

"Alyada, my sparrow, you really mustn't overreact so ... ALYADA!" He swayed, thumped the door once more for good measure and sank against it, left forearm flat against the upper panel and forehead propped a little above the peephole. "Alyada ... this isn't funny."

It was and it wasn't, Damant decided, given that Karza had soured his dignity as a result of having found another impressionable handmaiden upon whom to lavish his fading charms. Keti would likely not be impressed. He looked like death, with the splotchy mottled pallor of one who'd indulged all manner of intoxicants and was now living on the unhappy cusp of late-stage drunkenness and inevitable hangover.

"ALYADA!" Karza kicked the door and rebounded unsteadily away, his bleary eyes at last fixing on the approaching Damant. "Nothing for you here, Castellan ... just a small disagreement."

"Small disagreements seem to follow you," Damant made no effort to hide his contempt, "especially where young women are concerned. I suggest you go home."

"Home?" Karza blinked. "I haven't any shoes and the streets are heaving. I can't be seen like this."

"The streets are heaving because the Eternity Queen is blessing the

Redemptor's Feast. Perhaps you should attend. You look like you could use a blessing ... and redemption."

"Shouldn't you be there, *Castellan*? Instead of creeping along the corridor from the quarters of our delicious little high handmaiden." Karza leered and tapped his nose. "Aha! Courtly affairs. Don't worry. Your secret's safe with me. I hope she was appropriately ... grateful to you for clearing her name." The accompanying smile would have made sewer waste shrivel.

"You're disgusting."

The smile turned sly. "Refused you, did she? My sympathies, but maybe our lovely Yali needs something a little more ... spry. Would you consider an exchange of interests?" He glanced back at the door, which had, quite understandably, remained solidly closed. "Dear Alyada could use a little stern-faced authority in her life."

Damant stepped closer. He was sick of Tuzen Karza. Men of his grubby calibre had always existed and likely always would, but it was another thing for them to flourish in plain sight. "Take my advice, my lord," he said, his voice low and dangerous. "Stop talking and get yourself gone."

Karza shook his head in what he probably supposed was a sorrowful gesture. "What happened to you, Damant? We used to have such fun, you and I. Now you sound like my brother used to. A sanctimonious, superior—"

He made a wet choking noise as Damant took him by the throat and slammed him up against the wall. "Listen to me very, *very* carefully. You will stay away from Yali, now and for ever, or I will feed you all the stern-faced authority I possess alongside the remains of your teeth. Am I understood?"

Karza, splotchy complexion darker than ever as he fought for breath, scrabbled at Damant's fingers. Any reply he might have offered was lost in a wheezing splutter. Uncertain of so much of the recent past and enraged at even the possibility that he'd indulged in anything Karza might have considered *fun*, a piece of Damant yearned to squeeze off the count's odious head and thus guarantee at least a small improvement to Khalad's lot.

In the end, the arrival of a two-man redcloak patrol at the end of the corridor made the decision for him. He let Karza drop and stepped away. "Just remember what I said about the teeth."

If the two redcloaks had seen anything of his interaction with Karza, neither mentioned it as he stalked past. Likely they were as sick of his lordship's antics as everyone else. Yali was right. Some headaches were impossible to live with. One way or another, Damant swore he was done doing so.

Twenty-Nine

A dozen redcloaks stood sentry on the inner edge of the south gate, their spears held less as weapons and employed more as crutches in the face of onerous duty. The causeway beyond was clear, save for the two golden-skulled koilos standing sentry at its midpoint, their polished ember-saints' lamellar gleaming in the sun.

Damant's heart sank. They should have been here by now.

He set out towards the causeway, hoping that the quirk of its gentle rise simply hid what he wished to see. Halfway to the gate, a pair of redcloaks fell into step, one to either side.

"You used to understand punctuality." Golden mask and scarlet hood might conceal Rîma's face, but they'd no chance of disguising her wry voice.

Damant veered from the gate and looped back around the gentle, arid waves of the outer palace's sand garden. "I had things that needed saying," he murmured. "Any problems?"

"None," said Isdihar, the mask's echo not dulling her bitterness. "The guards barely glanced at the pass cards ye provided. When it became clear that the gateway hestics weren't going to immolate us, they lost interest. They've learned nothing from the uprising."

"Be glad of it while it serves us," said Rîma. "Is Yali safe?"

"For now," Damant replied. "She's not happy."

"I imagine not." She fell silent as a custodian patrol passed.

Neither spared them a glance. While Rîma's sword, buckled at her shoulder as was her way, was scarcely a standard redcloak armament – Isdihar's short scimitar and holstered shrieker were much more typical – it wasn't unknown for members of the Royal Guard to earn the right to carry weaponry of their choice. "But numbers will not avail us in this."

Reaching the end of the serpent-shaped topiary that marked the stone garden's boundary, they struck out along the flagstoned promenade towards the palace torch house. Though it had been days since the last Mistfall, and thus the torch house's previous burning, notes of lavender and juniper danced on the thin breeze. Rîma marched with the crisp stride of a born redcloak, Isdihar less so. Cloth and lamellar could conceal only so much – not least the fact that the Voice was a good three inches shorter than was generally permitted of recruits.

As they approached the high archway of the torch house's boundary wall, a custodian broke off from a hushed conversation with the driver of a blesswood-laden clatter wagon and hurried over and offered a ragged salute.

"Castellan?" The custodian's gaze lingered on Isdihar, but the silver *vahla* mask kept his thoughts – his suspicions? – hidden. "How may I serve you?"

Damant buried his worries beneath gruffness. "Inspection."

The custodian flinched, his attention snapping back to Damant's implacable stare. "Of course, sir ... but I'm afraid the security sweep has left everything out of order."

"I'll take that into account." Damant shot a meaningful glance at the clatter wagon, which was as battered and unlovely an example of its kind as he had ever seen. "But get that wreck under cover before the Eternity Queen returns. This is the Golden Citadel, not some Qersali slum."

"At once, Castellan."

The custodian offered a relieved bow and strode away, already hollering to his fellows on the boundary wall rampart and gesturing at the clatter wagon. Damant pressed on into the torch house tower, the skin at the nape of his neck prickling with sudden warmth as the sentry crest's hestic examined his soul-glyph.

"What was that about a security sweep?" asked Rîma as she set the outer door closed.

Damant craned his neck upwards. The torch house was an ancient design, with a single spiral stair serving the living quarters and fire platform high above, and a shorter straight stair leading to the storage cellars. No one in sight, but voices carried strangely in such spaces. "I don't know."

"Ye're the castellan," murmured Isdihar. "Ye're supposed to know everything."

"I've been busy." But she was right. He *should* have known. Which meant someone had kept it from him. It could have been one of his peers playing politics again, or simply a *gansalar*'s paranoia. With the Queen's Council under suspicion of conspiracy, the Royal Guard's commanders would be considerably less lax than the redcloaks watching the gates.

"Would we be wise to reconsider?" said Rîma.

"No," said Isdihar flatly. "We may not get another chance like this."

"She's right," said Damant. There was no telling the next time the Eternity Queen might be lured out of her sanctum. "We keep to the plan."

He led them into the storage cellar, whose organisation lay on a continuum between *disarray* and *firetrap*, with sacks, crates and boxes strewn or stacked in the most haphazard manner. An aged flame-haired sentry crest stood watch where the fifth arch met the wall, though the cracked glass of its prism betrayed just how long it had been since an ifrît had dwelled within. The wall below was piled high with bundles of seasoned pine branches – kindling for the torch house's blesswood flame, should it fail to light.

"Smartly now." Damant indulged a smile. "Get this lot moved aside."

Isdihar's golden mask hid her expression, but not her aggrieved tone. "Us? What of ye?"

He tugged at the collar of his uniform. "Castellans don't stoop to such things."

Rîma set to the task at once, hauling aside the bundled branches in the same fluid, contemplative manner in which she offered advice or cut throats. Isdihar stared at Damant, regal outrage battling practicality, and finally accepted her fate.

When the wall was clear, Damant traced a fingertip down from the sentry crest's perfect chin. Five bricks, Azra had said. One, two, three, four . . .

The fifth brick gave beneath his hand with a cough of dust. A section of wall otherwise indistinguishable from the rest swung inwards on a dark passageway.

Damant unclipped a small lumani lamp from his belt and started inside. "We'll close up behind us."

"What of all that?" Isdihar nodded at the kindling. "Will someone nae notice that it's moved?"

Damant cast a meaningful gaze around the cellar's disorder. "In this lot?"

They moved in silence through thick, choking dust, every breath stale with forgotten centuries and the gentle sway of spiderwebs the only promise of fresh air. The passageway soon became a low tunnel of mismatched brick- and blockwork, dotted with uneven archways and columns, broken occasionally by short stairways – more often by the sunken aftermath of long-ago subsidence. At times the going was narrow enough that Damant's shoulders brushed the walls, and at others wide enough that the lanternlight barely carried to its extent. Now and then, the grinding rumble of wagon wheels or the dull rhythm of marching feet above sent dust trickling from the uneven ceiling, warning that they were passing beneath a roadway; the scritch of tiny claws on stone reminded of vermin flourishing in the dark.

Damant kept careful tally of the passageways yawning out of the darkness, matching them to instructions he'd dared commit to nothing but memory. Confidence receded with every step. Doubt in his own memory, in Azra's directions – even her motives – grew. He had never believed himself claustrophobic, but it was one thing to make that claim in the open air and another to do so while walking in circles beneath the Golden Citadel, never again to feel the warmth of the sun …

He thrust a hand against the wall. The rough, scratchy brick helped restore reality to that increasingly unreal place.

"Ihsan?" murmured Rîma.

"I'm all right," he lied. "Just getting my bearings."

"That isn't what I meant." Even having lost him to the Eternity Queen's glamour for six months, Rîma knew him too well to be fooled. A point of frustration and solace both. "*Listen.*"

Frowning, he pinched his eyes shut. There. A scrape of metal on stone. Another. A shorter, sharper tap. The dull mutter of voices. Somewhere ahead, but distorted by distance and uncertain acoustics until it was impossible to know precisely where. Or *who*. It might just be sounds filtering through from the palace, but equally it could be redcloaks or custodians searching the passageways. He'd been careful to inform the Queen's Council of only the secret ways Mirela had used, and Azra had assured him that this run was entirely separate, but there were no guarantees the search hadn't spilled over.

"How much further?" asked Rîma.

"Two turns on the right, one on the left and then there should be some stairs with sunburst flagstones. Stay here. I'll take a look."

Rîma plucked the lantern from his hand. "*You* stay here. If a castellan doesn't dirty his hands hauling kindling, he certainly has no place down here."

He opened his mouth to argue that under the circumstances it would be entirely credible for him to be investigating the palace's secret passageways. He closed it again. Rîma wasn't just saving him from wandering the darkness alone. If there *was* trouble ahead, she was much more capable of settling it than he.

"Are you sure you wish to go through with this?" he murmured wryly.

The thin lumani light shaped a not-quite-smile – like Isdihar, she'd abandoned her redcloak mask to make it easier to navigate the gloom – then she plucked the lantern from his hand and vanished into the darkness, her footsteps barely a whisper.

Damant quickly lost track of how long Rîma had been gone – the passage of time being as suspect as anything else in that darkness – and fought the urge to stumble blindly after her. Isdihar's own impatient uncertainty filled the space between them with low, feathery breaths. Focusing on her discomfort made it easier to quell his own.

"Don't worry," he said, wary of his voice carrying. "Rîma knows what she's doing."

"I know," Isdihar replied, but the sense of her softened all the same. "May I ask ye something?"

A strange moment for a question, and an unusual – almost deferential – tone for one previously of royal rank. But then they were all skelders together now. "Of course."

"Why are you here? You couldae told us the route and let that be that."

He hesitated, but there could only ever be one answer. "Long before the Eternity Queen's glamour made me a slave, I let protocol do so. Laws are not the same as justice." Too late realising that the words framed a criticism of Isdihar's forebears. It had been *their* laws he'd enforced. "It's my duty to make amends."

"I hae known nothing but duty," Isdihar replied, distance in her voice separating them further though neither had moved. "I should nae have become the Voice so young, but after my mother died there was nae choice. The Eternity King needed someone to speak for him or Khalad would hae fallen apart. I speak for him still, word and deed. My life hae never been my own."

"What happened to your mother? The details never reached Tyzanta."

"The Obsidium Cult murdered her a week afore my sixth birthday," Isdihar replied in a savage whisper. "I have nae doubt that Katija's father was involved. My mother's blood held the secret he sought, ye see. The bridge 'twixt mortal and eternal."

"I'm sorry." Isdihar's mother's complicity in cruelty hardly lessened

305

the tragedy forced on a girl barely old enough to understand her loss. And who was to say if she'd prosecuted the Eternity King's will blindly, eagerly or despairing of any other choice. In the matter of bloody hands, Damant was in no place to judge.

But still there was something ... unsettling about a person's body being used for parts. Souls, he understood. That was normal. But the thought that Terrion Arvish had harvested and experimented with the blood of Isdihar's mother ...

"Khalad is a terrible place. I don't think my sire understands – under*stood*. He beheld naught but his duty to keep Tzal caged, and now ..." She drew down a deep breath, weightier than her years, the ache of it begging for comfort Damant knew not how to offer. "Now I hae duty of my own. I will see it done, even at the cost of my life."

Again, as at the Qabirarchi Palace, Damant caught the flash of steel amid the sorrow. So easy to admire Isdihar's quiet pride, her determination. Rîma had doubtless recognised it long before – she was always ahead of everyone else. What might Khalad have become if Vallant had succeeded in placing her on the throne? Perhaps the opportunity would arise again. He swore silently that Isdihar would survive the day, even if no other did.

The gentle glow of the lantern presaged Rîma's return. "There's been a partial collapse of a side tunnel into another immediately below. There's a work crew in *that* passage, bricking it up."

That made it part of the system Mirela had used. "Without anyone charting that passage above?" asked Damant.

"The hole isn't immediately apparent from their level," Rîma replied. "I listened in for a time. They just want the work done as quickly as they can and no more."

That was the problem with ruling through fear: it guaranteed compliance but stifled initiative. But Malis or one of her subordinates would be bound to inspect the work. When they did so, the labyrinth Damant now stood in would be revealed, but they'd be long gone by then. For better or worse.

306

They set off, moving faster than before by unspoken assent. Two turns to the right and one to the left later, a narrow passageway opened into what had been, unknowable years before, a grand stairway. Just as Azra had promised, the flagstones bore a stylised sunburst, the gilded detail still bright whenever the lantern light touched it.

"'Tis kin to Vallant's flag," murmured Isdihar.

"The ashborn worshipped the sun as fervently as Alabastra reveres the Stars Below," said Rîma. "Perhaps this is a holdover from their time, before Tzal sent fire from the Stars Below so that the cinderbloods could displace them."

Damant didn't care for the implied accusation. The ashborn – like the scaldera and Rîma's own people – had vanished into the past. Khalad's cities were built on the bones of those abandoned long before. "That can't be right. The Eternity King was a fireblood."

"Was he?" said Rîma. "Firebloods are the youngest of all, and at the very least Caradan Diar has been part of Khalad since Tzal was first caged."

Damant shook his head. "Firebloods are just cinderbloods with aspirations and inflated egos."

"I used to think that. I'm not so sure any longer. From the very start, firebloods suffered greatly from the lethargia while cinderbloods remain almost untouched. They look the same as one another, I grant you, but then so do you and I . . . and we are *not* the same." She twitched a shrug to rob the words of offence. "Every culture that has come and gone maintained that Nyssa fashioned them in her image. And what of Terrion Arvish's work with the aetherios tattoo? One daughter became a daemon while the other did not. An accident of experimentation, or something more? After all, Tanith's mother is a fireblood where Katija's was not."

"What are ye saying?" Isdihar spoke without raising her eyes from the sunburst flagstones.

Rîma sighed. "I don't know. Maybe I'm just a mad old woman seeing patterns where none exist, but I can't help but feel like there's *something*, some truth, that is so fundamental – so bound in with the fabric of our lives – that it's practically invisible. We can't see it because we're *part* of it. All I know is that Caradan Diar was no fireblood."

A mad old woman? She sounded it in that moment, her otherwise priestly manner gnawed from within by frustration. "How?" asked Damant.

"Because a piece of Isdihar doesn't belong to this realm, remember? The part that she owes to the lineage of Diar." She pursed her lips and gazed thoughtfully at Isdihar. "I wish I knew what it all meant. All I know is that Khalad's history is more lies than it is truth, and I wonder why."

"I've nae answers for ye." Isdihar pinched her eyes shut. "I wish I did. Ye must believe me."

"One problem at a time." Restored to composure, Rîma gazed upwards to where the stairs ended in a blank wall. "You are certain we're in the right place, Ihsan?"

"Only one way to be sure."

Turning his back on the others, Damant climbed the stairs to their furthest extent. Once again, Azra had spoken true: a corroded metal release catch sat concealed in a masonry hollow. It turned smoothly, allaying fears of a mechanism rusted through. With a whisper of hidden ropes and pulleys, the blank section of wall slid aside.

They made their way along the passage, the silent bas-reliefs of winged armoured women watching them with graven eyes. Anticipation shivered along Damant's arms as he raised his hands in the ritual gesture that would convince the motics to open the sanctum doors. A piece of him hadn't expected to get this far. Steeling himself, he passed inside.

Thirty

The sanctum doors rumbled shut.

Rîma stiffened, her hand going to her sword. "Something's wrong."

The heavy drapes to either side of the door billowed. Six redcloaks burst forth, three to each side. Having no time to go for sword or shrieker, Damant swung a fist at the nearest and doubled over wheezing as a gauntleted fist thumped into his belly. His eyes swimming with splotchy red and black, he heard Isdihar yelp, a redcloak bellow in pain and the clang of a sword hitting stone.

By the time his vision cleared, Isdihar stood deathly still, arms pinned by her sides by one redcloak and the blade of another's scimitar held at arm's length against her throat. Rîma stood in the shadow of one of the sanctum's free-standing bookcases. Her sword lay at her feet, discarded at the threat to the girl's life, and three redcloaks levelled their shriekers at her from paces away.

As a redcloak hauled Damant upright, a slow, sardonic handclap echoed about the room.

Malis Ethara stepped into view beyond the night-black stone of the throne immortal, the shadows of her self-satisfied expression length-ened by the magenta light of the soulfire column. Kastagîr followed a pace behind, his cloak swirling the sanctum's captive motes.

"It's a relief to see that my instincts aren't as atrophied as the Eternity

Queen believes." Malis walked a lazy half-circle about the sanctum perimeter, skirting the expansive bed and gilded dining table. "You've been so close to so many coincidences of late, Ihsan. Ardin's death. The attempt on Yennika's life. The assassin's capture ... Not at the heart, perhaps, but always near enough to make me wonder."

Failure bitter at the back of his throat, Damant couldn't even muster the vehemence to point out the gap between Malis's suspicions and the truth. For every act she'd named, save perhaps the last, he'd been deep in the Eternity Queen's glamour. But it didn't matter that wishful thinking more than fact had set Malis on her course. Not now.

"And then Igarî mentioned that you'd wanted the Eternity Queen to attend the Redemptor's Feast," Malis went on. "Not that she expressed it that way, of course. She was concerned that you'd attempt to take the credit. Always such a desperate, transparent little trallock; no wonder Alabastra is fading so fast. But it made me wonder why. Then I spoke to Faizâr and discovered we shared several suspicions. If you wanted the sanctum empty, I knew where you'd be. I'm afraid you'll be gone long before the Eternity Queen returns. There will be no assassination today."

Damant glared at Kastagîr, the bruises from his brawl with the koilos more livid in the sanctum's peculiar light. He felt somehow disappointed. The night of Mirela's pursuit, the captain had revealed a braver, nobler side of himself. A fleeting aspect, seemingly. As for Malis, she hadn't been *certain*, otherwise she'd have locked him up long ago ... or at least let the Eternity Queen into her plans. That meant that Yali was likely safe – at least for now – and there was still a chance for Isdihar and Rîma, if only he could find a way to create one.

"Your Eternity Queen – your *goddess* – is a fraud," he said. "Khalad will not survive her."

Kastagîr raised a hand to the level of his shoulder and clicked his fingers. Damant's knees cracked onto stone as his captor kicked his legs away and ground a shrieker's muzzle into his temple.

Malis gave a thin, self-satisfied laugh. "So it's apostasy as well as treason? Your execution *will* be memorable. My goddess *is* Khalad. My brothers and sisters of the kathari fought and died for her. I serve her in their stead, to whatever end she desires."

Her eyes gleamed in the backwash of the flames, matching her fervour. Zariqaz might have been falling ever faster to the Eternity Queen's glamour, but Malis was not among its victims. Her association with the Obsidium Cult was an open secret, but that she'd been one of its kathari, foot soldiers as fanatical as any Alabastran penitent, was news to Damant. The Eternity Queen had no need to seduce such souls. They were hers already.

"Ye wretched, deluded—" Isdihar hissed in pain as the scimitar twitched at her throat. A thin trickle of blood, black more than red, darkened her skin.

"Are you sure you wish to go through with this?" As ever, Rîma's words held the cold weight of a pronouncement of death, though Damant couldn't see how she was to keep that promise with three shriekers on her.

Malis shrugged. "It's already done. Captain Kastagîr, I'm content for the credit for their capture to go to you. A treacherous castellan, the fugitive Voice and a notorious rebel – yes, I've heard of you, Eskamarîma – quite the burnishing, even for a reputation like yours."

Kastagîr frowned. "You're certain?"

"Of course. It's enough for me to have served my goddess."

He approached Damant, his customary swagger even more pronounced as he drew his shrieker. "What happened? I never *liked* you, but I always thought you loyal."

Damant glared up at him. First Karza, now Kastagîr. It seemed that everyone in Zariqaz had seen something in him that didn't exist. The royal bodyguard was now merely paces away. Close enough, maybe, that Damant could twist clear of the redcloak's shrieker, pounce and . . . well, *die* most likely. Shot in the back. But it might give Rîma an opening to exploit.

He stared unflinchingly at Kastagîr, expecting at any moment another snap of the fingers to provoke another blow. "My eyes are open to what she is. Yours may be too, one day."

"Perhaps they already are."

Kastagîr raised his shrieker and fired in one smooth motion.

The redcloak with the scimitar at Isdihar's throat screamed and hit the floor, the orange flames from her blazing uniform muddying the sanctum's indigo shadows.

Recovering from astonishment a hair before his captor did, Damant flung himself backward and hooked a forearm behind her ankle. Her shrieker blazed as she fell, searing a charry black smear across the lazily turning silver and astoricum sphere high above their heads. Another shot rang out somewhere to his front, the thump of a falling body close behind. Then he was atop his captor, fist hammering with enough force to split knuckles. She slumped, wits gone. Breathing hard, he reached for his own shrieker.

A flurry of fading screams warned that it was already too late.

Rîma stood precisely where she had before, her sword naked in her hand and point-down against the floor. Her erstwhile captors lay slumped around her, the spreadeagled books dislodged from the shelves during the brief struggle become islands in a spreading pool of blood. For a woman like Rîma, a moment's distraction was a lifetime. Malis might have heard of her – might even have learned the complete form of her name – but she'd clearly not known enough to recognise that three redcloaks were in no way enough to challenge her.

The final redcloak lay dead at Isdihar's feet. Where Rîma's victims had fallen to a precision so immaculate that their wounds were not immediately apparent, this corpse bore a series of ragged, vicious gashes. Isdihar herself was breathing hard, her neck bloody from the scimitar's kiss, but she offered Damant a steady, determined nod.

Damant spun on his heel, knuckles creaking as he brought his shrieker to bear on Kastagîr. To his scant surprise, Kastagîr's was already levelled at him. Malis lay face-down at the foot of the throne immortal, one outflung arm protruding into the column of soulfire and the back of her robes charred and crusted.

"She tried to run rather than fight. Typical of a kathari." Kastagîr nodded at Damant's shrieker. "I *did* just save you."

"You did." Damant held his shrieker steady. Had the sound of the shots carried elsewhere in the palace? Unlikely, as the sanctum was deep and trammelled in stone, but the possibility remained. "Why?"

Kastagîr raised his free hand to his bruised face. "The koilos didn't give me all of these. Nor the ones that you can't see." His handsome features twisted, a grimace – a tear – chased away by an impassive mask no more convincing than a suddenly granite stare. "I hear the whispers. I know what everyone thinks I am to her, but she hasn't a scrap of love in her bones. What passion she has, she bends to cruelty."

No need to wonder who he meant, not after Damant had seen how the Eternity Queen had treated him the last time they'd been together in the sanctum.

"Then ye should have refused her. Or fled," said Isdihar sourly.

"There is no refusing her." Kastagîr's throat bobbed, his shrieker dipping. "I beg her to continue, even as she works a knife beneath my skin or sets burning brands to my flesh. The one time I found the strength to fight back, she ... twisted something inside me. I spent a week huddled in that corner, weeping without knowing why and wallowing in my own filth; beaten if I dared raise my eyes to look at her or defy her commands. Every meal since, I've eaten off her shoes. And if I displease her ..." He fell silent, his cheeks taut.

Damant glanced away, ashamed for himself as much as Kastagîr. No wonder he'd thrown himself into the koilos' path so readily. Physical strength was nothing to the Eternity Queen ... and it seemed that for all Rîma's claims, not all her glamours were incidental. Kastagîr was a special case. "Why? Why you?"

"She says ..." A stuttering breath forced itself past his lips. "She says I remind her of someone. She's never said who."

The suggestion sounded a clarion in Damant's memory. Though

the physical resemblance was far from perfect, Kastagîr's belligerent swaggering manner – at least, when the Eternity Queen's shadow was elsewhere – was all too familiar. "Her cousin Jorais. Yennika already killed him. It seems that wasn't enough for her."

Jorais had been Mirela's accomplice in Yennika's long-ago disgrace, joint architect of the systemic abuse and humiliation that had for a long time left her with a reputation worse than the most impoverished, shîm-addled street-nymph. That Kastagîr suffered so for tangential resemblance at last convinced Damant of the truth in Azra's claims of offering up the part of her that was Yennika to Tzal. Yennika's pain bundled up with Tzal's power. A bleak combination, and one that promised worse to come for Khalad if the Eternity Queen wasn't stopped.

Isdihar eased down the barrel of Damant's shrieker. "Ye hae naught to be ashamed of, Faizâr." She inclined her head, once again every inch the queen in waiting. "We are nae defined by choices we are powerless to make."

He nodded sharply and knelt, head bowed. "Thank you ... majesty," he murmured.

Rîma wiped her sword clean on a redcloak's corpse. "If we are to do anything to end this, it must be now."

Looking up, Kastagîr frowned. "How? The queen's not due to return for at least an hour."

Isdihar walked past him with barely a glance. "We were never here for her." She stepped around the low chaise and halted on the edge of the soulfire column, her face pinched and hesitant, the girl breaking through the cultivated mask of regal adulthood.

Rîma laid a gloved hand on her shoulder. "An hour can pass swiftly. If she returns, we are lost."

Isdihar stared down at Malis's corpse, lying at her feet. "I know. It's just that ..." She shook her head, determination returning to the cast of her brow. "Let it be done."

She plunged into the magenta flames. Her fingertips tracing the black stone of its armrests, she circled around to the back of the throne. Rîma kept pace, hand still on her shoulder.

Kastagîr rose, his expression weary but at last shorn of humiliation. "What is this, Damant? If you could access the sanctum, why not just kill the queen?" He glanced at Rîma. "From what I just saw, you'd only have needed her."

"Because that wouldn't kill Nyssa, only Yennika." The full truth about Khalad's three-faced goddess would wait. "She'd only possess someone else and we'd be no closer to freedom. You're not the only person she's broken. She just chose to keep you aware. We have to take away the source of her power."

Isdihar knelt behind the throne. At her touch, magenta light rippled across the backrest, leaving fading after-images of blocky cuneiform pictographs in its wake. The light faded and with it a square section of stone, located roughly level with the base of the occupant's spine, had they been seated. In the compartment behind sat a glittering multi-faceted prism as large as a skull, suspended in a spiderweb cradle of astoricum and silver. Millennia older than the lies of Khalad's recorded history, it nonetheless gleamed wickedly in the firelight, as bright as if a jeweller had only just finished polishing it.

"I've seen this before," breathed Rîma, her words suffused with surprise that was otherwise alien to her nature.

Isdihar, kneeling before her, flinched and stared up at her with hollow cheeks and a faraway stare. "Ye can't have."

"Not here," said Rîma. "Tadamûr. Beneath Amakala's throne. *My* throne."

Isdihar tensed, her lips drawn back and her eyes wild. "Rîma, I—"

The sanctum doors boomed open. A dozen redcloaks flooded in.

"Don't move!" roared their *gansalar*, safe behind a double rank of drawn shriekers. His masked gaze took in the carnage and his tone darkened. "Goddess willing, you'll last long enough to see trial."

Throat tight and careful to keep his hands well clear of a weapon, Damant took a long step in front of Isdihar, shielding her and Rîma with his own body. So the shots *had* carried? No. These redcloaks wore the insignia of the outer palace, not the inner. They didn't have the glyphs for the sanctum door.

He went still at a warning jerk of the *gansalar*'s shrieker and caught sight of Kastagîr a dozen paces away, motionless behind a free-standing bookcase, hidden from the redcloaks' sight. Steel glinted as Kastagîr eased his sword from its scabbard. However haunted his recent past, in the present he was still a warrior.

"It's safe now, lady," shouted the *gansalar*. "It's all just as you said."

Two figures approached through the shadowed doorway. One was broad-shouldered and robed, his gilded skull gleaming in the firelight. The other was gowned in gold, her dark hair twisted back in an unkempt bun and her green eyes shaded with remorse.

||I'm sorry, old man,|| signed Yali, ||but I couldn't let you do this.||

Thirty-One

The custodian yanked back Mirzai's head by a fistful of bloody hair and crowded close.

"Feel like talking yet, skelder?"

He rammed his fist into Mirzai's gut with the fury of a man determined to feel his knuckles touch brick. Mirzai sagged as much as the ceiling-strung chains about his wrists allowed. His shoulders screamed. What little breath he had left burst free of his lips in a spray of red-flecked spittle.

Bare feet scrabbling on the ash-thick floor of the custodium cell, he swayed madly to regain balance. "Fifteen turns," he murmured from a parched throat.

"You what?"

He stuttered a breath, ripe with the stench of sweat and copper. "Has to be fifteen turns, or the bolt . . . won't take." He met the custodian eye to *vahla* mask, defiance holding back the pain of old wounds and new. "Sorry. Weren't you asking . . . about how to secure a heating pipe?"

The custodian growled and punched him again.

"My mistake," Mirzai gasped, dredging a small satisfaction from the moment. The worst they could do was kill him. Almost be a relief after failing his mission. Failing Tarin. The cell's high slatted bars didn't let in much light, but even those thin slivers were enough to tell him that dawn had come and gone.

He glanced about the room, and saw his own failure mirrored on the faces of his fellow prisoners. Maxin looked the worst, one eye swollen shut and a livid burn from a shrieker's near miss visible through the rags of his shirt. Still, he'd broken a custodian's neck before they'd taken him. Vathi stared morosely at the floor. Aklia – who'd been dragged in by her heels barely an hour earlier – at the wall. All had taken their turn. The three custodians in the room had worked in shifts while the overseer had looked on from behind her green-striped *vahla* mask. No one had talked.

Mirzai just hoped that Tanith was still loose. Then there was a chance. He'd not gleaned much from the custodian's questions, but it was clear that the Ozdîri didn't know the extent of the sabotage, which meant the dhows *might* still be in port.

The custodian grabbed his hair again. "Don't look at them. Look at me."

He thumped a flurry of blows into Mirzai's gut, then drew back a fist level with his face.

"Enough!" The overseer held up a hand. "Take him up top. Let him feel the wind in his hair. Maybe that will jog his memory. And if it doesn't, over the side with him. The Zaruan can keep his secrets."

The interrogator stepped back, wiping a bloody hand clean on a rag. The other two custodians left the overseer's side. One trained her shrieker on Mirzai, who gritted his teeth and gathered what strength remained to him. Once his hands were free – if the key bearer blocked the shrieker's muzzle – there was a chance. A dreadful chance, but the river flowed where it would. Perhaps the Drowned Lady, if she existed, would look kindly on him. After all, she was a patron of lost souls and lost causes.

Unfortunately, the custodians had done this a hundred times before. The key bearer took as circuitous a route as the confines of the cell allowed and slipped behind Mirzai.

It was over. By shrieker or by gravity, his life was done. The realisation brought no despair, only exhilaration. For all that he'd lost, there was a piece of him that the custodians couldn't touch. They could only kill him.

He chuckled softly as the key bearer rebound the chains about his wrists. "Blood and freedom."

"Yeah, you'll be free all right." The interrogator flapped his hands in mimicry of wings in flight. "Free as a bird."

The key bearer shoved Mirzai in the back. "Move it."

A knock sounded on the cell door. "Overseer? New orders from the watch house."

The overseer waited for the key bearer and the interrogator to seize Mirzai's arms before she opened the door.

A fourth custodian entered from the darkened empty corridor and saluted. "High Overseer Jannir wants the prisoners. There's trouble brewing at Tyzanta and she needs the rest of the fleet under way." His cultured tone – one whose origins lay far afield from ash-swept Hazali – grew dry. "As I understand it, she's looking to take a personal hand in things. Two of them, bloody to the elbow."

A note of distaste crept into the overseer's voice as she glanced at Mirzai. "I see. You should have talked. At least going off the hangar canopy would have been quick." Her gaze snapped back to the newcomer, suspicion crowding her words. "Wait. What's wrong with your arm?"

The newcomer glanced down at his right sleeve and a silver hem darkened with blood. "Ah. That's unfortunate."

He swept out his arm in seeming apology. Something whispered in the gloom. The shrieker-armed custodian crumpled, clutching at the dagger buried hilt-deep in her throat.

"Take hi—"

The overseer collapsed spluttering as the newcomer slammed the edge of his hand between her gorget and *vahla* mask. He wheeled away, scimitar already free of its scabbard, and ran the interrogator through. Another dagger flew from his left hand and thunked into the key bearer's ribs. With a final lazy slice, he spared the overseer the torment of

319

her collapsed windpipe and tugged his mask clear, revealing a bald man with rich dark brown skin and a self-satisfied smile.

"How anyone sees out of those things I will never know."

Maxin grunted and stirred against his chains. "What are you doing here, mercenary?"

"My job."

"Of course she'd send you after us," said Vathi. "Lucky us."

The newcomer shrugged. "I can go."

"Please don't," said Mirzai, still too punch-drunk to tell if Vathi's suggestion was serious or simply Vathi being Vathi.

"Ah, manners." The newcomer scooped up the key from the body of its former bearer and turned his attention to the chains. "You must be new."

"I am." Mirzai rubbed at chafed and reddened wrists as the chains whispered free. "Who are you?"

The man offered a stiff bow from the neck. "My name is Hadîm . . ." he turned his attention to Aklia's chains, "and far from being sent after you, I was here before you arrived."

"*You* were Kat's contact?" said Aklia.

He shrugged. "She met my price."

"You might have sabotaged the silos yourself."

He sniffed, charm bleeding away into asperity. "I'm an artist. Grubbing around with machinery is work for glints like yourselves." Mirzai recalled how Kat had said that her contact wasn't technically minded. Hadîm's tone suggested that he wilfully elected to remain so. "I suggest you hurry. I was not a subtle man, and the streets are full of agitated folk. Four uniforms, four of you. Fortune provides."

Aches as forgotten as they were likely to be for some time, Mirzai stripped the key bearer and donned his robes, trying to ignore the places where they were warm and slippery with blood. Hadîm watched the door while the others changed into the lately masterless uniforms. His manner reminded Mirzai of Ravli, dead during the raid on Nyzanshar: watchful without being concerned, utterly focused on the moment at hand without seeming to care. A dozen like him and the battle for Araq, such as it was, would have gone very differently.

They filed out of the cell and into the custodium proper. Bodies lay everywhere: strewn across desks, at the foot of the stairwell – even at the entrance to the washroom. Hadîm stooped beside that particular corpse and retrieved a black-handled dagger from the small of its back.

"Ah. There you are." He returned Maxin's suspicious gaze with a scowl and shrugged. "Favourite dagger, you understand. Stay away from the windows."

Mirzai hastily withdrew to the centre of the room.

"What's happening out there?" asked Aklia, her voice dark with pain. Freed from her shackles, she held the left side of her body stiffly. That she was walking at all was a reminder of why the Qersali had resisted the armies of Khalad so long.

"Last I saw, your fleet had reached Tyzanta," said Hadîm.

"At least that part's going to plan," said Maxin, gingerly tugging his robes into place above his shrieker burn. "Have you seen Tanith?"

"I make it a point to avoid that amashti, but no."

Aklia and Vathi exchanged a guarded look. Not quite concern, but not so far distant either. For the second time in as many minutes, Mirzai's thoughts returned to Nyzanshar. Tanith had saved his life there. He'd certainly never have escaped Araq without her. "We need to find her."

"Not you too," sighed Maxin, with the aura of a man repeating a familiar conversation. "She's not as pretty inside as out, trust me."

Mirzai was too tired to glower. "I owe her."

"We came here to do a job. That comes first. She'll turn up, or she won't."

"And what will Kat say if she doesn't?" Mirzai demanded.

"Assuming any of us make it out of here to tell her?" Maxin said heavily. "She'll not like it, but she'll understand."

Mirzai scowled and nodded. Without the first idea of where to start looking for Tanith, there was little enough he could do alone.

Vathi flexed his wrist, winced and tore a strip of silk from the skirts of a corpse's robes to serve as a makeshift bandage. "What about the ships?" For the first time, frustration threatened to overwhelm his habitual fatalism.

"Still here, all but one. The high overseer's playing it safe." Hadîm grinned. "I think she's worried about her dhows blazing like Saint Qamfel's Day torches as soon as they break dock."

If only. "They *did* make a mess of the inspection chamber when they captured us," said Mirzai. The custodians had been particularly trigger-happy. "Probably can't piece together what we did."

Hadîm nodded. "For all they know, you've poisoned the whole system with blackfire damp."

"They'll be on the move soon," said Aklia. "Count Rashace will be screaming for every ship he can get. Angry fireblood beats out safety every time."

"Then we can still make this work," said Maxin.

"How?" said Vathi gloomily. "Some of us are barely walking. It's not like we can sidle up to those ships and pump them full of blackfire damp. And it's only a matter of time before someone finds this charnel house."

Hadîm folded his arms. "You're welcome."

Vathi ignored him. "They'll not bother to lock us up. They'll shoot us down or give us that flying lesson yon overseer was itching to give Mirzai."

"So we just do nothing, is that it?" said Aklia, passion overcoming her obvious pain. "Hole up here like rats in a sack while the Ozdîri burn down the fleet? There *has* to be something."

"There is," said Mirzai.

It depended just how deep into the mountain the silo pipework went. How backlogged and slipshod the dockside's maintenance crews really were. More than anything, if Silo Three had yet been drained. It *could* work. Probably. And even if it did, there'd be a cost. But what else was there? Thousands of lives, Tarin's among them, because if Kat died, there was no hope for him. That was worth a little courage, surely? Maybe the last courage.

One day you'll wake to find that the world is no longer the one you remember, and for all that you'll mourn the loss, it'll bring you clarity. Gallar had known she was going to her death at Nyzanshar. For the first time, Mirzai truly understood how she'd felt.

Uncertainty hardening to determination, he gestured towards the nearest window, the criss-cross of the hangar's lattice gates just about past the Ozdîri dhows. "Get to the watch house and close those lattice gates. It doesn't matter if the ships break mooring if they can't get clear of Hazali."

Hadîm arched an eyebrow. "I can find the harbourmaster. I'm very persuasive." He tossed his dagger up in the air and caught it by the blade, just in case anyone misunderstood his means of persuasion. "A touch of prism smashing and the gate will stay shut."

"And what happens then?" asked Vathi.

Mirzai pressed a hand to the comforting bulge of the serpent pendant concealed beneath his shirt. In his mind's eye he pictured Zephyr's glee at what he intended . . . and her horror at what it might cost. "Find a felucca small enough to slip through the spars and get out of here. I'll meet you back at the fleet."

"Why?" said Aklia. "Where will you be?"

"Silo control." That was the only part of the plan that bothered Mirzai. Once he was inside, it was simply a matter of levers and valves. Getting there was harder. If someone challenged him or saw through his disguise . . . But even if his part didn't work out, sealing the lattice gates *might* buy Kat the time she needed.

Maxin cracked his knuckles, a thoughtful expression on his face. "Want some company?"

"No." Some decisions you made only for yourself.

Maxin grinned. "Too bad. That was one of those rhetorical questions."

Thirty-Two

"At last!" crowed Hargo as the *Intemperate Wind* pulled below and aft of the *Tempest*. "Set best speed south and get me aboard the *Belligerent*. Emanzi is *not* taking the credit for my victory. Send a heraldic to Captain Qosa – the *Wind* can escort us."

Crouched double against her chains, indulging only the sparest breaths to lessen the blackthorn's grip on her thoughts, Tanith reflected that her stepfather was spending a fortune in heraldics where most would have relied on semaphore, but he'd never been one for thriftiness. For herself, all she cared about was that as the *Tempest* came about on its new heading relative to the wind, the clouds of blackthorn shifted with them. For the first time, she could breathe. More than that, she felt the creeping itch of her wounds beginning to close, her strength returning.

Now or never.

Slowly, she regained her feet. Flashes blazed in the distance as Kat's warships closed with the redcloak dhows. Beautiful, but for the men and women already dying amid the flames.

Tanith scowled, knowing she was prevaricating. No escaping what was coming. Just get it over with and have done.

She forced her arms down, ramrod straight, the muscles of her left locked tight from shoulder to wrist. Working the shackles' slender give to its utmost, she gritted her teeth, grabbed her left wrist tight in her right hand and yanked down with every scrap of returning strength.

With a gristly *crunch*, her shoulder ripped free of its socket. A hollow red roar of pain sent tears flooding across her cheeks. But the metallic whisper about her upper arms – of chains no longer tight enough to hold – made it grimly worthwhile. Her left shoulder a fused, throbbing lump, she twisted anticlockwise, winding the shackles' anchor rope about her legs and hips, bending low so that the shoulder chains' own belaying rope pulled the whole slithering mass clean over her head to clatter onto the deck.

"She's free!" The custodian at her rear reached for his shrieker.

Cries of alarm rang out, but Tanith kept her priorities straight. Her damaged shoulder screaming all the way, she spun clockwise, unwinding the belaying rope's embrace. It went taut, yanking her left arm to fire. She lashed out with a foot. The blackthorn brazier, its weighted base intended to resist the vagaries of the wind, gave reluctantly, but it gave.

It toppled and struck the deck with a hearty *clang*, scattering blackthorn ash and smouldering wood scraps into Hargo's path.

Her spirits rose as she drew down her first unguarded breath. Trapped on a skyship high above the ground? So what. Her shoulder feeling like a starving lion was chewing on it? Please. Outnumbered, six to one, without a weapon to her name?

With the blackthorn gone, she could work with that.

"A thousand tetrams to whoever brings her down!" bellowed Hargo.

A shrieker wailed. Tanith twisted aside. A heat haze traced the air and blasted a chunk of polished timber from the portside bulwark. She took a long step forward as a second shot screamed towards her, pulling the belaying rope tight across its path. It burst into charred, flaming scraps, its fragments hot against her forearms.

Shackles still heavy about her wrists, Tanith pounced before the custodian could fire a third. Her shoulder – her *good* shoulder, thank the Stars Below – thumped into his chest. His lower back struck the bulwark's edge and he vanished over the side with a thin wail.

Tanith's world turned red as a sailrider yanked on her dislocated arm. Screaming incoherently, she crushed him against the bulwark, smashed her shackles down on his head and ripped free.

She staggered away towards the mast. Beneath the pain, her shoulder itched like mad. It *wanted* to heal, but it couldn't because the bone wasn't in place.

Gritting her teeth, she braced her heels against the deck, pivoted and rammed her shoulder into the mast. The pain drove her to her knees, breathing hard and ragged, but the sensation of the bone snapping back into its socket? That was the sweetest satisfaction.

Warned by Hargo's desperate bellow, she turned about in time to see his scimitar flash. She ducked, and the blade *thunked* deep into the mast. Rolling clear, she scrambled back towards the quarterdeck, headlong towards the levelled muzzle of a custodian's shrieker.

"Help me!" she gasped. "You can see he's a madman! You have to protect me!"

Recent events made the words a lie, but that didn't matter. She just needed him to doubt, the better to let her glamour worm its way inside.

The custodian hesitated and was lost. He lowered his shrieker and pulled away his mask, head swaying as he wrestled with inexplicable doubt. Awash in the lavender scent of his soul, Tanith brushed the shrieker aside and clung to him. Her lips brushed his as the captain and the sole conscious sailrider bore down from the quarterdeck and Hargo's heavy footfalls thundered behind. Her stomach twitched as her victim's willpower melted. Her pulse quickened in anticipation of feasting on his soul. She hurt. She was bone-weary. More than that, she was angry at Hargo, at the world, at herself most of all.

She *deserved* this.

But she needed something else even more.

She pulled away and held out her shackled hands. "Set me free."

The custodian blinked and fumbled with the key, so addled that it took two attempts for him to set it cleanly in the lock.

"Thank you."

Tanith rammed her head forward. The custodian's nose crunched, his body limp even before he toppled. She grabbed for his scimitar. It slid free of its scabbard as its owner collapsed, shining bright beneath the sun.

She worked her left shoulder as Hargo and the other survivors advanced. The dull grind and pop of tendons pulling back into place fed soaring confidence. Two opponents for'ard of her and two aft, three scimitars and a boat hook. Not a shrieker in sight.

Such a shame.

The sailrider died first, belly opened east to west, his boat hook no match for a real weapon. Tanith's backswing half-severed the captain's sword arm and she ran him through before his scimitar clanged on the deck. The custodian was enough of an opportunist to launch himself at Tanith while her back was turned. His wild slash opened her still-healing shoulder to the bone, setting her arm ablaze with weeping indigo flame. She buried her blade in his gut and left it there, trapped in its prison of flesh as dying whimpers dragged both downwards.

That left Hargo.

"Daemon!" he roared, and swung two-handed at her head.

Catching the blade nearly cost Tanith three of her fingers. Hargo's haggard expression as she turned the scimitar aside, hand wreathed in the fire of her blood, was worth it.

"I think we're past name-calling, you and I," she said sweetly.

She twisted the scimitar from his grip and tossed it aside. Then she held up her hand, the blade's gashes already healing, so that he could see just how fleeting were the harms he'd inflicted.

"What I told you before, about my father hurting me more than you ever could? That was true." She stepped closer. "But we both know it wasn't for want of trying."

Hargo stumbled back, blood draining from his face as the portside bulwark cut off his retreat. He looked ten years older than he had moments before, the years between borne away on wings of fading hope. He'd had her at his mercy, beaten and shackled, and still she'd turned his prison to blood and terror. His greatest fear – one that had haunted him for a year, perhaps for her entire life – had come to pass, and had broken him cleaner than any sword stroke.

"I won't beg."

Far behind and below him, the deck of the *Intemperate Wind* crowded with custodians and sailriders, craning their necks to make sense of the commotion high above. The first shrieker shots whined out. Most dissipated before they reached the *Tempest*. Those that did barely scarred the gunwale.

"I don't need you to," said Tanith.

So often she'd imagined the torments she'd inflict when fate finally turned her way, all accompanied by the bloody tears of a dying and powerless man. Vengeance for herself. For her mother. For the weeping girl who'd scarcely understood why he'd beaten her so. Those fantasies had brought her joy in the very darkest of places ... but now the moment was here, she felt no delight, no yearning – nothing at all save impatience to have the deed done.

Brushing aside his boneless attempts to stop her, she gripped his head in her hands. "Khalad's suffered you long enough. So have I."

She held her glamour in check as she drank down the bitter lavender of her stepfather's wicked soul, offering neither solace nor mercy to dull the pain as she tore apart everything that he was and feasted on the scraps. No journey to the Deadwinds for Hargo Rashace. No prospect of rebirth at Nyssa's gracious command. Only the true oblivion of a damned soul. The amashti's gift to her prey.

For the first time in months, Tanith felt no guilt in the feeding. By the time she tipped the empty husk into the open skies, she felt free in a way she'd never imagined possible.

Shrieker fire still rippling uselessly up from the deck of the *Intemperate Wind*, she set her back to the dhow and crossed the corpse-choked deck to the *Tempest*'s wheels. The yacht's helmic took umbrage at her lack of glyph, but, soul-glutted as she was, she quashed its resistance with but a thought.

As the chastened ifrît unlocked the yacht's wheels, she stared at the battle raging to the south. She couldn't reach Kat in time to make a difference, nor had she the means of preventing the *Intemperate Wind* from doing so. But Hargo Rashace wasn't the only debt due.

Hauling on the lateral wheel, she brought the *Tempest* onto a heading back to Hazali.

The *Sadia's Revenge* shuddered as another cannon shot crashed against its portside bow. The shriek of shattering timber drowned all else, but the crackle of flame and the screams of the dying soon flooded back.

Kat grabbed at the quarterdeck balustrade. "We've got to get in closer!" She fought for breath as a thick waft of smoke overtook her. A full quarter of the ship was burning, from bowsprit to the stump of the foremast. Under control for now, but there was only so much water aboard to fight the fires. "They're pounding us to pieces out here!"

Get close, and they could tuck in beneath the *Belligerent*'s gun decks, lower than its shrieker cannons could depress.

"I'm trying!" Larsi leaned into the lateral wheel. "But we lost half our rudder sails three salvoes back, and most of what's left are jammed!"

The portside flank erupted as the surviving gun crews returned fire. Two of the three shots screamed across the skies and struck home against the *Belligerent*, hammering at the gentle bulge of the buoyancy tanks tucked against its keel. The foremost at last gave way, the puff of escaping eliathros lost at once into the stinging tarry smoke. Tattered sails blossomed along the dhow's flank as its captain let out more canvas to compensate. A small victory.

Not nearly enough.

Kat clung to the balustrade, the urge to leave her post and do something – *anything* – almost overwhelming. But if she went to fight the fires or help with the wounded, she'd lose what control of the broader battle she had left.

Control. What a joke. For all her planning, everything was coming apart. And all because half the redcloak fleet had arrived early. Her own ragtag warships had swarmed the first newcomer, insects stinging at a

329

lion's hide, punishing its captain's arrogance and leaving a masterless sinking wreck doomed to break apart on the plains. But that victory had cost her *Galadin's Lament*. Any two of the three remaining redcloak dhows could have picked apart the five battleworthy ships she had left. There'd never been much chance of victory, only of distracting the redcloaks long enough for the transports to empty Tyzanta.

With every passing second, the likelihood of doing even that faded further.

Far to starboard, a shrieker volley sheered away the topmast from *Amarid's Dream*.

You couldn't have known, breathed Caradan Diar. *But you can still win.*

"How?" she hissed. "How do I win *this*?"

Your tattoo binds you to the spirit world. Through it, the mortal world is yours to dominate. You did it before, at Athenoch.

Athenoch, where she'd wrested control of the koilos army Yennika had sent to destroy the city. But then she'd been drunk on the power of the Deadwinds. It had almost killed her in the moment, and again across the following months as omen rot's spasms had steadily squeezed the life out of her. For all that, she'd have gladly done it again. Though there were likely few koilos aboard the oncoming dhows, their crews relied on motics, helmics and above all shriekers to continue the fight. Control of those, and the battle was as good as over.

But the *Sadia's Revenge* was in no condition to go chasing the Deadwinds, and she'd no time to spare on the attempt. The only reason that the redcloaks hadn't overwhelmed them already was because they had to divide their efforts against several targets. Remove even a single ship, and looming defeat would become a rout.

You don't need the Deadwinds. You already have all that you need.

Kat felt his thoughts touch on Tarin's soul, entangled deep in the strands of her aetherios tattoo. A dozen times as potent as any ifrît. A hundred. Vibrant. Unaware. Helpless.

She gritted her teeth. "I promised to keep him safe."

How will you keep that promise if you die? Caradan Diar's graveyard whisper gained force and strength. *You are all connected, bound by invisible echoes of what once was. I will guide your hands. Show you how to spin that soul to a tether. What you did by instinct at Athenoch you can now do by design. One soul to save thousands.*

Tanith would have agreed, but then upbringing and nature had twisted her inside out long before she'd had a chance to know better. "No. If I do that, I'm no better than Tzal."

You make a distinction where none exists.

Of course he thought that. For millennia he'd treated Khalad like a gameboard, seeing only playing pieces and not people. But just as she had the day before, Kat had the sense of something half said – something he hadn't meant to say. "Maybe for you," she bit out.

"What was that?" called Captain Larsi.

Kat winced. "I—" She broke off as a shrieker shot screamed overhead. "I keep waiting for Vallant to show up and pull me out of the fire, like he used to." She'd hated it every time, but she'd have given anything to see the *Chainbreaker*'s black hull on the horizon. The promise of an earnest smile that maddened as much as it encouraged.

"You're Vallant now."

She grimaced. Vallant's uprising had called for terrible sacrifice, not always willing. He'd always survived . . . but then, the Bascari had *wanted* him to survive for much of that time. Did that even count? Had she inherited an impossible dream? "Thanks."

With a ripple of sails, the *Ancestral* slipped in abaft the *Sadia's Revenge*, adding its heavy fire to the uneven battle. One of the *Belligerent*'s rudder sails blazed bright as flames overtook it. A section of scarlet bulwark shattered, hurling redcloaks and sailriders overboard. Kat's hope, guttering since fires had taken root in the *Sadia's Revenge*, kindled anew. Though scarred from its battles with its fellow blockade ships, the *Ancestral* was a true warship, almost the equal of one of the redcloak dhows. It wasn't the *Chainbreaker*, but it would do.

"Captain Larsi!" she shouted. "Do we have steerage?"

"Aye, more or less!"

"Then get us in close and low." Kat cast about for the signalwoman. "Thank Captain Gorahm and tell him he's to follow—"

The pressure wave of a shrieker cannon shot sucked the words from her mouth and hurled her to the deck. Larsi just ... vanished, torn apart in a storm of blood and flame that scored a charred furrow across the quarterdeck and smashed both ship's wheels to matchwood. The deck dipped to starboard as the masterless *Sadia's Revenge* began to list.

Enough! roared Caradan Diar. *If you die, I die. I will* not *see my work undone. There is too much at stake.*

Kat felt him reach into the spirit world for Tarin's soul, the tendrils of his outer presence already bleeding through the protective web he'd taught Kat to build around it. Still on her knees and her eyes pinched shut, she dived after him and fought back with every scrap of self she could muster.

For a wonder Caradan Diar recoiled, the dark shimmer of his presence retreating before Kat's fury. She pursued him across their shared soulscape, severing the tendrils that had wormed through Tarin's outer halo. The boy's formless wave of gratitude washed over her, redoubling her determination.

Cease this pettiness! howled Caradan Diar. He was no longer her mentor – often distant, seldom kindly – but an ancient, deathless ifrît, bleaker than any qalimîri. *I do only what must be done.*

"No," gasped Kat, her eyes lidded and the deck rough beneath her palms. "I won't let you."

No longer in retreat, Caradan Diar bore down on Kat's soul-self, an oily cloud tinged with indigo flame. She convulsed as it touched her. Trembling with a hollow, harrowing sensation for which she had no name, she drew back and found herself entangled in her own tattoo. Its threads came alive, smothering sensation from the mortal world, drawing her soul – her ifrît – deeper into the soulscape as a facsimile of burning indigo and violet.

"Boss!" She barely felt Aldhad tugging at her arm. His voice was a whisper. "Are you hurt?"

Her reply fell leaden from numb lips. The mortal world lost colour as the tattoo drew tighter about her ifrît. She felt Caradan Diar reach for Tarin once again. Gathering her fading will, she matched herself against him. To her surprise, he drew back.

Very well, he breathed. *This was your choice.*

Buried in the spirit world's murk and strung up tight by her own tattoo, Kat watched in horror as her body seized Aldhad by the throat, the lad's eyes wide and desperate as he fought to break her grip.

Let him go! she screamed, the words silent even to herself, for she no longer commanded a body with which to speak. Everything that she was in the mortal world now belonged to Caradan Diar.

Aldhad went limp in Caradan Diar's – in *her* – grasp. Magenta light blazed in the spirit world's darkness as the Eternity King drained the lad dry, the strands of their shared aetherios tattoo rippling with soulfire.

"It's not enough." Kat felt her lips move in time to her usurper's rasp. "No matter."

Pale shapes unwound from Caradan Diar's outstretched hands, after-echoes of Aldhad's fractured soul. They swept across the deck, distended fingers grasping at sailriders' flesh – *through* their flesh – teasing, twisting, luring forth the flickering soulfire from within. As bodies hit the deck, that soulfire coalesced and redivided, sweeping onwards and outwards across the *Sadia's Revenge*, the gossamer wisps growing in number, picking the deck clean of living souls and spiriting their essence back to the one who'd called them into being.

NO! screamed Kat, her soul shivering and sick. Even sealed tight within her own tattoo, she felt the crackle of soulfire racing across her stolen skin, the rush of potential. She watched helpless as Caradan Diar raised hands wreathed in purloined flame, the cold fires rushing across her arms, her torso, her legs, until it swathed her head to toe.

"*This* is sacrifice," Caradan Diar snarled from Kat's lips.

He reached out her hand to the *Belligerent* and the world turned to fire.

Thirty-Three

Damant stared past the redcloaks to Yali, heartsick with failure. She'd not been under the Eternity Queen's influence long, or he, Rîma and Isdihar would never have gotten close to the sanctum. That made it a recent development, maybe even within hours. Her spirits, already low from recent imprisonment and sentence of death, eroded further by being left behind while her few remaining friends marched into danger.

Which meant it was his fault.

||"I'm sorry too,"|| he said.

Yali frowned, her eyes tight in the sanctum's flickering magenta firelight. Was she still in there? Was she aware of what she was doing, and why?

Not that it changed anything either way. Now it was either surrender or fight – the one disastrous, the other hopeless. Twelve redcloaks and Gloom's looming cadaverous presence. A tall order, even with surprise on their side.

"On your knees!" shouted the *gansalar*. "Do it!"

Without seeming to, Damant glanced at Kastagîr, still concealed behind the free-standing bookcase. No way to communicate – Yali would discern the meaning of the most discreet sign. He dared not turn to look at Rîma, but then he knew her answer better than his own. He could only guess at Isdihar's wishes, but in the end that scarcely mattered.

Rebels made their own hope.

And besides, treachery was a game for any number of players. Mirela Bascari's final lesson.

He cleared his throat. "These redcloaks have betrayed the Eternity Queen. Destroy them."

The *gansalar*'s shrieker dipped, his consternation carrying through his expressionless golden mask. "Enough games. Now—"

He broke off in a hacking splutter as Gloom hoisted him off his feet by way of a one-handed grip about his throat.

The other redcloaks froze, an almost comedic tableau but for the *gansalar* thrashing and breathing his last in Gloom's implacable grip. A shrieker flared. Gloom twisted about and the shot blazed into the *gansalar*'s back. He flung the corpse at the shooter, hurling both to the ground in a tangle of arms and legs. A ragged volley of shots wailed out, Damant and the others forgotten by fully half of the redcloaks. Gloom staggered as his chest turned to flame and bore down on the nearest redcloak.

Kastagîr rammed his shoulder against the bookcase. It shuddered and toppled outwards, burying the redcloak immediately behind in heavy timber and a shower of books.

The sanctum was plunged into darkness. For two, three heartbeats the deadfires of Gloom's eyes and the smoulder of the *gansalar*'s corpse were the only light. Then the flames roared back, only to gutter once more. Damant felt a hand on his shoulder.

"Keep Isdihar safe," said Rîma. Then she was gone into the darkness.

The soulfire column billowed bright again, offering a brief glimpse of her back-swung sword, blood spraying from its tip. Damant bolted for the throne immortal as the redcloak's dying whimper sounded, all but colliding with Isdihar in the dark. She had her hands flat against the prism and her eyes closed. Somewhere behind him, steel scraped on steel and a scream rang out.

"What's happening with the flame," he said, "that's you?"

He shielded his eyes as the light blazed back, but saw her nod. More, he marked the thick black lines writhing and pulsing like dark veins beneath her skin. "It won't last," she said tautly. "And Tzal's bound to notice."

"She'll be on her way anyway," Damant replied. "Yali will have warned her."

Isdihar nodded. "What happened tae the koilos?"

Damant crouched beside her, shoulders itching at the lack of cover. Through the carnage and the swirling Deadwinds motes he glimpsed Yali beside the sanctum door, kneeling in a ball, her hands wrapped over her head. More proof of a conflicted soul – the Yali he knew wouldn't have hesitated to pitch in.

"Absolute control is an illusion," he said. "Let's just say that I made sure his loyalties were *very* narrow." None of it would have been possible had Kastagîr remained loyal, given that circumstances had required they share joint control of Gloom, but fate had been kind.

Not that it had done Gloom any good. As the firelight flared back into being, he was on his knees part way between the throne and the door, armour smouldering and half his chest blown away.

"How long do you need?" asked Damant. They could still make their sacrifice count. They had to.

Isdihar gave a vicious shake of the head. "I dinnae know! I've never done this before."

At least the redcloaks were having a rough time of it. Eight were already down. Nine, really, if you counted the one Kastagîr had in a vicious headlock while he duelled another. Even as Damant took in the sight, Kastagîr feinted, swept his opponent's sword wide and planted a boot in the middle of her chest.

"Yours!" he bellowed. The woman shot backwards across the sanctum, narrowly missing the dining table, and died in a wet, rippling gurgle as Rîma ran her through.

Ten down.

Darkness rushed in, smothering the sharp crack of a breaking neck and the thump of a falling body.

Eleven.

A thunder of running feet sounded from the approach passageway. The light blazed back as redcloaks bearing the insignia of the inner palace burst into the sanctum, two koilos ember-saints towering in their midst. Another shrieker volley lit the returning darkness, charring stone and setting drapes alight. Rîma tipped the dining table onto its side and crouched behind its heavy timbers. Kastagîr ran the last of the outer palace redcloaks through. Sword still in the corpse's ribs and hand at the scruff of its throat, he braced the body as a shield as shots thumped home.

The bitter waft of cooking flesh filled the air.

In the light of the burning drapes, Damant caught sight of a redcloak taking aim.

"Down!"

He dived at Isdihar, breaking her connection to the prism and dragging her behind the throne. The shrieker shot meant for her instead slammed into his shoulder. His roar of pain drowned out the deadwood *crunch* of his breaking collarbone, the crackle of flame racing across his outer robes, reaching hungrily for the flesh beneath.

No longer subject to Isdihar's command, the soulfire column blazed back, brighter than ever.

Damant slumped against the throne, lost in a red-black world. Through lidded eyes, he glimpsed Isdihar tug away her cloak and smother the flames.

"Pouch . . ." he gasped. "Last breath."

She dipped, fingers working at his belt as shriekers wailed about them. The cool glass of a vial touched his lips. A stuttering breath drew the wisp of soul-stuff deep. The colours returned to the world, smothering the greater part of his pain with the euphoria peculiar to last breath.

Better.

His right arm was useless, the joint frozen and his fingers barely responding. He couldn't wield a sword nor aim a shrieker – if what he did with one could truly said to be *aiming* – but he could at least think again. For whatever that was worth.

"Thank you."

Isdihar rose high on her knees and immediately ducked as a shot whined overhead. "I need tae reach the prism! I'm so close."

No chance of that, not with the throne side-on to the sanctum door.

"Can't ... do anything if you ... get shot," Damant replied, every breath sending sparks of pain along his wounded arm. He tried not to think about the brittle stiffness of his skin, and what it meant.

"Then what?" Isdihar ground out, frustration ice-hot beneath her words.

Bracing his good arm against the side of the throne immortal, Damant twisted about and risked a glance around the side of the throne. Kastagîr, his shrieker's muzzle now propped under the armpit of his shield-corpse, was retreating across the sanctum, an advancing ember-saint a lurching bonfire as he loosed shot after shot into it.

On the other side of the doorway, Rîma eked every scrap of cover from the scattered furniture, moving from table to bookcase to planter pedestal with balletic grace, stalking victims as the redcloaks spread out through the room. Two of the new arrivals – having learned too late that the erstwhile queen of Tadamûr was little less than death incarnate – were already down. But her time was running out. The second ember-saint was bearing down, the paucity of space her enemy as much as any other factor.

Leaning back into the illusory safety of the throne immortal, Damant gritted his teeth and drew his shrieker. He couldn't be that much worse a shot with his left hand than his right, surely? "If I draw their fire, can you handle that koilos?"

Her lips a thin slash, Isdihar nodded. Whatever doubts had followed her to the sanctum, she'd plainly abandoned them since the shooting had begun.

"Good." Damant gripped his shrieker tight and twisted on his haunches. "On three. One ... two ... three!"

He rose up, dragging the dead weight of his right arm with him and trained the sights of his shrieker at a knot of redcloaks advancing towards the throne.

"THIS ENDS NOW!"

A cold wind blasted across the sanctum, felt not on the skin but in the soul. The Eternity Queen stood in the doorway; head high, arms spread and shoulders mantled with indigo flame to contest the magenta of the soulfire column and the rapacious orange of the burning drapes. Formless, nebulous ifrîti swirled across the sanctum. No longer half imagined as when Damant had last stood before her in that room, they tugged at the living with gossamer distended fingers and filled the air with wordless, muttered promises of belonging.

Yali screwed herself into an even tighter ball. Isdihar drove the heels of her hands into her eyes and dropped back behind the throne. The koilos froze. Redcloaks moaned as the pale spirits tugged at their arms, their clothes, shriekers falling dark and silent at their sides. Mewling and sobbing, Kastagîr sank to his knees, his eyes streaming with tears and his courage fled; the warrior of moments before reduced to a beaten cur as the Eternity Queen bent her will upon him.

Damant braced himself as the fading ifrîti caressed him, pleaded with him, commanded him. When their words and fingers burrowed deeper, numbing and cajoling, he rammed his wounded arm against the throne's backrest. Pain drove out what willpower could not. The spectral shadows retreated, only to swirl to the attack anew.

The burning koilos at last collapsed, a pace from the weeping Kastagîr. The redcloaks started forward once more.

Through lidded eyes, Damant saw Rîma stand tall, her eyes locked to the Eternity Queen's and her expression cold with fury. "I know now what you are," she said. "And what I was meant to be."

She thrust the point of her sword against the sanctum's flagstones. Dark shapes coalesced around her, no more real than the Eternity Queen's gossamer heralds, the echo of mask and robe more imagining than fact. These too Damant had seen before, but in that curious space between dream and waking when Rîma had freed him of the Eternity Queen's glamour. The dead of Tadamûr, or what remained of them.

They swept across the sanctum and cast themselves at the Eternity

Queen's heralds, their fickle forms collapsing into dark, swirling vapour as they made contact, steam and smoke coiling together and writhing for dominance. The redcloaks halted anew and swiped uselessly at the air, seeking to fend off something that existed beyond their reach.

The pressure on Damant's thoughts eased as battle joined, the ifrîti assailing his mind drawn away. He'd no clue as to the nature of Rîma's sudden revelation. He was glad only that it had struck. Beside him, Isdihar blinked. Shaking herself to something approaching awareness, she edged around the throne, making for the prism.

But as soon as it had begun, the balance of the battle shifted. The dead of Tadamûr slowly dissipated to dark skeins, fading into the pallid essence of the Eternity Queen's heralds. Rîma leaned into her sword, a face that seldom betrayed sorrow or pain contorted to a rictus of loss. Isdihar gasped, her eyes clamped shut as the whispers renewed.

Rîma was losing, and for the life of him Damant knew not how to help her. Even had he been confident of lining up a shrieker shot, the old dilemma remained: kill Tzal's body, and his spirit would simply claim another. Only Azra would die.

Azra . . .

The last of Tadamûr's dead wisped away, once more a memory. Rîma dropped to her elbows, her sword clanging against stone.

"Azra!" Damant shouted to be heard over voices he was certain existed only in his mind. "I don't know that you can hear me, but if you want to be free, it's now or never!"

The Eternity Queen rounded on him, her eyes shining with malice. "You fool! She has no power. She's just a voice in my dreams. That is the bargain she made!"

Damant ignored her, digging deep into what little reserves remained. "Tzal doesn't know you, Azra. Not like I do. Not like Kat does." He felt a heel for invoking Azra's distant love, but when your back was against the wall, any weapon was fair game. Besides, he'd no way to know if Azra could even hear him. "You were always Yennika's strength, even before you had a name. Make that strength count while you still can!"

"Yennika is nothing," bellowed the Eternity Queen, a dark male voice rippling beneath her sultry tones. "I am Tzal! I am Khalad! You have no power—"

She dropped into a puddle of golden skirts like a puppet with its strings cut, her indigo halo and her gossamer heralds blurring into nothing. When she spoke again, it was with Azra's voice, trembling but resonating with triumph and pride as she propped herself up on her hands.

"I ... can't hold her long," she gasped. "Whatever you're going to do, do it!"

Isdihar ran for the prism. The redcloaks for Isdihar. Rîma, sword in her hand once more, reached them first.

As fresh screams rang out, Damant staggered across the flame-scorched floor – past Kastagîr, still lost and weeping in his own private damnation – to kneel beside Azra. Her eyes glassy and pained, her breaths swift and shallow, she barely acknowledged him, her gaze instead fixed on the floor between her hands. Laughter lines deepened to wrinkles and the last black leached from her hair, leaving steel grey threaded with silver.

Setting aside his shrieker, he laid his hand atop one of hers. "You did good."

Azra laughed without humour. "You've no idea how nice it is to hear you say that," she murmured. "But I can't ... I can't stay. If you see Kat ... tell her I'm sorry."

Her expression slackened. The indigo halo flickered back into existence. He snatched his hand clear as the Eternity Queen met him eye to eye from inches away, a snarl on her lips.

"Oh Ihsan," she growled. "That's really the best you had? You will beg for Kastagîr's fate."

He felt it before he heard it: a thin whine on the edge of hearing dulled by age. The death cry of something ancient, trapped too long and desperate for release. It gathered strength and volume with the passing moments, rising to a deafening threnody, part bellow, part scream.

The Eternity Queen stared toward the throne immortal. "What have you done!" she howled.

Isdihar knelt once more at the back of the throne, the prism no longer in its cradle but in her hands. The darkness beneath her skin crazed her face like broken glass. As the other-worldly scream reached fever pitch, she met Damant's gaze, determined and yet repentant.

Somehow her simple whisper carried over the cacophony. "I'm sorry."

The prism shattered in an outrush of black light, sweeping Damant into silent darkness.

Thirty-Four

The torrent of magenta fire swept the *Belligerent*. Trapped in the darkness of her own hijacked soul, Kat felt every death.

Sailriders, redcloaks, koilos, ifrît – the flames smothered them all, pinching out souls as candle flames between finger and thumb. Echoes writhed beneath the spirit world's inky skies, the bright lights of the living turning dark against the heavy shadows of their dhow's hull. A moan of ecstasy and horror escaped Kat's lips as the thinning souls passed through a body no longer hers to command, the tattoo strands that held her ifrît captive dancing with stolen flame. Pieces of the dead brushed her soul, staining her with ambition and loss, their sorrows and joys. Through them, she glimpsed a world wider than she'd ever dreamed, felt a piece of herself touch upon the spires of Zariqaz and Phoenissa, the broken savannahs of Qersal, thick with the bright pinpricks of distant souls. Hers if she desired them.

It was a sense of completeness and belonging so profound that she recognised only a piece of it. It thrilled like nothing else, horrified like nothing could. It was power. *She* was power, bound to every living thing that crawled, walked or swam.

She wanted to be sick.

She felt her stolen body stagger as Caradan Diar wrestled with fatigue. Scattered soulfires vanished beneath a blanket of darkness. Dark shapes of skyships continued their majestic, brutal waltz beneath the spirit world's brooding skies, the brilliant discharge of shriekers engulfing souls by two and threes.

She slumped against the strands of her tattoo, breathing hard from memory and instinct more than need, for an ifrît knew nothing of mortality.

Desolate and heartsick, she stared down at herself. She'd always thought of ifrîti as shapeless, but hers retained a woman's form, diffuse and fluid with flickering flame. But then the ifrîti she'd known were dead, and she was alive ... wasn't she? Certainty faded, the connection – what she *hoped* was a connection – to flesh and sensation belonging more to memory than fact. The memory of her lungs ached against a yammering heart.

She *was* alive. She had to be.

LET ME OUT! The oppressed skies swallowed up her silent scream.

She tugged at the inky tattoo strands. They clung to her, viscous and tarry, their racing flames cold against her own.

Who's there? called a plaintive voice. *Please answer me.*

Kat twisted in the strands. A male ifrît, huddled within the web, his form more diffuse than hers, its flames translucent and restless. Tarin.

I'm here, she said, wondering if her words carried. *I can hear you.*

He gave a shuddering sigh. *Drowned Lady be praised.* Relief turned frantic. *I can't ... I can't see anything. Where am I?*

He couldn't see? Just how far had he faded? Caradan Diar had promised her that he wouldn't be aware. That he'd be safe. Not that Caradan Diar's promises held the value they'd once commanded.

What's the last thing you remember? asked Kat.

Araq was burning. I was burning ... Is Aethri ...?

Kat didn't know who Aethri was, but the pain in Tarin's words bridged the gap. So many had died at Araq. You couldn't save everyone, much as she wished it otherwise. *I'm sorry. I don't know.*

His ifrît darkened with sorrow. *I thought the river had taken me.*

That was something, at least. Ifrît were all emotion, no memory. How much longer would Tarin hold together? How long would *she* hold together, for that matter? What evils would Caradan Diar wreak in her name, wearing her face?

She couldn't allow it.

As her resolve took shape, she felt her mortal body stand tall. The strands of her tattoo came alive with flame as Caradan Diar reached out towards a second redcloak dhow. The spirit world blazed with soulfire as the hungry flames raced through its hull, snuffing out the lights of its crew one by one.

Even awash in the ecstasy and revulsion of expanded awareness, Kat felt Caradan Diar falter. The web dimmed and turned dark, its reserves of soulfire spent. The shadow-dhow limped on beneath brooding skies, its foredeck bright with souls ignorant of how close death had come to claiming them. Her body doubled over, its hacking bloody cough echoing across the spirit world. She shuddered, clinging tight to her anger until it passed.

Now or never.

Girding every scrap of her strength, she tugged again at the strands of her tattoo. Bereft of soulfire, they yielded, stretched, then tore free with a wet shimmering snap. Triumphant, Kat blazed deeper into the darkness, gathering the scraps of soulfire that had flickered free from the severed strands. Almost nothing, but it would be enough. It *had* to be enough. It was her body. Her life.

You cannot fight me, howled Caradan Diar. *You are nothing but a sliver of cold flame that thinks itself alive. A lie that believes itself the truth.*

The spirit world convulsed, the bow wave of his wrath scattering her ifrît's feeble flame across the darkness.

As she struggled to bind her dissipating soul-self together, Caradan Diar reached hungrily for the surviving souls aboard the *Sadia's Revenge*.

Tanith shuddered without knowing why as she brought the yacht speeding in towards Hazali. Guilt at killing her stepfather? She laughed the idea aside, but couldn't escape the feeling of something amiss.

Something *definitely* lay amiss at Hazali, though here the issues were decidedly mundane. The lattice gates were closed, the uppermost pair clamped tight around the prow of an Ozdîr warship that had chanced the shrinking gap and paid the price. The inner gantries were thick with redcloaks hauling on ropes as they tried to move by hand that which motics usually accomplished.

Cause for hilarity, under other circumstances. Cause for relief in those at hand, for it meant that Maxin and the others had completed the mission she'd soured. Only ... there was no way to get the yacht inside the hangar.

"Always has to be the hard way." Soothing the helmic with a burst of soulfire – the ifrît was a particularly twitchy example of its kind, and had needed constant reassurance – Tanith hauled back on the pitching wheel, aiming for the watch house and the empty customs dock, whose feluccas had been called away to the emergency at the lattice gates. If yon emergency had indeed been Maxin's doing, then that was as good a place as any to start looking. Assuming that the watch house's shrieker cannons didn't blow her out of the skies, of course, but it would take a brave custodian to lay a gun against Hargo Rashace's personal yacht.

Commotion further along the hangar caught her eye as she closed: three figures running along the gentle curve of the ash-buried canopy, the watch house to their backs. Shrieker shots flashed out from the custodian pursuit, gouging great plumes of ash into the skies.

Three figures, not four. But it was a start.

Tanith hauled on both the lateral and pitching wheels, the yacht's motics realigning the mainsail and outriggers. As the ship came about behind the pursuers, she left the helmic to chart a steady course and headed for'ard. The custodian she'd headbutted during her takeover stirred drunkenly from the deck and grabbed at her ankle.

She kicked his hand away without looking and cuffed him about the head. "Oh. A volunteer."

Sharply aware that she was running out of both time and distance, she yanked the end of the mooring line from its capstan, tied it fast around his ankle and grabbed his robes at scruff and spine.

"Wait!" he shouted. "No!"

She heaved him over the low bulwark. The capstan rattled merrily away as the mooring line played out. A dull thump from below, barely audible over the creak of rope and canvas, and the line went slack.

Shouts of alarm rang out as the pursuers on the canopy at last realised that the yacht was coming in too low. Tanith leaned out over the starboard bulwark to survey her handiwork and was rewarded by the sight of the keel's leading edge flinging a custodian aside. A second ducked too late and was swept off the canopy to plunge past the swarming feluccas at the lattice gates. The others dived clear, the first shrieker shots blazing skyward to contest Tanith's wild laughter.

As the yacht closed with the fleeing trio, she cupped a hand to her mouth and waved. "Hey, idiots! Rope!"

She jerked a thumb back towards the tethered custodian bumping along the canopy, transformed by circumstance from a worthless drag anchor to a deadweight that would make the rope climbable.

She had the fugitives aboard before the yacht cleared the canopy's distant end. Vathi and Aklia, both battered and beaten. Hadîm, his presence as much a surprise as his self-satisfied expression was not.

Tanith glared from one to the next, a chill in the pit of her stomach. "Where are the others?"

The door to the silo control room shuddered against the toppled tool cabinet, the cacophony of voices beyond undercut by an overseer's bellow. "Break it down! Drag those skelders out by their heels!"

Maxin wiped his brow with the back of his hand. A wasted effort, as both already glistened with his own blood, as did his sleeve and the left side of his robes. "This ... this could be going better." He swayed and fell against the wall, his fingers leaving a scarlet smear on filthy plaster.

"A fine time to say so." Mirzai threw his weight against the flywheel of Silo Three's distributor pipe. All around him, metal creaked and shook as the pressure shifted. Brass gauges twitched, vindicating precious minutes spent examining the wall-mounted flow diagram.

It *had* been going better until minutes before. No one had given them a second glance as they'd made their way down to the *Lumberfast*. The tanker's guard hadn't been quite so trusting, but the pier's remoteness and Maxin's talent for concentrated violence had settled that particular problem. A cursory check of the cargo pressure gauges had confirmed that no enterprising soul had simply pumped the blackfire damp back aboard from Silo Three, but that wasn't why Mirzai had insisted on the detour. A lifetime as an engineer had taught him the elegance of simplicity, and for such elegance they'd needed the uncured shrieker hidden beneath the wheelhouse floor.

The silo overseer, already run ragged by Ozdîri captains, had been in no mood for fresh arguments and had taken their uniforms at face value. Sadly, the same had not been true of the *real* custodians set as sentries in the control room. Mirzai had shot one. Maxin had handled the other two in rather more personal fashion, but the second had died harder than the first, the point of his scimitar slipping between Maxin's ribs to puncture his lung. Worse, the foreman had fled in search of help. They'd barely barricaded the door in time.

Mirzai darted back and forth along the pipe-encrusted rear wall, watching as the needles twitched and climbed, adjusting spigots and flow valves, encouraging the motic pistons to force the mix of eliathros and blackfire damp deeper into the dockside's maze of pipes. Not the eighty/twenty mix he'd proposed back on the *Sadia's Revenge*, but an altogether more provocative thirty/seventy, all driven under a pressure the silo pipework had never been designed to contain.

"It's building!" he shouted over the clamour at the door. "Won't be long now."

"Good," gasped Maxin. "I'd hate to miss it." He slid to the floor, hacking and spluttering. "Stinks in here," he wheezed.

"Yeah." Swept up in euphoria that had only a little to do with the rarefied atmosphere, Mirzai fought the urge to laugh. "This stuff will kill you."

Even without the sickly-sweet smell, the burnt-orange haze clinging to the rafters betrayed that the seals in the control room pipes were giving way. And if that was true, it would be true across the system. *If* he'd locked off the right pipes. *If* something didn't burst and vent the precious blackfire damp into the open air. Generations of Hazali engineers had installed pipes where they really shouldn't have. Eliathros distribution lines ran along the canopy underside before dropping down the mooring piers. Bulk-transfer pipelines piggybacked on support struts. Shortcut on top of shortcut, but Mirzai supposed they'd never considered that someone might flood the system with blackfire damp.

The door splintered. The overturned cabinet shuddered. The hinges held. This time.

A cluster of gauges edged into the red. The dial for Silo Three sank to its lower limit.

Mirzai snatched the uncured shrieker from among the scattering of filthy tools on the foreman's desk. He glanced at Maxin. "Sorry I dragged you into this."

Maxin was barely breathing and his skin had taken on a greyish tinge. "Didn't drag ... I followed. Knew ... how it would end." His sudden rumbling laugh spluttered into a blood-flecked cough. "The things we do ... for family, eh?"

Mirzai nodded. "For family." Would the river bring him to Midria and their grandfather? Would they welcome him or be dismayed? "Blood and freedom."

Whether to the river or the Deadwinds, Maxin had already gone.

Fingers clutched tight to his grandfather's pendant, Mirzai sank to his knees, his vision swimming and the cloying eliathros/blackfire mix clinging to every shallow breath. The remains of the door broke apart. Custodians crowded the space beyond, shoving and kicking at the cabinet.

One aimed a shrieker.

"Don't be a fool!" bellowed his overseer, shoving the weapon aside. "Do you want the whole place to go up?"

Laughing his last defiance, Mirzai staggered to his feet. "Behold, a new Age of Fire!"

He aimed his own shrieker at the roof and squeezed the trigger.

The hangar canopy erupted with a deafening roar, hurling glass, soot-blackened flame and a suffocating cloud of ash skyward. Tanith grabbed at the lateral wheel to steady herself as debris tore at the mainsail and peppered the hull. Astern, the watch house vanished into the growing hole in the canopy as those sections that the explosion hadn't blown outwards collapsed under their own weight.

"Would you look at that," murmured Aklia.

One of the dockyard's corroded buttresses ripped away from the mountainside in a rumbling spill of rock. With a yawning moan of abused metal, the entire eastern side of the dockyard sagged. Wooden piers tore free of their stanchions, hurling bodies and cargo into the wind. A lattice gate ripped away from its pillars with a jagged scream. And then, with a dull, angry rumble, what was left of the dockside – and a good chunk of the lower city – slid lazily down the mountainside. Those feluccas not caught up in the explosion scattered. The troop barges and dhows, still trapped behind the lattice gates and caged from above by the remnants of the canopy, were dragged down with the wreckage of their berths, their masts crushed and dark figures plunging from their capsized hulls.

Spluttering on a mouthful of ash, Tanith hauled on the lateral wheel, aiming the yacht's prow at the flame-flecked mass of half-collapsed buildings and seeping pipework still clinging to the mountainside.

Hadîm grabbed her arm. "What do you think you're doing?"

She glared at him and shook away his hand. "Going back for the others."

"Who do you think did this?" said Vathi. "They went after the central silo. They're gone."

She balled a fist to swing, but let it fall, her throat raw and swollen.

Kat hung in the darkness as Caradan Diar harvested the last of the sailriders aboard the *Sadia's Revenge*, helpless to do anything more than hold her ifrît-self together. Unable to weep, she screamed into the spirit world's void as cold flame rushed through her stolen body once more.

What's happening? said Tarin, his silent words hurried and pensive. *I don't understand.*

Someone I trusted is doing something terrible, Kat replied bitterly. *It's my fault, and I'm not strong enough to stop him.*

She'd always loathed how war called for the greatest good of the greatest number. Whether through malice or perceived necessity, Caradan Diar was winning the victory they needed, but at the cost of the lives of men and women who'd trusted her. How often had she clashed with Vallant about his cavalier approach to his followers' lives? This was worse.

How can I help? said Tarin.

You can't, Kat replied, taken aback not just by the immediacy of the reply, but also by his sudden confidence. *You can only get hurt.*

I think I already did. He pulled at the tattoo, his ifrît burning brighter than before. *I'm not an idiot, though I sometimes do idiotic things. I may not be dead, but I'm not alive either, am I?*

Kat hesitated. *No.* The last pinprick about the *Sadia's Revenge* blinked out. She felt her body shift as Caradan Diar reached out to the *Ancestral* in search of a fresher harvest. *This is a contest of souls. The only help you can give would drain you dry. I promised your uncle that I'd protect you.*

I understand. He paused. *Do it anyway.*

Kat gathered herself as tightly as she could. She didn't care at all for how dim her flames had grown. *Weren't you listening?*

My uncle's always saying that if we don't stand together then we stand for nothing.

351

Kat didn't reply, too busy chasing a possibility awoken by the words. *You were born to be a weapon*, Caradan Diar had said. *You all were.* And he was wielding the souls of his erstwhile allies *like* weapons, expending them callously in the pursuit of victory.

Caradan Diar, Eternity King – tyrant – had always taken what he needed, without thought to the cost. What if she didn't need to take from Tarin? What if she could just borrow? Join the strength of his soul to hers?

Buoyed by even that slender hope, Kat drifted to where her tattoo held him captive. *Maybe there's a chance I can do this without killing you, but I can't promise anything.*

Do it. Tarin's voice hardened. *Blood and freedom.*

Zephyr had claimed that Mirzai was a nobler man than he knew. A trait he'd apparently passed on to his nephew.

Kat reached out, the flames of her ifrît brushing his, merging with his. She felt the brightness before she saw it, a sudden warmth against the spirit world's chill. And then Tarin was gone, carried within her, what fading strength he'd still possessed joined to hers.

Kat launched herself into the darkness, striving again for the threshold between the worlds of the living and the dead. Caradan Diar turned his attention from the *Ancestral* and bent his oppressive will against her almost at once, rousing the soulscape to howling, treacherous currents.

Begone, he roared. *I do only what must be done.*

Even with Tarin's strength joined to hers, Kat's flame guttered. She dug deep and flung herself deeper into the storm. Layer by layer it peeled her apart, the spirit world's bright threshold falling further and into the distance.

Desperate, she reached down into the piece of herself she shared with Tarin, and found him barely a wisp, fading fast.

Send me to the river, he murmured. *I'm ready.*

No! It would make no difference now anyway. Had she a hundred, a thousand souls buttressing hers, perhaps she might have prevailed.

But Caradan Diar had once harnessed the Deadwinds to cage a god. It had been arrogance to fight him as an equal.

The spirit world's threshold dimmed. What remained of Kat's ifrît plunged back into the darkness, the clammy tendrils of her aetherios reaching up to claim her.

A woman's agonised death scream shook the soulscape to its ethereal foundations, echoing and redoubling across the darkness before crashing away as if it had never been. Caradan Diar's wordless cry filled the void, his grave-born voice thick with triumph, but rippling with loss.

Its backwash gathered up Kat's fading ifrît and swept her into darkness.

When she opened her eyes, she was kneeling on the quarterdeck of the *Sadia's Revenge*, flesh and blood once more. In the distance, Hazali burned, flames leaping skyward from the ruins of its hangar. Nearer to, two surviving dhows – one redcloak and one Ozdîr – fled south on every scrap of canvas they could muster, leaving Tyzanta to the battered ships of the rebel flotilla.

She clutched at her tattoo. Deep within the feeble magenta flicker she felt the weight of Tarin's soul, wispy but hale. She felt also the darker, ashen presence of Caradan Diar, slunk back to the depths of her soul to lick his wounds. In the moment of extinguishing her for good, he'd relented.

She blinked, numb and confounded. "Why? Why didn't you finish me?"

It no longer matters, he sighed. *Isdihar is dead. Khalad's fate is sealed.*

Kat remembered the scream that had shaken the spirit world, and recalled too the proud, determined face of Isdihar Diar, who'd gone willingly into the heart of Zariqaz, even knowing the risks.

As the wind carried cheers of victory from the *Ancestral* and *Amarid's Dream*, she stared across the ravaged, corpse-choked deck and wept.

Thirty-Five

The stars ruled the sky, but Athenoch's main square blazed with life and light. Kat had never seen so many people packed into the space between the blocky, patchwork stone buildings. Athenoch was an impossible city, trapped behind the Veil but kept safe by the black tower at its heart – or more accurately the slowly rotating silver and astoricum sphere the tower guarded. When Vallant had found it, all else had been rubble and ruin, the remnant of a city so different in architecture and design that it seemed not to belong to Khalad at all. Only in the Stars Below had Kat seen anything remotely alike, though at least Athenoch's embankmented river was of ordinary water, rather than the glimmerless black that wended through those buried streets.

Drumbeats sent revellers coiling through the bonfires. Someone had broached wine casques plundered from House Jovîna storehouses six months before, and its sweet, rich scent mingled with woodsmoke and the mouthwatering aroma of freshly roasted meat. All had something to celebrate. Long-term residents rejoiced at Zephyr's return and the restoration of their link to the world beyond the Veil. The Tyzantan refugees at new-found freedom. And the sailriders of the rebel fleet at triumph and survival. All beheld the future in the leaping flames. Kat only saw the faces of those they'd lost ... and all they had left to lose.

Azra had never felt further away.

Thus she sat alone on her balcony, legs stretched out across the floor, the hem of her skirts stirred by a cool breeze tinged with blesswood smoke, an untouched glass of wine at her side, and longed for . . . what?

It no longer matters. Isdihar is dead. Khalad's fate is sealed.

Zephyr had brought *Telthi's Pride* to the border of the Veil to guide the swollen fleet home, ropes daisy-chaining each ship to the next so that all might benefit from her uncanny ability to chart the gently glowing mists. Though even she struggled on this particular voyage: what should have taken less than a day stretched to almost five.

In a fit of rage at what he'd done to her and the crew of the *Sadia's Revenge*, Kat had buried the Eternity King as deep in her tattoo as she could, which it transpired was very deep indeed – there was no better tutor than first-hand experience.

But as she sat alone – at least, *physically* alone – in her cabin aboard the battered *Sadia's Revenge*, she had concluded that her erstwhile mentor's silence was of his own choice, not her imposition. No amount of cajoling or demand had lured him forth, and what little she could read of his soul was so tangled that it offered no insight. That he'd loved Isdihar she no longer doubted, but it was equally clear that something else lurked beneath the suffocating thunderheads of his sorrow.

The relief crew from *Amarid's Dream* had left her alone, their stolen glances and hushed words respectful, almost reverential. No one had wondered at how she alone of the original crew had survived the battle – they'd shown only relief that she'd done so. In her solitude Kat had nowhere to run from the memory of what Caradan Diar had done. Had used *her* to do. Or from the sick realisation that a piece of her had revelled in it.

Or the knowledge that, in the end, those deaths might count for nothing.

It no longer matters. Isdihar is dead. Khalad's fate is sealed.

The music quickened, shouts and handclaps urging the dancers on through the maze of leaping flames. As Kat raised her wine glass, she caught sight of Tarin sitting silently on the courtyard's edge. At least she'd kept that promise. Restoring his soul to his recovering body had been her first act on return to Athenoch. After, she'd lingered only long enough to ensure that last breath and surgeon's work would keep him from the Deadwinds. Though he was bandaged and unsteady – the walking cane propped between his feet would be necessary for weeks to come – he would live. More than could be said for his uncle.

The glass still distant from her lips, Kat closed her eyes and begged sleep to take her.

The apartment door creaked open. Tanith. It had to be. There was a furtiveness to her footfalls even when she wasn't sneaking around. "Most people knock."

"I'm not *people*." Tanith lounged with elbows propped against the balcony's iron balustrade, head thrown back so that her unbound hair dangled out over the courtyard as she peered skyward. "They're asking for you. They have been since we returned."

Kat scowled into her glass. "I'm not in the mood."

"Get in it. Or fake it. They need this and you need it. You're a hero. Enjoy it."

"A hero? That's what you think I am?"

"I didn't say I believed it . . ." Tanith levelled a sapphire stare at her, eyes shining with rare concern. "Kat, what's this really about?"

It no longer matters. Isdihar is dead. Khalad's fate is sealed.

She didn't know how to even *start* talking about that. But she had to, didn't she?

"It's . . . I . . ." Even as she tried to frame the explanation, something else slipped free. "I failed. And people are dead."

"I see." Tanith's tone made it clear that she didn't see at all. "Kat . . . it was a battle. We knew going in that some of us would die. Half the people down there are only alive because of you. You need to focus on that. We all do."

Kat watched her closely, puzzling at the unfamiliar note framing her final words. Tanith had never exactly possessed a moral core. Her nature as an amashti – a predator – didn't allow for it. A piece of her just didn't understand what it was to be mortal. Too many emotions cauterised by the flames of her daemonic blood. Sisters they might have been, but they were more different than alike.

"That's not what I meant." Kat hung her head, the words scraping at her throat. "During the battle, the Eternity King ... took control of me. He consumed the crew of the *Sadia's Revenge* and used their souls to snuff out a redcloak skyship. I couldn't stop him. You have to believe me."

Though the confession opened up wounds only recently closed, a piece of her felt lighter for speaking. Shame was always as much the secret as the deed.

"From what I heard of the battle, he probably saved your life," said Tanith.

Kat leapt to her feet, propelled by a hot rush of anger. "He *used* me."

"Maybe he did what was needed. The greatest good of the greatest number."

She turned away in disgust. "You sound like Vallant."

"And you sound like you always do: complaining that life isn't fair, even when others protect you from the worst of it."

"What's that supposed to mean?"

"Your little passenger handed you victory. Triumph without blame."

"Then why don't I recognise my reflection any more? Do you know what it's like to watch – no, to *feel* – yourself do something awful and be helpless to stop it?"

Tanith pushed away from the balcony. "You're asking *me*? At least you have the luxury of blaming someone else."

"You really think it's that simple?" Kat snapped.

"Isn't it? Did you fight him?"

"With everything I had." She didn't dare say that it hadn't been enough. Even *thinking* it made her feel twice the failure. A weapon wielded and set aside only because a long-dead hand had chosen to do so. "It doesn't change the fact that people died because of me."

Tanith narrowed her eyes. "You're not responsible for what the

Eternity King did, Kat. You were his victim. By all means be upset. Even better, be angry! Stars Below, be angry at me if it helps. But don't carry his guilt."

"I should have done more. Fought harder. It's not ..." Kat caught herself just in time, for all the good it did.

"Fair?" Tanith flashed a wry smile. "Life isn't, or I'd long since have gone to the Deadwinds. Is that what you want?"

Kat opened her mouth to argue and closed it without a word. Of course Tanith understood. Probably better than she did herself. For all that amashti hunger had driven her sister to do terrible things, she'd pursued plenty more out of choice. Kat had a monster inside her, though common cause had lulled her to its nature. Tanith *was* a monster, though she was trying so hard not to be. The reminder didn't dispel the guilt and horror that had held Kat in its grasp ever since Tyzanta – she knew that it would be with her as long as she lived – but she felt its hold slacken.

"Right now, or in general?" She offered a smile of her own to signpost the poor joke.

Tanith sniffed. "Maybe it's better that you don't answer." Her expression softened, hauteur fading to quiet understanding. "You didn't kill those people, Kat. He did. And if I know *anything* about my sister, she's going to learn from this. She won't let it happen again."

Kat sucked down a deep breath and rose to her feet. "You're damn right."

She faltered even as she spoke, uncertain how to keep that promise, and found herself staring down into the courtyard. At Tarin. Caradan Diar's first victim, had events unfolded as he'd wished. Had she not fought. She'd learned so much these past months, not least in matters of war. Caradan Diar had won because he'd understood the battlefield better than she, but in that victory he'd taught her a lesson she'd not soon forget. About herself. And about her limitations.

"I'm sorry for comparing you to Vallant," she said.

"You're the only one who thinks it was an insult." Tanith tapped the side of her head. "Vallant's been gone for months and still he has more of a hold on you than . . . *him*."

Kat snorted and caught another juniper whiff of blesswood, ordinarily so rare in Athenoch. Arms rigid, she braced her palms atop the balustrade. Below, a couple broke off from the dance, the younger man pointing excitedly at the balcony. Surprised to have glimpsed the legendary Katija Arvish, she supposed. Still she felt a fraud. With a last glance at Tarin, she turned her back to the leaping flames.

"You know what my first thought was when I heard that Mirzai had died?" she murmured. "That it didn't matter, because he'd helped save so many others."

"Maybe it's true." The uncertainty was back in Tanith's voice.

Kat scowled. "It's *exactly* what Vallant would have said, and at least he had the decency to keep new recruits alive for more than a couple of days. Mirzai deserved better. So did Maxin." She still couldn't believe that Maxin had gone. What was the saying? *No stronger friendship than one forged in conflict.* Maybe it was true. She'd half killed him at their first meeting, though he'd picked the fight. "He was always there when I needed him."

Tanith's lip twisted. "You didn't kill them, Kat."

"Oh, but I did." She laughed without humour. "I sent him to Hazali for the same reason I sent you: because I knew he'd get the job done. That trust killed him and Mirzai both. Tarin keeps asking to talk to me. How do I face him knowing that?"

Tanith regarded her in silence, lips pinched tight and her brow furrowed. "Because what went wrong at Hazali wasn't your fault . . . It was mine."

"I don't understand."

She turned away. "I don't want to talk about it." But she didn't leave.

"It's a bit late for that," Kat replied. "Tell me . . . please."

Tanith gave an aching sigh. "I wasn't there when they needed me."

"Nor was I."

She snorted. "You were leading a fleet to save thousands. I took it upon myself to kill my stepfather and got myself captured. But for Hadîm, they'd *all* be dead. All because no matter how I try, I'm still nothing but a sack of selfish appetites." Her shoulders wilted. When she spoke again, it was in a brittle voice. "You sent me to Hazali because you knew I'd get the job done? Well I didn't. Mirzai and the others got it done *despite* me."

No longer blinded by her own borrowed guilt, Kat at last realised that Tanith hadn't come looking for her to drag her down into the celebrations, but to seek absolution of her own from the only person she trusted to offer it. Another friendship forged in conflict, though Kat still didn't understand her as well as she should. Tanith was too wild, too impulsive, freer than Kat could ever imagine herself being. She'd no ties to Vallant's rebellion, no moral outrage. In fact, no morals at all so far as Kat could see. Just personal loyalty . . . to Kat herself, and to a handful of others. Maxin had not been among that handful, which left . . .

Kiasta.

"I didn't realise Mirzai meant that much to you," she said softly.

"He didn't," Tanith replied curtly. "I barely knew him, and for most of that time he was either under my feet or one of us was screaming . . . but he treated me as if I were normal. Do you know how rare that is?"

"I've some idea."

"I'm not like you. I've grown used to not recognising my reflection . . . so why does this hurt so much?"

She stood trembling and defiant, daring and begging Kat to offer an explanation. Unrepentant and appalled at having put such a piece of herself on display.

"Maybe it's because you're not just a sack of selfish appetites," said Kat. "Not any more."

Tanith clenched her fists, rigid as a mooring line. "I don't like it."

"It gets easier." Kat offered a lopsided grin she didn't feel but which Tanith needed to see. "And if I know *anything* about my sister, she's going to learn from this. She's not going to let it happen again."

Tanith snorted. "I feel like I've heard those words before."

"They were pretty good," said Kat. "They bore repeating."

"Right." Inch by inch Tanith unwound, the carelessness of manner and posture Kat so often envied banishing the brittle, almost fragile creature she'd recently been. "I suppose this is the part where we hug?" A defiant tone, but not entirely so.

"It doesn't have to be." Kat felt her smile falter. She'd never been comfortable with overt affection, one of many ways in which she'd been – she *was* – Azra's opposite. But it was more than that. Mirzai might have been able to set aside Tanith's daemonic nature, but try as she might, Kat could never quite manage to do so. Hypocritical, possibly. Unfair, certainly. But as Tanith herself had said, life wasn't fair.

Yes, it was definitely that, and not because her own emotions were becoming as calloused as she'd so often accused Vallant's of being.

Wasn't it?

A knock at the door spared her the need to examine that thought in greater detail.

She strode past Tanith into the sparsely furnished living room. "Come in?"

Fadiya Rashace entered as diffidently as her daughter Tanith had not, wary of intruding on another's privacy. In appearance she remained a prophecy of how that daughter would change with the coming years, her hair losing its lustre as silver overtook the grey and laughter lines weathering winsome beauty with the wisdom of a life lived. It didn't take a discerning eye to recognise how well Athenoch suited her. Freed from the prison her jealous husband had made of their house, she'd thrown herself headlong into her new life.

Almost from the first she'd offered leadership and guidance to the populace, always through example rather than imposition. Though officially the city answered to a council, hers had quickly become the firmest voice. Where Kat – and to an extent, Vallant before her – had shied away from the business of making Athenoch function as an actual city, under Fadiya's guidance efforts to reclaim the ruined streets had redoubled and the surrounding hillsides had thickened with crops and

361

livestock. She knew every name and every troubled heart. Her next challenge would be to integrate the Tyzantan refugees into a populace they outnumbered. There were no finer hands to accomplish the task.

Setting the door closed, she looked Kat up and down, then Tanith. "You both look as though you're about to burst into tears. Have you been arguing again?"

"No, *Mathami*," said Kat, using as ever the old Daric term of affection for a woman who was family and yet not. For all that Fadiya wasn't her mother, she'd raised her. "At least ... not in the way that you're thinking."

Tanith cuffed at her eye and glared at Kat, daring her to pass comment. "It's true."

"I see." Fadiya unconsciously echoed the same tone of polite disbelief with which Tanith had earlier uttered those words. "If this is about Hargo, I won't say that I'm pleased at how he left this world, but goodness knows Tanith had cause to act as she did."

Kat blinked. "She told you?"

"Almost at once." Fadiya arched an eyebrow, musical tone and wry smile robbing the following words of offence. "At least *one* of my daughters was in a hurry to see me."

"I'd a lot to do," Kat replied, more defensively than she meant to.

"To all appearances, most of them involve staring into the darkness and fretting over deeds long done." Fadiya shook her head. "You don't change. Always so serious. But you can't stay in hiding for ever, my dear *qori*."

Kat glanced from Tanith to Fadiya, feeling well and truly outflanked. Had mother and daughter conspired, hoping to wear her down? "I'm not coming down to the celebration. It'll be no good for anyone, least of all me."

"That's not why I'm here. There's something you need to see."

Athenoch's black tower was far enough from the revelry that the sounds of celebration were a distant murmur, the bonfires barely a

362

dull glow behind the city's restored buildings. Its foreboding aspect had earned the tower an unenviable reputation, further reinforced by those who claimed to hear voiceless whispers echoing beneath its honeycomb muqarnas ceilings. For Kat, it didn't help that the tower stood easily six times the height of the closest building – even in the dark, glancing out across its broad balconies to the distant silhouettes of the moored fleet set her stomach shivering. Of all Athenoch's residents, past and present, Rîma had been the only one who'd found comfort in the place.

Rîma. Leagues away in Zariqaz, her fate unknown. Yali too. Standing in the cold cross-breeze that cut across the sphere's open chamber, Kat missed them terribly. If Isdihar was dead, could there be any hope that they remained this side of the Deadwinds?

More friends sent to their deaths out of necessity. She really *was* turning into Vallant.

But some sights chilled the heart even more than the uncertain fate of those one loved.

At the centre of the chamber, the great silver and astoricum sphere hung motionless above its plinth.

"How long has it been like this?" asked Kat.

Fadiya shrugged. "It's hard to say. You know how everyone avoids this place. One of Yennal's boys came up here on a dare. Everyone thought he was lying to blunt his father's wrath."

"But not you?" asked Tanith.

"The only children who ever thought they could lie to me are in this room."

Tanith stared down at her feet. Kat suppressed a smile at the sight. Then she looked again at the sphere and even that small mirth slipped away.

"Maybe it doesn't mean what you think?" said Tanith.

Fadiya shook her head. "The boundary with the Veil has been shrinking inwards for nearly a week. That's why I've had blesswood burning. Perhaps a few inches a day, but it's getting faster. Gambling is a crime against common sense, but if I any longer commanded the wealth of House Rashace, I'd stake it all on the two being connected."

It no longer matters. Isdihar is dead. Khalad's fate is sealed.

"I think you're right," said Kat. "Only it's not two, but three."

"I don't follow."

"Isdihar Diar died almost a week ago. From the start, the Eternity King warned that we'd have no future without her. That can't be a coincidence." She held Fadiya's gaze, silently pleading that the older woman wouldn't question the details. Now was *not* the time to reveal that her body and soul were no longer entirely her own.

Fadiya paled. "The Voice is dead?"

Tanith shot Kat a glance. "No one else knows yet."

Fadiya murmured something unintelligibly Daric under her breath. "That poor child."

Tanith snorted. "Poor all of us if the Veil's on the move. We're sure it's not working?"

Kat stared up at the sphere. That she could even do so was all the answer she'd ever need. "Used to be I could barely stand in the same room as that thing without wanting to heave my guts up. Now? Nothing."

Except for creeping existential terror, of course. For as long as she could remember, Alabastra had preached that Caradan Diar had kept the Veil at bay. Even with the Eternity King dethroned, somehow he'd continued to do so. No more. Perhaps Isdihar had been more pivotal to the process than she'd understood. Perhaps Caradan Diar was punishing them for getting her killed. Perhaps anything. There came a point where understanding lost its importance. Even with the sphere inert, its astoricum would keep souls from fraying providing they stayed within the tower. But that would not save Athenoch's crops, or its livestock. Better to fade away, body and soul, than starve.

"How much blesswood do we have?" she asked softly.

"Enough for a few weeks," Fadiya replied. "Maybe a month, if the Veil doesn't grow hungrier."

"It will," said Tanith, with morose finality. "We have to evacuate."

"If it's happening here, it's happening everywhere," said Kat bitterly. "Most folk won't notice at first. They'll just think it's a particularly persistent Mistfall, but as the weeks pass and the blesswood runs out ..."

She fell silent, her mind so gummed that she could barely think. The more she strove to grasp the enormity of it all, the more impossible the task became. In her heart of hearts she'd never expected to survive the fight against Tzal, not after so many others had died. But she'd hoped that victory was possible, even if she didn't live to see it. Maybe she'd even hang on long enough to see Azra freed, if she was lucky. That had always been the greatest of her fool's hopes, holding her together through each new disaster. But this? This was the end of everything.

Are you happy, you miserable corpse? she raged silently. *Is this the future you wanted for your people?*

Caradan Diar shifted in the depths of her soul but gave no sign of having heard.

Deadwinds take him anyway.

Tanith was right: anger helped. It burned away the horror and kindled purpose. Possibility. Not much of one, perhaps, but it was better to attempt something and fail than cling to blesswood flames until they went out.

"*Mathami*, I need you to do something for me."

Still pale, Fadiya nodded. Firebloods didn't lightly succumb to horror and didn't linger there long. Those that were worthy of the title, at least. "Name it."

"Get every skyworthy ship provisioned for as long a voyage as can be managed – speak to Marida, she'll help. Make sure they're fit to sail on my return."

"Why, where will you be?"

Kat stared out into the starlit night, past Athenoch's streets and the celebrations of folk who didn't yet know that their world was collapsing, out to where the Veil's mists smudged the horizon. "I have to finish what Vallant started."

Thirty-Six

Amarid's *Dream* plunged through the mists, its smoke-stained lateen sail and lateral outriggers unfurled to steal every scrap of the Veil's impossible wind. The dhow was neither so fast nor so sleek as *Sadia's Revenge*. However, it had emerged from the Battle of Tyzanta unscathed but for a scorched bulwark where the other was little more than a battered hulk.

Given the tragedy of Vallant's last voyage, Kat had sought only volunteers for its reprise. She could have filled the dhow a dozen times over with those who stepped forward, but in the end had refused all but a bare crew of thirty – sufficient to manage the ship, but few enough to spare her conscience should the worst befall.

Tarin had been among the refused. At Fadiya's urging, Kat had finally spoken with him, though she'd little to offer the lad but her regrets. He'd borne them stoically and asked to join her crew in order to honour his uncle's sacrifice. She'd refused as gently as haste had permitted. With his injuries Tarin was in no condition to be anything other than a burden. All the same, she'd taken comfort from the boy's reluctance to blame her for Mirzai's death.

A lookout cupped his hands to his mouth. "Something off the starboard bow!"

The mists shifted. The jagged stone stump of a black tower loomed beyond the bulwark. Its uppermost storeys were long since gone, claimed by whatever disaster had left the remains canted at a fifteen-degree angle. Had it once housed a silver and astoricum sphere as Athenoch's did? Had another town nestled in its Veil-shadow? Not for the first time, Kat was struck by how little she knew about the Veil. Her whole life it had been a supernatural presence to be feared and cheated, not understood. The tower passed away aft and lingered for a time, memorial to a forgotten past, then the Veil swallowed it up as though it had never been.

"A good sign," said Zephyr, standing beside her at the ship's wheels. "Not far adrift now, are we."

Kat's ears pricked up at the certainty in her words. "Does that mean your memory's coming back?"

"Pieces. Glimpses. Dreams of terror and flame. The rest is gone for ever. Always the same, it is, when the mists wear *akîa* away." Zephyr scowled. "Treat with the Elders must we, and hope they will guide as they did before."

Hope. There it was again, the great illusion that brought salvation out of defiance. Kat shivered and looked her up and down, watchful for the telltale red glint to her eyes. Zephyr was always more diffuse behind the Veil than beyond it, but the difference was starker than memory recalled, her womanly form and gown gauzy against the greenish-white. Like Tanith, she was more soul – or *akîa*, as she called it – than was healthy. "Can you hold together?"

Zephyr's musical laugh danced away into the mists. "Afraid I'll become all hunger and no *akîa*? Nothing to fear, have you. Rooted am I in friendship and purpose." She raised a hand to her throat, her fingers reaching for a choker – and its red-gold brooch – no longer there. It and she had been inseparable until *Chainbreaker* had been lost to the mists. She dropped her hand to the wheel. "Miss the touch of astoricum, I do. The slivers in this ship sustain, but they do not comfort."

Kat empathised. Even with the Veil's hunger blunted by the precious scraps of astoricum embedded behind the ship's ifrîti prisms, it was impossible to ignore the skeins of mist clutching at body and soul. In time they'd both fade to nothingness as the Veil stole away sense of self and purpose.

She breathed deep, the nostalgia-laced scent a hundred downy claws seeking purchase in her lungs, and made another attempt to determine how long they'd been travelling. Time flowed strangely in the mists, the span of days calculable only after the fact, when sun or stars again shone overhead. Even astoricum couldn't keep the mists' influence wholly at bay.

Zephyr's unease went far deeper than her own. The rest of the crew, Kat included, were sailing into the unknown. Bad enough, but Zephyr was retracing a path already trodden. One that she'd survived where no one else had. Not all unknowns were equal, and not all horrors could be shared. "You didn't have to do this."

She arched the ghost of an eyebrow, her expression once again more sardonic than maudlin. "And what would you have done had I not?"

"That's not the point," said Kat. "You've lived in the mists your whole life. Even if the Veil claims Khalad, you'll be safe."

Zephyr shook her head. "Not so certain, am I. Colder have the mists become, more insistent. Or perhaps I feel my missing pieces keener for lingering in its grasp." She sighed, her extremities uncoiling to vapour, only to draw inward with her following breath. "And it matters little when all is spoken and more is done. I have lived in the mists, but they were never my home. When my family forsook me, I found another. Stand with them, will I, as surely as they would stand with me."

"Thank you," said Kat, surprised to hear her so sincere.

"And besides," Zephyr continued as if Kat hadn't spoken, "not so long ago my kind offered yours false hope of freedom. Anfai burned because of it. Sleep easier, I would, were that debt settled. Owe Mirzai that much, I do."

Another soul burdened by loss, but Zephyr had earned her sorrow. She'd known Mirzai better than any of them. "Speaking of sleep," said Kat, "you've been clinging to those wheels since we left Athenoch. Even you need to rest sometime."

"And how will you steer, *waholi*?" asked Zephyr, her voice rippling with more amusement than disdain. "Blind in the mists, you are."

Kat shrugged. "True, but this *waholi* has been paying attention." She levelled a pointed stare at the rope looped tight about the lateral wheel's uppermost spindle. "We've been locked off for some time now. You're letting the winds carry us in."

Zephyr raised her brows; surprised, perhaps even a little impressed. "If all goes well, straight to Xe'iathî we will come."

"Zee-ath-ee?" Kat echoed the unfamiliar word and knew even before a smile tugged at Zephyr's mouth that she'd botched the pronunciation. "That's where you're from?"

"Just a poor gust am I," said Zephyr. "Unfit even to wait at tables in so grand a place. But only with the Elders will we find help, so to Xe'iathî we must go."

"And I don't imagine the Elders will talk to me without you?" More than that, Kat wasn't at all certain she wanted to speak to *them*. Conversation with Zephyr was akin to walking blindfold and barefoot across a room scattered with iron scrap. The Elders were likely worse.

"Wore away what little patience they had, did Vallant." Zephyr offered a crooked smile. "That much I *do* remember."

Kat folded her arms. "Then it does us no good if you're bone-weary when we arrive." She met Zephyr's stare dead-on. Some figures of speech applied poorly to the vaporous Issnaîm. Kat wasn't even sure Zephyr *had* bones. "You know what I mean."

"I—"

"Get some rest." She twitched a one-sided shrug. "I'll touch nothing except to stop us hitting something we shouldn't, and even then I'll wake you at once."

With obvious reluctance, Zephyr stepped away from the wheels. "Hold you to that, shall I."

Halfway to the quarterdeck companionway she glanced back, features crowded with suspicion. Seeing that Kat had made no move towards the wheels, she drifted away out of sight.

369

Left alone, with no soul closer than the aftercastle lookout, Kat's thoughts drifted to those left behind in the mists. She'd no fears for Athenoch. Between Fadiya and Marida the evacuation could be in no better hands. There was always the possibility that some englamoured refugee might attempt to cause trouble in the Eternity Queen's name, but Kat was confident that Athenoch's custodians were equal to the task . . . and she'd lined Hadîm's pockets with a fortune in tetrams just in case they weren't.

More, she worried over her friends in Zariqaz, Rîma most of all. Did they know that the Veil was on the move? Zariqaz lay at the heart of Khalad, and the mists would claim all else before its golden spire at last succumbed, but succumb it would.

And what of this voyage, born of desperate hope more than expectation? It was said that there was no truer sign of madness than repeating an action and expecting a different result. The first attempt to breach the mists had already claimed Vallant and the *Chainbreaker* . . . What right did Kat have to hope for better? The striving seemed born of arrogance more than salvation.

As the hours slipped away, the arguments chased round and round in her head, bleaker with every repetition. She found herself unable to resist revisiting them, enraptured by the futility of it all.

This is your chance. Turn us around.

Her stomach tensed at the silent voice. So much for being rid of him. "So you *are* still there?" she murmured, too softly for the aft lookout to hear.

Evidently. Your attempt to imprison me was inventive, but you lack experience.

Better and better. Either he was brazening out humiliation – possible, but unlikely – or her one sanction against an increasingly unwelcome passenger was already worthless. "What do you want?"

I told you. Turn this ship around. Abandon this foolishness.

"Khalad is done, you said it yourself. The Veil is on the move."

Breaching the Veil offers no hope. It will only stir tragedy to disaster.

370

Did he sound *scared*? Maybe not. Kat couldn't imagine that mortal emotions held much sway over Caradan Diar. But something in his voice ... For all that she wanted to close her thoughts to him – if that was even possible – she couldn't discount the possibility of a danger hidden in her plan. "How? If it's so important, tell me."

You are not ready for that knowledge. At best, it will break you. At worst, it will mean the end of everything.

She snorted. "Why should I believe you?"

If you have no faith in my words, why trouble us both with questions? For all its silence, his voice blossomed to fill the mist-laced quarterdeck. *Turn back. Now.*

So he had nothing after all. Just veiled threats and the self-importance of a man too accustomed to getting his own way, afraid of what he had to lose. She'd known so many of those, and her days of falling blindly into line lay long in the past. "No. People are relying on me. I will *not* let them down."

Leadership calls for sacrifice.

"What have *you* sacrificed?" she hissed. "Tell me that. Not your body or your kingdom – you lost those by underestimating the Obsidium Cult! Same for your so-called duty to keep Tzal caged. As long as you've been crawling about my soul you've given nothing, *lost* nothing ... but you lecture me about sacrifice?"

YOU KNOW NOTHING OF MY SACRIFICES!

Kat staggered, his fury sweeping through her soul like a gale. More than fury. Loss. "Isdihar ... You knew she was going to die, even before Tyzanta. You planned it." She swallowed a bitter mouthful as one revelation followed another.

Isdihar accepted her fate. His temper had cooled, but the loss remained. *She understood what was required of her.*

Kat blinked, shaking with so much anger that it was all she could do to stand. "She didn't go to Zariqaz to break Tzal's connection to the Deadwinds, did she? You're responsible for what's happening with the Veil."

It was necessary.

"Necessary?" She didn't care that her bitter shout drew a curious glance from the aft lookout.

Tzal's bond to the Deadwinds cannot be broken, but his fire can be starved.

"Fuel? You're talking about the souls of everyone in Khalad!" The souls of those caught behind the Veil would never reach the Deadwinds. They would simply fade from existence, preventing Tzal from harnessing their soulfire but also denying them the possibility of rebirth. The idea was so vast, so monstrous, that just trying to put it into words set her stomach spasming. "During the Obsidium Uprising you *begged* me to save Isdihar. You told me her death would doom us. 'If she dies, the Cold Flame will take you all.' Your words. What was the point if you meant to destroy us anyway?"

I told you what you needed to hear so that you would protect her from the Obsidium Cult. For the first time he sounded simply old rather than timeless. *Her fate was not forgone. It was my hope that you and I could return Tzal to his cage and Khalad to what it was. But as the months passed, I came to realise that you lacked the will. Whatever you think of me, I loved Isdihar. I have loved all my daughters. I have mourned each one. I would have spared her this.*

"I'm sure that's of great comfort to her now." Awash in horror, Kat succeeded in filling the words with only a fraction of the intended venom. "Why support me at Tyzanta at all?"

To keep Tzal distracted and give Isdihar opportunity to fulfil her purpose.

"And because I was a fallback if she failed," she replied bitterly.

Easy to see how he'd conspired with Isdihar without her knowing. The Eternity King and his Voice had always shared a silent bond. Or perhaps, she thought sourly, Tyzanta hadn't been the first time he'd seized control of her body – merely the first time of which she'd been aware. She'd thought them allies, but in the end was she any less Caradan Diar's puppet than Azra was Tzal's? Before Tyzanta, Tanith

372

had tried to warn her that he was using her. Why hadn't she listened? "I had it right before, didn't I? I really was just a weapon to you."

I will not apologise for deeds done to correct your weakness. Tzal must not be free.

"He's already free, remember? You failed."

The Stars Below were merely the cage. Khalad is the prison. If you breach the Veil, he will follow.

"I won't let him."

What you intend is irrelevant. Turn the ship around. Bid farewell to those you love while you still can.

Kat folded her arms, disgusted that he could even *think* his words would sway her. More and more she felt like he was talking past her. Her father had been much the same before he'd faked his own death: so fixated on his obsessions that he'd lost sight of everything else – even his own daughter. Fitting in a way that the Eternity King had fallen prey to the same delusion. After all, her father had been the one to dethrone him.

"I'm done following your instructions."

Untrue.

The world and its mist-drabbed colours slipped away. Kat plunged into the spirit world of her aetherios tattoo, no longer mortal but ifrît. Caradan Diar's bleak soul rippled past her, rising as she fell, clawing for freedom with tongues of bright indigo flame.

Still plummeting, she grabbed at him, the magenta of her ifrît dabbling and darkening as it bled through his indigo flame. He brushed her aside and continued to rise. She fell faster, the first strands of her tattoo snaring her ankles, her shins, her knees . . .

No! she shouted.

Snared in the web of her tattoo, she felt her body straighten. "I offered you the chance to meet your end with dignity," Caradan Diar said with her voice. "You should have listened."

He reached for the rope securing the pitching wheel. With a rush of horror, Kat realised he didn't mean to turn the *Amarid's Dream* around, but to crash it behind the mists.

She felt her hand close around the rope.

Unseen impact swept her legs out from under her body, throwing it clear of the ship's wheels. She felt a sudden pressure on her back. Another about a wrist that both was and wasn't hers. The dull thud of her head striking timber. The rough scrape of the deck beneath her cheek.

"Back in your box, *your majesty*." Tanith's guttural Kaldosi vowels rippled through the spirit world. "I'm asking nicely."

Caradan Diar howled. The spirit world shuddered, its shadows retreating as a new, vibrant flame coursed across its skies. Exhaustion creaking behind every thought, Kat sank against the web of her tattoo as the fires of her ifrît guttered, drawn aloft by a hungry wind.

"You can't destroy me without killing her," the Eternity King snarled in Kat's voice.

"I know that," said Tanith, much too lightly for Kat's liking. "But I don't *need* her. How much do you need *you*?"

The spirit world dimmed. Kat blinked and found herself face-down against the deck, Tanith kneeling on the small of her back and her right wrist throbbing in an armlock. Gritting her teeth, she dragged Caradan Diar's resentful soul as deep into her tattoo as she could manage. She shuddered at the backwash of his pain. Whatever Tanith had done to him would keep him quiet, at least for a time. "He's gone. You can get off me now."

Tanith sprang lithely to her feet. The dress she'd worn for celebration had long since gone in favour of practical black leathers, her golden hair was braided in thick plaits and black powder darkened her eyes to pools of shadow. Tanith Floranz girded for battle.

Kat rolled to a sitting position and massaged her wrist. "Thanks."

"Your soul tastes disgusting, did you know that?"

"That's probably for the best. Thank you for watching over me."

Tanith shrugged as if it was nothing, but couldn't quite conceal a flush of pride. At her own suggestion she'd shadowed Kat ever since Athenoch, watching for any sign of the Eternity King's re-emergence.

She wasn't the only one watching her now. Both the aft and port lookouts were shooting her sidelong glances far less subtle than they believed. Her heart sinking, Kat resolved to let the rest of the crew in on the secret. They deserved the truth.

"I doubt it'll keep him quiet for long." Tanith helped her to her feet. "His soul . . . there's something different about it. I don't know if I could consume it even if I wanted to. He's probably right about the attempt killing you."

"It won't come to that." Kat swore silently that he'd not take her without a fight again, and wished she still had a deity to pray to.

"I heard part of the argument. Learn anything interesting?"

She hesitated, but Tanith more than anyone deserved the truth. "He's responsible for the Veil's collapse. He's so terrified of Tzal that he's willing to destroy Khalad and everyone in it."

"*Kiasta* . . ." breathed Tanith. "Are you sure we're on the right side?"

"I don't think we were ever on his side. I just hope there really is a realm beyond the mists." Even a wan smile took effort. "Otherwise I'm going to look twice the fool."

"There is," Tanith replied, her certainty the most solid thing about her. "Enna found her way home in the end."

Kat wished she'd met the woman. A high-ranking member of the Obsidium Cult, Enna had turned on them to save Tanith. But even before that she'd nudged Tanith away from her selfish, self-destructive path. But as to whether she truly hailed from beyond the Veil – much less had returned there – Kat had neither notion nor proof. "Then the Issnaîm will show us the way. They showed Vallant."

Tanith scowled. "You really think you can trust them?"

"Sail!" bellowed a lookout. "Sail off the port bow!"

Thirty-Seven

Kat ran for the port bulwark. A scrap of char-black sail and rigging showed through the coiling mist, on the threshold where greenish-white drowned everything. No flag in sight, not yet, nor a scrap of hull. "Reckon it's a drifter?"

Not all ships made it to the safety of a torch house when Mistfall descended. Crews claimed by the mist, they drifted masterless through the Veil until their buoyancy tanks failed.

The lookout spat over the side to ward off bad luck as the sail vanished. "Could be. Done well to stay aloft this deep, though."

"Sail to starboard!" roared another sailrider.

A chill shot along Kat's spine. One drifter was unlikely. Two at once was unheard of. "Crews to their guns!"

The lookout swallowed and ran for the watch bell mounted beside the ship's wheels.

"Wake Zephyr," Kat told Tanith, glad that the daughter of the Issnaîm had this once elected to sleep in a cabin and not, as was often her habit, on the watch platform atop the mainmast.

By the time a dozen sailriders had joined Kat on deck, scimitars, crossbows and shriekers ready in their hands, the starboard sail had vanished.

She beckoned to Bo'sun Yazar, a scrawny man of middle years, little less ragged than the tattered House Jovîna uniform he wore. "Make sure the shrieker cannons are primed, but no one shoots without my order."

Would shrieker cannons even work behind the Veil, or would the flame dissipate before reaching the target? It wasn't soulfire so far as she knew, but she'd never thought to ask. Yazar nodded and ran for the companionway, almost colliding with Zephyr and Tanith coming the other way.

Without waiting to be told, Zephyr drifted past Kat and slipped the restraining ropes from the ship's wheels. "Told me there was a sail, did Tanith."

Kat nodded. "At least two. Can't be both drifters."

"That they are not." Zephyr raised her voice. "Strike the sails! And be making no sudden moves!"

Sailriders hurried to comply without a glance at Kat for confirmation. Most were old hands and knew better than to question Zephyr's authority. With a rush of pulleys, the outriggers retracted. The mainsail furled to its yard, the canvas folds gathered tight by brail ropes. *Amarid's Dream* slowed.

A snatch of melodic, sorrowful song echoed through the mist. Its close, fluid harmonies stroked at Kat's heartstrings until they ached, a perfect match to the Veil's scent of squandered yesterdays. Even as it faded, Zephyr raised her own voice in reply, haltingly at first but with growing confidence, beautiful and terrifying. Not quite the song that had once lulled Tzal to slumber in the Stars Below, but near enough to awaken unhappy memories.

As Zephyr fell silent, Kat caught another glimpse of black canvas off to port, nearer than before. "Those are Issnaîm ships, aren't they?"

Zephyr nodded, her glossy white eyes pensive as they scried the mists. "Read our coming on the currents, did they. Deciding if we are friend or fodder. Take little, it will, to turn the one to the other."

Kat didn't care for how cheerless she looked, nor the uncertainty crowding her voice. "Then we'd better do all we can to convince them we're friendly." She turned to Tanith. "Head below. Tell Yazar to close the gun ports."

"You're sure about that?" asked Tanith.

Amarid's Dream had a respectable eight shrieker cannons, enough to hold its own against anything short of a redcloak war dhow, but getting into a firefight with the Issnaîm could only end badly. Win or lose, their search would be over. "No, but do it anyway."

Tanith nodded and ran for the companionway. Gasps rang out along the deck as another scrap of sail pierced the starboard mists.

"If we have to fight, what are our chances?" asked Kat.

"Slower than us, are they," said Zephyr, "and sluggish. Rely on surprise, they do. If dead they wished us, dead we'd already be."

"I thought your people never left the mists."

She laughed bleakly. "Think your kind are the only ones to quarrel among yourselves, do you?"

The starboard mists billowed apart and a vast dark shape swooped towards *Amarid's Dream*, so majestic and grotesque that it stole Kat's breath away.

The Issnaîm vessel wasn't a skyship as such things were reckoned in Khalad, where long centuries of nautical history had shaped both form and function to the trackless Cloudsea. Rather, it was the colossal, skeletal corpse of some winged beast twice the length of *Amarid's Dream*, its bones lashed tight by a web of ropes and a ridge of black lateen sails cresting its spine. Scraps of that same canvas formed the membrane of its rigid ossified wings and bloomed as spinnakers above and below. Rippling shadow formed a low bulwark across its upper ribcage and shoulder blades to form some semblance of a deck. A patchwork lattice of the same stretched fore and aft to support its serpentine neck and tail. Even in death, the narrow, reptilian skull retained a haunting nobility and a predator's leer. Kat had seen such a beast before, but only in her father's sketchbook, surrounded by scrawled facsimiles of cuneiform and scribbled passages claiming the goddess Nyssa had three faces rather than the accepted two.

"It's a drakon," she breathed, as wary awe descended across the deck.

"A drakon it *was*," Zephyr corrected bitterly. "Nothing but bones

378

and malice for thousands of years are they, yet still we refuse to let them rest."

The drakon wheeled about, its port wingtip yards from the starboard bow, and Kat at last saw the ungainliness to which Zephyr had alluded. Though its bones jerked and quivered as ropes slackened or went taut, the limbs remained unmoving. Wings that had once borne the creature aloft were now little more than pitching sails, adjusted by the tapestry of shadowy ropes. Kat's wonder bled away to pity. Whatever temperament the drakon had possessed in life, it surely deserved better than to be more than an ungainly, ramshackle skyship in death.

The second drakon emerged from the portside mists and swept past the prow, the wind of its passage tugging at Kat's hair. Along the main deck, sailriders clasped interlinked hands to their chests in the sign of the Flame, and gripped their weapons tighter.

"Keep your nerve!" called Kat.

A heavy mist-shadow fell across the deck as the first drakon yawed closer. A dozen Issnaîm crested its bulwark and descended to the quarterdeck of *Amarid's Dream*, hazy blossoms drifting on the Veil's impossible wind.

Zephyr at her side, Kat went to meet them. The foremost was a tall fellow with a neat black beard that glittered with the light of captive stars. He wore a high-collared coat the same bluish-white as his skin and bore at his waist a curved scabbard inlaid with red-gold astoricum. His form shifted and rippled as if it sprang more from imperfect memory than truth, but his glossy white eyes held no telltale red of *akia* in retreat, only ill-hidden surprise.

"What here have we?" he said, gazing at Zephyr. "Thought you lost to mists and madness, did we, Xepheri of Hollowhal."

"And very nearly I was, Scirran," she replied, "but seek the path again we must. Will you escort us to Xe'iathî, *nasaîm*?"

Scirran loosed a hearty baritone laugh. "So you can lead another *waholi* crew to their doom? Do you hate them so?" He looked on Kat for the first time. "A siren is she, and you a fool for ..."

His genial expression crowded with wrath. His scimitar glistened like silver ice as it left its scabbard, the metal as much the memory of a blade as his coat was of cloth. "What have you brought among us, outcast?"

The air glittered as the other Issnaîm reached for their weapons. Kat spread her arms, palms out, as her sailriders drew their own blades. "No! We need allies, not a fight."

Zephyr drifted between her and Scirran, anger lending her solidity. "No threat to you is she."

"No threat?" Scirran's eyes burned into Kat's. "Stained black is her *akîa*, withered and rotted."

Kat froze, the ghost of Caradan Diar's bitter laughter on the edge of her hearing. Not triumphant, not even amused, simply the weariness of a man confronted by the punchline of a tedious joke he'd long seen coming.

Zephyr gave a vicious shake of the head. "A soulweaver is she. You perceive the shadow of the dead she carries within."

Scirran snorted. "And what would a lowly menial know of it? Marked by the Betrayer she is! Praise the Drowned Lady that I should see this day. After all this time, avenged shall our people be." He glared at Kat anew. "You wish to see the Elders? Receive you gladly they shall, if briefly."

"Don't be so sure about that." Tanith's words issued from behind Kat, accompanied by a whisper of drawn steel. "A lot of terrible things could happen to a lot of people between now and then."

A throaty growl of agreement issued up from the main deck, warning of a situation sliding towards disaster. Kat pinched her eyes shut, Scirran's words and the Eternity King's reaction painting a bleak picture, even if the detail of the brushwork escaped her.

"Indeed they could." Zephyr brushed Scirran's scimitar aside with the flat of her hand and reached for her own.

Kat put her hand on Zephyr's shoulder. "No. He's right. There's something terrible in my soul. There has been for a long time. I should have told you. I should have told everyone." She breathed deep, guilt for what the Eternity King had done at Tyzanta – what he'd meant to do bare minutes before – returning fourfold. "But Athenoch can't afford this fight. Captain Scirran: is the word of an Issnaîm everything that Zephyr has led me to believe?"

"An aether caste of the first rank, am I." He glared at Zephyr. "Ten times a menial's slender honour is my word worth."

"Then promise my crew safe passage and you may bring me to your Elders."

Thirty-Eight

S ave for the redcloaks who brought bowls of suspect gristly stew and emptied his slops bucket, Damant saw no one for days. He knew the cell well enough, with its high barred window that barely allowed sunlight to touch the crumbling plaster walls but somehow ushered in enough wind to leave him shivering through the night. Even if he hadn't, the sour smell would have betrayed that he was in the bowels of the outer palace, where servants forever fought a losing battle to repair a sewer system never designed for the grandness of the buildings towering above.

Yes, he knew the cell: the immediate neighbour of the one that had lately held Mirela Bascari.

What he didn't know was how he'd come to be there.

He recalled the battle in the sanctum – in blurs of light and sound if not cohesive detail – but everything between Isdihar's scream and waking atop the thin mattress, barefoot and in shirtsleeves, was ... gone. What had become of Isdihar? Of Kastagîr? Of Rîma, most of all.

He'd spent the first day worried that the events were missing because the Eternity Queen's glamour had taken him once more. Logic eventually overwhelmed that concern. If he had become her thrall anew, she'd have had no reason to imprison him, and he no fears to entertain. On the third day, when his wounds had scabbed over and his aches retreated to dull and distant throbs, uncertainty festered to the notion that a great deal more time had passed since the sanctum than he'd first assumed. How would he know? How *could* he know? So much of his life had been a battle for order. The possibility of losing that control for a second time thinned the foul air, made every breath a rasping, harrowing effort.

In that hour it was Yali who saved him – or rather her unhappy example. Loneliness and doubt had finally worn away her resistance to the Eternity Queen's glamour. They would do the same to him, should he let them.

That realisation jolted him out of his downward spiral, and he forced himself to seek structure in his confinement. Purpose. Claim what order he could and sanity alongside. Even if Rîma was still free, he couldn't rely on her to be his salvation yet again.

Even in rags, he'd *that* much pride remaining.

From small sounds and hushed conversation beyond the bars, he divined that the other cells were empty. He noted the hours at which the guardroom – dimly heard along the corridor – changed shifts. Through lidded and weary eyes he examined the redcloaks who brought his meals and emptied his bucket. Two with drawn swords to preclude violence on his part while a third attended to the task. Only ... the shorter of the evening's duo moved with a distinct limp, her reactions notably slower. Not much of an opening, but desperation brought its own advantage – perhaps enough to wrest away a weapon. After that, it was "merely" a matter of overcoming the other two redcloaks without drawing attention ... and after *that*, all he need do was escape the dungeons, the palace, the Golden Citadel and then – most likely – Zariqaz itself.

But what else was there?

Fraying sanity aside, he'd a duty to help the others if he could – if they yet lived – and to warn Arvish that whatever plans she'd entertained were dead as dust. Or were they? Had Isdihar succeeded in those final moments? Was the Eternity Queen even now severed from the Deadwinds?

Irrelevant. When it came to a choice between the slow creep of insanity from being trapped in a cell and death in a possibly futile gesture, the second held far greater appeal.

So it was that by the time evening rolled around on the fifth day, Damant had made what preparations he could: a fistful of hoarded grit to fling into the face of the limping guard, and the slops bucket in ready reach for the other. Socially and otherwise unexpected nightsoil made a formidable impression.

It was therefore a great pity that the evening's footsteps resolved to five redcloaks, rather than the usual three. Led by a *sarhana*, no less. Damant gritted his teeth. With those numbers, already difficult odds steepened sharply. A pair of drawn shriekers lengthened them to impossibility. Rîma could likely have done it, but he wasn't Rîma.

Where was she?

"Bring him," snapped the *sarhana*.

Damant offered no resistance as the redcloaks shepherded him from the cell and up the steep dungeon stair. Not that cooperation forestalled the "encouragement" of the open-palmed shove or the strike of a boot against his calves – the usual indulgences of weak, vicious souls given licence. Had he ever been like that as a young custodian? He thought not – he *hoped* not – but those days seemed further in the past than ever.

A junction beckoned at the stairs' summit. A left turn beneath the statue of Nyssa Iudexas meant that they were bound for Sinners' Walk, and he for execution on the Golden Stair. It made any risk, any odds, acceptable. Worse than taking his last look at the setting sun with a koilos' flamberge at his neck was arriving there without a fight. He let himself stumble, his shoulders slumped. Mock weakness was a poor weapon, but the only one he had. Well, not *quite* his only weapon: he still had a fistful of grit clamped between his fingers. That and the steep stair behind might account for two of the guards if fortune was with him.

The *sarhana* turned right at the top of the stairs. Now thoroughly confused, Damant was still re-examining his potential fates when his escort marched him into the dimly lit dungeon chapel. Graven likenesses of ember-saints stared down from filthy, time-worn alcoves, the interplay of light and shadow from flickering lumani seeming to rouse their fleshless, hollow faces to motion.

The Eternity Queen stood at the altar, silver hair and golden dress shimmering and a deep indigo halo about her shoulders. "So good of you to join us, Ihsan."

A heavy boot struck the back of Damant's knee and he crashed to the tiles, his precious handful of grit rushing through his fingers. His fall stirred a pungent, eye-stinging swirl of grey tessence dust, the incense of yesteryear still musky with lavender and juniper. Coughing and spluttering, knees against tile and one hand braced against the floor, he cuffed at his eyes with the inside of his filthy sleeve.

When he lowered his arm, a bloodshot gaze met his from inches away.

Damant didn't recognise Kastagîr at first, not beneath the blood and grime caked into his hair and five-day stubble. Even without the filth, the witless watery stare and vacant broken-toothed smile was so unlike the proud man he knew. The rotten-meat stench of him grew sourer still as cracked lips split to a crazed, wheezing chuckle.

The Eternity Queen tugged on the golden rope leashed about Kastagîr's neck. "Faizâr, please. Show some manners."

He howled and scurried back to her side on hands and feet, the torn and soiled rags of what had once been his uniform stirring the incense dust anew. He yelped as she aimed a kick at him, finally coming to rest hunched and trembling against the altar, and gazed up at her in a blend of terror and adoration as his filthy broken-nailed hands pawed at her skirts.

"That's better," she said, talking to Damant and not the broken mess at her feet. "I think I prefer him like this, don't you?"

The air thickened with gossamer apparitions. Seductive pleading mutterings brushed at the back of Damant's thoughts. Distended, crooked fingers grasped at his arms, urging his soul to cast loose from his mortal body and embrace her glory. He clamped his eyes shut, blotting out the Eternity Queen even as she grew more vibrant, more beautiful. His soul became heavier in the darkness, but the whispers faded to nothing. When he opened his eyes, he found the Eternity Queen staring down at him, her brow furrowed.

"So she's still protecting you?" she murmured. "If only Amakala's line had showed this creativity in *my* service. I'd have been free of Caradan Diar long ago."

He knelt back and halted when the cold pressure of a scimitar's point touched his neck. Knowing that he'd no reason to fear slipping back under the Eternity Queen's control left him feeling better than he had since awakening in the cell. "I'm sorry to disappoint."

"Don't be. When you've existed for as long as I have, surprises are the rarest of luxuries. But I wanted to be certain, you see. I'd thought you might yet be useful, but alas it seems only as an example." She sighed. "Is there anything more wasteful than misguided ingenuity? You know my name, don't you? My *real* name."

She offered a sly smile. For all that her body was now of an age with Damant's, she was no less the Yennika Bascari he'd first met. Imperious and impish. But he knew at once that wasn't the name she wanted to hear. Not a good sign given the six witnesses, but he supposed that Kastagîr no longer counted for much of anything, and the five redcloaks were certainly deep in her glamour.

"Tzal," he replied stonily.

"Not Nyssa?" She flashed another smile. "How quickly faith unravels."

"Khalad will be free of you."

"Free of me? Darling, I *am* Khalad."

"I'm sure Caradan Diar used to say the same."

"He chose Nyssa to be my name, did you know? He thought a goddess would be more endearing than a god. More palatable. But believe me, mortal or divine, women are nothing but trouble."

She aimed another kick at Kastagîr, who prostrated himself and covered his head with his hands.

"Take Azra. I knew she was still in here, but not how much agency she'd stolen while I slept. She's gone ... at least in all the ways that matter. What's left of her is screaming as I peel the last of her secrets away. Who knows what I'll find?" She pursed her lips and stared off into the shadows of the chapel, her voice dropping to a conspiratorial murmur. "I should be used to having pieces of me rebel by now, but this feels different. It's so intimate. There's a thrill to it. You really have no idea."

More and more there was something off about the Eternity Queen's behaviour. Damant couldn't put his finger on it, but supposed fretful days behind bars had taken their toll. "Where's Rîma? Yali?"

Another shrug. "My high handmaiden has resumed her duties. As for the Tadamûri witch? Like you, she's to be part of tomorrow's spectacle. A reminder and warning to the masses. I would have preferred Caradan Diar's whelp to join you, but her little act of sabotage didn't leave enough to be worth the bother." Malice glinted behind the words. "I still keep finding scraps of ash in my sanctum."

Damant's heart sank as he thought back to his last – his *first* – real conversation with Isdihar Diar, in the tunnels beneath the palace. *Now I hae duty of my own. I will see it done, even at the cost of my life.* She'd known how it would end. She'd even tried to tell him.

"That poor, noble child." He swallowed, struck by the sense of utter loss at no longer having a deity to whom he could pray for comfort, or to commend a valiant soul. "But we did what we came to do. That counts for something."

"And what do you suppose that was?"

"Your days of siphoning souls from the Deadwinds are done. The next attempt on your life will be the last ... assuming your body lasts that long."

She laughed. "Is that the lie she sold you? Ihsan, I *am* the Deadwinds. We are one. Shake Khalad to pieces and still it and I will be bound. The siphonic prism in the throne immortal leached the Deadwinds not to sustain me but to hold the Veil at bay. That poor, noble child *used* you to bring about the end of the world. Her sire failed in his duty to imprison me, so she chose to lay waste to all that is. Very precocious."

He blinked, horror creeping through thoughts suddenly numbed. "I don't believe you."

"Would you like to see the sanctum? The sphere no longer turns. Its companions on the border will be fading, even the one in your precious Athenoch. When that happens, no amount of blesswood will save Khalad. The next time the pressure between the worlds shifts and Mistfall comes, we'll be done. It may take weeks or months, but Khalad will slip away, never to return."

Damant clenched his fists. Could it be true? Had Isdihar planned this from the start? Had Rîma? No ... Rîma wouldn't have had any of this. She wouldn't sacrifice the very people she professed to save. But Isdihar, borne down by duty ...

My life hae never been my own.

She'd tried to warn him. Why hadn't he listened? Because he'd been so desperate to strike a blow, to sweep away his own unwilling deeds, that he'd clutched at any straw. And now Isdihar Diar – who'd trembled with a determination too many went without their whole lives – was dead, and Khalad's battle against the Veil was dead alongside.

So why wasn't the Eternity Queen troubled? If the Veil swallowed Khalad, she was as lost as any of them.

"You don't seem concerned," he said, as evenly as he could manage.

"Futility is the mother of invention," she replied airily.

"That's not much of an answer." But then Tzal was divine, not mortal. Maybe the mists had no claim on him.

"It's all you're going to get. Khalad's evolution has taken so many strange paths, but I didn't expect this. My fault for seeking out surprises, I suppose. I find I'm not even that troubled by your treachery, darling. I should be, but I'm not. *That's* the part I find concerning. Isn't that strange?"

It wasn't to Damant, not now he'd had time to piece together all the little oddities of the Eternity Queen's behaviour. Her continued humiliation of Kastagîr. The self-congratulatory flourishes. The fact that he and Rîma were to be executed in spectacular fashion when glamour prevented much of the population from recognising or caring about spectacle. And then there was the *darling*: that little faux-affectionate flourish that Yennika and Azra had both used like common punctuation . . . but which the Eternity Queen had not prior to that day. Azra had once said that Yennika and Tzal were the same being. With Azra extinguished, it seemed that was truer than ever. That was worth a little hope. Maybe Nyssa was as infallible as the legends told. Maybe that was even true of Tzal. But Yennika? Yennika was far from perfect. It had never been enough for her to simply win; she had to be *seen* to have won.

Unfortunately, he didn't know how that helped him. "Then maybe you shouldn't have me executed?"

She knelt before him, incense ash dulling the golden shimmer of her skirts. "Oh Ihsan, you don't know how tempting that is. But an example must be set . . . one way or the other."

She leaned in and kissed him on the cheek, lingering long enough for her breath to warm his skin even as the cold indigo flames of her halo chilled his soul. Then she stood abruptly, yanked on Kastagîr's leash and glared past Damant to the *sarhana*.

"Take the traitor back to his cell." She smiled, her tongue darting across perfect teeth. "And make sure he falls down the stairs along the way."

Thirty-Nine

There was no meal that night, not that Damant would have felt much like eating even had one been presented.

True to their instructions, his redcloak escort had given him a hearty shove at the top of the dungeon steps, and on realising that he'd survived the descent with only bruises and a sharp crack on the head to his name, had remedied the dearth with boot and fist, reopening old wounds along the way. Unable to sleep, he lay on the bed as swollen flesh stiffened, every breath stabbing broken ribs into his left side, and watched a fat, crook-legged spider as it worked to expand its silken web in the corner between ceiling and wall.

Worse than anything was the knowledge of utter failure. He'd have gone gladly to execution had they severed the Eternity Queen's connection to the Deadwinds. Instead, he'd helped Isdihar destroy Khalad. It still seemed so unreal – a prospect too large for the mind to fully contain, much less understand – but he believed it. He felt it in every inch of his aching body. The Veil was coming for Khalad, and it was all his fault.

As midnight came and went, and the echo of conversation from the guardroom eased into silence, fortune found another avenue of torment.

"I wasn't sure I should believe it," murmured a voice outside the cell door. "Ihsan Damant, the terror of skelders from Zariqaz to Tyzanta, locked up, beaten down and marked for death."

Damant dragged himself upright and lurched towards the door. Tuzen Karza stood just beyond the bars, in what were for him quite sombre clothes, his attempt at impassivity undermined by the slight curl of a smile. "What do you want?"

"Perhaps I had to see this for myself. You have to admit, you're quite a sight . . . and quite a smell." Karza's smile broke cover. "Or perhaps—"

Damant's swollen knee buckled as he lunged, but momentum compensated for failing flesh. The straining fingers of his right hand skirted the bars and clamped about Karza's throat, choking him to silence. Damant gripped the door's crossbar with his left hand – rousing a chorus of pained complaint from his ribs, but pain was transitory and some deeds important – and yanked Karza face-first into the bars. The *clang* of the door in its frame drowned out sudden frantic spluttering.

"Get . . . off, you . . . fool," Karza wheezed. He locked his two hands around Damant's one, colour rising to his cheeks as he fought to pull himself free.

"Not a chance." Damant leaned in, his face as close to Karza's as the bars allowed. "This is one mistake I *can* set right."

How long until the sounds of the struggle made themselves known in the guardroom? Long enough for him to squeeze Karza's head off his shoulders, maybe?

Abandoning his attempts to prise Damant's fingers from about his throat, Karza braced his hands against the bars and tore free. Damant collapsed against the door as Karza caromed off the adjoining wall.

Still spluttering, he staggered upright and rubbed at his reddened throat. "That wasn't friendly. I've a good mind to leave you there."

His left hand, previously empty, held a heavy key. The smile returned to his lips, but this time with none of the hauteur that had so thoroughly earned Damant's contempt in past months. With a hundred tiny changes to posture and expression, Tuzen Karza melted away, leaving a haler – though not necessarily humbler – man in his place.

Damant slumped, his forehead braced against the cool angular iron of the bars. "You bastard."

"Be nice. I can still leave you there." Tatterlain set the key in the lock and made a half-turn, only to slap his forehead as the mechanism bit. "Almost forgot."

He fished in his pocket, produced the smooth metal sphere of an aether bomb and depressed its tiny plunger.

Damant shuddered, the rage of the unleashed ravati ifrît more imagined than felt as it spiralled unseen and upward towards the distant Deadwinds. The hestic above the door would already be in retreat, temporarily cowed by the ravati's passage, but so would many scores of others caught in its skyward path. Across the palace, lumani had already gone dark, motic-sealed doors would refuse to open ... even koilos might pause in their patrols. "Subtle."

Tatterlain turned the key. "You really *do* want to stay here, don't you?"

Damant lurched through the door. He sank heavily against the wall, shoulder screaming as the pressure on unhappy bones shifted. "I ... need a moment."

A good many moments. Maybe enough to last the rest of his life.

"Here." A vial of last breath glimmered as Tatterlain broke it under his nose. "It's not much, but it should get you moving."

Damant inhaled as deeply as his broken ribs allowed, the worst of his harms drifting off on lavender clouds even before the prickle faded from his nostrils. "Thanks."

Tatterlain shrugged. "I think of everything." He held up a cautioning hand as Damant made to push away from the wall. "Easy. Easy. Take that moment. There's a fair walk ahead. If it's any consolation, Rîma was in an even worse way. Her own fault, really. She does rather encourage folk not to take chances around her."

"She's alive?"

"For now. But isn't that all any of us can hope for?"

Damant nodded, his strength returning as pain melted away. "Some custodian I am. You had me completely fooled."

"I *am* Tuzen Karza. Did you doubt it?"

"It was a good performance." Which didn't assuage the feeling of foolishness for not having recognised it as such.

"That's not what I meant." His lips twisted in a scowl utterly unbefitting of Karza and only marginally less so of Tatterlain. "Tuzen Karza saw life as an endless parade of opportunities to imbibe, inhale, swindle or bed. But for some reason his brother Arazen loved him. He dragged him out of bawdy houses and gutters. Cleared his endless parade of debts. And how was he repaid? When the Phoenissan custodium came for him on trumped-up charges of corruption, Karza could have dispelled them with a word. After all, he was fourth in line for head of House Karza, while Arazen was illegitimate. He was too arrogant and too afraid. Arazen died in the mines. The better part of me died with him. When I finally sobered up, I sought out Vallant. It was what Arazen would have done had he not wasted his life tidying up after me. He lived to help others."

"I see." So much about Tatterlain made sense now, not least the crimes committed for Vallant in Karza's – his *own* – name. Like Azra, he'd imbued his former self with every loathed trait and mannerism, and every inch of blame besides. Only while Azra was Yennika Bascari as she could have been – perhaps *would* have been, but for her cousins' abuse – Karza was Tatterlain's true self. He wasn't the performance; *Tatterlain* was the performance. No wonder he'd remained untouched by the Eternity Queen's glamour. He'd already been living a lie. "I'm sorry."

Tatterlain shrugged as though the matter was nothing. "No tears for self-inflicted wounds. I confess I have found it far too easy to be myself of late." He offered a wan smile. "Rîma asked me to take up the old mantle and be her contingency. One does not lightly refuse her requests. It would have been easier if she'd kept me informed of her plans, but she's a daemon for secrets when the mood takes her."

Damant thought back to their last encounter, when he'd found Karza – Tatterlain's manner encouraged thinking of them as different people – hammering on a handmaiden's door. "That's why you were snooping around Yali's suite."

He nodded. "It did me no good. Eavesdropping on the deaf is a fool's hobby."

"Does Yali know?"

"If she did, we'd have been neighbours this past week." He shot a pensive glance along the corridor towards the guardroom. "Are you good to move?"

"No," Damant replied, "but we've pushed our luck too far already."

"I wouldn't worry about the guards," said Tatterlain. Even with cheer returning to his voice and expression, it did so without a trace of Karza's pompous self-regard. "I think of everything."

So it proved. The guardroom held not a waking soul, the soft breathiness of folk lost to the arms of sleep the only sounds within. Two sat sprawled at the table, face-down in half-finished meals. Another in a spray of pentassa cards. Only the last might have passed for conscious, and that was purely because he'd slumped backwards into his chair rather than forwards.

"Looks like some akori seed found its way into the stew," said Tatterlain. "What has Zariqaz come to when you can't even trust the serving staff?"

The guardroom held two other doors save the one by which they'd entered, one of which led up to the chapel in which the Eternity Queen had held her brief audience and thence to the palace proper. Tatterlain struck out for the other.

"Wait." Damant grabbed at his arm, regretting it as a thousand tiny daemons attacked his left side with daggers. Last breath was miraculous, but even miracles had their limits. "Wrong way."

Tatterlain levelled a patient stare. "My dear Damant, notoriety aside, you look and smell like a corpse. There are a dozen gates between here and the outside world. At least half of them are guarded, and after I let off that aether bomb, at least half of those guards will be on the lookout for trouble. But be my guest, have at it."

"Or?" Damant grimaced. *You look and smell like a corpse.* "You can't be serious."

"I am never anything other than sober, save in the course of duty."

Tatterlain in the lead, they passed through the door and descended a long straight stair, the tidemarks of discoloured stone betraying generation upon generation of buildings fashioned atop those that had come before. The air soured with every step, its rank and musty smell overpowering even Damant's unenviable odour. At last they reached a second door, this one edged with a greased leather baffle to ensure an airtight fit. Another identical door awaited just four paces along the floor's uneven stones. It was locked, but Tatterlain had a good many keys at his disposal that night.

As he hauled the door open, the stench redoubled. Thick with putrefaction, bodily waste and the rotting accretions of ages, it stifled even the memory of sweetness until a maggot itself would have gagged. In the tunnel beyond, a time-worn stone jetty projected into a viscous and turgid sewer flow, its contents mercifully hidden by shadows that the thin lumani prism atop the doorway had no hope of penetrating. A stack of tarred wooden coffins fronted the upstream edge of the jetty. Another sat, lid open, on the narrow slipway opposite. A corroded iron hoop jutted up and out from the base, pointing roofwards at a forty-five-degree angle.

"We've not had much rain of late," Tatterlain breathed, his elbow crooked across mouth and nose. "So as long as your heart doesn't give out in a burst of unbridled ecstasy at this wonderful bouquet, you should stay afloat long enough for a friend of mine to fish you out at the weir gate."

Damant eyed the coffin. Prisoners died in the dungeons all the time, and few rated the trouble of hauling them out through the palace. Better to set them afloat and let the current carry them into the clutches of bodymen and outcast shrivers in the Zariqaz Undertown. A fine escape route, so long as the current didn't falter, the coffin didn't sink or you weren't choked by the noxious air. But the alternative was a beheading on the Golden Stair.

"And you?" he spluttered.

"Unfinished business," Tatterlain replied. "Tuzen Karza abandoned his brother. Tatterlain doesn't leave anyone behind."

His bravado couldn't conceal the danger. The Eternity Queen would be rightly furious to discover her captives fled, and the circle of suspects was growing ever tighter. Karza aside, Igarî Bathîr was the only member of the Queen's Council in Zariqaz yet alive and undisgraced. There was every chance Tatterlain was returning to his death. Damant didn't waste breath pointing that out. Tatterlain surely knew it anyway.

He nodded heavily. "Let's get this over with."

He lay down in the slipway coffin, the tenuous light of the sewer cut off as Tatterlain dragged the lid into place and screwed it down. A heavy shove – the underside of the coffin grating alarmingly beneath Damant's back – and he bobbed into the current.

He lost track of how long he lay there in total darkness, the air growing thinner with every moment, and each lurch and dip of the coffin rousing fears of capsizing or sinking outright. He caught his breath as the coffin juddered against an unseen obstruction, the creak of timber and the dampness beneath his elbow the product – he hoped – of a frantic imagination.

Sounds echoed above and away. Footsteps. Laughter. The rumble of wheels on stone. All muted by the coffin's closeness, distorted by the acoustics of the sewer tunnel. The more fervently he tried to lie still, the more irresistible it became to convulse, to move – to do anything at all – even with the knowledge that to do so was to invite disaster.

The air grew stale and heavy in his lungs. He drifted in the dark, convinced beyond belief that the current had borne him under, his thoughts consumed by grim fascination as to whether he'd suffocate before he drowned – or, given the state of the sewer, choke.

With a hollow *boom*, the coffin struck something solid and slewed about. Unseen stone scraped away beneath. The lid gave way with an angry screech, levered back by the blade of a prybar, black against the overarching brick tunnel. His ears full of a weir's angry rush, Damant gulped down an approximation of fresh air and lurched upright, shaking uncontrollably.

A slender, pale-faced young woman stood beside the coffin, a lumani lantern in one hand and the prybar in the other. A wisp of flame-red hair showed beneath her hood, her green eyes watchful but unafraid as she helped him onto the algae-slick steps. The coffin bobbed against the sluice gate a moment longer, then the current drew it away towards the weir's frothy green-white crest, the rope and hook by which his rescuer had snared it snaking through the murk behind. Damant watched it go and knew with the certainty of stone that he'd never enter a confined space ever again.

The young woman grinned. "The weir nearly had you."

That voice. Just about the last he'd have expected to hear in a Zariqaz sewer: soft and collected, with impeccable cut-glass diction and just a hint of superiority. "Marida?"

She laughed, a sound more musical than the sewer deserved. "Not for some months now. She moved on once the isshîm lost its hold on me."

He heard the difference now. Even at her friendliest, Marida had always leavened her words with mockery or threat as the mood took her. This young woman had nothing of either. Her poise, her confidence – those she could only have learned from the ageless qalimîri who'd once worn her body. But her willowy beauty was all her own, the emaciation of her shîm addiction long months in the past. "Then what do I call you?"

She cocked her head, eyes scouring his for a glimpse of a joke. "Keti? We've met, remember? At conclave."

Damant tried to reconcile this refined, well-spoken young lady with the addled, infantilised trophy who'd hung so readily on Tuzen Karza's every word and favour, but he was too exhausted, too sore and – he increasingly suspected – too old. The skitter of an unseen sewer rat broke his reverie. "Forgive me. It's been a bad week."

Keti offered a smile as elegant as the rest of her. "I've a clatter wagon by the outfall. Let's get you somewhere safe ..." she looked him up and down, her nose wrinkling, "and to a bath."

Forty

The cage of crystal and woven light had once been a marvel, as had the room in which it stood, but in the present, thick black mould thickened the crystal walls, and filth crowded windows that had once been a dozen glittering shades of blue. From what Kat had seen, little of Xe'iathî was in better condition. It had the air of a place long forgotten, though it was plainly inhabited. Silent crowds had watched Scirran march her along webways of woven shadow chased by the same silvered crystalline light that formed the bars of her cage. Seemingly, that light held the entire city aloft. Zephyr had once said that the Issnaîm wove starlight and shadow. Seeing it made it no easier to believe.

As she paced back and forth across her cell, careful not to stray too close to the bars – the air around them hissed hot and cold, and she'd no desire to know what their light would do to unprotected flesh – Kat couldn't help but wonder about Xe'iathî's heyday. Like the drakons by which the Issnaîm charted the skies, the city was a relic of old glories, preserved beyond its time. It resonated with Rîma's tales of Tadamûr, whose traditions had worn its people thin. It wasn't hard to imagine why Zephyr had fled the mists for Khalad. For all its faults, the world beyond the Veil at least felt alive. Xe'iathî felt ... *impermanent*, as if it belonged neither to the mists nor the mortal world.

You should have heeded me, breathed Caradan Diar.

"Chatty again, are we?" The Eternity King was fainter than he'd been aboard the *Amarid's Dream*. Perhaps she'd finally managed to bind him . . . or he was feigning weakness as a prelude to more unpleasantness. "I'd think twice about getting assertive. You seem unpopular around here. I have to say, the title of 'Betrayer' suits you."

You speak from ignorance.

"Do I?" Kat took bleak enjoyment in the moment. Yes, she was helpless, but so was he. "You're an Issnaîm, aren't you?"

No, he said coldly. *I am the last lingering gasp of what they once were.*

Kat had heard similar snobbery from firebloods all her life. "So all this time you knew there was a way through the Veil."

There is nothing beyond the Veil but death.

"Fine words from someone who tried to kill me and my crew."

Your stubbornness left me no choice. Now we will both suffer.

"There's hope for my crew, and for our mission." If Scirran's word – and the mercy of his Elders – was equal to his lofty promises. "That's what matters."

You assume parity where none exists, sneered Caradan Diar. *The Issnaîm will not recognise you as an equal, and only equals can bargain.*

"I'll take my chances."

He fell silent, his arguments or his patience spent. Kat resumed pacing and attempted to align the new facts with what she already knew. Better that than worrying over the fate of Zephyr, Tanith and the others. The Issnaîm – or rather their forebears – had imprisoned Tzal behind the Veil, so in that sense it was unsurprising that Caradan Diar was of the same people. Zephyr's forebears had once *served* Tzal. In that context, the Eternity King's status of "Betrayer" could mean many different things.

The simplest reading lay in Khalad's none-too-distant past, as his suppression and seeming extermination of the Issnaîm was well documented . . . but that presumed a sliver of truth in a history riven by lies. More concerning was the possibility that he'd earned his title for imprisoning Tzal, which would mean that this faction of Issnaîm – both Zephyr and Scirran had spoken of a fragmented people – had remained loyal to the Cold Flame. Zephyr had always presented the Issnaîm legends in allegorical terms, not least among them the notion that the Veil was the skin of a silver pearl, fashioned from Tzal's own obsession. Had she done so to conceal her ancestors' complicity?

Back and forth Kat paced, frustration rising as time slipped imperceptibly away. Though the mists were calmer at Xe'iathî – in line with Zephyr's claims that the Issnaîm dwelled in the sheltered spaces of the Veil – still their nostalgia-scent muddled perception. But whether they passed swift or slow, every moment was one stolen from Athenoch's hopes.

She was thus relieved when the rippling shadow that served as the door to her jail parted, admitting three strangers. No, *two* strangers. The third was Zephyr, rendered almost unrecognisable in the first instance by the fact that she'd re-formed a usually revealing gown to a modest, high-collared dress that covered every inch of her save for head and hands, and in the second by her humble – almost servile – posture, her eyes downcast and her head bowed. Her star-flecked hair, unbound for as long as Kat had known her, was gathered to a tight ponytail by a clasp of silvered light. Her companions were as diffuse as the Issnaîm who'd crewed Scirran's drakon. Martial robes, naked swords and unfriendly expressions lent solidity that their forms lacked.

"To ask for your promise to come peaceably, am I," said Zephyr, her expression unreadable. "If given, the Elders will hear you."

Kat's heart ached to hear a voice usually so waspish and carefree grown so controlled and distant. "How are the others? Did Scirran keep his word?"

"Still aboard ship, hale and unharmed they are. Remain so, they will, until the Elders' judgement is made." The smallest hint of amusement touched Zephyr's voice. "All but gnawing the bulwark with impatience is Tanith."

Kat forced herself to relax. "Then I give my promise gladly."

Forefinger and thumb tucked to his palm, the nearer guard wove a dizzying gesture in the air. As the door to Kat's cell faded to nothingness, he produced a pair of wrist shackles from beneath his robes.

Zephyr's expression darkened. "Given her promise, has she."

"Marked by the Betrayer she remains," said the guard. "Worthless is her word."

She raised her head to a defiant stare. "Not to the Elders."

"Too long have you been gone, menial," snapped the other guard. "Forgotten your place, you have. Perhaps you are as *akîa*-rotten as she, and deserving of dissolution."

Zephyr went rigid, her lips pinched and her eyes awash in sudden terror.

Kat held out her hands. "It's all right, Xepheri." Whatever tension lay beneath Zephyr's interactions with her people, having her seem more of an outsider would only make things worse. "Lately I haven't been as in control of myself as I'd like. This is probably for the best."

The guard snapped the hot-cold shackles about her wrists.

You are a fool, breathed Caradan Diar as the guards led her from the jail.

The scent of the Veil rushed back full flood as Kat hit the open air, the essence of old memories clogging her throat and bringing tears to her eyes. Blinking them away, she followed the first guard out onto a walkway as broad as a Zariqaz road. Zephyr kept pace, gaze downcast once more, leaving the second guard to bring up the rear.

A sprawling palace of geometric crystal shimmered with silver light at the roadway's end, dwarfing lesser spiral-roofed buildings that huddled in twos and threes on smaller branches of the web, the outermost half-hidden by the mists. The shadows of the walkway seethed beneath Kat's every footstep, but they held firm enough, without the nauseating sway of the rope bridge they so closely resembled. Even so, Kat couldn't help but notice places where the web of light and shadow had grown dark, leaving jagged remnants of broken paths to jut blindly. The extent of Xe'iathî's web was perhaps twice the size of Araq, but the light touched barely a quarter.

Other Issnaîm kept their distance, drifting away onto side strands of the webway where opportunity allowed and dipping their gaze until the procession moved on. Those as soberly attired as Zephyr kept their eyes averted not from Kat alone, but also from more gaudily attired Issnaîm. Kat glimpsed some curiosity – especially in the younger faces – but not so much as there might have been. More proof that Vallant had been to Xe'iathî.

She glanced over her shoulder. *Amarid's Dream* was nowhere in sight, lost to the Veil. Hopefully not for ever, but the way her luck had been tracking, she wouldn't have laid a bent dinar as the stake. "I owe you an apology."

"Speak of it later, we will, if we can," said Zephyr without looking up.

Kat cast around for something else to say. Anything to keep Zephyr talking and in turn ease her own guilt. "It's a beautiful city."

"Once, long years ago, perhaps. Before we lost the art of weaving its light."

"What happened?"

"The Betrayer happened. Lured us into Khalad, did he, with promises of reconciliation. Let us settle long enough for time to pass and memories to fade. And all the while he dabbled in forbidden disciplines, the Dark of Creation and the stuff of souls."

So *that* was why the Issnaîm showed no sign of using ifrîti. "I didn't know you found it so abhorrent."

"Born to it are you. What is unnatural to us is part of your being." Zephyr's expression darkened. "But it made the Betrayer's armies unstoppable. Skyships blackened the Cloudsea. One by one, our cities fell. Drove us back to the mists, did he, to havens we no longer knew how to maintain. Clung here ever since, we have, and called it living, trusting to the light to preserve our *akîa*."

Another mystery resolved. Kat had wondered at the lack of astoricum in the haven, but Zephyr had always claimed that what little of the metal the Issnaîm possessed belonged to heirlooms, such as her long-lost brooch and Scirran's scabbard. They'd no need of such protections in Xe'iathî if the light shielded their souls. "I can't imagine any skyship besting those drakons."

"One alone could not, but drakons were always few. Now they are just memories lashed together with shadow-vine." Zephyr's voice darkened with bleak humour. "Be glad. Gives the Elders reason to listen, it does. Remember the power of shriekers, do the oldest. Afeared are they of hearing them speak above Xe'iathî."

Kat grimaced. No wonder the populace were so reserved. To her, *Amarid's Dream* was simply a warship. To the Issnaîm, it was a horror from myth. "I didn't mean it to be a threat."

Zephyr met her eye to eye, all pretence of humility gone. "*I* did. Knew from the first that leverage would be needed. Always strongest is the simple message."

"Then why did they allow our ship to come so close?"

Zephyr sniffed. "Pride is older than Khalad."

Kat considered as the sentiment hung on the air. Zephyr had always been a puzzle, and never more than now she was among her own people. For all that she pretended subservience, defiance seethed beneath. "The Eternity King's crusades happened centuries ago. Do the Issnaîm really live that long?"

Zephyr laughed without humour. "We do not live at all. Told you before, did I. Strangely flows time through the Veil. Trapped in it are we, fused in crystal; ageless and timeless while we remain, sustained by the radiance of our havens."

"I'm starting to see why you left," said Kat.

Zephyr snorted. "Never belonged here, did I. Menial caste I am, entitled to nothing but scrape and scorn. To fetch and carry while luminals scavenge the mists for figments of better days and aethers play at warrior to proclaim one another heroes."

And all of them blind to the ability of a woman they'd dismissed as a drudge, trapped by tradition that made the divide between fireblood and cinderblood seem trivial. If there was a pilot in Khalad to match Zephyr's ability, they'd yet to cross Kat's path.

"I'm sorry I didn't tell you about the Eternity King."

"Forgotten it is. Think yourself the only hoarder of secret shame, do you?" Zephyr shook her head. "At Anfai I was, when they greeted us like serathi bringing benison. Piled worth even on a menial caste, they did, for no one told them I was but a servant. Felt belonging there more than I did among my own, *ayin,* and still I abandoned them to burn when the aether caste withdrew. Long years it was, as things are reckoned beyond the Veil, before I found Vallant wearing away in the mist. The ghosts of Anfai demanded I save him. Changed me for ever, they did."

Kat had no notion what a "serathi" was, but had long grown accustomed to Zephyr dotting her speech with unfamiliar phrases. How strange the tides of history were. But for the massacre at Anfai, Zephyr would never have saved Vallant twenty years ago. How many people had lived and died on that crux of fortune? "Did Mirzai know?"

"Had no heart to tell him, did I. Now the moment is lost. But I will not let his death – nor Vallant's – count for nothing."

It was the first time that Kat had heard her admit aloud that Vallant was dead, rather than merely missing. "You weren't to know how things would end. For either of them."

"And did you, with the Betrayer?"

She grimaced. She'd asked herself that same question so many times since Tyzanta. "Without him, I'd be dead of omen rot. Maybe I should have let it take me." But had she done so, she couldn't have saved Tanith from becoming Tzal's host during the Obsidium Uprising. A perfect host. The evils he wrought through Azra were as nothing to what he could otherwise have achieved. The tides of history again. "All I can do now is make that choice count for better."

Zephyr laughed without humour and drifted closer. "Then trust to this: I will see Xe'iathî burn before I betray the memories of those I failed."

"Stand away from the prisoner, drab," barked the second guard.

Zephyr retreated, head once again bowed in pretence of subservience, leaving Kat to walk the rest of the way in silent contemplation. Did Zephyr anticipate her threat as a position of last resort, or necessity?

The procession entered the palace gates into a hall lined with ragged shimmering tapestries whose crystal threads had worn away, revealing the murky grey walls beyond. Shadows curled up through cracks in the tiled floor.

Passing through a final archway and its attendant guards, Kat found herself in a grand, roofless chamber whose far wall was dominated by three colossal statues that shone so brightly they seemed at first to be fashioned of Xe'iathî's silver light rather than crystal. All were female, the central one shrouded so that nothing showed of her face. The proud companion to her right rejoiced in a spill of flame-like hair, similar to that which graced so many likenesses of Nyssa, and held aloft an orb blazing fit to banish all shadows. The last figure appeared sterner than her sisters. She too held aloft an orb, but this was split down the middle, one hemisphere bright and the other dark.

The arrangement of the statues struck Kat as strange, but it was only as impatient guards ushered her and Zephyr towards the raised crystal thrones at their base that she realised the chamber had once held a fourth statue, sited between the shrouded woman and the bearer of the bisected sphere. Only the plinth now remained. Tzal for a guess – the treacherous god removed from sight and station for his transgressions.

There were four thrones in all – one per statue – each occupied by an Issnaîm of such great age that the stars barely glimmered in their ash-white hair. All held staves of coiling shadow. Other Issnaîm bore murmuring witness from a gallery ringing the upper wall, level with the statues' shoulders, while Scirran was a glowering, impatient presence hovering beside the rightmost throne.

The guards brought Kat and Zephyr to a halt just shy of the chamber's centre, marked by a scuffed circular tile three paces wide and bearing the flowing stylised image of an eye, etched in cold blues. Kat felt the Eternity King shift fitfully against her tattoo, his sense fearful and his strength but a sliver of what it had been aboard *Amarid's*

405

Dream. Tanith had hurt him more than she'd known. The realisation provoked a grim flush of triumph. For all his arrogance, Caradan Diar could be beaten.

Assuming that she survived what was to come. Triumph cooled to ice. Bound as she was to the Eternity King, anything that roused his fear should also concern her.

The guards bowed to the Elders and withdrew.

One of the Elders stirred in his throne. "By sun, moon and river do we greet you, Xepheri of Hollowhal." He glanced at Scirran. "Though we hear you bring one marked by the Betrayer to this haven."

Kat wondered at the caution in his voice – and at the invocation of the "moon", a word she'd heard Zephyr use but never explain.

Zephyr bobbed an ornate curtsey of a style long since fallen out of use in Khalad. "I do, out of need."

"It is no mere mark," said another Elder, aghast. "She bears the very essence of the Betrayer."

A shocked hush descended on the chamber.

"True, it is," said the third. "See him, do I. Burrowed deep within her *akia*."

"Unwilling is she," said the fourth. "A victim, deceived, as were we."

The first shook his head. "Unproven, is that." He gripped the armrests of his throne and leaned further forward to address Zephyr. "A gift far beyond your station is this, menial. Humbled and grateful are we."

Again Kat heard caution in his words, almost the suspicion of someone manoeuvring against a political opponent, though Zephyr was scarcely that.

Scirran drew himself up, his diffuse form gaining a measure of solidity. "If the Betrayer is here, by the strength of my word and the courage of my crew was he brought."

The soft murmur of conversation returned to the gallery. Her head still bowed, Zephyr's left cheek tightened, the adjoining eye twitching half closed.

"And rewarded you shall be," said the fourth Elder. "Generous beyond words is this gift. Enough that you may spare the menial the scraps from your table, good aether captain."

Thoughts racing behind an immobile face, Kat glanced again at Zephyr. Being presented as a gift was a very different proposition from the opportunity to petition that had been promised. From her increasingly agitated expression, Zephyr was of the same mind. From her silence, she'd no idea how to set the audience back on its proper course.

Kiasta. Time to take a risk.

"I am no gift," said Kat. "Xepheri brought me here because I need your help."

Again the gallery fell silent. Scirran glared at her with outrage, while Zephyr regarded her with unhappiness and the four Elders with disdainful curiosity.

"How remarkable," said the second, aggrieved. "It speaks. It's aware."

"So was the other," said the fourth.

"True," the second replied, her lip curling to a scowl. "Though more shrill is she."

Kat strove to ignore the unflattering comparison to Vallant. "I mean no offence, but the truth is important to my people … as I'm sure it is to you."

"As water to the river are lies to your kind," said the first Elder bitterly. "Did you collude willingly with the Betrayer?"

Kat hesitated. For all that she'd given no consent for Caradan Diar to lodge himself in her soul, the pact she'd struck in order to save her life could be considered collusion. Instinct warned against lying. "At first."

"Then chose your allegiance, you did. Why should we give you anything but death?"

It didn't escape Kat's notice that no one seemed interested in knowing her name or offering theirs. However low Zephyr lay in the Elders' sight, outsiders ranked lower still. Or perhaps it was the result of ingrained hatred. The Issnaîm had once fought and died for Tzal. Conquered for him. A scar so deep would throb throughout eternity.

"Because if you let my ship depart with what they need, then …"

Deep in her soul, Caradan Diar tensed. *I beg you ... do not do this.*

She ignored him, taking pleasure in the redoubled fear framing his words. "... then I offer myself and the Betrayer without a fight, to face whatever justice the sons and daughters of the Issnaîm see fit."

The chamber dissolved into uproar, hundreds of voices clamouring for dominance. The Elders leaned across their thrones and spoke among themselves, their words drowned out by the noise from the gallery above.

Zephyr surged to Kat's side, her expression stricken. "What *waholi* foolishness is this?"

Kat offered a wan smile. "Making my choice count for something better."

"Kill you, will they," Zephyr hissed, "just to be certain he's gone!"

"I thought they might," Kat said with a glibness she didn't feel. "But shrieker cannons won't solve this." Though they'd certainly play their part, even unfired. Even with the request taken in isolation, the Elders had no reason to agree – she was offering them something they already possessed – but fear of what *Amarid's Dream* might do in reprisal. "Do I have your promise?" she asked as the clamour at last faded.

"The word of a menial caste?" replied Zephyr sourly.

"Of a friend. I'm not what's important here." She sounded like Vallant, Kat realised. Earnest and cloying. Between his influence and Caradan Diar's baleful presence, just how much of her was left? "I'm trusting you and Tanith to carry on."

The first Elder's deep voice cut through the last of the hubbub. "Exactly what do you seek in exchange?"

Kat stared up at him and stifled a sigh of relief. "Passage to the realm beyond the Veil."

He exchanged a glance with the other Elders. "Xepheri already sought this knowledge. Beyond the boundary of obsidium towers and the pearl's shifting skin there is nothing but death."

There it was again, the reference to the pearl of obsession with which the Issnaîm's forebears had caged Tzal. Kat had heard Zephyr recount that story a dozen times, but this was the first occasion on which the black towers had featured in the tale.

"Lost to me it is," said Zephyr. "Devoured by the mists alongside my companions."

"Then learned nothing, have you," said the fourth Elder.

The first Elder silenced him with a look. "It is a short sail from here to the lesion in the Veil. Xepheri was not the first to seek the passage. No other has ever returned."

Was that a refusal or agreement? Kat wondered. "We've no choice. The Veil is devouring Khalad. We can't live within the mists as you do. Your legends of a realm beyond the Veil . . ." better not to mention that Caradan Diar had also spoken of it, "are our only hope. I know you've no reason to love my kind, but surely you can spare us a little mercy?"

The second Elder rubbed her chin. "A dangerous business, is sifting truth from legend. But if it is your wish to die, then we will not stand in your path." She turned a thoughtful gaze on Zephyr. "And you, daughter, whom death nearly claimed before – do you spurn the second chance fate has granted?"

Zephyr threw back her head and stood tall, the menial's stoop gone from her posture. "Stand with my friends, will I. Always."

"Delusion," said the third Elder. "You have been away from home too long. Your place is here."

"Even without friendship, a debt would I owe," said Zephyr. "A kindness to one who pulled me from the mist and restored me to *akia*."

"Ah." The caution that had haunted the first Elder's exchanges with Zephyr was at last gone from his voice. "Your memory troubles you still? Then stay. Time will heal the loss."

"My friends have no time, and so nor do I."

"And if fate does not spare you a second time?"

"Then I will pass into the Dark in good company, and pray that the Drowned Lady is kind."

"So be it, with a heavy heart." To Kat's way of thinking the first Elder's words were a poor match to his manner, which seemed more

409

relieved than sorrowful. She might have examined the thought further, except he then turned his glossy white gaze on her. "Prepared to make good on your part of the bargain, are you?"

Zephyr grimaced. "Kat . . ."

So much for seeing Azra again, but then there'd never really been much hope of that. Fairness was for children, and Kat had grown old that past year. "This is my choice. You're not to blame." She raised her voice, again addressing the Elders. "I'm ready."

"Then step forward," said the second Elder. "Pass into the Eye of Judgement."

With a final glance at Zephyr, Kat edged forward until she stood on the stylised eye. As one, the Elders struck their staves against the ground. Her vision flooded with brilliant silver-white light, drowning out all else. Even the repeated, rhythmic sound of the Elders' staves on tile felt distant – a faltering heartbeat, fading with every pulsing strike. There was only the light, and the fire rising within, kin to the touch of her shackles.

She clamped her eyes shut as the first spasm struck, a hot-cold fist squeezing her soul tighter and tighter, each pulse in time with the distant pounding of the staves.

Breaths ragged in her throat, she opened her eyes and saw a dark shape standing beside her. The Eternity King. Not the withered corpse she'd encountered in the sanctum of the Golden Citadel, nor a vaporous Issnaîm, but a man of flesh and blood, darkly handsome, garbed in gold and grey.

After all I've done for your kind, this is how it ends.

"You . . . used me," gasped Kat.

I saved you. That anything lives in Khalad is down to me. These mongrels sought to destroy you all, afraid of what you might become. I thought with guidance you might overcome what Tzal made of you. But it seems that cruelty is burned into the bone.

The light pulsed. The fist about Kat's soul squeezed tighter. She sank to her knees, eyes lidded against the pain, resentful that Caradan Diar spoke so lightly while her every word barely scraped past her lips. "You put . . . it there."

His form shifted and shimmered in the light. *I had hopes for you, Katija Arvish.* His voice turned bitter. *I return to the Dark of Creation a fool.*

"Not . . . a fool. Tyrant . . . dethroned." Every word was a laborious effort. "Leaders sacrifice. Your . . . words. We make this one . . . together."

You are all of the same flame. He was barely a shadow now, no more real than a candle's after-image. *You will serve Tzal whether you mean to or not.*

Unable even to kneel any longer, she slumped sideways, the tile floor cold and hard beneath her cheek. "I'll die . . . before that happens."

No. You won't.

Kat closed her eyes. She was already dead, burning from within, but it was worth it to know that the Eternity King would share her fate. Doubly so that their deaths brought hope for others.

Caradan Diar gave a last breathy sigh. The light blazed, rousing the inside of Kat's eyelids to a hot white glow.

The drumbeat fell silent. The light faded.

The pressure about her soul lessened, inch by shuddering inch.

A hand found hers in the darkness. "Kat? Kat, can you hear me? Over, it is."

Trembling, she opened her eyes. Zephyr was kneeling above her, face twisted with relief. Fumbling, Kat searched her soul for any trace of Caradan Diar and found none – just an annoying buzzing sensation, familiar but impossible to place.

"I . . . don't understand," she croaked as Zephyr helped her stand.

The first Elder peered down from his throne, expression unreadable. "Ignorance is no crime. No need to kill you here, have we. If you seek the Old Realm, death will find you soon enough."

Forty-One

"You're sure this is the right course?" asked Tanith.

"Certain of nothing, am I," Zephyr replied. "But this is the heading I was given."

Kat peered out into the mists, searching for some sign that the Issnaîm Elders hadn't steered them false simply to be rid of them. Wasted effort, for the seething clouds of greenish-white offered up nothing. With Xe'iathî far behind, the mists seemed angrier than ever, their clutch at soul and self more insistent than Kat had ever known. Instinct warned of something askew. From the hushed silence that ruled *Amarid's Dream*, the crew felt it too.

"I see something!" bellowed the prow lookout. "Dead ahead!"

Tanith on her heels, Kat took the companionway steps two at a time and bolted for the prow. As she passed the mainmast, her left ankle spasmed, threatening an unceremonious collapse.

Tanith grabbed her arm. "Graceful as ever."

"Some of us don't have your advantages," said Kat sourly to cover growing worry. She'd had three such attacks since *Amarid's Dream* had spread its sails, always afflicting the muscles on her left side. Too close to old memories for comfort. Not that Tanith looked much better. After days behind the Veil – for days it had surely been, though they were impossible to track – she looked paler than ever, her beauty increasingly luminous as her hunger grew. Another cause for concern.

"Always with the excuses," Tanith replied as they reached the prow. "Always . . ."

Far beyond the bulkhead, on the very edge of what was visible through the seething mists, danced a shimmer, black as starless sky. It pulsed and rippled, twisting lazily anticlockwise in one moment only to reverse in the next. Kat had never seen anything to match it, both hauntingly unreal and inescapably tangible. *The lesion in the Veil*, the Elders had said. This could be nothing else. A wound in the firmament of the mists.

"I guess that's what we're looking for." Her voice quickened with excitement. They'd found it. Against all odds, they'd actually found it!

"You think so, do you?" Tanith's wide-eyed awe undermined her sarcasm. She closed her eyes as if trying to catch a scrap of song across a crowded tavern. "It's . . . calling to me."

Kat stared at the shimmer, unable to look away. She felt its pull deep within, a need that had no name. Barely a whisper, but as undeniable as hunger. "And me. I don't— No!" She tore her gaze from the lesion to see Tanith standing on the bulwark, already tensing for a leap. Kat grabbed her belt and dragged her back down to the deck. "What were you thinking?"

Tanith pulled free and glowered. "I have to go to it! Don't you understand?"

Kat stepped away, taken aback by her sister's sudden fervency, her sapphire eyes wilder than she'd seen them in months.

Others joined them at the bulwark, Bo'sun Jazal among them. "Sail! No, two!"

Kat followed his pointing finger and saw the charred remnant of a lateen sail flapping mournfully against the mists, tethered to a mast canted nearly thirty degrees. A smaller sail – in scarcely better condition than the first – belonged to the same skyship: a black-hulled dhow lying on its starboard side atop a rippling expanse of white sand, its pinion sails crushed like matchsticks beneath its keel. Half its port bulwark was blasted away. What remained was charred to

413

a crisp. Stray rigging danced and dangled in the Veil's impossible winds, but the soot-soiled sunburst flag draped across the stern barely twitched. Dark patches of scattered wreckage marked the trail of the ship's demise.

"Stars Below," breathed Tanith. "It's the *Chainbreaker*."

"What happened?" asked the lookout.

Jazal gave a low whistle. "Found itself a fight."

"All the way out here?"

Kat spun about towards the helm, possibilities converging to cold, terrible certainty. The first Elder's strange behaviour towards Zephyr until her confession that she'd lost her memory. *No need to kill you here, have we.* In hindsight, the phrase was more sinister by far.

"Stand to your guns!" she shouted. "Zephyr! Bring us about! Full sail!"

Amarid's Dream banked sharply as Zephyr hauled on the lateral wheel.

The mists parted abaft. A drakon dived towards *Amarid's Dream*, fire already belching from its ossified jaws. Kat froze as the flame rushed towards her, a part of her wondering how something so long dead could produce such a thing. The air screamed. Tanith slammed her bodily to the deck as the section of bulwark by which they'd stood caught light. Three sailriders, the lookout among them, were caught in the blaze and swept overboard to the mercy of the mist.

The drakon plunged past the port bow. *Amarid's Dream* shuddered as the bones of an outflung wing raked its flank. Pallid eliathros wisped skyward, barely glimpsed through the angry flames raging across the portside deck. The deck lurched and dipped as the port buoyancy tanks failed. Ahead, the drakon steadied, spinnakers blooming as its pilot brought it about back around in an ungainly arc.

Kat ran for the quarterdeck. "If we take another hit like that, we're done!"

"Might be already," Zephyr replied, wrestling with an uncooperative wheel. "Burst our portside tanks, did they! The lateral rudder sails are burned through. Bold heroes all, the aether caste." The venom in her voice would have killed an ox.

A second drakon breached the starboard mists, fire already spilling from its long-dead maw. Zephyr set the pitching wheel spinning. Deck canting madly to port from the leak in the portside buoyancy tanks, *Amarid's Dream* dived. Kat grabbed at the quarterdeck balustrade, skin prickling as flame set the upper mast ablaze.

The starboard shrieker cannons wailed, the gunners firing without orders, but Kat could have kissed them all the same. Two shots passed harmlessly below the oncoming drakon. The third ripped through two of the ridgeline spinnakers and exploded against the shadowy bulwark, flinging Issnaîm sailriders into the mists. A third struck the cluster of ropes binding the starboard wing to the body. The shadow-stuff melted, hissing free of the bones they bound. As the remaining sails shifted to match the captain's doomed attempt to bank, the wing tore fully away. Kat cheered with her crew as the drakon plunged from sight, dragged down by the weight of its surviving wing.

The deck lurched beneath her feet, sinking a further ten degrees to port as another damaged buoyancy tank ruptured.

"Get us down!" she shouted, holding onto the balustrade for dear life.

"Glad you said that, am I," Zephyr replied, leaning into the lateral wheel. "*Up* is no longer an option."

A grinding crash sounded at the bow. The burning remnant of an aethersail, spars and all, swept over Tanith's head and back across the deck. It missed by inches the sailriders sheltering at the quarterdeck's rear and caromed off the aftercastle, away into the Veil.

"Lost the last of the rudder sails, we have!" shouted Zephyr.

"Hold onto something!" bellowed Kat. An unnecessary order, unheard over the roar of the flames and the wailing wind. Every sailrider still above deck was clinging to rope or bulwark for dear life. She peered up through the swirl of smoke and cinders that had once been the mainsail. The first drakon was already high overhead, warning of how far *Amarid's Dream* had plunged in a few short moments.

Beyond the prow – *below* the prow almost, given the *Dream*'s increasingly steep plunge – the wreckage-spattered sands of the Veil glistened. The *Chainbreaker*'s lifeless hull loomed in welcome.

Amarid's Dream struck the ground with the deafening roar of a dying forest, hurling a cloud of white sand skyward. Kat's last thought as the impact wrenched her free of the quarterdeck balustrade and swept her into black was that it was both fitting and unfair that she and Vallant had died exactly the same way.

Forty-Two

Ignoring his protesting bruises, Damant darted forward across the boarded-up warehouse, the flick of his wrist transmuting a head-height feint to a rising underarm slice. Rîma politely ignored the former and stepped into the latter, catching his blade on her own and shoving it aside. But she did so more slowly than Damant expected. Her pained wince – however brief – spoke to injuries not yet healed.

Worries concealed behind an impassive mask, he stepped back across the dusty floor and returned his scimitar to low guard. Rîma mirrored the gesture, but with a pronounced limp.

"You're faster than I remember, Ihsan."

A fine compliment. Except Damant knew it wasn't true. Rîma was slower. A *lot* slower. Testament to the torture she'd suffered at the red-cloaks' hands. To hear Keti tell it, they'd almost torn her apart. Not to aid interrogation, for they'd asked her no questions, but simply because they could.

For the first three days in the Karana Street safe house, she'd kept to her room while Keti tended her wounds – a task that required as much carpentry and metalwork as last breath. Rîma's withered body resisted harm better than ordinary flesh and blood, but broken bones required drilling and splinting. Damant had offered to help, but Keti had relayed Rîma's polite rebuff. Pride, he supposed. It was easier to let a stranger see you vulnerable than a friend.

With little else to occupy his time, he'd have patrolled the nearby streets had Keti not insisted that he make no attempt to leave for fear of attracting unwelcome attention. Recognising the good sense in her words – delivered with a mix of Marida's authority and Tatterlain's humour – he'd whiled away the days as best he could while Keti came and went at all hours, returning now and then with food, wine, and news of the outside world.

When Rîma had finally emerged, the black grave bindings that concealed her body neck to foot restored, he'd accepted her offer to spar out of boredom more than anything else. Tatterlain, besides being a liberator of persons, had also retrieved their weapons from the palace cells. It surprised Damant just how much the weight of his scimitar and his Qarradin-crafted shrieker made him feel more like himself, but not half as much as seeing Rîma reunited with her sword – once borne by the legendary Queen Amakala of Tadamûr.

Or it had until he'd realised how little she was herself. He'd seen her ailing before during her return to Tadamûr, but that had been a mental thing, her mind smothered by the city-soul that had consumed the spirits of her people. This was something else. He'd suspected it from the first clash of blades. After an hour's sparring, the chinks of daylight from the boarded windows turning grey as evening approached and his skin prickling with sweat, he was certain.

"We both know it's not me that's different," he said, his eyes on hers.

Her face – as ever the one piece of her showing above her grave bindings – bore no trace of its wounds. Last breath had healed it, just as it had frozen it in relative youth while the rest of her body shrivelled and hardened. "Perhaps I'm saving myself for something that matters."

She lunged, the point of her sword aimed at Damant's heart. He twisted aside and chased her back across the room with a flick of his scimitar. "Personally, I think you're going easy on me," he lied. "You'll have to be faster if you're to bring down the Eternity Queen. That's what you're meant to do, isn't it? It's what you said back in the sanctum."

At least, he *thought* that was what she'd said. Desperation had made his own memories less than reliable.

She lowered her sword. "So you remembered."

"I'm not so old that I forget things like that."

She offered a not-quite-smile, as she always did when he said such things. "Then I cannot hide from my failure."

"I don't understand. I saw what you did. You met her will to will. You—"

"I *failed*. Worse, I am the architect of that failure."

Damant let the point of his scimitar droop. "If you're talking about Isdihar – about what she did – she lied to all of us. I doubt that Caradan Diar gave her any choice."

"I was not, though she is seldom far from my thoughts. I meant Tzal. We speak of him as if he is a single entity when really he is a glut of souls."

That certainly tracked, given how completely he'd absorbed Yennika from Azra. That and his claim that he *was* the Deadwinds. Azra herself had suggested that Tzal wasn't truly whole. Perhaps he wasn't even alive as they understood it. But Rîma already knew that *he* knew that, so she had to be getting at something else. "Except for the dead of Tadamûr? You used them to counter his glamour." She arched an eyebrow in surprise. Damant's heart warmed at having surprised her. "I've seen a thing or two, you know."

"Indeed. But the host I commanded was not enough for anything other than delay. Their souls were too few and too thin. Tzal overwhelmed and consumed them."

"I don't see how that makes it your failure."

She scowled. "Their souls were too few because most were lost when I destroyed Tadamûr's city-soul. Too thin because they barely escaped my folly. We claim arrogance belongs to youth, and that selfishness flourishes best in a mind too unformed to know its place. Yet here I stand, she who destroyed our greatest weapon against Tzal because she could not bear to perform her duty."

Damant thought back to the sanctum. To the siphonic prism Isdihar had destroyed. Tadamûr's throne room had been fashioned to serve as a focus for the Deadwinds, and if that was so, then ... "Amakala created Tadamûr's city-soul as a weapon against Tzal?"

"More than a weapon. His *rival*. An artificial god ... and I destroyed it."

An artificial god. The harder Damant tried to grasp what that meant, or might entail, the faster his thoughts lost purchase. But one thing *was* clear.

"You had no choice! It was destroying you." The baleful pressure of Tadamûr's city-soul had broken Rîma even before she'd crossed its boundary, and hollowed her out so that she could better serve as its docile queen. "I know what I saw at your coronation. The city-soul might have given you the power to contest Tzal, but it would have robbed you of everything that drove you to confront him. You'd still be there now if Hadîm and I hadn't freed you, staring blankly into the darkness while your subjects bowed and scraped through half-forgotten ritual."

She spun on her heel, her back to him. "You don't know that."

"I know that if we were in the same situation again, right now, I'd act as I did before!" He broke off, knowing that he was shouting, and struck a more reasonable tone. "Maybe Amakala intended what you say, but it didn't work. Power without the will to wield it isn't really power at all."

She tilted her head, a strand of white hair slithering lower across her shoulder. "Tell me, Ihsan: when did you get so wise?"

"When I started keeping better company. Don't get too used to it."

At last, Rîma turned around. "I don't know that I believe you, but I will consider your words." She shook her head. "It doesn't change the fact that in trusting Isdihar, you and I have wrought Khalad's doom. Tzal almost doesn't matter any longer, not with the Veil closing in."

"Maybe not," he said slowly, fragments of their conversation taking on a new shape. "What if we had another siphonic prism?"

"And who would use it? It took me months to learn how to do what I did in the sanctum, and that was with Isdihar's guidance."

"Arvish can handle it," he said, surprised by his own certainty. "Assuming she's still alive."

"She lives. I would know otherwise. But it changes nothing. We *don't* have another siphonic prism, and we lack the knowledge or craft to make one."

"What about the one at Tadamûr?"

"The city is gone, buried beneath rock. No trace of it remains."

He stepped closer. "But there's a chance."

"No." Another not-quite-smile, this one bereft of warmth. "Do I strike you as someone who does something by half-measures, Ihsan?"

"Then what do we do?"

She sheathed her sword. "We make our peace with those we love and hope for a miracle."

"I've never been one to believe in miracles," he said gruffly.

"Then perhaps it is time you started."

He shook his head, frustrated by Rîma's fatalism but also at his own failure to dispel it. "I still don't understand why Tzal was so calm. If he's nothing more than a glut of souls, then the Veil will destroy him as readily as any of us."

"He said nothing of it at all?"

"Only that 'futility is the mother of invention'."

"He'd better be right, for all our sakes. Seldom has the struggle felt more futile."

Damant nodded, not yet ready to give up on Tadamûr's siphonic prism. If they could get back into the Golden Citadel, they could enter the Stars Below via the Qabirarchi Palace. There *might* still be a way to access Tadamûr's ruins. Perhaps not much of one, but anything was better than sitting around waiting for the redcloaks to find them or the Veil to devour everything. Of course, getting into the Golden Citadel would likely be difficult, but Damant suspected that Keti could arrange it . . . or Tatterlain, if he was still alive. Damant hadn't seen him since the sewer. Nor had Keti, so far as he knew. She'd proven as apt at deflecting questions as Tatterlain, or else had disarmed them with a wicked smile.

The door to the living quarters – in reality, a cluster of offices made barely habitable by furnishings – eased open, admitting the elusive Tatterlain. And he *was* Tatterlain, rather than Tuzen Karza. It wasn't just the lack of gaudy robes and make-up. He carried himself differently, the confidence quieter than the braggart's poise Damant had loathed so well.

He leaned against the door jamb, insouciance made flesh. "Not interrupting, am I?"

"Only an argument," said Damant.

"Then perhaps I should go away until it's over. I *hate* arguments."

"Don't you dare." To ensure that Tatterlain couldn't make good on his threat, Rîma swept across the warehouse and embraced him. "I should be furious with you for casting aside our only remaining advantage, but now that I see you, I haven't the heart."

"I've never seen much advantage in staying safe while my friends die," he replied.

She pulled away. "We weren't important."

"You were to me." For once he was utterly serious. "Contingencies are there to be used. Besides, there aren't many people left to have suspicions. Malis and Ardin are dead. Faizâr's a drooling imbecile on a leash—"

"Are Hargo and Emanzi back from Tyzanta yet?" asked Damant.

Tatterlain offered a sly smile. "That's right, you don't know. Kat cleaned Tyzanta out. Hargo's dead and Emanzi's hiding from dear Yennika's wrath in what's left of Hazali." He shook his head. "What times we live in."

Damant was glad to see a little joy return to Rîma's face. "Good for Arvish."

"Indeed. That leaves Igarî Bathîr and some rake named Tuzen Karza as the Queen's Council, and I'm afraid that as of this evening, Count Karza is no more." Tatterlain set his jaw. "Let him stay dead this time.

Let him be forgotten. And speaking of resurrections . . . I've seen reports from a place called Araq – one of those dust-blown towns out east – that suggest a certain veilkin . . ."

"Issnaîm," corrected Rîma, her brows beetled.

He waved the objection away and pressed on. ". . . a certain Issnaîm of our acquaintance isn't as lost as we thought."

"Zephyr's alive?" said Damant. Rîma was actually smiling now – the real thing, not the half-measure she usually favoured.

Tatterlain shrugged. "Maybe. Lots of strange things happen out east. Being honest? It's all more than a little bit confused right now. Zariqaz is . . . quiet. Too quiet. Half the people are walking around in a daze. It's like lethargia, but they're still upright."

"They're afraid for the future," said Rîma. "If the mists really are on the move, nothing like this has ever happened before. I take it the news *has* broken?"

"No avoiding that, what with the Eternity Queen having redcloaks scramble hither and yon evacuating those towns closest to the Veil. Just silt-holes so far, only a few hundred souls apiece. It's going to be horror once it hits Kaldos or Nassos."

Damant frowned. "That doesn't make sense. Tzal's spent months grinding the border towns to dust. Now he's saving the inhabitants?"

"It makes perfect sense," said Rîma. "He was killing them because it made him stronger. But every soul lost to the mist is one he can't consume. The Veil doesn't play favourites. It will swallow us all, him included."

"'Futility is the mother of invention.'" Damant thought back to his brief audience with the Eternity Queen in the palace dungeons. "Maybe she's expecting us to fix this."

Tatterlain snorted. "No wonder I always wanted to be royalty: wave a hand and watch something happen."

"It usually works," said Rîma.

"True, but assuming there's a way to stop the Veil eating everything, do we even want to?"

She glared at him. "How can you ask that?"

He held up his hands in defence. "Look, I've no more desire to die in the Veil than either of you, but the Issnaîm imprisoned Tzal for a reason. Stars Below, but after everything we've seen, we know they'd good reason to do it. Maybe it's better to let things end."

Damant shook his head. "Under Tzal, there's hope. There's none in the Veil. Azra gave her life so that we could escape. We owe it to her to keep fighting."

Tatterlain shrugged, unoffended. "I just wanted to be sure. Oh, by the way, I brought you a little something, but I'll need a hand bringing it in. Is Keti about? I haven't seen her."

"She went out around noon in search of more last breath," Damant replied. "Some of us aren't healing as fast as she likes. But I'm up to performing a bit of fetch-and-carry."

Tatterlain grinned. "I gladly accept your sacrifice. But mind your hands. She bites."

Forty-Three

The "she" in question turned out to be Yali: gagged, bound and blindfolded in the cargo cabin of the same battered clatter wagon in which Keti had brought Damant to the warehouse. Contrary to Tatterlain's warnings, she didn't bite – the filthy gag made that impossible – but she thrashed and kicked furiously as they carried her in from the covered loading dock to the largest of the living quarters. It took all three of them to lash her to a high-backed chair, and she still managed to leave the makings of a new bruise on Damant's cheek, courtesy of an elbow that struck home with far more impact than her bindings should have allowed.

Tatterlain folded his arms and surveyed their handiwork. With her wrists bound and ropes securing her to the chair at shoulder, elbow, thigh and ankle, Yali wasn't going anywhere. Not that it stopped her snarling and thrashing about with enough force to set the chair rocking. "Like I said, I don't leave anyone behind."

Damant watched Yali with no small discomfort. Her golden handmaiden's gown stood in stark contrast to her animalistic manner. Not the behaviour of a kidnap victim, but something darker. Fury born of glamour's devotion, or had the Eternity Queen broken her as she'd broken Kastagîr? "Bringing her here might not have been wise."

Rîma favoured him with an unhappy stare. "How can you say that?"

"Can you free her without Isdihar to help you?" Damant replied bluntly.

425

"I don't know." Reluctance creaked beneath her words. "Even if Isdihar were here, I couldn't be certain. When I broke Tzal's hold over you, I still commanded an army. All I have left are dregs."

Damant looked on the struggling Yali once more. At a face he'd only ever associated with kindness and humour now contorted with rage. In the end, the decision made itself. "Then let me be your army."

"I beg your pardon?" said Rîma.

"You said it before: the souls of Tadamûr were too faded to offer serious contest. I may be battered, but I'm still alive, and I'll be damned if I let Yali stay in his clutches a minute longer. When you freed me from Tzal, you put a piece of your soul into mine. Take a piece of me with you this time. I'll shake her loose."

Too late, he wondered if that was true. What if rather than breaking Tzal's hold on Yali, she instead brought him into her glamour?

Rîma narrowed her eyes. "Are you sure . . ."

". . . that I want to go through with this?" Damant gave a wry smile to accompany his passable impression. "No. But the Eternity Queen only got her hooks into Yali because I didn't trust her enough. I'm tired of watching the young suffer for my mistakes. You understand that, don't you?"

She nodded, her grey eyes heavy with long millennia. "More than you can know. Very well, let us try."

She stood behind Yali and extended her sword to Damant, holding it not by the hilt but halfway along the blade. "Place your hands on the steel. The echoes of its former bearers will guide us."

After a brief hesitation, Damant unholstered his shrieker and passed it to Tatterlain. "Just in case." Then he gripped the sword.

"Are you prepared?" asked Rîma.

He nodded, though he still wasn't certain what he was preparing *for*.

"Then we will begin . . . And Ihsan?" She gave a taut nod. "Thank you."

She laid her hand on the back on Yali's head.

Damant plunged into darkness.

*

426

Panicked, he spun about. Nauseous. Disoriented. The darkness held no landmark, no way to determine up from down. No sense of existence beyond the extent of his own self. There was only Rîma's sword in his hand, its metal cold in a place that knew neither chill nor warmth.

"Rîma!" The word vanished into the darkness, swallowed up and silent almost before he'd fully given it voice.

Already reeling, he stumbled, fell . . . and kept falling.

The Eternity Queen's laughter echoed around him.

A gloved hand found his. Another grabbed at his arm. A third. A fourth. Together they righted him. Four hooded, black-robed figures in golden masks. The dead of Tadamûr, or their dregs. They felt less real than they had before, wraithlike even in that impossible space. But they offered an anchor – a means of making sense of his surroundings. For the first time, he felt pressure beneath his feet. In the distance, a gangling brown-haired figure in a golden gown had her back to him.

"Yali!"

She offered no response. Damant set out towards her, the shadowy dead on his heels.

The darkness flared with bright magenta flame, and suddenly the Eternity Queen stood before him, her expression contorted with fury.

You will not have her! She's mine. Her snarl of anger cooled to a seductive smile. *Or perhaps you'd like to join her?*

He gripped the sword tighter. "Never again."

She swept out her hand. Fire scattered the dead of Tadamûr and drove Damant to his knees. Rîma's sword slipped from his grasp and spun away into darkness, swallowed by the abyss even as he scrabbled frantically to claim it.

The Eternity Queen stepped closer, golden dress and bronze skin wisping into magenta flames that billowed in a non-existent breeze. *Never is a very long time, Ihsan.*

She glowed brighter, brilliant in the darkness. Damant shrank away, cursing his arrogance. Already he felt the pressure of the Eternity Queen's will. Caressing. Probing. Soothing. He didn't have Isdihar's peculiar heritage or Rîma's ageless wisdom. He was just a mortal man, and an old one at that.

He'd been a fool to come into Tzal's clutches once more.

But it wasn't Tzal, was it? It was just a piece of him, split off to ensure that Yali remained englamoured. A piece of a god was not a god.

Stand up, Ihsan. He couldn't tell if the voice was Rîma's or his own, but he found strength in its certainty. *Make good on your promise.*

Trembling, he rose to his feet.

The Eternity Queen's eyes flashed. *I preferred you on your knees.*

"I'm done kneeling to you. I never should have started."

He swung a fist, the blow thick with every scrap of fear, of loss, of humiliation and of guilt – of guilt most of all. The Eternity Queen shimmered to nothing as his fist landed, cast to the non-existent winds. Breathing hard, Damant spun around, but he was alone. No dead of Tadamûr. No Eternity Queen. There was only Yali, staring at him with red-rimmed eyes.

||It's all right,|| Damant signed. ||I've come to take you back.||

But how? Rîma's sword had broken the final bond for him, but that sword was now lost. So he did the only thing he could, which was to throw his arms around Yali and hold her tight.

Damant awoke in an ungainly heap on the warehouse floor.

Tatterlain bent over him with an expression that might have been concern. "Can't stay down there all day. Things to do."

"Did it work?" Damant shook his head, but the cobwebs clung closer than ever. Even the smallest movement took effort; limbs and lungs alike swore that he'd been walking for days.

"See for yourself."

Tatterlain stepped away, revealing an unbound, tear-stained Yali signing frantically with Rîma. As Damant rose achingly to his feet, Rîma pressed a finger to her lips and pointed in his direction. Yali closed the distance between them and hugged him with enough force to drive the air from his lungs. She held the embrace for a long moment, shuddering with emotion, then stepped away, green eyes bright with remorse and joy.

||I'm sorry. I'm so sorry. I . . .|| She cuffed tears from her eyes and returned to what were for her stumbling signs. ||I tried to fight, but she was too strong.||

||It wasn't your fault,|| Damant replied. ||I should never have left you behind. Can you forgive me?||

Yali gaped. ||Me? Forgive you?|| She shook her head and laughed softly. ||You're a fool, old man.||

Tatterlain pouted. ||No hug for me?||

||You don't deserve one, letting me think that you were that awful rake! You *propositioned* me.|| Her obvious horror was final proof, had Damant needed any, that Yali was among those that Tatterlain had fooled.

Tatterlain spread a hand across his chest. ||Can you blame me? You're a lot prettier when you're not crying.||

Yali clapped her hands to her ears. ||I don't want to hear this!|| But there was at least a little colour in her cheeks.

Ensconced in a series of beaten-up armchairs, they spent the next hour bringing Yali up to speed with all that had happened since the sanctum, aided by a bottle of calvasîr Tatterlain had retrieved from the clatter wagon. He also brought in a large brown haversack, which he dumped at the foot of his chair without paying it obvious attention.

||Spoils from the palace?|| asked Yali.

||"Something like that,"|| he replied. ||"Our dear Eternity Queen won't miss it."||

Yali stared down into her glass. ||You're probably right. The Veil's all she's spoken about for days. That and Kat. She needs a new body. She's aged ten years since the sanctum. I don't think she's going to hold together much longer.||

||"Any sign of Azra?"|| asked Damant, his own glass untouched.

Yali shook her head. ||It's going to destroy Kat when she finds out.||

429

"She died a better woman than she lived," said Rîma. "There's comfort in that."

Tatterlain raised his glass aloft. "Here's to dying better than we've lived." When no one seemed eager to join his toast, he shrugged and drank.

"Is there anything you've heard that we can use? Anything at all?" Damant asked Yali. "You've been closer to the Eternity Queen than any of us."

No, I . . . Wait, there was something, but I don't know why it should matter. She took a sip, scowled and set the glass pointedly aside. More than once she muttered about the lethargia. About there being no point to it killing firebloods if it left cinderbloods free to destroy everything. "That's the problem with free will," she said once, "so I think we'll have less of it for a while."

"Sounds like another wave of arrests and spectacle executions," said Tatterlain.

"I don't think so," said Rîma thoughtfully. "In fact, I wonder if Tzal created the lethargia specifically to destroy the firebloods."

"That's absurd," said Damant.

"Is it? We know that Khalad has been home to many races over the centuries, and that each one perished when Nyssa – that is to say *Tzal* – sent fire from the Zaruan Mountains to birth a new Age of Fire, wiping away the old so that the new could prosper. Terrion Arvish believed that freeing Tzal from the Stars Below would unleash a new epoch. Perhaps it did. And just like before, the old order – in this case the firebloods – is being swept away."

Tatterlain poured himself another generous measure of calvasîr. "Even assuming he wants to keep you upstart cinderbloods around, why do my undelightful peers have to shuffle off? It doesn't make sense."

Belatedly Damant realised that Tatterlain – né Tuzen Karza – was himself a fireblood. "It does to Tzal. He'll have a reason, even if that reason's boredom or simple malice. I wish I saw how it helps us."

Rîma shrugged. ||"It may not. But it seems clear that even when he was trapped in the Stars Below, Tzal brought about the rise and fall of Khalad's civilisations. The ashborn, the scaldera – maybe now the firebloods, if the Veil doesn't end us all first – all of them ruled by Caradan Diar."||

Tatterlain tilted his glass towards her. ||"All of them except your people."||

||"Maybe even mine. It can't be a coincidence that Tadamûr and Zariqaz are so close together. I always assumed Zariqaz was founded second, but what if it wasn't? We assumed that the Alabastran church stole Amakala's likeness for Nyssa Iudexas, but what if it was the other way around? What if my ancestor strove to supplant Tzal in every way?"||

Damant frowned. ||"Then maybe the answer does lie in Tadamûr after all."||

||"I already told you, it's gone,"|| she replied angrily. ||"There's no city-soul, no siphonic prism. Nothing."||

||"I mean, if we really *want* a siphonic prism, we have one."|| Setting his glass aside, Tatterlain upended his haversack. Five fist-sized lumps of black glass tumbled onto the worn carpet, each glinting with half-melted silver and astoricum tracery. ||"I wouldn't say it was in peak condition, but we have one."||

Yali stared at him in wonder. ||How did you get this?||

||"That thing about the Royal Guard being incorruptible? Turns out it's really not true if you have enough tetrams to throw at the problem."|| He stared down at the remains. ||"Talk to any shriversman and they'll tell you that prisms shatter all the time, but they can be re-fused. The shape isn't really relevant – it's the material they're made out of. If all that's true, then a furnace and a little skill . . ."||

Damant grunted. ||"That can't be true, otherwise the Eternity Queen would already have had it repaired."||

||"Why should she even think it possible? She didn't make it. The Issnaîm, or at least their forebears, did that. It honestly may not have

431

occurred to her. If Rîma's right, then Tzal is more one to throw away and start over than patch things back together."||

||"That, or he isn't worried by the collapse of the Veil after all,"|| said Damant.

||"Futility is the mother of invention?"|| asked Rîma.

||"That's part of it, I can feel it in my bones. What I don't know is *why*."||

Yali frowned. ||Say you're right. Repairing that prism means finding a master shriver. They all work for Alabastra, which means they all work for the Eternity Queen.||

Damant considered. ||"Not necessarily. There's always Mezzeri – the woman who fixed up Mirela's hisser. She's a master shriver, or she was."|| He paced out his words, thinking as he went. ||"If Mezzeri repairs the siphonic prism, we have a bargaining chip. I doubt we can convince Tzal to return to the Stars Below, but we might be able to negotiate something."||

||"And even if we can't,"|| Rîma put in, ||"with the mists at bay, we'll be able to focus on Tzal again."||

Tatterlain gave a slow nod. ||"Where is this Mezzeri?"||

||"Tanleer Street,"|| said Damant. ||"Assuming she's not dead or in a custodium cell."||

||"Then we'll go tonight. It'll give Keti a couple of hours to get back and let the streets calm down."|| Tatterlain shot a glance at Damant. ||"Besides, some of us look like they could use a nap. But I'm thinking that Mezzeri can as easily make the repairs at Phoenissa, Galzanta or even Athenoch as here in Zariqaz. Let's get out while we can."||

||If she agrees to come,|| said Yali.

Tatterlain waved an airy hand. ||"I assume that we'll be at our most persuasive."||

||"The redcloaks will be watching the railrunner stations,"|| said Rîma. ||"And I doubt we can charter a skyship at this notice."||

Tatterlain knocked back the last of his calvasîr and began hauling the pieces of the siphonic prism back into his haversack. ||"It so happens that Tuzen Karza has a regular arrangement at Selesti Dock. A pleasure barge, discreetly outfitted, very private. No questions asked. He was planning on taking a turn around midnight. An apology to Keti, for what I understand were myriad infidelities. Loathsome fellow, but we might as well make him of use one last time."||

It didn't escape Damant's notice that Tatterlain was back to speaking of Tuzen Karza as another person. ||"Why do I get the feeling you've been one step ahead of us this whole time?"||

Tatterlain beamed. ||"Don't feel offended. I am in many ways a remarkable man."||

Forty-Four

A hand tugged on Kat's shoulder. "You need to wake up, sister. Set an example."

A hundred scrapes and bruises screamed for attention as Kat opened her eyes onto darkness. Questing fingers found a rough bandage tied about her temples. Bleary eyes latched onto Tanith, and behind her a dozen filthy and bloodied sailriders, squatting beneath the upturned curve of what had once been the port bulwark of *Amarid's Dream*. The remnant of the skyship's aft lay canted over, keel skyward and the deck propped clear of the sand by the mainmast's stump. The remains of the prow was separated from the rest of the ship by a dozen wreckage-strewn yards, the carriage of a shrieker cannon visible among bodies, shattered crates, severed ropes and fire-blackened timbers, some of them still ablaze. More figures sheltered beneath the prow, Jazal among them, faces tight.

Further out, the *Chainbreaker's* silhouette contrived to offer disappointment.

"Zephyr?" Ignoring protests from her aching limbs, Kat made to rise. "Where is she?"

The pressure of a vaporous hand held her in place. "Here am I. Stay down."

One hand braced against the bulwark's overhang, Tanith peered out skyward. "There's a drakon still up there," she said bitterly. "Probably waiting to see if there's anything worth finishing off. I don't understand why they didn't kill us at Xe'iathî."

"Because there is nothing beyond the Veil but death." Kat scowled. "If the Elders had killed us in plain sight, we'd just be dead. If we die out here, we become part of the myth. We're a warning."

"To who?" asked Tanith. "Who would possibly know or care?"

"My people," replied Zephyr softly. "Stop them seeking the Old Realm, it does. Keeps them reliant on the Elders. My fault, this is. I should have known. I should have remembered."

Kat shook her head. "You're not responsible for what the mists took from you. If it had been anyone else at the helm, we'd all be dead." She raised her voice so it would carry to the other survivors. They had to be angry, and with all they'd endured – all they'd lost – some among them might think of blaming Zephyr. "We owe you our lives."

Zephyr's lips thinned to a scowl, but she nodded. Kat empathised. Zephyr wasn't the only one at fault. She'd sensed something amiss back in Xe'iathî. Why hadn't she acted on it? Too busy running from trouble, she supposed. Hope and desperation were a toxic mix. Whatever else she'd become – whatever else others saw in her – a piece of her hadn't stopped running since she'd first fled her father's creditors. Maybe for the briefest time with Azra.

She grimaced the memory away.

"I think ... yes, they're moving off," said Tanith. "I guess we're no fun any more."

"So what?" growled a bearded sailrider Kat tentatively identified as Braban. "We've no ship. We're not going anywhere. The Veil's gonna take us."

A murmur of agreement rippled beneath the upturned deck. Kat clambered to her feet. A spasm racked her left side as she did so, squeezing the breath from her lungs and forcing her to clutch at Zephyr for support. She pinched her eyes shut until it passed. No. Not *this*. Not now, on top of everything else. She drove back despair with anger. At the Issnaîm, at Caradan Diar, at Vallant for getting her into this mess in the first place. At herself for letting him.

It could damn well wait. Tanith was right: she needed to set an example.

She fixed Braban with a stare as Jazal's group dribbled in to join the survivors. Eighteen sailriders left from a crew of thirty. All bloodied. Some limping. Others with livid burns.

"We're not done yet, but you're right: this ship's flying days are done and we've already been in the mists for too long – the astoricum won't keep us together for ever." She paused, more to catch her breath than for emphasis. She hoped it didn't show, or that it would at least be ascribed to injuries from the crash. "*Chainbreaker* looked reasonably intact. If any of its buoyancy tanks are still viable, we can transfer the last of our eliathros. Then all we need are sails. There'll be canvas in the *Chainbreaker*'s hold."

"That's if our starboard tanks didn't crack on impact," said Braban.

Kat nodded. "You're not wrong. But do you – do any of you – want to let the mists take you without a fight? We came here for a reason. We've lost friends getting this far. I don't mean to give up now." Another murmur rippled out, but this one defiant. Heads nodded, Braban's among them. "So let's get to work. Jazal? Dig out the astoricum from behind the winch assemblies. The motics can't help us now, and we'll need something to keep us together as we cross to the *Chainbreaker*. The rest of you, let's find out what the Issnaîm left us to work with."

Heads held higher, the sailriders bled away to their tasks. Kat exhaled, just a little.

"You sounded just like Vallant," Tanith breathed in her ear.

"Shut up." With an effort, Kat lowered her voice. "What about you?"

"What about *what about me*?"

"That display up on the deck. You were about to jump into the mists."

Tanith scowled. "Like I said, the lesion was calling to me." Scrunching her lips in discomfort, she paused. "I don't do well with instinct, but it's under control now."

436

Kat believed her, if only because she too no longer felt the pull of the lesion, though whether that would last when it was again in sight – for the moment, it lay hidden beyond the *Chainbreaker* – she couldn't be certain. "What about the rest?"

Tanith's scowl deepened. "I'm not going to start eating your crew, if that's what you mean."

"Then I need a favour ..." Kat glanced over Tanith's shoulder to the burned body of a dead sailrider. "Get an astoricum shard from Jazal and take the dead out into the mists. Let the Veil have them. We'll remember them as they were." Better for the bodies to fade than to be a drag on morale.

Tanith twitched a mirthless smile. "I get all the pretty jobs."

"As soon as there's something that needs a good stabbing, I'll be sure to let you know."

Tanith stared over to where Zephyr was busy helping a sailrider sift through a broken crate. "I could happily stab a lot of Issnaîm right now."

The search of the wreckage turned up a bounty in excess of expectation. Enough ship's biscuits and cured beef to last the denuded crew for better than a week, and four unsplit barrels of fresh water. Two of the three starboard buoyancy tanks had indeed survived intact, the third with a slow leak that Jazal plugged with scraps of greased leather. All eight shrieker cannons were serviceable, though the *Dream*'s ungainly demise had thrown them all from their carriages and shattered most of the ifrîti prisms that granted them flame.

With recovery well under way, Kat led Tanith, Zephyr, Braban and two sailriders named Halila and Qath out into the mists. Each carried a small haversack of food and a flask of precious fresh water. Everyone had an astoricum shard about their person, but Kat insisted that they be roped together as an extra precaution. With her at their head, they forged on into the mists.

To all appearances the *Chainbreaker* lay no more than a quarter-mile from the wreck of *Amarid's Dream*, but the Veil seemed determined to act against them. Three times they lost sight of the ship as the shifting skeins swallowed it up, on each occasion finding that they'd somehow headed out in the wrong direction entirely. Each time, they struck out again, Kat closing her ears to the hungry, weeping cries that echoed through the greenish-white.

"Children of the Issnaîm, they are," murmured Zephyr, "*akîa* lost and hunger upon them. Let us hope they do not catch our scent."

Was she speaking of the crew of the downed drakon, or of others stranded long ago? Kat didn't like to ask. Even with a scrap of astoricum clutched tight, Zephyr was growing ever more vaporous. How long before her *akîa* unravelled and the red glint touched her eyes?

They finally reached the canted-over *Chainbreaker* on their fourth attempt. Close up, it looked even more intact than at a distance. The ragged gash along its port buoyancy tanks and the trailing wreckage of its pinion sails reaffirmed how it had died, the ship crippled so cleanly and efficiently that Kat wondered just how many vessels lost on the border of the Veil had perished to aether caste sport. The foresail was largely intact, though the angle of the deck caused it to hang drunkenly from its stays.

Kat saw no sign of the crew as she clambered up the hummock of its port flank with the help of rope and grapnel, but nor had she expected to after so long. As she crested the remains of the port bulwark, the lesion in the Veil shimmered in the middle distance, not suspended in the distant skies as the mists' duplicitous perspective had first suggested, but touching the trackless sands. Again she felt the tug in her gut. As Tanith joined her at the bulwark, she shot her a questioning glance.

Tanith scowled with unspoken strain, but shook her head. "Does anyone else feel that?"

Braban paused in the act of belaying a rope to a broken section of bulwark. "Feel what?"

"Never mind," Kat replied. If the lesion spoke to her and Tanith alone, that made it another dubious benefit of their aetherios tattoos. Good and bad. Probably. There was always bad with the good. At least the grip of the mists had lessened on the approach to *Chainbreaker*, the astoricum of the ship working together with the shards they'd brought from *Amarid's Dream* to hold dissolution at bay. "Let's see what we have."

They divided into teams of two, Tanith and Halila checking the gun deck and crew quarters while Braban and Qath clambered down into the hold. That left Kat and Zephyr to check the surviving buoyancy tanks and steerage. The starboard tanks were indeed mostly intact. Better still, *Chainbreaker* sat but lightly on the sands – proof, as Zephyr put it, that she wanted to fly again.

"Looks like you deliberately grounded the ship in such a way as to make it easier to refloat," said Kat, as they climbed the ropes back up to the quarterdeck. Or *Kat* climbed, at least. Zephyr simply floated alongside, looking more vaporous all the while.

"Wish I could recall any of it, do I," she replied, a catch in her throat. "Someone should remember them."

Though her phrasing suggested that she was speaking of the crew, it was clear that Vallant was uppermost in her mind. For all the mockery that passed between them, or perhaps because of it, they'd always been inseparable. Zephyr had saved Vallant at his lowest ebb, betrayed by those he'd served and lost in the Veil that had claimed his wife and daughter. For most of the time she'd known them, Kat had assumed that they were simply another pair of Rîma's "old souls", reunited across reincarnation. However, with it now being clearer than ever that the Issnaîm sat apart from the promise of rebirth, she for the first time entertained the idea that their bond was something much more commonplace.

"I never thanked him," she said. Pride made the words stumble, but some things were better said late than never. "He was arrogant, insufferable and right more often than anyone should be, but he was a better friend than I ever knew."

Zephyr offered a sad smile tinged with wickedness. "Cannot tell you, can I, the number of times I wanted to throw him overboard. But life without him has no colour. Made the impossible seem real, did he … as do you, at your best."

439

Kat grunted the compliment away. "If it remains impossible, then what does it matter?"

"Because in a world that takes and trammels, to *give* is the greatest kindness and hope is the finest treasure."

Uncertain how to respond, but feeling ever so slightly less a fraud, Kat threw herself into checking the ship's wheels and steerage lines. The latter led her from the quarterdeck, through the gun deck and finally to the dingy, suffocating confines of the aft orlop.

While the lateral rope survived as little more than charred, knotted lengths caught in the pulleys, the pitching line was an untouched rope of a slender gauge more commonly used to reef a sail.

"Tried to make repairs, someone did," said Zephyr, "but the mists took them first."

Kat blinked to clear watering eyes. The *Chainbreaker*'s lumani having faded long ago, she'd had to fashion a makeshift torch from canvas scraps, and the acrid smoke stung her eyes terribly. "Let's get back to the others."

Returning to the main deck, she perched as comfortably as she could against the base of the aft mast and stared out towards the shimmering, flickering lesion – the promised gate to the Old Realm. Salvation, maybe. But more and more, she felt as though there was something else at play. When she closed her eyes, she could almost see the shape of it, even hear voices whispering of it in the dark. Had the Eternity King spoken any truth at all, or had he merely told her what he'd wanted her to hear? And the Issnaîm ... Had the centuries distorted an age-old undertaking to cage Tzal into an imperative to prevent anyone at all from leaving the prison Khalad had become?

"There's something we don't understand about all this," she murmured.

"Want to go back and ask the Elders, do you?" said Zephyr.

Kat stared at the lesion. Did it really offer salvation? What if the Elders had acted out of a misplaced sense of kindness, and some terrible fate awaited beyond? The mists made monsters of the Issnaîm, if they had neither silver light nor astoricum to protect them. Would the lesion – or the Old Realm beyond, if it existed – do worse to Kat and her kind? "Maybe."

"No truth will they willingly give. Had their chance, did they."

Kat glanced at a carriageless shrieker cannon thrown clear during the crash. For the first time, she recognised the depression in the sands beneath it. The last trace of a man or woman, pinned in place until death or the Veil took them. "Then I'll speak in a voice that they can't ignore."

A muffled cry issued up from the companionway. It wasn't until another followed on its heels that Kat recognised Braban's voice and made sense of the words.

"There's something in here with us!"

She took the steps as fast as the *Chainbreaker*'s awkward angle allowed. Her acrid makeshift torch revealed Braban kneeling a dozen yards from the hold's aft companionway, Halila crumpled and unconscious beside him. Qath held a makeshift torch while Tanith had a wicked dagger in hand, her eyes scanning the mess of crates and barrels of the deeper hold. Heavy ropes still held much of the cargo lashed to the inner hull, but enough had shaken loose to leave the footing lousy with wreckage.

Kat crouched beside Halila. Blood matted her hair to her scalp, but she was breathing. "What happened?"

Braban shook his head. "We were checking for supplies when something came out of the darkness and swung at me." He glanced down at Halila and grimaced. "Hali shoved me clear, more fool her."

"What was it?" snapped Tanith, her focus still on the darkness.

"Didn't see." He clenched and unclenched a fist. His eyes were wide and frantic in the torchlight. "But it was fast and angry."

"Not one of mine gone to etravia, was it," said Zephyr. "Slashed and bloody would you both be."

The words didn't noticeably soothe Braban. Perhaps that was due to the odd note of pride with which they'd been offered.

Kat drew her sword and nodded to Tanith. "Let's take a look."

"I thought you'd never ask," she replied dourly.

Bracing her feet against the deck's slope as best she could, Kat edged into the darkness, torch high and scimitar extended. After a dozen yards, the wreckage-strewn clearway between the cargo divided about a towering netted bundle of sail canvas lashed to the ceiling and floor, creating two narrow corridors between the uneven crates. Disdaining Kat's mortal need for torchlight, Tanith nodded right and headed down the associated passage. Stepping over the remnant of a crate that had come unmoored, Kat headed left.

Wet, ragged breaths whispered out to challenge her soft footfalls. Shadows shifted in the flickering torchlight, imagination conjuring monstrous shapes that retreated when her eyes were on them and flowed back when they were not. Trusting to her hearing more than her eyes, Kat pressed on. The corridor of crates narrowed and twisted to her left.

A snarl rippled as she rounded the corner. The shadows shifted.

She ducked as something large and fast swung out. It whistled over her head, more felt by its backwash than seen, shattering the flank of a crate with a dull crunch.

Breathing hard of air suddenly rancid with stale sweat, she lashed out with a foot, more instinct than intent, and struck something solid but yielding. It went backwards in a gasping rush and sprawled across a barrel, the baulk of charred timber that had been its makeshift club clattering from an outflung hand.

Greasy yellow-orange light spilled across a matted, overgrown beard and wild, bloodshot eyes. A torn and filthy uniform, kin to the one Kat herself wore. As he toppled off the barrel onto all fours, she glimpsed a length of black ribbon lashed about his right wrist, a scrap of silver and red-gold shining in the torchlight.

Kat blinked, her thoughts at last catching up to the evidence of her eyes. "Vallant? . . . Vallant, it's me. It's Kat."

A wet growl in his throat, he reached blindly for his weapon.

Kat lowered her scimitar. "Bashar . . . I'm not going to hurt you."

All well and good, except she doubted his intent aligned with hers. There wasn't even a scrap of recognition in those eyes. No glimpse of intellect or self. The red-gold at his wrist. Zephyr's brooch. Its precious astoricum, more substantial than anything else aboard *Chainbreaker* or *Amarid's Dream*, had kept his body whole behind the Veil these past months, but what of his soul? You lost more than *akîa* in the mists. Had it torn gaps in his memory, or was he so broken and charged with adrenaline at having his refuge invaded that he wasn't thinking straight? Did he even remember her?

"I'm here with Zephyr. You remember Zephyr, don't you?"

He screwed up his face. "Gone ... Lost ..." He pressed the brooch to his chest, the words dredged up from somewhere deep and half remembered. "Went for help ... Mists took her, all red-eyed ... weeping." He sagged, face lined and distraught.

Was she getting through? Was there at least a *piece* of Vallant left? "She's here."

Growling, he pounced. Kat sidestepped his downward swipe and collapsed to one knee as a spasm racked her lungs. Wheezing like a woman twice her age, she saw his second attack too late. The baulk chimed a glancing blow off her skull, driving her the rest of the way to the deck.

Behind Vallant, the shadows shifted.

"Don't ... hurt him," she gasped, and spat blood onto the deck.

Tanith rushed out of the darkness. In one smooth motion she gathered Vallant up by the throat and slammed him into a crate, then rammed her forehead into his to scatter what little remained of his wits.

The slope of the deck made getting the unconscious Vallant and Halila up to the captain's cabin challenging, a problem solved by fashioning a stretcher from broken timber. Before long, both were wedged as comfortably as could be managed: Vallant in his cot, and Halila across the long chaise in the outer quarters.

"Head back to the *Dream*," Kat told Braban and Qath. "Bring whatever last breath survived the crash, and tell Jazal I want him here. Let's get this old heap skyworthy."

As they left, she passed up Tanith's obvious "we need to talk" scowl and crossed to the cot, where Zephyr had one of Vallant's hands clasped in both of hers, the soft spill of an Issnaîm lament lending sweetness to the air. She'd not left his side from the moment they'd brought him out of the hold.

Her song fell silent as Kat approached. "My fault, this is. Never should I have left him."

Kat stared down at Vallant, wondering if she should be happy that he was alive or sorrowful at his condition. Six months, alone for most of it, subsisting off rations that had survived the crash. The numbers didn't add up. Even if the mists hadn't taken him, starvation or thirst should have done so. But then numbers seldom tallied cleanly in the mists. If they'd favoured good fortune over ill for a change, she'd take it.

She rubbed the swelling on her brow from where he'd struck her. Another lump to join the one earned during the crash. "You're the only reason he's still alive." She nodded at the brooch, still wound about his forearm. "My guess is that you left it with him and went to find help."

Zephyr's expression slipped into the faraway look that had become habit when she scried forsaken memories. "Or felt my *akîa* fading, I did. Wanted to spare him that horror."

All red-eyed ... weeping, Vallant had said. Kat decided that Zephyr could be spared that information. "He's alive. That's what matters." She hoped it was true.

The faraway look hardened. "A reckoning there must be for this."

"Stay with him," said Kat. "Make sure he doesn't hurt himself."

"Or anyone else," put in Tanith from the far wall. "Kat ..."

Kat sighed. "I know. Later." Beyond the ruin of the aft windows, half a dozen silhouetted figures were emerging from the mists. "Work to do first."

To her surprise, Tanith didn't argue the point, so she passed out onto the main deck and waited for Jazal and his sailriders to join her.

"Heard you had some trouble," he said warily.

"Something like that." Kat briefly explained all that he'd missed. Even now, Vallant's name was a charm, rousing Jazal and the others to determination she'd not seen since they'd first breached the Veil. He'd been back barely any time at all, and already he overshadowed her. Good. She'd never wanted the job in the first place. "I want *Chainbreaker* aloft. The starboard buoyancy tanks are intact, steerage is repairable and the holds full of spares. Pull apart the *Dream* if you have to, but get us skyborne again. Can you do it?"

Jazal's cheek twitched. "It'll take time."

"We're none of us going anywhere," she said. "Well, I am. You're not."

"I hear you. Wait . . . what?"

Kat pointed at the lesion, shimmering away in the mists. "We came a long way to find out if that leads anywhere. If I'm not back by the time you're ready to sail . . ." What? Return home and cling to Athenoch until the Veil swallowed it? Sail round and around in circles until the mists took them? Follow her blindly into whatever horror had claimed her? "If I'm not back, look to Zephyr for your orders."

Jazal nodded. "Right you are, boss."

Kat retrieved her haversack from where she'd slung it over the ship's wheels and confirmed that everything was in place. Food for a day or two, all things being equal. It would have to do. Heaving it up onto her shoulder, she made a controlled abseil to the alabaster sands.

To her complete lack of surprise, Tanith was waiting for her, arms folded. "Slinking off without me, are you?"

"How can I when you're right here?" asked Kat.

Tanith favoured her with an old-fashioned look. "The omen rot's back, isn't it?"

So she *had* seen. "One last gift from Caradan Diar," Kat replied bitterly. "Turns out he never cured me at all, he was just holding it at bay. I was going to tell you."

"Sure you were."

She sighed. "I have to do this. One way or another, I'm already dead. Better to die knowing than wondering."

"I'm coming with you. Don't try to stop me."

Kat smiled, glad beyond words and surprised to be so. "Wouldn't dream of it."

Side by side they set out into the mists, heading always toward the shimmering black lesion. This time, the capricious Veil made no attempt to throw them off course, or perhaps the lesion's very nature made that impossible. Every step brought them closer, until the air hissed and spat and the surface of the lesion resolved to shifting black platelets, each one like a skin of ice barely formed across a puddle, offering no reflection and scraping against one another under the influence of some unseen current.

"The Black River . . ." murmured Tanith, her fingertips outstretched almost to the point of making contact, "flowing beneath the world."

Kat tilted her head. There *was* something curiously fluid about the surface. "More Anfaian legend?" Except that wasn't right, was it? Anfai's heresy had begun with the Issnaîm, maybe even with Zephyr herself.

"I've seen it, Kat," Tanith replied, deadly serious. "In the Stars Below. This isn't that, but I think it's something similar. A door to another place."

"Maybe this wasn't a waste of time after all," said Kat, but she made no move to touch the lesion.

"You're sure it's a good idea?"

"I used to," Kat replied, unable to look away. "But what did the daughters of Terrion Arvish ever know about good ideas?"

She held out her hand. After the briefest of hesitations Tanith took it.

With a deep breath, Kat stepped forward.

Forty-Five

A less than gentle tug on Damant's shoulder woke him into darkness. Rolling over, he stared blearily up at a thoughtful-looking Tatterlain. "What is it?"

"Pull yourself together and meet me in the crosswalk."

Tatterlain slipped away, and Damant began the laborious process of easing his bruised and protesting body out of the sagging bed. He pulled on his skelder's garb – it still felt strange not to be wearing a uniform – and padded as gently as he could to the enclosed, dust-laden crosswalk that spanned Karana Street, linking the offices in which they slept to the main body of the warehouse.

Tatterlain was a shadowy figure halfway along, standing beside the single remaining glass pane in an otherwise boarded-up run of windows. He pressed a warning finger to his lips. "Here."

"What is this?" Gruffness was more habit than intent. Damant had long since decided that Tatterlain's concerns were very much his own. "What time is it?" The air held the chill of night, but Zariqaz cooled quickly once the sun went down.

"A little before eleven if the guildhall clock can be trusted," murmured Tatterlain. He stepped back from the window. "Tell me what you think."

Karana Street looked much as most such thoroughfares did at that hour, with intermittent passers-by and a good number of conversation circles transacting dubious business where the shadows were deepest. "I don't see it."

"Give it a moment."

Damant did, and at last realised what had spooked Tatterlain so. Folk engaged in illicit trades kept their eyes on the street to guard against custodians, or on one another in anticipation of a double-cross. Here, everyone in sight was watching the warehouse. They weren't even being subtle about it. The shadows were home to at least a hundred watchers, their number swelling all the time as occasional passers-by peeled off to join them. "*Kiasta*."

Tatterlain's grin lacked his usual flair. "Someone's spent too much time with Kat." Seriousness returned. "This is bad, isn't it?"

The groups of watchers grew further, fed by newcomers. Not everyone who transited through Karana Street joined the vigil. A good half kept walking, but Damant saw no obvious pattern to those who remained. There were more than a few skelders garbed and girded for dubious business, but also soot-blackened factory labourers, painted street-nymphs, guildsmen and gaudy-robed firebloods – even an archon in pristine white robes. As he watched, a couple divided, the man striding towards the nearest vigil while the woman trailed behind, tugging at his sleeve, expression carrying angry tone through the still air though her words were lost. Turning back, the man levelled a flat stare, and at last she stalked away into the night, while he joined his new companions in staring at the warehouse.

It didn't make any sense – or rather, it didn't make any sense Damant wanted a part of. "Is Keti back?"

"No." Tatterlain's reply rippled with concern. "That's why I'm worried."

Damant nodded, a new ache added to a heart already heavy with them. "Wake the others. I'll keep watch."

Tatterlain returned a few minutes later with a dishevelled Yali and a watchful Rîma in tow, the former in close-fitting skelder's gear and the latter in her duster coat and broad-brimmed hat.

"Here." Tatterlain, now with the haversack containing the remains of the siphonic prism across his shoulder, handed Damant his weapons and a heavy coat.

He tugged them into place and wondered just how much of his shrieker's charge remained. ||"What's the best way out?"||

||"Back through the warehouse."||

||Through the warehouse?|| Yali scowled. ||They're *watching* the warehouse.||

||"We're not leaving through the front gate,"|| said Tatterlain patiently. ||"There's a hidden door into the old belltower. From there, we can get onto what's left of the district wall. We'll drop down into Hannam Street and cut into the alleys."||

||We'll still be in full view once we're up there.||

Rîma cleared her throat. ||"In my experience, most folk don't look up unless they've a reason."|| She turned to Tatterlain. ||"Are you leaving a note for Keti?"||

Tatterlain winced. ||"Under the circumstances, I thought it better not to. She's a clever girl."||

||"Then we'd better get moving,"|| said Rîma. ||"You lead. I'll bring up the rear."||

They descended into the warehouse, Tatterlain a dozen paces in front and moving like a skittish cat. Damant travelled with his shrieker drawn, Yali with a long dagger in her hand. Rîma followed unconcernedly. After a few moments of industry with a dummy brick, a hidden catch and a rope-and-pulley, Tatterlain had the door to the belltower open.

The space beyond was pitch black and thick with refuse – the tower had been derelict for a decade before the Obsidium Uprising. Damant resolved not to think about the filth squelching under his hands as he climbed blindly up the spiral stairs. By and by, musky air gave way to the smoke-chased Zariqaz night, the star-flecked square of an open doorway beckoned, and he was at last out onto the walls.

"Stay low," whispered Tatterlain, "just in case someone *does* look up."

Thirty feet below and barely that back across the warehouse's sunken, gappy rooftop, Karana Street was thicker with watchers than ever. Even as Damant crouched behind the parapet, a column of twenty redcloaks came marching down from the direction of Tosla Street. At their *gansalar*'s command, they drew their weapons and fanned out towards the warehouse gate. Almost as one, the watchers strung out to form a silent cordon around both the warehouse proper and the office bay on the other side of the street.

"I don't believe it," breathed Tatterlain.

Even in the darkness, Damant read the denial in his face. "Remember what the Eternity Queen said to Yali about having less free will for a while? That's what we're looking at." His stomach churned. Bad enough to have been made a semi-willing participant in Tzal's schemes, but this? Had Tzal always possessed this ability? *Futility is the mother of invention.* Perhaps that was as true of gods as mortals. "He's not leaving things to chance any more."

"You don't know what you're saying," Tatterlain hissed.

"I know better than any of us, except Yali."

"The whole city could be like this."

Damant thought back to the couple's one-sided argument. "I doubt it. At least, not yet."

Tatterlain gripped the parapet edge and with obvious effort tore his gaze from the street. "Is this what happened to Keti?"

Damant tried not to think about that deft, personable young woman being smothered by Tzal's glamour. She'd risked everything to save him and Rîma both. She deserved better. "Who's to say?"

The lingering effects of Marida's possession had shielded the girl from glamour for months . . . Had she at last succumbed to Tzal's rising power? Or had she simply been swept off the streets and broken by more conventional means? That *something* had befallen her, Damant didn't doubt, given the surety with which Tzal had moved against the warehouse.

If Keti had fallen to the glamour, were any of them safe? Rîma owed her protection to the dead of Tadamûr, but Damant had seen for himself that their power was spent, or as near as made no odds. He assumed that he and Yali were immune, having escaped the Eternity Queen's shadow once already, but was that true? As for Tatterlain, he'd been a man of two minds for as long as he'd been in Zariqaz. It might not be enough any longer.

Tatterlain tensed, his expression that of a man with both minds made up.

Damant grabbed his shoulder. "You can't go back for her."

Tatterlain glowered at him. "She trusted me."

"We don't even know if she's still alive."

He shoved Damant's hand away, his lips almost a snarl. "I can't abandon her."

"You think *I* want to?" There was more than one way to lose someone to the Eternity Queen, and if Tatterlain went marching back to the warehouse, there was every chance that'd be the last they saw of him, too. "We're not abandoning her. She was taken from us. Make it count for something. You've been at this far longer than I have, you *know* that's how it works."

Tatterlain sagged, the fight leaving him as quickly as it had come. "You're a bastard, Damant . . ."

"I hear that a lot."

". . . but you're right."

"I hear that a lot too." Sometimes he wished he didn't.

Yali appeared in the doorway, Rîma close behind. ||What's happened?||

Damant shared a glance with Tatterlain. ||"Nothing that won't keep. We'd better get moving."||

Heads low, they made their way along the narrow rampart until its decaying frontage met the blank gable of a half-collapsed factory, and navigated their way down to ground level. From there, they slipped into the alleyways that made a maze of the district's southern reaches, passing unremarked amongst street skelders and alley rats readily dissuaded from mischief by a twitch of Damant's shrieker or Rîma's sword.

Damant took the fact that no one attempted to stop them as proof that the Eternity Queen still couldn't see what others saw. Influence – and orders – had to pass from one person to the next. Omnipotent perhaps, but not yet omnipresent.

Tanleer Street was much as he remembered it, the residents huddling for warmth around bonfires running its length. By now hypersensitive to the bearing of others, Damant caught no shortage of curiously blank looks, but those who dwelled in the wreckage of Tanleer Street had more reasons than glamour to distance themselves from reality.

Shrieker concealed beneath his coat and his skin crawling whenever a gaze lingered on him too long, he skirted the outer edge of a bonfire and approached the wooden pillars and leaded windows of Mezzeri's shop. As before, the door – now showing signs of recent repair – was locked. As before, the act of trying the handle drew inexpertly concealed interest from the nearest bonfire.

Damant set his back to the bonfires. ||Yali? Can you get that open?||

She rolled her eyes. ||Don't insult me, old man.|| Taut signs and restless eyes belied her humour.

"You and I will go inside," he told Tatterlain softly as Yali turned her attention to the lock. He shifted his gaze to Rîma. "Make sure we're not disturbed, but be gentle. They're children, they know not what they do."

Rîma flashed a not-quite-smile, but like Yali her eyes were troubled. "And if they are not just big bearded children with troubled minds and loutish manners, but hands of the Eternity Queen?"

Of course she knew. She was always ahead of him. "Then I'd appreciate a warning."

She inclined her head. "As you wish."

Yali stepped away from the door and offered a subdued curtsey. ||Fast enough for you?||

||Always.||

The shop was as jumbled as before, though the details were different as wares came and went in the pursuit of its owner's dubious trades.

But the bitter aromatic of pipe leaf still hung on the air, still sweet with recent burning rather than the dryness of old ash. Mezzeri was still around. Or *had* been around recently.

"Perhaps you should have knocked," breathed Tatterlain.

"Perhaps." In Damant's experience, knocking just gave a person of interest the opportunity to become a fugitive. On the other hand, he couldn't discount the possibility that he was still thinking like a custodian, rather than the skelder he now irrevocably was.

"Mezzeri?" he called. "It's Damant. I just want to talk."

Silence. On the upside, no sound of running feet as she beat a retreat to back door or bolthole. And there was a watchfulness in the darkness.

He tried again. "If you're half as connected as someone in your ... profession should be, you'll know I'm a fugitive. You're far more threat to me than I am to you."

"Nice," muttered Tatterlain. "Put ideas in her head, why don't you?"

Damant stepped deeper into the gloom. The statue of Nyssa Iudexas stared down at him with passionless eyes. "You know something's wrong, Mezzeri. You used to be a shriver. You're more sensitive to souls than most. In fact, I'll bet you knew that there was something wrong with me the last time I was here ... which means you know that there isn't any more. Aren't you just a *little* curious as to what I have to say?"

The shadows shifted. Mezzeri slid out from between two groaning shelf cabinets, a custodium-issue shrieker unswerving in her hands. She looked older, her eyes tighter and the lines etched deeper in her face.

"You want to talk? So talk."

"I need to get something from my friend's bag," said Damant, careful to keep his hands away from his shrieker. "May I?"

Not a muscle twitched in Mezzeri's face. Her gun hand could have been carved from stone. "You might want to be careful."

Taking assent and threat as implied, Damant fished a chunk of the siphonic prism from Tatterlain's haversack and tossed it to Mezzeri.

She caught it cleanly, her eyes widening in wonder. "Where did you get this?"

"That's my business. Can you repair it?"

"It's aetherglass. I've only ever seen a splinter. They used it in the oldest prisms." She blinked, her attention as much on the fragment as Damant. "And by oldest, I mean thousands and thousands of years."

"Can you repair it?"

"Maybe. If you have the rest and I had a furnace."

Her eyes were shining with artificer's wonder: that undeniable and unquenchable joy at having something remarkable at hand. Damant had once felt that way about justice. No, the *law*. He still felt for justice as he always had, but the two were not the same. "We'll get you to one."

"What? No!" She blinked and stepped back, the shrieker raised. "I'm not going anywhere with you."

Damant pursued. Custodian's instincts were good for something even now, and they were screaming that Mezzeri knew just how precarious her situation was. "It's us or the palace dungeon. We've been attacked once tonight. One way or another, the Eternity Queen's going to find out we were here. Believe me when I say she's getting less trusting by the day."

Mezzeri glowered. "Thanks a lot."

"There's a desperate tyrant on the throne. The Veil's closing in. You fix that prism and we have a chance of doing something about at least one of those things. Otherwise we're all dead."

The door creaked. Yali and Rîma slipped inside.

"The crowd's getting restless," said Rîma. "*Karana Street* restless."

Mezzeri's expression grew even more pinched. Yes, she knew what was at stake. She just needed another push.

"Decision time, Mezzeri," said Damant. "Do you have anyone you care about? This is your chance to save them from what's coming. But if we leave without you, that's it."

"My daughter lives at Sumarand." The shrieker dropped. "I need to gather a few things. Tools and such."

Damant nodded. Sumarand lay far to the east. Likely the Veil had already swallowed it, leaving the city's finite supply of blesswood the only thing keeping Mezzeri's daughter alive. "Tatterlain will help."

Tatterlain sniffed. "Nice. I used to be somebody in this town, you know?"

Mezzeri shook her head. "If you want to be useful, there's a trapdoor in the back room. Get it open and secure the ladder. It'll take us straight into the Underways." The Underways were the forgotten remnants of streets buried underfoot by new construction. A labyrinth of tunnels, artificial caves and half-collapsed buildings, they were the haunt of skelders, shîm-heads and fugitives of all kinds. She nodded at Rîma. "If it's as bad out there as she says, I'm not going out the front."

Tatterlain glanced at Rîma for confirmation – Damant didn't take offence, he'd have done the same. Receiving a slight nod in return, he tapped Yali on the shoulder and threaded his way between the shelves towards the rear of the shop. Mezzeri ducked behind the counter. The metallic crackle of a safe's combination dial rose to challenge Damant's increasingly shallow breaths.

He peered out of the window. Rîma was right about it being like Karana Street. Too many motionless people. Too many blank stares, all of them directed at the shop. He shuddered away a chill. "If Tzal *is* expecting us to fix this mess, why is he working so hard to stop us?"

"Perhaps a tyrant's instinct to dominate outweighs even self-interest," murmured Rîma.

He shook his head. "All those people. They were normal when we arrived."

"The most sensitive to his commands feel it at a distance," said Rîma. "That's why the watchers at Karana Street held off as long as they did. Vigilance was all that Tzal was able to compel. I doubt they even knew what they were watching for, or why. But as more succumb, the more irresistible he becomes, feeding off them, steering them, growing stronger as the radius of his influence expands. He can't control a mere handful of the englamoured, but if that handful becomes a gathering, becomes a crowd ..."

Damant thought back to how the arrival of the redcloaks had galvanised the watchers at Karana Street. If Tzal had tightened his control over anyone in Zariqaz, it would be the members of the Royal Guard. "It's like an avalanche. It builds fast and crushes everything in its path, but leaves everything uphill untouched."

She nodded, her gaze still on the bonfires beyond the glass. "Yes, that's precisely it."

"How do you know?"

Her eyes narrowed in pain. "Because the city-soul of Tadamûr did this to my people."

He shook his head. "I saw Tadamûr. The rituals, the trappings of days past. Everyone caught in a rut of old habits because that's what they remembered. It's not the same."

"Because the city-soul longed to maintain past glories. It wasn't malevolent, just misguided. Tzal's desires are very different."

Damant looked on the street – on the men, women and children– with fresh eyes. By the time Rîma destroyed the city-soul, there had been almost nothing left of its victims. "Is there any saving them?"

"I can't say. We're all connected, more than you know. Old souls tangled so tight that we can't see what's real any longer. Lies within lies within lies ..."

Damant had the distinct impression that she wasn't really talking to him any longer. "What do you know that I don't?"

She offered a wintry smile. "That would be a list entirely too long to recount. But as to all this? I don't *know* anything. I have glimpses and guesses. If I'm wrong, then it is kinder to spare you the burden of my fancies."

"And if you're right?"

"Then saying nothing is kinder still."

For the first time, Damant realised that the malaise he'd seen in Rîma since their escape from the palace was as much in her mind as her body. What had she seen when she'd matched wills with Tzal?

He was about to ask her when Mezzeri surfaced from behind the counter, a knapsack at her shoulder. "Let's get going before I change my mind."

"I . . ." Damant turned to Rîma, questions still seething, but she had already gone. Beyond the window, the first redcloaks entered Tanleer Street, a koilos a forbidding presence in their midst. As the unenglamoured citizens scattered from the bonfires, the watchers stiffened, purpose hardening in their flame-lit faces. The leading edge of the avalanche was upon them. Questions would wait. "Agreed."

They descended into the Underways, Damant expecting to hear the door of the shop crunch open with every rung of the ladder that passed away beneath his feet. In the end, the echo of the same didn't overtake them until they were a good quarter-mile distance through the uneven, sloping tunnel. By then the myriad options for pursuit – the Underways in that part of Zariqaz were a notorious honeycomb – offered sufficient protection that Damant permitted himself to relax.

But only a little.

Forty-Six

Tatterlain led the way through lichen-lit tunnels and buried graveyards, the *drip-drip* of water run-off and breached sewer pipes echoing through the darkness. He never hesitated when a choice of routes presented itself, be it a half-collapsed stairway or an undignified scramble through a rubble-choked archway, but pressed on with the confidence of a man who'd long ago memorised every twist and turn.

Damant was glad to have the burden of guidance fall on other shoulders. His joints screamed their disapproval at what was becoming a long and tortuous journey. Nor did the musty texture of the air help his aching lungs. Fortunately, those few ne'er-do-wells and predators that took an interest as they passed soon lost enthusiasm when they realised their erstwhile prey was well armed.

Rîma stayed close to Mezzeri throughout, likely as much to guard against the woman bolting as to act as her protector.

By and by, they passed through a hole in gaping brickwork and into a rubble-choked storm drain, and then by means of a corroded ladder emerged into an alley. Dizzyingly high overhead, the Golden Citadel gleamed in the starlight, no longer beautiful to Damant's way of thinking, but watchful and sinister. Downhill, the alley emptied out onto an empty cobbled plaza. There, behind a crumbling adobe wall – the span beyond the gate half hidden behind a wooden scaffold and canvas tarpaulins – lumani lanterns made crooked shadows of carracks and barges tied up at Selesti Dock's crowded jetties.

||"I don't like this,"|| murmured Tatterlain. ||"These docks supply half the lower city. They never sleep, even at this hour."||

Rîma twitched a shoulder. ||"The bridges behind us are burning."||

||"I know."|| His rakish smile fooled no one. ||"A poor attempt at being responsible."||

||I can take a look?|| said Yali.

||"We'll all go,"|| Damant said firmly. ||"Split up now and we're doing the Eternity Queen's work for her."||

They set out again, Rîma in the lead and Damant taking up position as Mezzeri's watchdog. As they approached the alley mouth, shadows shifted beneath a jettied roof. A hand reached for Tatterlain. "Wait, you—"

Rîma grabbed the stranger's arm at the wrist and spun him face-first into the alley wall with his captive wrist hitched up between his shoulder blades. "Quiet now. There are terrible things abroad this night."

Tatterlain tapped her on the shoulder. "It's all right. This is Kanad. It's his barge we've come looking for."

Rîma let him go and stepped back. "My apologies. It has been a trying night."

"And more to come." Kanad massaged his wrist, his unfavourable stare rendered all the more saturnine by sallow cheeks and a neat full beard. "Docks are locked down, every ship tied up tight and the crews dismissed. There are four koilos at the gate and a redcloak cordon further up the street. I don't know how you got this far."

Tatterlain shrugged as Rîma signed a translation for Yali. "I'm resourceful."

"Not enough to get the *Celedine* out tonight you're not." Kanad shook his head. "However you got here, you'd better go back."

Damant scowled. It couldn't be coincidence that Selesti was sealed up tight. They hadn't outstripped the pursuit from Tanleer Street after all. Tzal had already known where they were heading.

Tatterlain's eyes touched closed. "I'm sorry, Keti." His words were barely a whisper.

"I take it we're not leaving," said Mezzeri acidly.

||"We're leaving."|| Damant borrowed the ghost of his former authority and jerked his head towards the alley mouth and the wall of Selesti Dock. ||"We go through whatever's in our way."||

"Through four koilos?" said Kanad. "Are you mad?"

Damant unholstered his shrieker. "You can come with us and maybe you'll live, or you can stay here and probably die." He shrugged as if the choice didn't matter, though without Kanad – and his soul-glyphs to command the barge's helmic – the chances of taking sail were vanishingly small.

||"Where's your sense of adventure?"|| said Tatterlain. ||"It can't be worse than what happened at Ansaross."||

"Getting out of Ansaross nearly killed us both," said Kanad.

Tatterlain grinned. ||"But it didn't. And we didn't have Rîma with us back then."|| He frowned and cast about. ||"Where *is* Rîma?"||

Damant turned on his heel, but saw only a Rîma-shaped space where she'd stood moments before.

Yali pointed towards the alley mouth. ||She left while you were pontificating.||

Tatterlain stiffened. ||"I do *not* pontificate."||

Rîma was already halfway across the plaza to the dockyard gate, her sword drawn and held low at her side, its tip brushing the cobbles. Damant shook away a chill of premonition. Even at her best, one koilos was Rîma's match, and she was at far from her best.

Even as he ran after her, she swept up her sword to the salute and called out to the koilos, "You deserve better than this. I'm sorry."

They lurched towards her as one, lamellar scales shifting beneath the starlight. Their ripple-bladed flamberges, each as tall as Damant, gleamed in the backwash of the flickering indigo flames of their eyes. Rîma had judged her angle of attack to perfection, forcing the first koilos to meet her head-on while the others were trailing behind. As it hacked down, the flamberge steel gleaming, she pirouetted aside, her own blade scattering scales from the armour at its waist.

Damant skidded to a halt and levelled his shrieker.

Invisible flame screamed across the plaza, bursting to blazes of hungry orange against the already battered adobe wall, a patch of cobblestones and – for a mercy – the shoulder of the rearmost koilos. Rîma forgotten, it pivoted on its heel and lurched headlong towards him, its charred left arm hanging uselessly from a shattered shoulder and its trailing sword striking sparks from the cobbles.

Damant held his ground and aimed anew. He squeezed the trigger. With a feeble whine, a shimmering heat haze gathered about the muzzle and dissipated to nothing.

The koilos screamed with all the force the shrieker had not and picked up speed.

Damant bolted, aiming not for the dockyard, but cutting across the gate and sprinting for the thicket of crossbeams, braces and pillars supporting the repair scaffold. A glance over his shoulder confirmed the koilos' dogged pursuit. A clamour of bells from the dockyard approach warned that the outbursts of shrieker and enraged koilos had not gone unmarked.

Already tiring from the trek across the city, he missed his footing on reaching the scaffold's outer edge. He caromed painfully off a timber upright in a flailing attempt to keep his balance, and stumbled on, snatching dangling ropes and flapping canvas from his path. He didn't dare glance behind. It was enough that the koilos' lumbering footfalls were drawing ever closer. All that mattered was leading the pursuit further from the dockyard gate, further from the others.

Cursing his stumbling legs, he forged on, ragged breaths burning his lungs. He ducked under a diagonal cross-brace and seconds later heard the rotten *crunch* as the koilos simply ploughed its way through.

Warned by a combination of the koilos' screech and the sudden draught at his neck, he threw himself into a dive, skinning his elbows through his silk sleeves. A dull *thunk* sounded above his head as steel

461

met a thick timber column. Spluttering on a mouthful of bitter dust, he rolled over just as the koilos yanked the flamberge free in a shower of splinters.

With no time to get clear, Damant aimed the recalcitrant shrieker along his prone body. "Now or never, you hear me? Or it's both of us."

Arvish always swore that shriekers didn't perceive enough of the mortal world to hear speech, but maybe this one did, or had perhaps in the intervening moments regathered enough of itself for one final shot. A heat haze seared the air. The koilos' chest exploded into fragments. With a thin whine, it toppled backwards and collapsed against a cross-brace. The scaffold gave an unhappy groan, grit trickling down between the planks of the upper walkway.

Damant clambered upright. Twenty pairs of scaffold pillars back towards the dockyard gate – he'd run far further than he'd realised – Rîma had her sword braced at grips and tip against a flamberge's strike while Yali hacked again and again at the koilos' back. Kanad was face-down on the cobbles, still moving but with a bloody gash across his forehead. The koilos towering above him held a thrashing Tatterlain high by the throat.

No sign of Mezzeri. Fled, Veil take her.

Ignoring Tatterlain's desperate kicks, the koilos flung him at Yali, taking both down in a tangle of arms and legs. In the same moment, Rîma slid her sword aside. As her opponent stumbled, she spun about, sword reversed and her back to the koilos' armoured chest. With both hands again about the grips, she rammed the point of the blade backwards past her hips. It burst clear of the koilos' spine in a spray of lamellar scales and gilded bone, then ripped sideways to cut the baleful cadaver almost in half.

Then the fourth koilos crowded the far end of the scaffold, leaving Damant eyes for nothing else.

Too bone-weary to run, he raised his shrieker. The ifrît, now well and truly spent, didn't even manage a feeble heat haze. Accepting the inevitable, Damant thrust the shrieker into its holster and drew his scimitar. It felt heavier than it had even earlier that day. Or perhaps his years were at last catching up with him. No matter. He'd sought to be a distraction. He could be one still.

"Damant! Get down!" shouted Mezzeri.

He'd barely glimpsed her standing midway between him and the koilos when a glittering *something* left her hand: too bright to be an ifrît prism, a swirl of magenta seething against the multifaceted exterior. A crystal tetram, bursting with volatile soulfire.

Damant flung himself backwards in the same moment the tetram struck the dockyard wall. The deafening backrush of the explosion bore him to the ground, the brief rush of fire filling the air with the stink of burning dust and bone. A gout of flame-wreathed smoke swallowed the koilos. Then with an almighty clatter, the central section of the scaffold gave way, burying it beneath an avalanche of broken timber and metal fixings.

Eyes streaming against the smoke and hacking fit to cough up a lung, Damant stumbled clear of the remains of the increasingly unstable scaffold.

"Over here!" Mezzeri lay a dozen paces away, pinned by debris at shoulder and ankle.

Collapsing to one knee, Damant helped her drag the wreckage free and stagger upright. "I thought you'd abandoned us."

"I did. I changed my mind. Cost me a fortune."

Damant eyed her knapsack. *Tools and such*, she'd said when emptying her safe, and plainly lied. A crystal tetram was worth enough to begin a new life ... or save one, as it turned out. "Thanks."

"You just better not be lying, that's all ... Ah!" She collapsed against him as her ankle buckled. Gingerly she made another attempt to stand unaided, only to meet the same result. "Great."

The final koilos was at last down, head struck away and Rîma standing in what appeared to be silent prayer at its side. Alone of anyone Damant had ever met, she felt a kinship with the things and greeted their destruction with remorse. Kanad was on his feet, albeit groggily. Only Tatterlain was still down, Yali kneeling at his side. Her brief flurry of signs assured Damant that he was only unconscious, not dead. Which would have been less concerning but for the bells still chiming out through the night and the silent watchers gathering along the dockyard approach. The redcloaks of the cordon could only be moments away.

Mezzeri's arm about his waist, Damant took her weight and set out for the others.

Rîma greeted him with a shallow bow. "I told you I was saving myself for something important."

"You did." But Damant didn't miss the pained note in her voice, nor the stiffness with which she carried herself. He turned his attention to the groggy Kanad. "Are you fit to sail?"

He offered a pained nod. "If the alternative's staying here, yes. But it'll take a little time to get ready."

Damant eyed the dockyard approach with growing unhappiness. ||"Yali, go with him. Take Mezzeri with you. Get the barge ready to cast off. Rîma will handle any troublemakers along the way."||

Rîma nodded. ||"And you?"||

||"I'll bring Tatterlain. Meet me once you've cleared their path."|| Arms already aching at the prospect, he glanced down at Tatterlain, whose temple sported a florid sunburst bruise. ||"But help me up with him first?"||

With Rîma's help, he hoisted Tatterlain up over his shoulder.

Even the hobbling Mezzeri outpaced him on the long journey down the main jetty, towards a gaudy red and gold hull barely visible in the starlight. Before long he was alone, flanked by silent, blocky cargo carracks, their foredecks thick with half-unloaded cargo and their hatches battened down. With every laboured breath, Damant strove to forget his aching shoulders and focused on putting one foot in front of the other. Then again. And again.

A scrape of steel sounded from the darkness ahead. A thin, fading scream as some luckless soul fell foul of Rîma. The wind shifted, carrying with it the murmur of the approaching crowd and the tramp of running feet.

Damant was perhaps halfway to the barge when a stumble warned him that his weary legs would not be ignored for ever. Shoulders creaking, he eased Tatterlain off his shoulder and into a sitting position against a bollard. He dropped to one knee. He just needed a moment. Maybe two. Enough to stop his lungs burning and his knees trembling.

A hundred yards along the jetty, the barge's mainmast inched a juddering arc as ropes hauled it upright. As far again in the other direction, the first silhouettes of pursuit crowded the inner gate. Redcloaks and the same mishmash of civilians as had closed on the Karana Street warehouse, armed with scimitars, cudgels and spars of broken scaffolding.

Running feet presaged Yali's breathless arrival. She skidded to a halt beside Tatterlain. Rîma crouched next to Damant, her expression crowded with concern.

Yali stared at the oncoming crowd, her eyes tight. ||Another two minutes, Kanad says.||

Damant shook his head. "We don't have two minutes," he said, too tired to sign. It was all an equation of vying timings now. Time for Kanad to get the barge skyworthy. Time for the crowd to close the distance. The one wasn't equal to the other.

"You don't." Rîma stood up. "But you will."

||No!|| said Yali, her expression aghast. ||They'll tear you apart.||

"She's right." Damant rose, head and heart at loggerheads. Both recognised what Rîma intended; one stolid in its acceptance, the other screaming. Logic versus friendship. The Deadwinds take logic anyway. "We came this far together. We finish it the same way."

Rîma shook her head, a fleeting fond smile turning ancient and unyielding. "Ihsan . . . Earlier today you asked if I was tired of watching the young suffer for my mistakes, but you are not old as I am old." She reached up to her shoulder. Her sword whispered free of its scabbard.

465

"I have lived long and made more mistakes than I can count, but I have never once regretted standing by my friends. I will do so one last time. Do me the honour of respecting it."

Yali thrust herself between them, eyes blazing. ||I won't let you do this!||

Rîma shook her head and signed something too fast for Damant to follow. Eyes pinched shut, Yali subsided and embraced her, face buried in her shoulder, then stepped away.

Damant lost the battle to hold back his tears almost at once. Old souls, bound together through all the changings of the world. He'd never really believed it until that moment, but now it meant everything. "Until the next life, Eskamarîma."

"Until then."

With a last not-quite-smile, she turned on her heel and stalked to meet the approaching crowd.

With Yali's help, Damant hoisted Tatterlain to his feet as the crowd's murmur became a roar. Each with an outflung arm across their shoulders, they set out towards the barge, their unconscious comrade no longer the weightiest burden. Halfway there, Rîma's voice rang out beneath the stars, its edge every bit as keen as the blade of her sword.

"Are you sure you wish to go through with this?"

Damant risked a glance over his shoulder and saw her sweep her sword to a salute. She sprang forward, a shrieker shot plucking at her duster coat. A redcloak died under her blade and she pirouetted to parry another. The roar of the crowd thickened with screams.

Awash with the useless urge to go back, Damant somehow forged on towards the barge. The sail billowed free of its brails as he reached the gangplank, the skyship already drifting from its mooring. Leaving the helmic to keep the barge in place, Kanad met them at the gunwale and helped Yali haul Tatterlain aboard.

"Where's the other one?" asked Mezzeri as Damant clambered after him.

He couldn't even see Rîma any longer – only a mass of bodies and glinting steel atop a blood-soaked jetty. "She's not coming. Get us moving."

Kanad ran for the wheelhouse. Motic winches hissed. Ropes creaked as lateral outriggers unfurled, speeding the barge away from Selesti Dock. Damant found Yali at the prow, her gaze towards the horizon and her arms wrapped tight about herself. He squeezed her shoulder and saw the reflection of his own stricken heart in her eyes.

||What did she say to you?|| he signed with faltering hands.

Yali pinched her eyes shut. ||That tyranny cannot be defeated by cruelty, only through sacrifice. A message for Kat, she said.||

Unable to find any answer worth the breath, Damant said nothing at all.

Forty-Seven

"Rîma!"

Kat lurched bolt upright, heart hammering and cold sweat matting her shirt to her back. Darkness bled away into the warmth of pine-green tent panels lit from without by the sun; into the rich scent of hot linen and beeswax. But as the last jumbled strands of nightmare faded, the dread lingered, sustained by the undeniable sense that a piece of her was missing. *Old souls bound together across lifetimes.* Rîma's claim, proven in the bleakest way possible.

"I'm sorry ..." she mumbled, hands clutched to her chest as if pressure might ease the grief thick in her throat. "I should have been there."

But *why* hadn't she been there? She stared around the tent's bare furnishings, crafted in an unfamiliar style from a dark polished wood and finished with leather and thick pelts. Her boots lay atop the fleeces serving as the floor. Her battered coat sat neatly folded on a low stool.

Where was she?

She pinched her eyes shut, grief displaced by present need. The Veil. Xe'iathî. The treachery of the Issnaîm. Vallant. Entering the lesion with Tanith, and then ... nothing. She twitched the thick blanket aside. Still fully clothed but for boots and coat. Whoever had brought her here – wherever *here* was – had at least respected her privacy, even if they'd taken her pack and her scimitar. She saw them now – guards or jailers? – dark shapes against the sunlit canvas, spears thin silhouettes in their hands.

Where was she? Qersal? If her crew had found her unconscious in the mists, that would be the nearest hope of help. Or … She blinked, a muscle twitching in her gut as excitement stirred.

Maybe she wasn't in Khalad at all.

She spun her feet clear of the mattress and grasped the edge of the bed as her vision blurred. Even in the gloom, the colours seemed richer, the fragrances stronger, the blanket softer, the chatter and clatter beyond the tent somehow crisper than sounds had any right to be – as if her whole life a wall had existed between her senses and the world, and that wall was no longer there. Tanith's friend Enna had spoken of that as well, hadn't she? Claimed that everything in Khalad was sealed behind magenta glass.

It took Kat a moment to recognise the burst of stuttering, relieved laughter as her own. It had worked. She was in the Old Realm, beyond the Veil. And she *belonged* here. She felt it as firmly, as inescapably as she'd felt the pull of the lesion back in the mists.

The Old Realm was *real*. Let the Veil take Khalad, Tzal and everything within. There was still hope … even if Rîma would never know it.

But where was Tanith?

She pushed away from the bed, the pressure on her senses easing as the remnants of sleep left her. No sooner had she reached her feet than the tent flaps parted and a warrior strode in.

Even without the straight sword buckled at his waist and the golden scale armour atop his green silk robes – which must have been sweleringly uncomfortable in the dry heat of the tent, let alone under the open sun – there could have been no other way to describe him. His skin was a shade richer than Kat's own bronze, his thicket of black curls as yet ungreyed by the onset of middle age. He bore his broad-shouldered frame proudly and straight-backed, his hazel eyes appraising, but not unkindly: a man taking the measure of the unknown without malice.

469

More than that, he moved like Rîma – which was to say that he moved with Rîma's confidence, rather than her grace – as if he was simply fulfilling actions ordained long ago.

He offered Kat a shallow bow and a deep-voiced greeting. She eyed him warily. Daric she spoke fluently, and even her Qersi had improved sufficiently in recent months that she could pick out key phrases, but here she recognised nothing of detail or form. The warrior narrowed his eyes in thought and spoke again, the sounds different but no less impenetrable.

She shook her head. "I'm sorry, I don't understand."

He brightened, if an understated raising of the eyebrows could be said to be such. "Then I believe this should serve, *savim*."

His pronunciation didn't quite match what Kat was used to – the vowels were shallower and the words more clipped – but he was understandable enough, save for what she took as a closing honorific. "Yes, I think it will."

"I forget my manners." His lips twitched, the hint of a chagrined smile briefly disrupting an otherwise impassive expression. He bowed again. "My name is Halvorn Jamar, and it is my honour to serve the emperor as a havildar of his guard."

More unfamiliar words, though the first pairing clearly constituted his name. The question now became how much to tell him. As little as possible. At least until she knew more. "Kat," she replied. "I'm afraid I don't know how I arrived here. My memory's full of holes."

"There is little reason you should. One of my patrols found you at the roadside just after dawn, dead to the world. I apologise for the poor accommodations, but an army encampment seldom offers luxury."

Kat elected not to tell him that the "poor accommodations" were a good bit more comfortable than most of the places she'd lived. "What about Tanith ... my sister?" She scowled, realising that her attempt at clarification was nothing of the sort. "She was travelling with me."

"We saw no one else."

A hundred terrible fates rose behind her eyes. What if Tanith hadn't come through the lesion? What if she was still in the mists, perhaps lost, maybe unconscious? Would her scrap of astoricum keep her together long enough for the others to come looking? Or had she passed through to the Old Realm only to have tragedy befall her? Unlikely, perhaps – in matters of jeopardy, Tanith was more often the peril than the victim – but with Rîma's loss still heavy in her heart, Kat felt the possibilities all too keenly.

She started forward. "I need to find her."

Jamar raised a calloused hand but made no move to touch her. Standing foursquare in the entrance to the tent, the combination of muscle and scale was as good as a locked door. "You need to eat. Rest. This is unkind country in which to meet with misfortune, *savim*. You are fortunate to be alive."

Kat pulled on her boots. "All the more reason to find Tanith."

"And how will you do so? The plains fold strangely out here, so close to the desert. Zaifîr and worse than zaifîr roam at will. Can you defend yourself?"

Caution warned against brashness. Caution be damned. "If you give me back my sword."

He considered for a moment, then inclined his head. "Perhaps you could. But how then will you find your sister? Can you tell the signs of her passage from those belonging to another?"

Kat winced. Of course she couldn't. She was a city rat. "Perhaps I'll learn."

"Perhaps you will." Somehow Jamar managed to offer appeasement without sounding condescending. "But the sun is at its height and this is no time to go searching for anything at all. However, if you would be so good as to tell me what your sister looks like, I will see if she can be found."

Kat hesitated. Distrust had become more than instinct – it was baked into her soul. However, she didn't even know how to retrace her steps to where she'd been found. "We don't look much alike. She's younger than me. Blonde, with fair skin. She's also a little ... wild."

471

An epithet of kindness more than accuracy. "She'll cooperate if she knows I'm safe."

Probably.

"I see." Jamar's tone suggested that he'd read more into Kat's words than she'd have liked. "You are my guest, *savim*. Give me your word you are not fleeing justice, and are no enemy of my emperor, and you will have mine that neither you nor your sister will face harm here."

Fleeing justice? Both the Eternity Queen and the Issnaîm would likely claim that she was, but their opinions were of little account ... and she could scarcely feel enmity to this "emperor", whoever – or whatever – it was. And besides, it was increasingly apparent that she needed Jamar's help, not just to find Tanith but also to retrace her steps back into the Veil. If she – or indeed anyone else – was to have any hope of a future in the Old Realm, it had to begin with trust.

"You have my word." Uncertain if there was a specific ritual response to such a request, Kat settled for speaking with all the solemnity she could muster. "And my trust."

Jamar inclined his head. "I shall strive to prove worthy of them. Place your faith in my soldiers, *savim*. There are worse things in the desert than women, however wild. And I insist you eat something. Though I must apologise in advance ..."

Kat smiled, hoping that if her body relaxed, her soul would follow suit. "Because an army encampment seldom offers luxury?"

"Indeed. Though I trust you will find our food filling enough."

The guards snapped to attention as Jamar left the tent. Kat followed haltingly as her newly delicate senses adjusted to the blazing midday heat. The encampment comprised forty or so tents nestled in a hollow of sun-bleached grassland, ringed by a ruptured crown of slate outcrops too unevenly set to be anything other than a natural formation. A narrow-ramparted wooden palisade patched the gaps in the rocks, completing the somewhat cramped fortification. It wouldn't have lasted more than a few minutes against a barrage of shrieker fire, but then no one she saw carried such weapons, instead favouring long curved bows that looked to be larger cousins of those used by Athenoch's hunters. Nor did she see any trace of clatter wagons like those that would have accompanied redcloaks to war – though one corner of the stockade did hold a dozen timber horse-drawn carts of a sort seldom used in Khalad for anything other than ceremony.

Jamar gestured for her to sit at a run of benches beneath an awning at the encampment's centre. As he vanished into a nearby tent, Kat stared up at the flag fluttering overhead, its emerald field and silver owl – a heraldry entirely unknown to her – a reminder of how little she knew of this world. She'd have to learn, certainly, but not now. All that mattered was keeping Jamar's cooperation until she could find Tanith and return to the others. The last thing she needed was a fight. Though there were few enough soldiers in the encampment – the rest presumably being out on patrol – both men and women were cast from the same unyielding mould as Jamar himself.

The food – fresh bread and a bowl of spiced, sweet stew – was palatable enough, though the latter's taste didn't match the promise of its aroma. Nor did Kat immediately feel the benefit, even though it had surely been long hours since any food had passed her lips. It was hard to feel sated when observed so closely. Not counting those of Jamar, who sat across the bench from her with a bowl of his own, there were never fewer than three pairs of eyes upon her. Apparently trust only went so far. On the other hand, Jamar hadn't said that he trusted her, for all that she'd said *she* trusted *him*.

And of course, even she'd been lying.

"I've given word for your sister's description to be passed to the patrols," he said.

"Thank you," Kat replied between spoonfuls. "I don't recognise this place. Did you bring me far?" As was increasingly becoming habit, she framed the question in a way that she hoped wouldn't arouse suspicion.

Jamar gazed at her curiously, but without threat. "Perhaps a quarter of a league."

473

"That can't have been fun in this heat." Even beneath the awning – and in a loose shirt, no less – she was sweltering.

"You were in need." He set his already empty bowl aside. "You chose an unhappy time to walk these borderlands. The Ithna'jîm are always restless when a full moon graces the heavens. Perhaps they don't like the truth it reveals."

"Truth isn't always pleasant." Kat matched his unconcerned manner as best she could. It didn't escape her that Jamar had, mostly without seeming to, posed a question of his own while answering hers. *Ithna'jîm.* Where had she heard that word before? Jamar had infused it with enmity but not hate, although she was starting to think that he seldom roused himself to such extremes of emotion. Not that it made him any less dangerous. Considerate wasn't the same as placid. Fortunately, whatever the Ithna'jîm were, he'd not taken her for one. Or had he? She increasingly had the sense that he was playing out a net and its folds were closing about her all the time. And then there was that other word again. *Moon.* A name that sometimes graced Zephyr's speech.

"You never told me where you were heading," he said.

Kat felt the net inch tighter. A little truth was needed. "My people are looking for a new home. We've travelled a long way east. My sister and I came on ahead." Better to imply that those who followed her were still further out than Jamar's patrols. It was truer than he could know.

"On foot?"

"Lately, yes." She'd seen no more evidence of skyships than shriekers, so obfuscation seemed sensible.

"Horseback would have perhaps been wiser."

Another veiled question, but also an opportunity for a grace note to underline her good character. "Not if we didn't want to steal."

Jamar's cheek twitched in what Kat was starting to suspect was the closest he came to showing disgust. "Your thanes are always squabbling, but it's the people who suffer." His expression turned contemplative. "Do all of your people speak Britonisian as well as you?"

474

Britonisian was presumably his name for the language. *Thane*, another unfamiliar word. Jamar had imbued it with the weight of a title, but the longer their conversation went on, the less confident Kat was in her reading of it. Was this another trap? She might have lucked into some existing status quo, but she'd no way of knowing finer details. Even asking the name of the realm Jamar served – which by implication did not belong to the language he spoke – would undo her half-truths. "Most of us get by."

He nodded, thoughtful. "Then your timing – whatever hardships caused it – might be apt. The prince is due ..." His eyes tightened with concern as he glanced at a grand tent set back from the neat rows of its smaller cousins. "Overdue, in fact. The borderlands are fertile and sparsely inhabited. If you're prepared to meet tithes of service and taxes, he may grant you leave to settle."

Kat matched Jamar's thoughtful look with one of her own, uncertain if his offer represented another tightening of the net. "It's been a long time since anyone showed us that sort of kindness."

"I make no promises," he replied drily. "The prince is young, but he possesses a glimmer of his father's wisdom ... on his better days."

Could it really be as easy as that? She set aside her bowl, unable to face eating anything more even though she didn't feel remotely full. "Thank you, I—"

A sudden spasm shook her left side, locking muscles tight and squeezing the breath from her lungs. Hacking and gasping, she pitched forward, her right cheek bouncing to rest against the table's wooden top. Through blurring vision, she saw Jamar jump to his feet, heard him bellow something in an unfamiliar language.

Little by little pain receded and sensation returned, the first shallow breaths alongside.

Jamar loomed above her. "Don't try to move, *savim*. I've sent for the surgeon."

"I'm all right," she wheezed, her cheek still resting against wood. Had the omen rot ever been this bad before? There came a point when all pain blurred.

"I fear that you are lying." A dull rumble of humour removed the words' offence.

Kat braced her hands against the table and pushed herself into a rubbery sitting position. "There's nothing he can do. This is just something I have to live with." And die with, most likely, now that Caradan Diar was no longer holding the omen rot back. "I'm not infectious, if that's what worries you. It's just . . . part of who I am."

Jamar nodded and waved away a white-robed figure on the edge of her still-blurry eyesight. "If that is what you wish, but—"

A bellow from the palisade cut him off. The encampment shook to the tramp of boots as golden-armoured soldiers rushed to the eastern rampart.

"What is it?" asked Kat.

"Sky-shadow," replied Jamar, thoughtful more than concerned. "The Ithna'jîm have come to take another look at us."

Kat followed his gaze to the dark speck rushing closer across the cloudless sky. Moment by moment it resolved from a speck to a blob, to outflung wings, a long neck and a sinuous tail. A drakon. Not one of the ossified and abused corpses that the Issnaîm pressed to service as skyships, but a living, breathing beast of flesh and blood, with charcoal-black scales. As it swooped nearer, she glimpsed riders kneeling along its spine, though it was still too far distant to tell if they were lashed into place with rope or by some other means.

"They won't bother us. No one wants to die for a few worthless rocks." Jamar spoke with all the concern of a man watching a cat basking in the sun. The same couldn't be said of his soldiers, whose alarmed cries needed no translation. "Forgive me, *savim*."

He bellowed up at the rampart. At once, the soldiers recovered a measure of martial deportment. Long bows were unslung, arrows nocked and quivers looped by their straps over the split logs of the palisade. Still half a mile out and a good four hundred feet in the air, the drakon did a lazy barrel roll and belched a cloud of smoke-tinged flame skyward.

"And if they don't agree?" said Kat, captivated by the drakon's serpentine majesty. Zephyr had been right – the undead remnants the Issnaîm commanded were nothing to the living. Would she be pleased to know that the creatures still thrived in service to other masters? Kat's father would have loved the sight, and she was almost sorry he wasn't there to see it until she remembered that he'd been a deceitful, terrible man.

"Then we will remind them that our arrows are sharp and fly true." In another man, Jamar's words might have come across as boastful, but from him they were matter-of-fact.

Kat suddenly remembered where she'd heard the word *Ithna'jîm* before. Tzal had once used it of Zephyr. Ithna'jîm. Issnaîm. The words were the same, she realised with a start, the one softened over millennia of isolation until it became the other. Final confirmation, had she needed it, that this was indeed the homeland of the Issnaîm . . . and of Tzal himself.

She blinked, and found Jamar staring at her with his familiar maybe-concern maybe-suspicion.

"Why are you here, if no one wants to die over a few rocks?" she said, hoping to deflect his interest.

"Because the emperor looks to his southern border and wonders if the land is still as cursed as legend tells." He stared again at the distant drakon, already winging its way back east. "And because a warrior does not always get to die where he wishes."

His words cast a less than favourable light on the possibility of the prince allowing Athenoch's refugees to settle. Who better to defend contested borderlands than indebted outsiders who would not be missed?

She squinted up at the sun, now markedly into its westward decline. "If the excitement's over, would you take me back to where you found me?" She offered a winning smile. "I'm sure your patrols will do their best, but Tanith's my sister: it could be that I recognise something they might miss."

"What if you suffer another attack?" asked Jamar.

"Then leave me where I drop or carry me back ... but I have to do this."

"Very well."

It took less than a minute in the saddle for Kat to truly appreciate just why Khalad preferred clatter wagons, railrunners and skyships to horses. Her mount, a sturdy dappled gelding, stank of sweat, jolted her bones with every step along the uneven roadway, and worse, drew angry black flies as readily as any torch house attracted moths. But it was at least well trained, content to walk along beside Jamar's own steed with little input from Kat herself. Jamar's horse was somewhat larger and more heavily built, as suited its rider, and Kat pitied anyone who had to stand firm against the two while they closed at the gallop. Her scimitar, since returned to her, felt like a toothpick before such a prospect.

Soreness and stench aside, the westward ride was companionable enough. The plains, while as dry as any to be found in Khalad, had their own rugged beauty, the yellowed waist-high grasses dotted with thorn patches and occasional vulture-haunted trees with gnarled boles and cloud-like leaf canopies. That beauty turned increasingly arid as the plains stretched south through the shimmering heat towards the desert.

They travelled in silence, Jamar's quiet interrogation in abeyance and Kat lost in her own thoughts. She tried to tell herself that she'd imagined Rîma's death, or misinterpreted a nightmare. Unthinkable that a woman who'd witnessed a hundred thousand years of history unfold – who'd saved Kat's life more times than she could count – was gone. But more impossible still was to deny the hollow ache in her heart that hadn't even begun to fade. And what had become of Tanith? Would she know of her own sister's death with half the certainty with which she'd accepted Rîma's?

The road dipped towards a narrow reed-choked lake that stretched away far to the south. Midway between the northern shore and the road, a pair of towering black stone stumps reached crookedly towards the sky. Despite the heat, skeins of mist drifted across the surface of the water, sometimes obscuring it completely. But nowhere was it as thick as between the two stumps, which, as Kat's horse trotted closer, she saw were no natural rock formation but the uprights of a broad archway that had long since lost its crown.

"Here." Jamar brought his horse to halt opposite the archway and swatted away a cloud of inquisitive midges. "The grass remembers, even if you do not."

Kat dismounted with all the grace of a falling brick and stared at the hollow of crushed stalks. "Good for the grass."

"Better that you collapsed here than on the other side. The mists are old magic. They'd have swallowed you up without a trace."

Kat nodded and made her way further along the road, doing her best to ignore the wails for attention from saddle-sore flesh. Mists and old magic. It couldn't be a coincidence, not after Jamar had spoken of the land being cursed. As she drew closer, she made out the familiar shapes of Issnaîm cuneiform on the stones. More, telltale edging stones protruded from the grass, bounding a vanished roadway that had once served the gate.

She stared again at the mists, which carried both the unmistakable greenish-white tinge and the nostalgia-laden scent of the Veil. They filled the space between the stumps and clung to the lake's western shore, as if they were leaking through from another place, only to burn away in the sunshine. The grasses between the stumps were crushed in several places, as were those on the approach to the road. She crouched, triumph warming her heart ... a boot print. And the indentations: too many for one person, but not for two. Tanith *had* made it through the lesion.

Not bad for a city rat.

Kat gazed into the mists, her skin crawling at the prospect of diving back in. More than her skin. Every inch of her screamed that she should turn her back on the arch and run for the horizon: a primal fear, stronger than anything the Veil had provoked in months, and so distinct that it barely felt like her own.

Jamar dismounted. "I told you, that's a forbidden place. If she's gone that way . . . well, you have my regrets, *savim*."

A shout drew Kat's attention east. A man in bloodied golden armour stood on the roadway's gentle crest. He was leading a white horse by its reins and walking with the stumbling steps of one near exhaustion. Another man lay slung across the horse's saddle, a dead weight in armour stained the colour of rust.

Jamar, displaying a turn of speed she'd never have suspected he possessed, swung up into his saddle and galloped towards him. By the time Kat caught up, he had his boots on the ground once more and was deep in conversation with the newcomer, a man a good fifteen years his junior – younger than Kat herself, if she were any judge – black-haired and green-eyed. Not yet as rugged and weather-worn as Jamar, but well on the way. A flurry of questions and replies rattled between them, interspersed by the younger man taking gulps from the waterskin Jamar pressed into his hand.

"What's happened?" asked Kat. "Who is he?"

The younger man glowered at her, provoking another quickfire exchange. A hint of a scowl flickering across his face, Jamar bowed heavily and turned to Kat, his voice uncharacteristically hard. "He is Prince Edric, second in line to the imperial throne. He and his escort were attacked earlier today . . . by a blonde woman with blue eyes. Two men died keeping her from the prince. A third will be lucky to live until moonrise." He laid his hand on his sword. "You and I will speak again, and this time I will have the truth."

Forty-Eight

They came back for Kat as night fell, to a new tent markedly less comfortable than the old. It had no furniture save the low stool on which she sat – just an empty square of bare earth, bereft of temptation or opportunity. The rope about her wrists further diminished the opportunity for mischief, had she been so inclined. The presence of Jamar, standing arms folded between her and the flaps, reduced it almost to nothing. Prince Edric – his bloody armour exchanged for a green and black silk robe that shimmered in the lanternlight – stood a little behind and to Jamar's side.

"It is my hope that you will cooperate," rumbled Jamar. Even now, with slain comrades and a wounded prince – Kat had plenty of experience when it came to concealing injuries out of misplaced pride, and Edric's stiff-legged entrance hadn't come close to fooling her – he was reason itself. Even so, she noted that the "*savim*" honorific was no longer in evidence. "You are a stranger. You spat on your word and my hospitality. You are linked by blood to an attack on the imperial heir. No law of mortals or gods will protect you. Only the truth."

"The truth is that she and her sister are assassins." Edric's command of the language wasn't half as confident as Jamar's, but he was fluent enough. He'd none of Jamar's reserve, but Kat supposed she couldn't blame him. "Her life is already forfeit. Likely they're witches too. The one who attacked me moved almost too fast for the eye to follow. She bled flame."

Awash with concern at the first hint that Tanith had been injured in

481

the confrontation, Kat almost missed Edric's brief scowl, one she could have sworn was directed not at her, but himself. Guilt over the dead men, most likely.

"Perhaps, my prince, but even assassins have motives." Jamar turned his attention back to Kat. "As I said, only the truth will serve you now."

"And if you don't like that truth?" asked Kat.

"Your situation is unlikely to worsen," he said drily, "but the choice remains yours."

"This is a waste of time," snapped Edric. "Her guilt is proven."

His eyes on Kat's, Jamar shook his head. "Forgive me, *savir*, but it is merely inferred. It would set a poor precedent if we held others accountable for the actions of their siblings."

The air in the tent, already cooling with night's onset, chilled further as Edric regarded Jamar with an unfriendly expression. "Ask your questions."

Jamar bowed. "As you command, my prince."

Kay looked from one to the other. Joint interrogations were a common enough tool among custodians, with one questioner offering a sympathetic ear while the other issued threats. This had the feel of something different. A younger man steeped in authority but lacking experience, resentful of his underling's wisdom? There could be something to exploit there. Execution at their hands was the least of her concerns. It would at least be faster than the painful decline omen rot promised. She'd suffered another attack before Jamar and his prince had returned, one that had twisted her inside and out. They'd only grow worse. But she still had a chance to make her life count for something – for the people of Athenoch, if not for Tanith.

"I already told you the truth," she said, pre-empting any question Jamar might have. "Most of it. We really are looking for a new home."

A muscle twitched in Edric's cheek. "You've a strange way of going about it."

Kat shifted on her stool in a failed attempt to ease the pressure on her saddle-sore skin. Edric increasingly reminded her of a woman she'd left months in the past. Just how much younger than her was he? What did that say about who she'd been when she'd first met Vallant?

Jamar grunted. "You claim to have travelled from the west, but you clearly don't belong to those lands. You don't speak their tongues."

Kat re-examined their initial conversation. Just how many snatches of languages had Jamar attempted before he'd settled on one comprehensible to them both? He'd known she was lying almost from the first. And yet ... he'd still treated her like a guest and not a prisoner – at least until Tanith had ruined all that – which meant that even now there was a slim possibility she wasn't among enemies. Well, not *entirely* among enemies. Edric looked ready to run her through.

"How is the man you saved?" she asked him.

"Kalar will live, if the Goddess is kind," Edric replied stiffly.

"I'm glad."

"Of *course* you are."

No bridges to be built there, not that Kat had expected otherwise. Though she'd addressed the prince, she'd meant her words for Jamar. "I'm sorry I misled you, but I had my reasons." She took a deep breath. "We're not from the west. At least, not *your* west. We come from a place beyond the mists."

"Impossible," said Edric.

Jamar's expression flirted ever so briefly with surprise before settling to its customary impassiveness. "The prince is of course correct." But his tone invited her to continue.

Kat cast about for something, *anything* that might serve as leverage. "The ruins where you found me ... do they have a name?"

"They once belonged to the city of Kha'ladria," Jamar replied, "before the Ithna'jîm civil war tore their empire apart."

In her mind's eye, Kat again walked the city in the Stars Below, a city of the same black stone as the mist-shrouded archway. "And there are legends, yes? One day the mists just swallowed up the city and its people, and when they cleared, the place was gone?"

"Every child knows them," said Edric with barely contained

impatience. "The Ithna'jîm at last tired of Tzal's cold flame. They turned on him and destroyed him."

Kat stifled a grimace. She was piecing it together as she went, but there was no way to prove that she wasn't simply parroting what was to them commonplace myth. "They *imprisoned* him. Only he wasn't the only one they trapped. We've lived out our lives there for generations, but now the prison is failing. The mists are closing in. Escape is our only hope. This is our real home. I *belong* here. I felt it as soon as I woke up."

"Recounting a new variation on a centuries-old story offers little in the way of proof," said Jamar.

Kat felt the blood drain from her cheeks. Only *centuries*? That couldn't be true. Rîma had lived for a hundred thousand years, and Khalad had been old when she was young. But then time flowed strangely in the Veil, and Khalad itself was little more than a bubble in the mists, like the city in the snow globe her father had treasured. Had he known, even then? Yet another secret that a less selfish man might have shared.

"Perhaps." For the first time Edric sounded thoughtful. "But it's not a new variation."

Jamar frowned. "My prince?"

"There's something similar recorded in the imperial library, though I doubt many have read it. My family lost pride in the past a long time ago." Edric glared at Kat, his voice hardening. "But even if everything you've said is true, it doesn't excuse your sister's actions."

Again, the guilty self-directed frown for his companions' deaths. For all his intemperance, Edric was likely a good man, or would mellow to become one. As for Tanith ... well, that was complicated, and always had been.

"She's not wicked ... but she is unwell," said Kat, choosing her words carefully. Honesty was all well and good, but throwing around words like *daemon* wouldn't help anyone. "You could say that we both share the same illness, but it takes her very differently."

Edric shook his head bitterly. "Unwell? She approached out of the reeds, begging for our help. Oldran was suspicious at once. I should have

484

listened, but I . . . she . . ." He swallowed. "When she got close, her beauty fell away . . . Oldran was the first to die. I ran her through, but she must have struck my wits away. When I awoke, Kalar was the only other one still living, and just barely."

Kat closed her eyes, the gaps in the story clear for all Edric's attempts at concealment. Tanith's glamour had taken him, and then, when she'd gotten close enough to scent his soul, hunger had overcome her. How could she have been so careless? She had to have known how close she was to losing control . . . Or perhaps not. Sensation was so different on this side of the lesion, so much stronger. And then there was one other piece to the puzzle.

"She didn't ask you to help *her*, did she?" she murmured. "She told you that her sister had collapsed, was maybe dying."

"I don't remember," he said, defensively.

"I believe you," she told him. Those who survived long enough to emerge from Tanith's glamour seldom had a reliable memory of events. "This isn't your fault."

Edric stiffened. "Should I care what you think?"

But she saw in his eyes that he did. A good man with a shrouded memory would care very much. He'd probably even have helped Tanith, had circumstances been different.

The tent flaps parted, wafting in bitter campfire woodsmoke. A soldier entered and clasped a fist to her chest in salute. Jamar's expression tightened as she issued her report, while what little friendliness Edric had attained vanished as if it had never been. Further exchanges rattled back and forth, and then the soldier retreated into the growing commotion outside.

Jamar regarded Kat grimly. "They found Oldran's body in the reeds." His lower lip curled in disgust. "Half-eaten. At first they thought hyenas had been at it, but the wounds are wrong."

Kat's gut tightened. It didn't make sense. It couldn't be Tanith. Even at her wildest, only the soul of her prey mattered – physical food did nothing to sate her hunger. "Where is she?"

"She's made a lair of the lake shore," said Edric. "If she's there, we'll run her to ground."

They meant to kill her, Kat thought dully. She couldn't bring herself to blame them. Nor would Tanith – the woman she *remembered* as being Tanith – if she was so far gone to her amashti hunger that she couldn't be brought back. But even if they did kill her – even if they *could* – how many more would die along the way?

"If she's like this, you're all in danger. I'll help you find her. She'll listen to me."

For the briefest moment she felt Jamar's doubt as an almost physical presence: a pressure she could neither describe nor explain, unyielding but with the prospect of malleability. Almost like an ifrît, waiting to be coaxed by a soul-glyph.

Edric uttered three taut words in his own language, breaking the spell, then swept from the tent without a backwards glance.

Jamar lingered long enough to offer Kat a conflicted look. "I'm sorry, *savim*."

Kat sat alone in the greasy circle of lanternlight as hoofbeats rose and faded outside the tent. The elation of hours before was little more than a memory. The fate that had overtaken Tanith was bad enough, but the knowledge that her actions had scattered any hope for the people of Athenoch tinged the tragedy with bleakness that left Kat wanting to weep. Even if Edric consented to her release, he'd never trust her, and by extension never trust her fellow refugees. Too many lies had been told and too much blood spilt.

She closed her eyes but found no solace in the darkness, only the disappointed stares of those she'd failed.

No. Not failed. Not yet. Saving Edric meant saving Tanith, and vice versa.

The encampment was deathly quiet. Likely there were only a handful of soldiers left. And she didn't have to fight all of them, not if she was careful – just the one spilling a fire-cast shadow against the tent. Maybe not even that one, if her luck held.

She rose from her stool and moved it directly beneath the tent's peak, and thus directly below the oil lantern suspended from the cross supports. It was a simple enough design, similar to those she'd seen in the poorer parts of Tyzanta: a brass reservoir and wick holder crowned by a hexagonal brass cage, sealed with glass.

Working as quickly as she dared, she unhooked the lantern. Biting her lip against the growing pain from the hot glass beneath her fingertips, she dropped to the floor, set the lantern on the stool . . . and froze at the sound of movement outside.

She held her breath until the guard stamped his feet and settled once more, then turned her attention to the lantern. With her wrists bound, it took three attempts and several burned fingertips to unscrew the cage from the base, leaving a naked flame to which she offered up the rope. After a seeming age – and a pair of livid burns at her wrists to match those already itching her fingers – her restraints burned through, leaving her hands free.

Increasingly aware how much time was slipping away, Kat turned her attention to the sides of the tent. All were pegged down too close to the ground to let her wriggle clear and too securely to uproot without creating a commotion.

One option left.

She set the remains of the lantern aside, picked up the stool by two of its legs and moved to stand to the left-hand side of the flaps.

"Help!" She filled her voice with urgency to bridge any language gap and hoped her guard was the only one close enough to hear. "The tent's on fire!"

The guard burst through the flaps. Kat brought the stool crashing down towards his head. At the last moment he spun around, his right forearm raised to take the blow. He barely staggered as the stool shattered. His open-handed punch to Kat's gut drove her to the floor. He had the point of his sword at her throat before she'd chance to rise.

Failure thick in the back of her throat, she stared up at his impassive face. Violence had failed. Only the slender hope of reason remained. "Your prince is riding to his death."

The guard stared down, offering no clue that he'd heard her words, much less understood them.

"Please," said Kat. "Let me save him."

She felt a pressure between them, as she had with Jamar at his departure, only this time it gave. The guard stepped away, swaying drunkenly and blinking like a man struggling to hold onto his thoughts. Then he straightened and stood aside, leaving a clear path to the tent flaps. Kat stared at him, triumph curdling. She'd seen it too many times before, in Tanith's company and at the fall of Tyzanta. The man was smothered by a glamour. *Her* glamour. But she couldn't *do* that.

Or at least she hadn't, until now. What did that mean? Nothing good, she felt sure, because little in the life of Katija Arvish ever ended for the best. The food that offered no satisfaction. The glamour. Signs that something inside her was changing, or was being changed by her presence in the Old Realm. Making her more like Tanith, and making Tanith more like . . . what?

She gritted her teeth. It would wait.

As she'd hoped, the encampment had emptied, leaving a bare handful of guards at gate and palisade. Choosing the ladder furthest from any of them, Kat climbed to the rampart, slipped over the wall and ran westward across the plains, careful always to keep the road in sight as much as overcast skies allowed. Few stars showed, though far to the north a light shining behind the clouds roused them almost to pearlescence. As soon as the dark shadow of the encampment was lost, she cut across the road and mirrored its course from the south.

She hurried on, running until her knees shook and walking only as long as it took them to recover, praying all the while that omen rot would leave her be. A quarter of a league, Jamar had said. It felt three times that in the dark, with the prospect of death to come or perhaps already past.

At last, she spotted pinpricks of lamplight in the distance. Twenty or so, moving steadily westward. The mist-shrouded remnants of the arch came into view soon after, black even against the night. The lanterns and the dark shapes that bore them were a chain of artificial fireflies bobbing to scatter reflections across the surface of the lake.

Kat urged her legs to fresh effort, skirting the misty arch and its nostalgia stench for fear of awakening nausea. As she splashed on into the reeds the air came alive with soft silver light, not nearly as bright as day but brighter than starlight – enough to reveal the soldiers converging along the western shore. She saw Jamar part way along the southern line. Edric was one of the four lantern-bearers to the north, advancing on a tree-crowned rocky outcrop with swords drawn. Two hundred yards distant, no more.

Still running, her trousers clammy to the thigh and mud sucking at her boots, Kat stared north towards the break in the clouds, and the pale white disc sitting proudly against the inky sky – a cold sun, drowning the plains in a pale echo of daylight. Was this the moon of which Zephyr had sometimes spoken, in whose name the Issnaîm had greeted her? She'd seen it before, sculpted above Athenoch's lintels and in the grim architecture of the city in the Stars Below.

Mud slithered away beneath her left foot. Flailing for balance, she slipped sideways in a spray of water, all but dunking herself.

As she fought for balance, a magenta shimmer caught the corner of her eye. She twisted about, birthing fresh ripples and distorting the image anew. Little by little the water settled, the sheen of the lake restored. A woman stared up at Kat – or rather the hazy approximation of one – her being a blaze of magenta and indigo flame that rippled and folded back in on itself only to billow outward with the rhythm of the breeze. Heart in her throat, Kat splashed away, scattering the apparition to ripples once more. As she did so, she caught sight of her own hand in the moonlight: no longer flesh and blood, but seething flame – an ifrît made manifest in the mortal world.

She stared in horror as her reflection re-formed, Jamar's words from earlier that day echoing through her thoughts. *The Ithna'jîm are always restless when a full moon graces the heavens. Perhaps they don't like the truth it reveals.* Zephyr too had spoken of the moon as a revealer of truths. What did it mean?

Trembling, she drew back her shirtsleeve and gazed down at her aetherios tattoo. The spidery lines sat dark and brooding – almost malevolent – against the fires of her "skin". Sick and shaking, she pressed her hands together and watched the leaping flames of her fingers bleed one into the other. Her reflection in the lake mimicked every movement, her expression calmer than her doppelgänger's racing thoughts.

Kat hated her for that.

You are nothing but a sliver of cold flame that thinks itself alive, Caradan Diar had said. *A lie that believes itself the truth.*

She'd thought it nothing more than a contorted insult, offered to prove his cleverness. But it had been more, hadn't it? So many times she'd had the sense that he'd spoken freer than he'd intended, but not about *this*.

Another memory surfaced. Another glimpse into truths the Eternity King had meant to keep from her. *You are all of the same flame. You will serve Tzal whether you mean to or not.*

She had the shape of it now, if not the detail. A vast ineluctable truth as close to perfect despair as anything she'd ever known. She sank to her knees in the water, borne down by it, smaller than she'd ever felt in her life. No wonder she felt as though she belonged here. She did . . . and yet she did not.

The moon disappeared behind a cloud. Kat's flames dimmed with the fading of the silver light, restoring her to the self she'd always known. The lie that believed itself the truth.

Everything she believed was a lie.

A scream sounded further along the bank. Shouts rang out. Four lanterns become three, bright against the restored darkness.

The sight jarred her from her stupor. Tanith was still her sister. Her responsibility.

Water streaming from her clothes, she dragged herself out of the mud, blotted out everything but the need to put one foot in front of the other, and *ran*.

She was halfway to the outcrop when three lanterns became two. Twenty yards out when a scream and a tinkle of breaking glass left only one. She was close enough now to see them plainly atop the outcrop, lit by the backwash of the surviving lantern: Edric and Tanith. Roosting sparrows scattered from Edric's path as he stumbled backwards through the trees, sword in hand and his face a rictus of terror. Tanith was a nightmare given form, smeared with gore and seeping indigo flame from a dozen wounds. She scrambled across rock and root on all fours as often as not, her skin waxy and haggard, her eyes sunken to black-rimmed pits.

With a mad, throaty laugh, she sprang, Edric's desperate sword-thrust slipping past her waist as she bore him down onto the rocks. The *thud* of skull striking stone carried out across the water. The lantern slipped from his lifeless hand and rolled to rest against a tree root.

Kat splashed past a half-submerged woman in golden armour, the blood pinkish where it curled into the water. "Tanith!"

Tanith's head jerked up, blood-matted once-golden hair brushing at her shoulders. Her sunken eyes met Kat's, bereft even of recognition. She looked away at once, lips parting as she lowered bloody teeth to Edric's throat.

"No!" Kat slammed into her, bearing her away into the lake.

Tanith keened, thrashing and biting, as the water swamped them. Her nails gouged a bloody furrow in Kat's cheek. "Let me go!" she shouted, the words more shriek than speech. "Let me go!"

Kat flung her arms about her sister and tried not to think about how much stronger Tanith was. "Never," she gasped. "Do you hear me?"

The moon broke through the clouds and they turned to flame, Tanith's indigo blaze ragged and smouldering black at its edges. Still Kat held her tight until their fires mingled, not warm as flame should be, but icy cold.

"The hunger's tearing me apart," croaked Tanith, her struggles dimming as her voice turned listless. "These people . . . they have nothing to ease it, no matter how deep I dig. I can still taste them . . . bitter metal at the back of my throat."

That explained the half-eaten corpse, though Kat wished it hadn't.

"I couldn't . . . help myself," Tanith breathed. "I'm slipping away . . .

When I come back, pieces of me are missing. It's this place ... this horrible, horrible place."

"No, it's not," Kat replied, cradling her sister's head against hers. "It's us. We shouldn't be here."

The moonlight faded and they were flesh and blood once more, though Tanith's belonged more to others than herself. Shouts rang out in the middle distance as the rest of the searchers closed.

"Let me go, Kat," said Tanith, trying to pull away. "Please." She sounded lost, almost frail. In the short time since she had entered Kat's life, she'd mocked, threatened, raged, joked, sometimes offered contrition and even fleeting remorse. But she'd never sounded so heartsick and broken as at that moment.

"I already told you no."

"That's not what I meant." She drew down a shuddering breath. "I can't live like this, Kat. Just let me go."

A lump formed in Kat's throat as the voices grew nearer, the unfamiliar shouts now directed at her. "I can't."

There had to be a way to help. Had her aetherios tattoo held any soulfire, she could have shared it, but what reserves she'd carried from Athenoch had long since gone into the mists. Or had they?

You are all of the same flame. It had to be good for something. Ever since her father had first inked her tattoo, it had been a tool for taking, because he'd beheld the world as something to be plundered. She'd learned that from him ... but maybe she'd learned wrong.

Still holding Tanith's thin body close, she unravelled a piece of her own soul, just as Caradan Diar had done to so many others at Tyzanta, and breathed it into Tanith.

Her sister shuddered in her arms, her breathing steadying as her muscles relaxed. Colour and firmness returned to her cheeks; not yet the winsome beauty she'd been, but a far cry from the hollowed creature of recent memory.

Behind Kat, the sloshing footsteps came to a halt.

"Kindly turn around, *savim*," rumbled Jamar.

Her lips pinched tight, Kat disentangled herself from Tanith and complied. She found herself facing not just Jamar, but six of his warriors also. All save he held a naked sword. A seventh knelt beside the prone Edric and offered Jamar a shallow nod.

"Is he alive?" asked Kat.

"He is," said Jamar, his expression unreadable. "Do you expect my thanks?"

"No." So he *had* seen, or had at least seen enough. "But I'm hoping you'll let us leave."

"Say that I did." He folded his arms. "Where would you go?"

Kat hesitated, but there was only one possible answer. Even now, part of her yearned to stay, but she knew not to trust it. Embracing that urge would be a betrayal of who she was – or at least who she'd tried so hard to be. "Home, for however long it lasts."

She didn't want to think about the implications of her words. Her heart was already too full as it was.

Jamar's monolithic stoicism cracked to something halfway between wariness and horror. "What *are* you?"

So he'd seen *that* part as well. "I don't know," she lied. "But I won't fight you." She glanced back. Tanith was still hunched over in the water, her eyes fixed on something only she could see. "Neither of us will."

They stared at each other in silence, a piece of Kat almost hoping that he'd put them to death. Better that, in its way, than to face the enormity of what awaited her back in Khalad. Perhaps Tanith had been right. Perhaps it was better just to let go.

"You saved my prince's life," said Jamar at last. "I give you yours in trade. Never return."

Kat exhaled. For better or worse, the choice was made. "Don't worry. I can't."

Forty-Nine

Eyes dead ahead to avoid triggering an attack of vertigo, Kat stepped lightly from the low gunwale of the *Chainbreaker*'s felucca and onto the quayside of crystalline light. A line of twenty Issnaîm warriors surged forward, silverlight swords drawn and expressions as hard as those of vaporous beings could be. A half-mile out to her left, barely visible through the shifting mists, its sails tattered and patchwork repairs pale against its battered black hull, *Chainbreaker* continued on its lazy arc around Xe'iathî's perimeter.

"What have you done?" howled the foremost Issnaîm. "Tear you apart for this, will Scirran!"

Kat folded her arms and held her ground as the tendrils of acrid black smoke from Xe'iathî's buildings coiled into the mist. Whatever the Issnaîm used to fashion their settlements, it burned well. "Scirran won't be joining us. Turns out those drakons of yours aren't so dangerous when you can see them coming."

She glanced back at Zephyr, standing at the felucca's helm. If she was at all concerned to see a tenth of Xe'iathî burning, she hid it well. Not a surprise. She'd wanted to crew the *Chainbreaker*'s cannons herself. In the end, she'd relented only because another's claim was greater than hers.

Kat bit back the last of her guilt. The burning buildings had already been derelict and the Issnaîm didn't need to know that between the crash and its recent rematch against Scirran's drakon, *Chainbreaker* had only three functioning shrieker cannons and a handful of spare prisms to power them. Most had been salvaged from *Amarid's Dream*. "I want to speak to the Elders."

"Nothing to say to you, have they!" retorted the Issnaîm.

"This isn't a negotiation." Kat forced herself to stay calm. Reason was more unsettling than bluster in moments like this. "Twice we came to you in friendship. Twice now your Elders betrayed us." She pointed to the *Chainbreaker*. "They *will* see me … or my ship will take Xe'iathî apart piece by piece."

Chainbreaker's flank belched flame. The shot wailed past the shimmering webwork spires of the Elders' palace and vanished into the mists. Kat hoped it had been meant as a warning. For all that rest had done him the world of good, Vallant still had a certain … wildness about him.

The lead Issnaîm's expression crumpled. "Take you to the Elders, will I."

Kat breathed a soft sigh of relief. Razing Xe'iathî wouldn't solve anything. It would only punish the innocent alongside the guilty. However, the Issnaîm couldn't have known that. She felt no victory at their capitulation. It brought her closer to a truth that she didn't want to hear.

She started forward. "Good. Let's get this over with."

It took less than an hour for the Elders to confirm everything she had feared.

Kat spent the early hours of the westward voyage alone at the *Chainbreaker*'s prow, the impossible Veil-born wind tugging at her hair. The rest of the crew left her to it for the most part, having picked up on her mood either by direct observance or whispered warning. Not exactly the stuff of leadership, but she was drowning and had no notion of what she might do or say that wouldn't simply drag everyone else down with her. It had been hard enough telling the others that there was no salvation for them beyond the lesion. Telling them *why* would take more than she had to give.

Tanith was the only person who might understand, but Tanith was in even worse shape. For all her offhand comments about eating people to survive, it was one thing to devour the insubstantial glory of another person's soul, and quite another to taste their blood at the back of your throat. Kat knew her sister well enough by now to recognise that it wasn't what she'd done in the Old Realm that troubled her as much as what she *might* do now that they'd returned home.

They were neither of them the same as they'd once been. Several times since returning to the *Chainbreaker*, Kat had felt the temptation to wield her new-found glamour. More than that, she felt the dark throb of Tzal's presence far to the north and west as plainly as if it were a wound in her side.

She gripped the bulwark as omen rot clamped tight about her heart and lungs, the pain turning the greenish-white mists of the Veil a muddy red-black. She almost welcomed it now. Better to know that an end was coming. That whatever happened next, she wouldn't have to live with it.

She'd more or less regathered herself when a wisp of lavender soul-scent warned of Vallant's approach, reminding her that she'd more than one reason for seeking solitude.

"If I didn't know better, I'd say you were avoiding me." Clean-shaven and wearing a fresh uniform – his olive skin scrubbed and his curls cropped close – he again looked and sounded like himself ... so long as you didn't linger on the eyes, which were as restless as Kat knew her own to be. Nearly fifty souls had taken ship with him six months before. To lose them all was a heavy toll, even by his standards. And then there was the matter of his seclusion in the mists. How much time had passed for him while six months had crawled past in Khalad? It had to be like waking from a dream to a nightmare.

"And everything's always about you, isn't it?" Kat replied.

"The benefit of notoriety, as I hear you've had good reason to learn, these past months." He drew down a deep breath. "Thank you."

"For finding you? That was an accident."

"I'm sure." His reply held an echo of humour. "No ... I meant for holding things together while I was gone. I always knew you would."

"Then why thank me?"

"Because I have some idea what it took from you. Most don't and never will."

He didn't know the half of it. But he would. "If you're hoping for an apology for the things I've called you in the past, you're going to leave disappointed." Sparring with Vallant was too old a habit to leave behind, even if he seldom fought back. She almost felt grateful. Something, at least, was still the same.

"As it happens, you looked like you needed a friend. Do I qualify?"

And just like that, she wanted to thump the earnestness off his face. "You do. Whether either of us likes it or not."

He stared off into the mists. "So what happened out there? I'll ask if no one else will."

A piece of her ached to tell him. The rest, wiser by far, elected not to. "It'll have to wait until we return to Athenoch. I only have it in me to tell the story once."

She expected him to argue. Instead he simply nodded. "As bad as that?"

Worse. "Do you mind if I ask something?"

"You're in command for now. Ask what you like."

Kat narrowed her eyes, unsure if he meant it. Especially the bit about being in command. "Why didn't you cross through the lesion when you had the chance?"

"It wouldn't let me." He scowled away memories. "I don't remember much, but I do remember that. It was like pushing against glass."

And yet it had opened freely for her and Tanith. Kat stared down at her aetherios tattoo and felt her father laughing at her from beyond the Deadwinds. Or was it simply another coincidental "benefit" of his work to free Tzal from his prison in the Stars Below? She doubted she'd ever know. "I see."

Vallant regarded her thoughtfully. "I'm certain that I don't. However, I will promise you one thing, Kat: whatever's eating away at you, it's not your problem alone. We're all in this together."

They were indeed, for all the good that did them.

Fifty

When *Chainbreaker* docked at Athenoch, there was no mistaking that the Veil was closer than ever. Even with blesswood burning at every corner of the city, the pine-forested hills and crop fields were little more than the stuff of imagining. More pervasive was the air of defeat. For years, Athenoch had been a refuge. No more. Under Fadiya's leadership, every ship in the town had been made as skyworthy as limited resources allowed . . . but they had nowhere to go.

Zephyr left almost at once, taking the *Chainbreaker* to gather news of the wider realm. Feeling ever more a failure, Kat promised to hold a conclave as soon as was practical. Rebuffing all attempts at companionship, she passed her time in the highest chamber of Athenoch's black tower arranging and rearranging the puzzle pieces in the hope of finding any configuration that offered respite from her abiding misery.

Chainbreaker returned as night fell, sufficiently ahead of schedule to rouse her curiosity. Thus she was waiting at the docks when Yali, Tatterlain and Damant disembarked, alongside a stranger named Mezzeri.

Still heartsick from Rîma's death – that she had died on her own terms offered some solace – learning of Azra's final fate knocked Kat sideways once more, not least because she hadn't felt Azra's passing as she had Rîma's. After everything they'd shared – everything they'd endured and sacrificed for one another – did their bond really mean so little? Guilt became frustration and frustration a smouldering anger that gave her the strength to claw her way out of despondency. Better still, Mezzeri's presence – and the reason for it – at last offered at least the *possibility* of a way forward.

Vallant – damn him – had been right, just like he always was. They *were* all in it together.

Kat called the conclave an hour after nightfall the following day, its attendance limited to those she trusted with her secrets and her life – Vallant, Damant, Zephyr, Yali, Tatterlain, Fadiya, Hadîm and Marida. Tanith declined to attend. However, as the conclave formed beneath the black tower's motionless silver and astoricum sphere, hers wasn't the only face absent in the guttering light of the oil lanterns. Rîma. Maxin. Amarid. His sister Jaîna. Azra. Azra most of all.

They mattered still. They *all* mattered. Kat would find a way through this, however imperfect, for them and for the thousands who'd made Athenoch their home.

Armed with that certainty, she took her place in the circle. She felt her left hand trembling and clamped it shut. ‖"I'll make this as simple as I can, but nothing I say here can leave this room. You'll understand why by the time I'm done."‖ It was in fact the main reason for choosing the tower as the meeting point, rather than the conclave hall by the river. No one would climb all those stairs out of simple eavesdropping curiosity. ‖"The realm of Zephyr's ancestors is real. But it can never be our home."‖

Zephyr exchanged a glance with Vallant. ‖"Why? Are the people hostile?"‖

‖"Not so I saw. In fact, those Tanith and I met were kinder than we deserved."‖ Kat dug deep for words that didn't want to be spoken. ‖"The problem is with us – or with everyone except you, *nasaîm*. We're not who we thought we were. We are all Tzal … or at the very least, we're pieces of him. I always thought that hope was the greatest lie. Turns out there's nothing true about us at all."‖

The room went silent, broken only by the wind clutching at the tower's balconies. Damant and Marida looked thoughtful. Hadîm wore the self-satisfied smile that seldom left his face. The remaining expressions were curiously similar: sympathy with a touch of sorrow.

Vallant cleared his throat. ||"Kat . . ."||

Here it came.

||". . . you've been under a lot of pressure—"||

She cut him off with a sharp, chopping Simah sign. ||"Don't."|| She'd hoped it would get easier once the words were out in the open. No such luck. ||"This is hard enough already. Let me speak. If you've the strength for it, we can argue when I'm done."||

Vallant opened his mouth to speak and closed it again as Fadiya arched her eyebrows. Damant's gaze didn't leave Kat for a moment.

||"We're all ears, Kat."|| Tatterlain winced and pinched finger and thumb together in a Simah apology for Yali. ||"Figuratively."||

Yali barely acknowledged the words. Like Damant, she'd eyes only for Kat.

Kat nodded her thanks. ||"The Issnaîm have a tradition of something called a moon. It's . . . a pale reflection of the sun and its light reveals truth. We don't have it here, but in the Old Realm . . ."|| she swallowed, ||"it showed me what I really am. Tanith too. Not flesh and blood, but flame. Tzal's flame."||

||Perhaps it was just a glamour,|| said Yali. ||A different world might mean different magics.||

||"I wish I could believe that, but we didn't just *look* different. We were becoming something different. I englamoured someone, almost without trying. Like it was second nature. And Tanith . . ."|| She shook her head. Tanith had enough to worry about without getting into those gory details. ||"She was different, too."||

She left unsaid that those changes had followed them from the Old Realm. She'd suspected as much at the first scent of a lavender soul and the need it had awoken. Confirmation had come with breakfast that morning, the bread and figs ashen on her tongue.

Her lips pressed tight, Fadiya gave the shallowest of nods. A sign perhaps that mother and daughter had spoken more than Kat had realised.

"I appreciate a good story," said Hadîm languidly, "and that's all this is: a good story. It's not proof of anything."

"Not by itself, no. But then I remembered something that Caradan Diar told me." Kat glanced around the conclave circle. Fortunately, it seemed *that* awkward truth had already propagated, sparing her the explanation. "He said we were all of the same flame, and that we would serve Tzal whether we meant to or not."

"I imagine that the Eternity King said a great many things," said Tatterlain. "Few of them true."

Kat shook her head. "You don't know how much I hoped for that, but the Issnaîm confirmed it. There's more to their legend of Tzal than Zephyr knows. One that generations of their Elders kept secret, even from their own kind. Unable to free himself from his prison, Tzal split a portion of himself into countless lesser flames, hoping that many minds might find a solution where one could not. Think of it: generation upon generation multiplying, prospering, learning new skills, new ideas, and passing them on to the next. All unknowingly working towards a goal Tzal couldn't achieve for himself. Caradan Diar was so terrified of Tzal escaping that it turned him into a tyrant, and that tyranny only made things worse." She recalled the Eternity King's dying words. "He thought that by controlling us he could ... I don't know, redeem us, maybe? He died a monster, but in a strange way he cared about us."

No, that wasn't right, was it? He'd had hopes for them ... but hopes of what? She could almost see it – had glimpsed it on the edge of her vision for days – but it remained stubbornly beyond sight.

"And in the end, he and Isdihar decided that it was safer to pull everything down," said Yali.

"Him, certainly," Damant put in. "The more I think about it, the more I think she obeyed him out of fear. I think she even tried to warn me."

"Oh good," said Tatterlain, grimacing. "More guilt."

Damant shrugged, his face hard. ||"It's a perennial crop hereabouts."||

Vallant shook his head. ||"Kat, I can't go along with this. You're saying we're not real."||

Zephyr laid a hand on his shoulder. ||"Not saying that at all, is she. You may be of Tzal, but you are not him. A piece of you, he is, as all your ancestors are a piece of you. Nothing more."||

||"Not here, maybe,"|| said Kat, ||"but out there, in the Old Realm? We're a seed sown and nourished to become something terrible. If even one of us gets out, Tzal gets out. Everything he's done here – everything he did to Zephyr's ancestors – he'll do again."||

Yali fixed her with a stare little more charitable than the one Vallant had offered. ||Kat, can you hear yourself? This is mad.||

Kat saw the doubt in her eyes. ||"That doesn't mean it isn't true. We've always believed that Nyssa created us in her own image. Looked at one way, that's all this is."||

"Futility is the mother of invention," murmured Damant.

||"What was that?"|| asked Marida, her black qalimîri eyes glistening beneath a frown.

He stood straighter. ||"Something the Eternity Queen said. I thought she was talking about the Veil's advance, but it works here as well."||

Vallant narrowed his eyes. ||"Ihsan, you're not buying into this?"||

||"I've seen some of what Kat describes."|| Damant understood all right. Kat saw it in his eyes. ||"Time and again, the Eternity Queen asserted that she was Khalad, *was* the Deadwinds. She even talked about the sensation of having pieces of her rebel. I put it down to arrogance. I know better now. Tzal didn't control me. He stole the piece of me that might have fought him."||

Yali hung her head. ||And me.||

||"And Ardin, and probably more others than we'll ever know."|| Damant grunted. ||"Rîma restored me. Ever since, I've been able to see something of how the glamour works. Kat's right. We're all connected. But it's changing. What the Eternity Queen did to me is not what she's doing in Zariqaz now."||

502

Tatterlain rubbed his generous chin. "The mob that chased us from the city *were* different. Blank-eyed and obedient, barely distinguishable from koilos."

"They weren't like that because of something Tzal put in them, but because of what he removed," Damant agreed heavily. "The Eternity Queen boasted of stripping away free will, and she has, as easily as you or I would fold a hand behind our backs. Part of them is now part of her. A truth so fundamental to the fabric of our lives that it's practically invisible, as Rîma said. One that it would be kinder not to know. I'd say this qualifies."

Vallant shook his head, his vacant eyes on the motionless silver and astoricum sphere overhead. "I don't believe it."

Damant twitched a mirthless smile. "You think I want to, Bashar?" It was the first time Kat had ever heard him use Vallant's given name. "However outlandish, facts remain facts. Arvish has the right of it."

She shot him a grateful look. There was no question that Damant was with her now; Tatterlain and Yali too, judging by their expressions. More than that, he'd given shape to what had been formless conjecture. But still she couldn't shake the sense that she was missing something important.

Fadiya held up a hand level with her chin in the old fireblood custom of securing a moment in which to speak. "But we're not the first civilisation in Khalad. Our cities are built on the ruins of those laid down by the ashborn, the scaldera…" she glanced at Hadîm, "…others."

"Failed attempts, maybe," said Damant. "So Tzal sent fire from the Stars Below to wipe the slate clean and start over. Rîma thought he was busy doing the same thing right now with the lethargia. So do I."

"Assuming you're right," said Marida, "why a sickness and not more fire?"

"Maybe he lacks the power to do so," said Kat. "Khalad has never been more populous. More people means less of Tzal to go around. And the mists have claimed so many over the centuries. Every scrap they steal diminishes him."

||"I don't think it's that,"|| said Damant. ||"Drowning Khalad in fire would have been the end of us cinderbloods as well. Maybe he recognised that we had the potential to achieve what he wanted."||

Fadiya, one of only two firebloods in the room, grimaced but said nothing. Tatterlain, being the other, simply shrugged.

Hadîm's smile broadened to something unfriendly. ||"How deliciously arrogant."|| As one of Rîma's people – perhaps the *last* of Rîma's people – he'd reason to take offence, Kat supposed. ||"What makes you so special?"||

||"Because we don't give up,"|| Damant said bluntly. ||"Firebloods like winning, but they like an easy life even more. They embrace structure and play it for all it's worth. But if you push us, we push back harder. Rîma once told me that the ashborn were innocent, peaceful. No use to Tzal. Perhaps the same was true of the scaldera. And your people ...?"||

Hadîm was no longer smiling. "We unmade ourselves through indolence and self-importance," he murmured. "Tzal had no need to sweep us away."

||"Not quite,"|| said Damant, as Tatterlain signed a translation of Hadîm's words for Yali. ||"Queen Amakala destroyed you while searching for a means to fight him. The city-soul of Tadamûr was to have been her weapon."||

||"Do you really believe that?"|| asked Marida.

||"Rîma did,"|| he replied, his signs as stiff as his voice. ||"That's enough for me. She held her own against the Eternity Queen for a time and all she had to work with were the dregs that latched onto her when Tadamûr fell. She died thinking that in destroying Tadamûr, she'd failed us all."||

||That's why the Eternity Queen's been so cruel, even when it made no sense,|| said Yali. ||Provoking the Qersali, oppressing the border towns ... She kept squeezing us tight, so that finding a way through the Veil was our only hope.||

The corner of Tatterlain's cheek twitched the unhappy frown of a man accepting an unpalatable fact. ||"And when the Veil began claiming the borderlands, she started the evacuation."||

||"Exactly,"|| said Damant. ||"The souls of the dead find their way back to Tzal. Those lost to the Veil are gone for ever. It wasn't kindness, but self-preservation."||

Kat nodded. There was a bitter energy to the conclave now, the momentum building with every word spoken. ||"Vallant couldn't cross the lesion into the Old Realm, but Tanith and I could, which means that our tattoos – which my father created by building on the work of generations of Obsidium cultists – made it possible. I suspect that we could find a way to bring others with us, given time."|| She counted off the points on her fingers. ||"But even getting that far meant meeting the challenge of the Veil. It required finding friendship with a daughter of the Issnaîm – the same people who'd once tried to wipe us out in order to prevent that very escape."||

||"In other words, there's a lot could have gone wrong with Tzal's plan,"|| said Tatterlain.

Kat shook her head. ||"It never was a plan, not the way you mean. My father claimed to hear Tzal's – or rather *Nyssa*'s – voice. Maybe he wasn't the only one. I certainly did, or thought I had. Maybe we've all been influenced to lesser or greater degrees even if we don't know it. But for the most part I think Tzal just set us running and waited to see how it played out."||

Fadiya's cheeks paled. ||"Katija . . . if what you're saying is true, there could already be pieces of him in the Old Realm. The seed, as you put it, may already have taken root."||

||"Or maybe the Issnaîm never succeeded in banishing him fully, I know. But that doesn't change anything for us. Zephyr's ancestors fought to save their world from Tzal's tyranny. We've no right to risk undoing their work."|| Kat straightened, surprised at how easily her next words flowed. ||"I won't allow it. Neither will Tanith."||

||"Nor I,"|| Zephyr said softly. ||"Let the lesion remain hidden for ever."||

"Humour me on one point," said Hadîm. "You saw yourself as flame, not flesh and blood. But why flesh and blood at all? There's no one here to fool. If everything you say is right, we wouldn't know any better."

"Trapped by the past, is Tzal," said Zephyr. "Made you thus, did he, to mirror the body he once wore."

"That, or he was hoping to deceive not those in Khalad, but beyond," said Tatterlain. "Trust me, infiltrating your enemy's a lot easier when you look how they expect."

The conclave lapsed into a far from comfortable silence.

"This is all very interesting," Vallant didn't sound at all sincere, "but I'm not hearing anything that helps us."

"Take comfort in the fact that Tzal would now seem to be as much Yennika as Yennika is Tzal," said Damant. "She always had the arrogance of the divine, and it was always her greatest weakness. Perhaps she's made it his, too."

Hadîm's lips twitched in a bleak smile. "Our options would seem to be tyranny or death. Not the stuff of which battle cries are made."

"It isn't even death," said Fadiya. "If true, the only way we can hurt Tzal is to say our goodbyes and give ourselves to the Veil."

But there *was* something else. Kat was increasingly certain of it. Something that Caradan Diar had intended before she'd proven herself unwilling to be as ruthless as he'd needed. She felt certain that Damant had offered a piece of the puzzle, but her heart and mind were too full to narrow it down. That left only the plan that was barely a plan at all.

She flexed her fingers to ward off stiffness. "Thanks to Tatterlain, we've an option somewhere in between. Mezzeri has repaired the siphonic prism from the throne immortal. Tzal needs Khalad just as much as we do. We offer a trade: the means to restore the balance of the mists in exchange for concessions. It won't be freedom, but we'll survive."

Tatterlain winced. "Tzal doesn't strike me as the bargaining kind."

"He will if the alternative is the mists winnowing him away piece by piece."|| The gleam in Marida's glossy black eyes added malice to her words. ||"If we accelerate that process, he'll bargain."||

Damant glared at her. ||"You're talking about driving innocents into the Veil."||

Marida folded her arms. ||"This isn't a time for sentiment. We—"||

Yali stamped her foot to cut her off. ||Then what's the difference between us and Tzal? Tyranny cannot be defeated by cruelty, only through sacrifice.||

Kat stared at her. ||"What was that?"||

||It was the last thing Rima said to me.||

Tyranny cannot be defeated by cruelty, only through sacrifice. Yali had misunderstood, but it didn't matter. Not now. There *was* another way forward. Kat saw it, blazing bright as any torch house.

Vallant cleared his throat. ||"Can you give us the room? Kat and I need to have the argument she promised."||

Kat's heart sank as she met his gaze, his eyes as hard as she'd ever seen them. *You're in command for now*, he'd said aboard the *Chainbreaker*. There could only be one place this was going. She clenched her left hand tight as another precursor to an omen rot tremor struck.

Tatterlain started towards the stairs. Hadim shrugged and followed, the others drifting away in ones and twos. Only Damant showed no sign of moving. "Arvish?"

"It's fine," she replied, her voice as steady as she could manage. "We haven't had a shouting match in six months. I've missed it."

The twitch of a lip in an otherwise impassive expression told her he didn't believe her, but he left all the same. He, at least, trusted her.

Vallant stared in silence until the footsteps faded from the stairs, his ordinarily earnest face grim. "Twenty years I've been fighting to free Khalad. Twenty years. It's cost me more friends than I can count, and now you want to us to give up? I tell you, Kat, I'd rather die with a sword in my hand than be party to that."

Kat swallowed away a sour taste. "You can't be serious."

"Can't I? We still have ships. Men and women to crew them. From

507

everything Damant says, the redcloaks are spread thin. There's never been a better time to attack Zariqaz."

Kat's heart sank further. "You can't destroy Tzal with swords and shriekers, Bashar. You heard Damant: you'll be lost as soon as you get close."

He shook his head. "Ihsan was always prone to caution. If he can resist, so can I."

She flung a hand towards the balcony edge and the night-shrouded dock. "Maybe you can, but what about your crew? And even if they could, you can't *kill* Tzal, only his body." It was still easier not to think of him as the Eternity Queen. That meant thinking of Azra. "He exists as long as we do. He'll just take a new host. You'll have won *nothing*."

"Assuming you're right about any of this. You may have convinced the others, but I'm not there yet."

He hadn't listened at all, had he? Or else he was too arrogant to accept the gap in his understanding. So much had passed him by while he'd been trapped in the mists: the world he remembered was no longer the one any of them were living in. Or maybe, Kat thought dully, he hadn't recovered half as much of his sanity as she'd first thought.

"You think I want this?" she snapped. The fingers of her left hand twitched as she closed on him. "You think I don't wish I could fix it all by waving a sword around? It won't work, Vallant. We have to try something else."

"Why?" he demanded tautly. "If we're not real, why bother?"

Was he thinking of his wife, his daughter? Their deaths had launched his crusade. Their memory had held him together. Could you love an illusion? This fear, at least, Kat understood, for it had been uppermost in her mind for days.

"Because they're real to *me*." She rattled through the words so fast it left her short of breath. "*You're* real to me. However we began, we have value. We matter. We think and feel. *Kiasta*, that Tzal appals us is proof of that. We are not what is done in our name."

508

"Then what?" he shouted, hands clenched level with his chest. "What is there left for us to do? Tell me that!"

Kat took an involuntary step back, his anguish and rage a wall between them. "We change the world. As much as we can and for as long as we're able."

Vallant sagged, fury bleeding away from a face suddenly years older. "You sound like Rîma."

"Maybe. But they're your words."

He shook his head, a man adrift in memories. "Then maybe I sound like Rîma too."

Kat laid her hand on his arm. So easy to forget that Vallant had known Rîma far longer. He'd never be free of her shadow. "Vallant, I—"

The world pitched sideways and drowned in red, all sensation driven out by the fist squeezing at her heart and lungs, by the pain of muscles spasming fit to shatter bones. Kat heard herself screaming, the sound ever more distant as red bled away into a cold, clinging black.

Consciousness returned slowly, her heart yammering and every muscle in her body jangling. She felt cold tile beneath her splayed legs and Vallant's warmth at her back, his arms around her, holding her upright. "Easy, Kat. I have you."

She forced down a breath, the air like needles in her lungs. Another. With chagrin she recalled her shortness of breath and twitching fingers. Signs she couldn't afford to overlook. And her collapse . . . If the disease had progressed so far, she didn't have long. Days, maybe.

But just maybe it was long enough to change the world one last time.

"I thought your omen rot was cured," murmured Vallant.

"We both thought wrong." She swallowed. "It's not important now."

"Maybe it's important to me."

"Even though I'm not real?"

"Even though."

She heard his wry smile and managed one of her own. "Vallant . . . There *is* something else we can try. I didn't have a chance to tell the others, but I can't do it without your help. It's not perfect . . ."

509

"But nothing is where you and I are concerned." He sighed. "I'm listening."

Feeling her strength return, Kat turned around, the better to see his eyes and so that he might see the truth shining in hers. There was risk to this, but worse would be to let him fly off into the night to a battle he couldn't win. United, they had a chance.

She laid it out as plainly as she could, piecing together everything she'd learned, and everything she hoped to achieve. Spoken aloud, it sounded fanciful, but Vallant listened without interruption until she was done.

"I'll have to think about it." He didn't appear convinced, but he at least looked thoughtful. "But Kat ... you need to come clean with the others about what you're facing. Don't leave mourning their only recourse."

"I know, but there's so little time."

"Make some," he said softly. "If any of this is real, you owe them that."

Midnight came and went before Kat finally made it to bed, bone-weary and soul-frayed beyond anything that omen rot had to offer. But she clung to consciousness long enough to explain everything to Tanith, and went to sleep with hope clutched close. Vallant had listened. He *had* to have listened, otherwise it made everything a lie.

She woke at dawn to the soft, insistent pressure of Tanith's hand on her shoulder. "Vallant's gone. Damant says he left an hour before dawn."

Still groggy, Kat swathed herself in blankets and staggered to the apartment's balcony. Athenoch's makeshift dock sat empty beneath the bright morning sun. *Chainbreaker* was gone. So were *Timmara's Sword* and *Bescal's Wake* – every warship they had left.

"Of course he is," Kat replied. "Did Damant say where?"

"Zariqaz."

Sailing straight into Tzal's arms. Six hundred souls gone with him.

Uncertainty churning in her gut, Kat nodded and stared at the empty skyline.

Fifty-One

Ragged from the exertion of a sleepless night as much as omen rot's steady advance, Kat arrived at the dock a little after noon. Thanks to the efforts of what few experienced sailriders Vallant had left behind, *Telthi's Pride* was already straining at its mooring lines. The high-prowed carrack was neither fast nor formidable, having spent its recent years as a cargo scow hauling provisions back to Athenoch from beyond the mists. But all being well, it would be all she needed. Eyes dead ahead for fear that a single glimpse down between the creaking hull and the uneven dockyard would spur vertigo to ruin, she pressed a hand to the peeling green paint of the *Pride*'s hull. Neither it nor she were all that they once were, but that didn't mean they couldn't still serve.

Omen rot gripped her tight as she pulled back her hand, dimming the sun and sending every muscle in her left side into spasm. Strong hands caught her at waist and elbow as her knees buckled, holding her upright until the attack faded.

"Please don't throw yourself off the dock in plain sight of the city," said Tatterlain, with an airy smile. "It's bad for morale, and that's already low enough as it is."

Kat blinked away the last of the darkness and offered a wan smile. "It wasn't intentional. There's not as much of me to go around as there used to be."

"All the more reason that you should let me come," he replied, suddenly serious.

"You're needed here. Vallant's gone, and one way or another, I won't be coming back." She shrugged, stifling a wince as the motion pulled on unhappy muscles. "Fadiya sees around more corners than most, but she lacks your . . ."

He raised an eyebrow. "Flair for creative interpretation?"

"Let's call it that, yes."

"Could be handy, that, if you're negotiating with a baleful god."

Kat hesitated. She'd never been good at farewells, mostly because she spent more of her life glad to see the back of people than pleased to see them. But she wasn't that woman any longer – omen rot was the least of it. And Tatterlain was the oldest of her new friends, though she'd never have known he'd become so at their first meeting in that cramped Bascari clatter wagon, carrying her to execution. "Did I ever thank you for saving my life?"

"I'm sure it came up."

Which meant she probably hadn't. "Would you walk with me the rest of the way?"

He crooked his elbow for her to take. "A stroll in the sunshine with a beautiful woman? I'd be a fool to refuse."

More creative interpretation at work, for what beauty Kat might have admitted to was now in full retreat behind puffy, dark-ringed eyes, a greyish tinge overtaking her bronze skin. Between that and her stumbling steps, she'd no longer any need to come clean with others about her worsening condition, which had made the ensuing conversations easier to begin but harder to bear. Even so, she took Tatterlain's arm in hers and allowed him to lead her the rest of the way to the *Pride*'s gangplank, where the others were waiting.

"Arvish." Damant nodded a greeting, his effort to hide his discomfort appreciated despite its failure. Kat doubted she'd have done better in his place. "Everyone else is already aboard. Join us when you're ready."

It was a small enough crew. Hadîm, Tanith, Yali, Damant himself, and just enough sailriders to make the voyage possible. "Thank you."

He beat a grateful retreat up the gangplank, leaving Kat alone with Tatterlain and one other: the woman who was the closest thing she had ever had to a real parent, whose attempts to hold back her tears were about as successful as Damant's had been to conceal his discomfort. Kat untangled herself from Tatterlain and took her first unsupported steps. They were easier than she'd expected. Good.

"You're sure you'll find your way through the Veil without Zephyr?" asked Fadiya.

Zephyr had gone with Vallant, and there was no telling when she'd return. Or even *if* she'd return. "It's hard to explain, but I can *feel* Tzal," said Kat. "I have done ever since we returned from the Old Realm. If I follow that feeling, the mists won't keep me."

"I suppose it's no use asking you not to go?" said Fadiya.

"What did Tanith say when you asked her, *Mathami*?" Kat replied.

"That she'd too much to atone for to stay." Fadiya shook her head wistfully. "I just got you both back, and now I'm losing you again."

Kat took one of Fadiya's hands in both of hers. "I don't know what to say." Only three paths now beckoned. Either the omen rot would kill her, Tzal would kill her or . . . Well, she didn't want to think about the alternative.

Fadiya drew herself up, the fireblood matriarch coming to the fore. "I do." She laid her free hand atop Kat's, her watery gaze unblinking. "You are everything your father wasn't. You couldn't be better."

Discomfited as ever by an honest compliment, Kat stared past Fadiya's shoulder and out over Athenoch. It really was a beautiful city. Worth fighting for. Worth dying for. "I had a lot of help."

Fadiya softened to a smile. "As it should be. I only wish you'd had more from me."

Kat embraced her, lingering until the lavender of Fadiya's soul became more temptation than comfort. "Goodbye, *Mathami*."

*

The Veil was even more turbulent than on the return from the Old Realm. Kat clung to the ship's wheels, holding *Telthi's Pride* on course as best she could, steering always towards the aching throb beyond the unseen horizon. For a blessing, omen rot let her be save for occasional spasms in her left arm and shoulder. Even so, by the time the mists peeled back onto darkened skies and the nostalgia-scent of the Veil faded, she was sodden with sweat and shaking with effort.

"My turn." By way of reinforcement, Hadîm laid a hand on the lateral wheel and levelled a polite stare. "You should rest."

Rest alone wouldn't cut it any longer, but Kat nodded anyway. With the Veil behind them, they no longer needed the beacon of Tzal's baleful presence. Besides, she didn't know where they were headed, not precisely. Hadîm did. With a nod of thanks, she left the *Pride's* wheelhouse and began her descent of the quarterdeck companionway. Halfway down, omen rot swept her into darkness, the dull thump of elbow and spine barely felt through the aching, breathless haze.

"She won't make it." Damant's voice drifted through the darkness.

A hand found hers and squeezed. "She will," Tanith replied. "She'd better. So if you've nothing helpful to say, find something helpful to *do*."

Heavy footfalls tracked away. By the time Kat's eyelids deigned to prise themselves apart, she and Tanith were alone at the base of the companionway. With her sister's help, she propped herself up into a sitting position. "He didn't mean it like that," she said softly. "Rîma's death hit him harder than he'll admit. He's not good with feeling helpless."

Tanith snorted. "And I am?"

"You're different. You understand."

Tanith scowled, but gave a slow nod. "How are you feeling?"

The *Pride* began to climb, shimmering aethersails blossoming along its flanks ready to catch the Deadwinds. As smooth a deployment as any she'd seen, save for when Zephyr was at the helm ... but then if Hadîm was anything, he was a man who took pride in perfection.

Kat considered. Beyond her aching bones, the hunger was growing.

With one thing and another, she wasn't certain there was enough of her left to control it. "I'm afraid . . . I'm afraid I'm not entirely myself."

Tanith offered a wintry smile. "You're right, I do understand."

"What about you?"

The smile vanished, replaced by the evasive look Kat had come to know so well. But even that faded before Tanith spoke, lost behind stoicism that suited her better than it should. "In the Old Realm . . . I've lost control of myself before, but never that badly. I can still taste the blood." She stared out over the bulwark to where the first Deadwind motes danced against darkened skies. "The next time will be worse. It's like . . ."

"Like something inside you has awoken and has no intention of going back to sleep."

Tanith nodded distractedly. "That's exactly it. I'm not an amashti any more, or at least I don't think I will be for much longer. I'm becoming something else." She paused. "When you found me in the Old Realm, I told you I can't live like this. That part hasn't changed. It's not right. *I'm* not right. It seems I've completely lost my taste for eating people," she finished wryly.

Kat winced. "There's still the Deadwinds."

Tanith gave a vicious shake of the head. "It's not the same for me as it is for you. Any ifrît I consume is gone for good. Snuffed out for ever so that I can cling to life. It's not . . ." She broke off, at last catching up with Kat's earlier words. "Kat, I'm so sorry."

"It's all right." It wasn't, not really, but nor was it Tanith's fault. The glamour. The scent of lavender whenever people got close. The ash in her mouth when she tried to eat. The hunger that was growing steadily stronger. Tanith might not have been an amashti any longer, but there was still one aboard the *Telthi's Pride*. "It's not like I'll have to live with it long."

Tanith grimaced. "I preferred it when I didn't care about people."

It was a lie, of course. As a fugitive, she hadn't had cause to think of others as anything other than food. The world had hated her, so she'd hated it back. But little by little, she'd found her place in Khalad just as Kat had found hers. "If you don't want to be part of this, you don't have to. I'll find another way."

The grimace melted into a gentle sneer. "Sure you will. You'll collapse on top of Tzal and he'll be so mortified that he'll agree to your every demand." She shrugged. "One way or another, my time's coming to an end, just like yours. I'd like people to think well of me afterwards, if only a little."

Kat forced a smile. "I'll think well of you."

"You don't count. You're my sister."

The sky thickened with indigo and magenta motes. Vibrant. Tantalising. Flames coursed along Kat's left forearm as her aetherios tattoo drank in the soulfire. Excitement tugged at her gut as hunger sharpened to need. Distant enough to resist for now, but for how much longer? Tanith was right: it was no way to live. "Will you help me to my cabin? I should try to get some sleep."

Tanith's throat bobbed, her eyes on the dancing motes. She'd not fed since the Old Realm, and the scraps of soul Kat had shared with her had to be running thin. "Of course."

An insistent shake drew Kat back to the waking world. Yali stood beside the narrow cot, her face tight with the same concern that had become a fixture of Kat's existence. Tanith was right. Life was easier when you didn't care about people, but it was also easier when people didn't care about you, not least because it didn't leave you feeling as though you'd let everyone down.

Kat hauled the thin drape away from the porthole. Grey skies beckoned. On the horizon, the spire of Zariqaz gleamed dully through the cloud. ||Are we at Tulloq yet?||

||We've been tied up a few hours,|| Yali replied. ||Damant and Hadîm are out looking for a way down. Tanith's standing watch.||

Of course Tanith didn't trust the sailriders to do so. Kat swallowed a claggy mouthful that, taken alongside the grey morning, told her she'd been asleep far longer than she'd meant to. Trust was a thinning resource all over.

||You should have woken me.||

Yali shook her head, defiant. ||You need your sleep, honest and true.||

Hard to argue with that. Even breathing was an effort. More than that, she could feel the Deadwinds ifrîti seething in the depths of her tattoo, their emotions boiling closer to the surface of its soulfire than she was accustomed to. Close enough that she could feel their wordless voices pressing against her thoughts. Another new experience, and decidedly unwelcome even though Kat knew the cause. Had she left herself so weak that even a fragmented ifrît might challenge her for control?

Better not to think about that. ||Any problems?||

||A redcloak felucca wanted to board us. Hadîm handled it.|| A faraway look stole over Yali's expression. ||He's almost as good as Rîma.||

No need to ask what she meant. A patrol felucca held three or four crew. No obstacle for Hadîm. ||Did you tell him so?||

||He didn't seem to think it was a compliment.||

Kat stifled a smile. For someone like Hadîm, *almost* as good as Rîma was the worst of all possible insults. ||Did he ask what it would cost?||

||Not a word. Should he?||

||He always has before.||

Yali shrugged. ||Damant seems to think he's doing all this out of principle. He also said something unkind about that probably being a new experience for him.|| She pursed her lips. ||Kat . . . you're sure this is a good idea? The Eternity Queen's been searching for you ever since the Obsidium Uprising. Now you're walking straight into her clutches.||

||Would that be so bad? I'm damaged goods. What better way to trap her than in a broken body?||

Yali narrowed her eyes, hurt more than unfriendly. ||Don't say that. You don't know what it's like.|| She shook her head. ||I just hope she's feeling humble enough to meet your terms.||

Kat snorted. ||If Damant's right, she's practically Yennika Bascari

517

reborn, without Azra's redeeming features. She doesn't know what humility is. She's probably convinced that she's in control, even now.||

Yali nodded. ||There was smoke over Zariqaz when we arrived. What do you suppose happened to Vallant?||

Kat's chest tightened in a way that had nothing to do with omen rot. So there *had* been a battle. At least a piece of one. ||It'll be over by now, one way or another.||

||Why didn't you stop him? We both know you could.||

By englamouring him, in other words. ||If I had, I'd be just like Tzal. And who knows, maybe he was right and I was wrong.|| And then there was the other reason. The one that she hadn't dared tell anyone other than Tanith. They'd only think her mad. Probably they'd be right.

||Can your ego take that?|| asked Yali.

||I'll shrivel on the spot. Then he'll give me that earnest smile of his and tell me it wasn't my fault. I'll have no option but to kill him.||

||Fair. Very fair.|| Yali tilted her head. ||Are you up to eating something?||

||No. But I'll try.||

By the time Damant and Hadîm returned, Kat was feeling almost alive. Clean clothes helped rather more than the bowl of cold stew, but she forced the latter down knowing that it didn't have to feel like it was doing her any good so long as it did so. She even managed to descend the rope ladder from the *Pride*'s bulwark without help, though she felt Yali's eyes on her with every rung that passed away behind.

That she had to do so at all was because there wasn't anything resembling a quayside at Tulloq. Never a thriving settlement, it comprised a handful of squat, unlovely buildings and the austere headstocks of a mineworking, all of it abandoned for over a year and draped in a cursed reputation that had discouraged even the most determined scavengers. But no curse had laid Tulloq low. The miners had stumbled on the buried outskirts of Tadamûr, and paid the price.

||"Rîma did a thorough job collapsing the city,"|| said Damant. ||"But there's still a way through to the Stars Below."||

Hadîm nodded. ||"It will not be easy."||

Yali shrugged. ||When is it ever?||

Leaving *Telthi's Pride* to the care of its crew, they set out. Hadîm and Damant led the way, the latter taking little trouble to conceal the fact that he didn't entirely trust the former and growing increasingly irritable when it became equally clear that Hadîm didn't care. They travelled light, with only the thinnest supplies, their weapons and the haversack containing the reforged siphonic prism. Even through the canvas it felt cold to the touch, hungry for whatever soulfire it could steal. Tanith refused to go near it, so Yali bore it alongside her haversack of supplies.

Hadîm's prophecy of a difficult journey fulfilled itself almost at once. Though the motic ifrît powering the mineshaft elevator possessed just about enough soulfire to lower them into the depths, the passageways beyond were a labyrinth of collapsed tunnels and treacherous chasms – scars from when Rîma had extinguished the city-soul and destroyed Tadamûr. Navigating what remained levied a cost tallied in grazed skin, fraying patience and every yard of rope they'd brought with them.

Kat suffered two further blackouts during the descent, the second coming so close to pitching her into a yawning chasm that Damant insisted on supporting her the rest of the way. It made the going easier, but his proximity brought with it the lavender scent of his soul. It grew more distracting with every step.

Eventually the rock peeled back about an archway and the gloom yielded to a thousand, thousand glittering lights that might have been impossible stars, or could simply have been seams of precious stones buried in distant rock. Far below Kat's feet, the fragments of the winding stair upon which she stood met a broad road leading into a dark, silent city. In the distance, a column of magenta and indigo soulfire seethed and spiralled among the jagged crown-like ruins of an ancient temple – the same soulfire column that graced the Eternity Queen's sanctum. The Stars Below and the city of Kha'ladria that was.

"I'd forgotten how beautiful it was," murmured Tanith.

Kat let Damant lower her to a sitting position on a smoothed-off rock. She didn't see the beauty. It reminded her of too many failures for that, and might yet earn others before the day was done.

||"I suppose this is where we part ways,"|| said Hadîm.

Kat nodded. He was the only one who hadn't beaten Tzal's glamour – she and Tanith had done so in that very city when the god had first broken free. To have him go any further was as good as putting a weapon in the Eternity Queen's hand. But they'd never have found the route to the Stars Below without him. ||"It is. Thank you."||

||"All part of the service. I wish you the best for your negotiations."|| He offered Damant a sharp nod, received a grudging one in return, then heaved his pack onto his shoulder and vanished back through the archway.

||Do we rest or go on?|| asked Yali.

Kat glanced at Tanith, who shrugged. ||"Let's get it over with."|| She clambered to her feet, not keen to begin the trek, but too conscious of ailing reserves to chance any delay.

They descended into the city, Damant again insistent on supporting Kat and she too weary to argue. Tanith led the way, a drawn scimitar gleaming with the light of distant fires.

||"We're being watched,"|| said Damant as they entered the austere, statue-less streets.

||"I know,"|| Kat replied.

||Could it be aethervores?|| asked Yali.

Tanith gave a sharp shake of the head, her expression full of disgust at old memories. ||"Father killed them all, otherwise we wouldn't be in this mess."|| The aethervores – the corrupted remains of the Qabirarchi Council – had been Tzal's jailers.

The throb of Tzal's presence had been growing in Kat's thoughts from the moment they'd entered the Stars Below. No surprise, given that they were directly beneath Zariqaz. ||"The Eternity Queen has set watchers. Not really a surprise."||

More than that, she'd hoped for it. Between the Eternity Queen's witless thralls, custodians or "loyal" citizens hungering to collect a bounty, they'd never have made it through the city streets. Kat had never expected to get as far as the elevator serving the abandoned Qabirarchi Palace – the main thing had always been for the Eternity Queen to become aware of their presence before ambition or greed could cost them precious time that neither Kat nor Athenoch had. Their only hope lay in meeting her face to face and hoping that self-interest would carry the day.

She raised her voice to as close to a shout as she could manage. "Tell the Eternity Queen that Katija Arvish has come to bargain." It echoed back to her from the austere buildings, distorted and unfamiliar. "Tell her she'd better be quick," she finished softly.

As they drew nearer the temple mound, they halted on the stone embankment of a winding river for a brief meal of twice-baked bread and salted meat. The river itself was the only curve in a city that was otherwise all straight lines. No ripple showed on its surface; no reflection of the distant fires or the glittering stars.

||"I wish Mirzai could have seen this,"|| said Tanith. ||"Maybe it is his Black River after all, home of the Drowned Lady."||

Yali frowned. ||I thought Zephyr said it was only a myth.||

||"I don't think she knows one way or another. Not really."||

Kat hoped that Zephyr had possessed the good sense to leave Vallant to his fool's errand as soon as *Chainbreaker* had broached the mists. ||"A goddess who bears the innocent to safety and the guilty to judgement? It sounds like another interpretation of Nyssa to me."|| Nyssa Benevolas, aspect of mercy, and stern Nyssa Iudexas, who judged wayward souls. Queen Amakala had influenced the stories of the latter. To have heard Rîma talk about it, she'd even loaned her likeness. ||"A distorted goddess for a distorted world."||

||"Maybe,"|| said Damant, his one-handed signs slow and careful. ||"But the last time I was here, I nearly drowned in that river. I thought I saw a woman reach down to pull me to the surface. Told myself after that it was just one of those bas-reliefs fashioned into the embankment ... Maybe it wasn't."||

||"Divine intervention?"|| Tanith looked up from the water and levelled a wicked smile. ||"For you?"||

Damant shrugged. ||"This would be the place for it, wouldn't you say?"||

Tanith's smile vanished. "Maybe."

The final approach to the centre of Kha'ladria began in silence, each lost in their own thoughts and Kat increasingly without the breath to offer them aloud, even if she'd wished to. Here and there, misshapen bodies lay in puddles of stinking slime, their white-gold robes dark with dust and their waxy white skin peeling from translucent bones. A year on, nothing but time had feasted on the dead aethervores. The same couldn't be said of the elite kathari soldiers of the Obsidium Cult, whose flesh had long since been gnawed to the bone by vermin.

"Told you." Tanith spat on one of the aethervores and struck out towards the long causeway that led to the Qabirarchi elevator.

Kat barely heard her. ||"Do you feel that?"||

Tanith frowned. ||"Feel what?"||

Pushing away from Damant, Kat gazed towards the temple mound and the column of flame swirling above. ||"She's here."||

Without waiting for a reply, she made for the ruins, stumbling steps gaining strength at the prospect of making an end of things even as apprehension tightened her throat. As she passed through the outer ring of stone, she saw her, standing straight-backed against the coiling flames, golden gown and silver hair shining in the backwash and a flicking halo of magenta light playing across her shoulders. The Eternity Queen. Alone, save for the ragged and filthy figure hunched on all fours beside her, drool dripping from a cracked grin and eyes twitching vacantly.

"Kastagîr," murmured Damant. "Kinder to kill him."

||"That's why she didn't,"|| said Kat. ||"Stay here."||

She advanced through the remains of what had once been the temple's inner sanctum.

"You don't know how pleased I am to see you, darling," called the Eternity Queen. "I knew you'd come back to me."

Lungs aching and her legs sore, Kat halted a half-dozen paces away and looked her up and down. It was a long moment before she was certain it was really Azra, Tzal had worn her so thin. Fifty years gone to dust in barely a year. "Don't. I know you're not Azra. You're just wearing her shape."

The words were as much a reminder to her as a warning to the Eternity Queen. She'd thought she'd been ready for this moment – to treat with the creature that had stolen away the only woman she'd ever loved. She wasn't. Not even a little.

"I stood in the light of the moon," she said, striving for strength in certainty even though her voice trembled. "I know the truth. I know who you are and what I am. We'll return the siphonic prism so you can repel the mists. You'll free the souls that you hold in thrall. You'll allow Khalad to return to what it was and go back to playing at goddess. Not a prisoner, but an idol of worship. I've a feeling you'll enjoy that."

The Eternity Queen licked her lips and stepped closer. "So masterful, darling."

Kastagîr's broken grin leered wider.

"I've had good teachers," said Kat.

The Eternity Queen shrugged. "This is a realm of thousands upon thousands of souls. If the mists take me, they take them too."

Kiasta, she really was Yennika in word and deed. That supercilious self-assurance. That assumption that she was in control. All to the good as far as Kat was concerned. That arrogance had led Yennika to make plenty of mistakes in her time. Hopefully she'd afflicted Tzal with the same flaw. "They will," Kat replied, her voice hard. "But they deserve better than your rule."

The Eternity Queen stooped and ran her fingers through Kastagîr's filthy hair. "You demand a great deal. Why should I agree? If you're hoping for the great Bashar Vallant to pull you out of this, I'm afraid you're going to be disappointed. He's seeing the world *very* differently."

Kat swallowed a lump from her throat. It always hurt to hear the inevitable, even if you'd planned for it as best you could. "Because if you don't, we'll destroy the prism so completely that it can never be restored." She paused, glad that Yali couldn't hear her. "And because I'll surrender to you without a fight. Poor ..."

Don't think of her as Azra ... Don't think of her as Azra ...

"... poor Yennika's wearing thin." Kat raised her left arm so that the flames from her aetherios tattoo played over her fingers. My father made me for this. You need me."

"I see." The Eternity Queen offered Yennika's finest oily smile. "And what's to stop me from going back on any arrangement?"

"A year ago, in this very place, you told me that a bargain with the divine binds all parties."

The smile broadened. "I think I start to see what she saw in you ... It does, darling. It does." The Eternity Queen's expression turned hard as stone. "So I don't make them lightly. And I certainly don't bargain for what is already mine."

She gave a sharp snap of her fingers. The shadows of the outer temple came alive with dead-eyed figures: custodians, skelders, redcloaks, men and women in aprons and overalls, Gutterfield rags and formal gowns. An army drawn from all walks of life – whatever biddable souls had been closest to hand when the Eternity Queen had resolved to enter the Stars Below. Dragging a struggling Yali and Damant with them, they formed a circle of unseeing bodies around Kat and the Eternity Queen, blocking all possible escape.

One, a man in a severe black uniform with a stubby mace looped at his belt, walked past Kat without acknowledgement. Kneeling before the Eternity Queen, he laid Yali's haversack – the haversack containing the precious siphonic prism – at her feet and gazed up with blank-faced adoration.

"This belongs to you, my queen," said Vallant.

Fifty-Two

Kat fought to contain a rising sense of panic as the Eternity Queen's thralls forced Yali and Damant to their knees. Even the finest plan could be swiftly overtaken by events, and hers had barely qualified as even being good. It had simply been the only option to hand beyond outright surrender and despair. She'd always considered hope to be the lie that bound them together through thick and thin. Now hope was all they had.

Tanith was still free and the Eternity Queen hadn't noticed.

Better keep it that way.

"It's not much of an army." Even *sounding* defiant was an effort. "You look terrible."

The Eternity Queen drew closer in a swish of golden skirts. "This body can only hold so much of what I am. I thought it might do better – after millennia of imprisonment I'm not everything I used to be – but apparently not." She let Kastagir's leash fall and brushed Kat's cheek with the back of her hand. "Happily, you've brought me a replacement, darling."

Kat flinched. "Don't call me that."

His leash now running free, Kastagir sat back on his haunches and chuckled wheezily.

"Please." The Eternity Queen drifted away, shaking her head. "You were made for me. The perfect bridge between mortal and divine. Your father served me better than I could have hoped."

525

Kat met her stare. "You might not find me as comfortable as you'd like." As if to prove the point, her vision swam. She felt the fingers of her left hand twitch.

"Yes, I can smell the omen rot on you from here. I know that was your plan, darling." The Eternity Queen arched a perfect eyebrow. "Vallant told me. You shouldn't blame him. He'd nothing else to lash out with, not after I took his followers from him one by one. He was desperate. He'd have told me anything for even the *possibility* of their freedom."

Kat glanced at Vallant, still kneeling beside the siphonic prism's haversack. After what isolation behind the Veil had done to him, no one could have expected him to face failure in silence – especially when the cost was borne by others. "He'd have died for any of them. So would I."

"That's the difference between us, darling. Numbers make me stronger. They only multiply your weaknesses."

"I used to think that," Kat replied stiffly, her brow damp with sweat. Even standing was becoming an effort. "I was wrong."

If only she could have spared Yali and Damant all this, but they'd never have let her make the journey without them. And whether she'd liked it or not, she doubted she'd have gotten even this far had they stayed in Athenoch.

The Eternity Queen threw back her head in a theatrical sigh. "You can't imagine what it's like to be trapped in this body. It's blind to everything but its mortal senses. But you? You'll open everything to me. I'll know everything you know. That *all* of you know. You stood in the light of the moon and so will I. Omen rot doesn't concern me. The Dark of Creation is poison to you, but it made me what I am."

A sour taste gathered at the back of Kat's tongue. She'd not considered the possibility that Tzal might be able to unpick her memories once he possessed her. As soon as he did, the path through the Veil would be laid bare. She strove for defiance to mask a growing sense of disaster.

"It doesn't look like much from here." Damant choked off a grunt as one of his captors buried a fist in his gut.

The Eternity Queen snorted. "You sound like my divine siblings. You're wrong, as they were wrong."

Siblings? The Issnaîm divinities, Kat supposed. Or those worshipped in the Old Realm, if they were not one and the same. Had she erred in rushing to confront Tzal when she should have sought allies further afield?

Shadows shifted in the ruins beyond the soulfire column.

No. She had everything she needed, despite everything.

She squeezed her left hand tight and forced a grin. "Vallant wasn't desperate. He told you what he wanted you to hear. What *I* wanted you to hear."

The Eternity Queen froze, her expression suddenly brittle. "What's that supposed to mean?"

Kat spread her arms wide, inviting an embrace. Everyone was watching her now: the Eternity Queen with suspicion, Damant and Yali as if she were mad and the thralls with blank-eyed stolidity. Good. "Why don't you come and find out? Like you said, you'll know everything I know. Unless . . ." The word thinned to a spluttering wheeze as her lungs faltered. "Unless you're afraid."

The Eternity Queen stared, her magenta halo darkening to a rich indigo. "Afraid . . . of you? You're nothing but a scrap of errant flame, helpless and alone."

But she didn't sound certain.

"I might be many things," said Kat, "but I'm not helpless . . . and I will never be alone."

Deadwind motes swirling around her, Tanith leapt through the soulfire column. She slammed into the Eternity Queen, bearing her face-first to the broken flagstones. Kneeling astride her, she pinned her wrists to the ground.

"Get her off me, you fools!" shrieked the Eternity Queen. "Get her—"

Kat felt it before she saw it: the distant, insistent tug that was precursor to Tanith's feeding. A flickering flame more imagined than seen gathered about Tanith's hands and the Eternity Queen's wrists.

Its colour deepening from anaemic greys to pallid magenta, it rippled upwards, racing along Tanith's forearms. She threw back her head, lips frozen somewhere between ecstasy and disgust.

The Eternity Queen screamed. A deep, jarring wail that set Kat's bones on edge without ever troubling her ears. The soulfire column guttered, its shadows lengthening. The Eternity Queen's halo dimmed. Another gathered about Tanith's shoulders, fed by stolen soul-stuff.

Vallant lunged at Tanith, but she was already moving. Leaving the Eternity Queen in the dirt, she shoved him aside and snagged the siphonic prism's haversack by its straps.

As more thralls converged on her from all sides, she shot Kat a taut nod and bolted for the circle's edge. Redcloaks ran to block her path with scimitars drawn, but they might as well have meant to contain the wind. Steel gleamed in Tanith's hand, the dry, dusty air of the Stars Below suddenly rich with the hot copper of spilled blood. Then she was gone into the dark once more, carrying the siphonic prism further out of the Eternity Queen's reach with every stride.

Vallant made to help the Eternity Queen rise. She shoved him aside and flung out a hand towards Tanith's fading footsteps. "After her!"

Dozens of thralls peeled from the circle's edge and ran in pursuit. Dozens more remained. Too many to fight even had Damant and Yali been free. Even so, Damant tried to pull away from his captors, and received another gut punch for his trouble. By contrast, Kat realised that Yali was watching her with a thoughtful, almost calm expression. She *knew*. And if Yali had figured it out, then it was only a matter of time before the Eternity Queen did too.

Or maybe not. Arrogance had always been the strongest card in their hand. Tzal's ... and Yennika's. Yennika had enough arrogance for a dozen gods.

The soulfire column stuttered back to life, regaining a portion of its former radiance. The Eternity Queen staggered towards Kat, flame seeping from her eyes and shoulders. She was frailer than ever now, made angular as shrunken skin drew tight across her bones. "You really think she'll escape?"

"You're not looking well." Even those few words took all the breath Kat had. Everything depended on those next few moments, the desperate plan she and Vallant had cooked up not least. A plan to which only Tanith was privy in all its details. Everything else had been misdirection, to keep the Eternity Queen off balance, to feed the arrogance that had always been Yennika's downfall.

"It will pass," said the Eternity Queen, her voice gaining granite as she recovered her balance. "Yennika has served her purpose, but you and I will remake this world."

She turned towards the soulfire column.

Kat's flash of triumph was smothered by the realisation that it could all still fall apart. Tanith had left the Eternity Queen weaker than the other would have admitted, but if she bathed in the soulfire column and replaced what she'd lost, then it was all over.

She gritted her teeth. Now or never. "Yes, we will."

Summoning her last scraps of strength, she lurched forward and embraced the Eternity Queen.

She plunged into the spirit world, the Stars Below remade in shades of rippling darkness. Tzal's gravid, baleful soul blazed all around her, bleak and smothering, vaster than she could ever have imagined. A hundred times more oppressive than Caradan Diar's spirit. A thousand. Even as she made contact, her blood turned to ice. Tzal's cold flame crackled through her, peeling her own tiny, ailing soul apart a single wisp at a time.

You cannot defy me. Tzal's disdain rippled across their shared soul-scape.

Don't count on it. Kat's reply was barely a whisper by comparison, a breath of breeze stolen by a gale.

She reached deep into her aetherios tattoo, drawing every scrap of soulfire harvested from the Deadwinds and weaving it into her being. Despair blackened the unseen horizon. Even weakened, Tzal was so much stronger, his defences impregnable. What had she been thinking to contest a god, let alone cage him?

But even as her ifrît sank into smothering black, magenta pinpricks blazed to life all around her: the echoes of herself she'd woven through the unknowing sailriders of Vallant's fleet, safeguarding pieces of herself inside their souls in a mirror of what she'd once done for Tarin. It had taken almost the whole of that last night in Zariqaz, reduced her to barely a memory of herself within her own body. All for a gamble that when Tzal stole away the sailriders' free will, he'd absorb those pieces of her alongside, too gluttonous – too arrogant – to recognise what she'd done.

Yali's idea, though she didn't know it. *What's the difference between us and Tzal?* she'd asked. Nothing more than that between the cinderbloods and their fireblood oppressors: power and the will to wield it; the courage to stand tall and fight.

The greater risk had been that the act of absorption would rob Kat's echoes of their identity. That they would no longer truly be her any longer. But as ever more lights shimmered into being around her, that fear melted away in a flare of determination.

So much of what Tzal had thought himself was actually *her*. With Tanith having devoured a great measure of the rest, he was weaker than he'd ever been. Better, he was off balance. There was a chance. Not much of one perhaps, but the best she was going to get. He'd thought her dying, beaten. Dying? That was true – even in the spirit world, she felt her body spasming and convulsing against stone, its pain a red wail across her thoughts. Beaten?

Not a chance.

She didn't need to breach Tzal's defences. So much of her was already inside him.

And she wasn't alone.

Kat called the sundered pieces of herself home. They flocked to her in a murmuration of thought and colour, the slipstream drawing the gauzy ifrîti of Vallant's sailriders in their wake, some aware and pulsing with defiance, others simply gathered to her light and aching to be free. A piece of Vallant, alive with all the pride and the defiance that had kept him together through long years of rebellion, blazed to her side. He stared at his ifrît's echo of a hand, his sense pulsing with wonder and horror. Then he closed his fist, his flames rushing bright with purpose.

We're with you, Kat. We're all with you.

More ifrîti lit the darkness. Not Vallant's sailriders – others taken by Tzal, some of them vestigial and half digested, a few too stubborn to fade. Keti. Kastagîr. Countless more whose names she didn't and would never know, the plundered scraps of a thousand souls rallying to the hope of freedom as lost souls in Khalad ever had.

Kat felt Tzal's rush of panic as she bound herself back together – still only a spark beside a god's chill inferno, but no longer a single spark alone; one at the head of an army.

You were born to be a weapon, Caradan Diar had told her. *You all were.* In the light of the Old Realm's moon, she'd taken that to mean that they were Tzal's weapons against his jailers, and perhaps that was true. But any hand could wield a weapon, had it strength and purpose. After a lifetime in the light, the unwilling ifrîti at the core of Tzal's being knew nothing of the spirit world, but thanks to her aetherios tattoo – her father's legacy – Kat had walked it since girlhood. Thanks to Caradan Diar, she even knew how to fight there. She'd learned much from her friends, but her enemies had taught her far, far more.

Time to end it.

Assailed from without and within, Tzal's cold flame contracted. Its outer tendrils coiled to nothing as the swarm of bright motes pressed close. Kat bent her will upon them, not commanding but *guiding*, weaving a cage of light fit to cage a sullen, desperate god. She barely felt her body collapse, its pain slipping from her thoughts as its breathing slowed. She didn't need it any longer.

Enough of this!

Tzal's throaty howl shook the spirit world. Kat braced herself as his rage buffeted her ifrît. She lost ground inch by inch, his desperation tipping the balance even as she realised her mistake in forsaking her anchor to the mortal world. Body and soul were stronger together than apart. Worse, she'd severed her connection to her aetherios tattoo and its precious reserves of soulfire. Tzal wasn't the only one who could fall prey to arrogance.

His howl thickened to rich, wet laughter as he stripped away the outer layers of Kat's light. A hundred ifríti blinked out. As many more bled away into his resurgent flame, absorbed in an eyeblink. A battle barely in Kat's favour to begin with yawed towards disaster.

Swathes of the cage of light blinked out. The cold flame surged.

Kat plummeted, her ifrít quenched by his cold flame. Frantic, she cast about for any glimmer of light to redress the balance – any scrap of soulfire.

She found nothing; saw nothing but indigo flame – felt nothing but its numbing embrace. She searched for Vallant . . . for anyone . . . But what motes remained were scattered across the soul-scape. One by one they winked out.

It is done, rumbled Tzal, the exhaustion quivering beneath his words no consolation at all. *But a piece of you will always live on through me. Take solace in that.*

Even as he spoke, Kat felt something give. Not in what remained of her ifrít, but in the increasingly distant darkness: a shift in Tzal's unfathomable depths as something broke free and soared towards her, its ifrít a diffuse and crackling mass on the brink of dissolution, but incandescent with emotion. Tzal's smothering indigo recoiled, fatigue no longer concealed by bravado. For the first time, Kat realised just how close she'd run him. Victory and defeat teetered on a dagger's edge.

The new-come ifrít grew dim as it drew close enough for recognition, reserves spent in the effort to break free of its cage. Kat's own flames blazed brighter, fuelled by impossible joy. No. Not impossible. Of course Tzal hadn't really destroyed her. He'd never willingly give up a piece of himself. He'd just admitted it. Instead he'd buried her deep, but not nearly deep enough.

Take my hand, darling, said Azra. *We were always better together than apart.*

Kat reached out for her, their flames mingling and running together. And somewhere in the distance, Tzal screamed.

Damant tore free as the hands holding him slackened. No one tried to grab him again. Spinning on his heel, he saw the reason why. The temple mound was strewn with senseless and semi-conscious bodies, the latter with hands clutched to their heads while they groaned like men and women lost to a nightmare.

Twisting his shrieker from an erstwhile captor's unresisting hand, Damant glanced at Yali – the only other person still upright. ||"What just happened?"||

She shook her head. ||I don't know . . . Kat!||

Damant followed her gaze. Arvish and the Eternity Queen lay a pace apart on the threshold of the soulfire column, motionless. He skirted a motionless Kastagîr and closed the distance in a dozen strides.

Yali reached them first, skidding to her knees beside Kat in a spray of dust. Her tug at her shoulder provoked no response. Drawn expression turned heartsick as fumbling fingers found no pulse. ||She's gone.||

Damant gave a taut nod, and willed away a rising swirl of emotion. *Inevitable* was one thing in contemplation, another in the moment. He was too weary and confused to start reconciling how he felt about that. At least Vallant looked to be breathing. He'd figure out how he felt about that later too. As for the Eternity Queen . . .

She lay face-down in a spill of silver hair, fingers twitching and her shoulders rising and falling in time with fitful breaths. Damant looked from her to Arvish and back again, a low growl in the back of his throat. He had the muzzle of his shrieker pressed to the back of the Eternity Queen's skull before he realised that something had broken inside him. On reflection, he decided that he didn't care.

His fingers tightened on the trigger.

Tanith stepped neatly around him and ripped the shrieker away in the same moment he fired, the weapon clattering to rest among the pillars of the outer sanctum and the bolt of invisible flame wailing away towards the distant stars.

"*Kiasta*, what are you playing at?"

He glared at her. "We've tried everything else. At this point I didn't see the harm."

"I thought custodians were trained to check their target before opening fire." The siphonic prism haversack still slung over her shoulder, she dropped to her knees and carefully brushed the hair from the Eternity Queen's face. "Don't you make me look a fool, or I'll kill you myself," she murmured.

The Eternity Queen's eyelids fluttered. Glossy black eyes found Damant's and tightened in recognition. "Were you going to shoot me, Damant?"

He frowned. Even accounting for the frailty of a body worn almost away, the voice wasn't right. Azra. Yennika. Tzal. The Eternity Queen. Whatever name she wore – whatever her mood – there was always music in her words. In meter and tone she now sounded like someone else. Wry, but with an edge of suspicion that never quite faded. And then there was the matter of the eyes. The jet-black sclera and iris of a qalimîri: a soul in a body not its own. "Arvish?"

With Tanith's help she rose, dust spilling from her golden gown. She cracked a weary not-quite-smile. "Not exactly." She tapped a finger to her temple. "It's a little crowded in here."

Tanith narrowed her eyes. "Azra?"

"And Kat. And Tzal." The woman with Yennika Bascari's face stared blankly across the sanctum. "He didn't do as good a job at containing us as he thought. He's already squirming around, trying to get free. He won't. We won't let him." She spoke the final words with a coldness that made Damant shudder.

Yali stumbled to her feet, her expression crowded with suspicion. ||Explain. Now.||

||"The . . ."|| She stared down at trembling fingers that refused to form anything but the muddiest signs, and abandoned the attempt. "The aetherios tattoo made Kat a perfect host for Tzal, but it also gave us the means to turn his power against him. We think that *maybe* Caradan Diar was trying to show us that. Everyone who followed Vallant to Zariqaz carried a piece of us alongside. Tzal thought he was making himself stronger by englamouring them, but they weren't his, they just didn't know how to fight. A sleeping army waiting to be woken. By the time Tanith was done with him, there were just enough of them to make a difference."

Even with that explanation Damant felt none the wiser, but one thing he *did* understand. ||"So the prism . . . the negotiation . . ."|| he said after Tanith had finished signing a translation for Yali. ||"All of it was a lie?"||

"We knew that Tzal would never bargain in good faith . . ." she stared down at Kat's corpse, expression unreadable, "but the prism is vital. Someone has to hold back the mists, just as someone needs to keep Tzal imprisoned."

Yali pursed her lips, betrayal and relief fighting for her expression. ||This was always your plan?||

"Parts of it. The rest we had to improvise. Nothing ever works out how you'd like." She stared up at the soulfire column. "We have to go. Only the Deadwinds can sustain us now, and once we enter, we can't leave. Go. The city will be waking. A new Age of Fire awaits."

Tanith nodded and slid the siphonic prism from its haversack. ||"What about Vallant? The others?"||

"He'll recover. *Most* will recover. It will be like a dream."

||"And how do we explain what happened?"|| asked Damant.

She shrugged, Arvish's not-quite-smile broadening to the sly grin that Azra had always worn so well. "Tell them that the Eternity Queen was an imposter; Nyssa has reclaimed what was hers . . . and that she will be watching."

||"A three-faced goddess,"|| he murmured. Ancient heretics had always claimed that Nyssa possessed three faces. Merciful Nyssa

Benevolas, stern Nyssa Iudexas … and the hidden face that was Tzal. The faces would be different now, but the legend would go on.

"Exactly," said Nyssa. "Sometimes the past *is* prophecy after all. Kat's father hoped she'd be the vessel of the goddess reborn. He gets his wish."

||So you're going to rule?|| asked Yali.

Nyssa shook her head. "Caging Tzal will take everything we have. Khalad deserves to find its own way. You'll have to decide what happens next."

Yali's eyes were full of tears. ||But you'll be alone.||

Nyssa took her hands and squeezed them tight. "No. Never alone. Judgement and forgiveness. The promise of rebirth must be kept." She embraced Yali and held her tight. "You will see us again, all of you … but hopefully not for a long, long time."

Stepping away from Yali, she took the siphonic prism from Tanith. "Be good, little sister. And Ihsan?" The faintest trace of Azra's musical laughter danced beneath the words. "Thank Vallant for us when he wakes."

She clutched the prism to her chest and walked into the soulfire column, unsteadily but with purpose. The flames blazed brighter and brighter, indigo surrendering to magenta and growing hotter still. Damant's final glimpse was of her standing in the heart of the fire, prism raised high above her head. Then the flames flared to a brilliant, searing white, and she was gone.

In the End

The merciless sun beat down from a cloudless sky, rousing the sandstone walls of the Golden Citadel to blinding brilliance. Though he was ensconced in the palisaded shadows atop the gatehouse rather than in the grand courtyard, Damant's breathing was shallower than he'd have liked, the dry heat thick at the back of his throat a reminder of why he'd always striven not to be caught outdoors in such weather.

The last chime rippled away into the heat haze, unremarked by the growing crowd. A space that could perhaps have held a thousand people in comfort now had twice that jammed shoulder to shoulder between the gatehouse's scarlet banners and the inner stairway. More were arriving all the time. Unfolding history was an irresistible lure. For the first time in written history, Khalad had no monarch. Firebloods and cinderbloods alike had come to witness what would happen next.

His thoughts wandering to no certain purpose, Damant stared across the crowds, past the cordon of spears at the foot of the stairway and up at the inner palace, the roof of the conclave hall just visible in the middle distance. The gritty crunch of a footstep on the stairs brought him back to the moment.

Vallant joined him at the inner rampart, his arms folded loosely at his back. "You didn't get invited?"

Damant grunted. "As it happens, I did. I thought they'd do better without me."

The first conclave of the new ruling council had begun at dawn. It would likely stretch well into the night and retire with much left undone. But you had to start somewhere. Even the council's membership wasn't yet wholly settled. Fadiya and Marida represented Athenoch's former rebels. Yali and Tatterlain brought a degree of continuity from the old regime – the latter definitely as *Tatterlain*, and not Tuzen Karza: a new beginning of a more personal sort. In this, he was ably abetted by Keti, who was now no longer presented as a shîm-addled mistress, but recognised as a watchful protégée.

Igarî Bathîr still held her rank, mostly from the unspoken acceptance that Alabastra would have a role to play in what came next, and it was far better that role be taken by a woman more concerned with status than actual ambition. What had become of Emanzi Ozdîr no one knew, though there was talk of a mutiny at Hazali. Beyond that, a handful of firebloods notable for their distance from the Eternity Queen's reign were under consideration, as were several guildmasters and cinderblood civic leaders. Damant suspected that when the dust had settled, council membership would stretch well into double figures. All to the good as far as he was concerned. If he'd learnt nothing else in recent years it was that the ambrosia of power was safer diluted.

"Did you indeed?" said Vallant, deadpan. "What a coincidence."

"Don't tell me the great Bashar Vallant turned them down?"

"He never existed, as you know full well. There was only a man who tried his best to make things better. He never did quite manage it." Vallant shook his head. "I think it's time for old men to move on, don't you?"

Damant elected not to point out that Vallant was somewhat younger than him. Age wasn't just a tally of years, but a roster of burdens borne and battles lost. Vallant had a claim to more of those than most. More than that, he'd not been quite the same following the final confrontation with Tzal – as if a piece of him were missing, somehow. He wasn't the only one. It was a rare soul who'd fallen to the Eternity Queen's glamour and emerged untouched. Too many had never awoken at all. Whole districts of Zariqaz had become open tombs, the surgeons unable to do anything more for the afflicted than ease their soulless shells into death. "Old and useless?"

"Never that." Vallant offered a sly smile, recognising the jibe for what it was. "Who will be the new council's castellan if not you?"

"Kastagîr."

The smile vanished. "I'm all for reconciliation, but wasn't he just a little too close to the old regime? In all ways possible, in fact."

"The same could be said of either of us. He's a brave man and he stood with us when it counted." Damant shrugged, his eyes on the cordon protecting the inner palace, its members notable for the absence of their golden masks and scarlet cloaks. "The redcloaks have a poisonous reputation, and well earned. But if we don't want another civil war, they have to be dismantled carefully. One of their own at the head of the process will help."

Vallant offered a slow nod. "So you're still thinking like a politician?"

"I'll be glad to leave it behind. Maybe that's why I'm out here and not up there."

He chuckled softly to himself. "How are things in the Stars Below?"

"The last of the ember-saints are in place. Anyone who treads the Stars Below looking for trouble will soon wish they'd chosen more wisely." It had been Tatterlain's idea to make true the old myths of Nyssa's fabled palace. Now a host of koilos stood silent guard over their ersatz goddess, unanswerable to mortals so long as they were within the perimeter of the temple mound. Nothing short of an army could reach the base of the soulfire column any longer. "The old sanctum will become a shrine, open to all who seek Nyssa's wisdom ... Who knows? Maybe they'll get an answer."

"If there's anyone to give it."

Damant noted the uncertainty in Vallant's voice. In part, he shared it. He'd spent weeks in the Stars Below supervising the shriversmen's installation of the ember-saints but in all that time had caught no sign of Nyssa. Maybe he wasn't supposed to. Maybe she was in the Deadwinds.

But she was still *somewhere*. Reports from the border insisted that the Veil was actually retreating. For the first time in centuries, Athenoch was part of the world once more. So were many other places, lost so long that even scholars didn't know their names.

Nyssa. It still felt unreal, but it was easier than thinking of her as Arvish … or Azra. Those names didn't belong to her any longer, just as she didn't any longer belong to the world.

"There is," he said at last. "Otherwise we're in for a world of trouble."

Vallant's cheek twitched. "You really think she – *they* – can keep Tzal imprisoned?"

Damant mopped his brow with his sleeve. The cool air of the Stars Below had never been more appealing. Not so long ago, the very thought of being reliant on Azra for anything would have been laughable, but in the end she'd outgrown the resentments and horrors that had shaped her. Besides, it wasn't Azra alone, was it? She and Arvish had always been a formidable combination. Maybe it would be enough. "I don't know that what we think changes anything."

"In all matters save one." Vallant braced his hands on the inner rampart and leaned out. "Tzal made us for a purpose, but that purpose doesn't define us. We are all of us the choices we make and the deeds we do. That much hasn't changed."

Damant stared down at the crowd, envious of their ignorance. He knew the truth would haunt him for as long as he lived, as it would Vallant, despite his proud words. The rest of Khalad could be spared that burden. Some truths were kinder kept secret. "It mustn't."

Vallant offered what might have been a sympathetic look. "Did you ever think it would end like this?"

"End? This is a beginning. Let's hope we're worthy of it."

He nodded. "We have to be. Too many have died."

History would likely never record the final tally. Between the advance of the mists, the redcloak atrocities on the border and souls snuffed out in the final struggle, it was impossible to sift the missing from the dead. But Damant knew that Vallant didn't mean them. His losses stretched back decades. Tythia and Sadia, his wife and daughter – dead as a consequence of Damant's long-ago actions, though he'd never meant for it to happen. Amarid. Jaîna. Maxin. Telthi. Bescal. Galadin. Timmara. Ardin Javar. Rîma. There were others, of course. Hundreds of bodies scattered across two decades of hopeless rebellion. But Rîma most of all.

Damant nodded at the crowds. "What do you suppose she'd have said to see this?"

It spoke volumes that Vallant didn't need to ask who he meant. "That we should stop moping and enjoy the moment. Then she'd give us a *look*, to warn us against the foolishness of arguing."

"We'll see her again," murmured Damant. "If there's one thing I believe now, it's that."

Vallant nodded. "What's a few lifetimes between friends?"

They stood in an almost comfortable silence, watching as the crowd swelled further. Song broke out beneath the western colonnade and spread outwards as new voices took up the simple refrain. A prayer to Nyssa.

"Zephyr tells me you're leaving for Athenoch tonight," said Damant. Unwilling to be parted from Vallant again, no matter the risks, she'd stayed at his side through the fleet's opening skirmish with Zariqaz's defenders – even when the *Chainbreaker*'s crew had fallen to the Eternity Queen's glamour. They'd found her in the palace dungeon after Tzal's defeat, furious but unharmed. She likely wouldn't have stayed that way for long. Of everyone in Khalad, she alone held the secret of the lesion to the Old Realm. Tzal would have stopped at nothing to wrest it from her.

Vallant turned his back on the crowd and crooked a wry smile. "I think it's better that the shadow of the great Bashar Vallant falls a long way from Zariqaz. And you, I believe, are bound for Tyzanta? Still called to chase down ne'er-do-wells even now, is that it?"

Damant grunted. "I'll be happy never to lift a sword or shrieker ever again. I'd like to try building something while I've still the strength for it."

"Then I suppose this is goodbye." Vallant turned to leave, but checked himself without taking a step. Standing a little straighter, he turned around, the irritating earnestness he'd worn since his time as a custodium recruit under Damant's command on full display. "But if I've learned anything, it's that fate has a way of bringing us back together." He paused, his lips a thin slash. "Ihsan . . . what happened to Sadia and Tythia wasn't your fault. If this is our last parting, I want it to be as friends. Kat and I, we never quite made it work."

A weight that Damant had carried so long that he'd almost forgotten its existence melted away. Though their enmity had eased once he'd left Bascari service, he'd long since accepted that particular wound was not for closing. He knew he'd never fully understand what it had cost Vallant to speak those words. "You were there when you needed each other." He forced the reply out through a throat grown suddenly tight. "I'd say you did well enough."

Vallant offered another wry smile, the glint in his eye betraying that he recognised a deflection when he heard it. "Perhaps I'm a little jealous that she did what I couldn't?"

"Don't be. She needed you to push her, just like I needed her to push me. We're all in this life together. We always were. It's just that some of us take a while to realise it."

Vallant held out his hand. "Remember that. Athenoch is closer than it used to be. If you need me, I'll be there." He spoke the words lightly enough, but their promise weighed more than stone.

"Likewise."

They shook hands and parted, Vallant down the gatehouse stairs and Damant to the rampart edge. Far below, Zephyr threaded her way through the crowd to Vallant's side. Ignoring the gawping onlookers, she kissed him, then, with a wild burst of musical laughter, led him away past men and women who would one day tell their grandchildren of the time they saw not only saw the great Bashar Vallant, saviour of Khalad, but also a veilkin.

Damant waited until they'd gone from sight, then made his own way down to the courtyard. Though he didn't relish it, he'd one last farewell of his own to make.

He found Tanith sitting on a crumbling patch of the Black River's embankment in the Stars Below, the skirts of her white dress dangling in the water. She'd barely visited the surface since Arvish had ... well, since whatever had happened to Arvish. Damant still didn't really have a word for it.

Yali had blamed Tanith's distance on guilt. Tatterlain had suggested that she'd wanted to stay close to the soulfire column and thus her sister. Both played their part, Damant suspected, but he'd known her longer than most and understood her better.

She looked up as he approached, the cloth-wrapped bundle he'd retrieved from his quarters tucked under his left arm. "I thought you'd forgotten."

He halted behind her, his eyes on the soulfire column coiling and dancing on the distant hilltop. At the dark shapes of koilos silhouetted among the broken crown of the temple mound. "I don't forget anything ... but I am sometimes delayed."

She nodded, distant. Even in the peculiar light of the Stars Below, she looked terrible, her eyes sunken and her features sharp and hungry. But Damant only saw her thus with his eyes. In all other ways she exuded a terrifying beauty, irresistible perhaps, save to those who'd broken free from a stronger, more insidious glamour. Even so, a piece of his soul longed for her to look upon him with desire. "The conclave?"

"Vallant. He'd something he needed to say." It would have been cruel to speak to Tanith of absolution. "The conclave are still arguing ... One more thing they can manage without me."

A smile haunted her lips. "So he's gone?"

"Back to Athenoch. With Zephyr. She means to press him into helping Tarin track down the rest of Anfai's exiles. Whatever happens in Zariqaz, they'll have a home in Athenoch, should they want it." He offered a grim smile. "I don't think Vallant knows that yet."

"What's life without a few surprises?" She dabbled a hand in the water. It offered up no ripples worth the name. Featureless. Implacable. "It's time I left too. If I push it any further, people will die. I don't want that."

She'd not fed since the confrontation with Tzal. What she'd torn from him had sustained her for a time, but for the past week she'd grown a little more terrible and a little more beguiling every day.

"There's always the Deadwinds."

Her vicious shake of the head spilled golden tresses across her shoulders. "How can I? Every scrap of soul I touch is torn apart for good. Feeding on strangers was bad enough, but in the Deadwinds I can't pick and choose. It could just as easily be friends, gone for ever because I can't control my appetite. Mirzai. Rîma . . . Even you, one day. I thought I'd stopped being a monster, but some things aren't for us to choose."

"I wish there was something I could do."

She laughed without humour. "The only thing you can offer is the one thing I have to refuse. I only fed on Tzal because Kat told me she couldn't beat him otherwise. Do you know how many souls I sent to oblivion in that moment?"

Damant tried not to think about the empty husks that had littered the Zariqaz streets. "No."

"Liar." Even the small fondness in her accusation was enough to set his heart racing. "You were always kind to me, from the first moment we met. I wish I'd deserved it."

"I'd say you got there in the end."

She shook her head, not seeming to have heard. "I was never part of this world, not really. My father made sure of that. The best thing I can do now is to leave it. I can't even kill myself. My soul loose in the Deadwinds? It will be a banquet. I will become the cruellest of qalimîri."

He grimaced, her nascent glamour little to do with his unease. "It might not happen that way. Your soul might find its way to Nyssa. She'll help you."

She stared down into the water. To where her reflection should have been. "You didn't see me in the Old Realm. Kat did, and even she didn't really understand. Tzal spoke of the Dark of Creation. I felt its presence from the moment I set foot in there. It is hunger, Ihsan. Appetite unceasing. In the moonlight, Kat saw me as a creature of flame, but I saw myself as nothing at all. A hole in the world that could never be filled, not by love, nor friendship, nor purpose. If we are Tzal and he is us, then I'm more like him than I am like you. If we're reunited in Nyssa's light, even for a moment, it might give him the strength to free himself . . . or else I might become him."

"You don't know that."

She sat back, her eyes not on the river but on the soulfire column on the temple mound. "I don't, but even the possibility makes me want to curl up and weep."

A piece of Damant's heart broke to hear her so dejected. "Kat can handle it."

"She could *never* handle me." Pride shone through the words, leavened by a sliver of humour. "I have something else in mind."

"The river."

She nodded. "Mirzai told me that it bears lost souls to the Drowned Lady, who offers protection to those in need and calls down vengeance on those who make them so. I'm no longer sure which I am. I don't suppose it matters, if she stops me from hurting anyone else."

"Even if this *is* that river, what you just described still sounds like Nyssa Benevolas and Nyssa Iudexas by other names." But Damant's objection was rote, born of frustration at not being able to soothe away Tanith's pain. Even as he spoke, he recalled his own experience in the river's clutches: a lost and floundering soul, guided to the shore by a gentle smile and a slender hand. "What if you're wrong?"

"Then I'll drown, and we'll find out which of us is right about Kat being able to handle me. But at least I'll have tried to rise above what I was born to be."

We are all of us the choices we make and the deeds we do. Vallant was right. Again. Maybe Tanith would rise above her nature, Drowned Lady

545

or no. Azra had managed it. "What about your mother? You should at least say goodbye."

"I have. You're the last."

"I don't understand why. But then I don't understand why you wanted me here."

Tanith rose and at last turned to face him, her sodden skirts trailing water across the shattered stones. "Because I knew you'd want a chance to talk me out of it." Sapphire eyes shining, she reached out to touch his face, only to snatch her hand back and pinch her eyes shut. "And ... because I don't think I can go through with it without anyone to see me off."

That at least Damant understood. Pride cut both ways. It was harder to go back on a decision in plain sight of others. "Rîma once asked me to bear witness for her."

Eyes still shut tight, she chanced a smile. "You must have an honest face."

"That is perhaps the kindest way to describe it," he said heavily. Certainly not handsome, if it ever had been. Too many years had rolled over him for that, all of them filled with disappointment and cudgels.

"There are worse things to be remembered for than kindness." Steeling herself, she leaned in close and placed the most chaste of kisses on his cheek. "Goodbye, Ihsan."

"Here." He untucked the bundle from beneath his arm and held it out. "For the journey."

Tanith levelled an unfriendly stare. "You knew, didn't you? You let me say all that, and the whole time ..."

He shrugged. "I *was* a custodian, once upon a time."

She unwound the cloth, scowl fading to consternation as steel gleamed. "Rîma's sword?"

"I found it in the Eternity Queen's sanctum. I think she took it as a trophy."

"I can't take this." She shook her head. "It should stay with you."

"It's my great hope never to lift a sword ever again," said Damant evenly. "Not so long ago it held Rîma together when nothing else could. Maybe it will do the same for you."

Tanith opened her mouth to speak, but settled for a nod. Then, with growing confidence, she retraced her steps to the river's edge, aiming for the point where the embankment crumbled to a rubble slipway. She waded out into the river until the water reached her waist, and turned to face the bank once more. Eyes closed, she clutched the sword to her chest, lay back, and let the current take her.

Damant remained on the bank as the river bore her away, a white petal drifting on glimmerless black, at peace for the first time since they'd met.

He watched until she was gone – though so pervasive were the shadows in the Stars Below that he couldn't be certain if the currents dragged her down or merely out of sight – then began the long walk back to the causeway and the sunlit world. As he passed the temple mound, he glanced up at the soulfire column and fancied he saw Nyssa standing at its heart, offering a nod of approval. But perhaps it was just a trick of shadow and flame.

Thus did Ihsan Damant leave the Stars Below and its three-faced goddess for the last time. In the years to come, his leadership saw Tyzanta rise from its ruins to become the jewel of eastern Khalad once more. And in all those years, just as he'd hoped, he never again lifted a sword or a shrieker.

And then, just before the end, he saw Rîma once more.

Glossary

Note that the Daric language of Khalad commonly employs a cir-cumflex to lengthen and lend emphasis to vowels. Thus "î" is pronounced "ee" and "û" is pronounced "oo".

Cinderblood	One born to the lower class
Fireblood	One born to the upper class
Ifrît(i)	Fragment(s) of soul, shackled to service
Lock charmer	One accomplished in opening locks without benefit of a key
Skelder	Broad-ranging term for criminals and the societally undesirable
The Deadwinds	Vortex of soul-laden winds, centred on the city of Zariqaz
The Veil	The ever-hungry mists at Khalad's border
Adobe	A brick made of sun-dried straw and clay (also buildings constructed thereof)
Alabastra	State religion of Khalad
Amashti	Soul-sucking daemon

Archon	Member of the Alabastran priesthood
Astoricum	Mythical metal, also known as oreikhalkos
Ayin	Issnaîm expression of dismay
Azasouk	A grand marketplace
Blesswood	Sanctified timber burned in torch houses
Custodian	Keeper of the law
Custodium	Body tasked with enforcement of the law
Daric	Primary language of Khalad
Dhow	Large lateen-rigged military skyship
Felucca	Small lateen-rigged skyboat
Gansalar	Redcloak commander
The Golden Stair	Approach to the Eternity Queen's palace
Helmic	Ifrît that governs guidance
Hestic	Protector ifrît
Hierarch	Senior Alabastran priest
Isshîm	Illicit narcotic
Issnaîm	Race better known to the people of Khalad as "veilkin"
Kiasta	A mild Daric curse word
Koilos	Preserved indentured servant
Last breath	A restorative harvested from the recently dead

Lumani	Ifrît that provides illumination
Mistfall	The descent of unnatural mist
Mistrali	Seasonal rainstorm
Motic	Ifrît that governs simple mechanisms
The Obsidium Cult	Supposedly mythical (and secret) society
Oreikhalkos	Mythical metal, also known as astoricum
Pyrasti	Flame ifrît
Qabirarchi Council	Assemblage of hierarchs
Qalimîri	A deathless, parasitic soul
Qori	Term of affection in Daric, roughly equivalent to "daughter"
The Queen's Council	Governing body of Khalad, subordinate to the Voice
Railrunner	Steam engine governed by ifrîti
Redcloak	Soldier of the Royal Guard
Sailrider	Crew member on a skyship
Sarhana	Redcloak veteran
Savir/Savim	Honorifics issued in a far-off land
Shrieker	Flame-based weapon, powered by an ifrît
Shriversman	Craftsman responsible for the dissection of souls
Skirl	Slang term for an annoying youth
Simah	Widespread sign language

Talent wisp	Distilled essence of deceased talent
Tessence	Distilled soul
Torch house	Beacon that burns back the mists of the Veil
Trallock	A shiftless and unreliable individual, too focused on their own pleasures
Undertown	A city's lowest (and most insalubrious) levels
Vahla	Spirits who escort the guilty to judgement
Veilkin	What the people of Khalad call the Issnaîm
Waholi (impolite)	Issnaîm word for outsiders
Xanathros	A high temple
Xe'iathî	A lost city of light and shadow
Zol'tayah	Ruler of the Qersali people

Acknowledgements

You made it! Sit down, have a cup of tea and relax. Evil is vanquished, hope is renewed and maybe – just maybe – everything will be all right for a little while. Not for ever, perhaps, but for now . . . and that's all any of us can expect.

If you've come with me this far, you're probably bored of me harping on about the incredible support I receive not only from my wife, Lisa, but also from my agent, John Jarrold. I make no apologies for belting out the same words to a slightly different tune. This book – this whole series – wouldn't have seen the light of day without them. And of course mention should also be made of my editor, James Long.

My final fulsome thanks I offer to Christina Begerska, Greg Jones and Michael Geary, whose enthusiasm and encouragement has helped carry me to this final page.

What comes next for Khalad? For me?

Who knows.

You find your place, or one is found for you.

The search continues.

extras

about the author

Matthew Ward has frequently been accused of living in worlds of his own imagination, though really he lives near Nottingham with his extremely patient wife and several attention-seeking cats.

Find out more about Matthew Ward and other Orbit authors by registering for the free monthly newsletter at orbitbooks.co.uk.

if you enjoyed

THE LIE THAT BINDS THEM

look out for

THE SHADOW
OF THE GODS

by

John Gwynne

The Greatest Sagas are written in blood.

A century has passed since the gods fought and drove themselves to extinction. Now only their bones remain, promising great power to those brave enough to seek them out.

As whispers of war echo across the land of Vigrið, fate follows in the footsteps of three warriors: a huntress on a dangerous quest, a noblewoman pursuing battle fame, and a thrall seeking vengeance among the mercenaries known as the Bloodsworn.

All three will shape the fate of the world as it once more falls under the shadow of the gods.

CHAPTER ONE

ORKA

The year 297 of Friðaröld, The Age of Peace

"Death is a part of life," Orka whispered into her son's ear.

Even though Breca's arm was drawn back, the ash-spear gripped tight in his small, white-knuckled fist and the spearhead aimed at the reindeer in front of them, she could see the hesitation in his eyes, in the set of his jaw.

He is too gentle for this world of pain, Orka thought. She opened her mouth to scold him, but a hand touched her arm, a huge hand where Breca's was small, rough-skinned where Breca's was smooth.

"Wait," Thorkel breathed through his braided beard, a cold-misting of breath. He stood to her left, solid and huge as a boulder.

Muscles bunched in Orka's jaw, hard words already in her throat. *Hard words are needed for this hard world.*

But she held her tongue.

Spring sunlight dappled the ground through soft-swaying branches, reflecting brightly from patches of rimed snow, winter's last hoar-frost kiss on this high mountain woodland. A dozen reindeer stood grazing in a glade, a thick-antlered bull watching over the herd of cows and calves as they chewed and scratched moss and lichen from trunks and boulders.

A shift in Breca's eyes, an indrawn breath that he held, followed by a burst of explosive movement; his hips twisting, his arm moving.

The spear left his fist: a hiss as sharp iron sliced through air. A flush of pride in Orka's chest. It was well thrown. As soon as the spear had left Breca's grip she knew it would hit its mark.

In the same heartbeat that Breca loosed his spear, the reindeer he had chosen looked up from the trunk it had been scraping lichen from. Its ears twitched and it leaped forwards, the herd around it breaking into motion, bounding and swerving around trees. Breca's spear slammed into the trunk, the shaft quivering. A moment later there was a crashing from the east, the sound of branches cracking, and a form burst from the undergrowth, huge, slate-furred and long-clawed, exploding into the glade. The reindeer fled in all directions as the beast loped among them, oblivious to all around it. Blood pulsed from a swarm of wounds across its body, long teeth slick, its red tongue lolling, and then it was gone, disappearing into the forest gloom.

"What . . . was that?" Breca hissed, looking up at his mother and father, wide eyes shifting from Orka to Thorkel.

"A fell-wolf," Thorkel grunted as he broke into motion, the stealth of the hunt forgotten. He pushed through undergrowth into the glade, a thick-shafted spear in one fist, branches snapping, Orka and Breca following. Thorkel dropped to one knee, tugged a glove off with his teeth and touched his fingertips to droplets of the wolf's blood, brushing them across the tip of his tongue. He spat, rose and followed the trail of wolf-blood to the edge of the glade, then stood there peering into the murk.

Breca walked up to his spear, the blade half-sunk into a pine tree, and tried to pull it free. His body strained, but the spear didn't move. He looked up at Orka, grey-green eyes in a pale, muddied face, a straight nose and strong jaw framed with crow-black hair, so much like his father, and the opposite of her. Apart from his eyes. He had Orka's eyes.

"I missed," he said, his shoulders slumping.

Orka gripped the shaft in her gloved hand and tugged the spear free.

"Yes," she said as she handed Breca his spear, half-an-arm shorter than hers and Thorkel's.

"It was not your fault," Thorkel said from the glade's edge. He was still staring into the gloom, a thick braid of black, grey-streaked hair poking from beneath his woollen nålbinding cap, his nose twitching. "The fell-wolf startled them."

"Why didn't it kill any of those reindeer?" Breca asked as he took his short spear back from Orka.

Thorkel lifted his hand, showing bloodied fingertips. "It was wounded, not thinking about its supper."

"What did that to a fell-wolf?" Breca asked.

A silence.

Orka strode to the opposite end of the glade, her spear ready as she regarded the dark hole in the undergrowth from where the wolf had emerged. She paused, cocked her head. A faint sound, drifting through the woodland like mist.

Screams.

Breca joined her. He gripped his spear with both hands and pointed into the darkness.

"Thorkel," Orka grunted, twisting to look over her shoulder at her husband. He was still staring after the wounded wolf. With a last, lingering look and shake of his fur-draped shoulders he turned and strode towards her.

More screams, faint and distant.

Orka shared a look with Thorkel.

"Asgrim's steading lies that way," she said.

"Harek," Breca said, referring to Asgrim's son. Breca had played with him on the beach at Fellur, on the occasions when Orka and Thorkel had visited the village to trade for provisions.

Another scream, faint and ethereal through the trees.

"Best we take a look," Thorkel muttered.

"Heya," Orka grunted her agreement.

Their breath misted about them in clouds as they worked their way through the pinewoods, the ground thick and soft with needles. It was spring, signs of new life in the world below, but winter still clung to these wooded hills like a hunched old warrior refusing to let go of his past. They walked in file, Orka leading, her eyes constantly shifting between the wolf-carved path they were following and the deep shadows around them. Old, ice-crusted snow crunched underfoot as trees opened up and they stepped on to a ridge, steep cliffs falling away sharply to the west, ragged strips of cloud drifting across the open sky below them. Orka glanced down and saw reed-thin columns of hearth fire smoke rising from Fellur, far below. The fishing village sat nestled on the eastern edge of a deep, blue-black fjord, the calm waters shimmering in the pale sun. Gulls swirled and called.

"Orka," Thorkel said and she stopped, turned.

Thorkel was unstoppering a leather water bottle and handing it to Breca, who despite the chill was flushed and sweating.

"His legs aren't as long as yours," Thorkel smiled through his beard, the scar from cheek to jaw giving his mouth a twist.

Orka looked back up the trail they were following and listened. She had heard no more screams for a while now, so she nodded to Thorkel and reached for her own water bottle.

They sat on a boulder for a few moments, looking out over the land of green and blue, like gods upon the crest of the world. To the south the fjord beyond Fellur spilled into the sea, a ragged coastline curling west and then south, ribbed and scarred with deep fjords and inlets. Iron-grey clouds bunched over the sea, glowing with the threat of snow. Far to the north a green-sloped, snow-topped mountain range coiled across the land, filling the horizon from east to west. Here and there a towering cliff face gleamed, the old-bone roots of the mountain from this distance just a flash of grey.

"Tell me of the serpent Snaka again," Breca said as they all stared at the mountains.

Orka said nothing, eyes fixed on the undulating peaks.

"If I were to tell that saga-tale, little one, your nose and fingers would freeze, and when you stood to walk away your toes would snap like ice," Thorkel said.

Breca looked at him with his grey-green eyes.

"Ach, you know I cannot say no to that look," Thorkel huffed, breath misting. "All right, then, the short telling." He tugged off the nålbinding cap on his head and scratched his scalp. "All that you can see before you is Vigrið, the Battle-Plain. The land of shattered realms. Each steppe of land between the sea and those mountains, and a hundred leagues beyond them: that is where the gods fought, and died, and Snaka was the father of them all; some say the greatest of them."

"Certainly the biggest," Breca said, voice and eyes round and earnest.

"Am I telling this tale, or you?" Thorkel said, a dark eyebrow rising.

"You, Father," Breca said, dipping his head.

Thorkel grunted. "Snaka was of course the biggest. He was the oldest, the father of the gods; Eldest, they called him, and he had grown monstrous huge, which you would, too, if you had eaten your fill each day since the world was born. But his children were not to be sniffed at, either. Eagle, Bear, Wolf, Dragon, a host of others. Kin fought kin, and Snaka was slain by his children, and he fell. In his death the world was shattered, whole realms crushed, heaved into the air, the seas rushing in. Those mountains are all that is left of him, his bones now covered with the earth that he ruptured."

Breca whistled through his teeth and shook his head. "It must have been a sight to see."

"Heya, lad, it must have been. When gods go to war, it is no small thing. The world was broken in their ruin."

"Heya," Orka agreed. "And in Snaka's fall the vaesen pit was opened, and all those creatures of tooth and claw and power that dwelled in the world below were released into our land of sky and sea." From their vantage point the world looked pure and unspoiled, a beautiful, untamed tapestry spread across the landscape in gold and green and blue.

But Orka knew the truth was a blood-soaked saga.

She looked to her right and saw on the ground the droplets of blood from the injured wolf. In her mind she saw those droplets spreading, growing into pools, more blood spraying, ghostly bodies falling, hacked and broken, voices screaming . . .

This is a world of blood. Of tooth and claw and sharp iron. Of short lives and painful deaths.

A hand on her shoulder, Thorkel reaching over Breca's head to touch her. A sharp-drawn breath. She blinked and blew out a long, ragged sigh, pushing the images away.

"It was a good throw," Thorkel said, tapping Breca's spear with his water bottle, though his eyes were still on Orka.

"I missed, though," Breca muttered.

"I missed the first throw on my first hunt, too," Thorkel said. "And I was eleven summers, where you are only ten. And your throw was better than mine. The wolf robbed you. Eh, Orka?" He ruffled Breca's hair with a big hand.

"It was well cast," Orka said, eyeing the clouds to the west, closer now. A west wind was blowing them, and she could taste snow on that wind, a sharp cold that crackled like frost in her chest. Stoppering her water bottle, she stood and walked away.

"Tell me more of Snaka," Breca called after her.

Orka paused. "Are you so quick to forget your friend Harek?" she said with a frown.

Breca dropped his eyes, downcast, then stood and followed her.

Orka led them on, back into the pinewoods where sound was eerily muted, the world shrinking around them, shadows shifting, and they climbed higher into the hills. As they rose the world turned grey around them, clouds veiling the sun, and a cold wind hissed through the branches.

Orka used her spear for a staff as the ground steepened and she climbed slick stone that ascended like steps alongside a white-foaming stream. Ice-cold water splashed and seeped into her leg-bindings and boots. A strand of her blonde hair fell loose of her braid and she pushed it behind one ear. She slowed her pace, remembering Breca's short legs, even though there was a tingling in her blood that set her muscles thrumming. Danger had always had that effect on her.

"Be ready," Thorkel said behind her, and then Orka smelled it, too.

The iron tang of blood, the stench of voided bowels.

Death's reek.

The ground levelled on to a plateaued ridge, trees felled and cleared. A large, grass-roofed cabin appeared, alongside a handful of outbuildings, all nestled into a cliff face. A stockade wall ringed the cabin and outbuildings, taller than Orka.

Asgrim's steading.

On the eastern side of the steading a track curled down the hills, eventually leading towards the village of Fellur and the fjord.

Orka took a few steps forwards, then stopped, spear levelled as Breca and Thorkel climbed on to the plateau.

The stockade's wide gates were thrown open, a body upon the ground between them, limbs twisted, unnaturally still. One gate creaked on the wind. Orka heard Breca's breath hiss through his lips.

Orka knew it was Asgrim, broad shouldered and with iron-grey hair. One hairy arm poked from the torn sleeve of his tunic.

A snowflake drifted down, a tingled kiss upon Orka's cheek.

"Breca, stay behind me," she said, padding forwards. Crows rose squawking from Asgrim's corpse, complaining as they flapped away, settling among the treetops, one sitting upon a gatepost, watching them.

Snow began to fall, the wind swirling it around the plateau.

Orka looked down on Asgrim. He was clothed in wool and breeches, a good fur cloak, a dull ring of silver around one arm. His hair was grey, body lean, sinewed muscles showing through his torn tunic. One of his boots had fallen off. A shattered spear lay close to him, and a blooded hand-axe on the ground. There was a hole in his chest, his woollen tunic dark with crusted blood.

Orka kneeled, picked up the axe and placed it in Asgrim's palm, wrapping the stiffening fingers around it.

"Travel the soul road with a blade in your fist," she whispered.

Breca's breath came in a ragged gasp behind her. It was the first person he had seen dead. Plenty of animals; he had helped in slaughtering many a meal for their supper, the gutting and skinning, the soaking of sinew for stitching and binding, the tanning of leather for the boots they wore, their belts and scabbards for their seaxes. But to see another man dead, his life torn from him, that was something else.

At least, for the first time.

And this was a man that Breca had known. He had seen life's spark in him.

Orka gave her son a moment as he stood and stared wide-eyed at the corpse, a flutter in his chest, his breath quick.

The ground around Asgrim was churned, grass flattened. A scuffed boot print. A few paces away there was a pool of blood soaked into the grass. Tracks in the ground led away; it looked like someone had been dragged.

Asgrim put someone down, then.

"Was he the one screaming?" Breca asked, still staring at Asgrim's corpse.

"No," Orka said, looking at the wound in Asgrim's chest. A stab to the heart: death would have come quickly. And a good thing, too, as his body had already been picked at by scavengers. His eyes and lips were red wounds where the crows had been at him. Orka put a hand to Asgrim's face and lifted what was left of his lip to look inside his mouth. Gums and empty, blood-ragged sockets. She scowled.

"Where are his teeth?" Breca hissed.

"Tennúr have been at him," Orka grunted. "They love a man's teeth more than a squirrel loves nuts." She looked around, searching the treeline and ridged cliff for any sign of the small, two-legged creatures. On their own, they could be a nuisance; in a pack, they could be deadly, with their sharp-boned fingers and razor teeth.

Thorkel stepped around Orka and padded into the enclosure, spear-point sweeping in a wide arc as he searched.

He stopped, stared up at the creaking gate.

Orka stepped over Asgrim into the steading and stopped beside Thorkel.

A body was nailed to the gate, arms wide, head lolling.

Idrun, wife to Asgrim.

She had not died so quickly as her husband.

Her belly had been opened, intestines spilling to a pile on the ground, twisted like vines around an old oak. Heat still rose from them, steaming as snow settled upon glistening coils. Her face was misshapen in a rictus of pain.

It was she who did the screaming.

"What did this?" Thorkel muttered.

"Vaesen?" Orka said.

Thorkel pointed to thick-carved runes on the gate, all sharp angles and straight lines. "A warding rune."

Orka shook her head. Runes would hold back all but the most powerful of vaesen. She glanced back at Asgrim and the wound in his chest. Rarely did vaesen use weapons, nature already equipping them with the tools of death and slaughter. There were dark patches on the grass: congealed blood.

Blood on Asgrim's axe. Others were wounded, but if they fell, they were carried from here.

"Did men do this?" Thorkel muttered.

Orka shrugged, a puff of misted breath as she thought on it.

"All is lies," she murmured. "They call this the age of peace, because the ancient war is over and the gods are dead, but if this is peace . . ." She looked to the skies, clouds low and heavy, snow falling in sheets now, and back at the blood-soaked corpses. "This is the age of storm and murder . . . "

"Where's Harek?" Breca asked.